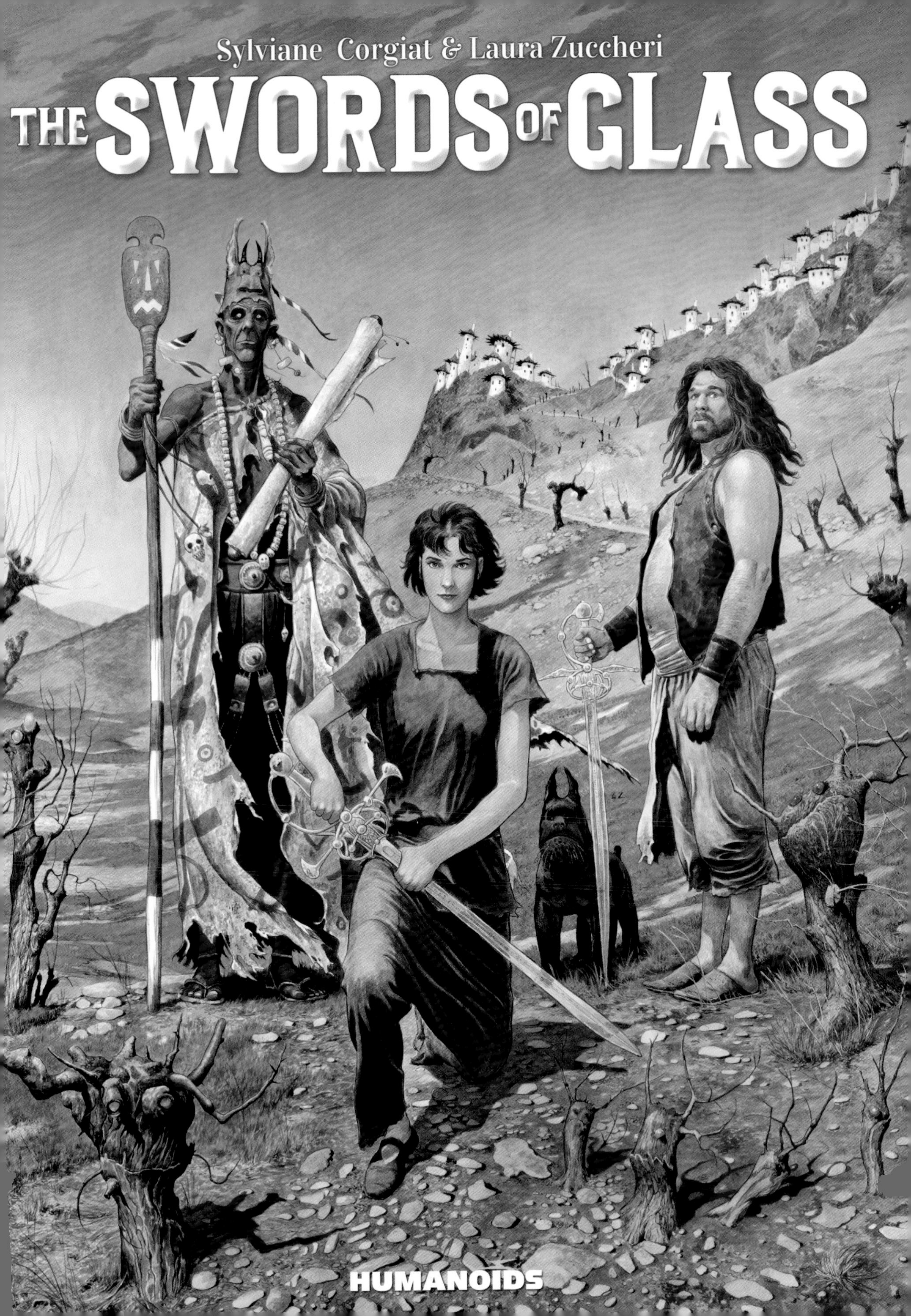
Sylviane Corgiat & Laura Zuccheri
THE SWORDS OF GLASS
HUMANOIDS

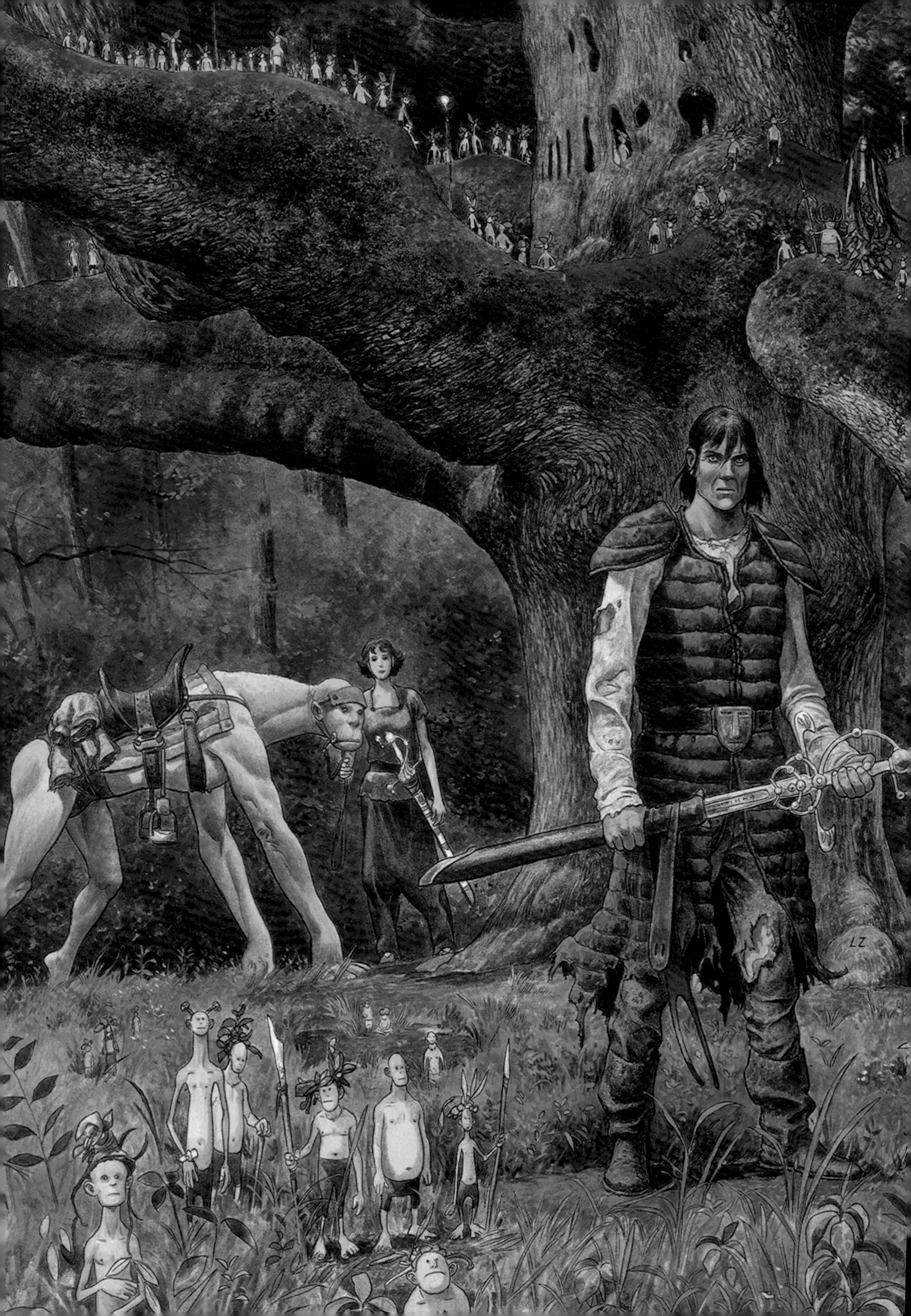

SYLVIANE CORGIAT
Writer

LAURA ZUCCHERI
Artist

LAURA ZUCCHERI (pages 5 to 150)
SILVIA FABRIS (pages 151 to 204)
Colorists

QUINN and **KATIA DONOGHUE**
Translators

ALEX DONOGHUE
TIM PILCHER
U.S. Edition Editors

JERRY FRISSEN
Book Designer

Fabrice Giger, Publisher

Rights & Licensing - licensing@humanoids.com
Press and Social Media - pr@humanoids.com

THE SWORDS OF GLASS.
This title is a publication of Humanoids, Inc. 8033 Sunset Blvd. #628,
Los Angeles, CA 90046. Copyright © 2015 Humanoids, Inc.,
Los Angeles (USA). All rights reserved. Humanoids and
its logos are ® and © 2015 Humanoids, Inc.

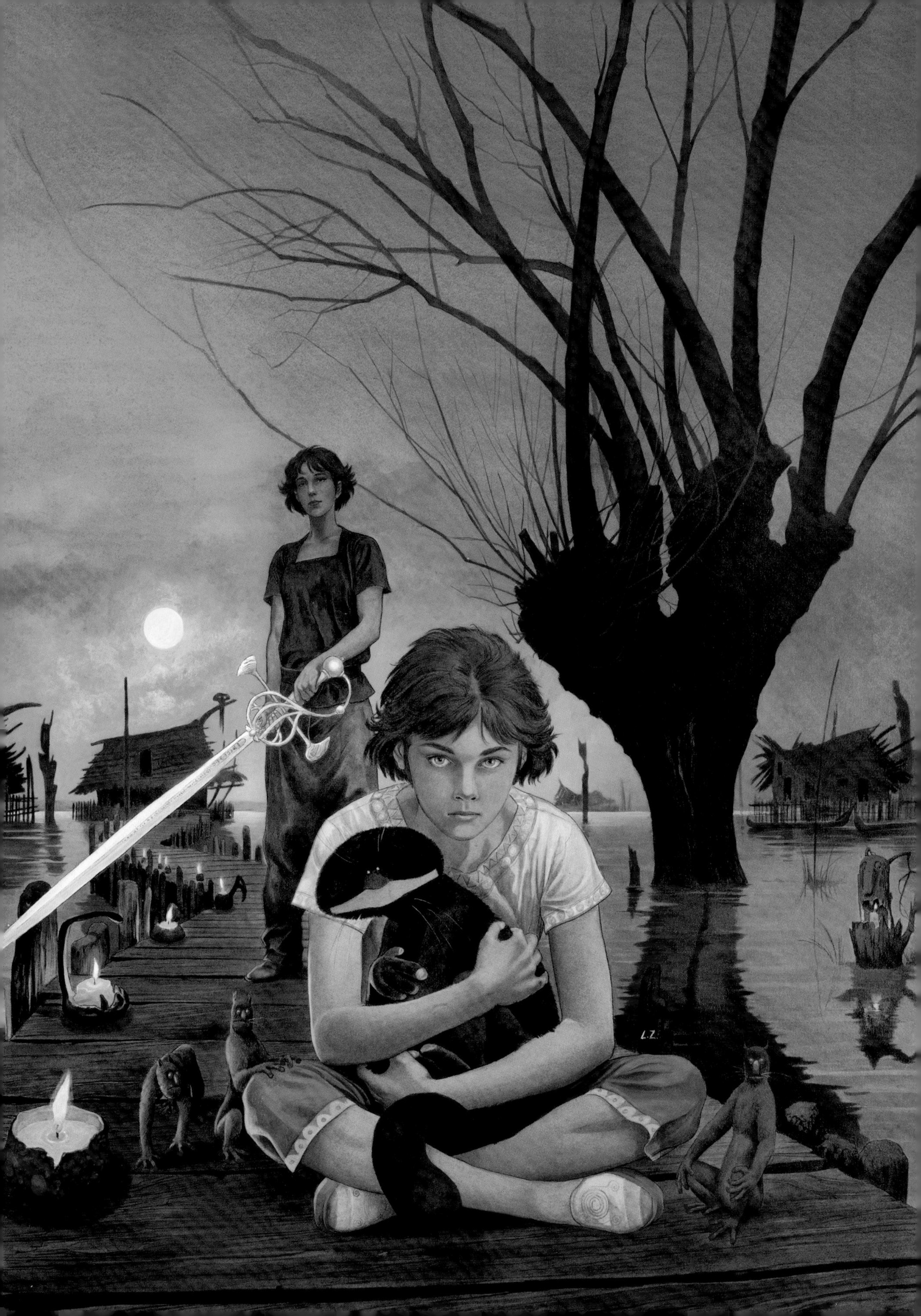
L.Z.

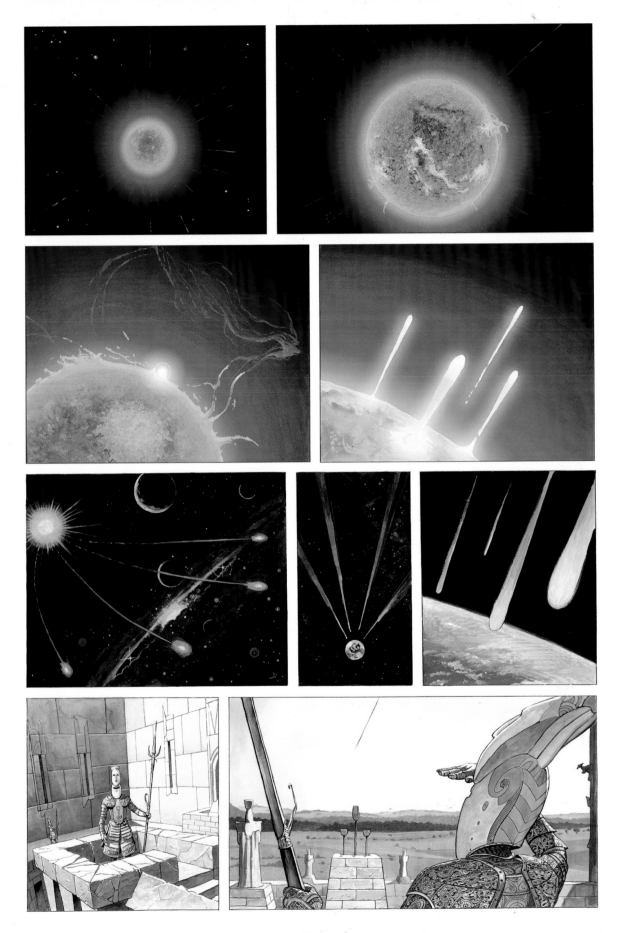

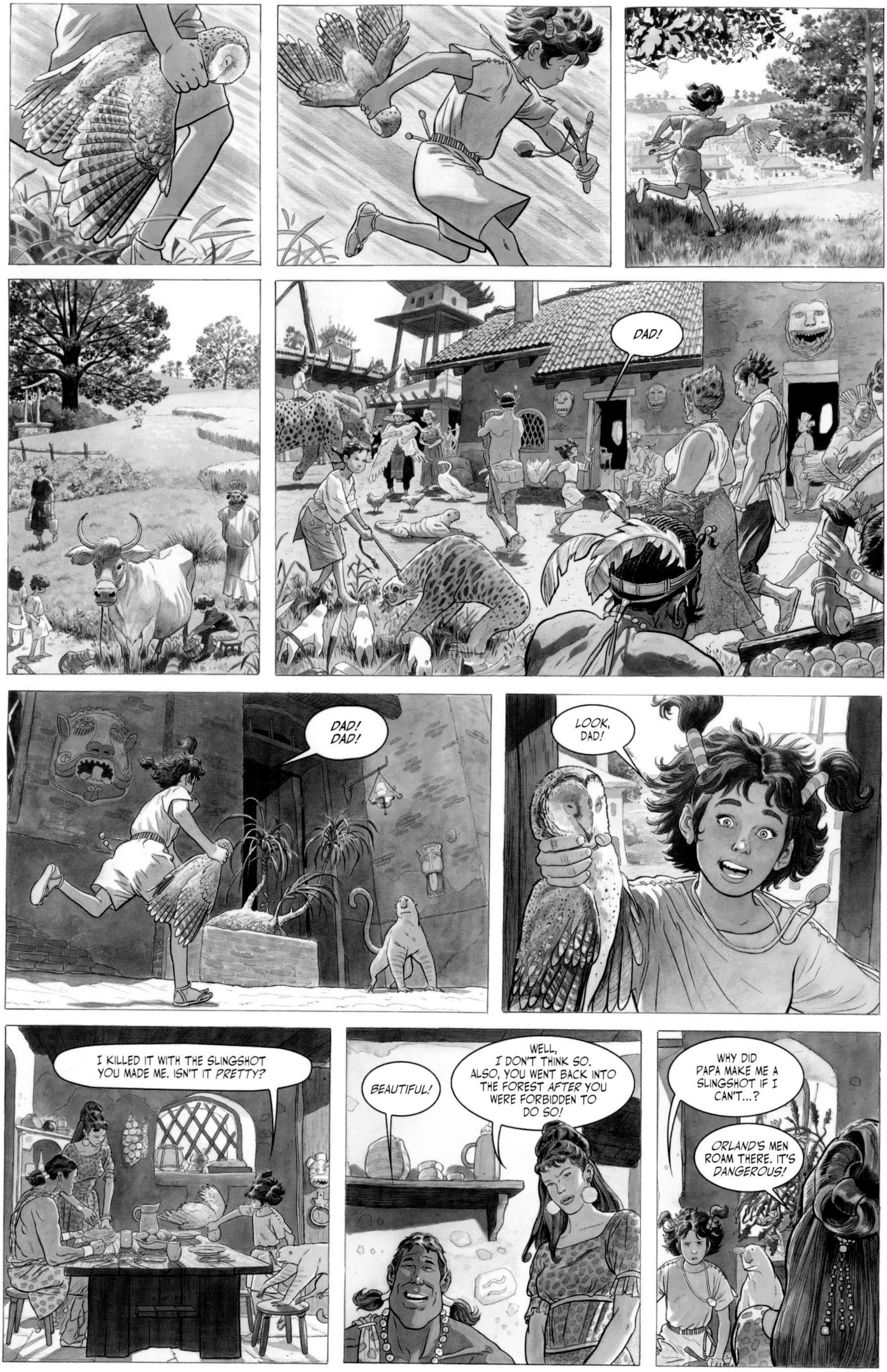
DAD!
DAD! DAD!
LOOK, DAD!
I KILLED IT WITH THE SLINGSHOT YOU MADE ME. ISN'T IT *PRETTY?*
BEAUTIFUL!
WELL, I DON'T THINK SO. ALSO, YOU WENT BACK INTO THE FOREST *AFTER* YOU WERE FORBIDDEN TO DO SO!
WHY DID PAPA MAKE ME A SLINGSHOT IF I CAN'T...?
ORLAND'S MEN ROAM THERE. IT'S *DANGEROUS!*

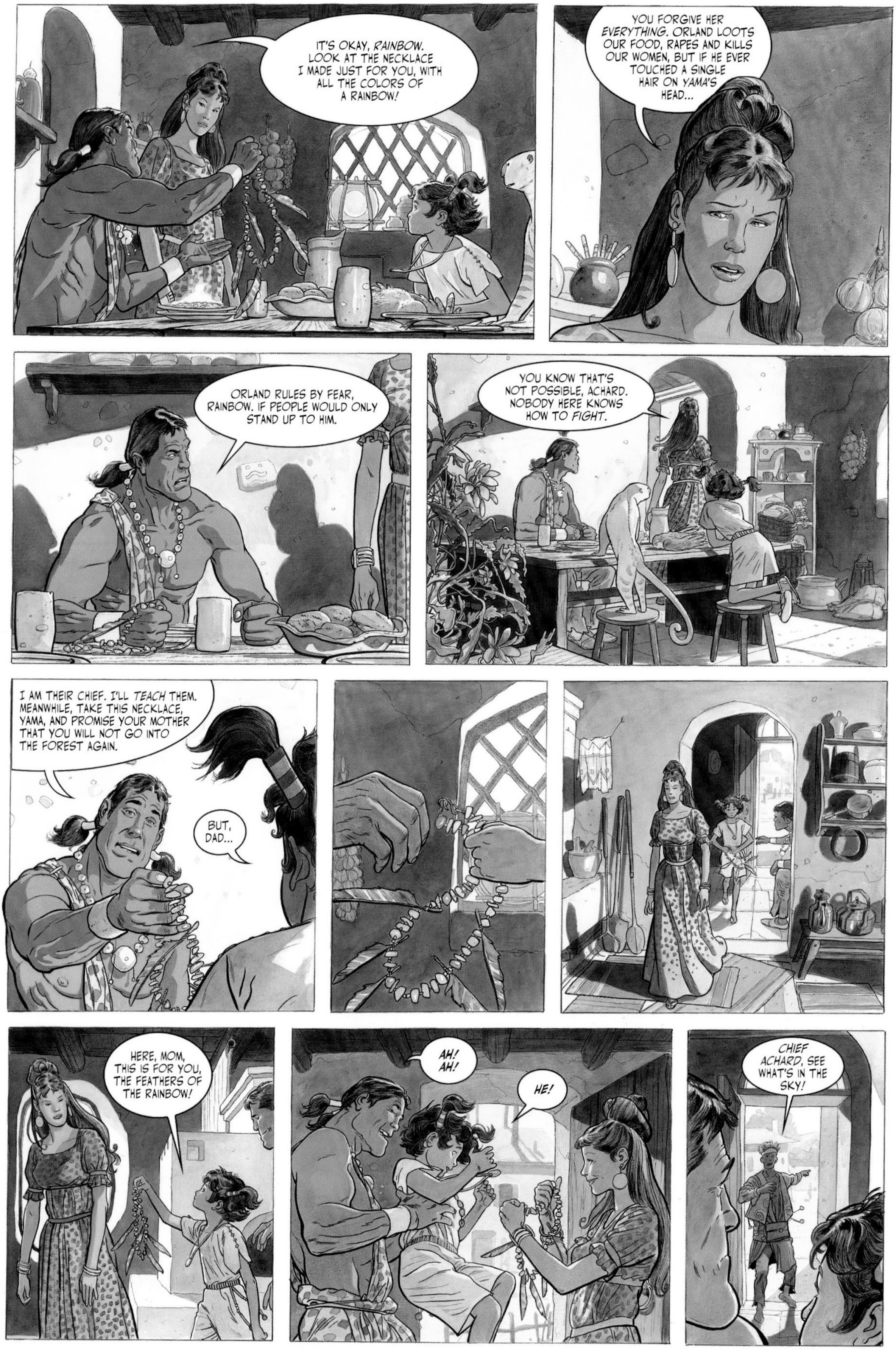
IT'S OKAY, RAINBOW. LOOK AT THE NECKLACE I MADE JUST FOR YOU, WITH ALL THE COLORS OF A RAINBOW!
YOU FORGIVE HER EVERYTHING. ORLAND LOOTS OUR FOOD, RAPES AND KILLS OUR WOMEN, BUT IF HE EVER TOUCHED A SINGLE HAIR ON YAMA'S HEAD...
ORLAND RULES BY FEAR, RAINBOW. IF PEOPLE WOULD ONLY STAND UP TO HIM.
YOU KNOW THAT'S NOT POSSIBLE, ACHARD. NOBODY HERE KNOWS HOW TO FIGHT.
I AM THEIR CHIEF. I'LL TEACH THEM. MEANWHILE, TAKE THIS NECKLACE, YAMA, AND PROMISE YOUR MOTHER THAT YOU WILL NOT GO INTO THE FOREST AGAIN.
BUT, DAD...
HERE, MOM, THIS IS FOR YOU, THE FEATHERS OF THE RAINBOW!
AH! AH!
HE!
CHIEF ACHARD, SEE WHAT'S IN THE SKY!

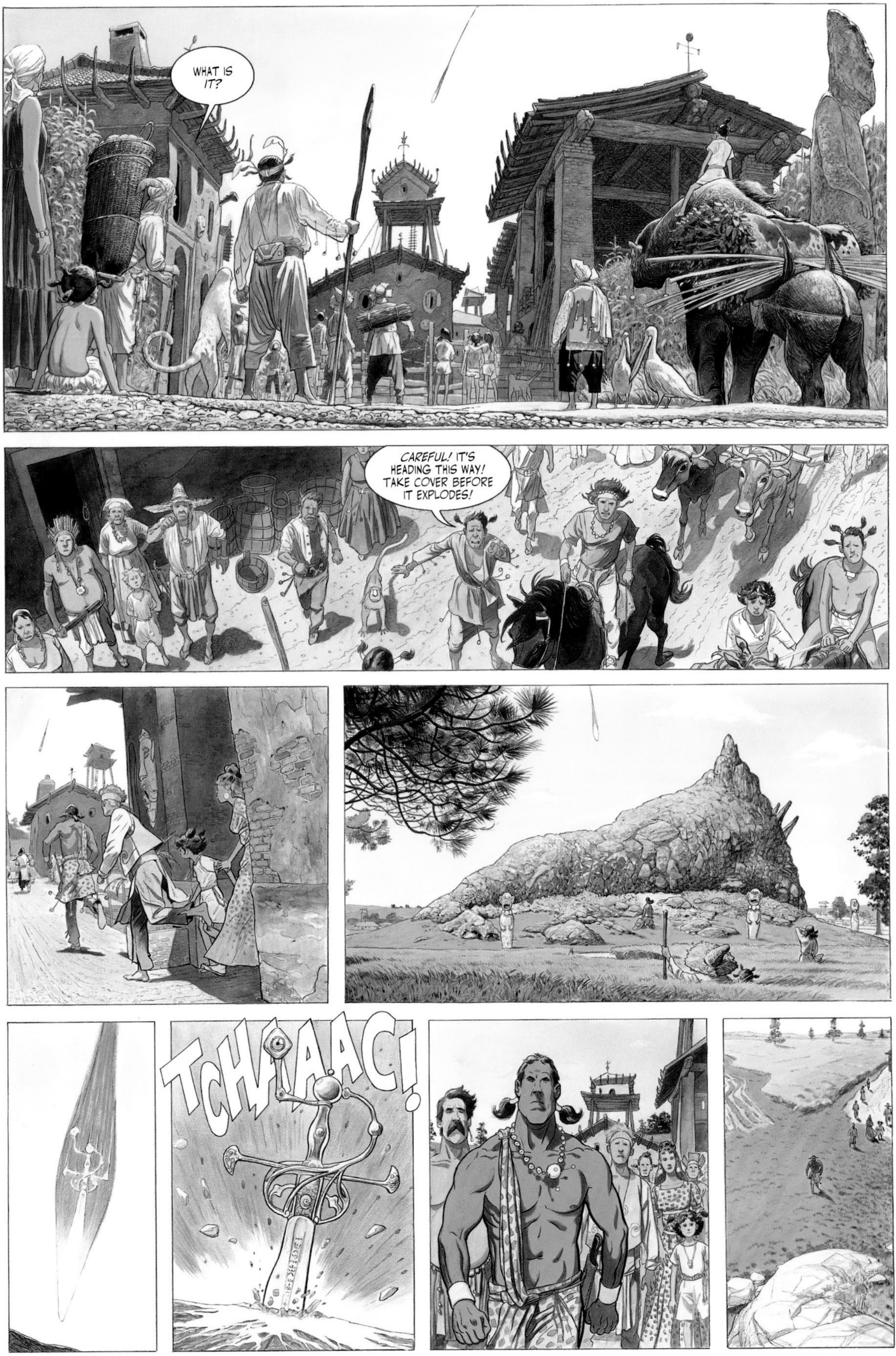
WHAT IS IT?
CAREFUL! IT'S HEADING THIS WAY! TAKE COVER BEFORE IT EXPLODES!
TCHAAAC!

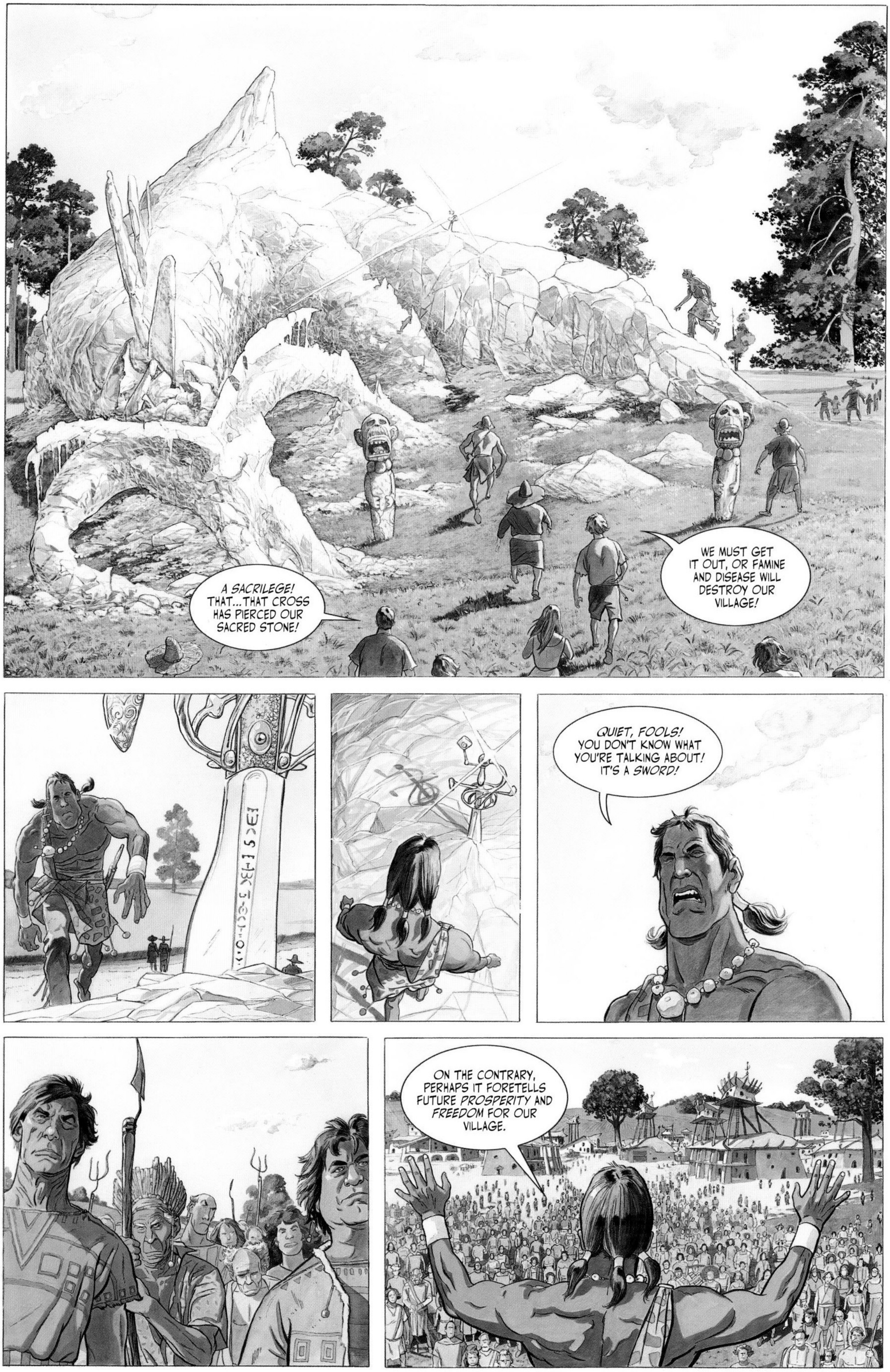
A SACRILEGE! THAT...THAT CROSS HAS PIERCED OUR SACRED STONE!
WE MUST GET IT OUT, OR FAMINE AND DISEASE WILL DESTROY OUR VILLAGE!
QUIET, FOOLS! YOU DON'T KNOW WHAT YOU'RE TALKING ABOUT! IT'S A SWORD!
ON THE CONTRARY, PERHAPS IT FORETELLS FUTURE PROSPERITY AND FREEDOM FOR OUR VILLAGE.

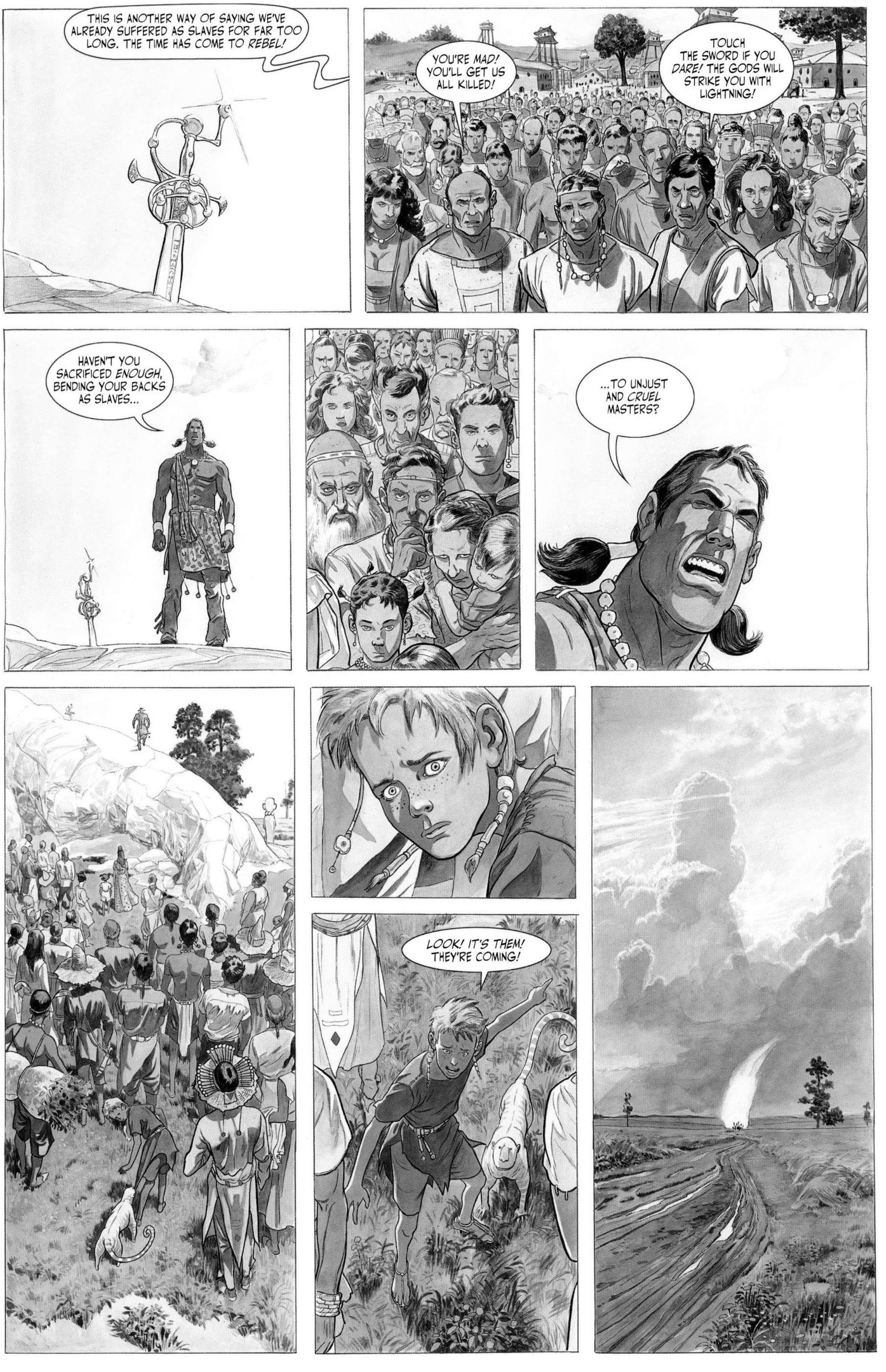
THIS IS ANOTHER WAY OF SAYING WE'VE ALREADY SUFFERED AS SLAVES FOR FAR TOO LONG. THE TIME HAS COME TO *REBEL!*
YOU'RE *MAD!* YOU'LL GET US ALL KILLED!
TOUCH THE SWORD IF YOU *DARE!* THE GODS WILL STRIKE YOU WITH LIGHTNING!
HAVEN'T YOU SACRIFICED *ENOUGH*, BENDING YOUR BACKS AS SLAVES...
...TO UNJUST AND *CRUEL* MASTERS?
LOOK! IT'S THEM! THEY'RE COMING!

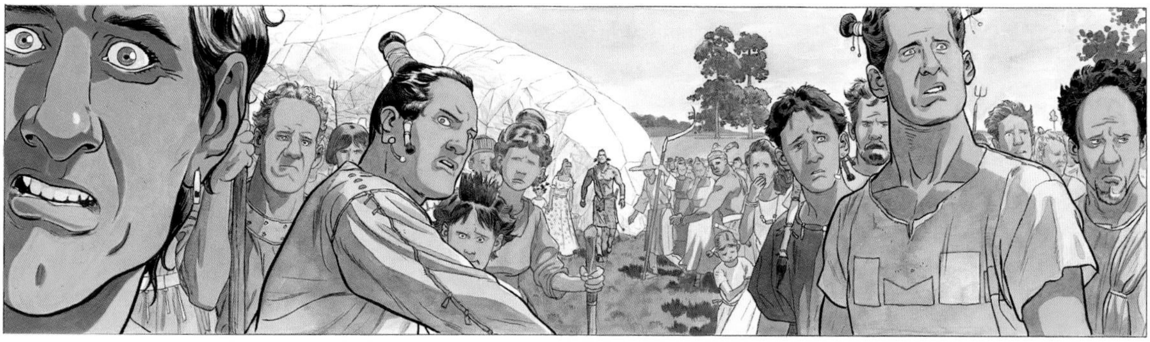

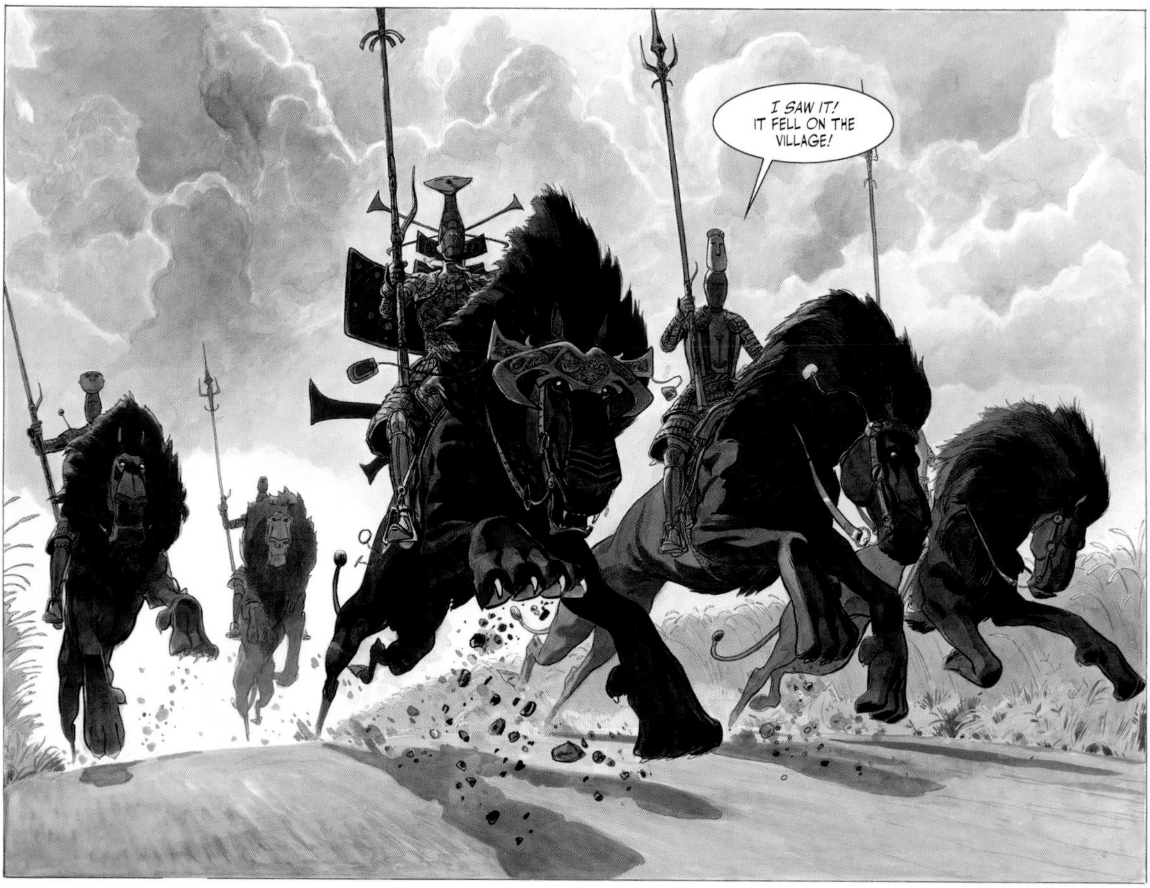
I SAW IT! IT FELL ON THE VILLAGE!

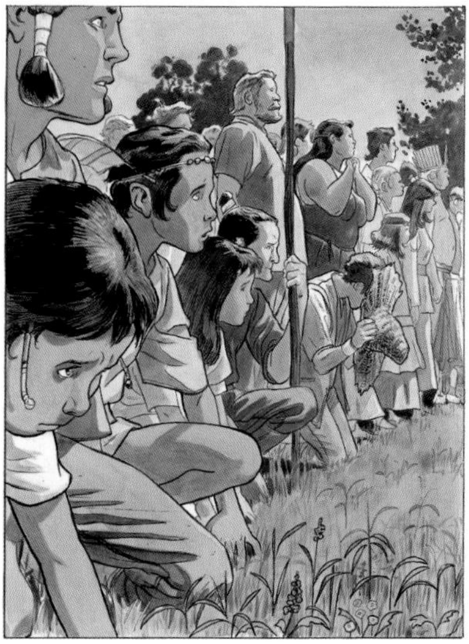

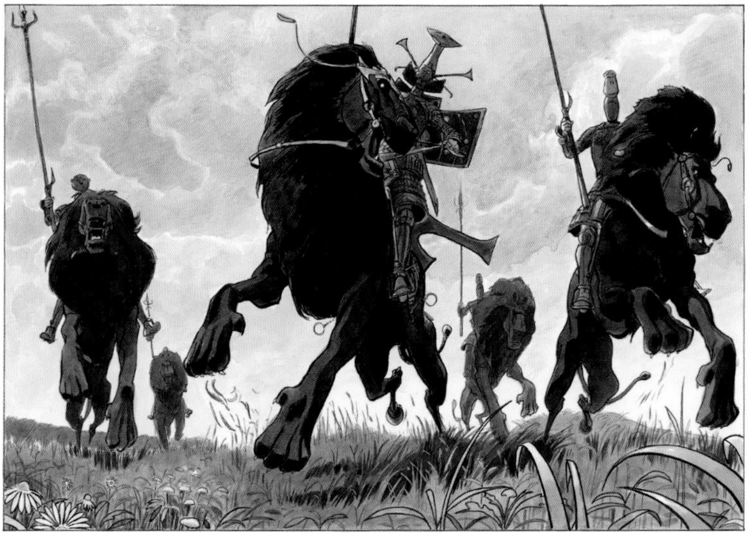

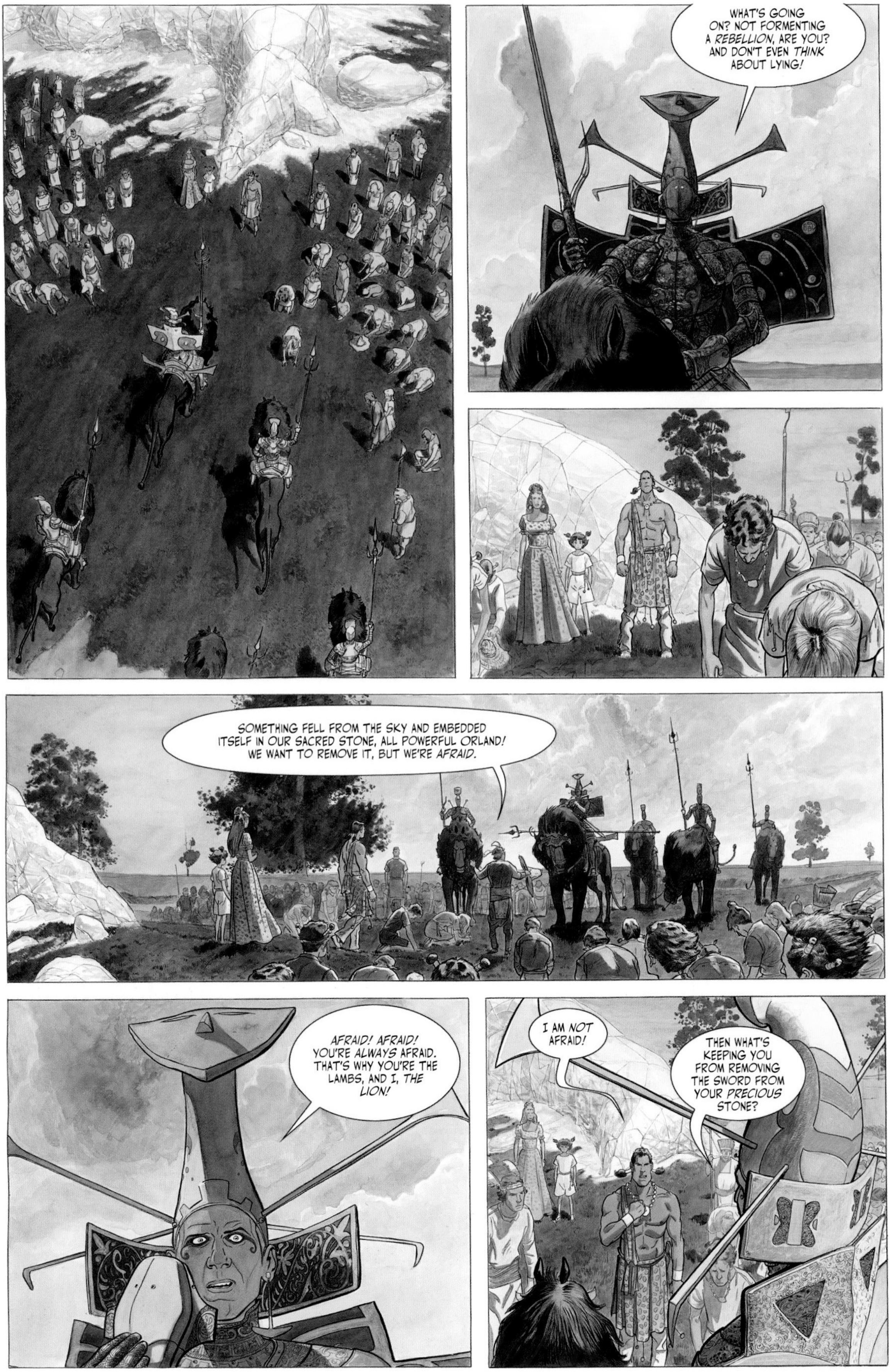
WHAT'S GOING ON? NOT FOMENTING A *REBELLION*, ARE YOU? AND DON'T EVEN *THINK* ABOUT LYING!
SOMETHING FELL FROM THE SKY AND EMBEDDED ITSELF IN OUR SACRED STONE, ALL POWERFUL ORLAND! WE WANT TO REMOVE IT, BUT WE'RE *AFRAID*.
AFRAID! AFRAID! YOU'RE *ALWAYS* AFRAID. THAT'S WHY YOU'RE THE LAMBS, AND I, *THE LION!*
I AM *NOT* AFRAID!
THEN WHAT'S KEEPING YOU FROM REMOVING THE SWORD FROM YOUR *PRECIOUS* STONE?

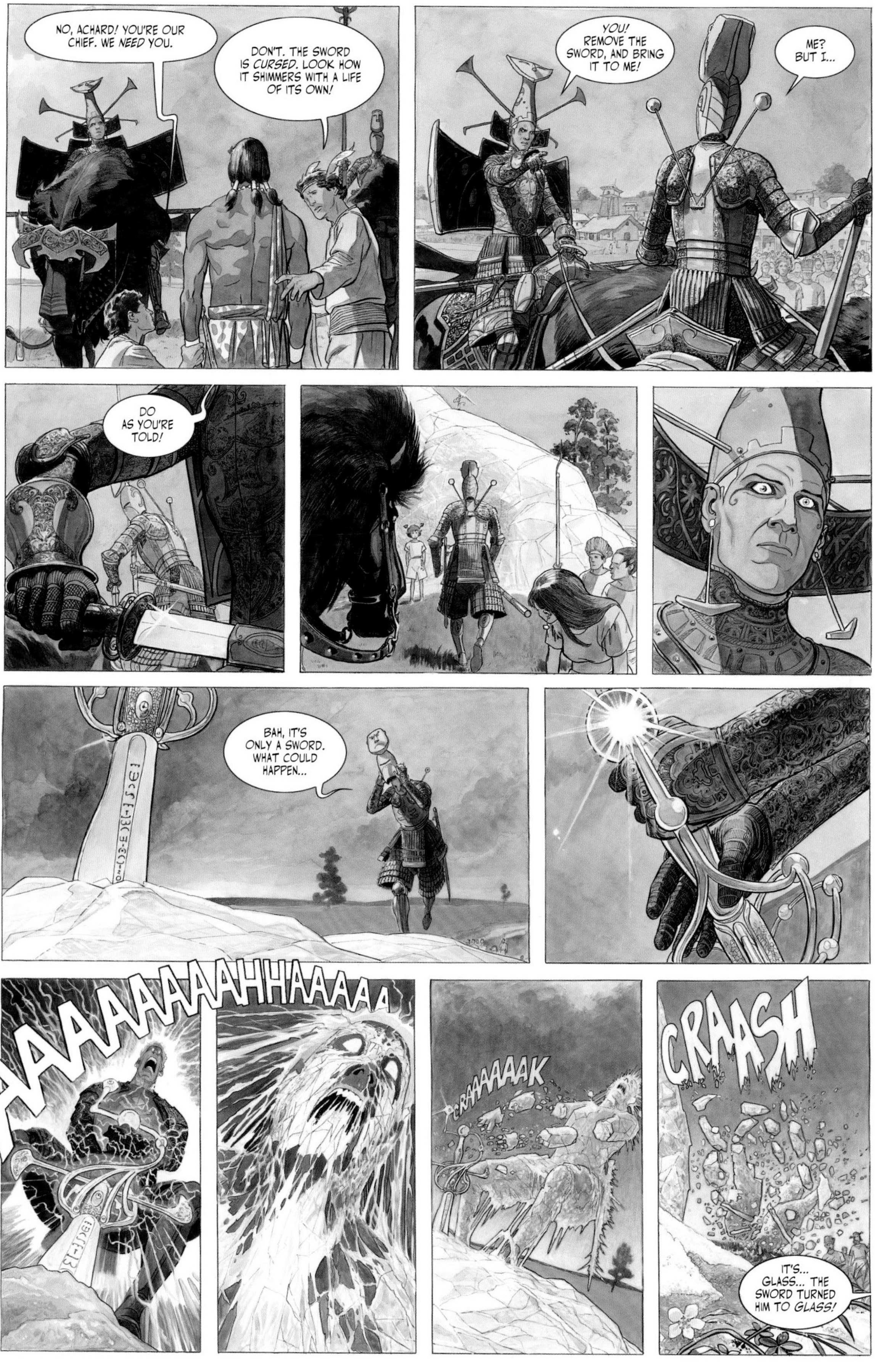
NO, ACHARD! YOU'RE OUR CHIEF. WE *NEED* YOU.
DON'T. THE SWORD IS *CURSED*. LOOK HOW IT SHIMMERS WITH A LIFE OF ITS OWN!
YOU! REMOVE THE SWORD, AND BRING IT TO ME!
ME? BUT I...
DO AS YOU'RE TOLD!
BAH, IT'S ONLY A SWORD. WHAT COULD HAPPEN...
AAAAAAAAHHAAAAA
CRAAAAAK
CRAAASH
IT'S... GLASS... THE SWORD TURNED HIM TO *GLASS!*

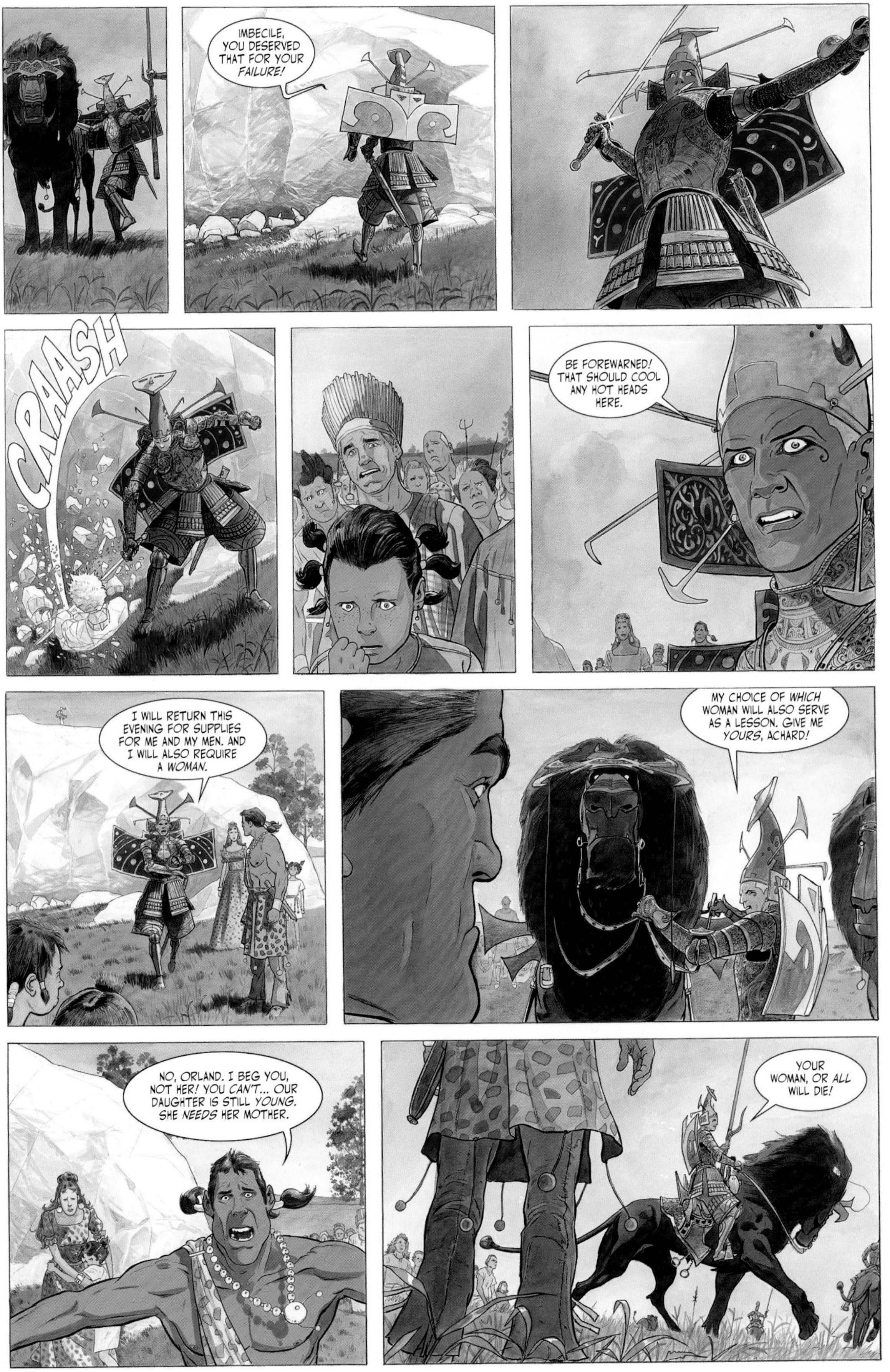
IMBECILE, YOU DESERVED THAT FOR YOUR FAILURE!
CRAASH
BE FOREWARNED! THAT SHOULD COOL ANY HOT HEADS HERE.
I WILL RETURN THIS EVENING FOR SUPPLIES FOR ME AND MY MEN. AND I WILL ALSO REQUIRE A WOMAN.
MY CHOICE OF WHICH WOMAN WILL ALSO SERVE AS A LESSON. GIVE ME YOURS, ACHARD!
NO, ORLAND. I BEG YOU, NOT HER! YOU CAN'T... OUR DAUGHTER IS STILL YOUNG. SHE NEEDS HER MOTHER.
YOUR WOMAN, OR ALL WILL DIE!

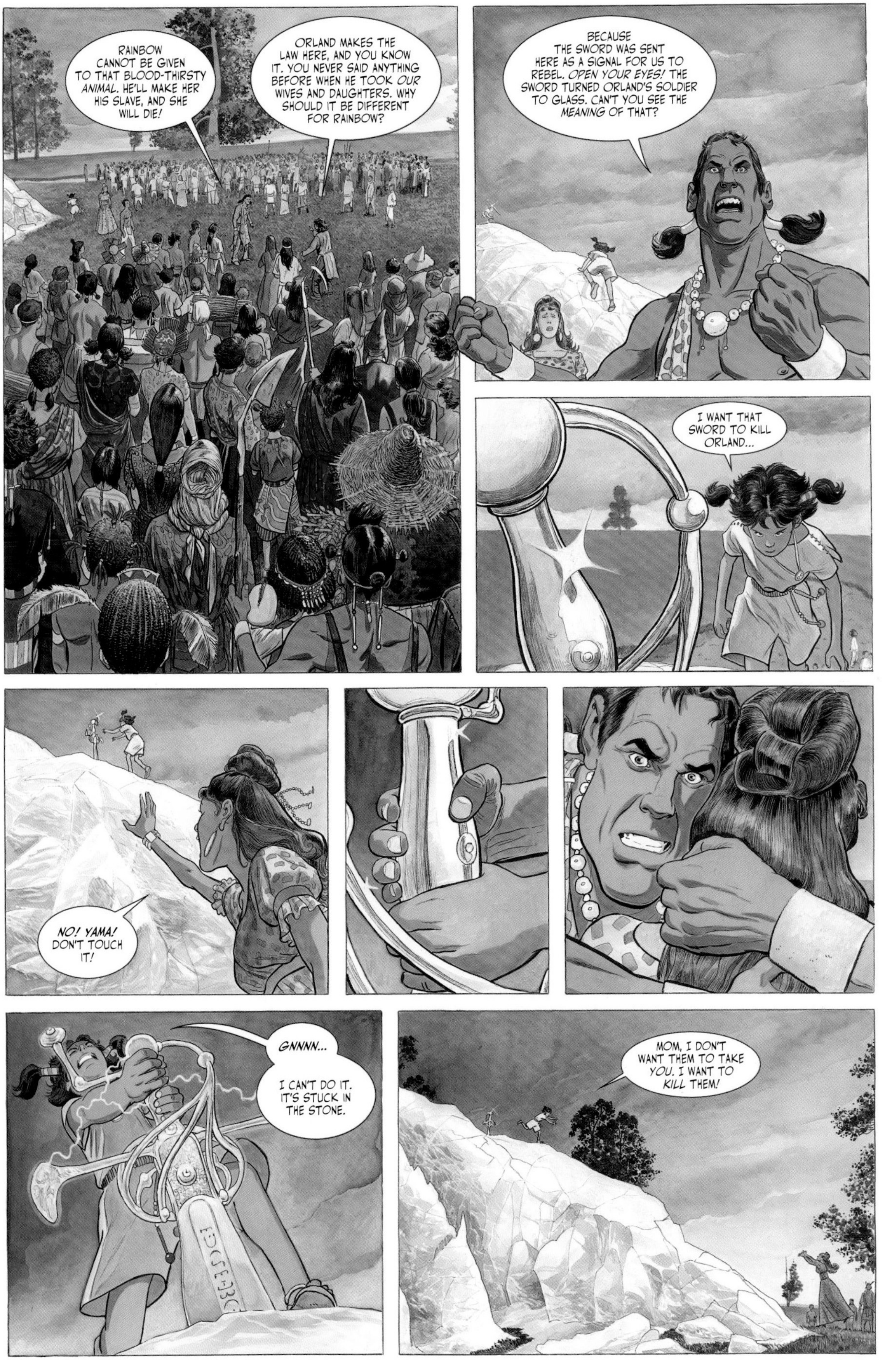
RAINBOW CANNOT BE GIVEN TO THAT BLOOD-THIRSTY *ANIMAL*. HE'LL MAKE HER HIS SLAVE, AND SHE WILL DIE!
ORLAND MAKES THE LAW HERE, AND YOU KNOW IT. YOU NEVER SAID ANYTHING BEFORE WHEN HE TOOK *OUR* WIVES AND DAUGHTERS. WHY SHOULD IT BE DIFFERENT FOR RAINBOW?
BECAUSE THE SWORD WAS SENT HERE AS A SIGNAL FOR US TO REBEL. *OPEN YOUR EYES!* THE SWORD TURNED ORLAND'S SOLDIER TO GLASS. CAN'T YOU SEE THE *MEANING* OF THAT?
I WANT THAT SWORD TO KILL ORLAND...
NO! YAMA! DON'T TOUCH IT!
GNNNN...
I CAN'T DO IT. IT'S STUCK IN THE STONE.
MOM, I DON'T WANT THEM TO TAKE *YOU*. I WANT TO *KILL* THEM!

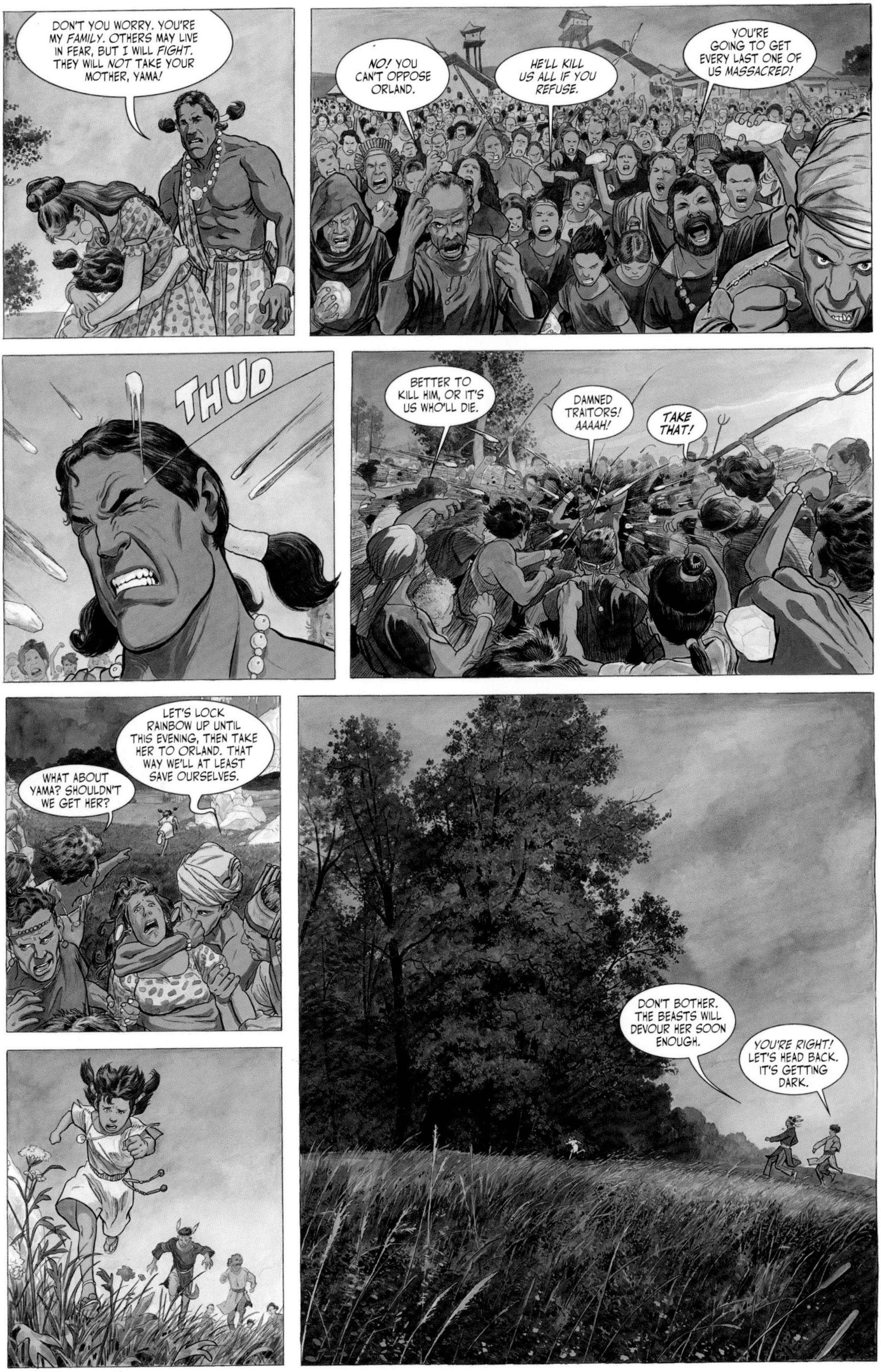
DON'T YOU WORRY. YOU'RE MY *FAMILY*. OTHERS MAY LIVE IN FEAR, BUT I WILL *FIGHT*. THEY WILL *NOT* TAKE YOUR MOTHER, YAMA!
NO! YOU CAN'T OPPOSE ORLAND.
HE'LL KILL US ALL IF YOU REFUSE.
YOU'RE GOING TO GET EVERY LAST ONE OF *US MASSACRED!*
THUD
BETTER TO KILL HIM, OR IT'S US WHO'LL DIE.
DAMNED TRAITORS! AAAAH!
TAKE THAT!
LET'S LOCK RAINBOW UP UNTIL THIS EVENING, THEN TAKE HER TO ORLAND. THAT WAY WE'LL AT LEAST SAVE OURSELVES.
WHAT ABOUT YAMA? SHOULDN'T WE GET HER?
DON'T BOTHER. THE BEASTS WILL DEVOUR HER SOON ENOUGH.
YOU'RE RIGHT! LET'S HEAD BACK. IT'S GETTING DARK.

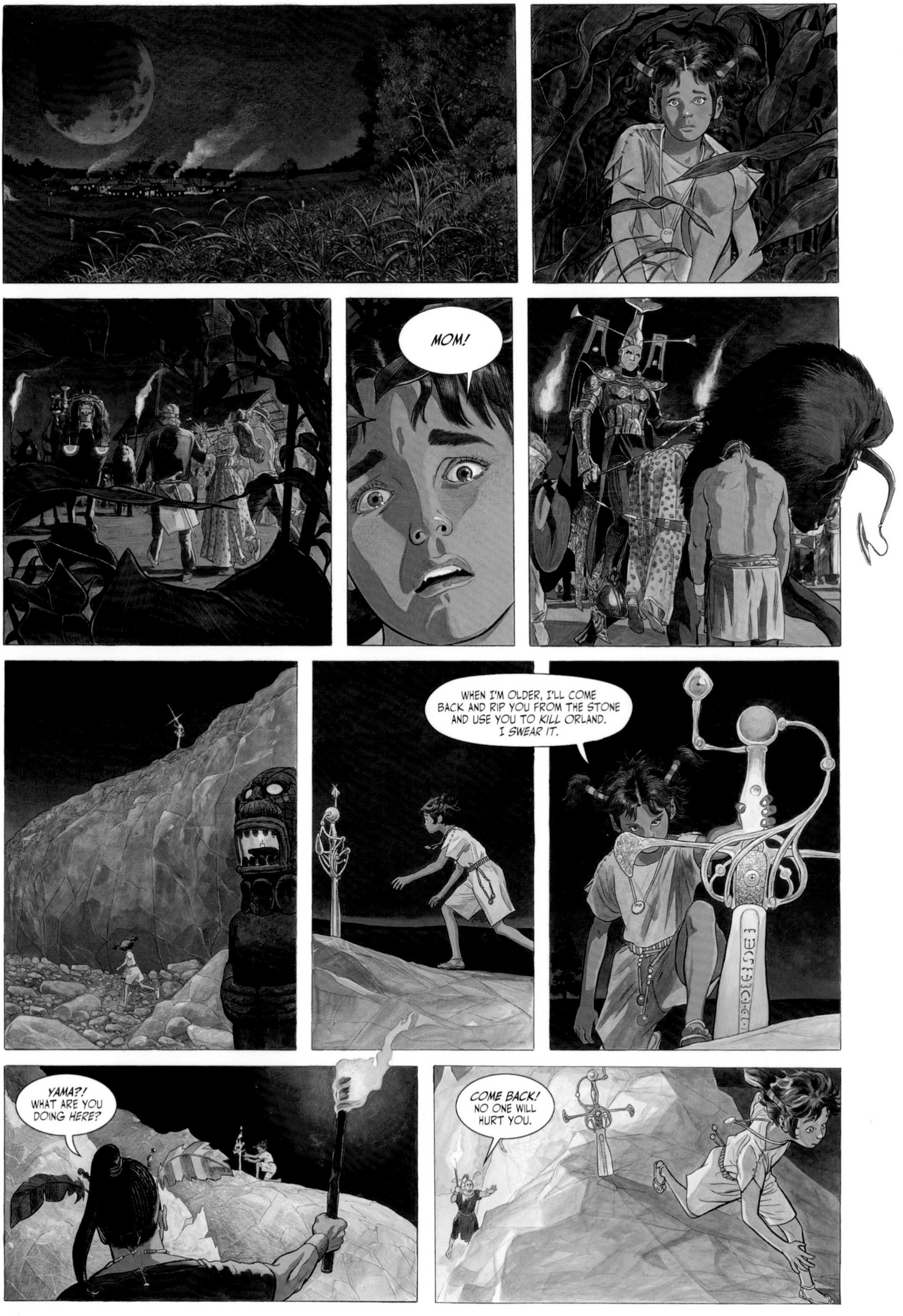
MOM!
WHEN I'M OLDER, I'LL COME BACK AND RIP YOU FROM THE STONE AND USE YOU TO KILL ORLAND. I SWEAR IT.
YAMA?! WHAT ARE YOU DOING HERE?
COME BACK! NO ONE WILL HURT YOU.

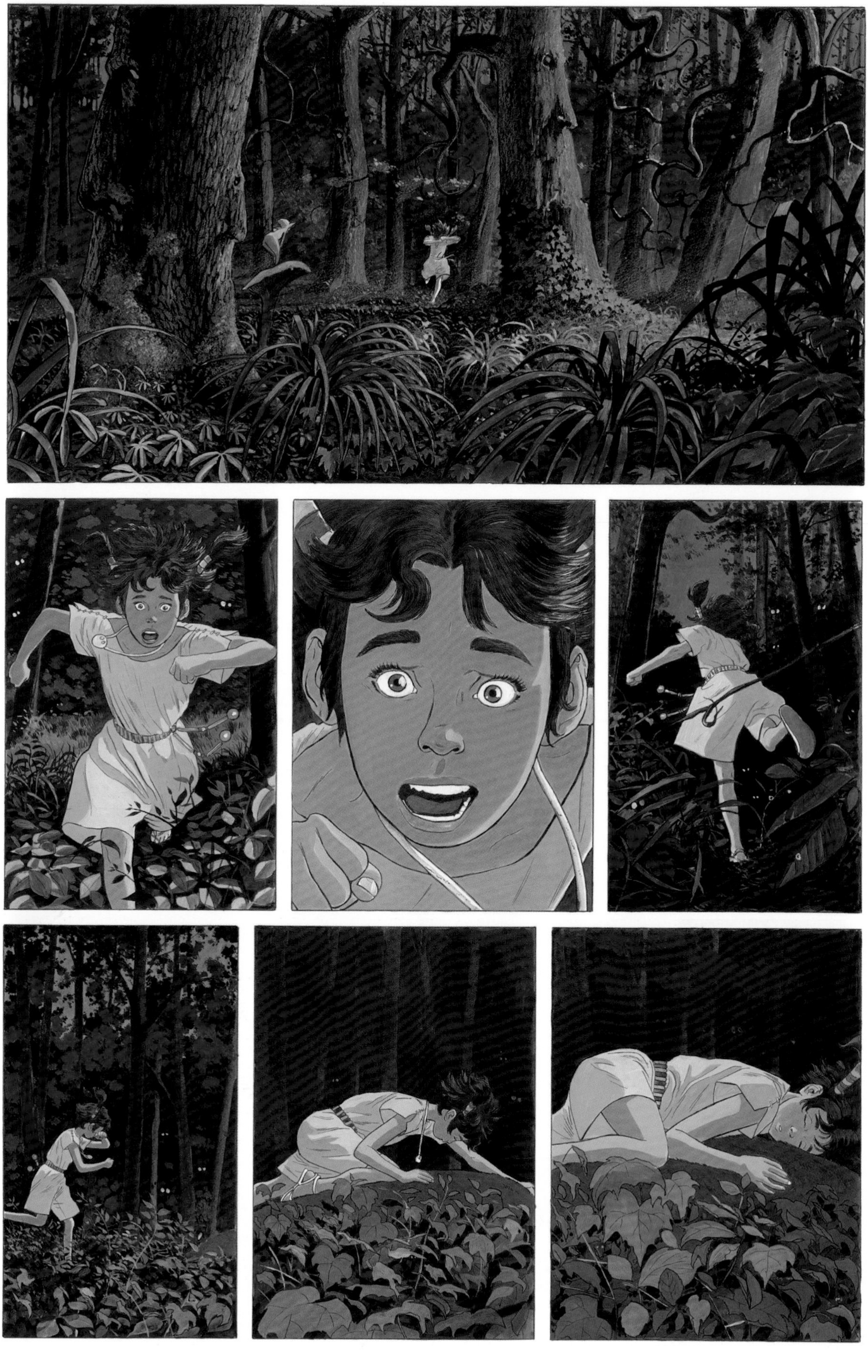

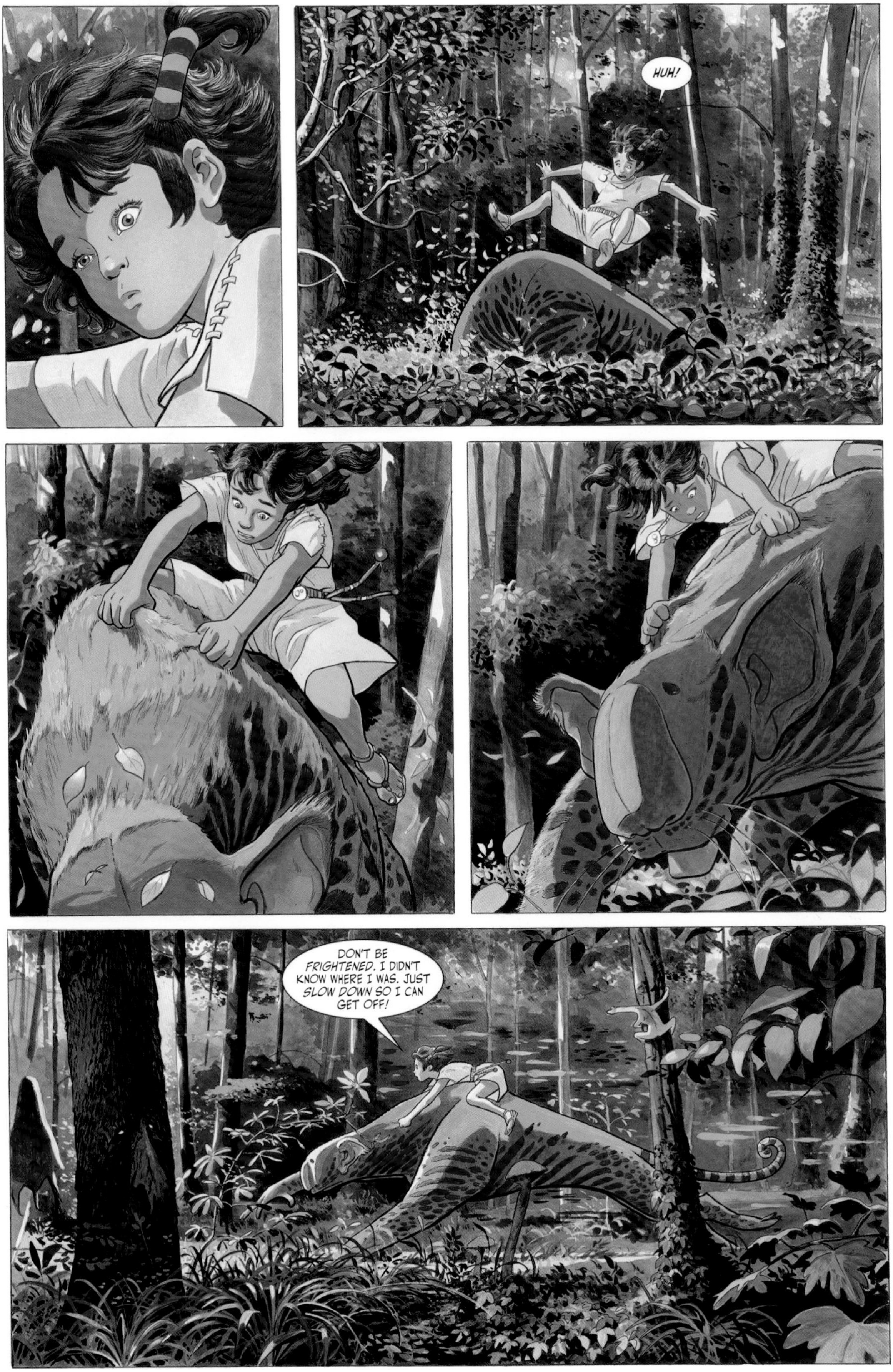
HUH!
DON'T BE FRIGHTENED. I DIDN'T KNOW WHERE I WAS. JUST SLOW DOWN SO I CAN GET OFF!

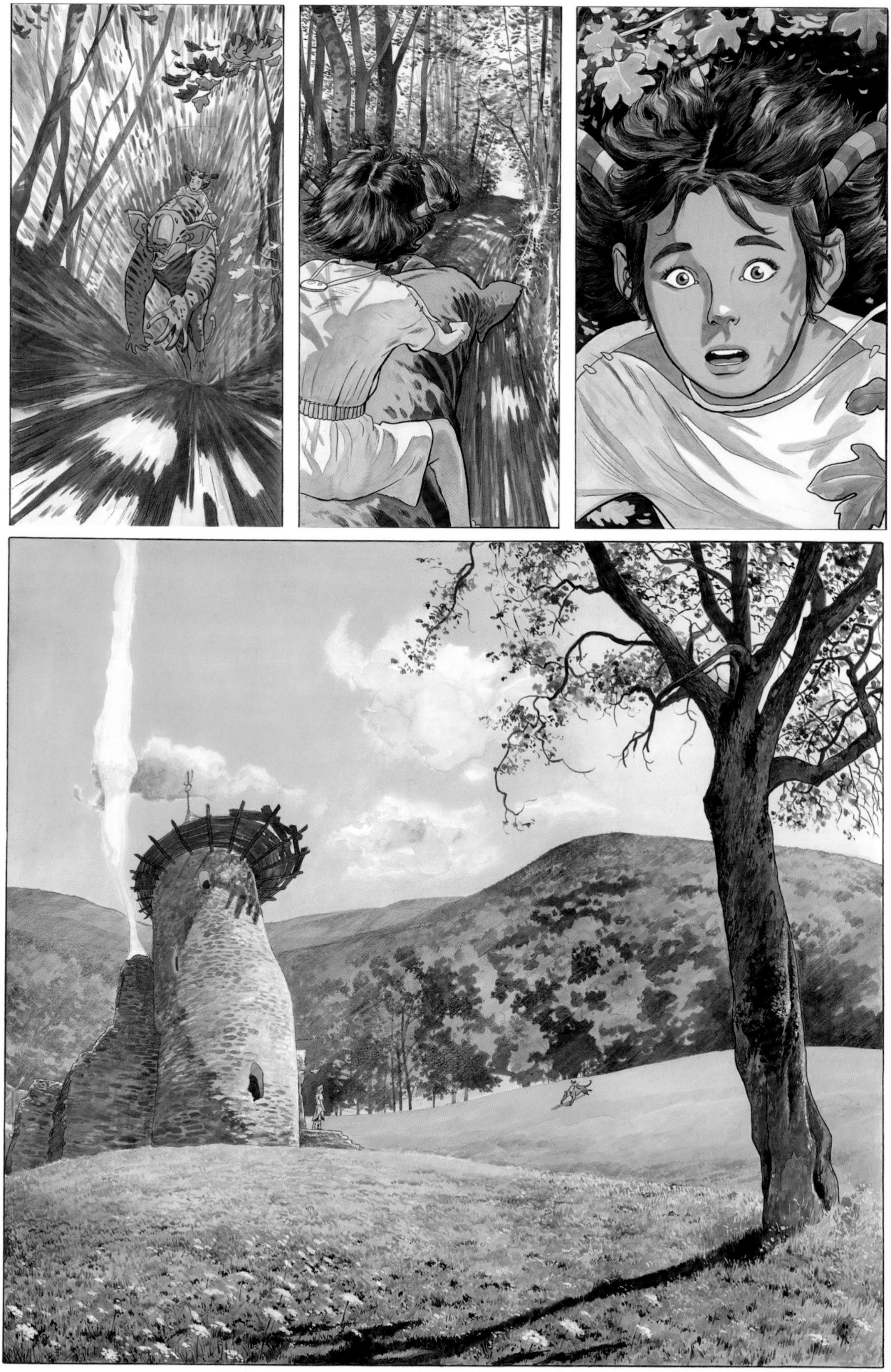

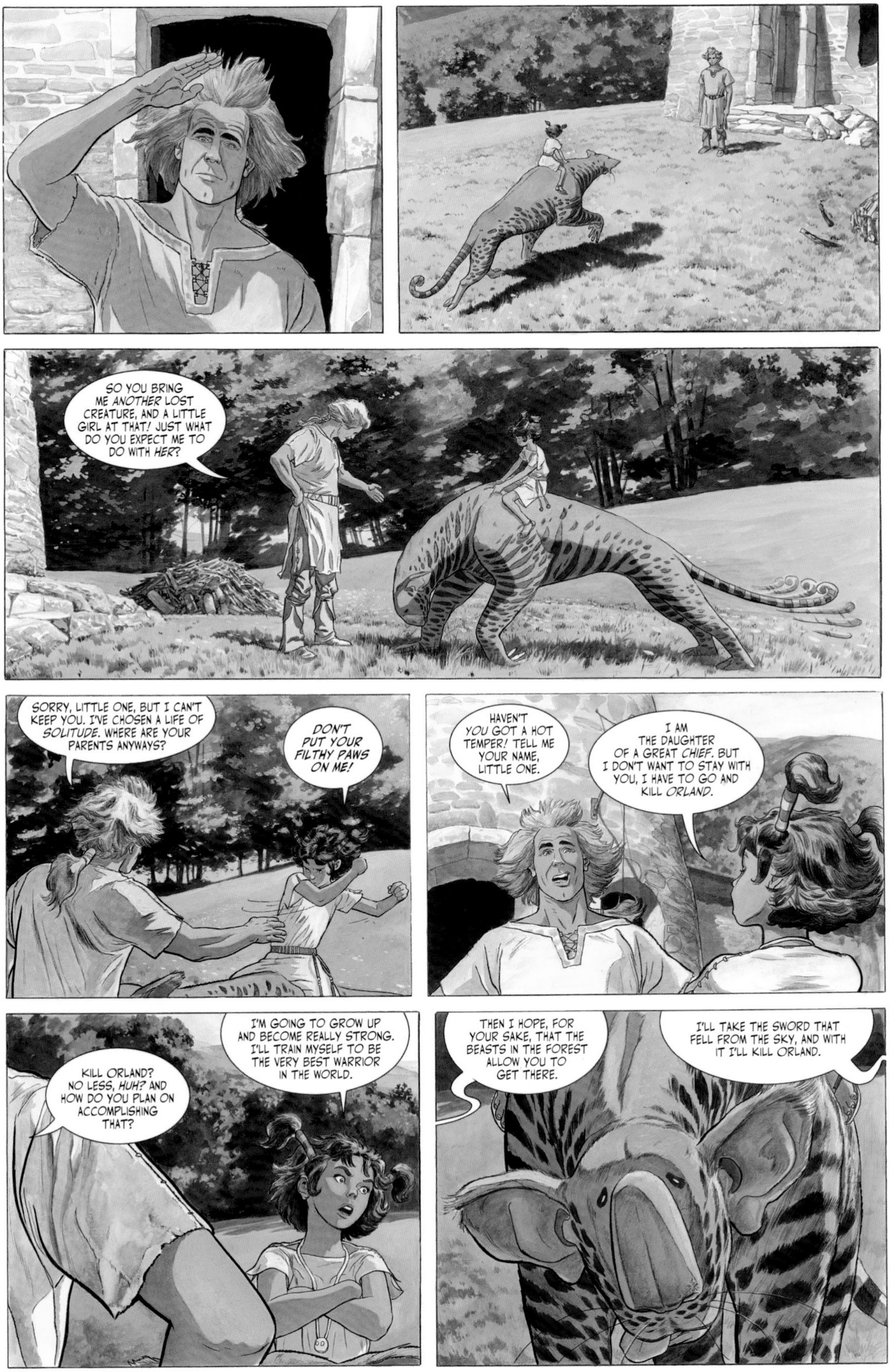
SO YOU BRING ME ANOTHER LOST CREATURE, AND A LITTLE GIRL AT THAT! JUST WHAT DO YOU EXPECT ME TO DO WITH HER?
SORRY, LITTLE ONE, BUT I CAN'T KEEP YOU. I'VE CHOSEN A LIFE OF SOLITUDE. WHERE ARE YOUR PARENTS ANYWAYS?
DON'T PUT YOUR FILTHY PAWS ON ME!
HAVEN'T YOU GOT A HOT TEMPER! TELL ME YOUR NAME, LITTLE ONE.
I AM THE DAUGHTER OF A GREAT CHIEF. BUT I DON'T WANT TO STAY WITH YOU, I HAVE TO GO AND KILL ORLAND.
KILL ORLAND? NO LESS, HUH? AND HOW DO YOU PLAN ON ACCOMPLISHING THAT?
I'M GOING TO GROW UP AND BECOME REALLY STRONG. I'LL TRAIN MYSELF TO BE THE VERY BEST WARRIOR IN THE WORLD.
THEN I HOPE, FOR YOUR SAKE, THAT THE BEASTS IN THE FOREST ALLOW YOU TO GET THERE.
I'LL TAKE THE SWORD THAT FELL FROM THE SKY, AND WITH IT I'LL KILL ORLAND.

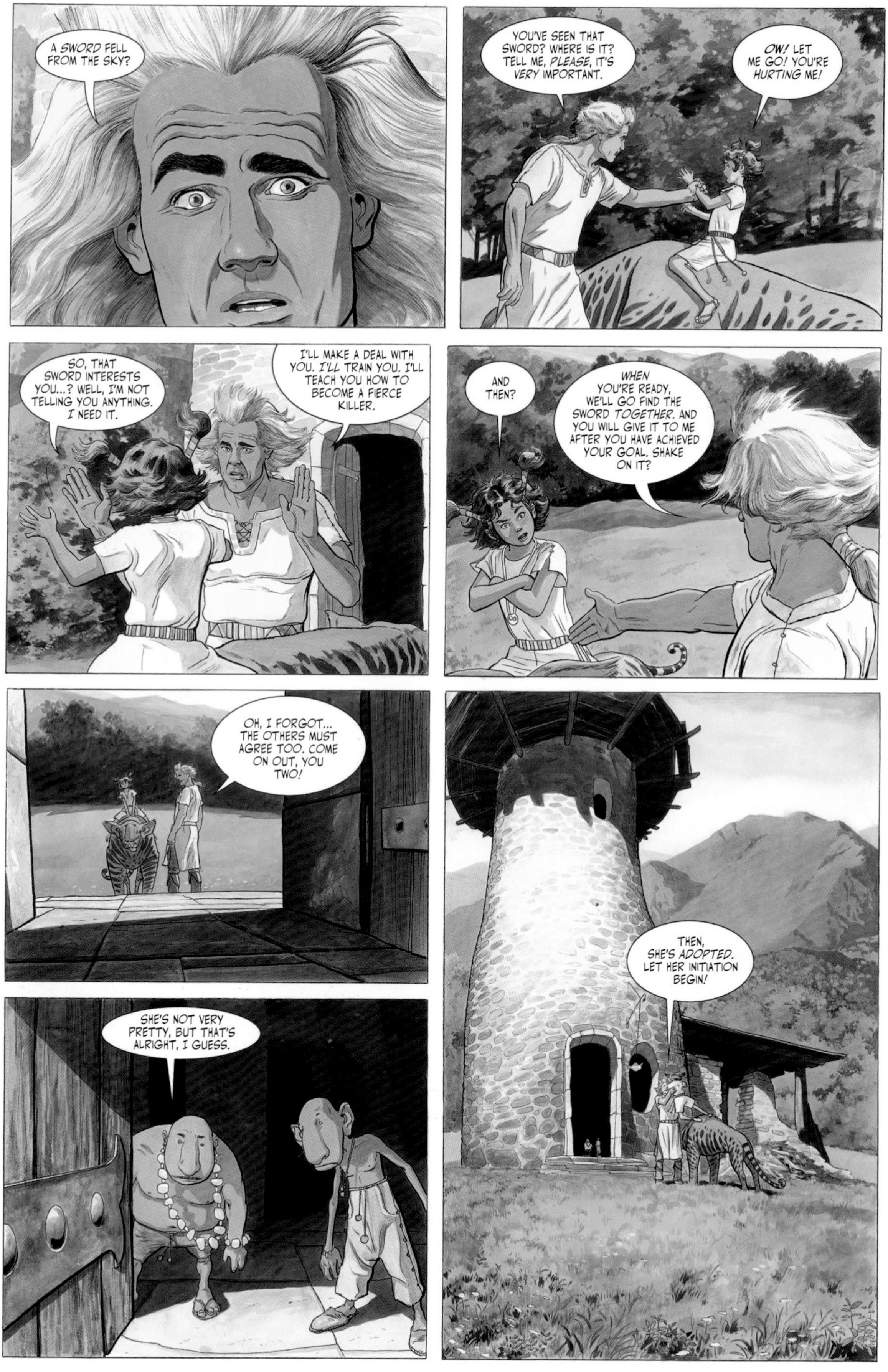
A SWORD FELL FROM THE SKY?
YOU'VE SEEN THAT SWORD? WHERE IS IT? TELL ME, PLEASE, IT'S VERY IMPORTANT.
OW! LET ME GO! YOU'RE HURTING ME!
SO, THAT SWORD INTERESTS YOU...? WELL, I'M NOT TELLING YOU ANYTHING. I NEED IT.
I'LL MAKE A DEAL WITH YOU. I'LL TRAIN YOU. I'LL TEACH YOU HOW TO BECOME A FIERCE KILLER.
AND THEN?
WHEN YOU'RE READY, WE'LL GO FIND THE SWORD TOGETHER. AND YOU WILL GIVE IT TO ME AFTER YOU HAVE ACHIEVED YOUR GOAL. SHAKE ON IT?
OH, I FORGOT... THE OTHERS MUST AGREE TOO. COME ON OUT, YOU TWO!
SHE'S NOT VERY PRETTY, BUT THAT'S ALRIGHT, I GUESS.
THEN, SHE'S ADOPTED. LET HER INITIATION BEGIN!

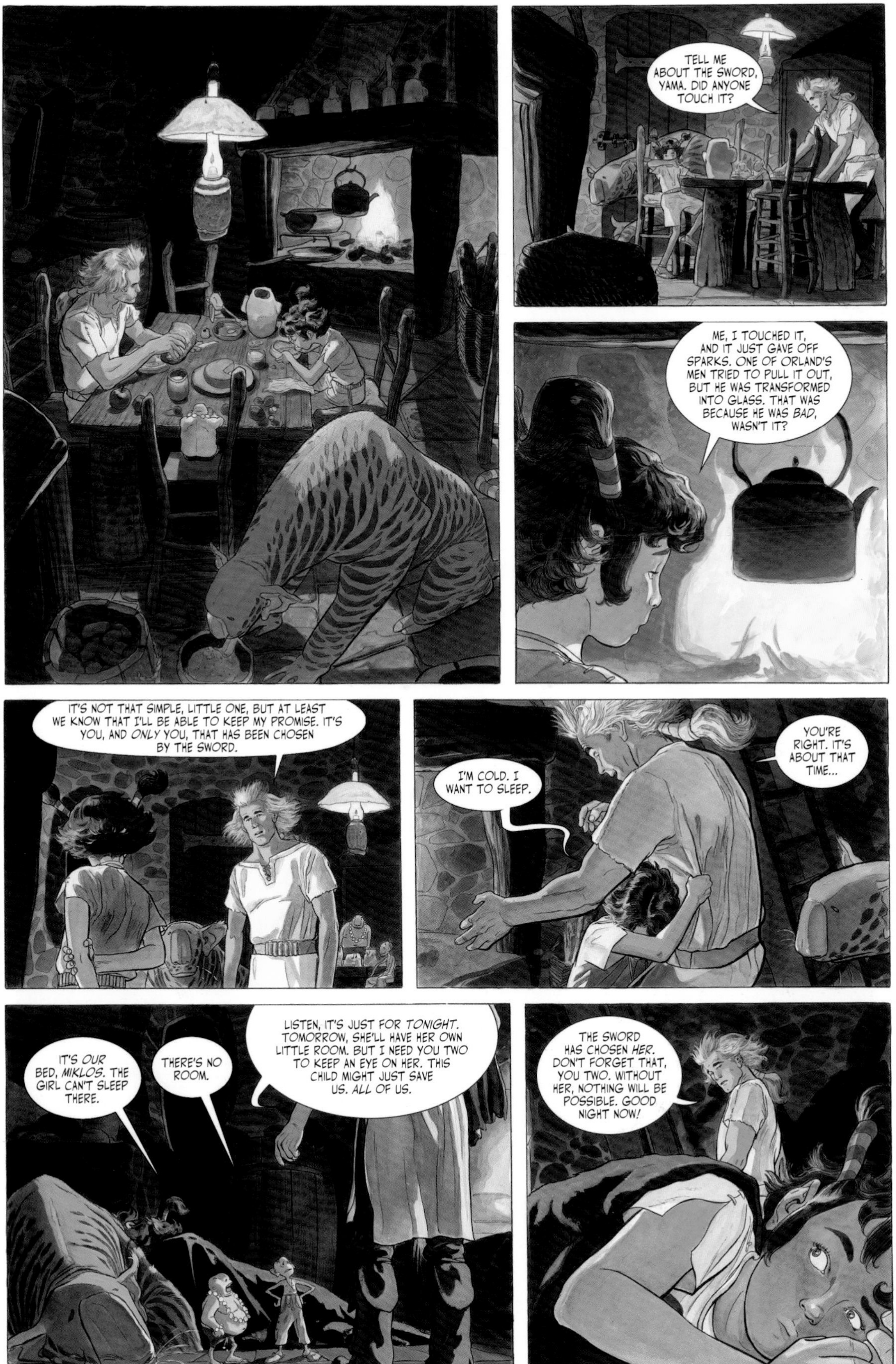
TELL ME ABOUT THE SWORD, YAMA. DID ANYONE TOUCH IT?
ME, I TOUCHED IT, AND IT JUST GAVE OFF SPARKS. ONE OF ORLAND'S MEN TRIED TO PULL IT OUT, BUT HE WAS TRANSFORMED INTO GLASS. THAT WAS BECAUSE HE WAS *BAD*, WASN'T IT?
IT'S NOT THAT SIMPLE, LITTLE ONE, BUT AT LEAST WE KNOW THAT I'LL BE ABLE TO KEEP MY PROMISE. IT'S YOU, AND *ONLY* YOU, THAT HAS BEEN CHOSEN BY THE SWORD.
I'M COLD. I WANT TO SLEEP.
YOU'RE RIGHT. IT'S ABOUT THAT TIME...
IT'S *OUR* BED, *MIKLOS*. THE GIRL CAN'T SLEEP THERE.
THERE'S NO ROOM.
LISTEN, IT'S JUST FOR *TONIGHT*. TOMORROW, SHE'LL HAVE HER OWN LITTLE ROOM. BUT I NEED YOU TWO TO KEEP AN EYE ON HER. THIS CHILD MIGHT JUST SAVE US. *ALL* OF US.
THE SWORD HAS CHOSEN *HER*. DON'T FORGET THAT, YOU TWO. WITHOUT HER, NOTHING WILL BE POSSIBLE. GOOD NIGHT NOW!

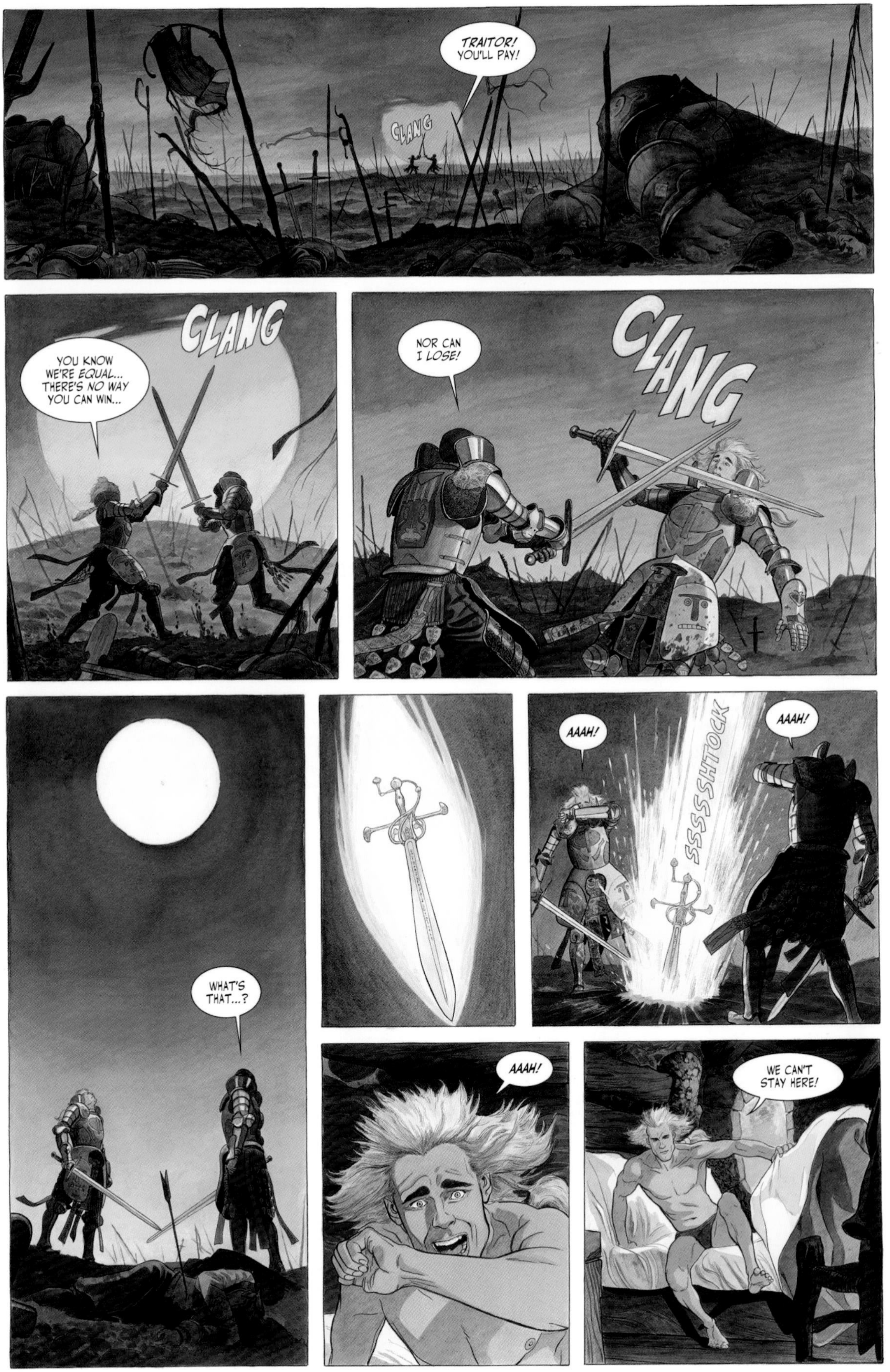

TRAITOR! YOU'LL PAY!
CLANG
YOU KNOW WE'RE EQUAL... THERE'S NO WAY YOU CAN WIN...
CLANG
NOR CAN I LOSE!
CLANG
WHAT'S THAT...?
AAAH!
SSSSSHTOCK
AAAH!
AAAH!
WE CAN'T STAY HERE!

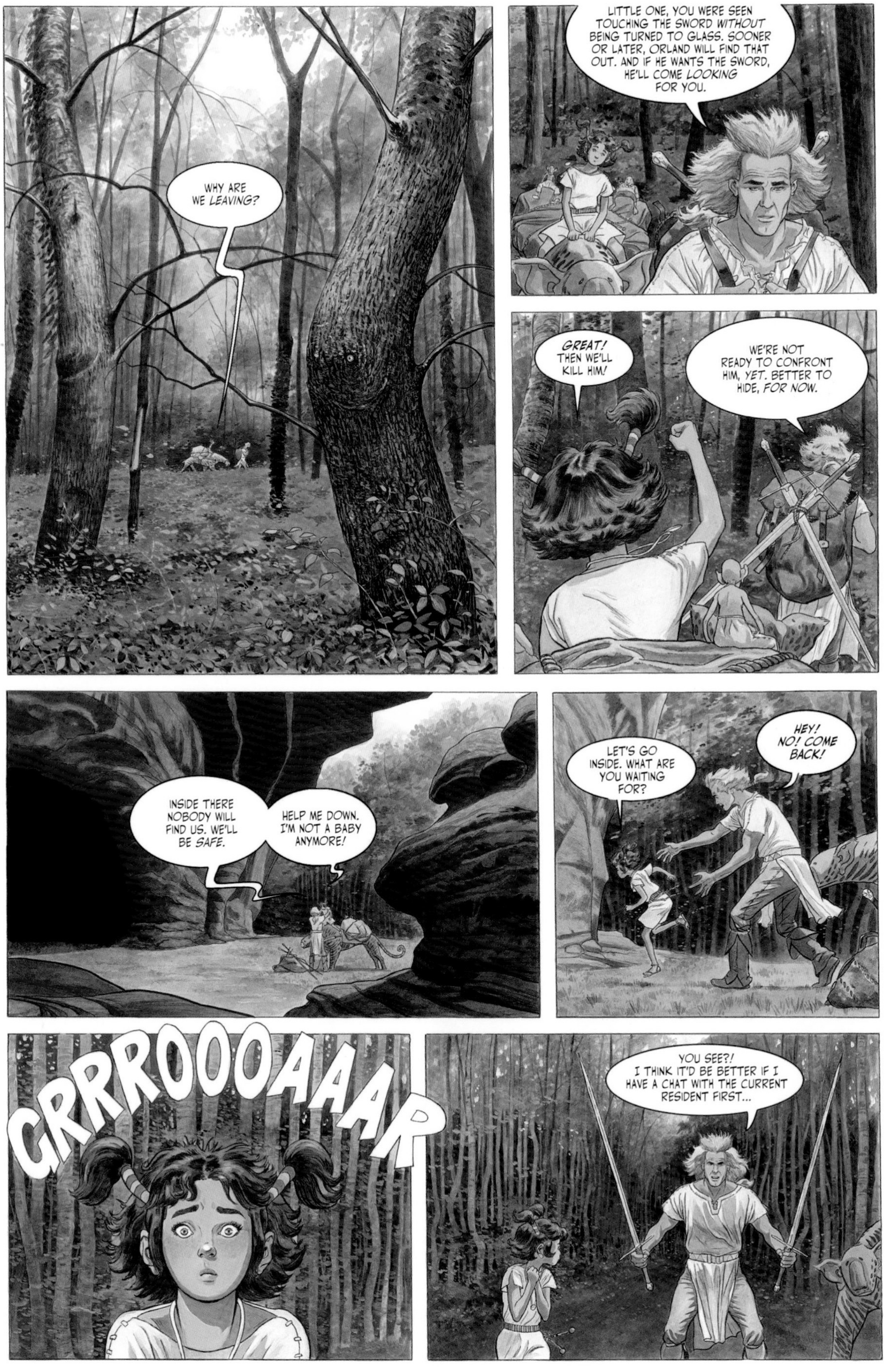
WHY ARE WE *LEAVING?*
LITTLE ONE, YOU WERE SEEN TOUCHING THE SWORD *WITHOUT* BEING TURNED TO GLASS. SOONER OR LATER, ORLAND WILL FIND THAT OUT. AND IF HE WANTS THE SWORD, HE'LL COME *LOOKING* FOR YOU.
GREAT! THEN WE'LL KILL HIM!
WE'RE NOT READY TO CONFRONT HIM, *YET*. BETTER TO HIDE, *FOR NOW*.
INSIDE THERE NOBODY WILL FIND US. WE'LL BE *SAFE*.
HELP ME DOWN. I'M NOT A BABY ANYMORE!
LET'S GO INSIDE. WHAT ARE YOU WAITING FOR?
HEY! NO! COME BACK!
GRRROOOAAAR
YOU SEE?! I THINK IT'D BE BETTER IF I HAVE A CHAT WITH THE CURRENT RESIDENT FIRST...

GROOOAAARR

WE CAN FIND SHELTER ELSEWHERE!

STAND BACK, LITTLE ONE, AND *WATCH!* FOR FIVE YEARS, I'VE BEEN ITCHING TO KICK THIS BIG BLOCKHEAD'S BUTT!

WATCH CLOSELY, YAMA, THIS IS YOUR FIRST LESSON ON HOW TO TRIM THE BEARD OF A MONSTER!

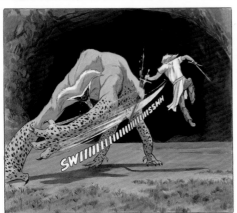

SWIIIIIIIIISSHH

FROO?

PEEK-A-BOO! HERE I AM!

HAH!

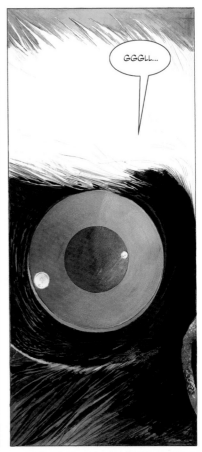

GGGLL...

OUFF! HE'S A REAL HEAVYWEIGHT! COME ON, EVERYBODY, WE'RE MOVING IN. WE JUST SCORED *FOOD* FOR THE WHOLE WINTER.

WOW! YOU'RE A REAL HUNTER! MY DAD COULDN'T HAVE DONE BETTER!

YOU'LL SEE. IT'S *DELICIOUS.*

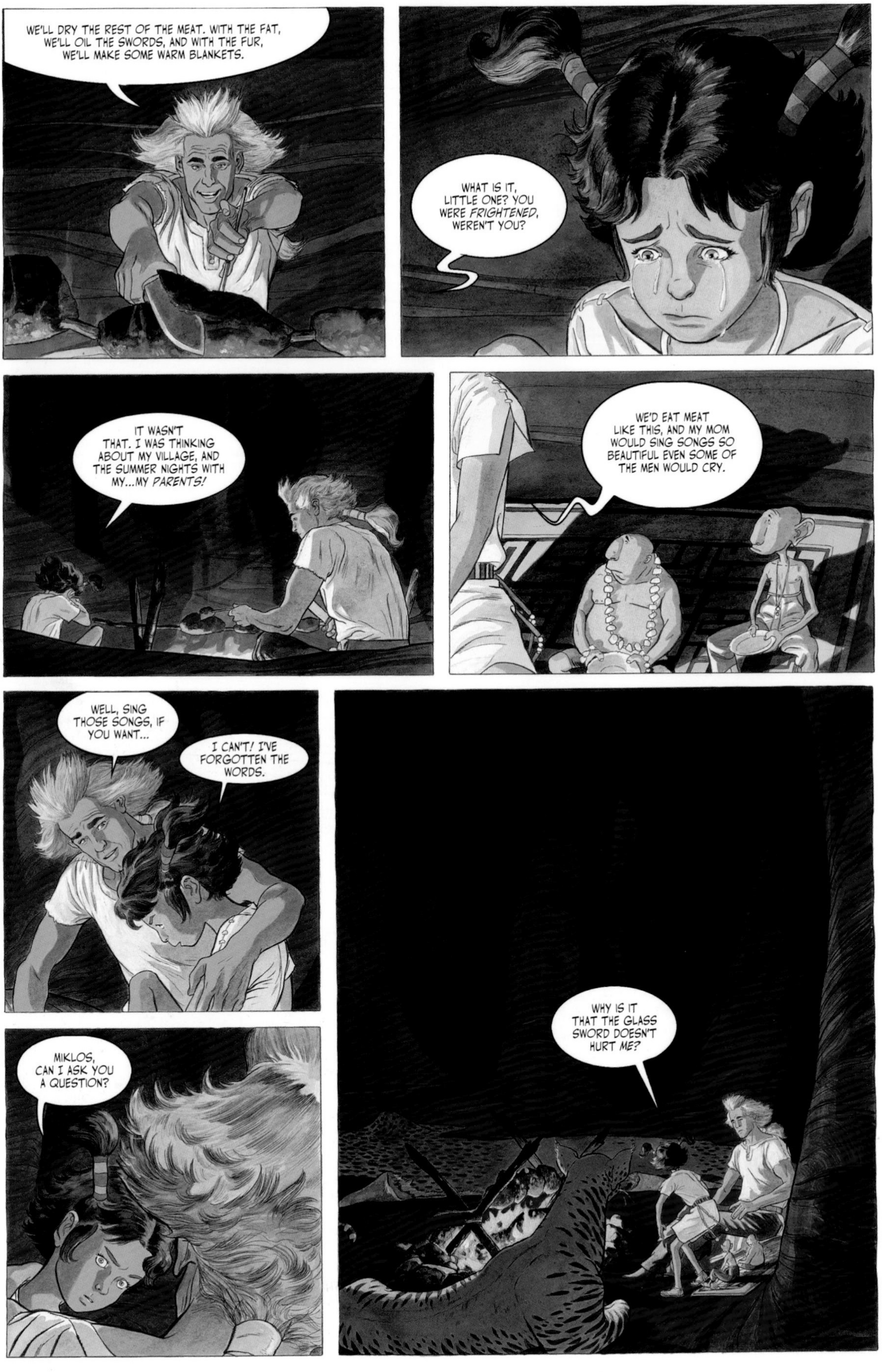
WE'LL DRY THE REST OF THE MEAT. WITH THE FAT, WE'LL OIL THE SWORDS, AND WITH THE FUR, WE'LL MAKE SOME WARM BLANKETS.
WHAT IS IT, LITTLE ONE? YOU WERE FRIGHTENED, WEREN'T YOU?
IT WASN'T THAT. I WAS THINKING ABOUT MY VILLAGE, AND THE SUMMER NIGHTS WITH MY...MY PARENTS!
WE'D EAT MEAT LIKE THIS, AND MY MOM WOULD SING SONGS SO BEAUTIFUL EVEN SOME OF THE MEN WOULD CRY.
WELL, SING THOSE SONGS, IF YOU WANT...
I CAN'T! I'VE FORGOTTEN THE WORDS.
MIKLOS, CAN I ASK YOU A QUESTION?
WHY IS IT THAT THE GLASS SWORD DOESN'T HURT ME?

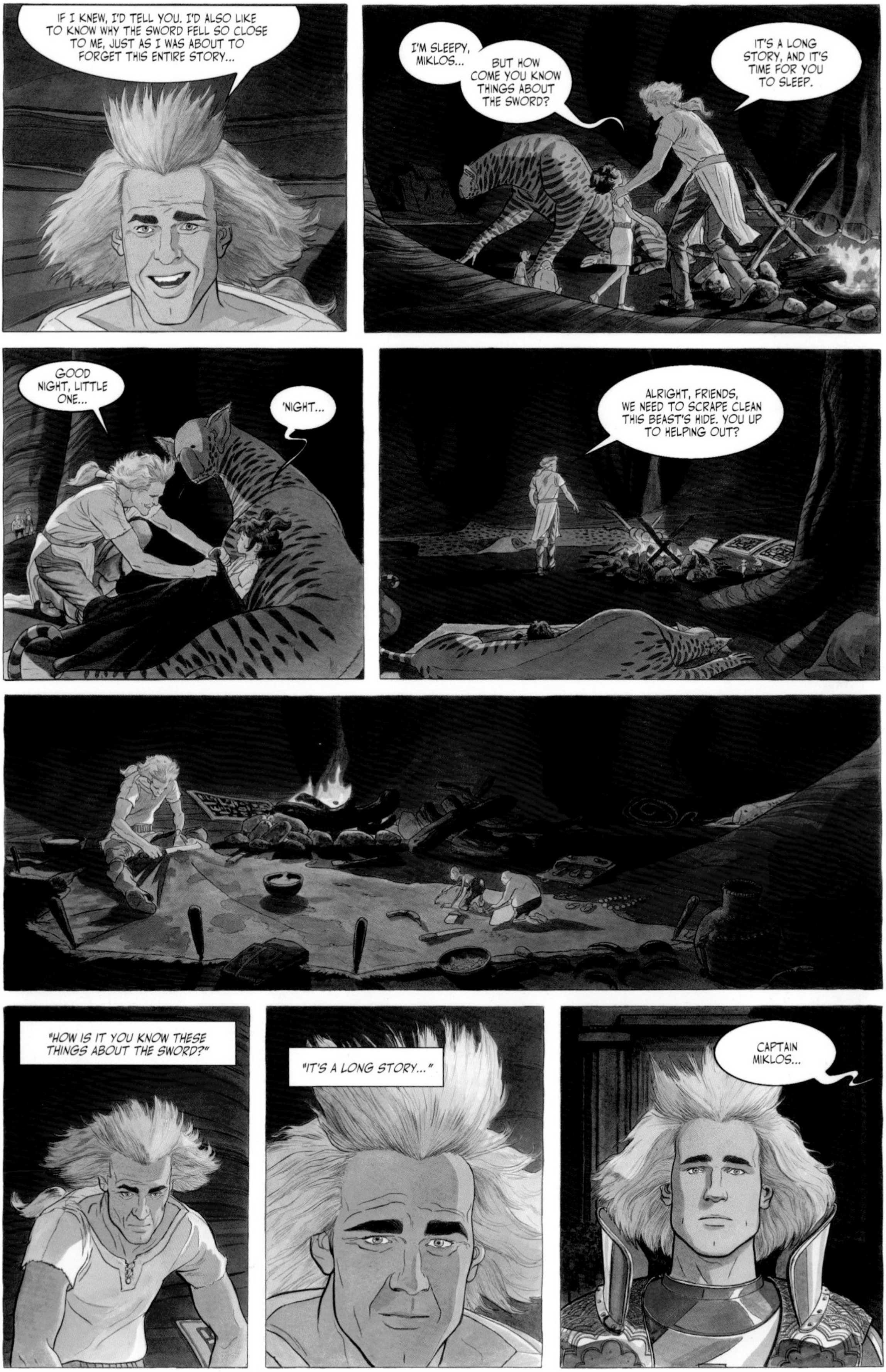
IF I KNEW, I'D TELL YOU. I'D ALSO LIKE TO KNOW WHY THE SWORD FELL SO CLOSE TO ME, JUST AS I WAS ABOUT TO FORGET THIS ENTIRE STORY...
I'M SLEEPY, MIKLOS...
BUT HOW COME YOU KNOW THINGS ABOUT THE SWORD?
IT'S A LONG STORY, AND IT'S TIME FOR YOU TO SLEEP.
GOOD NIGHT, LITTLE ONE...
'NIGHT...
ALRIGHT, FRIENDS, WE NEED TO SCRAPE CLEAN THIS BEAST'S HIDE. YOU UP TO HELPING OUT?
"HOW IS IT YOU KNOW THESE THINGS ABOUT THE SWORD?"
"IT'S A LONG STORY..."
CAPTAIN MIKLOS...

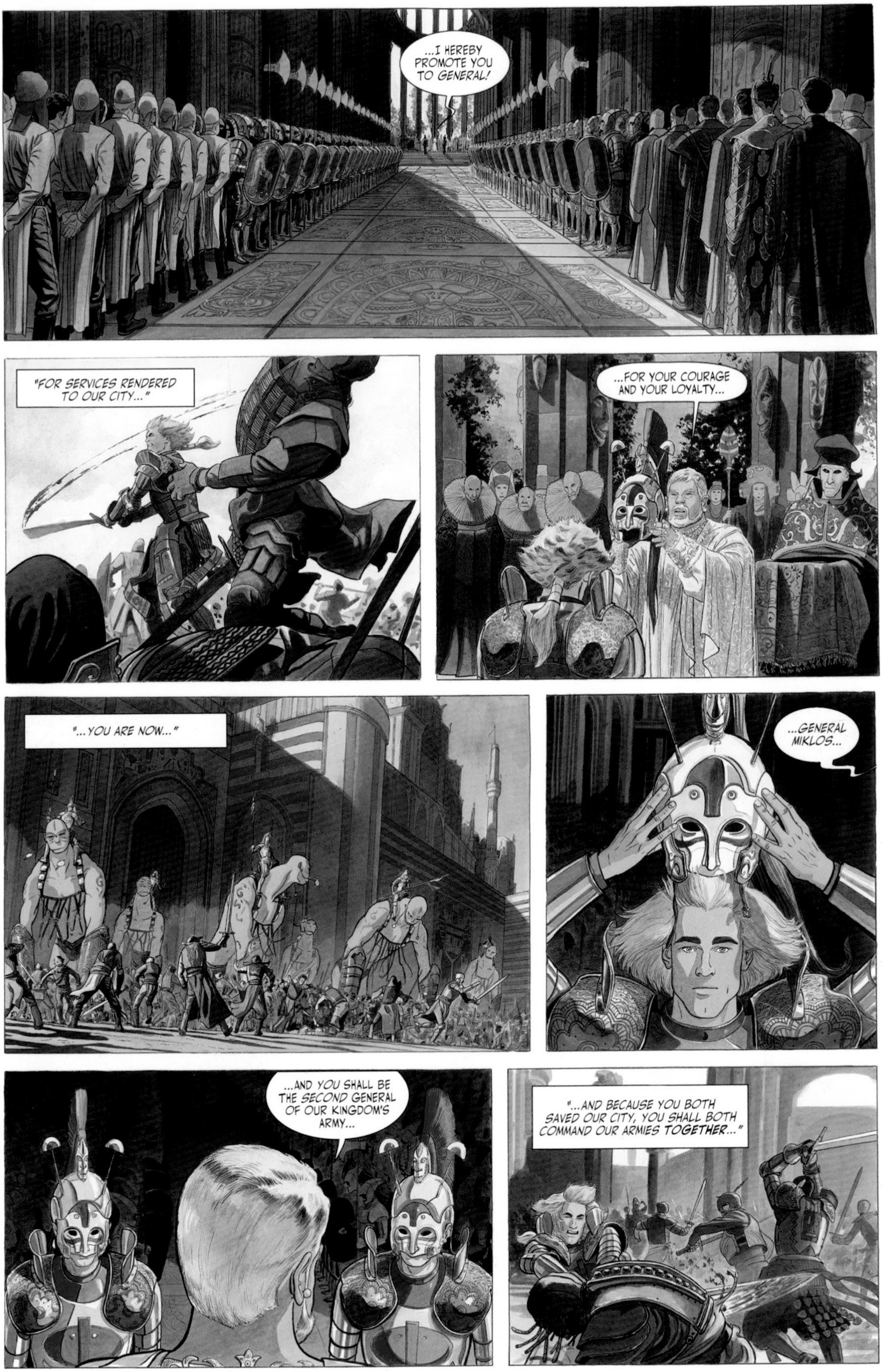
...I HEREBY PROMOTE YOU TO GENERAL!
"FOR SERVICES RENDERED TO OUR CITY..."
...FOR YOUR COURAGE AND YOUR LOYALTY...
"...YOU ARE NOW..."
...GENERAL MIKLOS...
...AND YOU SHALL BE THE SECOND GENERAL OF OUR KINGDOM'S ARMY...
"...AND BECAUSE YOU BOTH SAVED OUR CITY, YOU SHALL BOTH COMMAND OUR ARMIES TOGETHER..."

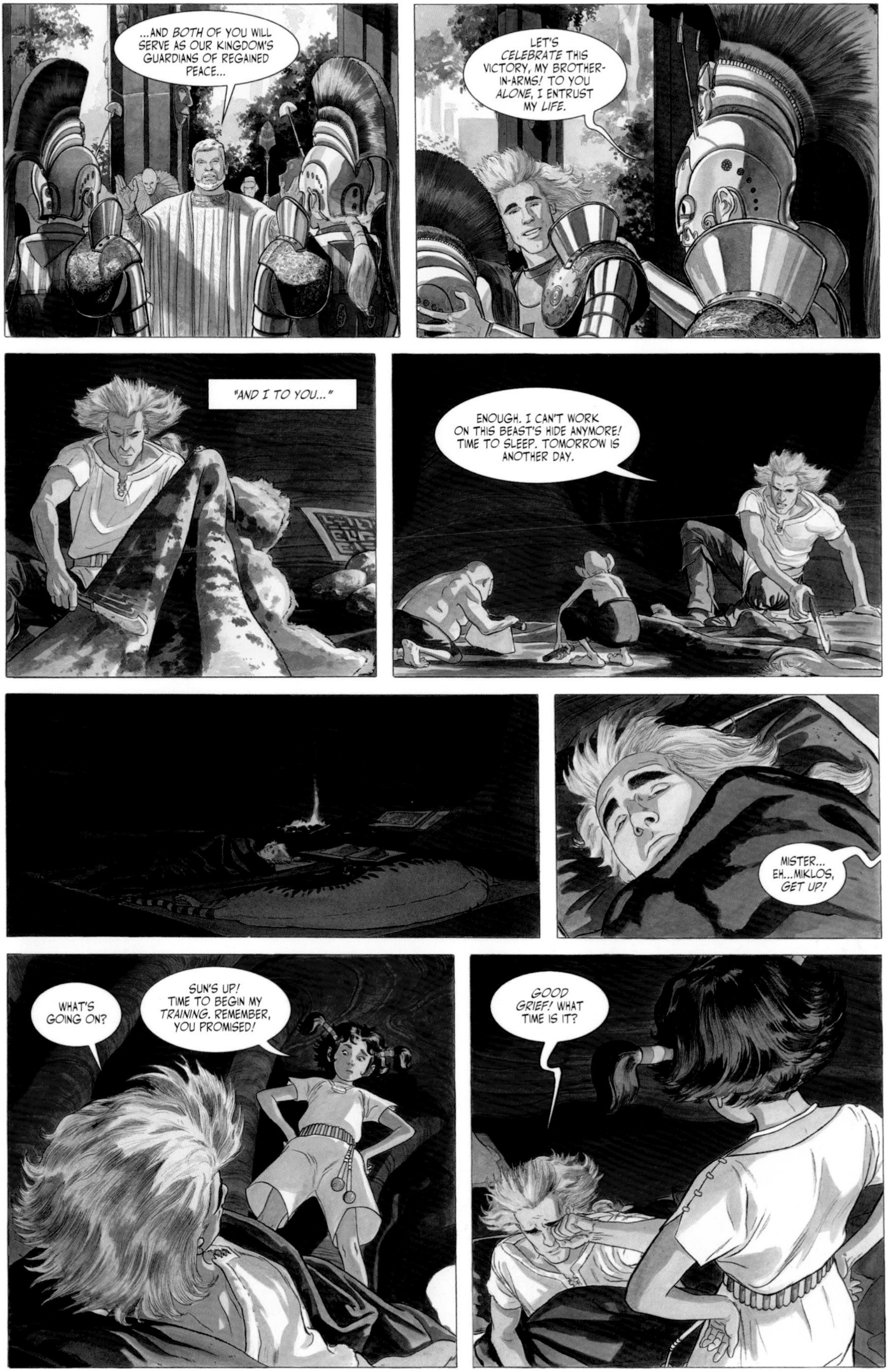
...AND BOTH OF YOU WILL SERVE AS OUR KINGDOM'S GUARDIANS OF REGAINED PEACE...
LET'S CELEBRATE THIS VICTORY, MY BROTHER-IN-ARMS! TO YOU ALONE, I ENTRUST MY LIFE.
"AND I TO YOU..."
ENOUGH. I CAN'T WORK ON THIS BEAST'S HIDE ANYMORE! TIME TO SLEEP. TOMORROW IS ANOTHER DAY.
MISTER... EH...MIKLOS, GET UP!
WHAT'S GOING ON?
SUN'S UP! TIME TO BEGIN MY TRAINING. REMEMBER, YOU PROMISED!
GOOD GRIEF! WHAT TIME IS IT?

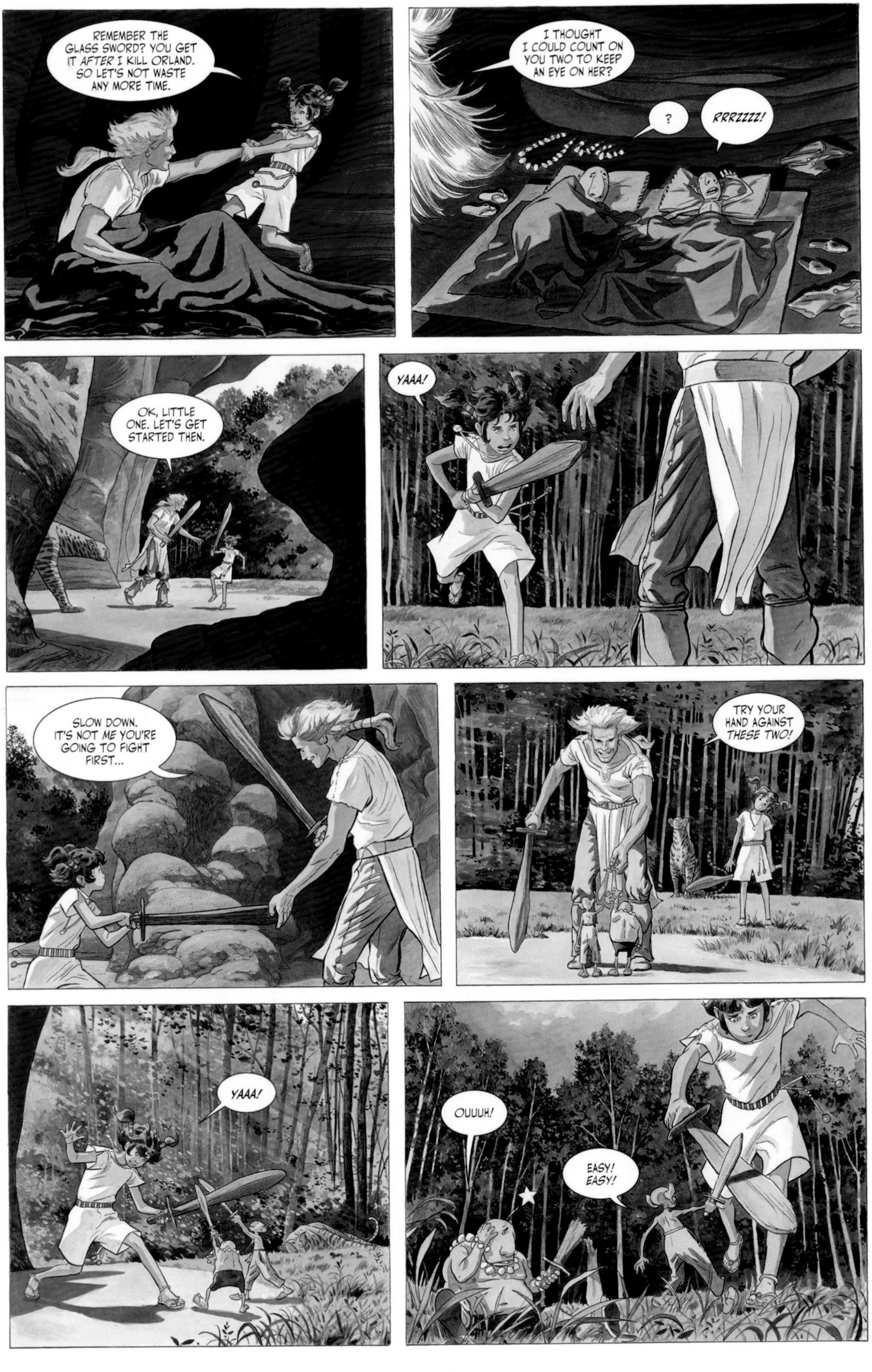

REMEMBER THE GLASS SWORD? YOU GET IT *AFTER* I KILL ORLAND. SO LET'S NOT WASTE ANY MORE TIME.
I THOUGHT I COULD COUNT ON YOU TWO TO KEEP AN EYE ON HER?
?
RRRZZZZZ!
OK, LITTLE ONE. LET'S GET STARTED THEN.
YAAA!
SLOW DOWN. IT'S NOT ME YOU'RE GOING TO FIGHT FIRST...
TRY YOUR HAND AGAINST *THESE TWO!*
YAAA!
OUUUH!
EASY! EASY!

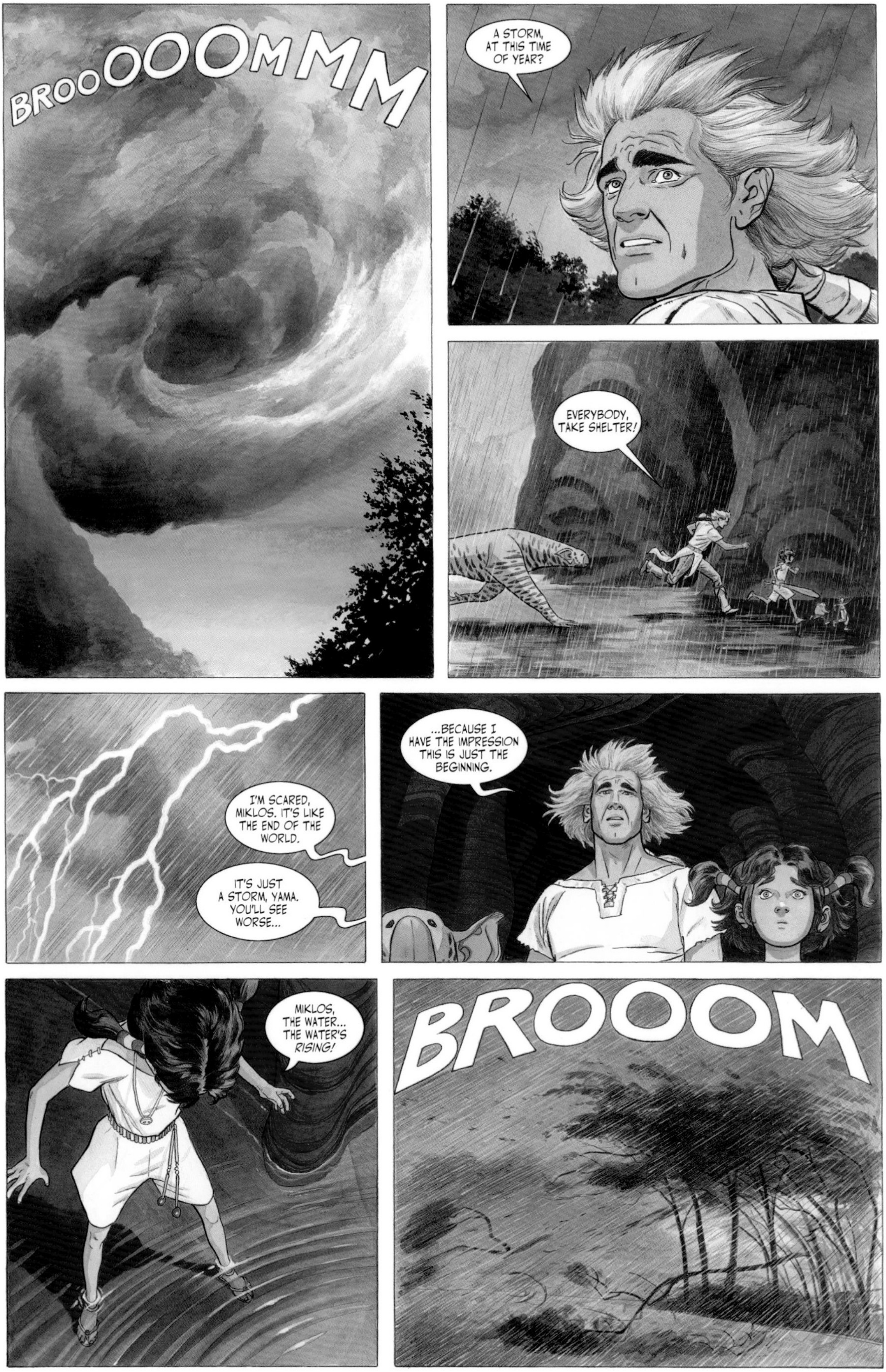
BROOOOOMMMM
A STORM, AT THIS TIME OF YEAR?
EVERYBODY, TAKE SHELTER!
I'M SCARED, MIKLOS. IT'S LIKE THE END OF THE WORLD.
IT'S JUST A STORM, YAMA. YOU'LL SEE WORSE...
...BECAUSE I HAVE THE IMPRESSION THIS IS JUST THE BEGINNING.
MIKLOS... THE WATER... THE WATER'S *RISING!*
BROOOM

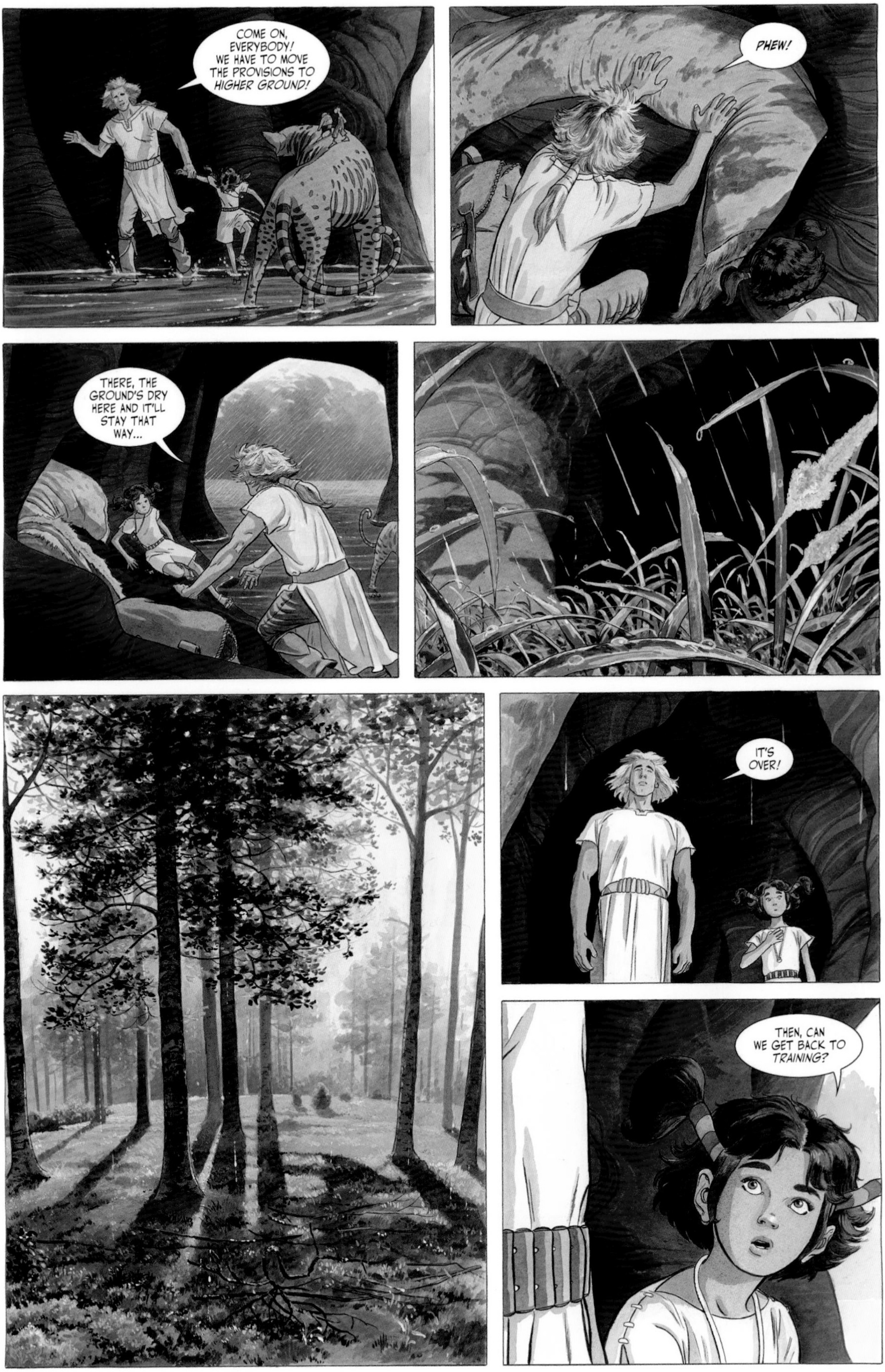

COME ON, EVERYBODY! WE HAVE TO MOVE THE PROVISIONS TO HIGHER GROUND!
PHEW!
THERE, THE GROUND'S DRY HERE AND IT'LL STAY THAT WAY...
IT'S OVER!
THEN, CAN WE GET BACK TO TRAINING?

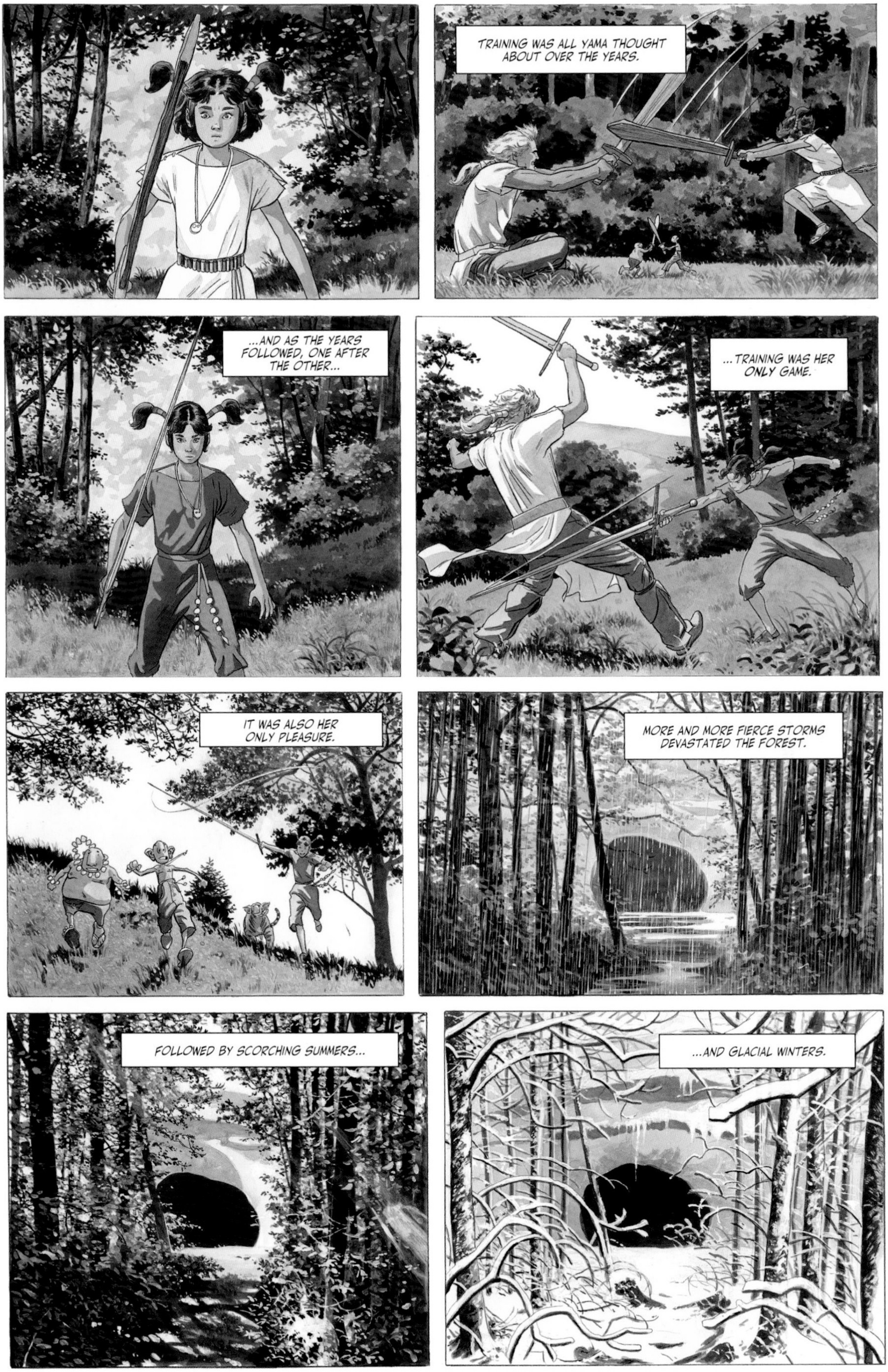
TRAINING WAS ALL YAMA THOUGHT ABOUT OVER THE YEARS.
...AND AS THE YEARS FOLLOWED, ONE AFTER THE OTHER...
...TRAINING WAS HER ONLY GAME.
IT WAS ALSO HER ONLY PLEASURE.
MORE AND MORE FIERCE STORMS DEVASTATED THE FOREST.
FOLLOWED BY SCORCHING SUMMERS...
...AND GLACIAL WINTERS.

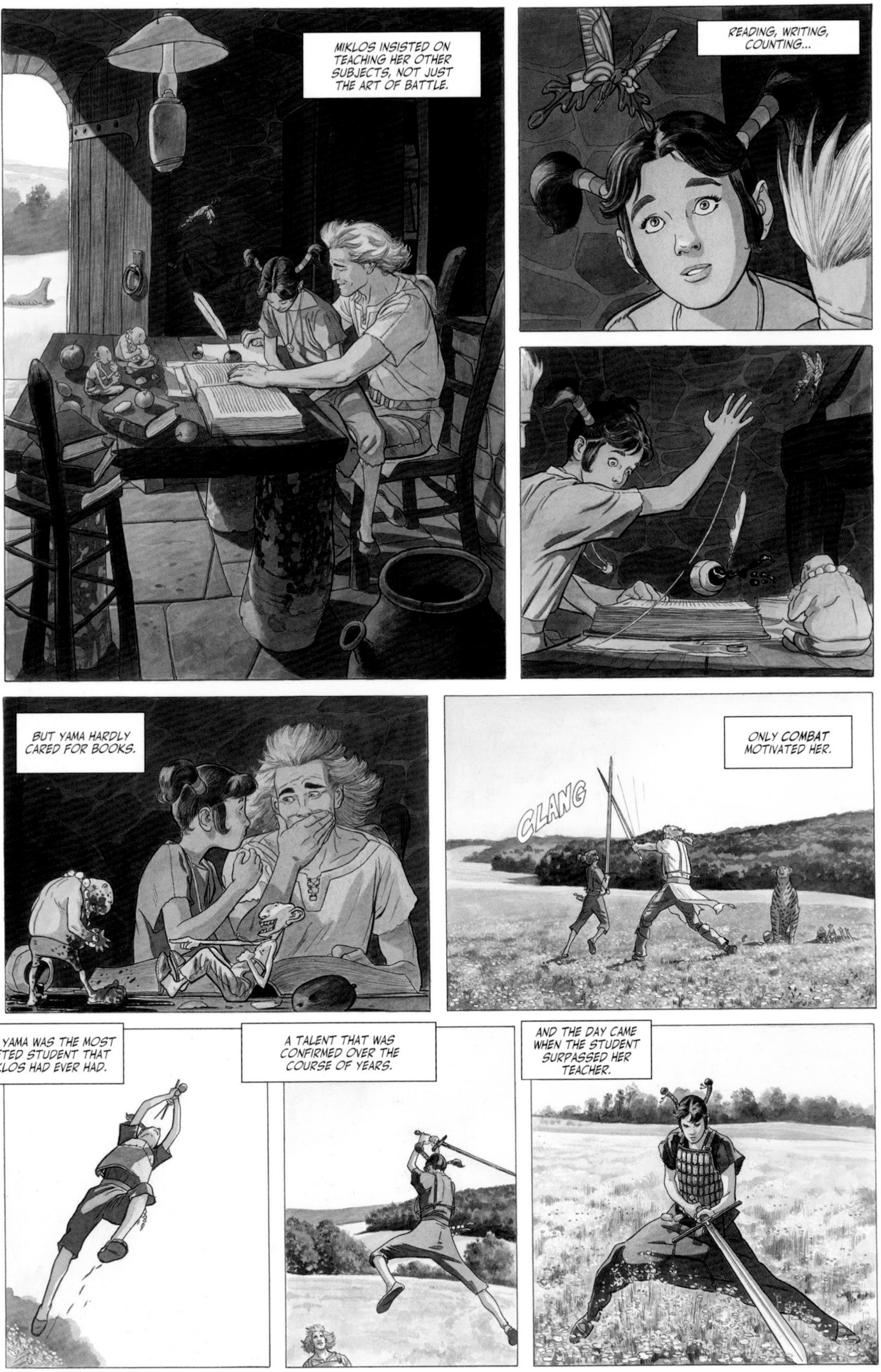
MIKLOS INSISTED ON TEACHING HER OTHER SUBJECTS, NOT JUST THE ART OF BATTLE.
READING, WRITING, COUNTING...
BUT YAMA HARDLY CARED FOR BOOKS.
ONLY COMBAT MOTIVATED HER.
CLANG
AND YAMA WAS THE MOST GIFTED STUDENT THAT MIKLOS HAD EVER HAD.
A TALENT THAT WAS CONFIRMED OVER THE COURSE OF YEARS.
AND THE DAY CAME WHEN THE STUDENT SURPASSED HER TEACHER.

ALTHOUGH MANY MONTHS PASSED BEFORE THE TEACHER COULD FINALLY ADMIT IT.

HA!

STOCK

AAH!

YOU'RE BEATEN! ADMIT IT!

HA! HA!

THERE'S STILL *ONE* MORE LESSON YOU HAVE TO LEARN!

OH!

I TOLD YOU BEFORE, NOT TO WASTE TIME TALKING. IT'S *YOU* THAT GETS TO DECIDE WHETHER YOU WON OR NOT. NEVER ASK YOUR ADVERSARY!

BROOUUMM

LET'S HEAD BACK. WEATHER'S GETTING UGLY!

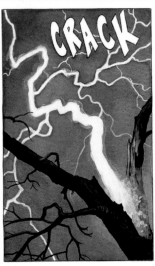

CRACK

THEY'RE COMING TOO OFTEN NOW. WE'RE NOT GOING TO BE ABLE TO WAIT MUCH LONGER.

WHAT DO YOU MEAN?

WE LEAVE TOMORROW TO FIND THE SWORD.

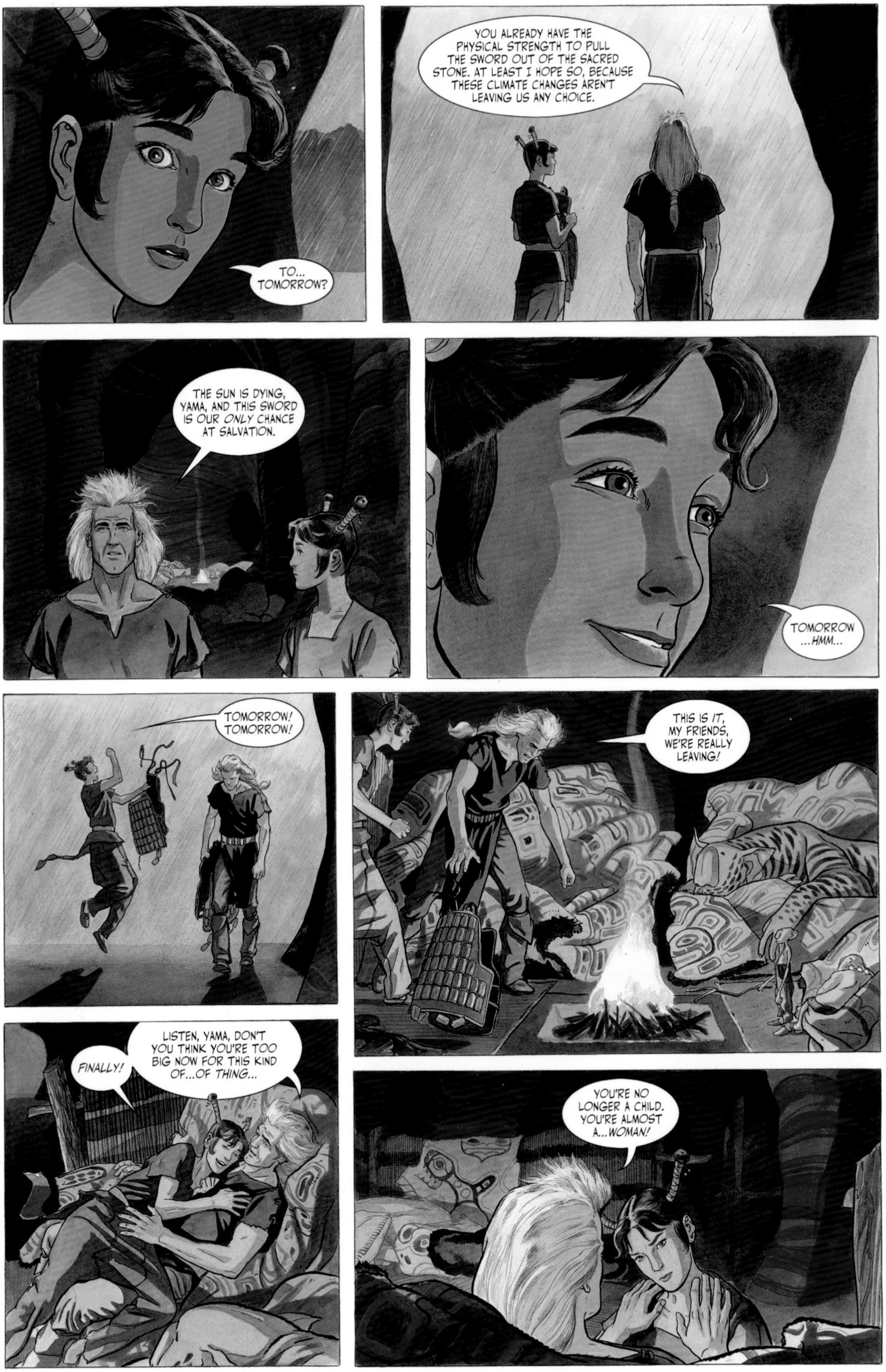
TO... TOMORROW?
YOU ALREADY HAVE THE PHYSICAL STRENGTH TO PULL THE SWORD OUT OF THE SACRED STONE. AT LEAST I HOPE SO, BECAUSE THESE CLIMATE CHANGES AREN'T LEAVING US ANY CHOICE.
THE SUN IS DYING, YAMA, AND THIS SWORD IS OUR ONLY CHANCE AT SALVATION.
TOMORROW ...HMM...
TOMORROW! TOMORROW!
THIS IS IT, MY FRIENDS, WE'RE REALLY LEAVING!
FINALLY!
LISTEN, YAMA, DON'T YOU THINK YOU'RE TOO BIG NOW FOR THIS KIND OF...OF THING...
YOU'RE NO LONGER A CHILD. YOU'RE ALMOST A...WOMAN!

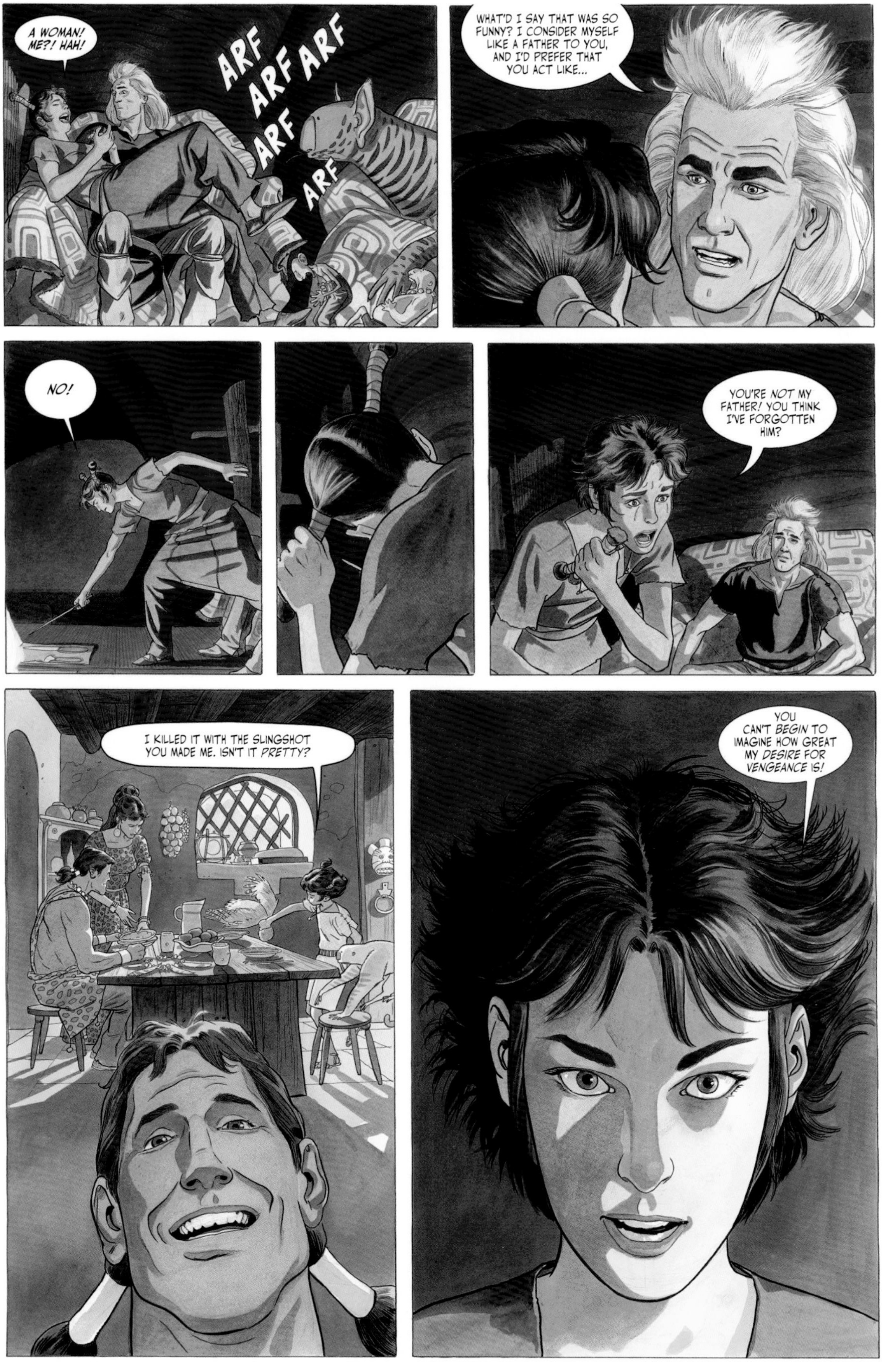
A WOMAN! ME?! HAH!
ARF ARF ARF ARF ARF
WHAT'D I SAY THAT WAS SO FUNNY? I CONSIDER MYSELF LIKE A FATHER TO YOU, AND I'D PREFER THAT YOU ACT LIKE...
NO!
YOU'RE NOT MY FATHER! YOU THINK I'VE FORGOTTEN HIM?
I KILLED IT WITH THE SLINGSHOT YOU MADE ME. ISN'T IT PRETTY?
YOU CAN'T BEGIN TO IMAGINE HOW GREAT MY DESIRE FOR VENGEANCE IS!

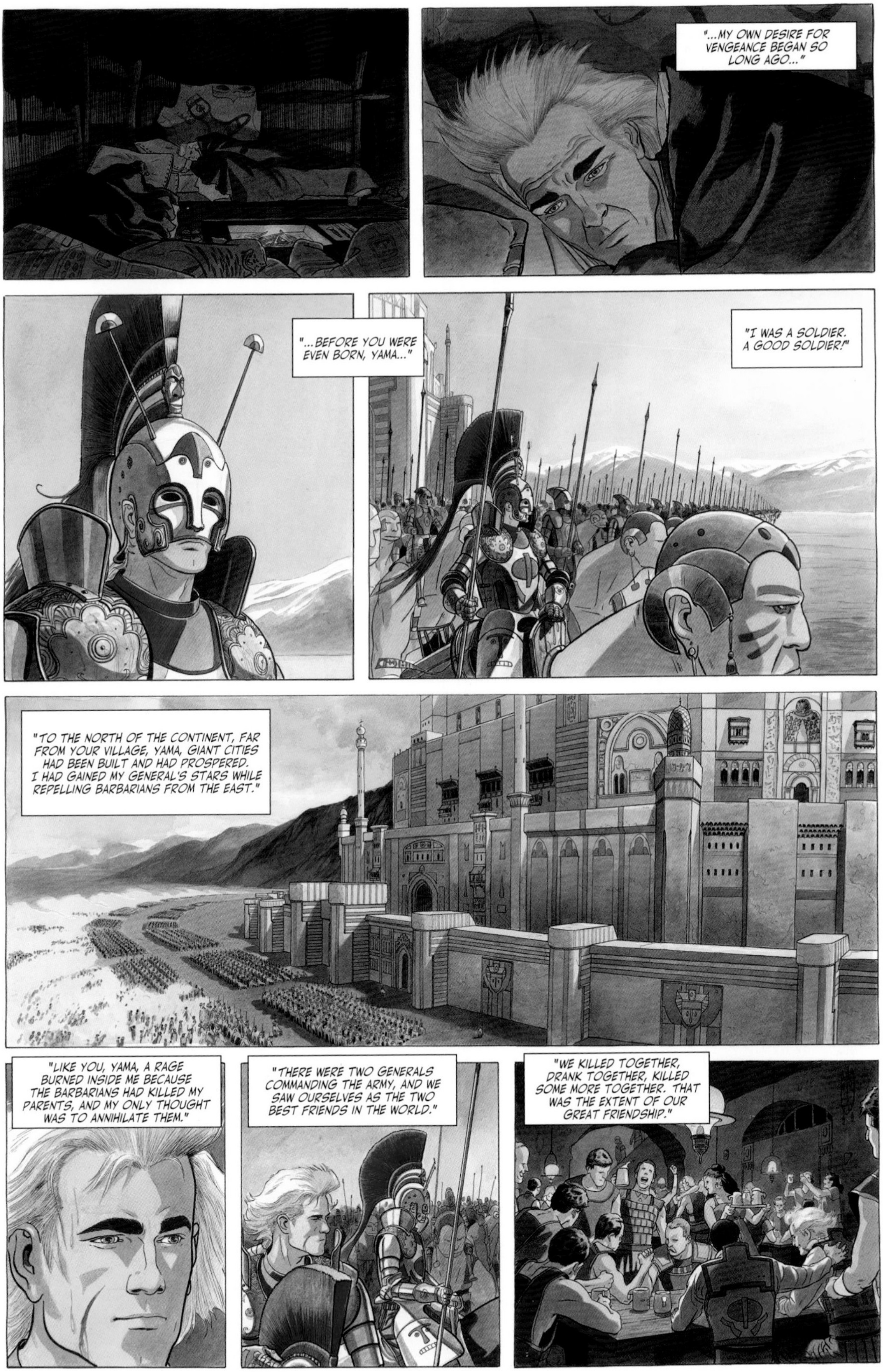
"...MY OWN DESIRE FOR VENGEANCE BEGAN SO LONG AGO..."
"...BEFORE YOU WERE EVEN BORN, YAMA..."
"I WAS A SOLDIER. A GOOD SOLDIER."
"TO THE NORTH OF THE CONTINENT, FAR FROM YOUR VILLAGE, YAMA, GIANT CITIES HAD BEEN BUILT AND HAD PROSPERED. I HAD GAINED MY GENERAL'S STARS WHILE REPELLING BARBARIANS FROM THE EAST."
"LIKE YOU, YAMA, A RAGE BURNED INSIDE ME BECAUSE THE BARBARIANS HAD KILLED MY PARENTS, AND MY ONLY THOUGHT WAS TO ANNIHILATE THEM."
"THERE WERE TWO GENERALS COMMANDING THE ARMY, AND WE SAW OURSELVES AS THE TWO BEST FRIENDS IN THE WORLD."
"WE KILLED TOGETHER, DRANK TOGETHER, KILLED SOME MORE TOGETHER. THAT WAS THE EXTENT OF OUR GREAT FRIENDSHIP."

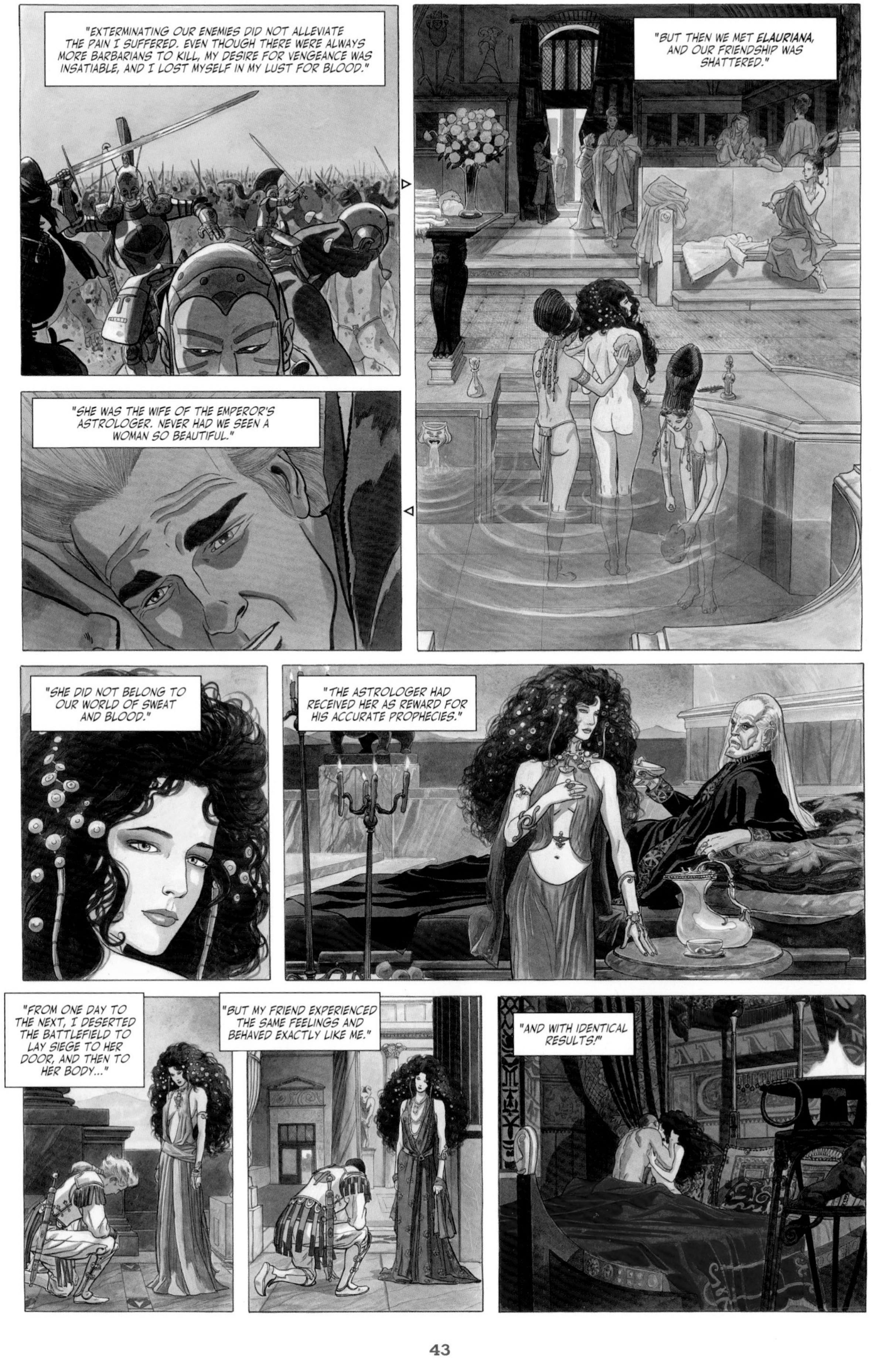
"EXTERMINATING OUR ENEMIES DID NOT ALLEVIATE THE PAIN I SUFFERED. EVEN THOUGH THERE WERE ALWAYS MORE BARBARIANS TO KILL, MY DESIRE FOR VENGEANCE WAS INSATIABLE, AND I LOST MYSELF IN MY LUST FOR BLOOD."
"BUT THEN WE MET ELAURIANA, AND OUR FRIENDSHIP WAS SHATTERED."
"SHE WAS THE WIFE OF THE EMPEROR'S ASTROLOGER. NEVER HAD WE SEEN A WOMAN SO BEAUTIFUL."
"SHE DID NOT BELONG TO OUR WORLD OF SWEAT AND BLOOD."
"THE ASTROLOGER HAD RECEIVED HER AS REWARD FOR HIS ACCURATE PROPHECIES."
"FROM ONE DAY TO THE NEXT, I DESERTED THE BATTLEFIELD TO LAY SIEGE TO HER DOOR, AND THEN TO HER BODY..."
"BUT MY FRIEND EXPERIENCED THE SAME FEELINGS AND BEHAVED EXACTLY LIKE ME."
"AND WITH IDENTICAL RESULTS!"

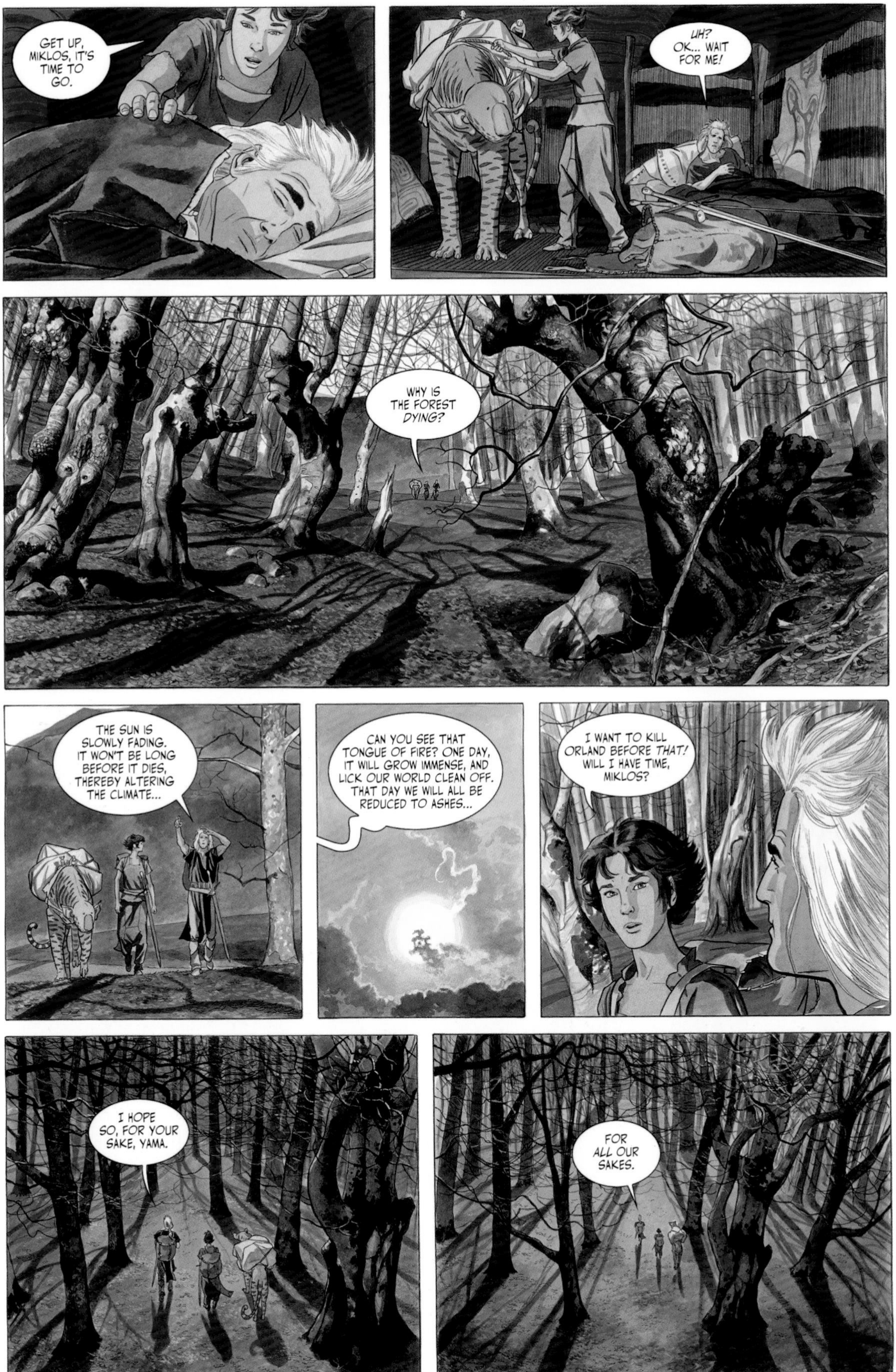
GET UP, MIKLOS, IT'S TIME TO GO.
UH? OK... WAIT FOR ME!
WHY IS THE FOREST DYING?
THE SUN IS SLOWLY FADING. IT WON'T BE LONG BEFORE IT DIES, THEREBY ALTERING THE CLIMATE...
CAN YOU SEE THAT TONGUE OF FIRE? ONE DAY, IT WILL GROW IMMENSE, AND LICK OUR WORLD CLEAN OFF. THAT DAY WE WILL ALL BE REDUCED TO ASHES...
I WANT TO KILL ORLAND BEFORE THAT! WILL I HAVE TIME, MIKLOS?
I HOPE SO, FOR YOUR SAKE, YAMA.
FOR ALL OUR SAKES.

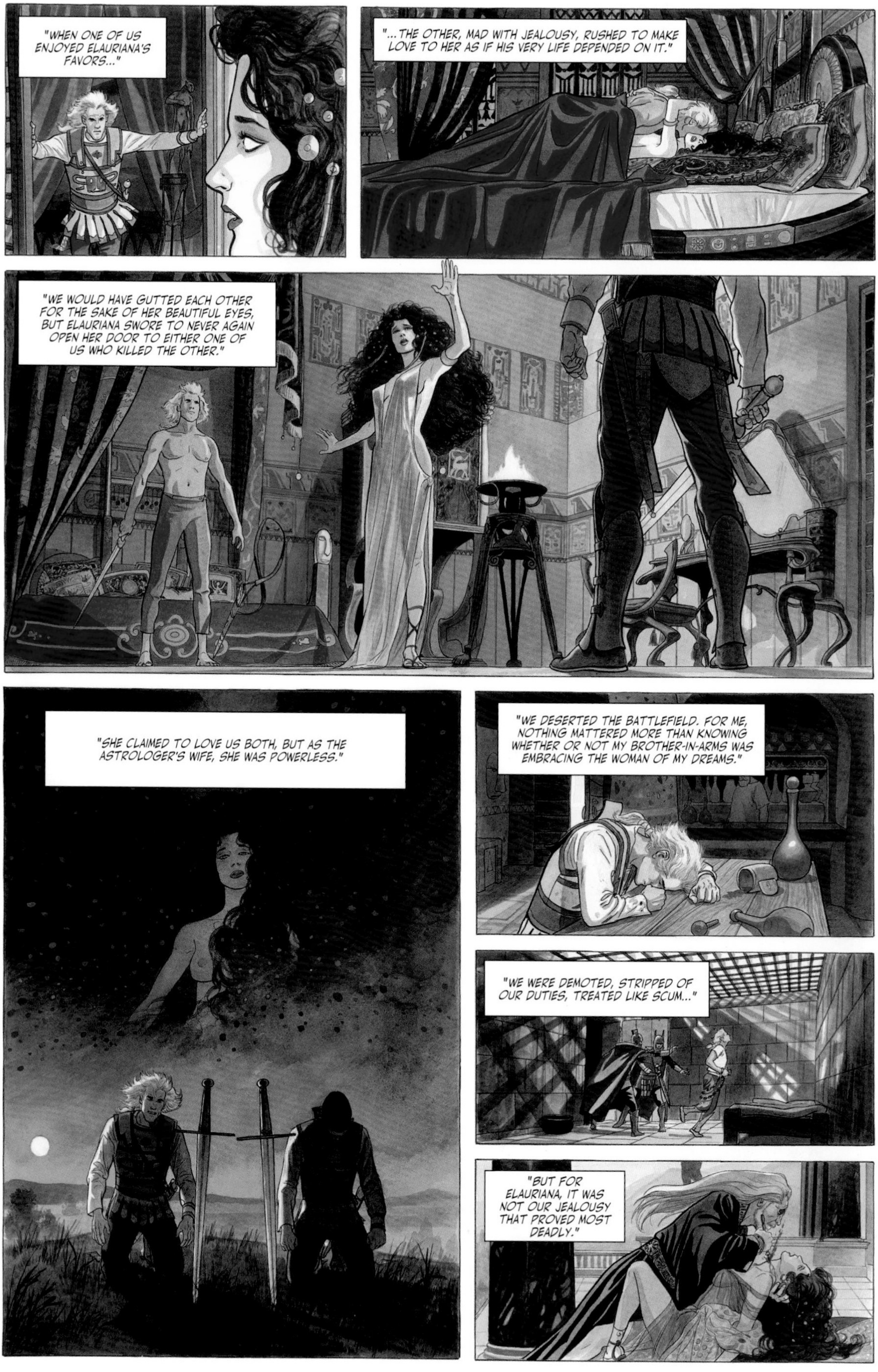
"WHEN ONE OF US ENJOYED ELAURIANA'S FAVORS..."
"...THE OTHER, MAD WITH JEALOUSY, RUSHED TO MAKE LOVE TO HER AS IF HIS VERY LIFE DEPENDED ON IT."
"WE WOULD HAVE GUTTED EACH OTHER FOR THE SAKE OF HER BEAUTIFUL EYES, BUT ELAURIANA SWORE TO NEVER AGAIN OPEN HER DOOR TO EITHER ONE OF US WHO KILLED THE OTHER."
"SHE CLAIMED TO LOVE US BOTH, BUT AS THE ASTROLOGER'S WIFE, SHE WAS POWERLESS."
"WE DESERTED THE BATTLEFIELD. FOR ME, NOTHING MATTERED MORE THAN KNOWING WHETHER OR NOT MY BROTHER-IN-ARMS WAS EMBRACING THE WOMAN OF MY DREAMS."
"WE WERE DEMOTED, STRIPPED OF OUR DUTIES, TREATED LIKE SCUM..."
"BUT FOR ELAURIANA, IT WAS NOT OUR JEALOUSY THAT PROVED MOST DEADLY."

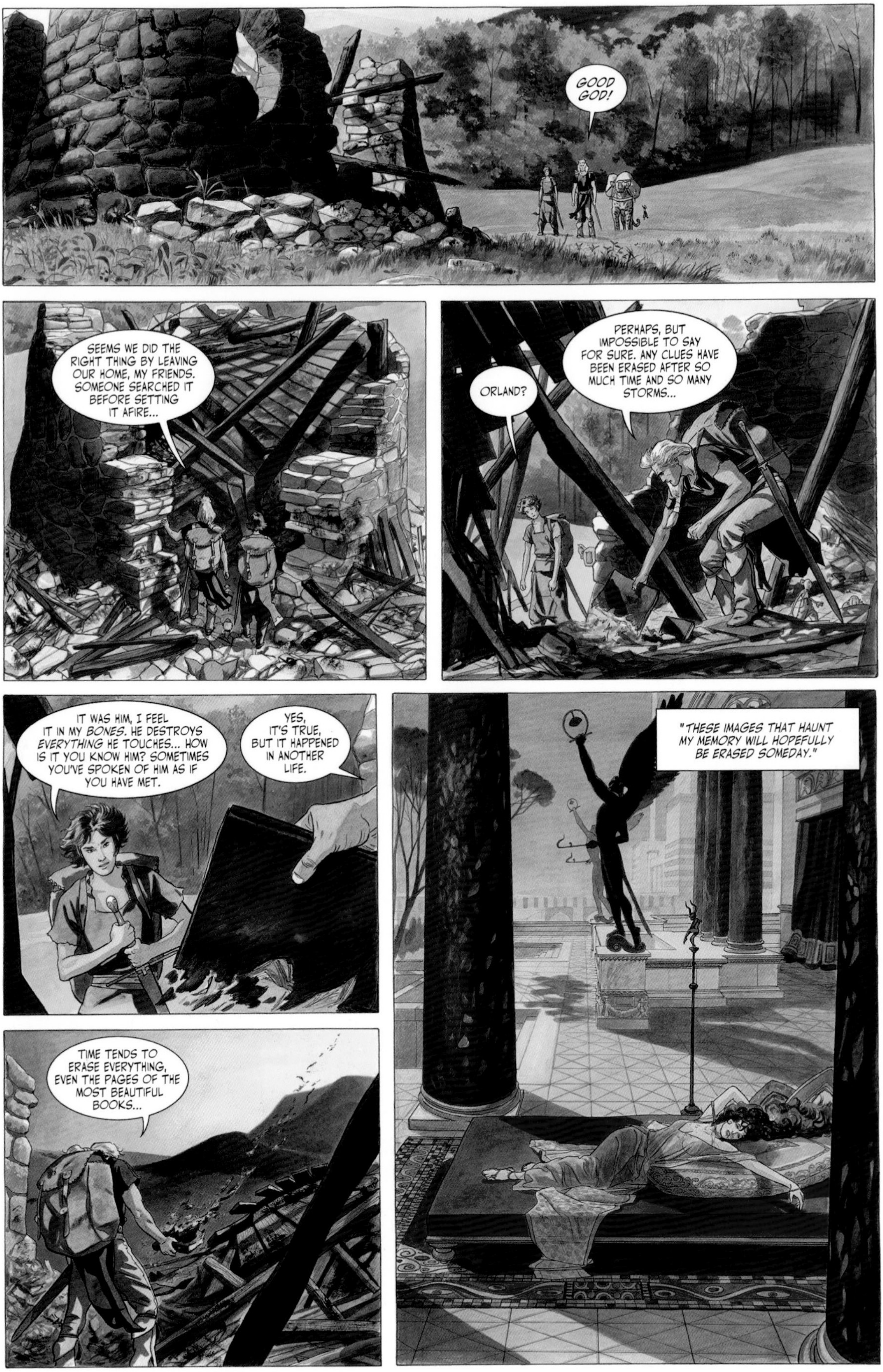
GOOD GOD!
SEEMS WE DID THE RIGHT THING BY LEAVING OUR HOME, MY FRIENDS. SOMEONE SEARCHED IT BEFORE SETTING IT AFIRE...
ORLAND?
PERHAPS, BUT IMPOSSIBLE TO SAY FOR SURE. ANY CLUES HAVE BEEN ERASED AFTER SO MUCH TIME AND SO MANY STORMS...
IT WAS HIM, I FEEL IT IN MY BONES. HE DESTROYS EVERYTHING HE TOUCHES... HOW IS IT YOU KNOW HIM? SOMETIMES YOU'VE SPOKEN OF HIM AS IF YOU HAVE MET.
YES, IT'S TRUE, BUT IT HAPPENED IN ANOTHER LIFE.
TIME TENDS TO ERASE EVERYTHING, EVEN THE PAGES OF THE MOST BEAUTIFUL BOOKS...
"THESE IMAGES THAT HAUNT MY MEMORY WILL HOPEFULLY BE ERASED SOMEDAY."

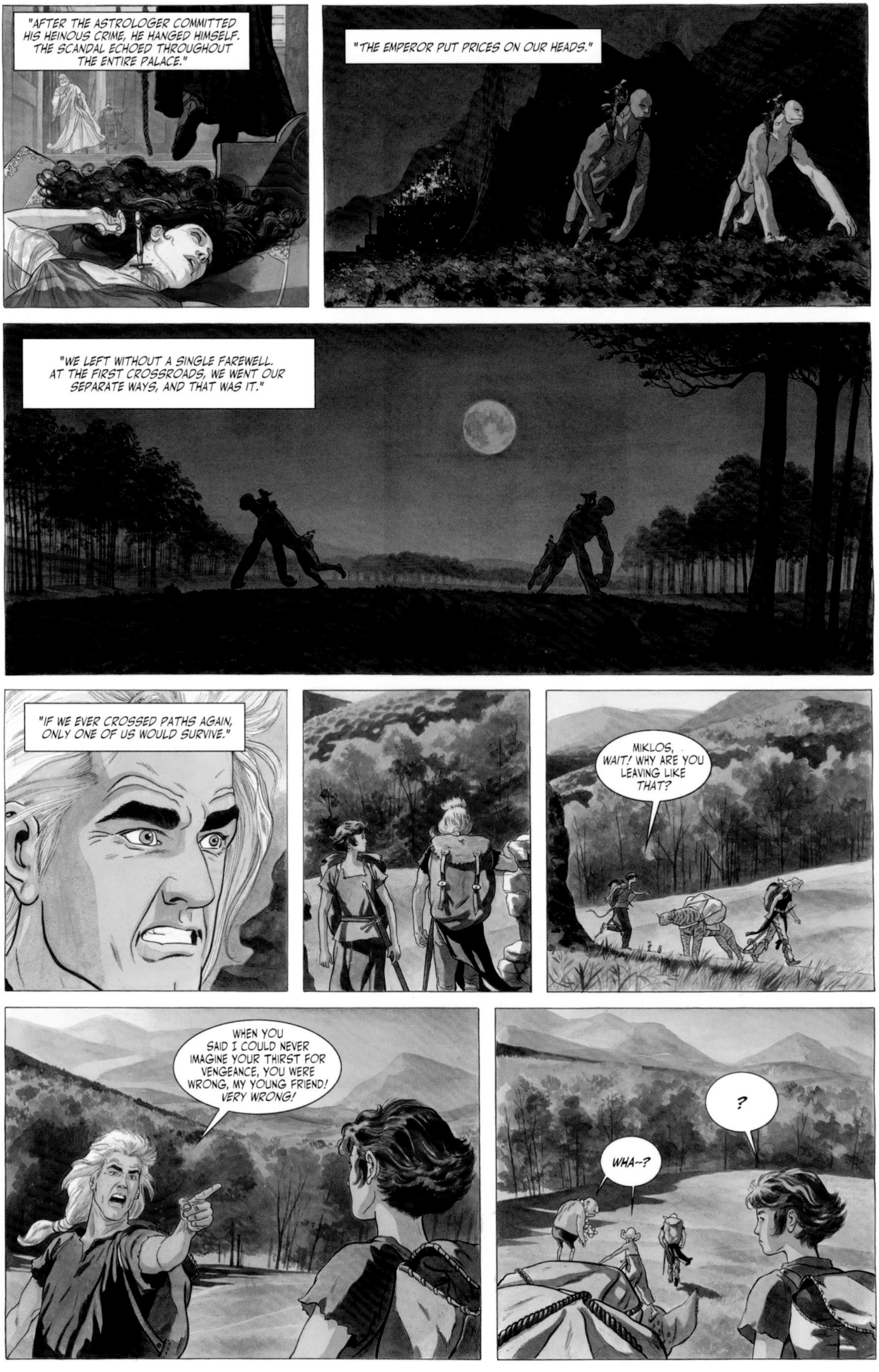
"AFTER THE ASTROLOGER COMMITTED HIS HEINOUS CRIME, HE HANGED HIMSELF. THE SCANDAL ECHOED THROUGHOUT THE ENTIRE PALACE."
"THE EMPEROR PUT PRICES ON OUR HEADS."
"WE LEFT WITHOUT A SINGLE FAREWELL. AT THE FIRST CROSSROADS, WE WENT OUR SEPARATE WAYS, AND THAT WAS IT."
"IF WE EVER CROSSED PATHS AGAIN, ONLY ONE OF US WOULD SURVIVE."
MIKLOS, WAIT! WHY ARE YOU LEAVING LIKE THAT?
WHEN YOU SAID I COULD NEVER IMAGINE YOUR THIRST FOR VENGEANCE, YOU WERE WRONG, MY YOUNG FRIEND! VERY WRONG!
?
WHA--?

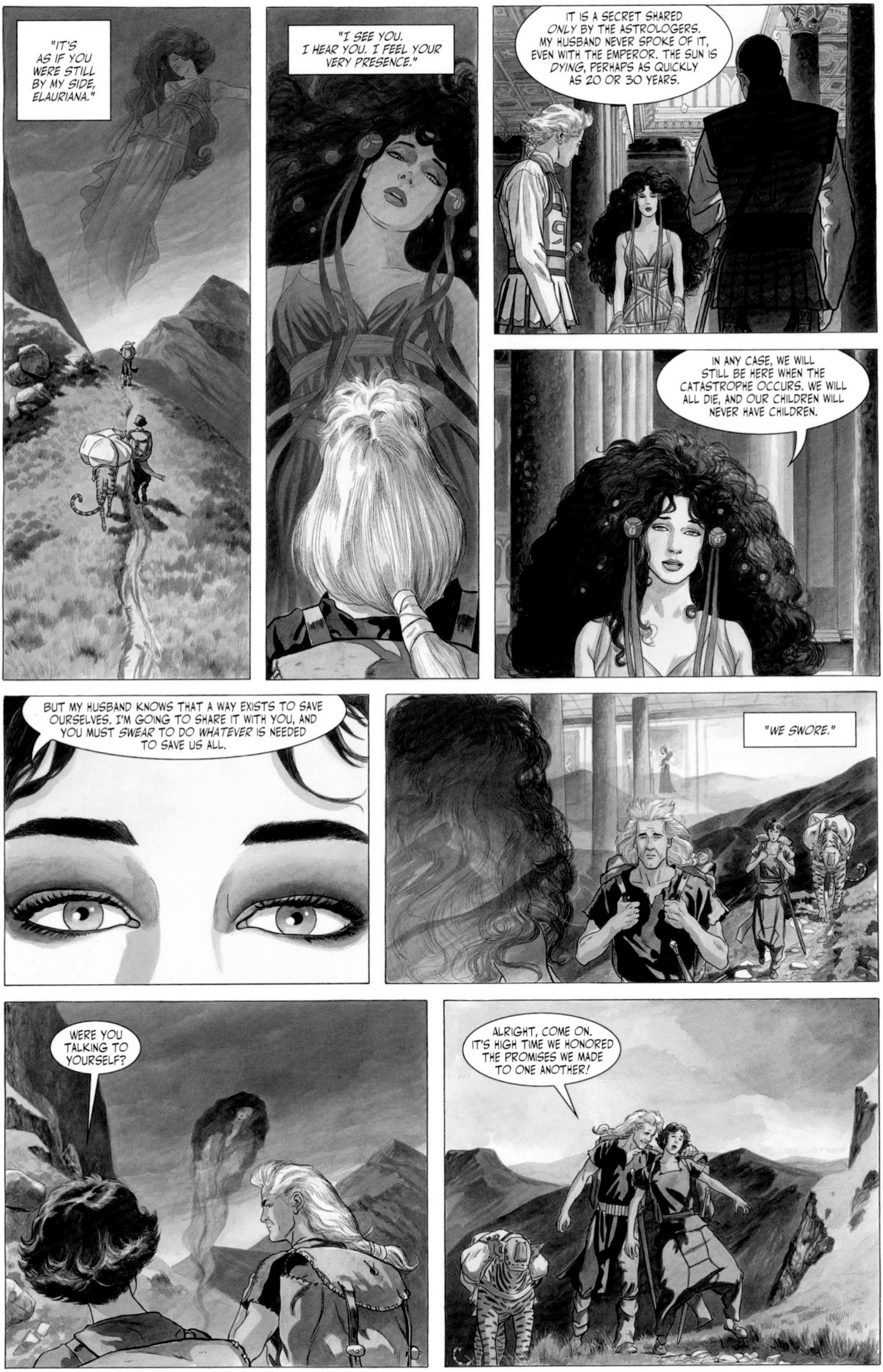
"IT'S AS IF YOU WERE STILL BY MY SIDE, ELAURIANA."
"I SEE YOU. I HEAR YOU. I FEEL YOUR VERY PRESENCE."
IT IS A SECRET SHARED ONLY BY THE ASTROLOGERS. MY HUSBAND NEVER SPOKE OF IT, EVEN WITH THE EMPEROR. THE SUN IS DYING, PERHAPS AS QUICKLY AS 20 OR 30 YEARS.
IN ANY CASE, WE WILL STILL BE HERE WHEN THE CATASTROPHE OCCURS. WE WILL ALL DIE, AND OUR CHILDREN WILL NEVER HAVE CHILDREN.
BUT MY HUSBAND KNOWS THAT A WAY EXISTS TO SAVE OURSELVES. I'M GOING TO SHARE IT WITH YOU, AND YOU MUST SWEAR TO DO WHATEVER IS NEEDED TO SAVE US ALL.
"WE SWORE."
WERE YOU TALKING TO YOURSELF?
ALRIGHT, COME ON. IT'S HIGH TIME WE HONORED THE PROMISES WE MADE TO ONE ANOTHER!

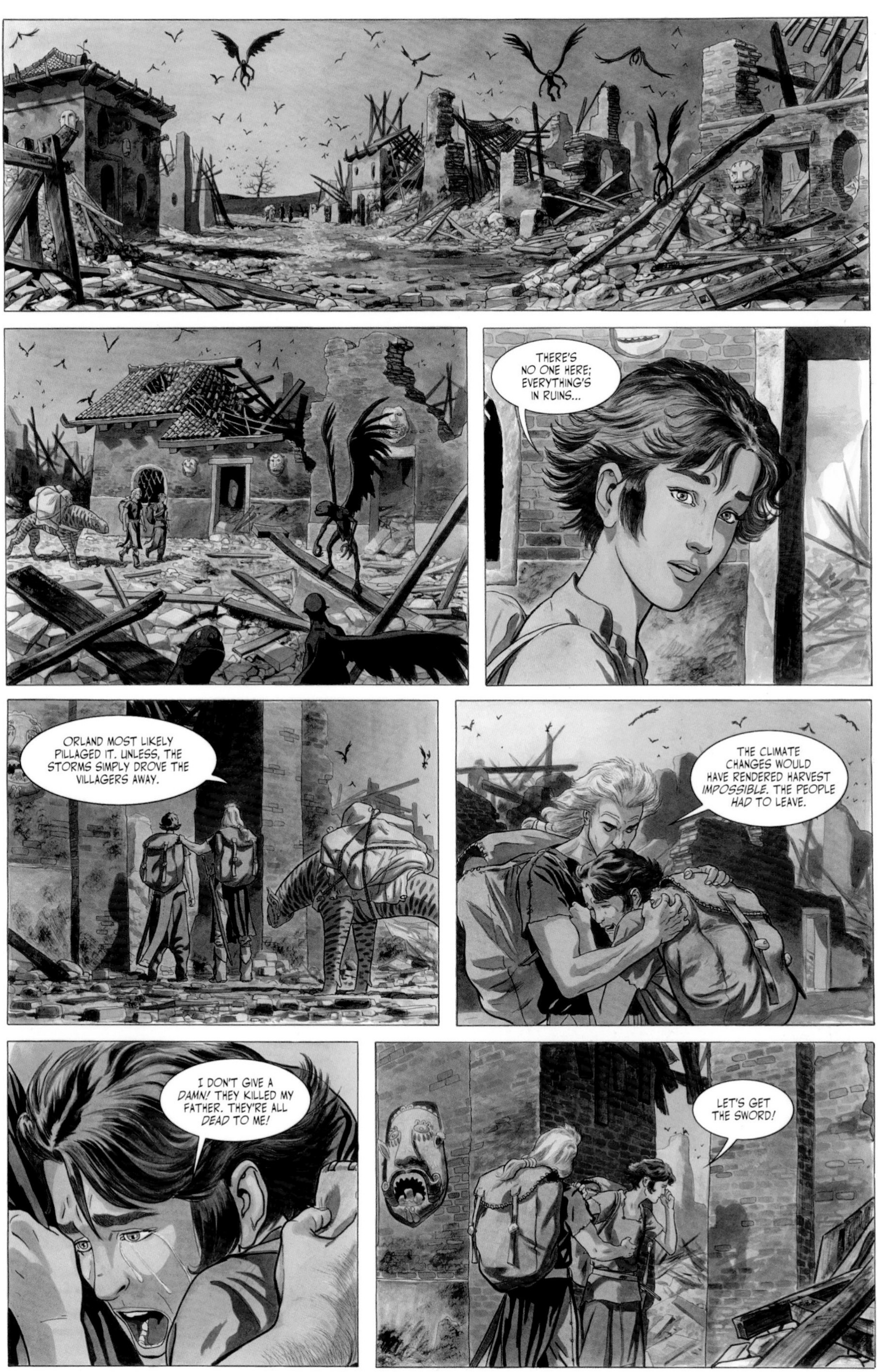
THERE'S NO ONE HERE; EVERYTHING'S IN RUINS...
ORLAND MOST LIKELY PILLAGED IT. UNLESS, THE STORMS SIMPLY DROVE THE VILLAGERS AWAY.
THE CLIMATE CHANGES WOULD HAVE RENDERED HARVEST *IMPOSSIBLE*. THE PEOPLE HAD TO LEAVE.
I DON'T GIVE A *DAMN!* THEY KILLED MY FATHER. THEY'RE ALL *DEAD* TO ME!
LET'S GET THE SWORD!

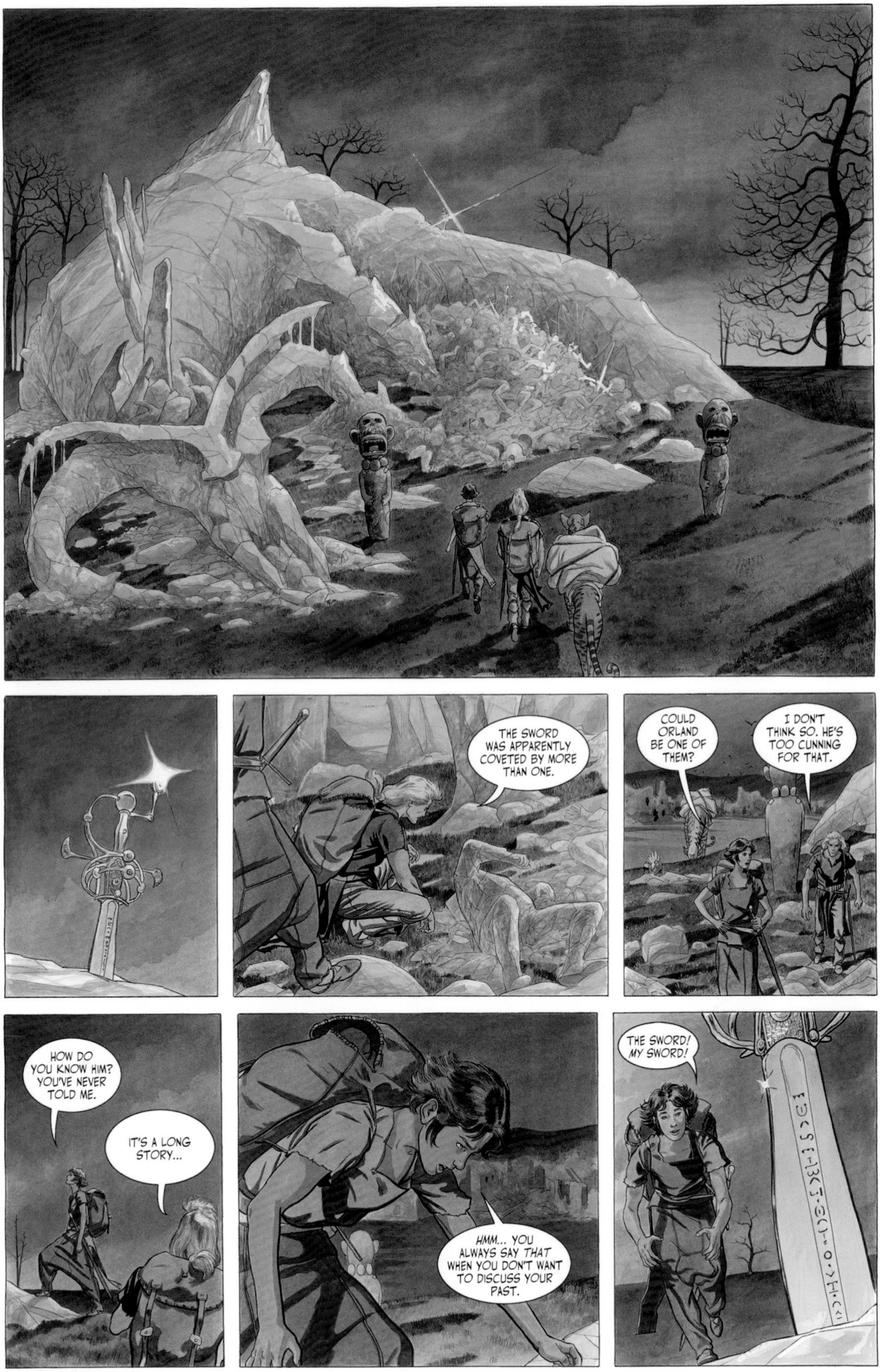
THE SWORD WAS APPARENTLY COVETED BY MORE THAN ONE.
COULD ORLAND BE ONE OF THEM?
I DON'T THINK SO. HE'S TOO CUNNING FOR THAT.
HOW DO YOU KNOW HIM? YOU'VE NEVER TOLD ME.
IT'S A LONG STORY...
HMM... YOU ALWAYS SAY THAT WHEN YOU DON'T WANT TO DISCUSS YOUR PAST.
THE SWORD! MY SWORD!

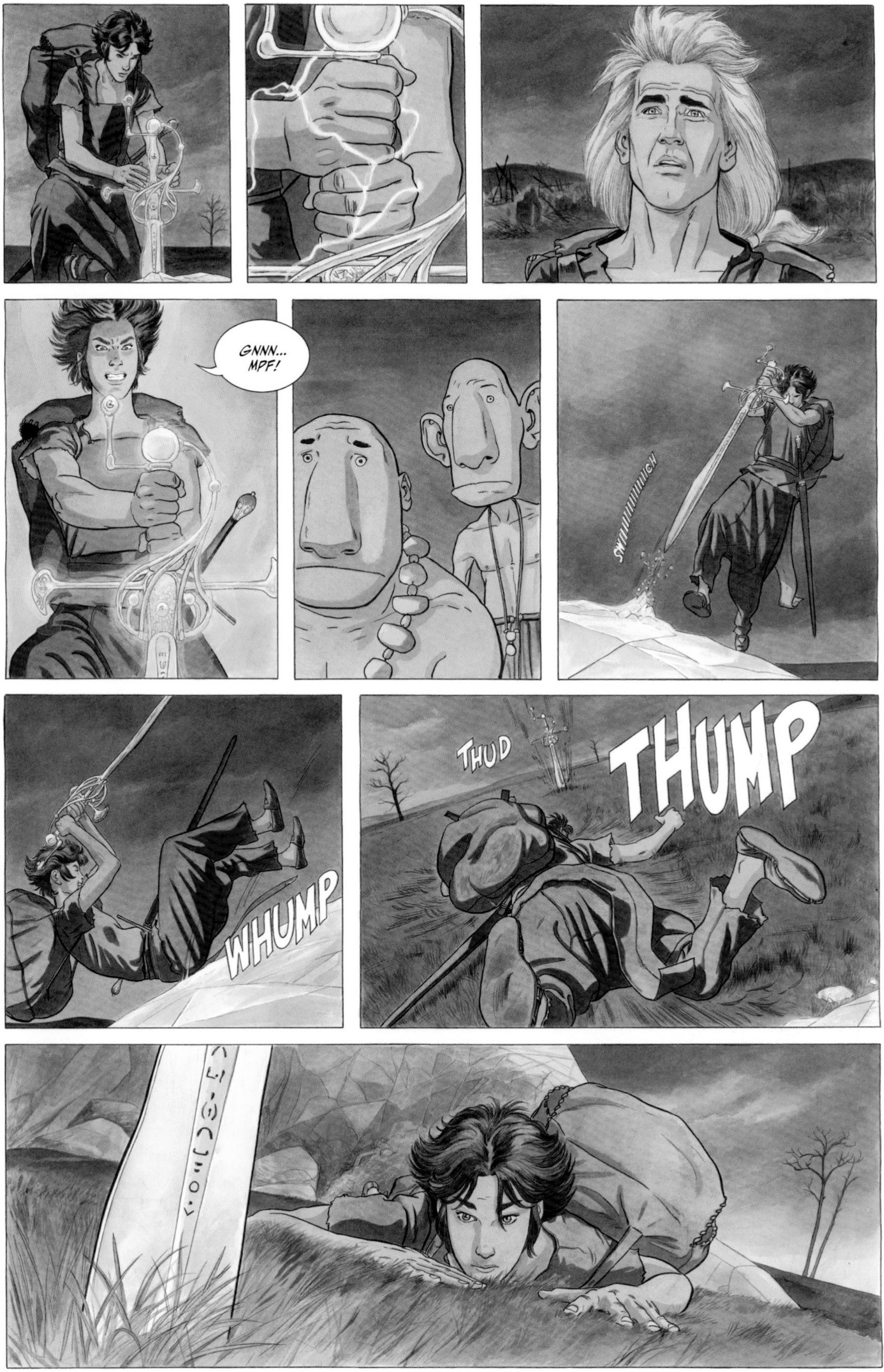
GNNN... MPF!
SWIIIIIIIIIIIICH
WHUMP
THUD
THUMP

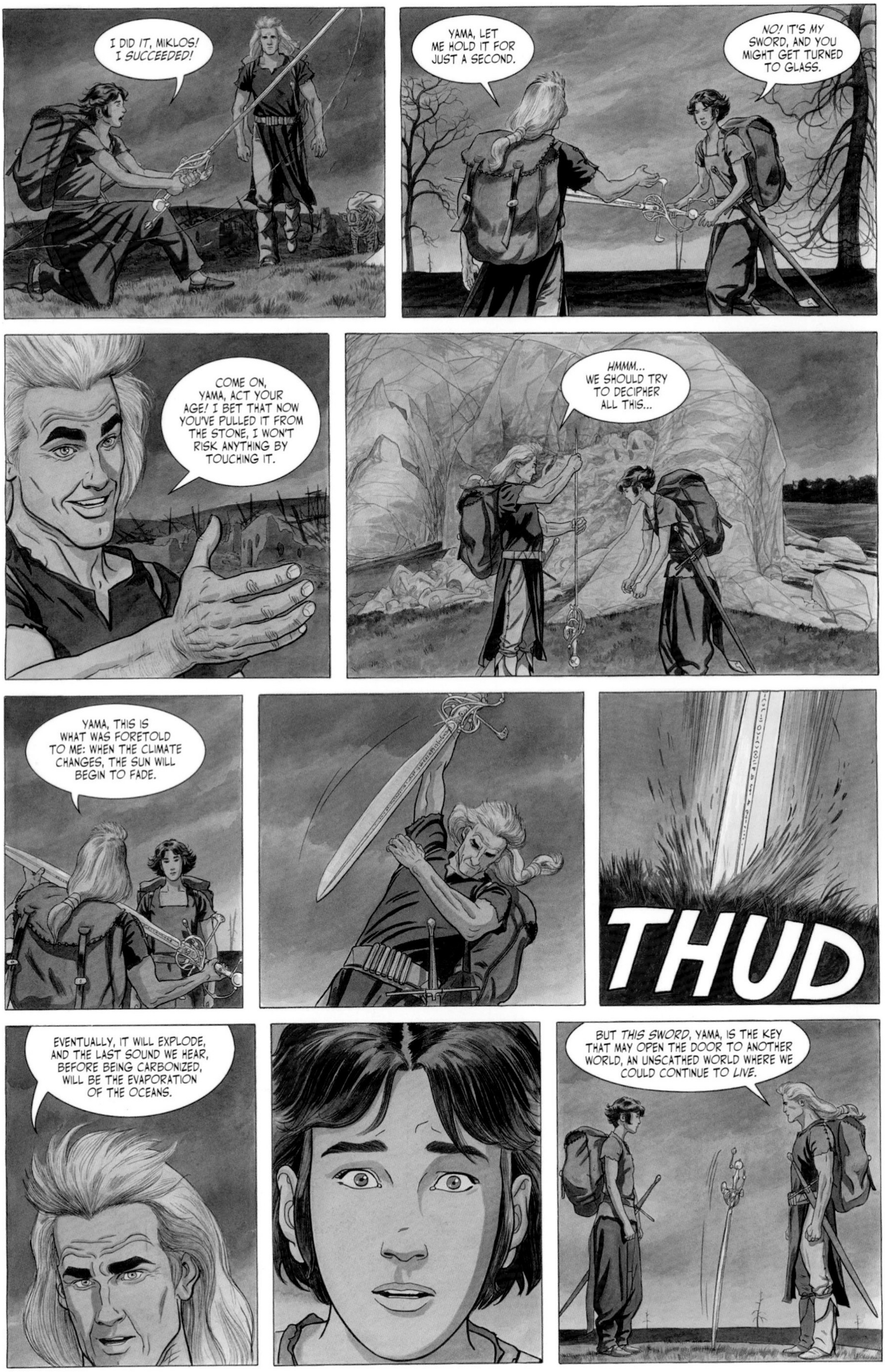
I DID *IT*, MIKLOS! I *SUCCEEDED!*
YAMA, LET ME HOLD IT FOR JUST A SECOND.
NO! IT'S MY SWORD, AND YOU MIGHT GET TURNED TO GLASS.
COME ON, YAMA, ACT YOUR *AGE!* I BET THAT NOW YOU'VE PULLED IT FROM THE STONE, I WON'T RISK ANYTHING BY TOUCHING IT.
HMMM... WE SHOULD TRY TO DECIPHER ALL THIS...
YAMA, THIS IS WHAT WAS FORETOLD TO ME: WHEN THE CLIMATE CHANGES, THE SUN WILL BEGIN TO FADE.
THUD
EVENTUALLY, IT WILL EXPLODE, AND THE LAST SOUND WE HEAR, BEFORE BEING CARBONIZED, WILL BE THE EVAPORATION OF THE OCEANS.
BUT *THIS SWORD*, YAMA, IS THE KEY THAT MAY OPEN THE DOOR TO ANOTHER WORLD, AN UNSCATHED WORLD WHERE WE COULD CONTINUE TO *LIVE*.

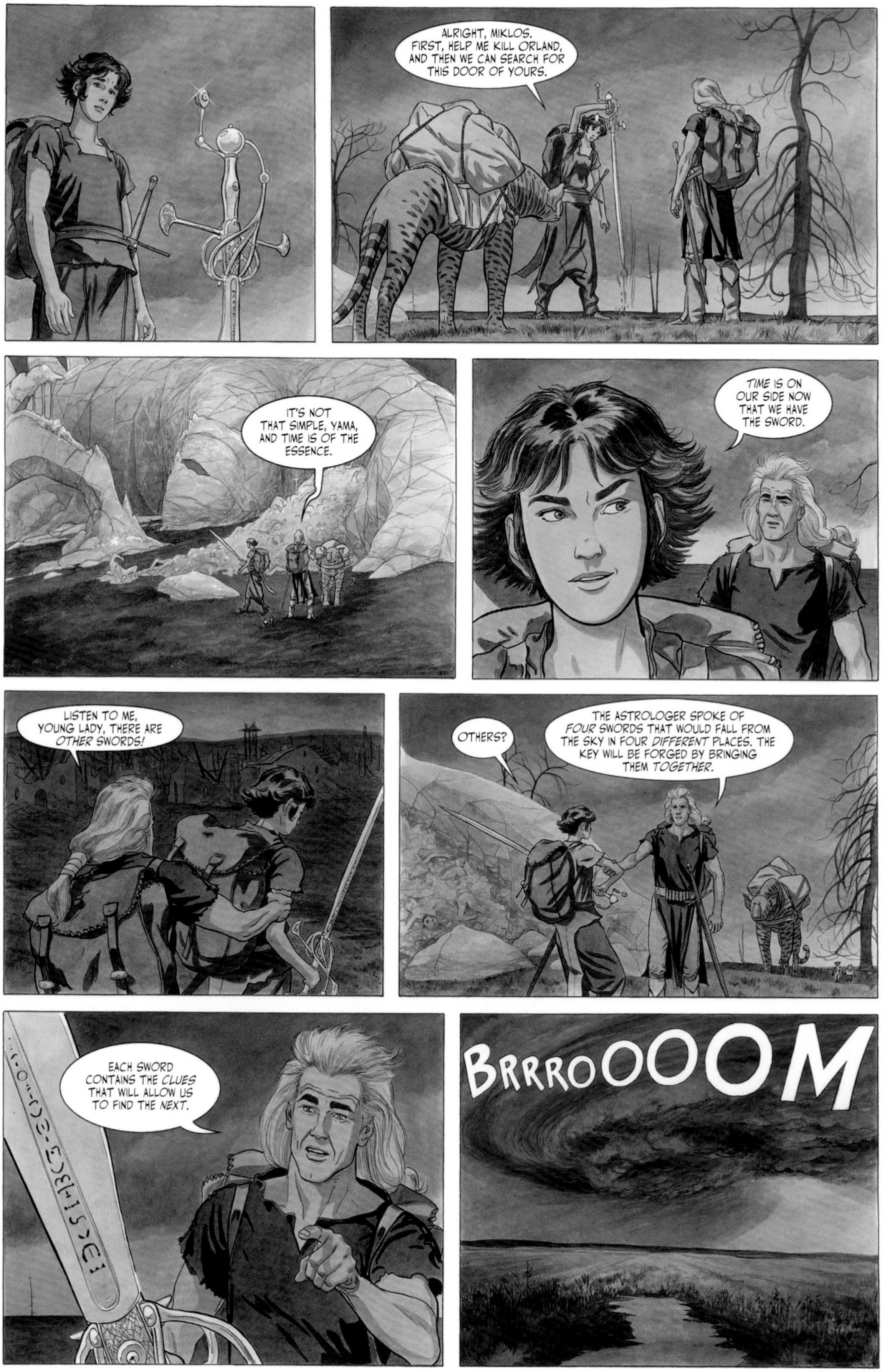
ALRIGHT, MIKLOS. FIRST, HELP ME KILL ORLAND, AND THEN WE CAN SEARCH FOR THIS DOOR OF YOURS.
IT'S NOT THAT SIMPLE, YAMA, AND TIME IS OF THE ESSENCE.
TIME IS ON OUR SIDE NOW THAT WE HAVE THE SWORD.
LISTEN TO ME, YOUNG LADY, THERE ARE OTHER SWORDS!
OTHERS?
THE ASTROLOGER SPOKE OF FOUR SWORDS THAT WOULD FALL FROM THE SKY IN FOUR DIFFERENT PLACES. THE KEY WILL BE FORGED BY BRINGING THEM TOGETHER.
EACH SWORD CONTAINS THE CLUES THAT WILL ALLOW US TO FIND THE NEXT.
BRRROOOOM

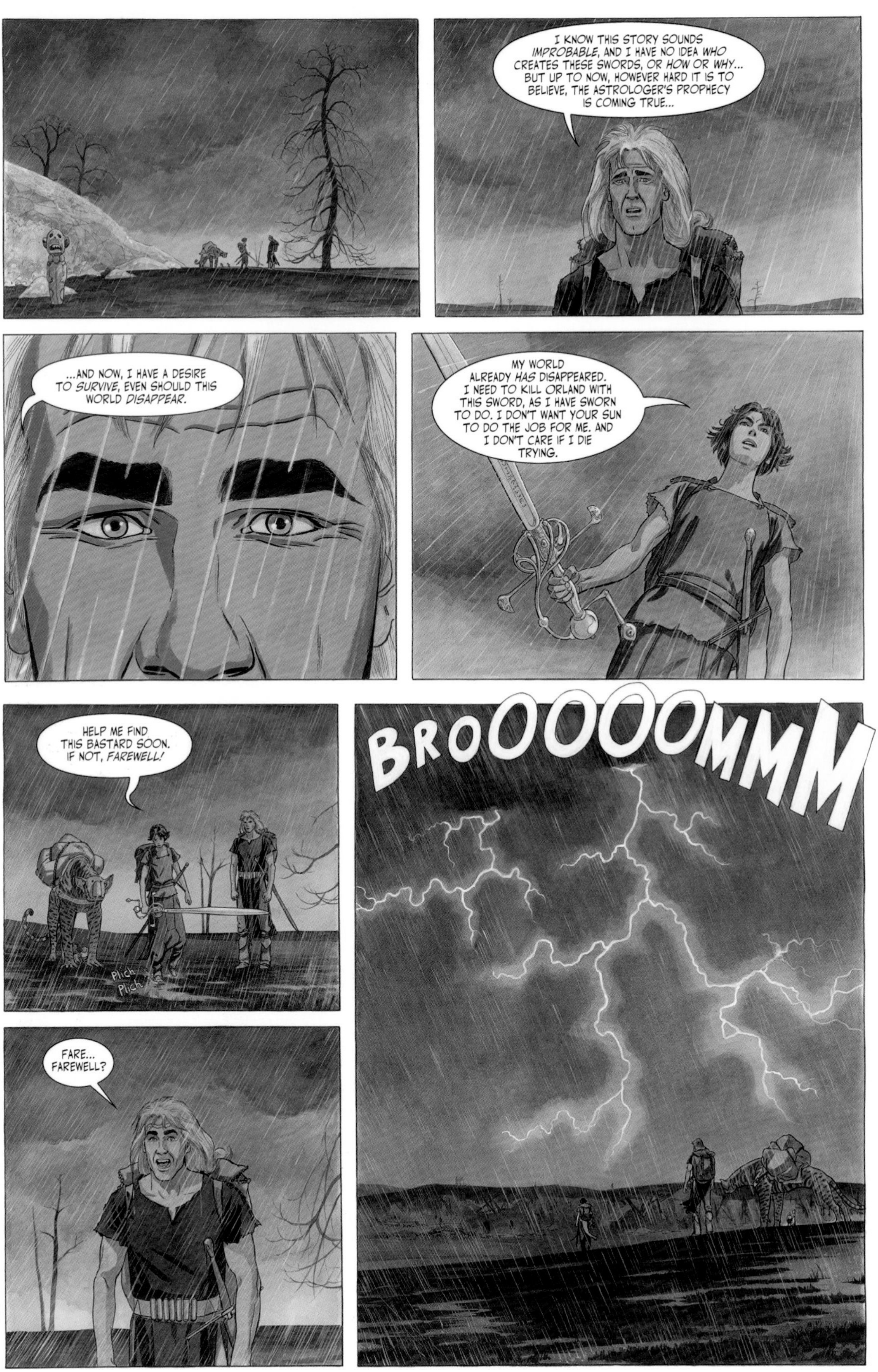
I KNOW THIS STORY SOUNDS *IMPROBABLE*, AND I HAVE NO IDEA WHO CREATES THESE SWORDS, OR *HOW* OR *WHY*... BUT UP TO NOW, HOWEVER HARD IT IS TO BELIEVE, THE ASTROLOGER'S PROPHECY IS COMING TRUE...
...AND NOW, I HAVE A DESIRE TO *SURVIVE*, EVEN SHOULD THIS WORLD *DISAPPEAR*.
MY WORLD ALREADY *HAS* DISAPPEARED. I NEED TO KILL ORLAND WITH THIS SWORD, AS I HAVE SWORN TO DO. I DON'T WANT YOUR SUN TO DO THE JOB FOR ME. AND I DON'T CARE IF I DIE TRYING.
HELP ME FIND THIS BASTARD SOON. IF NOT, *FAREWELL!*
Plich Plich
FARE... FAREWELL?
BROOOOOMMM

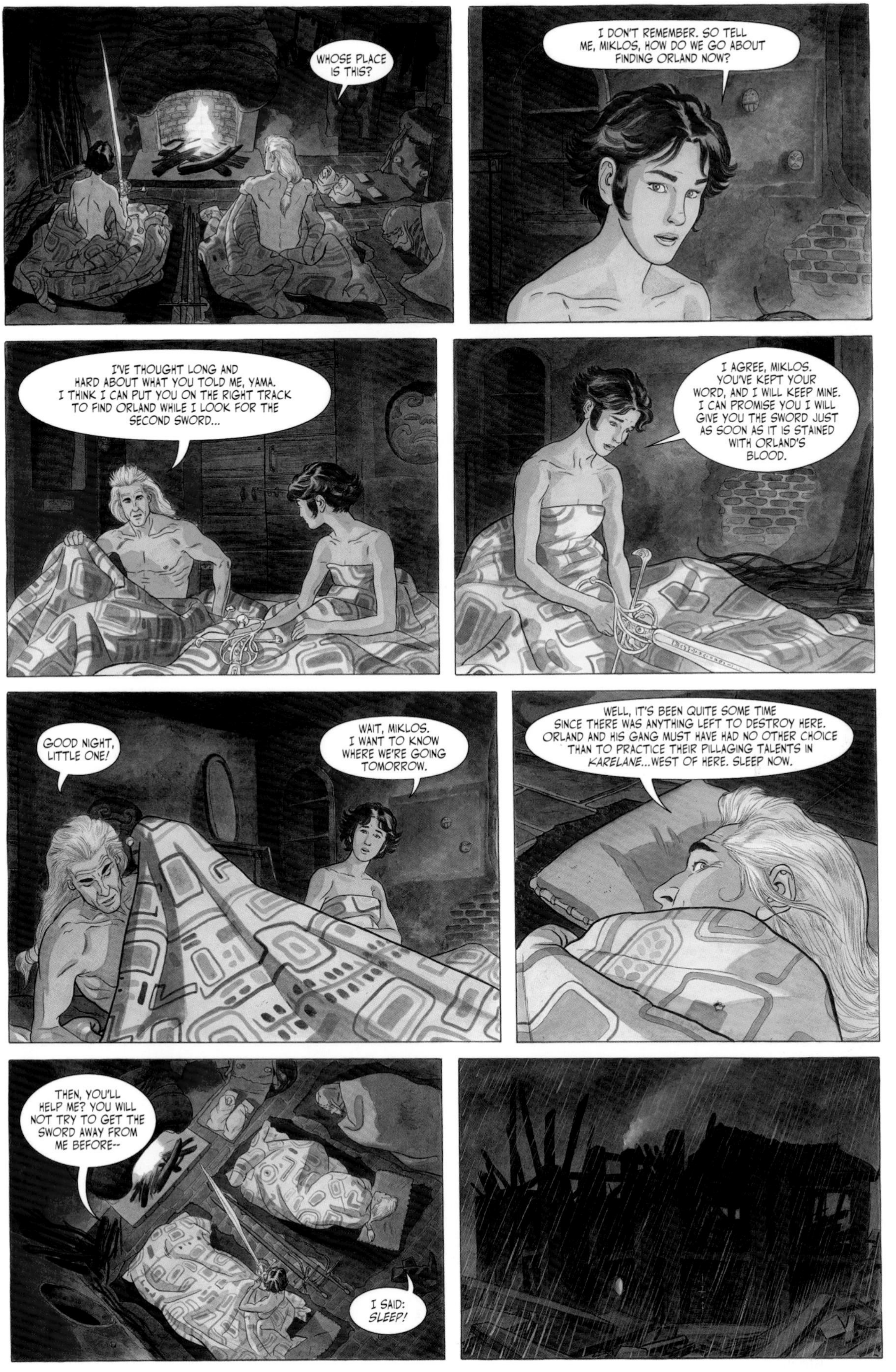
WHOSE PLACE IS THIS?
I DON'T REMEMBER. SO TELL ME, MIKLOS, HOW DO WE GO ABOUT FINDING ORLAND NOW?
I'VE THOUGHT LONG AND HARD ABOUT WHAT YOU TOLD ME, YAMA. I THINK I CAN PUT YOU ON THE RIGHT TRACK TO FIND ORLAND WHILE I LOOK FOR THE SECOND SWORD...
I AGREE, MIKLOS. YOU'VE KEPT YOUR WORD, AND I WILL KEEP MINE. I CAN PROMISE YOU I WILL GIVE YOU THE SWORD JUST AS SOON AS IT IS STAINED WITH ORLAND'S BLOOD.
GOOD NIGHT, LITTLE ONE!
WAIT, MIKLOS. I WANT TO KNOW WHERE WE'RE GOING TOMORROW.
WELL, IT'S BEEN QUITE SOME TIME SINCE THERE WAS ANYTHING LEFT TO DESTROY HERE. ORLAND AND HIS GANG MUST HAVE HAD NO OTHER CHOICE THAN TO PRACTICE THEIR PILLAGING TALENTS IN *KARELANE*...WEST OF HERE. SLEEP NOW.
THEN, YOU'LL HELP ME? YOU WILL NOT TRY TO GET THE SWORD AWAY FROM ME BEFORE--
I SAID: *SLEEP!*

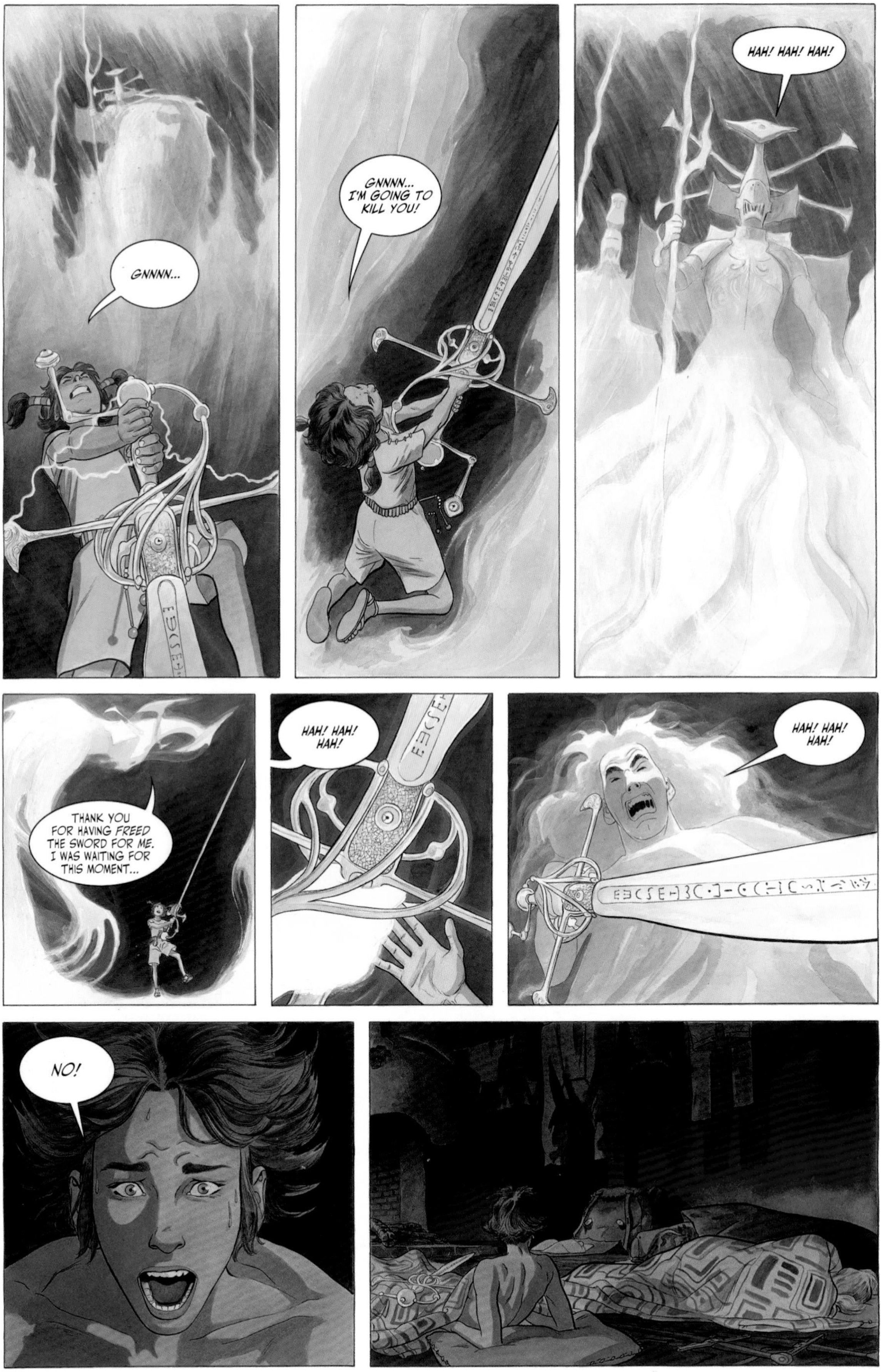
GNNNN...
GNNNN... I'M GOING TO KILL YOU!
HAH! HAH! HAH!
THANK YOU FOR HAVING *FREED* THE SWORD FOR ME. I WAS WAITING FOR THIS MOMENT...
HAH! HAH! HAH!
HAH! HAH! HAH!
NO!

GET UP, QUICK! SHE'S GONE!

MMMH? WHAT'D YOU SAY?

YAMA'S GONE. WITH THE SWORD!

GOOD GOD! SHE DID WHAT? BUT WHY?

I'D SAY IT'S BECAUSE YOU DON'T INSPIRE *TOTAL* CONFIDENCE. HEY!

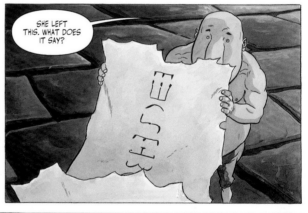

SHE LEFT THIS. WHAT DOES IT SAY?

SHE'S COPIED THE INSCRIPTIONS ON THE SWORD FOR ME. HER MESSAGE IS CLEAR. TO EACH HIS OWN WAY!

WHERE DOES THAT LEAVE US THEN?

WE HAVE TO FIND HER *RIGHT AWAY.* BY HERSELF, SHE HASN'T A CHANCE...

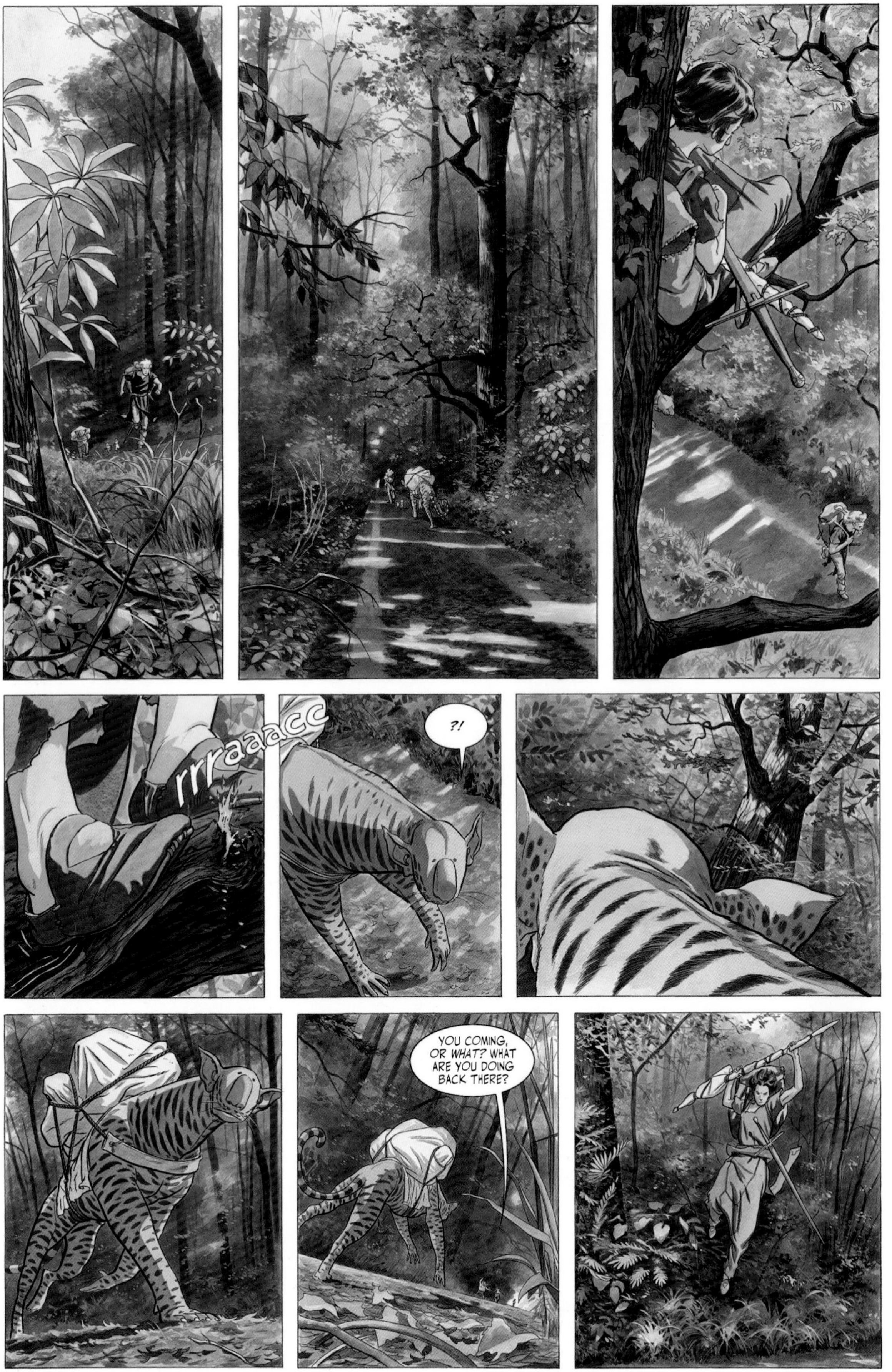
rrraaacc
?!
YOU COMING, OR WHAT? WHAT ARE YOU DOING BACK THERE?

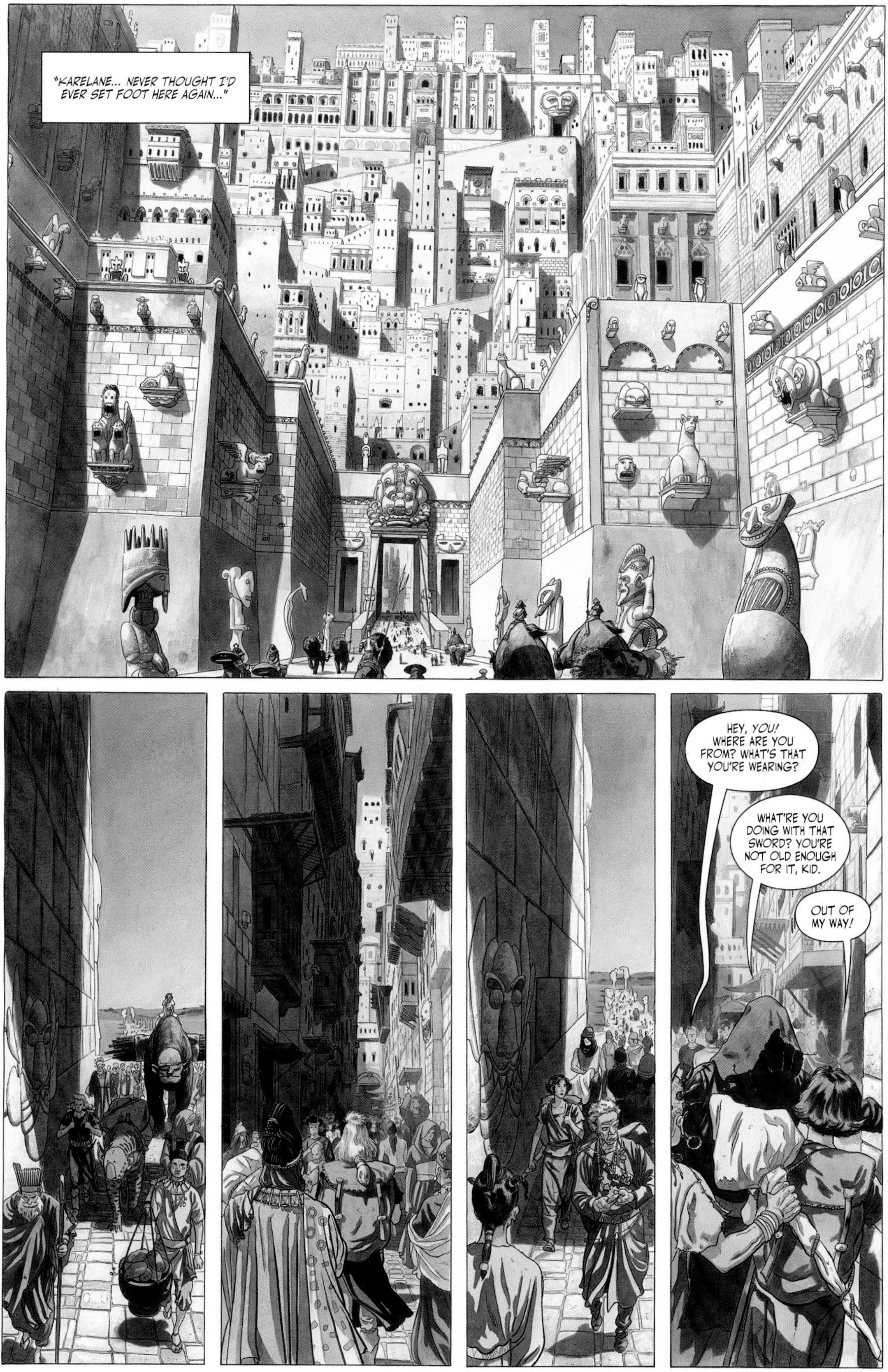
"KARELANE... NEVER THOUGHT I'D EVER SET FOOT HERE AGAIN..."
HEY, YOU! WHERE ARE YOU FROM? WHAT'S THAT YOU'RE WEARING?
WHAT'RE YOU DOING WITH THAT SWORD? YOU'RE NOT OLD ENOUGH FOR IT, KID.
OUT OF MY WAY!

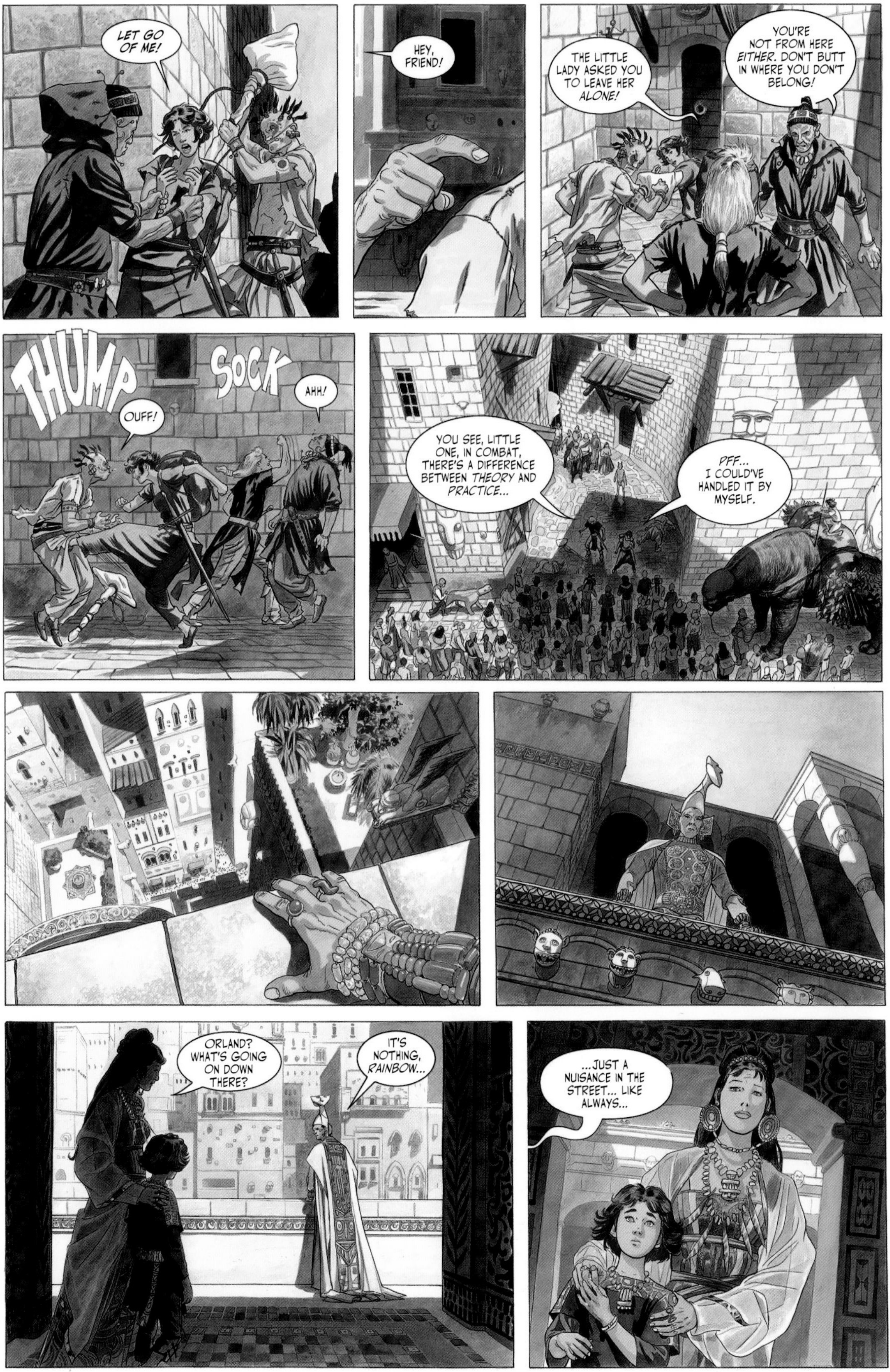

LET GO OF ME!
HEY, FRIEND!
THE LITTLE LADY ASKED YOU TO LEAVE HER ALONE!
YOU'RE NOT FROM HERE EITHER. DON'T BUTT IN WHERE YOU DON'T BELONG!
THUMP
SOCK
OUFF!
AHH!
YOU SEE, LITTLE ONE, IN COMBAT, THERE'S A DIFFERENCE BETWEEN THEORY AND PRACTICE...
PFF... I COULD'VE HANDLED IT BY MYSELF.
ORLAND? WHAT'S GOING ON DOWN THERE?
IT'S NOTHING, RAINBOW...
...JUST A NUISANCE IN THE STREET... LIKE ALWAYS...

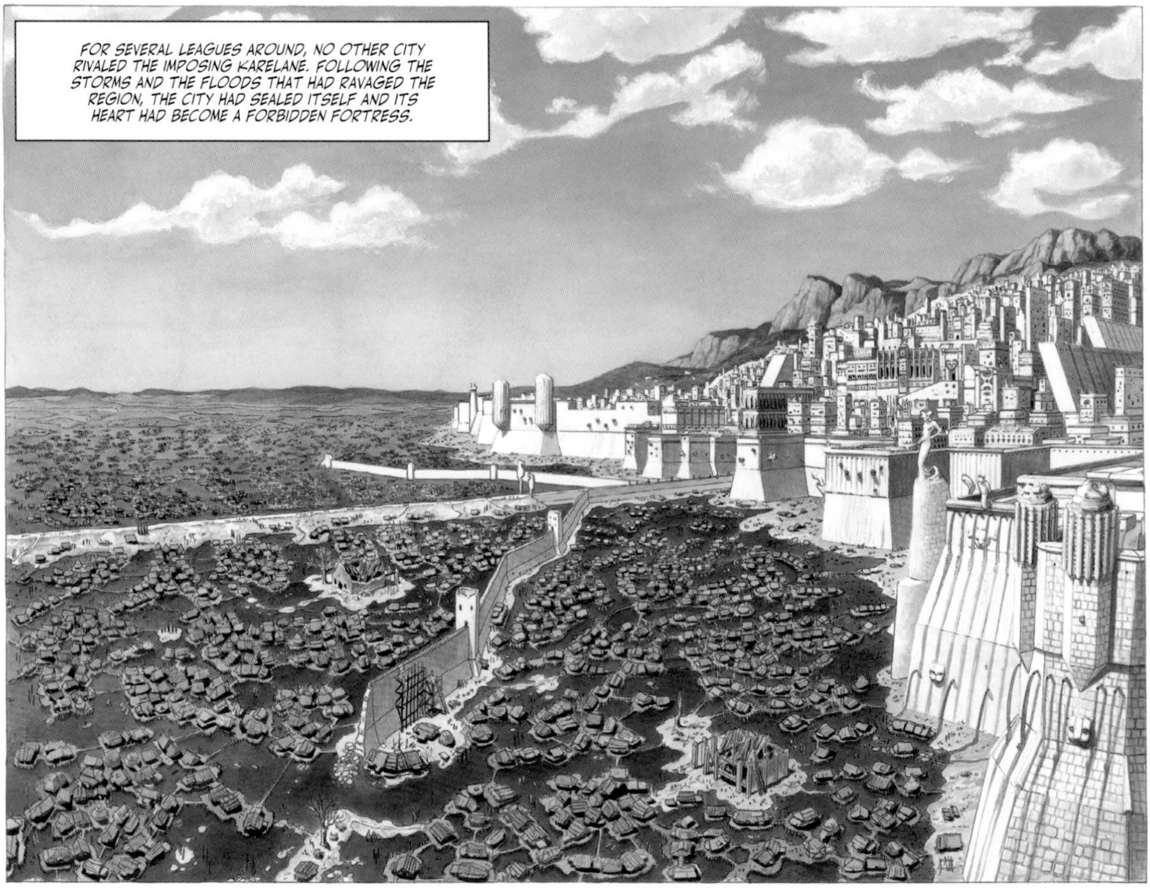
FOR SEVERAL LEAGUES AROUND, NO OTHER CITY RIVALED THE IMPOSING KARELANE. FOLLOWING THE STORMS AND THE FLOODS THAT HAD RAVAGED THE REGION, THE CITY HAD SEALED ITSELF AND ITS HEART HAD BECOME A FORBIDDEN FORTRESS.
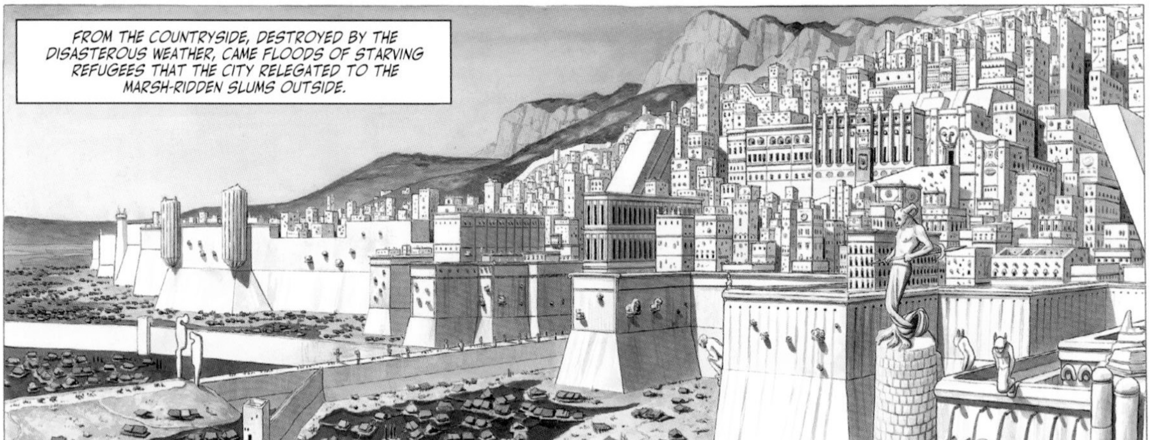
FROM THE COUNTRYSIDE, DESTROYED BY THE DISASTEROUS WEATHER, CAME FLOODS OF STARVING REFUGEES THAT THE CITY RELEGATED TO THE MARSH-RIDDEN SLUMS OUTSIDE.
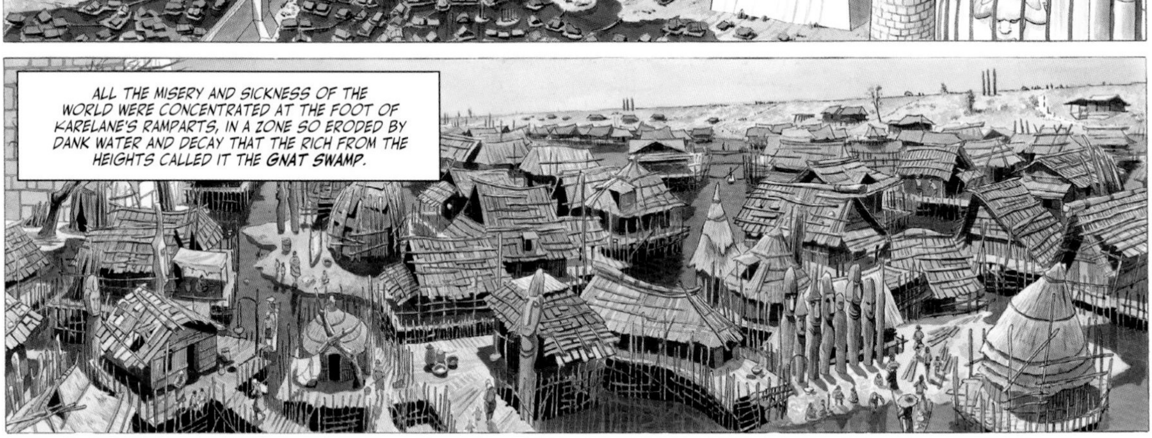
ALL THE MISERY AND SICKNESS OF THE WORLD WERE CONCENTRATED AT THE FOOT OF KARELANE'S RAMPARTS, IN A ZONE SO ERODED BY DANK WATER AND DECAY THAT THE RICH FROM THE HEIGHTS CALLED IT THE GNAT SWAMP.

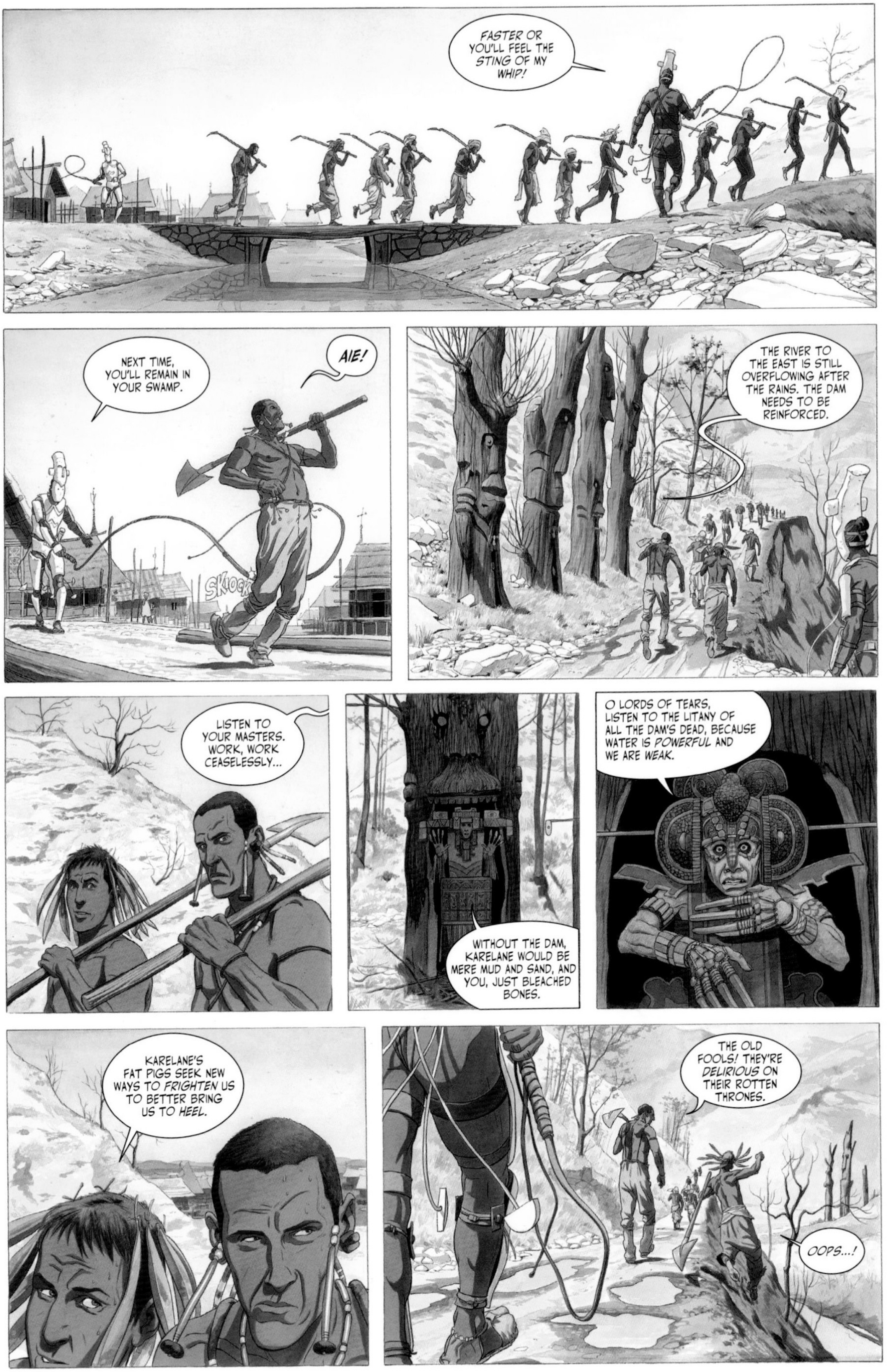
FASTER OR YOU'LL FEEL THE STING OF MY WHIP!
NEXT TIME, YOU'LL REMAIN IN YOUR SWAMP.
AIE!
SKIOCK
THE RIVER TO THE EAST IS STILL OVERFLOWING AFTER THE RAINS. THE DAM NEEDS TO BE REINFORCED.
LISTEN TO YOUR MASTERS. WORK, WORK CEASELESSLY...
WITHOUT THE DAM, KARELANE WOULD BE MERE MUD AND SAND, AND YOU, JUST BLEACHED BONES.
O LORDS OF TEARS, LISTEN TO THE LITANY OF ALL THE DAM'S DEAD, BECAUSE WATER IS POWERFUL AND WE ARE WEAK.
KARELANE'S FAT PIGS SEEK NEW WAYS TO FRIGHTEN US TO BETTER BRING US TO HEEL.
THE OLD FOOLS! THEY'RE DELIRIOUS ON THEIR ROTTEN THRONES.
OOPS...!

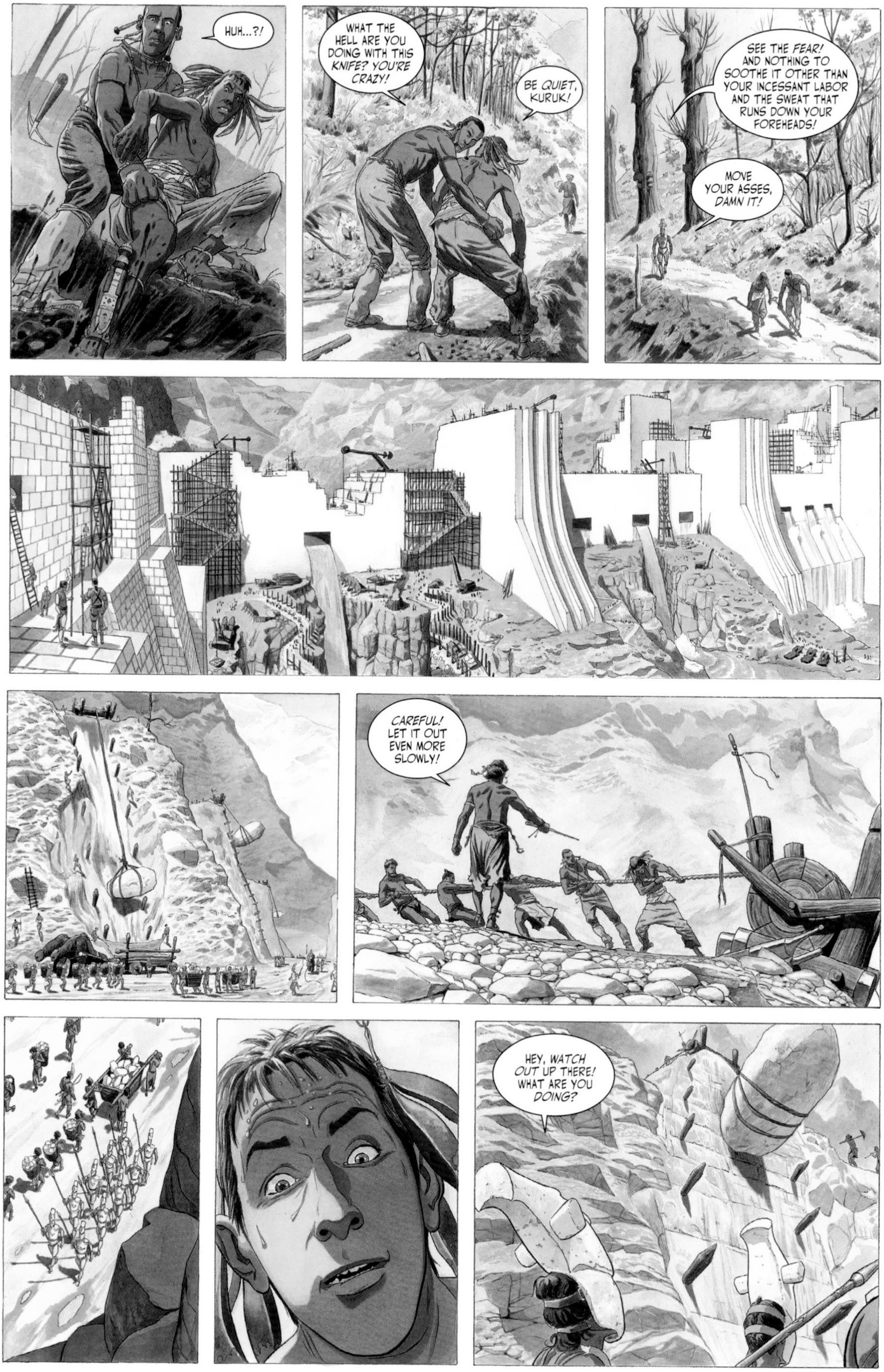
HUH...?!
WHAT THE HELL ARE YOU DOING WITH THIS KNIFE? YOU'RE CRAZY!
BE QUIET, KURUK!
SEE THE FEAR! AND NOTHING TO SOOTHE IT OTHER THAN YOUR INCESSANT LABOR AND THE SWEAT THAT RUNS DOWN YOUR FOREHEADS!
MOVE YOUR ASSES, DAMN IT!
CAREFUL! LET IT OUT EVEN MORE SLOWLY!
HEY, WATCH OUT UP THERE! WHAT ARE YOU DOING?

NO, NO, STOP! THEY'RE GOING TO SLAUGHTER US ALL.

SNACK

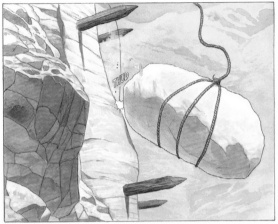

OUGH!!

WHAT THE...

HELP!

NO!

COME ON, QUICK, RUN. THEY'RE GOING TO KILL US!

NO, WE HAVE TO FIGHT BACK. THE TIME TO REVOLT IS NOW...

GENERAL ORLAND! GNATS HAVE KILLED TEN OF OUR MEN.

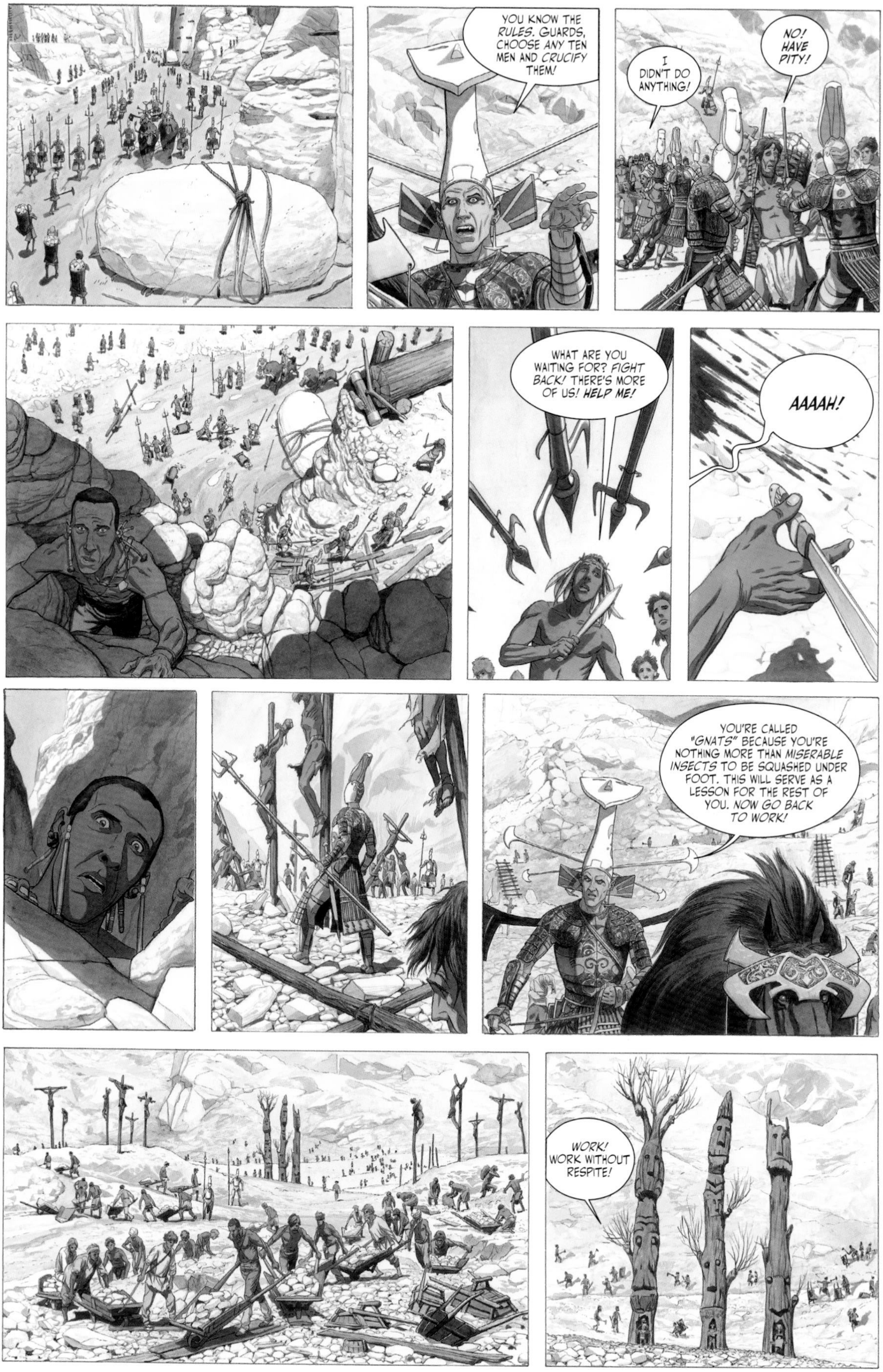
YOU KNOW THE RULES. GUARDS, CHOOSE ANY TEN MEN AND CRUCIFY THEM!
I DIDN'T DO ANYTHING!
NO! HAVE PITY!
WHAT ARE YOU WAITING FOR? FIGHT BACK! THERE'S MORE OF US! HELP ME!
AAAAH!
YOU'RE CALLED "GNATS" BECAUSE YOU'RE NOTHING MORE THAN MISERABLE INSECTS TO BE SQUASHED UNDER FOOT. THIS WILL SERVE AS A LESSON FOR THE REST OF YOU. NOW GO BACK TO WORK!
WORK! WORK WITHOUT RESPITE!

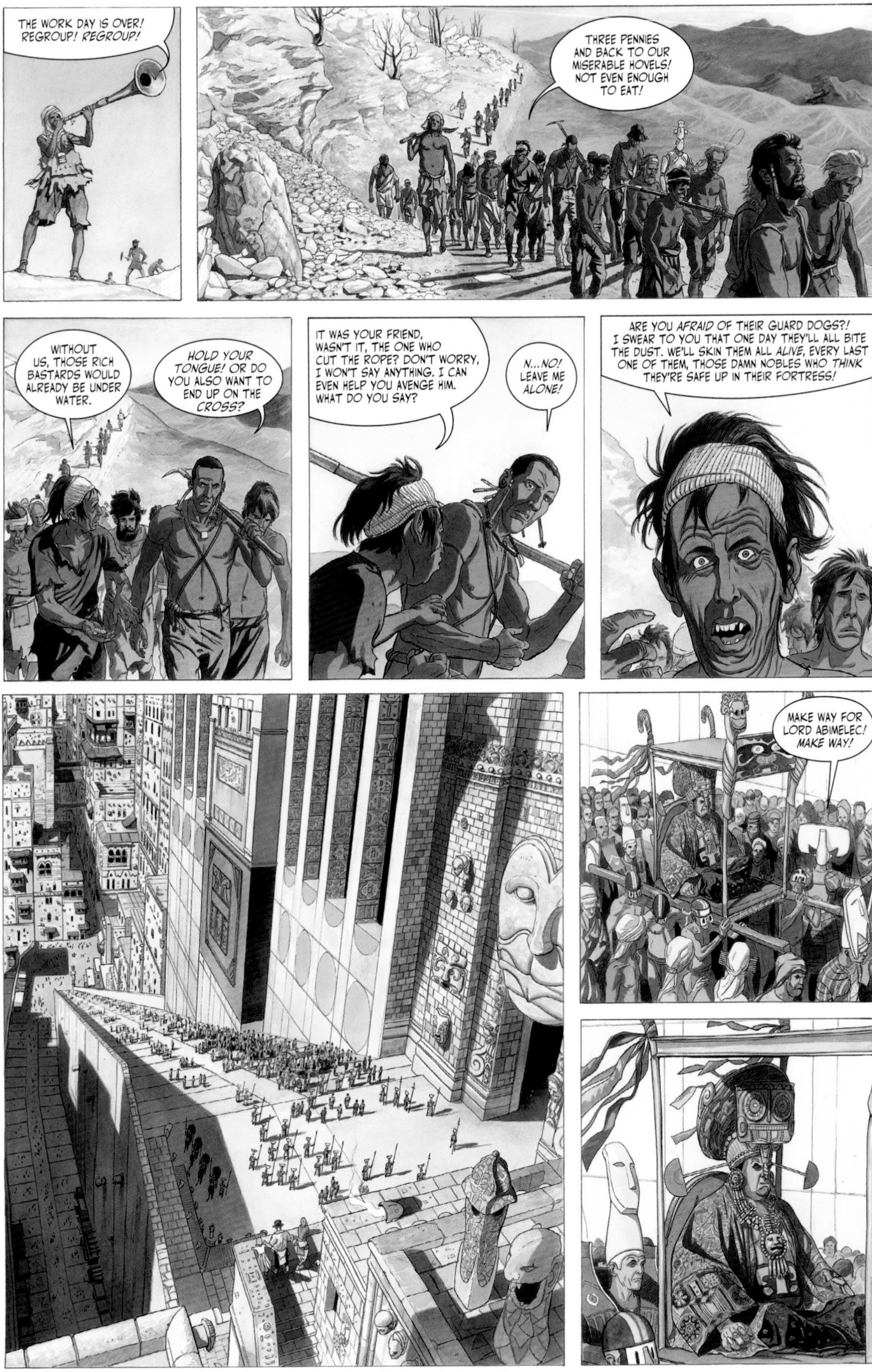
THE WORK DAY IS OVER! REGROUP! REGROUP!
THREE PENNIES AND BACK TO OUR MISERABLE HOVELS! NOT EVEN ENOUGH TO EAT!
WITHOUT US, THOSE RICH BASTARDS WOULD ALREADY BE UNDER WATER.
HOLD YOUR TONGUE! OR DO YOU ALSO WANT TO END UP ON THE CROSS?
IT WAS YOUR FRIEND, WASN'T IT, THE ONE WHO CUT THE ROPE? DON'T WORRY, I WON'T SAY ANYTHING. I CAN EVEN HELP YOU AVENGE HIM. WHAT DO YOU SAY?
N...NO! LEAVE ME ALONE!
ARE YOU AFRAID OF THEIR GUARD DOGS?! I SWEAR TO YOU THAT ONE DAY THEY'LL ALL BITE THE DUST. WE'LL SKIN THEM ALL ALIVE, EVERY LAST ONE OF THEM, THOSE DAMN NOBLES WHO THINK THEY'RE SAFE UP IN THEIR FORTRESS!
MAKE WAY FOR LORD ABIMELEC! MAKE WAY!

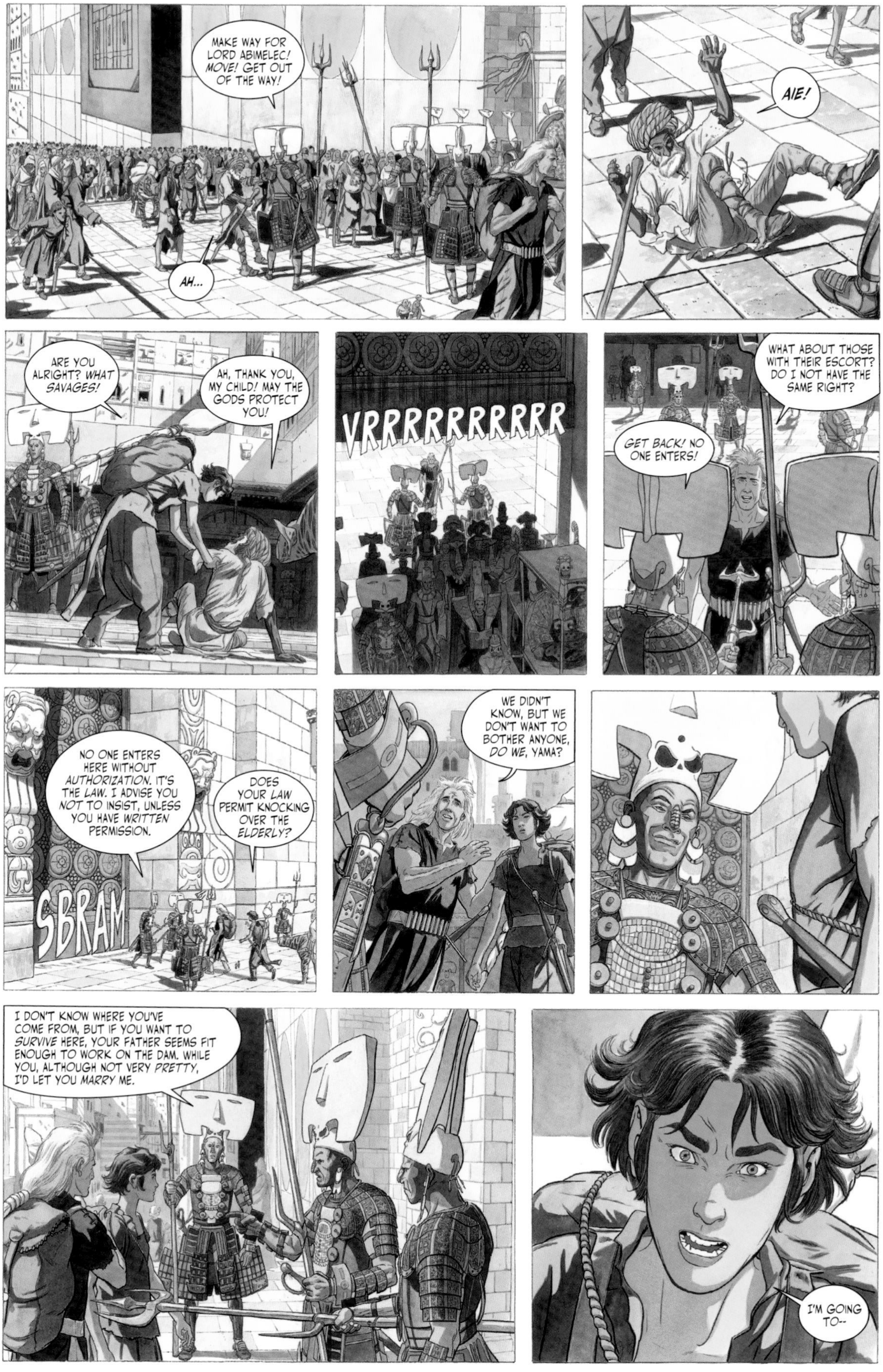

MAKE WAY FOR LORD ABIMELEC! MOVE! GET OUT OF THE WAY!
AH...
AIE!
ARE YOU ALRIGHT? WHAT SAVAGES!
AH, THANK YOU, MY CHILD! MAY THE GODS PROTECT YOU!
VRRRRRRRRRR
WHAT ABOUT THOSE WITH THEIR ESCORT? DO I NOT HAVE THE SAME RIGHT?
GET BACK! NO ONE ENTERS!
NO ONE ENTERS HERE WITHOUT AUTHORIZATION. IT'S THE LAW. I ADVISE YOU NOT TO INSIST, UNLESS YOU HAVE WRITTEN PERMISSION.
DOES YOUR LAW PERMIT KNOCKING OVER THE ELDERLY?
SBRAM
WE DIDN'T KNOW, BUT WE DON'T WANT TO BOTHER ANYONE, DO WE, YAMA?
I DON'T KNOW WHERE YOU'VE COME FROM, BUT IF YOU WANT TO SURVIVE HERE, YOUR FATHER SEEMS FIT ENOUGH TO WORK ON THE DAM. WHILE YOU, ALTHOUGH NOT VERY PRETTY, I'D LET YOU MARRY ME.
I'M GOING TO--

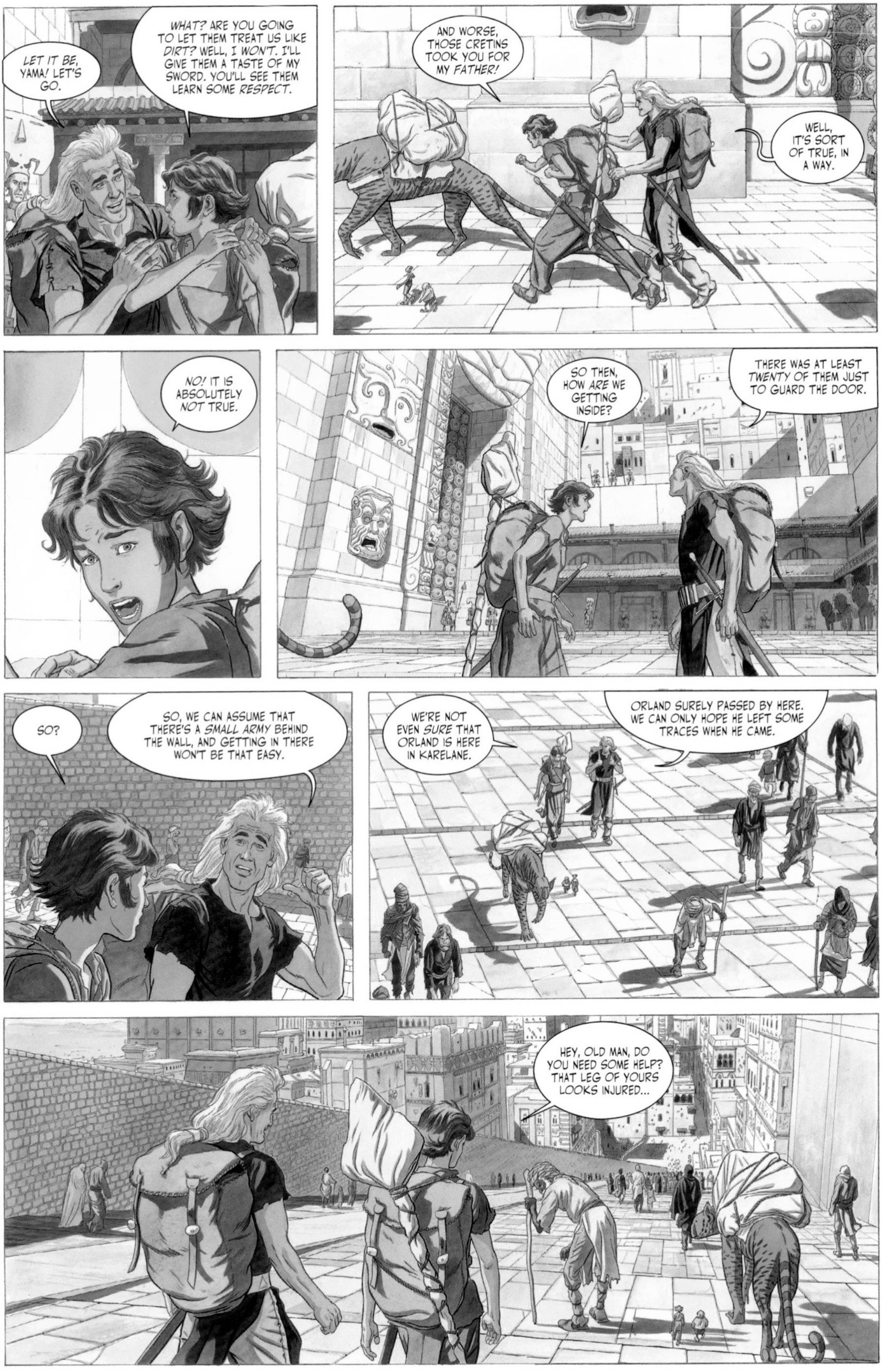
LET IT BE, YAMA! LET'S GO.
WHAT? ARE YOU GOING TO LET THEM TREAT US LIKE DIRT? WELL, I WON'T. I'LL GIVE THEM A TASTE OF MY SWORD. YOU'LL SEE THEM LEARN SOME RESPECT.
AND WORSE, THOSE CRETINS TOOK YOU FOR MY FATHER!
WELL, IT'S SORT OF TRUE, IN A WAY.
NO! IT IS ABSOLUTELY NOT TRUE.
SO THEN, HOW ARE WE GETTING INSIDE?
THERE WAS AT LEAST TWENTY OF THEM JUST TO GUARD THE DOOR.
SO?
SO, WE CAN ASSUME THAT THERE'S A SMALL ARMY BEHIND THE WALL, AND GETTING IN THERE WON'T BE THAT EASY.
WE'RE NOT EVEN SURE THAT ORLAND IS HERE IN KARELANE.
ORLAND SURELY PASSED BY HERE. WE CAN ONLY HOPE HE LEFT SOME TRACES WHEN HE CAME.
HEY, OLD MAN, DO YOU NEED SOME HELP? THAT LEG OF YOURS LOOKS INJURED...

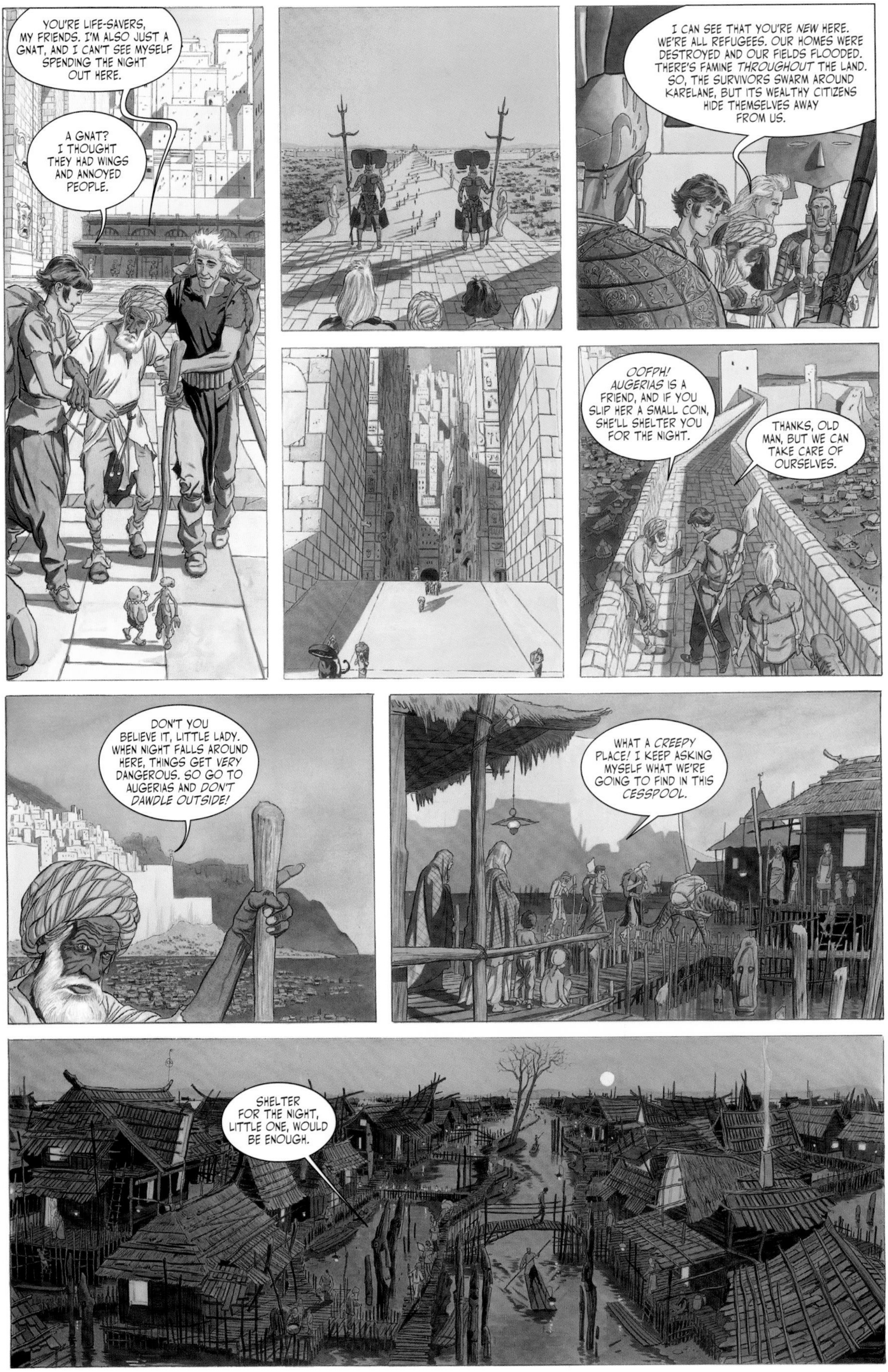
YOU'RE LIFE-SAVERS, MY FRIENDS. I'M ALSO JUST A GNAT, AND I CAN'T SEE MYSELF SPENDING THE NIGHT OUT HERE.
A GNAT? I THOUGHT THEY HAD WINGS AND ANNOYED PEOPLE.
I CAN SEE THAT YOU'RE NEW HERE. WE'RE ALL REFUGEES. OUR HOMES WERE DESTROYED AND OUR FIELDS FLOODED. THERE'S FAMINE THROUGHOUT THE LAND. SO, THE SURVIVORS SWARM AROUND KARELANE, BUT ITS WEALTHY CITIZENS HIDE THEMSELVES AWAY FROM US.
OOFPH! AUGERIAS IS A FRIEND, AND IF YOU SLIP HER A SMALL COIN, SHE'LL SHELTER YOU FOR THE NIGHT.
THANKS, OLD MAN, BUT WE CAN TAKE CARE OF OURSELVES.
DON'T YOU BELIEVE IT, LITTLE LADY. WHEN NIGHT FALLS AROUND HERE, THINGS GET VERY DANGEROUS. SO GO TO AUGERIAS AND DON'T DAWDLE OUTSIDE!
WHAT A CREEPY PLACE! I KEEP ASKING MYSELF WHAT WE'RE GOING TO FIND IN THIS CESSPOOL.
SHELTER FOR THE NIGHT, LITTLE ONE, WOULD BE ENOUGH.

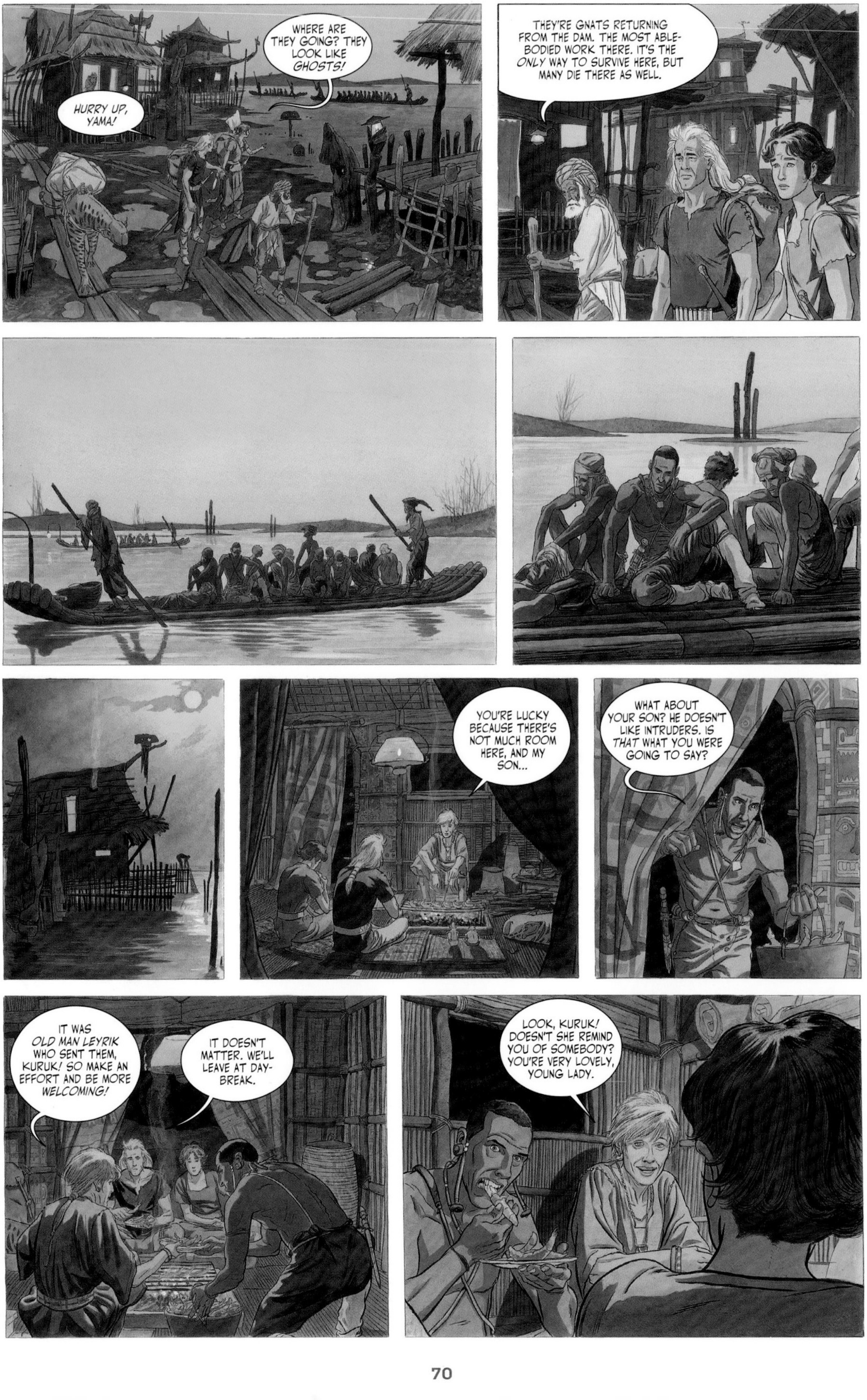
HURRY UP, YAMA!
WHERE ARE THEY GOING? THEY LOOK LIKE GHOSTS!
THEY'RE GNATS RETURNING FROM THE DAM. THE MOST ABLE-BODIED WORK THERE. IT'S THE ONLY WAY TO SURVIVE HERE, BUT MANY DIE THERE AS WELL.
YOU'RE LUCKY BECAUSE THERE'S NOT MUCH ROOM HERE, AND MY SON...
WHAT ABOUT YOUR SON? HE DOESN'T LIKE INTRUDERS. IS THAT WHAT YOU WERE GOING TO SAY?
IT WAS OLD MAN LEYRIK WHO SENT THEM, KURUK! SO MAKE AN EFFORT AND BE MORE WELCOMING!
IT DOESN'T MATTER. WE'LL LEAVE AT DAY-BREAK.
LOOK, KURUK! DOESN'T SHE REMIND YOU OF SOMEBODY? YOU'RE VERY LOVELY, YOUNG LADY.

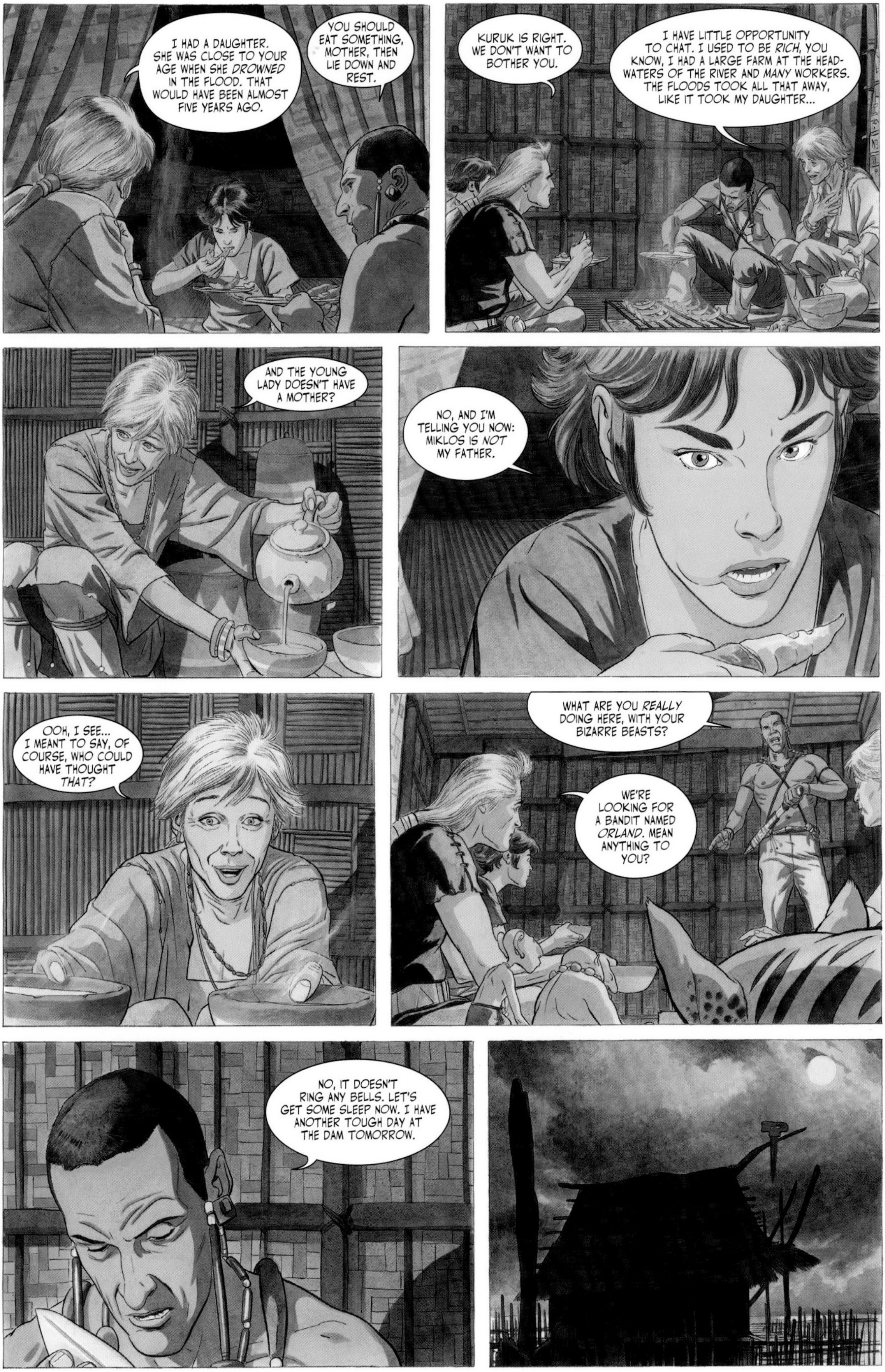

I HAD A DAUGHTER. SHE WAS CLOSE TO YOUR AGE WHEN SHE *DROWNED* IN THE FLOOD. THAT WOULD HAVE BEEN ALMOST FIVE YEARS AGO.
YOU SHOULD EAT SOMETHING, MOTHER, THEN LIE DOWN AND REST.
KURUK IS RIGHT. WE DON'T WANT TO BOTHER YOU.
I HAVE LITTLE OPPORTUNITY TO CHAT. I USED TO BE *RICH*, YOU KNOW, I HAD A LARGE FARM AT THE HEAD-WATERS OF THE RIVER AND *MANY* WORKERS. THE FLOODS TOOK ALL THAT AWAY, LIKE IT TOOK MY DAUGHTER...
AND THE YOUNG LADY DOESN'T HAVE A MOTHER?
NO, AND I'M TELLING YOU NOW: MIKLOS IS *NOT* MY FATHER.
OOH, I SEE... I MEANT TO SAY, OF COURSE, WHO COULD HAVE THOUGHT *THAT*?
WHAT ARE YOU *REALLY* DOING HERE, WITH YOUR BIZARRE BEASTS?
WE'RE LOOKING FOR A BANDIT NAMED *ORLAND*. MEAN ANYTHING TO YOU?
NO, IT DOESN'T RING ANY BELLS. LET'S GET SOME SLEEP NOW. I HAVE ANOTHER TOUGH DAY AT THE DAM TOMORROW.

LOOK HOW THE NIGHT MAKES THE WORLD APPEAR LIKE IT WAS BEFORE!

THE GNATS ARE MORE AND MORE NUMEROUS. THEY'LL END UP SINKING US, SIRE.

SO MUCH THE BETTER, YOU *IDIOT!* WHEN THAT DAY COMES, WE'LL BE LONG GONE AND FULL OF RICHES.

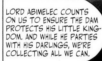

LORD ABIMELEC COUNTS ON US TO ENSURE THE DAM PROTECTS HIS LITTLE KINGDOM. AND WHILE HE PARTIES WITH HIS DARLINGS, WE'RE COLLECTING ALL WE CAN.

AND WHAT WILL HAPPEN WHEN THE DAM IS *FINISHED?* ABIMELEC WILL GET RID OF BOTH HIS WORKERS AND US.

THEY SAY THAT OUT WEST, LIFE IS STILL WORTH LIVING. SHOULDN'T WE LEAVE THIS CITY WHILE THERE'S STILL TIME?

HERE OR THERE, CHAOS IS STILL THE SAME, BUT HERE IT'S EXTREMELY *PROFITABLE!* WE WERE NOTHING MORE THAN STARVING *MERCENARIES,* AND NOW LOOK AT WHAT I'VE DONE FOR US! WHAT ARE YOU WORRIED ABOUT, YOU *MISERABLE IMBECILE?*

GENERAL ORLAND, WE'LL STAY BY YOUR SIDE, NO MATTER WHAT HAPPENS.

SOMEONE'S COMING, GENERAL!

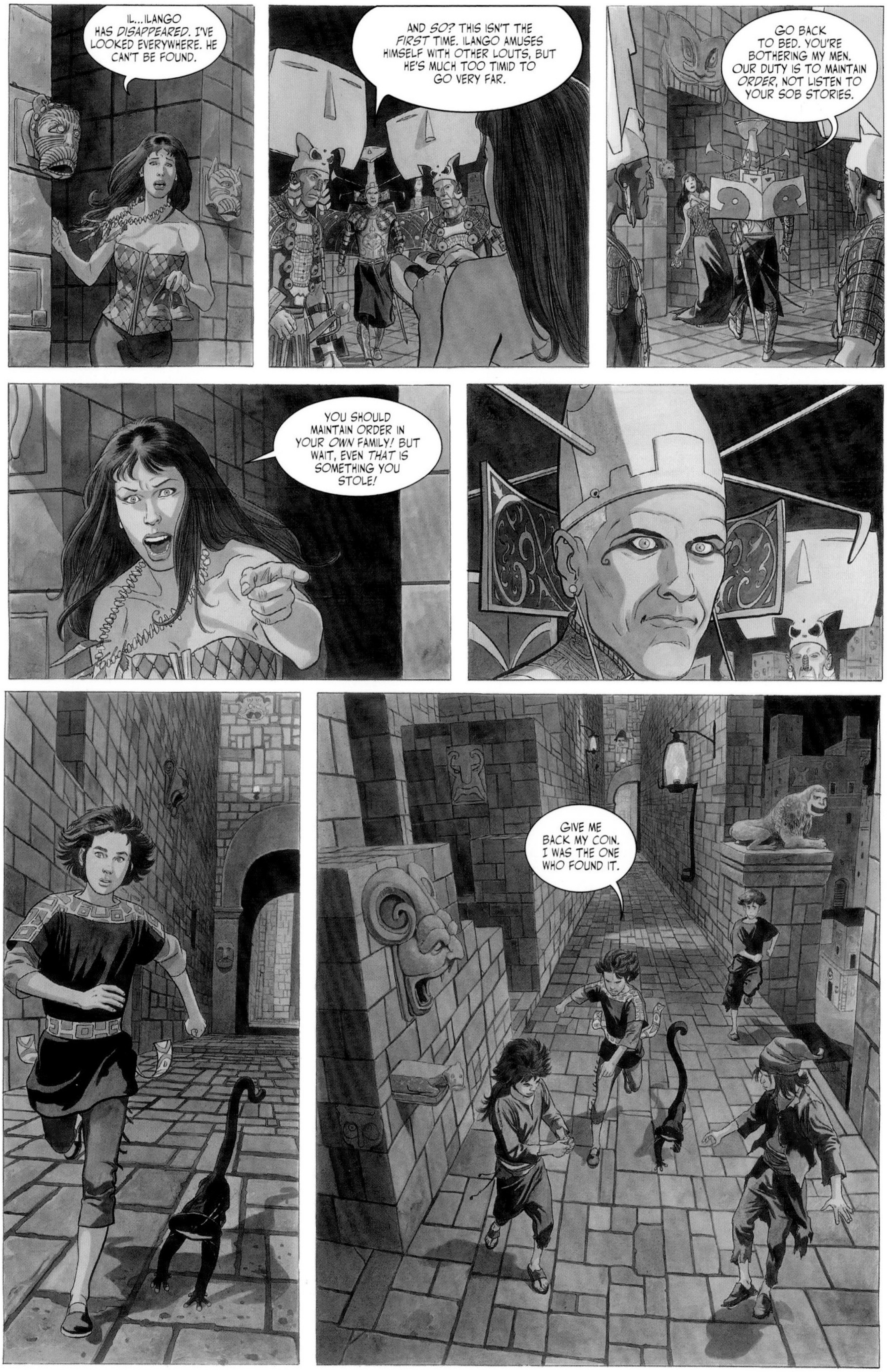
IL...ILANGO HAS *DISAPPEARED*. I'VE LOOKED EVERYWHERE. HE CAN'T BE FOUND.
AND *SO?* THIS ISN'T THE *FIRST* TIME. ILANGO AMUSES HIMSELF WITH OTHER LOUTS, BUT HE'S MUCH TOO TIMID TO GO VERY FAR.
GO BACK TO BED. YOU'RE BOTHERING MY MEN. OUR DUTY IS TO MAINTAIN *ORDER*, NOT LISTEN TO YOUR SOB STORIES.
YOU SHOULD MAINTAIN ORDER IN YOUR *OWN* FAMILY! BUT WAIT, EVEN *THAT* IS SOMETHING YOU STOLE!
GIVE ME BACK MY COIN. I WAS THE ONE WHO FOUND IT.

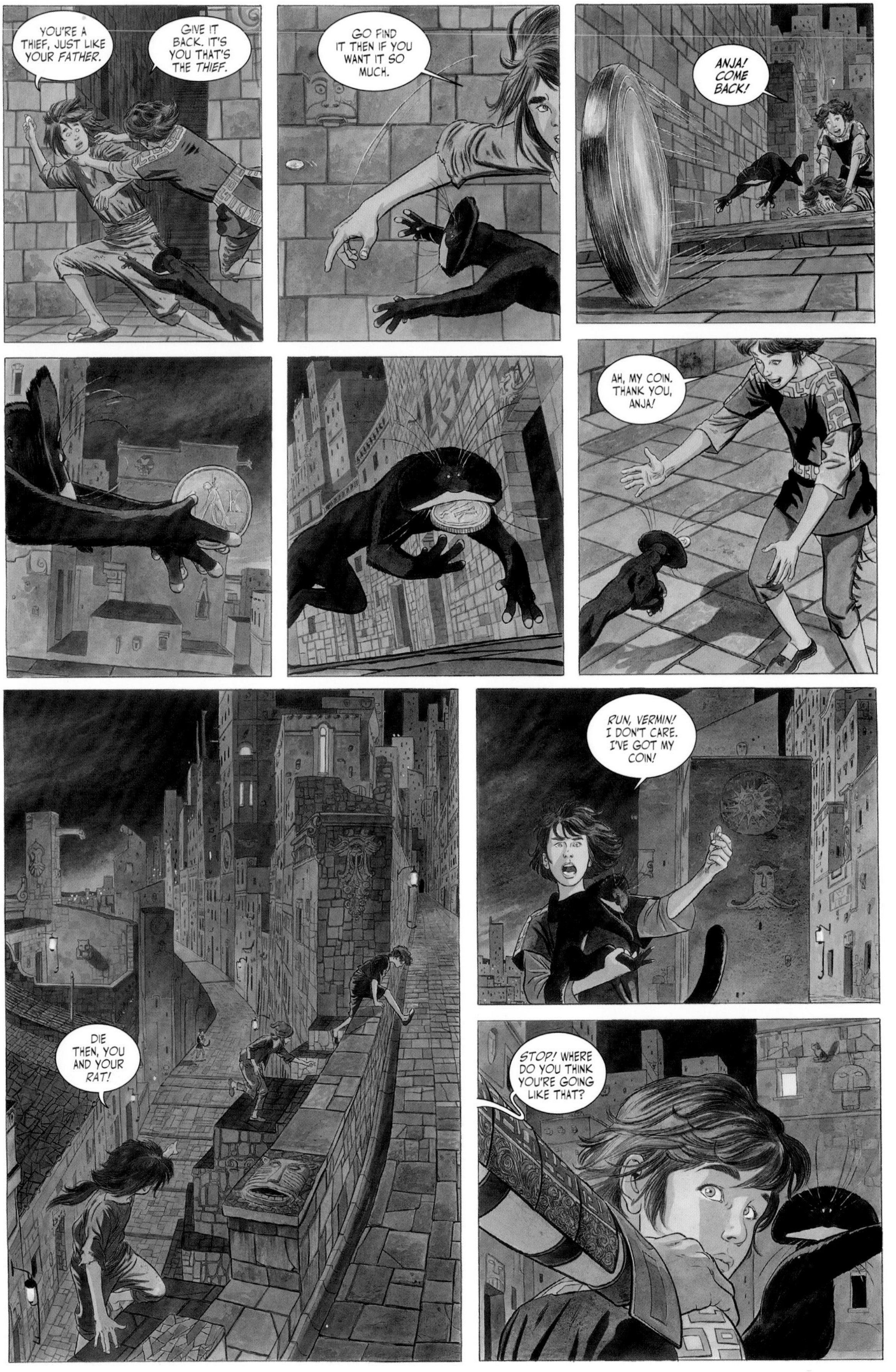
YOU'RE A THIEF, JUST LIKE YOUR FATHER.
GIVE IT BACK. IT'S YOU THAT'S THE THIEF.
GO FIND IT THEN IF YOU WANT IT SO MUCH.
ANJA! COME BACK!
AH, MY COIN. THANK YOU, ANJA!
DIE THEN, YOU AND YOUR RAT!
RUN, VERMIN! I DON'T CARE. I'VE GOT MY COIN!
STOP! WHERE DO YOU THINK YOU'RE GOING LIKE THAT?

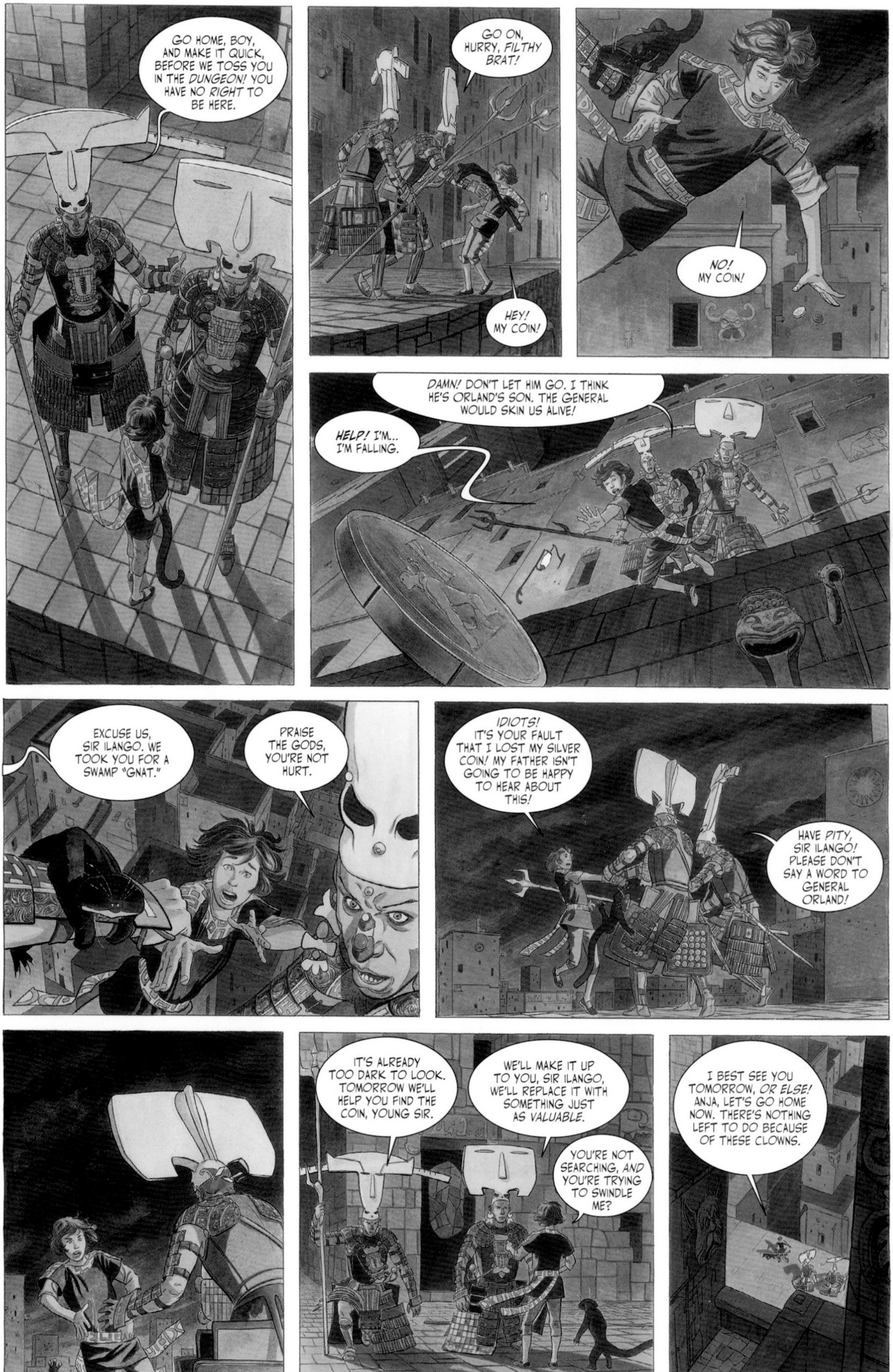
GO HOME, BOY, AND MAKE IT QUICK, BEFORE WE TOSS YOU IN THE *DUNGEON!* YOU HAVE NO *RIGHT* TO BE HERE.
GO ON, HURRY, *FILTHY BRAT!*
HEY! MY COIN!
NO! MY COIN!
DAMN! DON'T LET HIM GO. I THINK HE'S ORLAND'S SON. THE GENERAL WOULD SKIN US ALIVE!
HELP! I'M... I'M FALLING.
EXCUSE US, SIR ILANGO. WE TOOK YOU FOR A SWAMP "GNAT."
PRAISE THE GODS, YOU'RE NOT HURT.
IDIOTS! IT'S YOUR FAULT THAT I LOST MY SILVER COIN! MY FATHER ISN'T GOING TO BE HAPPY TO HEAR ABOUT THIS!
HAVE *PITY,* SIR ILANGO! PLEASE DON'T SAY A WORD TO GENERAL ORLAND!
IT'S ALREADY TOO DARK TO LOOK. TOMORROW WE'LL HELP YOU FIND THE COIN, YOUNG SIR.
WE'LL MAKE IT UP TO YOU, SIR ILANGO, WE'LL REPLACE IT WITH SOMETHING JUST AS *VALUABLE.*
YOU'RE NOT SEARCHING, *AND* YOU'RE TRYING TO SWINDLE ME?
I BEST SEE YOU TOMORROW, *OR ELSE!* ANJA, LET'S GO HOME NOW. THERE'S NOTHING LEFT TO DO BECAUSE OF THESE CLOWNS.

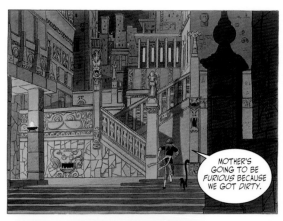

MOTHER'S GOING TO BE *FURIOUS* BECAUSE WE GOT *DIRTY*.

HURRY, ANJA, BUT DON'T MAKE A SOUND. WE HAVE TO GET BACK WITHOUT BEING HEARD.

ILANGO?

DEAR COUNTRY SPRITES! DEAR FOREST GENIES! PLEASE DON'T LET HIM TURN OUT LIKE HIS *FATHER!* I BEG YOU.

DON'T WORRY, MAMA. I'LL SOON HAVE ENOUGH GOLD AND SILVER SO WE CAN *LEAVE*.

WHAT ARE YOU *SAYING?* DON'T BE SO SILLY. WHAT WERE YOU UP TO?

ONE DAY, WE'LL ESCAPE, AND DAD WILL *NEVER* FIND US. TELL ME AGAIN ABOUT THE LAND WHERE YOU ONCE LIVED.

YOUR FATHER CAN'T BE *SO* BAD IF HE GAVE ME THE MOST BEAUTIFUL OF GIFTS, *YOU*.

AND *THAT*, WAS THAT ALSO A GIFT?

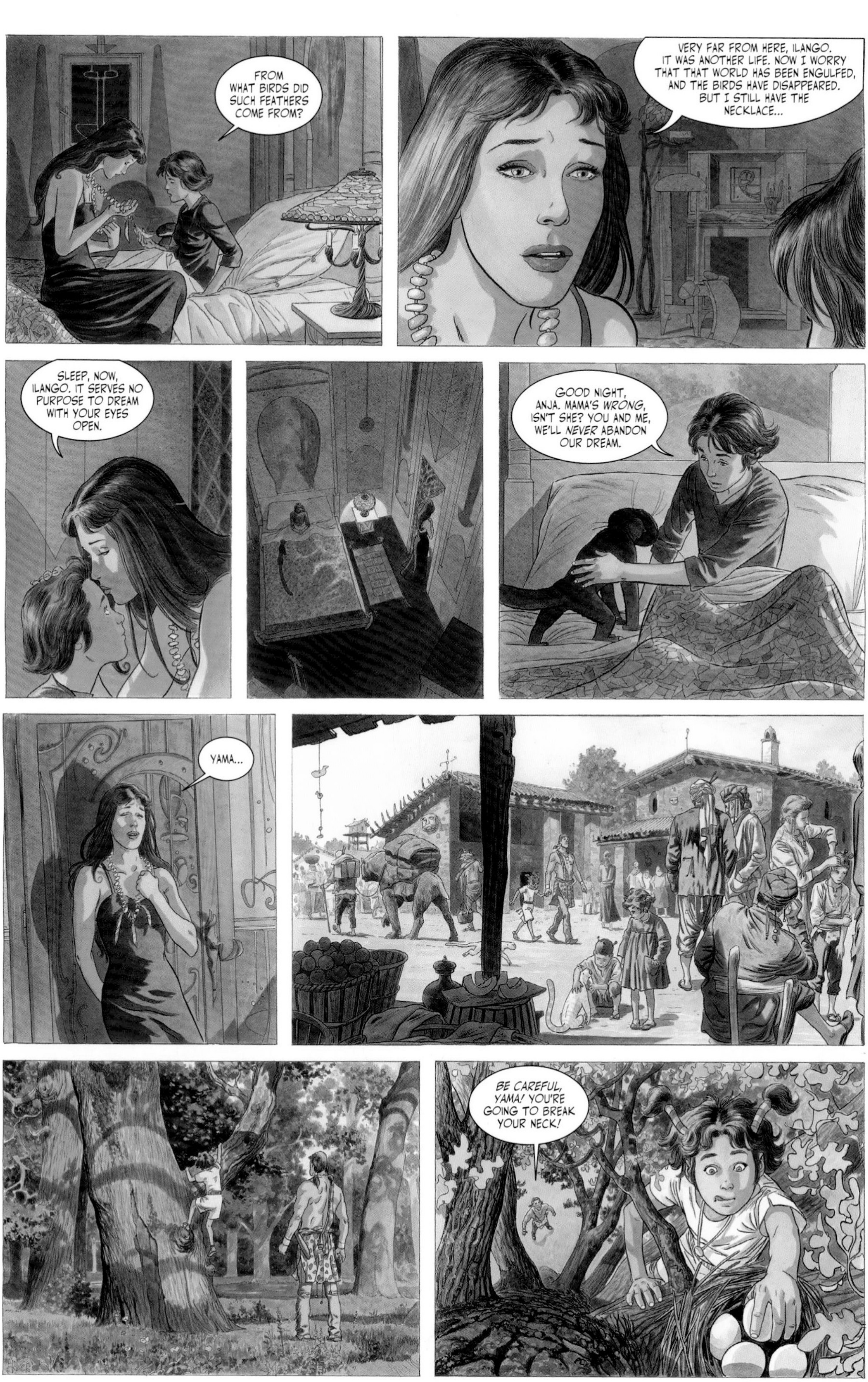
FROM WHAT BIRDS DID SUCH FEATHERS COME FROM?
VERY FAR FROM HERE, ILANGO. IT WAS ANOTHER LIFE. NOW I WORRY THAT THAT WORLD HAS BEEN ENGULFED, AND THE BIRDS HAVE DISAPPEARED. BUT I STILL HAVE THE NECKLACE...
SLEEP, NOW, ILANGO. IT SERVES NO PURPOSE TO DREAM WITH YOUR EYES OPEN.
GOOD NIGHT, ANJA. MAMA'S *WRONG*, ISN'T SHE? YOU AND ME, WE'LL *NEVER* ABANDON OUR DREAM.
YAMA...
BE CAREFUL, *YAMA!* YOU'RE GOING TO BREAK YOUR NECK!

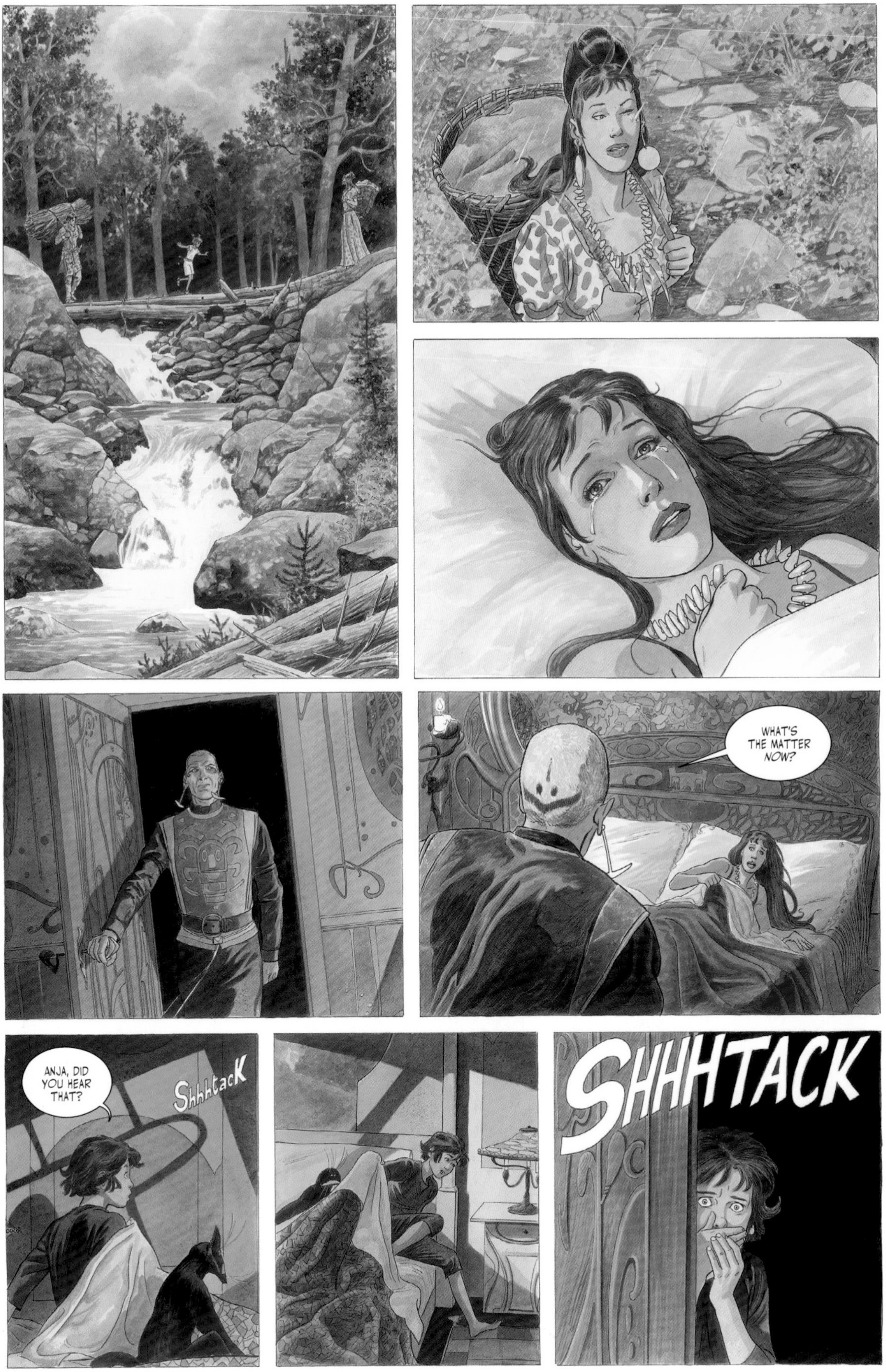
WHAT'S THE MATTER NOW?
ANJA, DID YOU HEAR THAT?
ShhhtacK
SHHHTACK

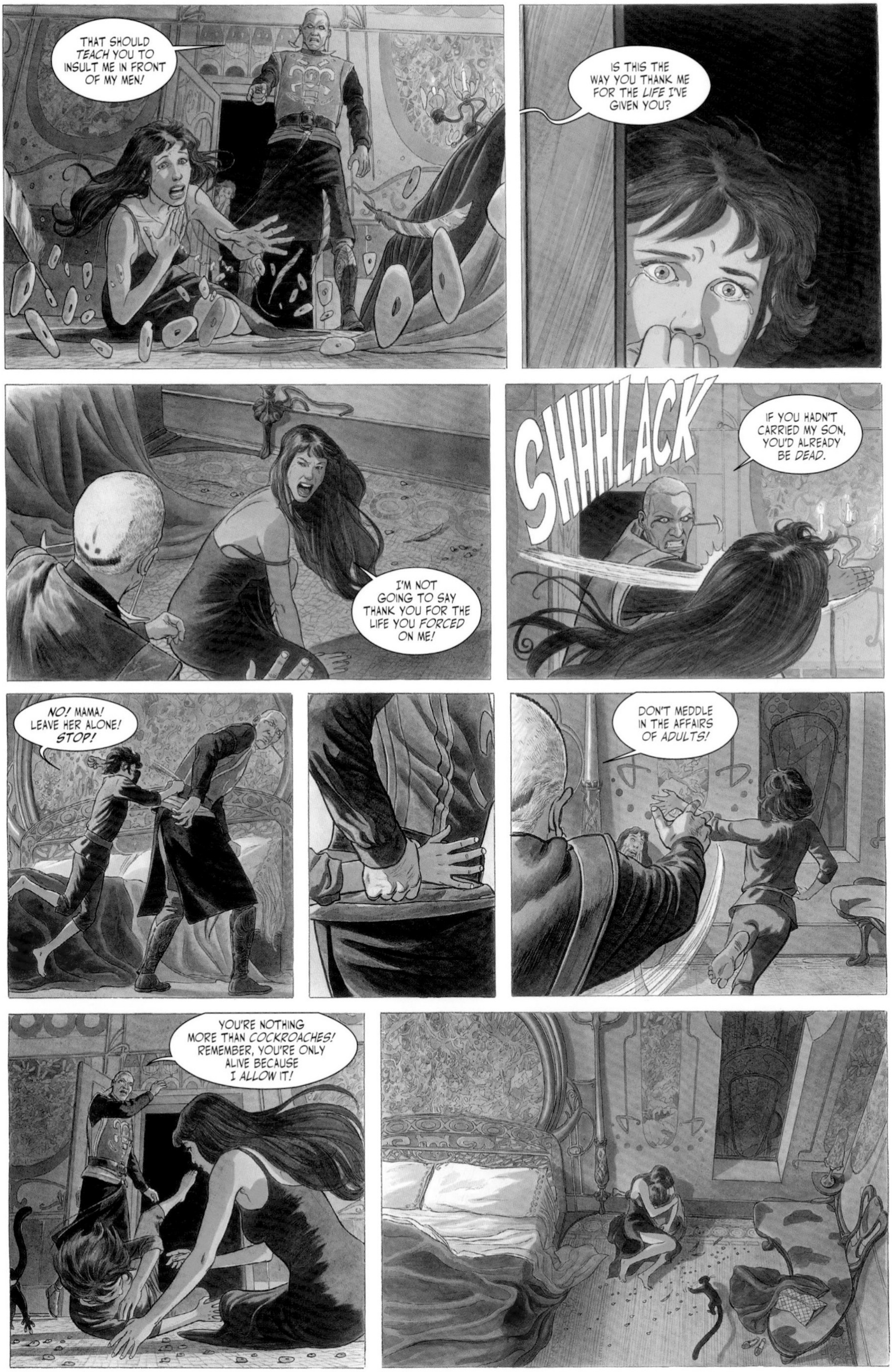
THAT SHOULD TEACH YOU TO INSULT ME IN FRONT OF MY MEN!
IS THIS THE WAY YOU THANK ME FOR THE LIFE I'VE GIVEN YOU?
I'M NOT GOING TO SAY THANK YOU FOR THE LIFE YOU FORCED ON ME!
SHHHLACK
IF YOU HADN'T CARRIED MY SON, YOU'D ALREADY BE DEAD.
NO! MAMA! LEAVE HER ALONE! STOP!
DON'T MEDDLE IN THE AFFAIRS OF ADULTS!
YOU'RE NOTHING MORE THAN COCKROACHES! REMEMBER, YOU'RE ONLY ALIVE BECAUSE I ALLOW IT!

SOON THERE'LL BE NOTHING LEFT TO EAT.

DON'T WORRY, I THINK I'LL BE ABLE TO SELL ALL THIS QUICKLY.

THE STRANGERS' LITTLE *BEASTS* WOULD FEED US FOR A FEW DAYS.

TAKE THIS AS WELL! YOU'LL BE ABLE TO MAKE A BIT OF MONEY OFF IT.

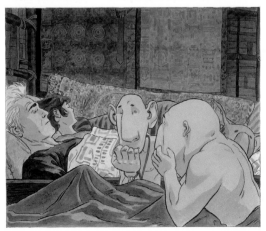

MIK...MIK... MIK...

WAK... WAKE...WAKE UP, QUICK!

WHAT? WHAT THE...?

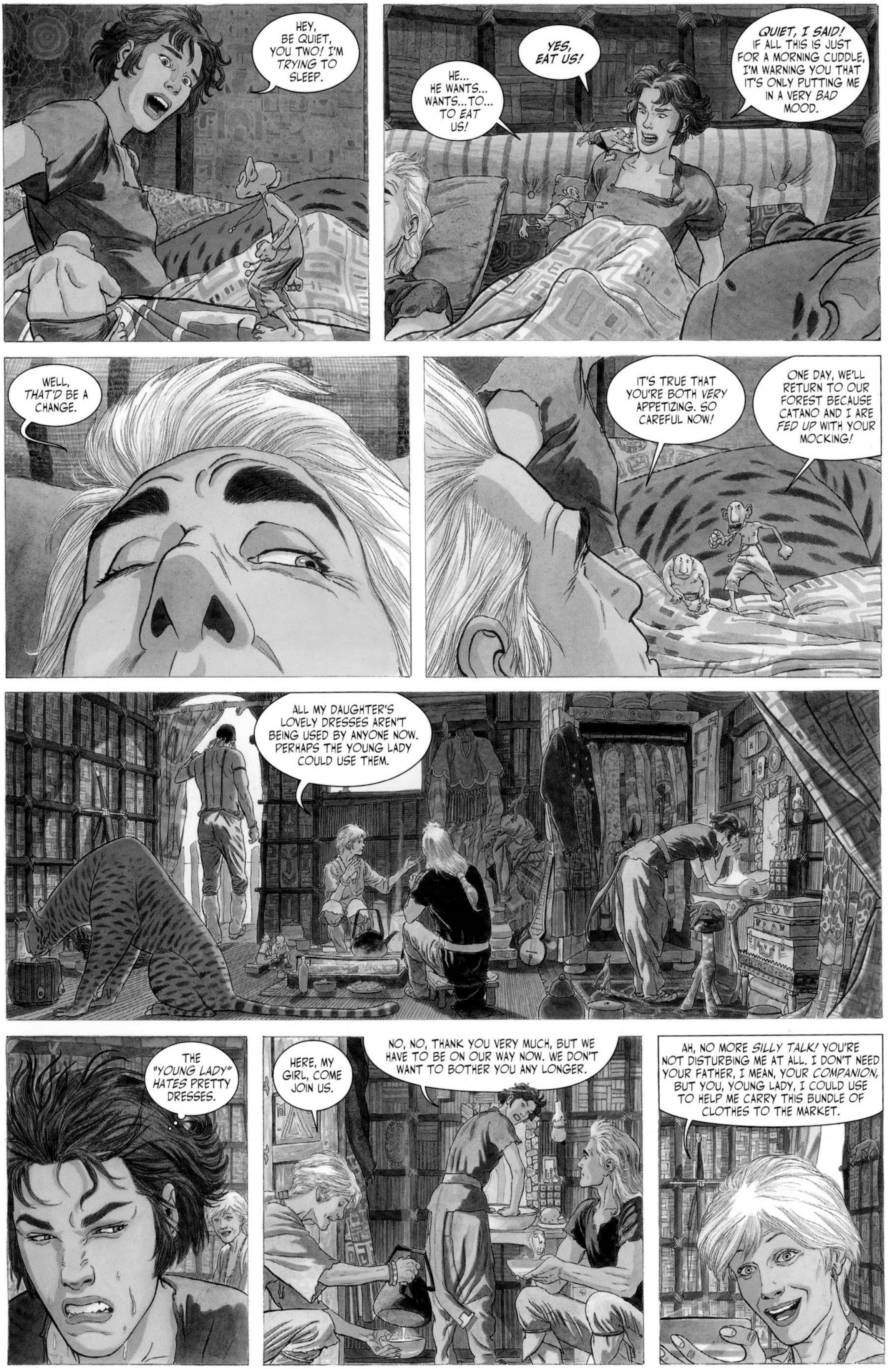
HEY, BE QUIET, YOU TWO! I'M TRYING TO SLEEP.
HE... HE WANTS... WANTS...TO... TO EAT US!
YES, EAT US!
QUIET, I SAID! IF ALL THIS IS JUST FOR A MORNING CUDDLE, I'M WARNING YOU THAT IT'S ONLY PUTTING ME IN A VERY BAD MOOD.
WELL, THAT'D BE A CHANGE.
IT'S TRUE THAT YOU'RE BOTH VERY APPETIZING. SO CAREFUL NOW!
ONE DAY, WE'LL RETURN TO OUR FOREST BECAUSE CATANO AND I ARE FED UP WITH YOUR MOCKING!
ALL MY DAUGHTER'S LOVELY DRESSES AREN'T BEING USED BY ANYONE NOW. PERHAPS THE YOUNG LADY COULD USE THEM.
THE "YOUNG LADY" HATES PRETTY DRESSES.
HERE, MY GIRL, COME JOIN US.
NO, NO, THANK YOU VERY MUCH, BUT WE HAVE TO BE ON OUR WAY NOW. WE DON'T WANT TO BOTHER YOU ANY LONGER.
AH, NO MORE SILLY TALK! YOU'RE NOT DISTURBING ME AT ALL. I DON'T NEED YOUR FATHER, I MEAN, YOUR COMPANION, BUT YOU, YOUNG LADY, I COULD USE TO HELP ME CARRY THIS BUNDLE OF CLOTHES TO THE MARKET.

IF WE CAN BE OF ANY HELP, WELL, THEN OF COURSE...

GO AHEAD, YAMA. AS FOR ME, I'LL CONTINUE SEARCHING. BE NICE TO THE LADY, OKAY?

BE CAREFUL WITH THE SOLDIERS. BY NIGHT, THE RATS ARE THE ONES TO LOOK OUT FOR, BUT DURING THE DAY, IT'S THE SOLDIERS WHO PREY ON US.

LET'S GET READY TO GO.

DON'T MOVE... YOU HAVE THE LOVELY HAIR OF A PRINCESS, MY DEAR.

PITY THAT A CERTAIN OAF HASN'T THE EYES TO NOTICE IT.

THE OAF IN QUESTION LOOKS AT YOU WITH LOVING EYES, BUT THE EYES OF A FATHER INDEED.

YEAH... I THINK HE JUST FINDS ME UGLY.

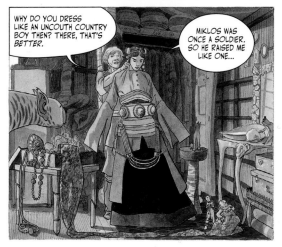

WHY DO YOU DRESS LIKE AN UNCOUTH COUNTRY BOY THEN? THERE, THAT'S BETTER.

MIKLOS WAS ONCE A SOLDIER. SO HE RAISED ME LIKE ONE...

WOW...! IS THAT REALLY ME?

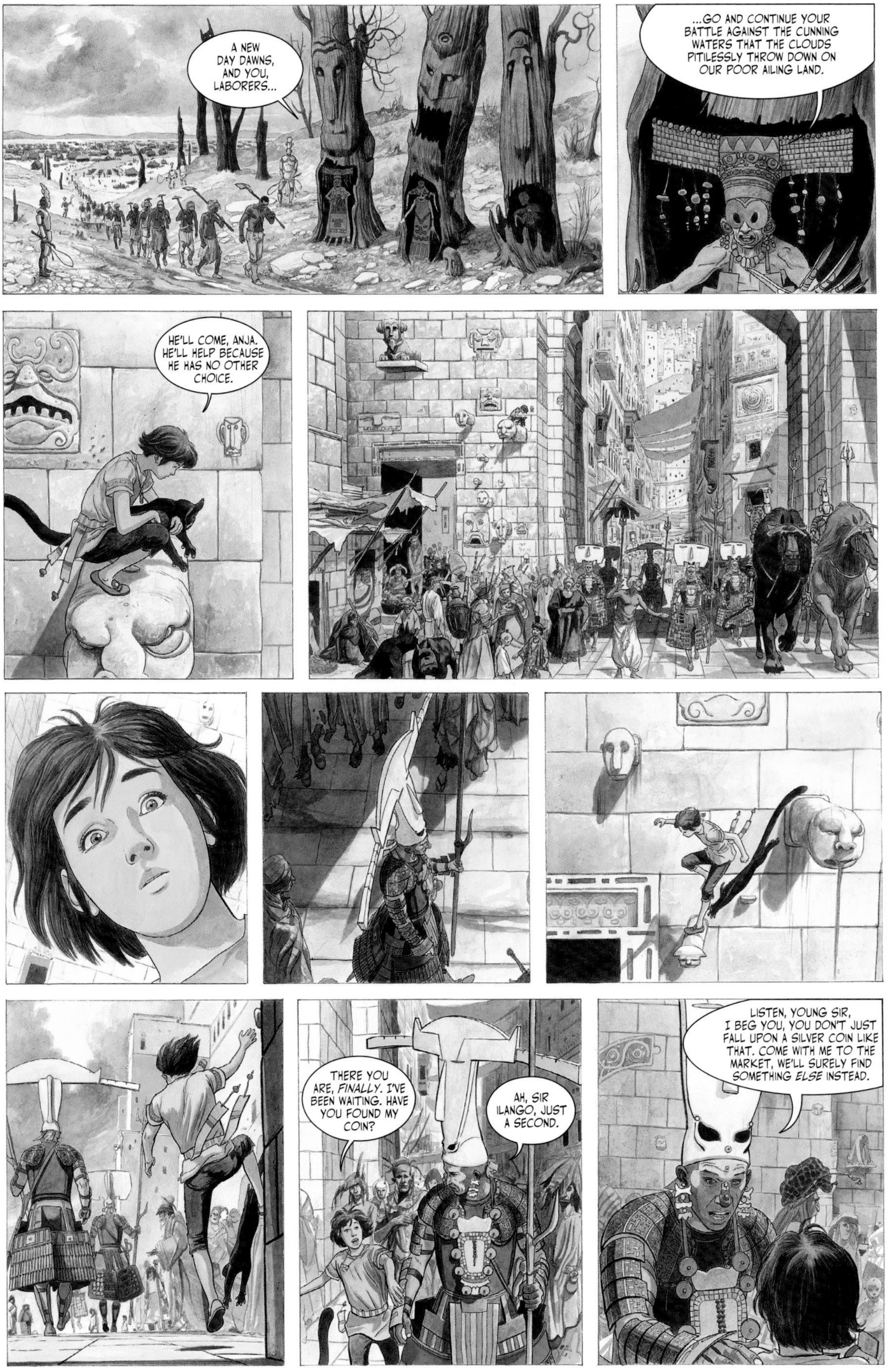
A NEW DAY DAWNS, AND YOU, LABORERS...
...GO AND CONTINUE YOUR BATTLE AGAINST THE CUNNING WATERS THAT THE CLOUDS PITILESSLY THROW DOWN ON OUR POOR AILING LAND.
HE'LL COME, ANJA. HE'LL HELP BECAUSE HE HAS NO OTHER CHOICE.
THERE YOU ARE, *FINALLY*. I'VE BEEN WAITING. HAVE YOU FOUND MY COIN?
AH, SIR ILANGO, JUST A SECOND.
LISTEN, YOUNG SIR, I BEG YOU, YOU DON'T JUST FALL UPON A SILVER COIN LIKE THAT. COME WITH ME TO THE MARKET, WE'LL SURELY FIND SOMETHING *ELSE* INSTEAD.

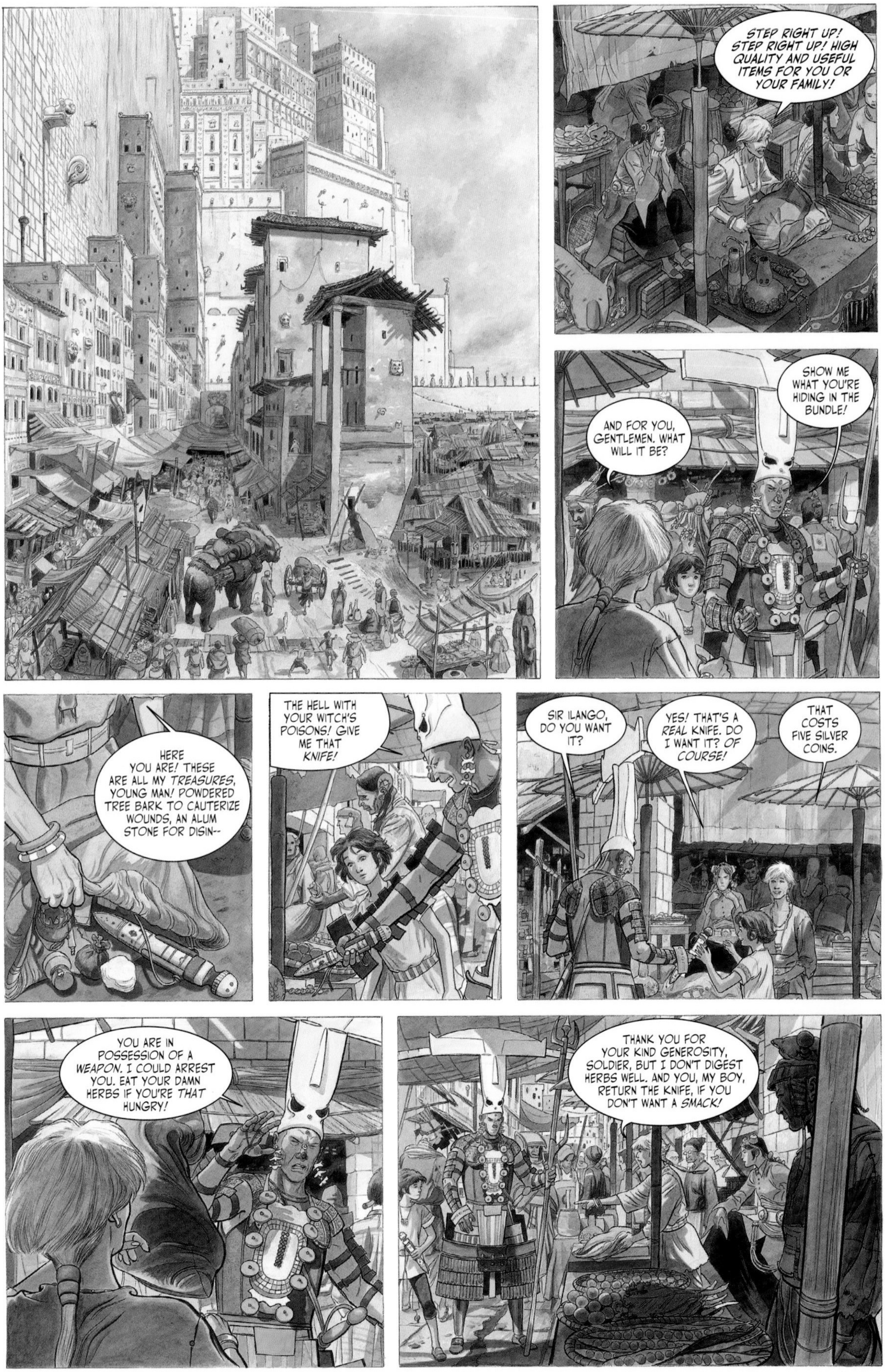
STEP RIGHT UP! STEP RIGHT UP! HIGH QUALITY AND USEFUL ITEMS FOR YOU OR YOUR FAMILY!
AND FOR YOU, GENTLEMEN. WHAT WILL IT BE?
SHOW ME WHAT YOU'RE HIDING IN THE BUNDLE!
HERE YOU ARE! THESE ARE ALL MY TREASURES, YOUNG MAN! POWDERED TREE BARK TO CAUTERIZE WOUNDS, AN ALUM STONE FOR DISIN--
THE HELL WITH YOUR WITCH'S POISONS! GIVE ME THAT KNIFE!
SIR ILANGO, DO YOU WANT IT?
YES! THAT'S A REAL KNIFE. DO I WANT IT? OF COURSE!
THAT COSTS FIVE SILVER COINS.
YOU ARE IN POSSESSION OF A WEAPON. I COULD ARREST YOU. EAT YOUR DAMN HERBS IF YOU'RE THAT HUNGRY!
THANK YOU FOR YOUR KIND GENEROSITY, SOLDIER, BUT I DON'T DIGEST HERBS WELL. AND YOU, MY BOY, RETURN THE KNIFE, IF YOU DON'T WANT A SMACK!

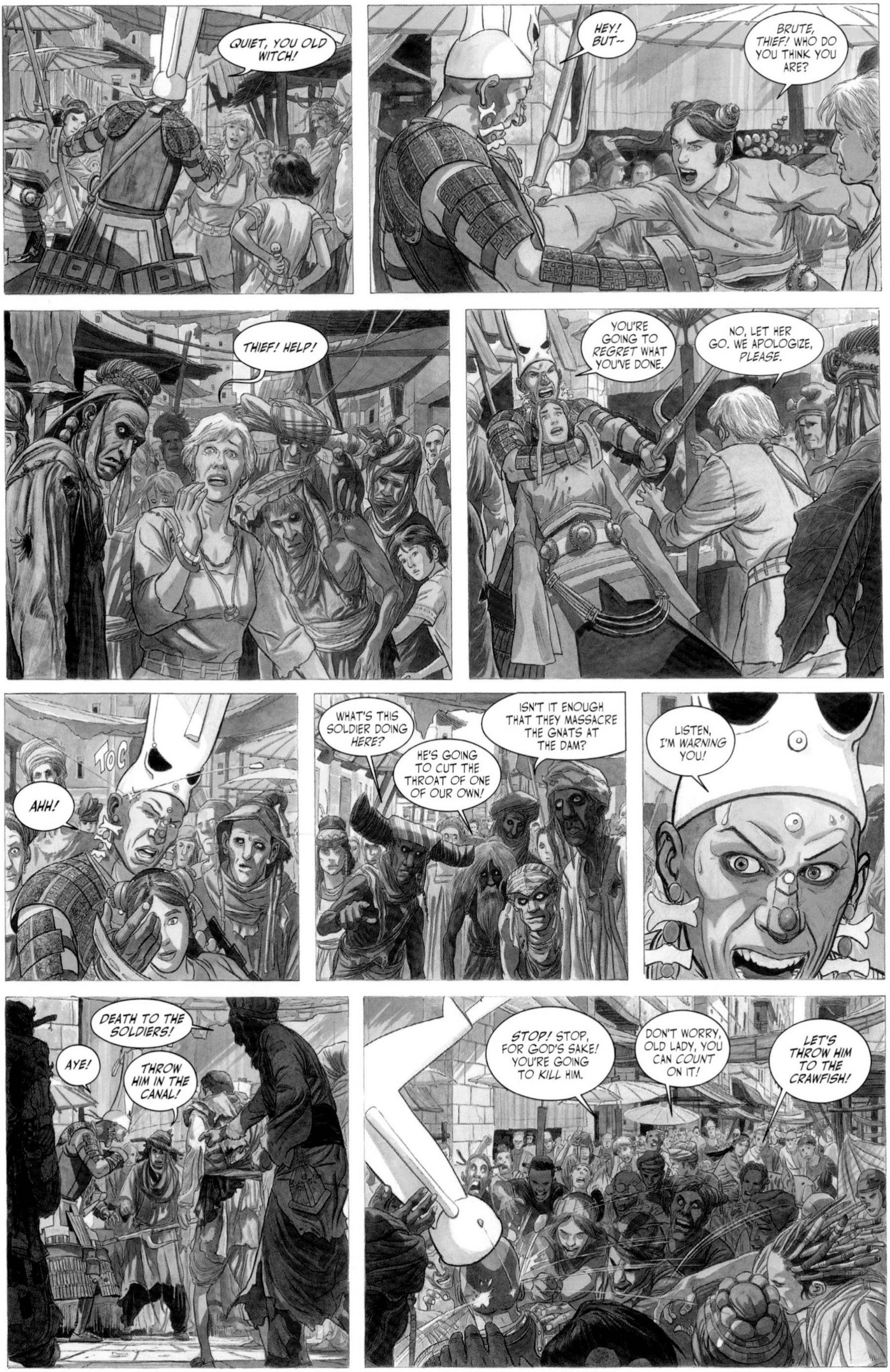
QUIET, YOU OLD WITCH!
HEY! BUT--
BRUTE, THIEF! WHO DO YOU THINK YOU ARE?
THIEF! HELP!
YOU'RE GOING TO REGRET WHAT YOU'VE DONE.
NO, LET HER GO. WE APOLOGIZE, PLEASE.
TOC
AHH!
WHAT'S THIS SOLDIER DOING HERE?
HE'S GOING TO CUT THE THROAT OF ONE OF OUR OWN!
ISN'T IT ENOUGH THAT THEY MASSACRE THE GNATS AT THE DAM?
LISTEN, I'M WARNING YOU!
DEATH TO THE SOLDIERS!
AYE!
THROW HIM IN THE CANAL!
STOP! STOP, FOR GOD'S SAKE! YOU'RE GOING TO KILL HIM.
DON'T WORRY, OLD LADY, YOU CAN COUNT ON IT!
LET'S THROW HIM TO THE CRAWFISH!

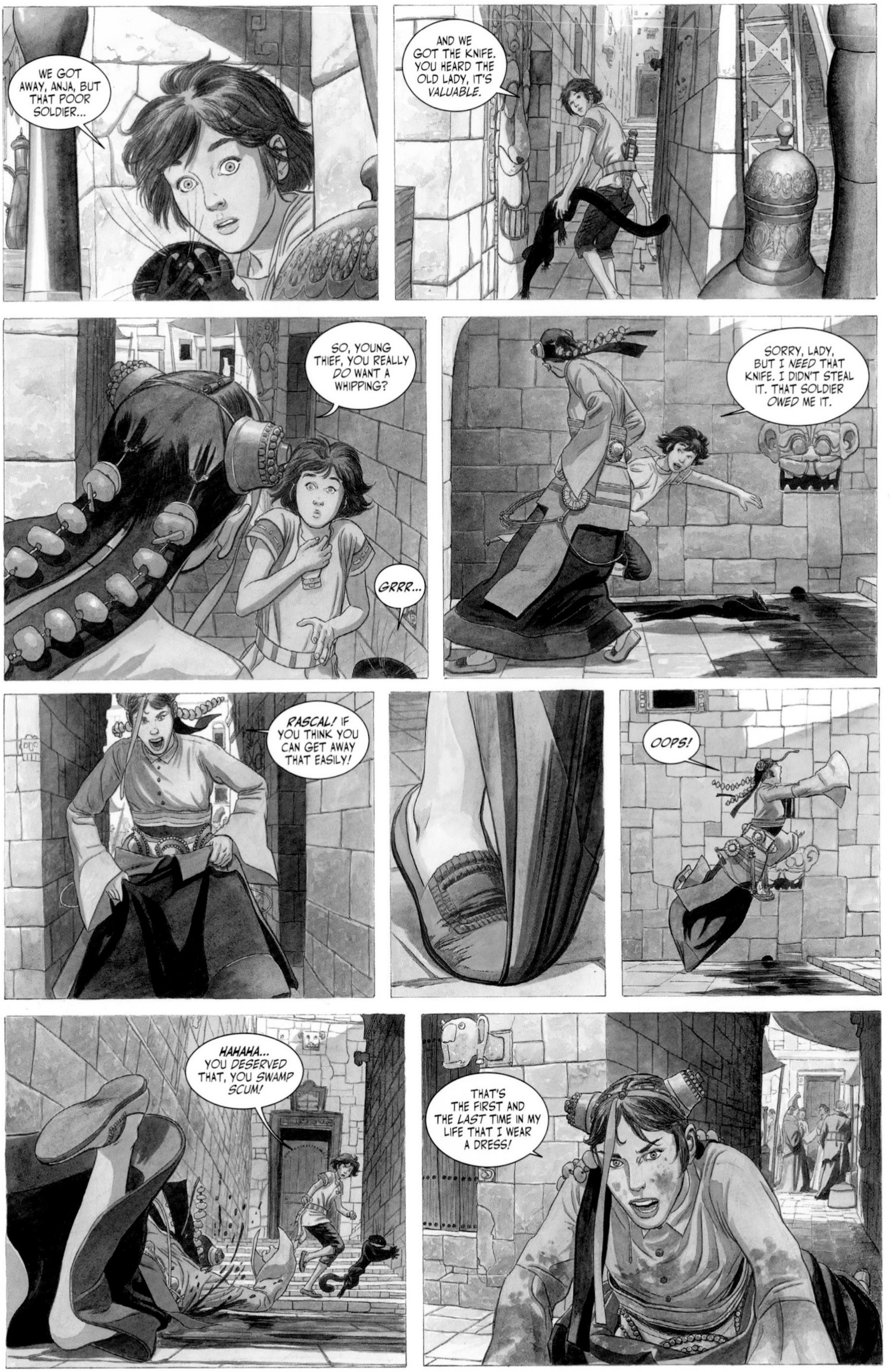
WE GOT AWAY, ANJA, BUT THAT POOR SOLDIER...
AND WE GOT THE KNIFE. YOU HEARD THE OLD LADY, IT'S VALUABLE.
SO, YOUNG THIEF, YOU REALLY DO WANT A WHIPPING?
GRRR...
SORRY, LADY, BUT I NEED THAT KNIFE. I DIDN'T STEAL IT. THAT SOLDIER OWED ME IT.
RASCAL! IF YOU THINK YOU CAN GET AWAY THAT EASILY!
OOPS!
HAHAHA... YOU DESERVED THAT, YOU SWAMP SCUM!
THAT'S THE FIRST AND THE LAST TIME IN MY LIFE THAT I WEAR A DRESS!

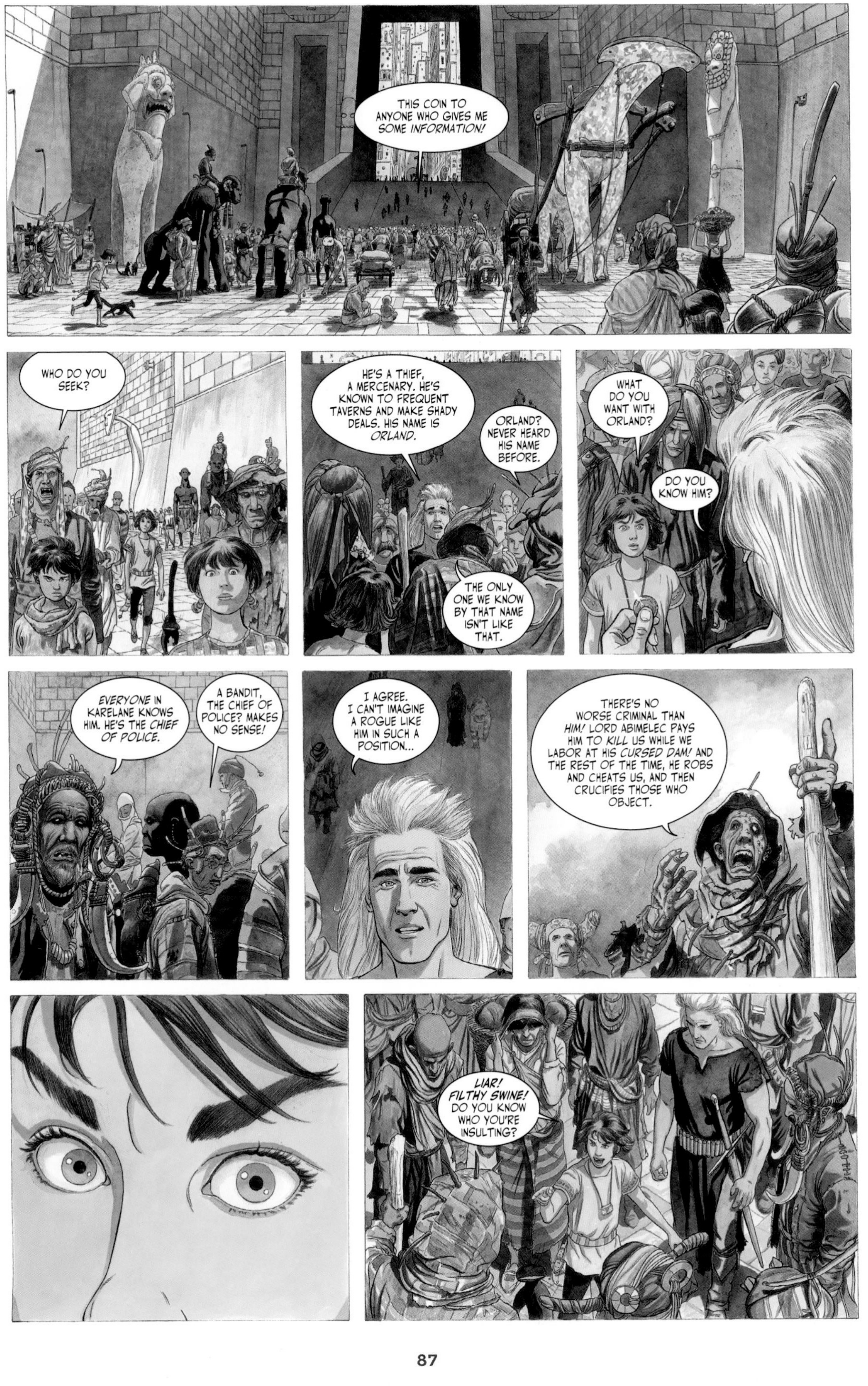
THIS COIN TO ANYONE WHO GIVES ME SOME *INFORMATION!*
WHO DO YOU SEEK?
HE'S A THIEF, A MERCENARY. HE'S KNOWN TO FREQUENT TAVERNS AND MAKE SHADY DEALS. HIS NAME IS *ORLAND.*
ORLAND? NEVER HEARD HIS NAME BEFORE.
THE ONLY ONE WE KNOW BY THAT NAME ISN'T LIKE THAT.
WHAT DO YOU WANT WITH ORLAND?
DO YOU KNOW HIM?
EVERYONE IN KARELANE KNOWS HIM. HE'S THE *CHIEF OF POLICE.*
A BANDIT, THE CHIEF OF POLICE? MAKES NO SENSE!
I AGREE. I CAN'T IMAGINE A ROGUE LIKE HIM IN SUCH A POSITION...
THERE'S NO WORSE CRIMINAL THAN *HIM!* LORD ABIMELEC PAYS HIM TO *KILL* US WHILE WE LABOR AT HIS *CURSED DAM!* AND THE REST OF THE TIME, HE ROBS AND CHEATS US, AND THEN CRUCIFIES THOSE WHO OBJECT.
LIAR! FILTHY SWINE! DO YOU KNOW WHO YOU'RE INSULTING?

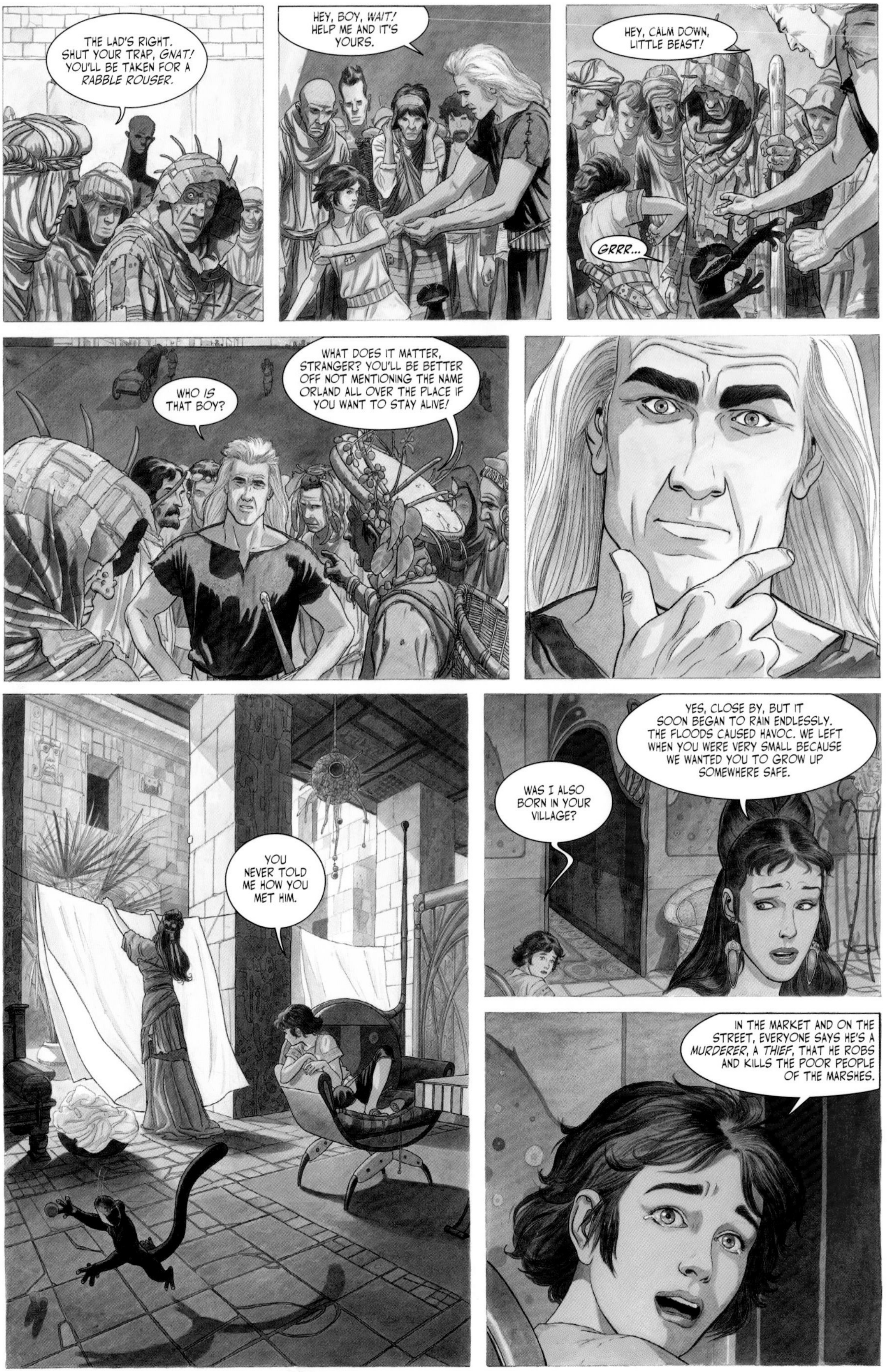
THE LAD'S RIGHT. SHUT YOUR TRAP, *GNAT!* YOU'LL BE TAKEN FOR A *RABBLE ROUSER.*
HEY, BOY, *WAIT!* HELP ME AND IT'S YOURS.
HEY, CALM DOWN, LITTLE BEAST!
GRRR...
WHO *IS* THAT BOY?
WHAT DOES IT MATTER, STRANGER? YOU'LL BE BETTER OFF NOT MENTIONING THE NAME ORLAND ALL OVER THE PLACE IF YOU WANT TO STAY ALIVE!
YOU NEVER TOLD ME HOW YOU MET HIM.
WAS I ALSO BORN IN YOUR VILLAGE?
YES, CLOSE BY, BUT IT SOON BEGAN TO RAIN ENDLESSLY. THE FLOODS CAUSED HAVOC. WE LEFT WHEN YOU WERE VERY SMALL BECAUSE WE WANTED YOU TO GROW UP SOMEWHERE SAFE.
IN THE MARKET AND ON THE STREET, EVERYONE SAYS HE'S A *MURDERER*, A *THIEF*, THAT HE ROBS AND KILLS THE POOR PEOPLE OF THE MARSHES.

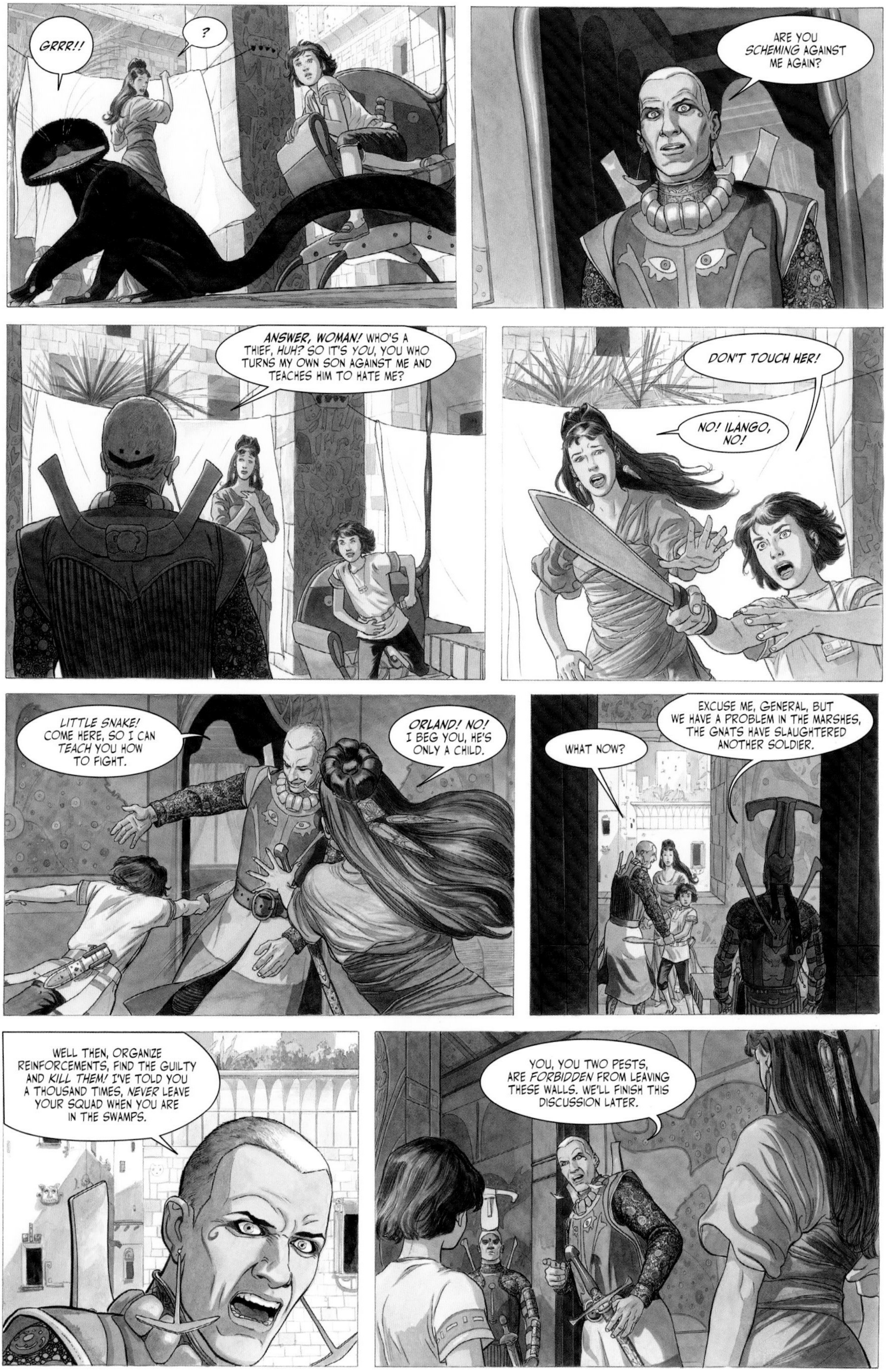
GRRR!!
?
ARE YOU SCHEMING AGAINST ME AGAIN?
ANSWER, WOMAN! WHO'S A THIEF, HUH? SO IT'S YOU, YOU WHO TURNS MY OWN SON AGAINST ME AND TEACHES HIM TO HATE ME?
DON'T TOUCH HER!
NO! ILANGO, NO!
LITTLE SNAKE! COME HERE, SO I CAN TEACH YOU HOW TO FIGHT.
ORLAND! NO! I BEG YOU, HE'S ONLY A CHILD.
WHAT NOW?
EXCUSE ME, GENERAL, BUT WE HAVE A PROBLEM IN THE MARSHES, THE GNATS HAVE SLAUGHTERED ANOTHER SOLDIER.
WELL THEN, ORGANIZE REINFORCEMENTS, FIND THE GUILTY AND KILL THEM! I'VE TOLD YOU A THOUSAND TIMES, NEVER LEAVE YOUR SQUAD WHEN YOU ARE IN THE SWAMPS.
YOU, YOU TWO PESTS, ARE FORBIDDEN FROM LEAVING THESE WALLS. WE'LL FINISH THIS DISCUSSION LATER.

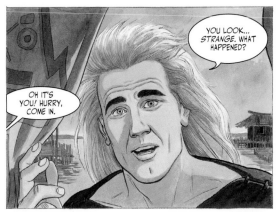

OH IT'S YOU! HURRY, COME IN.

YOU LOOK... STRANGE. WHAT HAPPENED?

A SOLDIER HAS BEEN LYNCHED IN THE MARSHES AND NOW THE GNATS FEAR REPRISALS.

MAY THE GODS INSURE NO ONE BLAMES US.

BUT WHY US, AUGERIAS? WE HAVEN'T DONE ANYTHING!

DO YOU REALLY THINK THE SOLDIERS GIVE A DAMN?

AND WHAT'S WITH THE OUTFIT?

I WAS FED UP LOOKING LIKE A COUNTRY BOY. AND YOU DIDN'T SEE ME BEFORE I FELL IN THE MUD PUDDLE!

IS THAT THE GETUP YOU EXPECT TO WEAR WHEN YOU CONFRONT ORLAND?

YOU'VE FOUND HIM?

IF IT IS HIM, IT WILL BE VERY DIFFICULT TO GET TO HIM.

BUT WE HAVE TO BE ABSOLUTELY SURE IT'S HIM.

OH YEAH? AND HOW WILL YOU BE SURE WHEN YOU CAN'T EVEN SEE WHAT'S *RIGHT* IN FRONT OF YOU?!

90

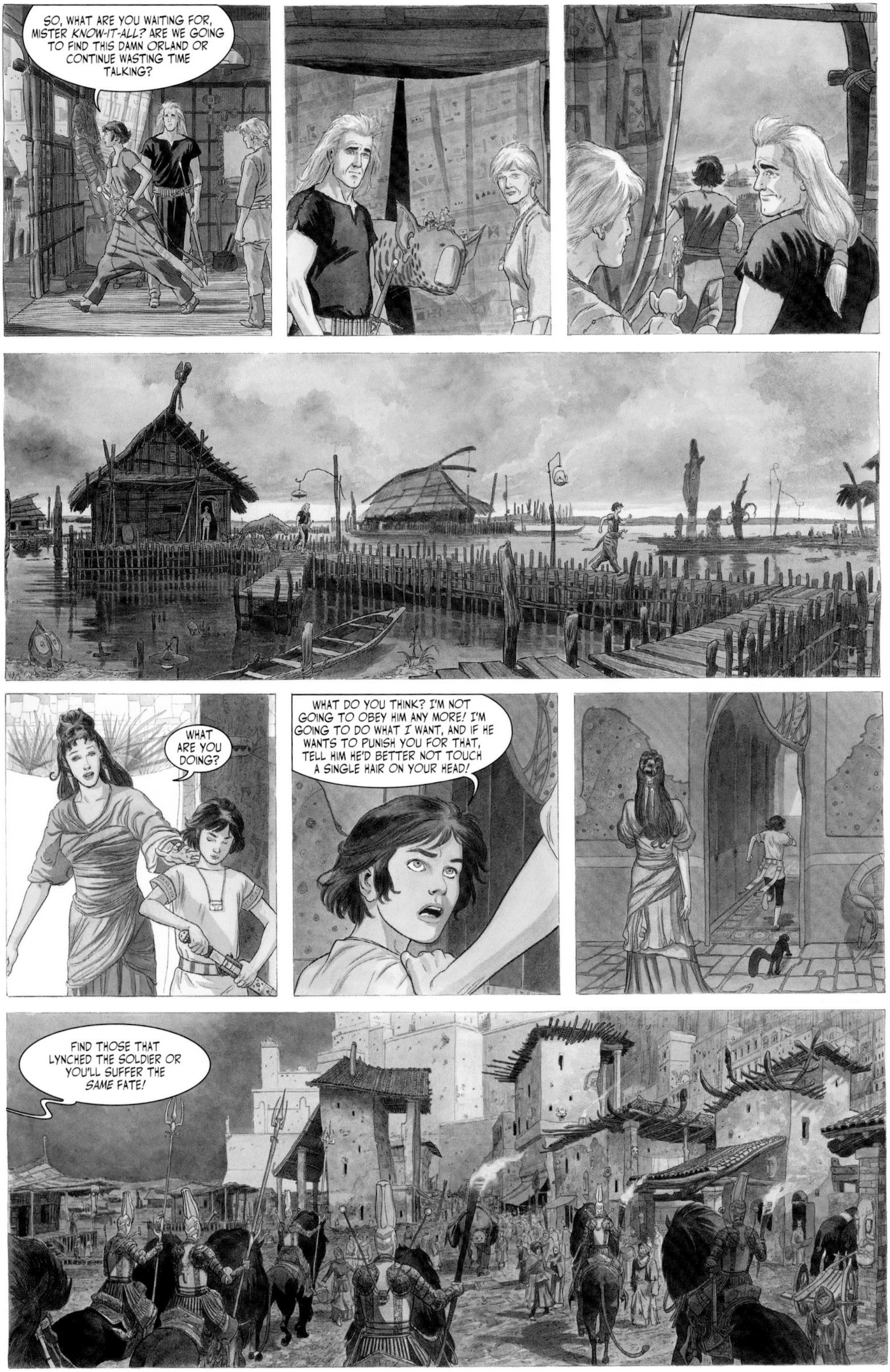
SO, WHAT ARE YOU WAITING FOR, MISTER KNOW-IT-ALL? ARE WE GOING TO FIND THIS DAMN ORLAND OR CONTINUE WASTING TIME TALKING?
WHAT ARE YOU DOING?
WHAT DO YOU THINK? I'M NOT GOING TO OBEY HIM ANY MORE! I'M GOING TO DO WHAT I WANT, AND IF HE WANTS TO PUNISH YOU FOR THAT, TELL HIM HE'D BETTER NOT TOUCH A SINGLE HAIR ON YOUR HEAD!
FIND THOSE THAT LYNCHED THE SOLDIER OR YOU'LL SUFFER THE SAME FATE!

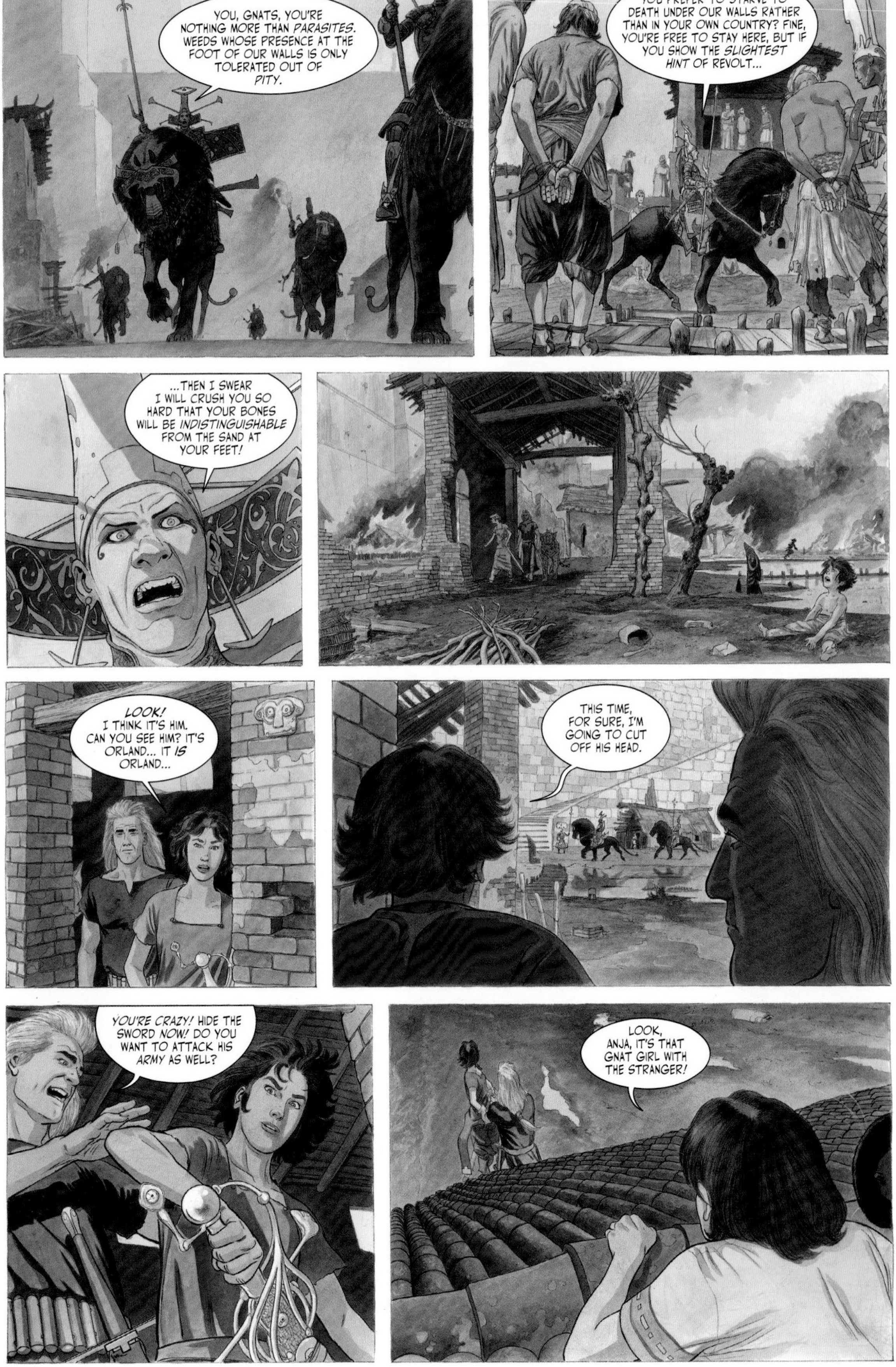
YOU, GNATS, YOU'RE NOTHING MORE THAN PARASITES. WEEDS WHOSE PRESENCE AT THE FOOT OF OUR WALLS IS ONLY TOLERATED OUT OF PITY.
YOU PREFER TO STARVE TO DEATH UNDER OUR WALLS RATHER THAN IN YOUR OWN COUNTRY? FINE, YOU'RE FREE TO STAY HERE, BUT IF YOU SHOW THE SLIGHTEST HINT OF REVOLT...
...THEN I SWEAR I WILL CRUSH YOU SO HARD THAT YOUR BONES WILL BE INDISTINGUISHABLE FROM THE SAND AT YOUR FEET!
LOOK! I THINK IT'S HIM. CAN YOU SEE HIM? IT'S ORLAND... IT IS ORLAND...
THIS TIME, FOR SURE, I'M GOING TO CUT OFF HIS HEAD.
YOU'RE CRAZY! HIDE THE SWORD NOW! DO YOU WANT TO ATTACK HIS ARMY AS WELL?
LOOK, ANJA, IT'S THAT GNAT GIRL WITH THE STRANGER!

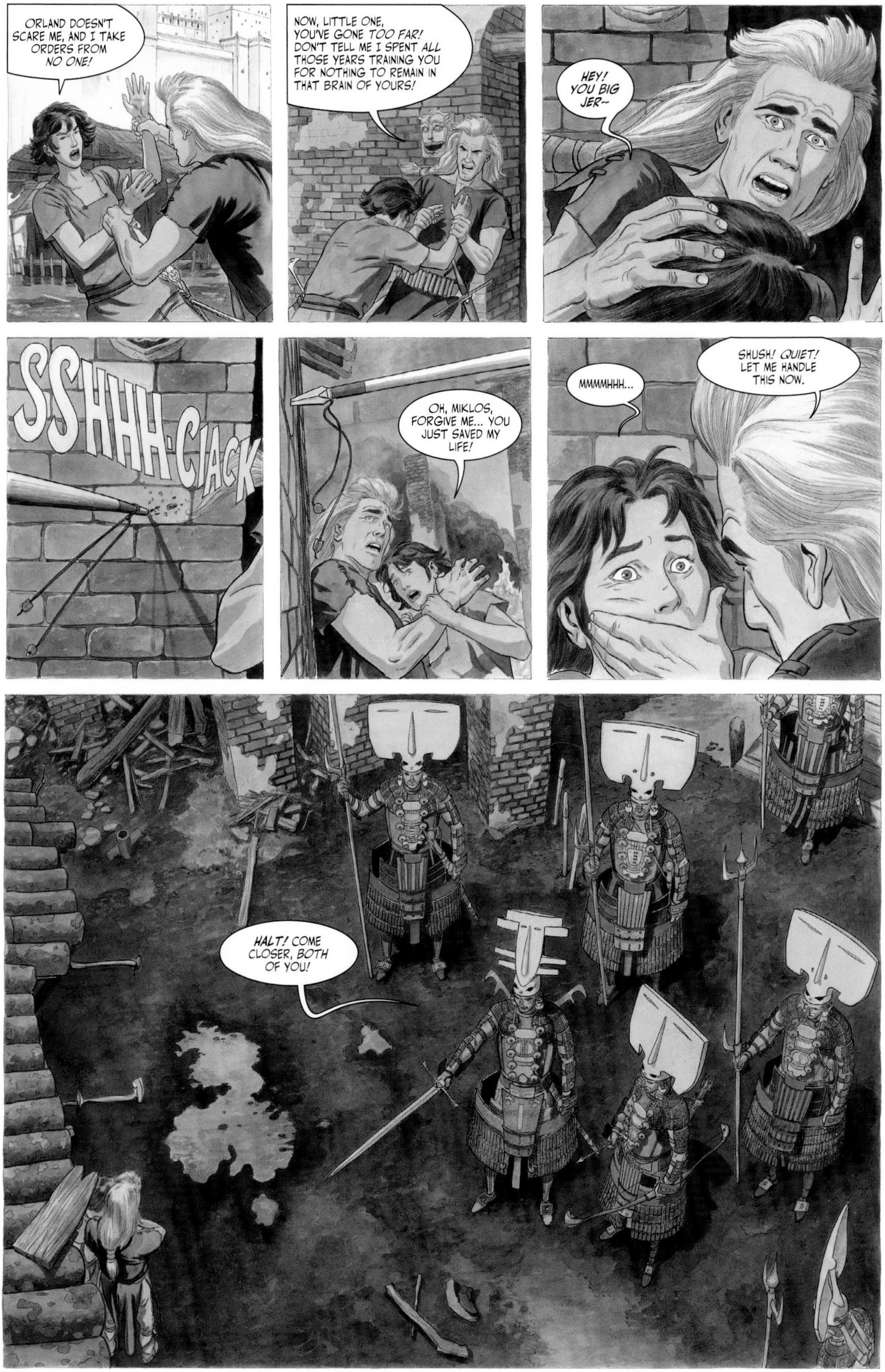

ORLAND DOESN'T SCARE ME, AND I TAKE ORDERS FROM NO ONE!
NOW, LITTLE ONE, YOU'VE GONE TOO FAR! DON'T TELL ME I SPENT ALL THOSE YEARS TRAINING YOU FOR NOTHING TO REMAIN IN THAT BRAIN OF YOURS!
HEY! YOU BIG JER--
SSHHH-CIACK
OH, MIKLOS, FORGIVE ME... YOU JUST SAVED MY LIFE!
MMMMHHH...
SHUSH! QUIET! LET ME HANDLE THIS NOW.
HALT! COME CLOSER, BOTH OF YOU!

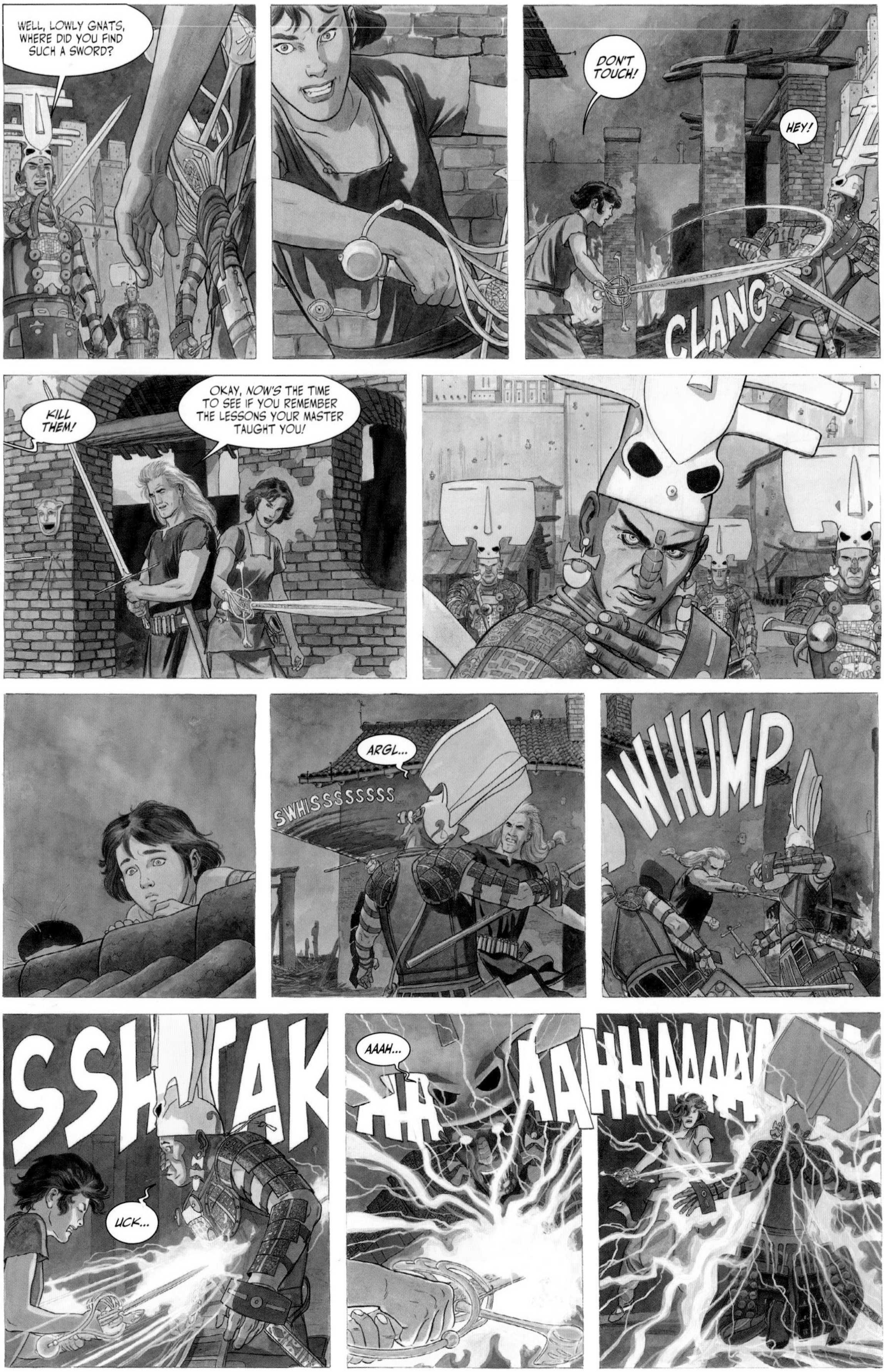
WELL, LOWLY GNATS, WHERE DID YOU FIND SUCH A SWORD?
DON'T TOUCH!
HEY!
CLANG
KILL THEM!
OKAY, NOW'S THE TIME TO SEE IF YOU REMEMBER THE LESSONS YOUR MASTER TAUGHT YOU!
ARGL...
SWHISSSSSSSS
WHUMP
AAAH...
UCK...

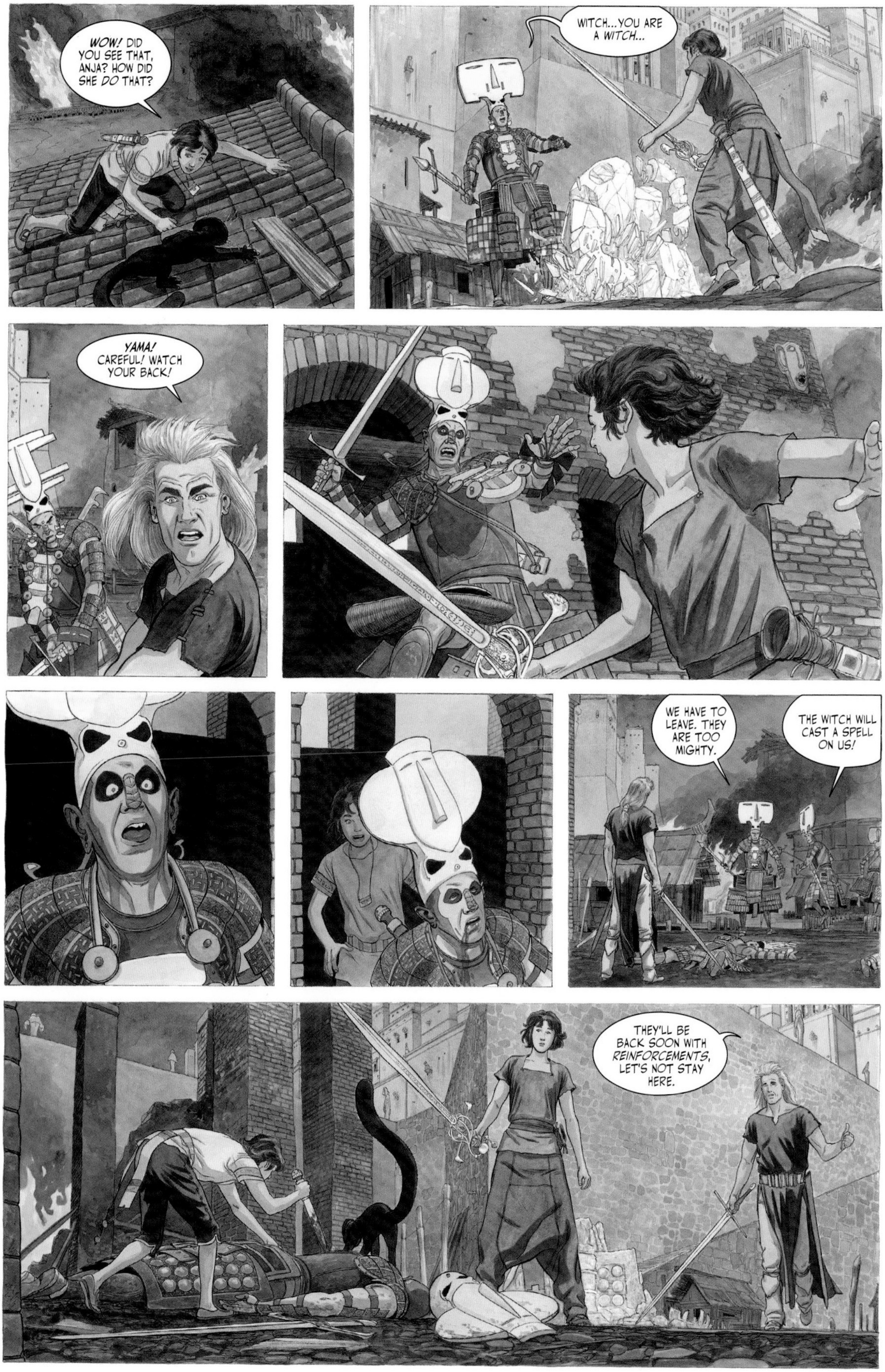
WOW! DID YOU SEE THAT, ANJA? HOW DID SHE DO THAT?
WITCH...YOU ARE A WITCH...
YAMA! CAREFUL! WATCH YOUR BACK!
WE HAVE TO LEAVE. THEY ARE TOO MIGHTY.
THE WITCH WILL CAST A SPELL ON US!
THEY'LL BE BACK SOON WITH REINFORCEMENTS, LET'S NOT STAY HERE.

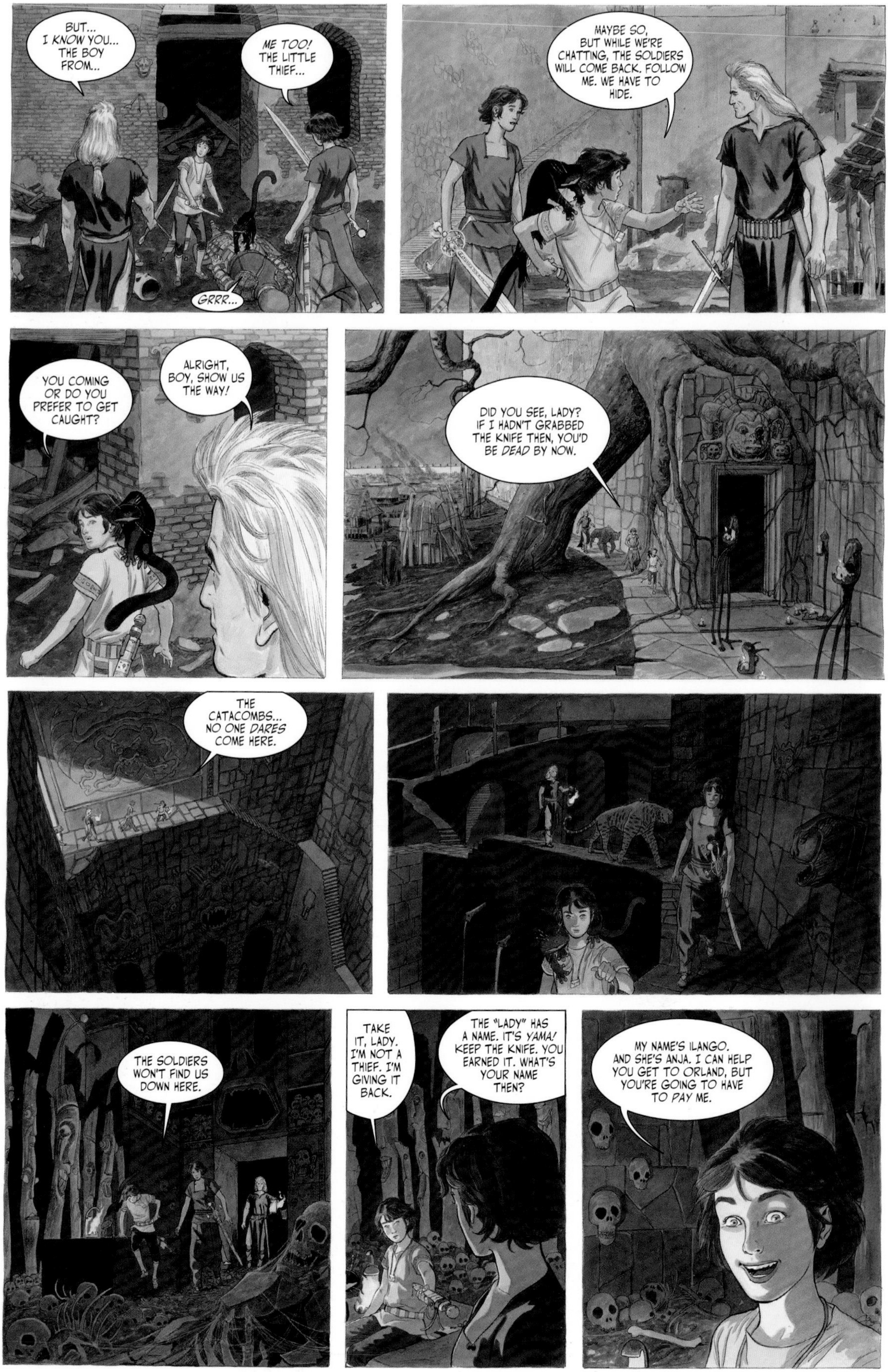
BUT... I KNOW YOU... THE BOY FROM...
ME TOO! THE LITTLE THIEF...
GRRR...
MAYBE SO, BUT WHILE WE'RE CHATTING, THE SOLDIERS WILL COME BACK. FOLLOW ME. WE HAVE TO HIDE.
YOU COMING OR DO YOU PREFER TO GET CAUGHT?
ALRIGHT, BOY, SHOW US THE WAY!
DID YOU SEE, LADY? IF I HADN'T GRABBED THE KNIFE THEN, YOU'D BE *DEAD* BY NOW.
THE CATACOMBS... NO ONE *DARES* COME HERE.
THE SOLDIERS WON'T FIND US DOWN HERE.
TAKE IT, LADY. I'M NOT A THIEF. I'M GIVING IT BACK.
THE "LADY" HAS A NAME. IT'S *YAMA!* KEEP THE KNIFE. YOU EARNED IT. WHAT'S YOUR NAME THEN?
MY NAME'S ILANGO. AND SHE'S ANJA. I CAN HELP YOU GET TO ORLAND, BUT YOU'RE GOING TO HAVE TO *PAY* ME.

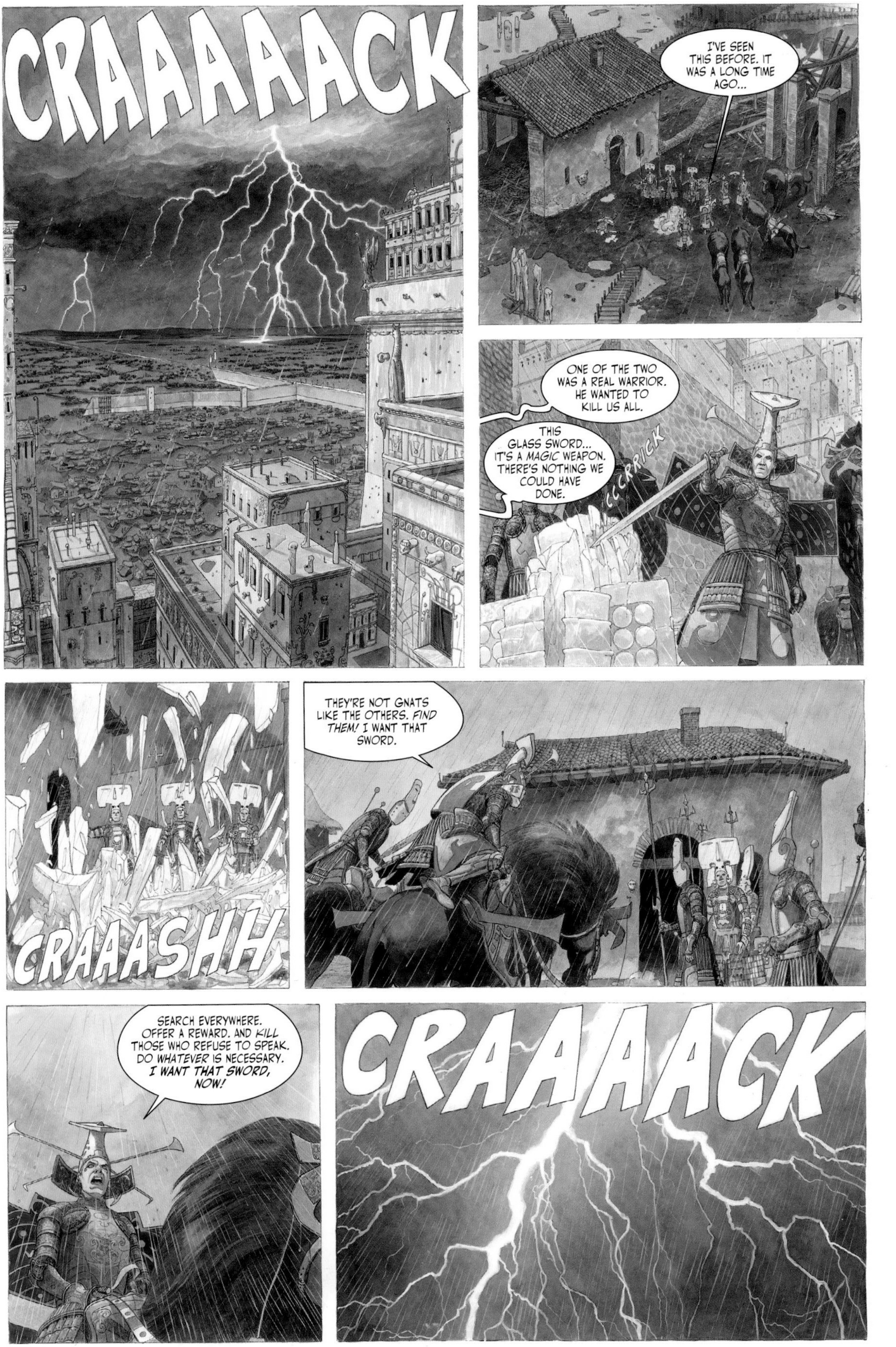
CRAAAAACK
I'VE SEEN THIS BEFORE. IT WAS A LONG TIME AGO...
ONE OF THE TWO WAS A REAL WARRIOR. HE WANTED TO KILL US ALL.
THIS GLASS SWORD... IT'S A *MAGIC* WEAPON. THERE'S NOTHING WE COULD HAVE DONE.
CCCRRICK
CRAAASHH
THEY'RE NOT GNATS LIKE THE OTHERS. *FIND THEM!* I WANT THAT SWORD.
SEARCH EVERYWHERE. OFFER A REWARD. AND *KILL* THOSE WHO REFUSE TO SPEAK. DO *WHATEVER* IS NECESSARY. ***I WANT THAT SWORD, NOW!***
CRAAAACK

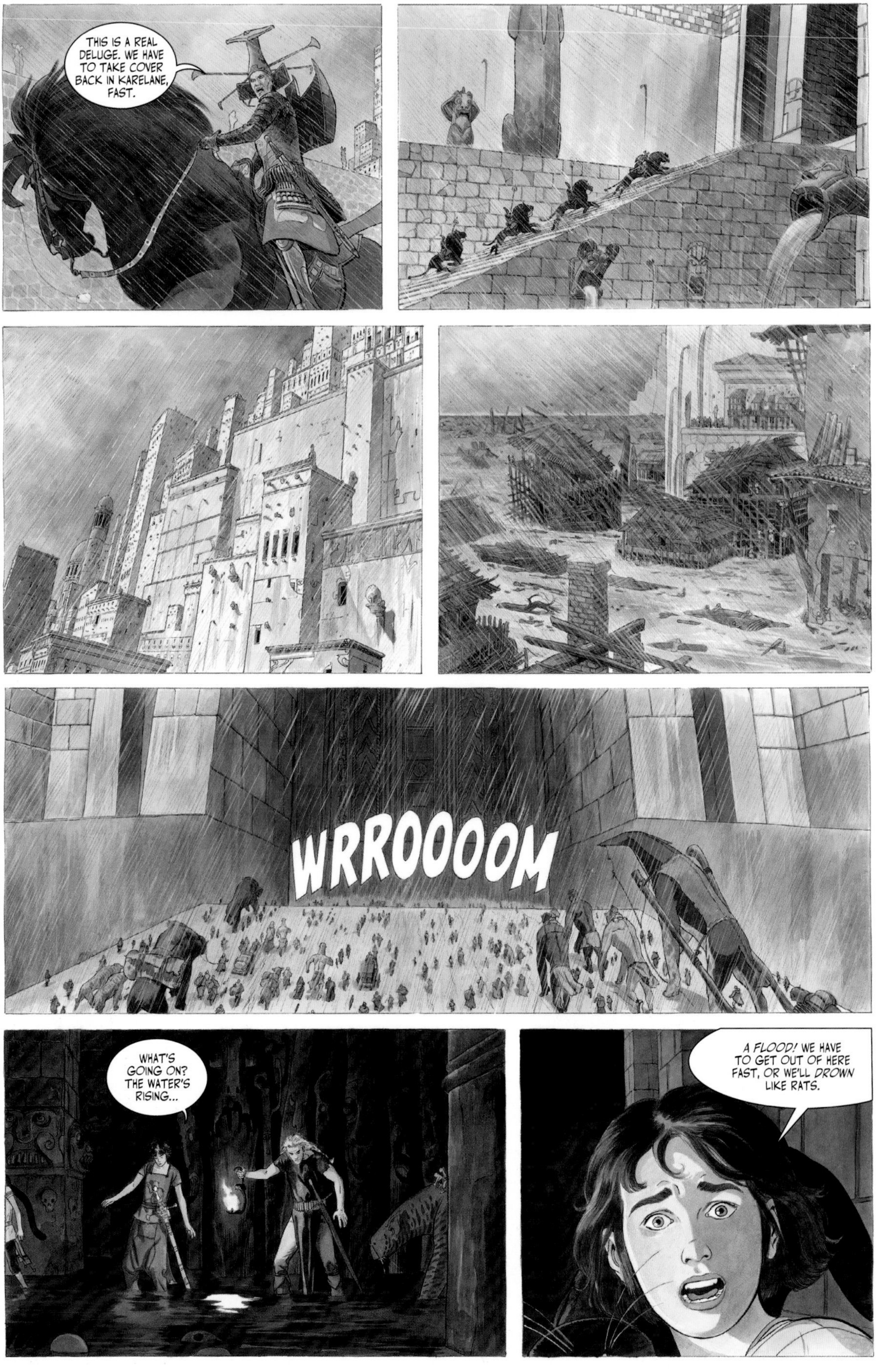
THIS IS A REAL DELUGE. WE HAVE TO TAKE COVER BACK IN KARELANE, FAST.
WRROOOOM
WHAT'S GOING ON? THE WATER'S RISING...
A *FLOOD!* WE HAVE TO GET OUT OF HERE FAST, OR WE'LL *DROWN* LIKE RATS.

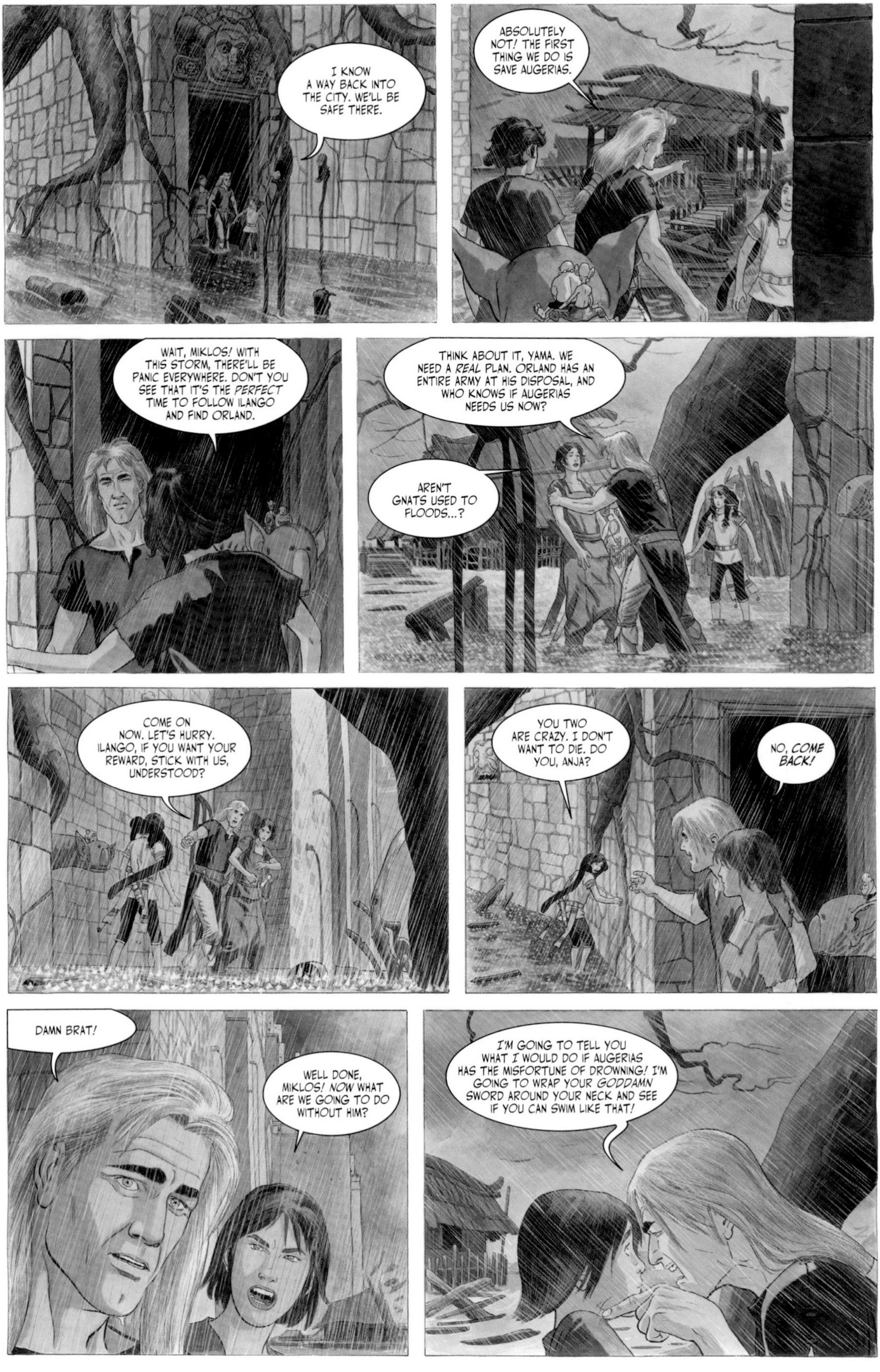
I KNOW A WAY BACK INTO THE CITY. WE'LL BE SAFE THERE.
ABSOLUTELY NOT! THE FIRST THING WE DO IS SAVE AUGERIAS.
WAIT, MIKLOS! WITH THIS STORM, THERE'LL BE PANIC EVERYWHERE. DON'T YOU SEE THAT IT'S THE PERFECT TIME TO FOLLOW ILANGO AND FIND ORLAND.
THINK ABOUT IT, YAMA. WE NEED A REAL PLAN. ORLAND HAS AN ENTIRE ARMY AT HIS DISPOSAL, AND WHO KNOWS IF AUGERIAS NEEDS US NOW?
AREN'T GNATS USED TO FLOODS...?
COME ON NOW. LET'S HURRY. ILANGO, IF YOU WANT YOUR REWARD, STICK WITH US, UNDERSTOOD?
YOU TWO ARE CRAZY. I DON'T WANT TO DIE. DO YOU, ANJA?
NO, COME BACK!
DAMN BRAT!
WELL DONE, MIKLOS! NOW WHAT ARE WE GOING TO DO WITHOUT HIM?
I'M GOING TO TELL YOU WHAT I WOULD DO IF AUGERIAS HAS THE MISFORTUNE OF DROWNING! I'M GOING TO WRAP YOUR GODDAMN SWORD AROUND YOUR NECK AND SEE IF YOU CAN SWIM LIKE THAT!

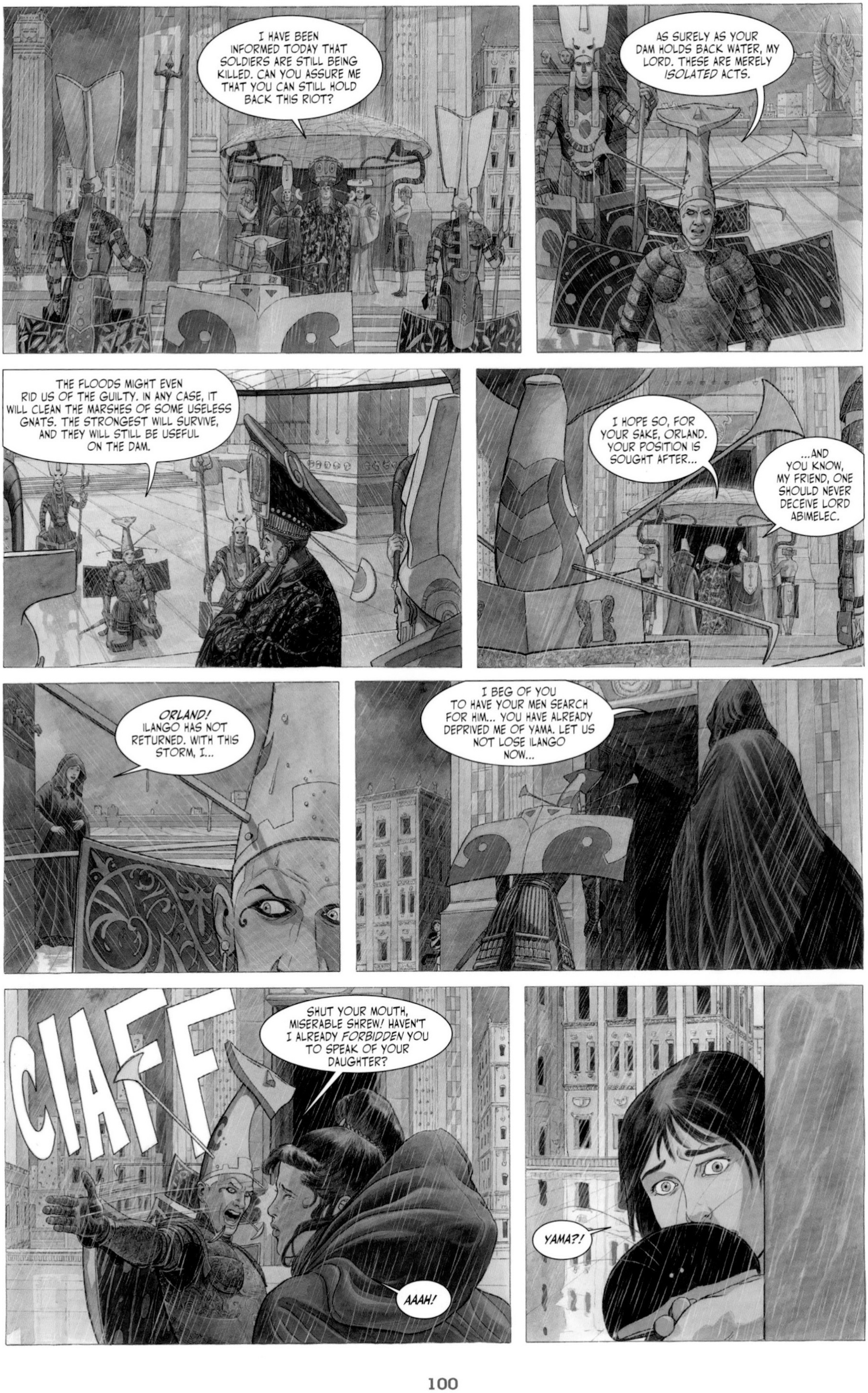
I HAVE BEEN INFORMED TODAY THAT SOLDIERS ARE STILL BEING KILLED. CAN YOU ASSURE ME THAT YOU CAN STILL HOLD BACK THIS RIOT?
AS SURELY AS YOUR DAM HOLDS BACK WATER, MY LORD. THESE ARE MERELY *ISOLATED* ACTS.
THE FLOODS MIGHT EVEN RID US OF THE GUILTY. IN ANY CASE, IT WILL CLEAN THE MARSHES OF SOME USELESS GNATS. THE STRONGEST WILL SURVIVE, AND THEY WILL STILL BE USEFUL ON THE DAM.
I HOPE SO, FOR YOUR SAKE, ORLAND. YOUR POSITION IS SOUGHT AFTER...
...AND YOU KNOW, MY FRIEND, ONE SHOULD NEVER DECEIVE LORD ABIMELEC.
ORLAND! ILANGO HAS NOT RETURNED. WITH THIS STORM, I...
I BEG OF YOU TO HAVE YOUR MEN SEARCH FOR HIM... YOU HAVE ALREADY DEPRIVED ME OF YAMA. LET US NOT LOSE ILANGO NOW...
CIAFF
SHUT YOUR MOUTH, MISERABLE SHREW! HAVEN'T I ALREADY *FORBIDDEN* YOU TO SPEAK OF YOUR DAUGHTER?
AAAH!
YAMA?!

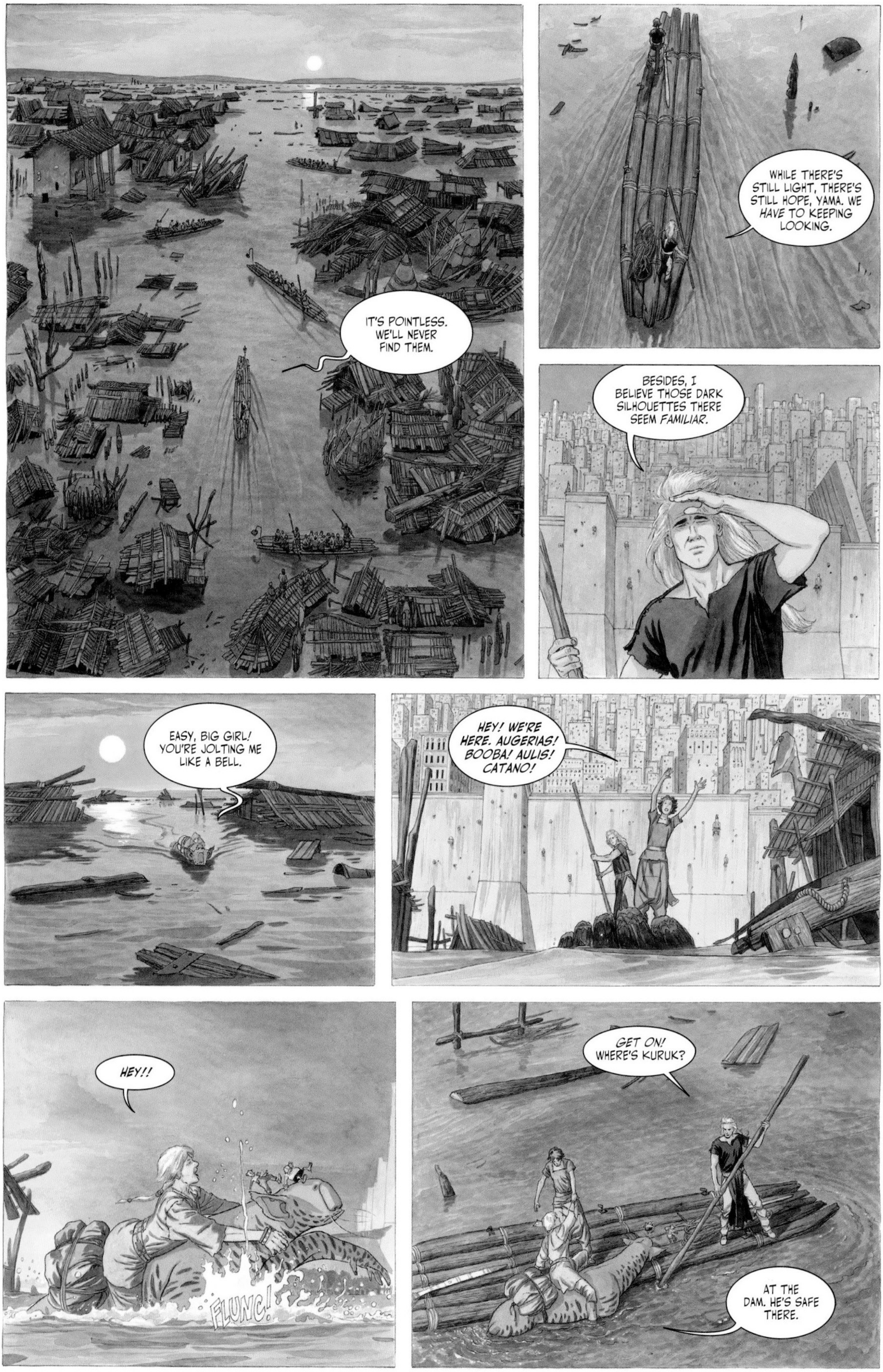

IT'S POINTLESS. WE'LL NEVER FIND THEM.
WHILE THERE'S STILL LIGHT, THERE'S STILL HOPE, YAMA. WE *HAVE* TO KEEPING LOOKING.
BESIDES, I BELIEVE THOSE DARK SILHOUETTES THERE SEEM *FAMILIAR*.
EASY, BIG GIRL! YOU'RE JOLTING ME LIKE A BELL.
HEY! WE'RE HERE. AUGERIAS! BOOBA! AULIS! CATANO!
HEY!!
FLUNC!
GET ON! WHERE'S KURUK?
AT THE DAM. HE'S SAFE THERE.

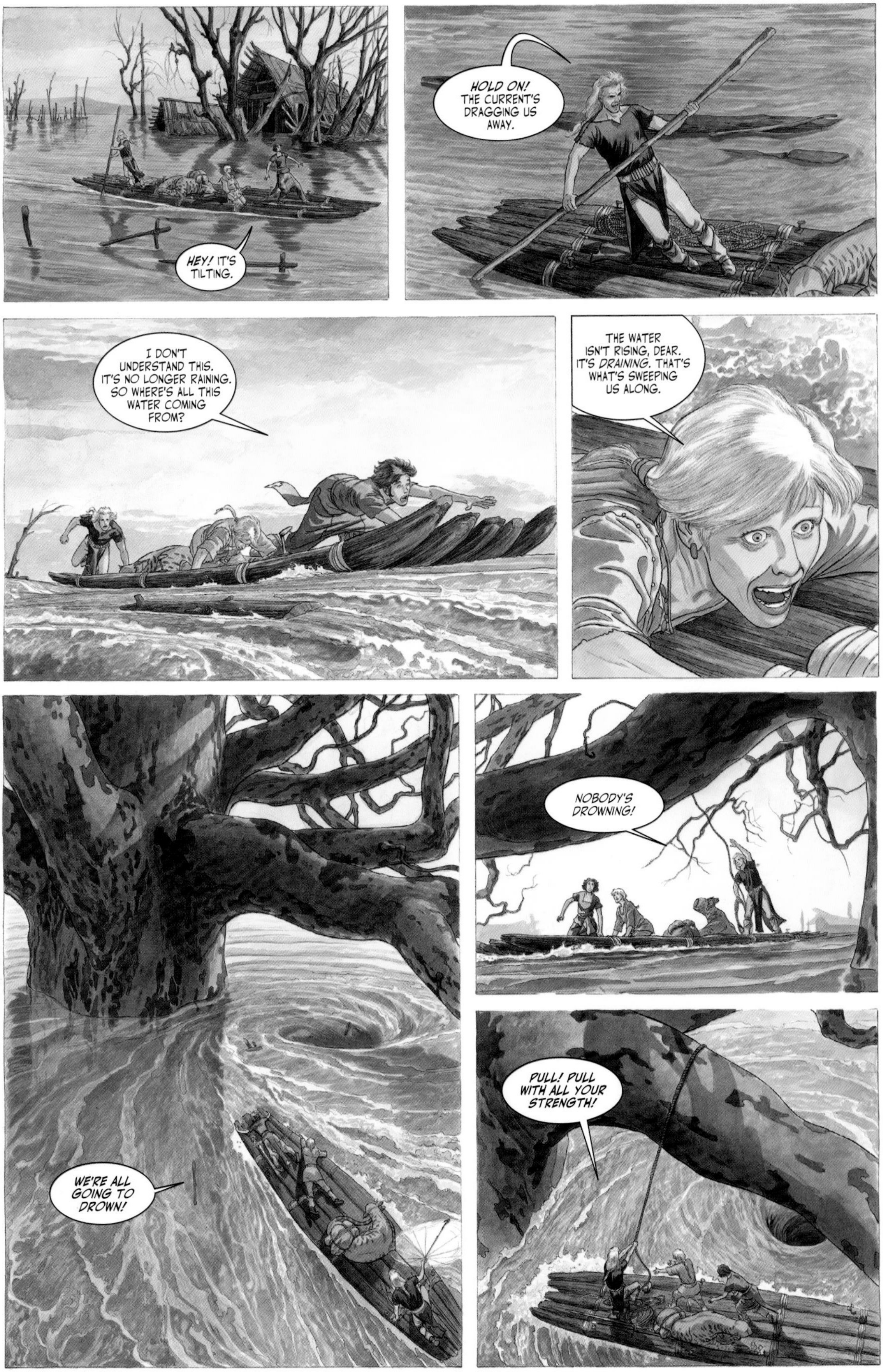
HEY! IT'S TILTING.
HOLD ON! THE CURRENT'S DRAGGING US AWAY.
I DON'T UNDERSTAND THIS. IT'S NO LONGER RAINING. SO WHERE'S ALL THIS WATER COMING FROM?
THE WATER ISN'T RISING, DEAR. IT'S DRAINING. THAT'S WHAT'S SWEEPING US ALONG.
WE'RE ALL GOING TO DROWN!
NOBODY'S DROWNING!
PULL! PULL WITH ALL YOUR STRENGTH!

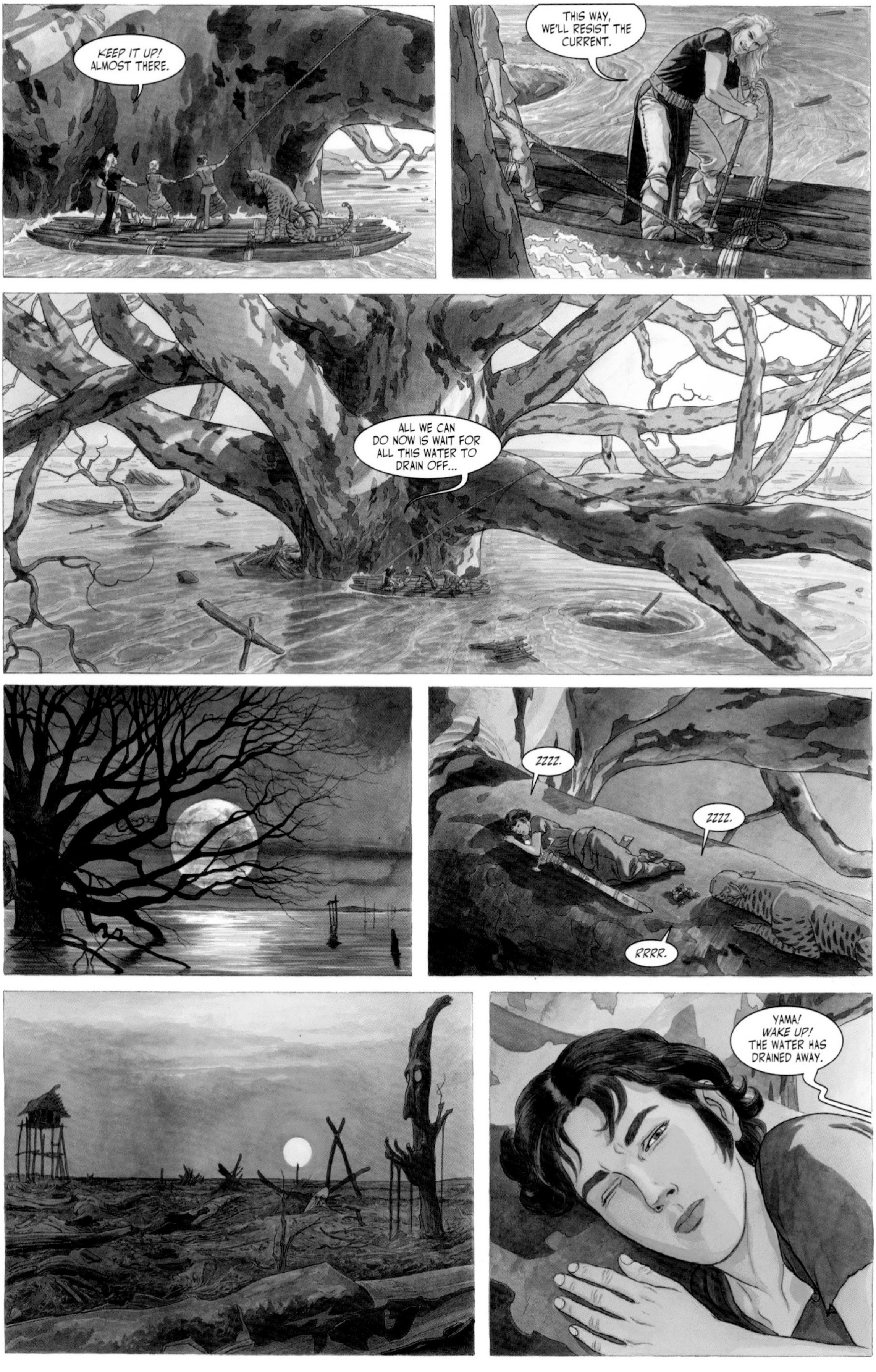
KEEP IT UP! ALMOST THERE.
THIS WAY, WE'LL RESIST THE CURRENT.
ALL WE CAN DO NOW IS WAIT FOR ALL THIS WATER TO DRAIN OFF...
ZZZZ.
ZZZZ.
RRRR.
YAMA! WAKE UP! THE WATER HAS DRAINED AWAY.

YAWN

OH OH! HELP!

CAREFUL! DAMN IT! THE GROUND IS SWOLLEN WITH WATER.

SPLASH

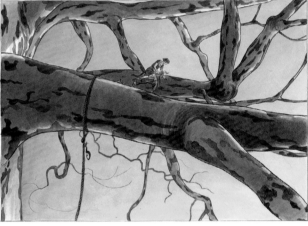

THE DELUGE IS OVER, FOR NOW. EVERYTHING WILL HAVE TO BE REBUILT ALL OVER AGAIN.

LET'S TRY TO FIND WHERE MY HOUSE STOOD. MY SON KURUK MUST BE SEARCHING FOR ME THERE.

HEY, YOU TWO THERE, WITH THE SWORD!

DON'T MOVE A MUSCLE! YOU'RE BOTH UNDER ARREST.

IT'S THEM, CHIEF.

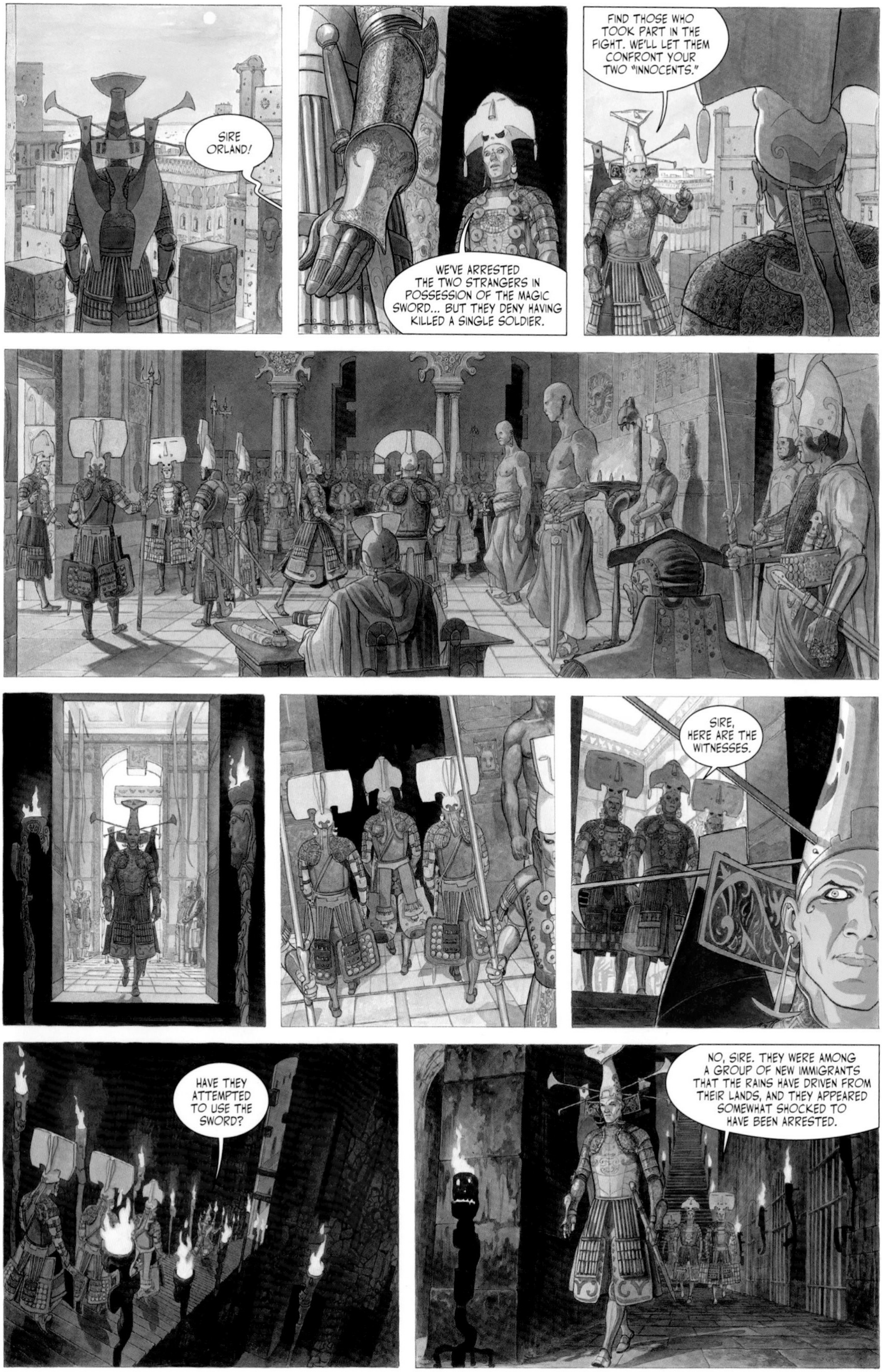
SIRE ORLAND!
WE'VE ARRESTED THE TWO STRANGERS IN POSSESSION OF THE MAGIC SWORD... BUT THEY DENY HAVING KILLED A SINGLE SOLDIER.
FIND THOSE WHO TOOK PART IN THE FIGHT. WE'LL LET THEM CONFRONT YOUR TWO "INNOCENTS."
SIRE, HERE ARE THE WITNESSES.
HAVE THEY ATTEMPTED TO USE THE SWORD?
NO, SIRE. THEY WERE AMONG A GROUP OF NEW IMMIGRANTS THAT THE RAINS HAVE DRIVEN FROM THEIR LANDS, AND THEY APPEARED SOMEWHAT SHOCKED TO HAVE BEEN ARRESTED.

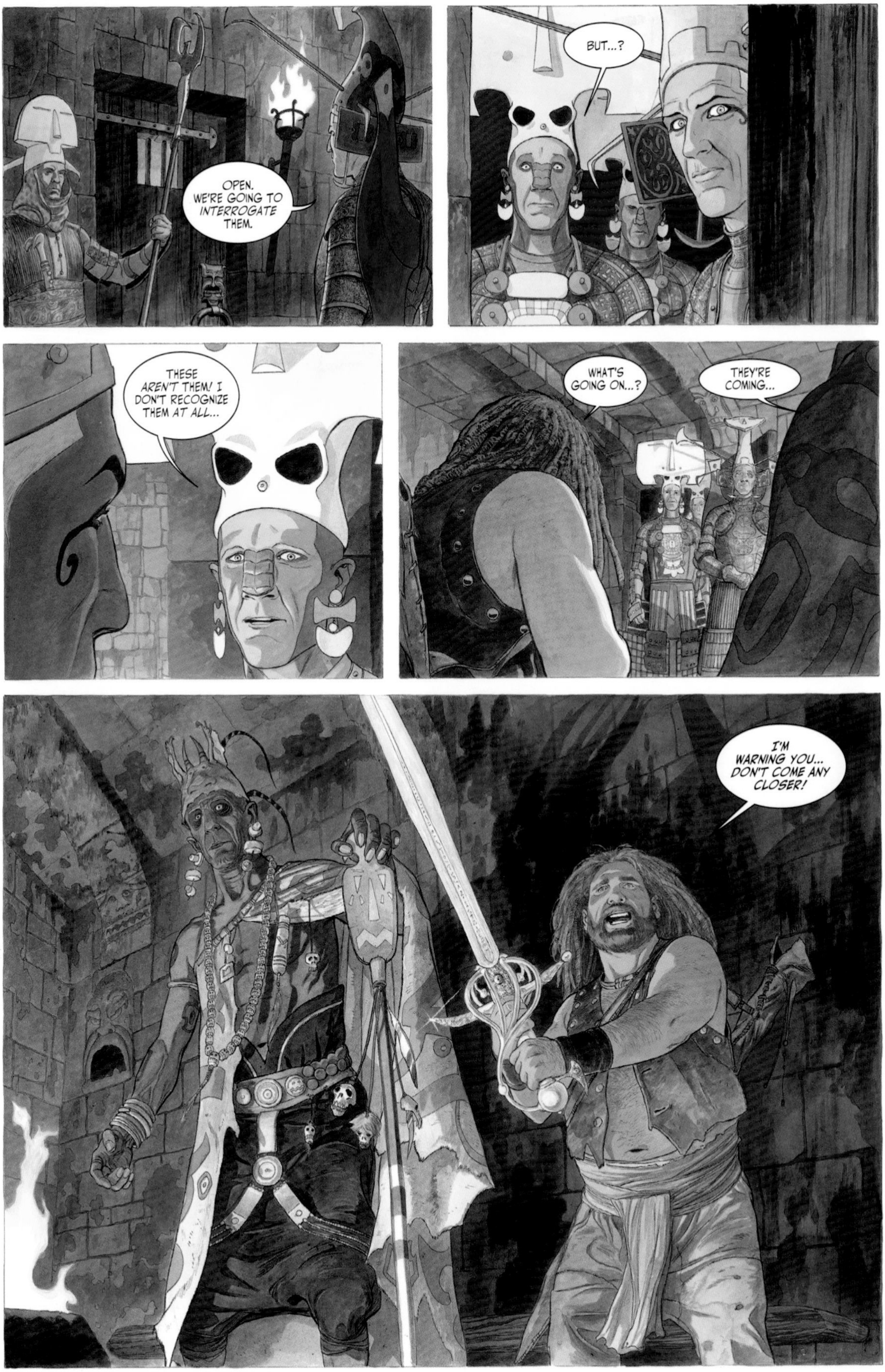
OPEN. WE'RE GOING TO INTERROGATE THEM.
BUT...?
THESE AREN'T THEM! I DON'T RECOGNIZE THEM AT ALL...
WHAT'S GOING ON...?
THEY'RE COMING...
I'M WARNING YOU... DON'T COME ANY CLOSER!

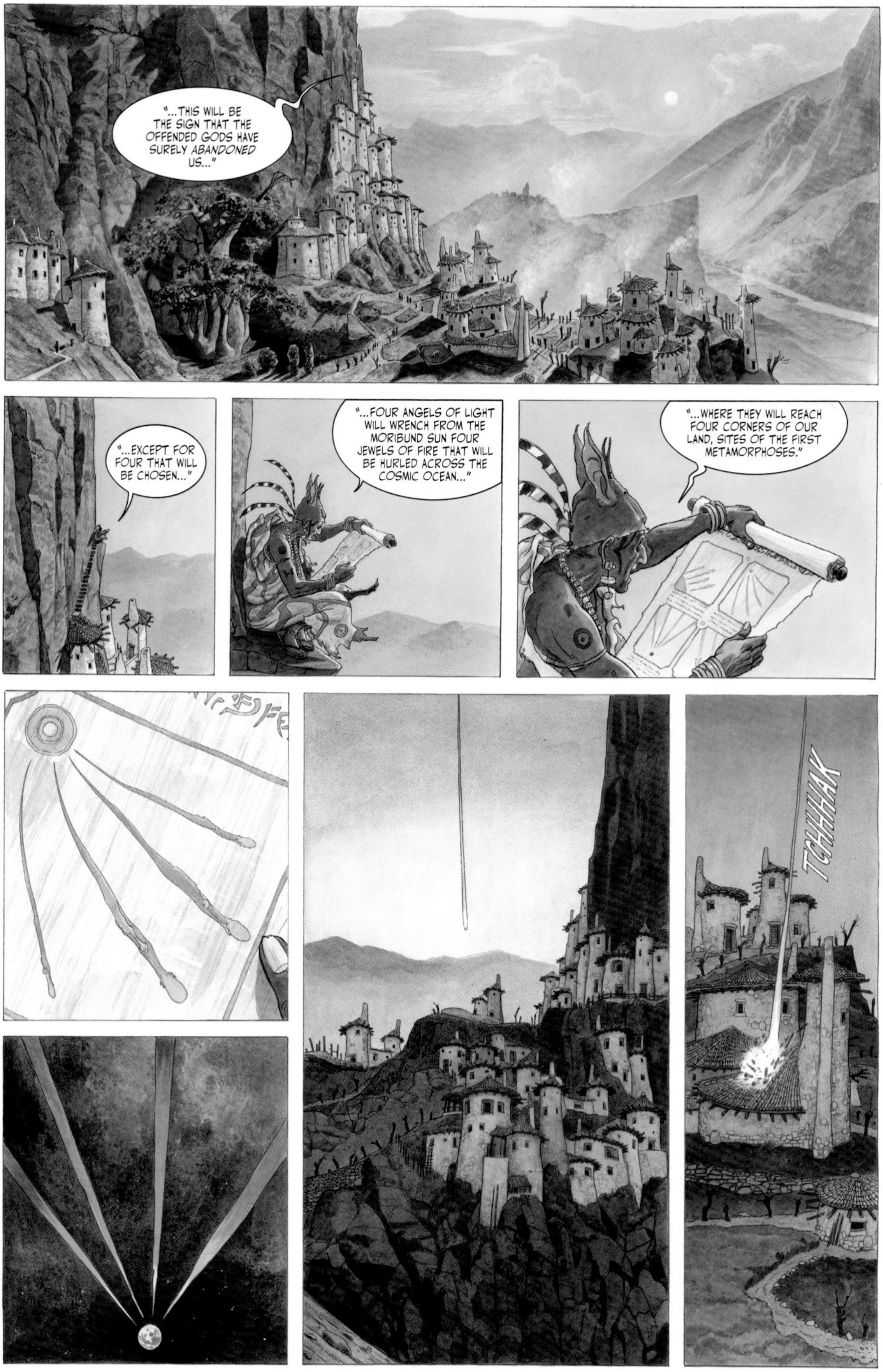
"...THIS WILL BE THE SIGN THAT THE OFFENDED GODS HAVE SURELY ABANDONED US..."
"...EXCEPT FOR FOUR THAT WILL BE CHOSEN..."
"...FOUR ANGELS OF LIGHT WILL WRENCH FROM THE MORIBUND SUN FOUR JEWELS OF FIRE THAT WILL BE HURLED ACROSS THE COSMIC OCEAN..."
"...WHERE THEY WILL REACH FOUR CORNERS OF OUR LAND, SITES OF THE FIRST METAMORPHOSES."
TCHHHAK

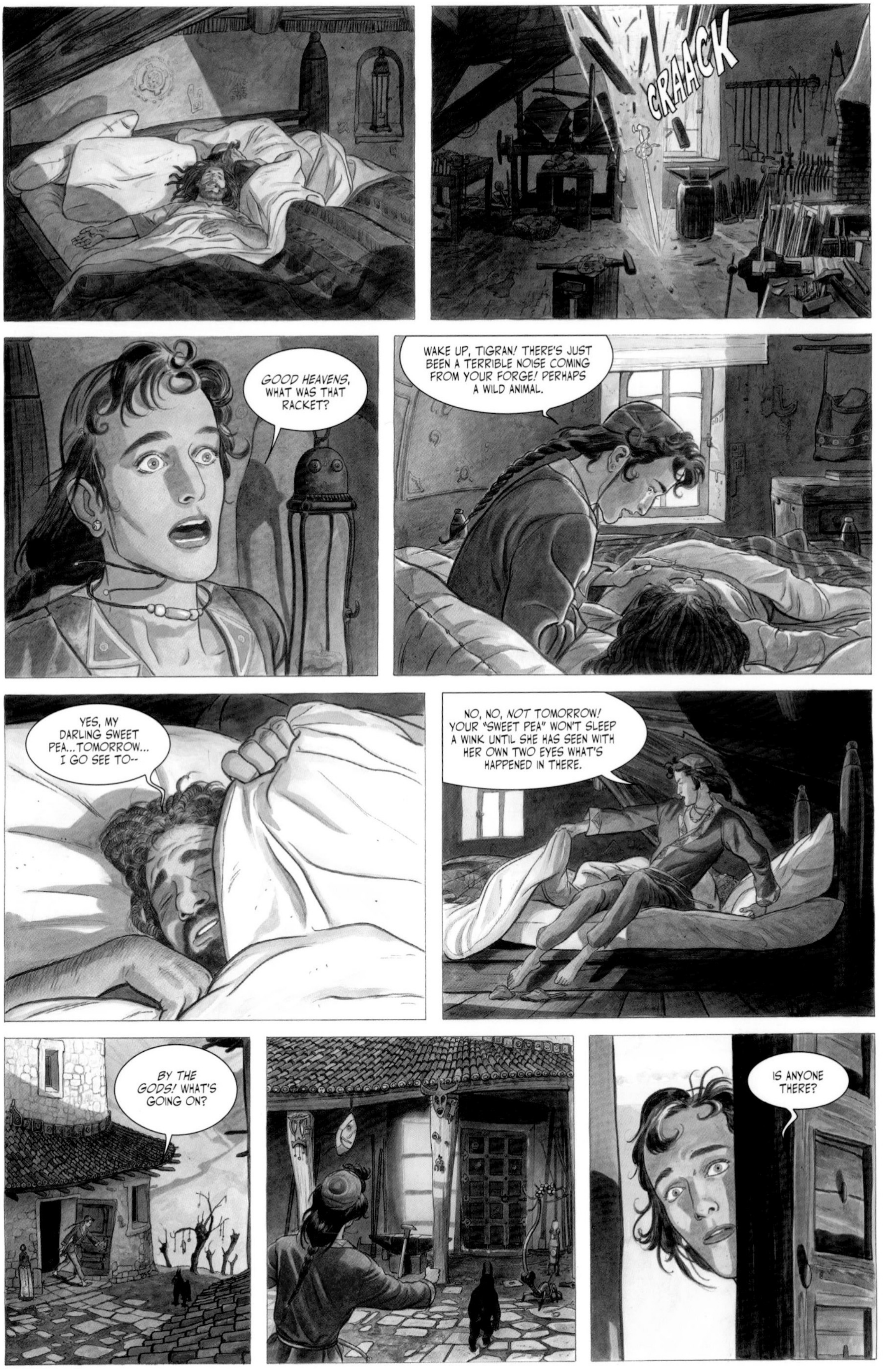
CRAACK
GOOD HEAVENS, WHAT WAS THAT RACKET?
WAKE UP, TIGRAN! THERE'S JUST BEEN A TERRIBLE NOISE COMING FROM YOUR FORGE! PERHAPS A WILD ANIMAL.
YES, MY DARLING SWEET PEA...TOMORROW... I GO SEE TO--
NO, NO, NOT TOMORROW! YOUR "SWEET PEA" WON'T SLEEP A WINK UNTIL SHE HAS SEEN WITH HER OWN TWO EYES WHAT'S HAPPENED IN THERE.
BY THE GODS! WHAT'S GOING ON?
IS ANYONE THERE?

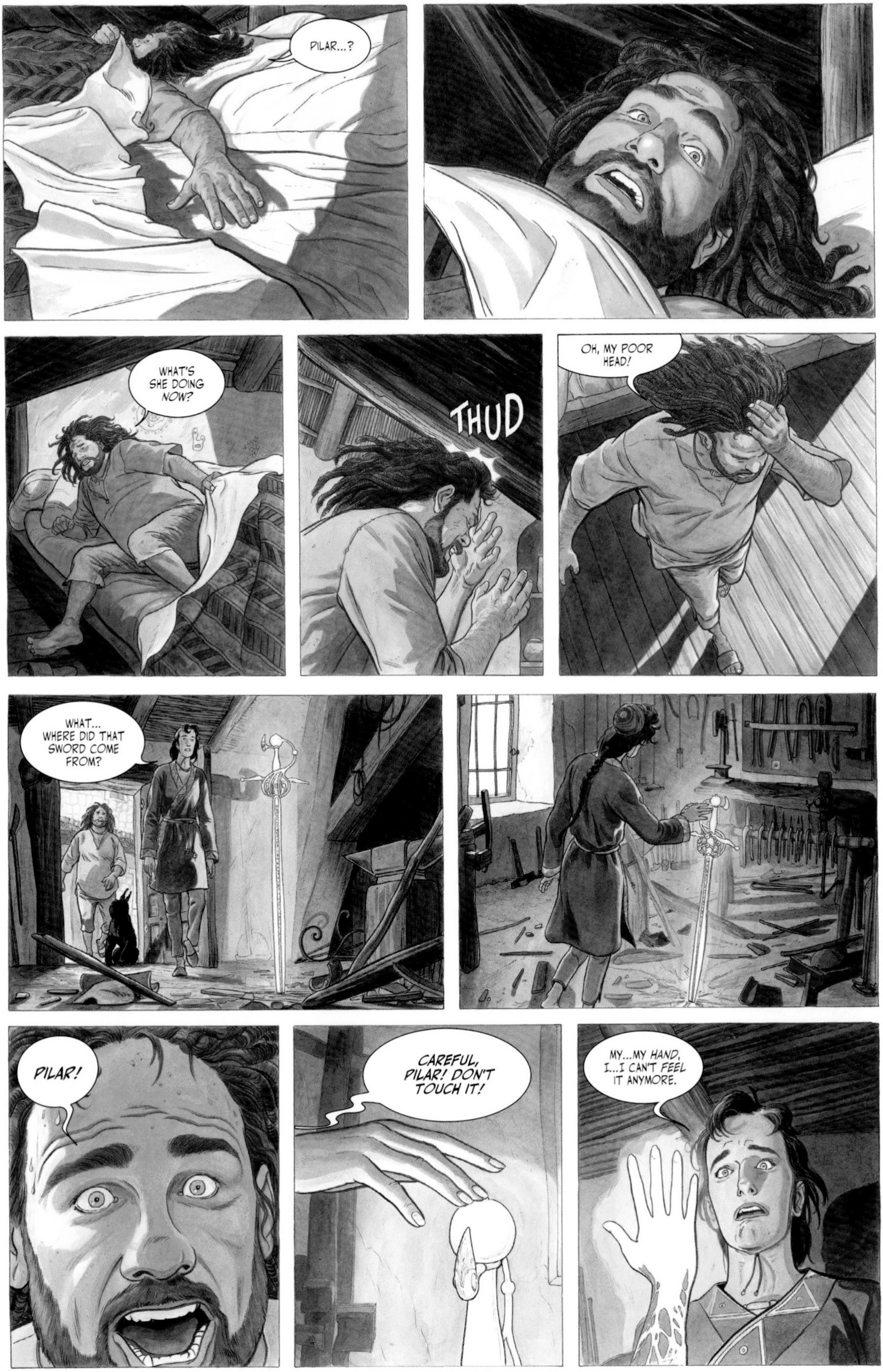
PILAR...?
WHAT'S SHE DOING NOW?
THUD
OH, MY POOR HEAD!
WHAT... WHERE DID THAT SWORD COME FROM?
PILAR!
CAREFUL, PILAR! DON'T TOUCH IT!
MY...MY HAND, I...I CAN'T FEEL IT ANYMORE.

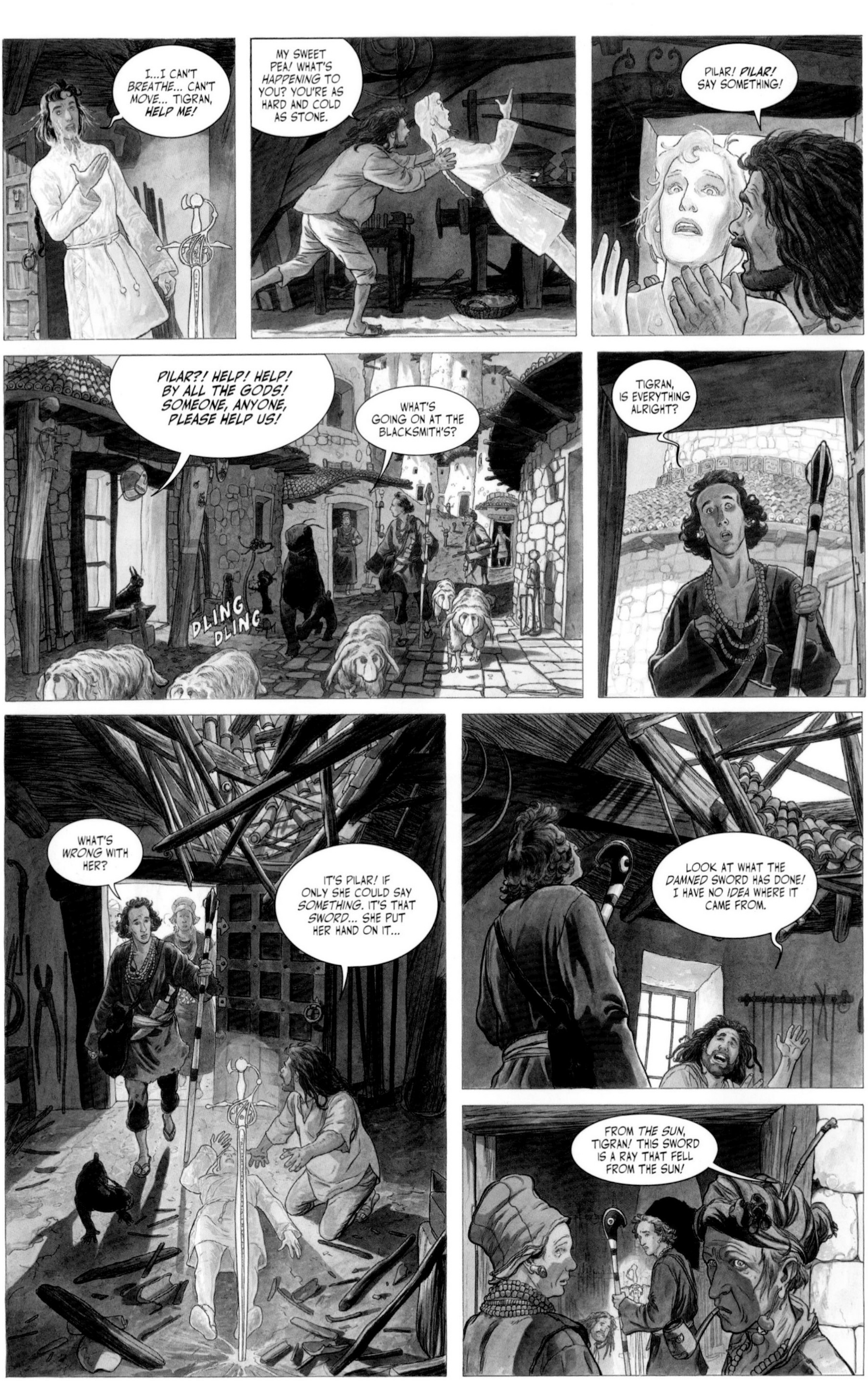
I...I CAN'T BREATHE... CAN'T MOVE... TIGRAN, *HELP ME!*
MY SWEET PEA! WHAT'S *HAPPENING* TO YOU? YOU'RE AS HARD AND COLD AS STONE.
PILAR! *PILAR!* SAY SOMETHING!
PILAR?! HELP! HELP! BY ALL THE GODS! SOMEONE, ANYONE, PLEASE HELP US!
WHAT'S GOING ON AT THE BLACKSMITH'S?
DLING DLING
TIGRAN, IS EVERYTHING ALRIGHT?
WHAT'S *WRONG* WITH HER?
IT'S PILAR! IF ONLY SHE COULD SAY *SOMETHING*. IT'S THAT *SWORD*... SHE PUT HER HAND ON IT...
LOOK AT WHAT THE *DAMNED* SWORD HAS DONE! I HAVE NO *IDEA* WHERE IT CAME FROM.
FROM *THE SUN*, TIGRAN! THIS SWORD IS A RAY THAT FELL FROM THE SUN!

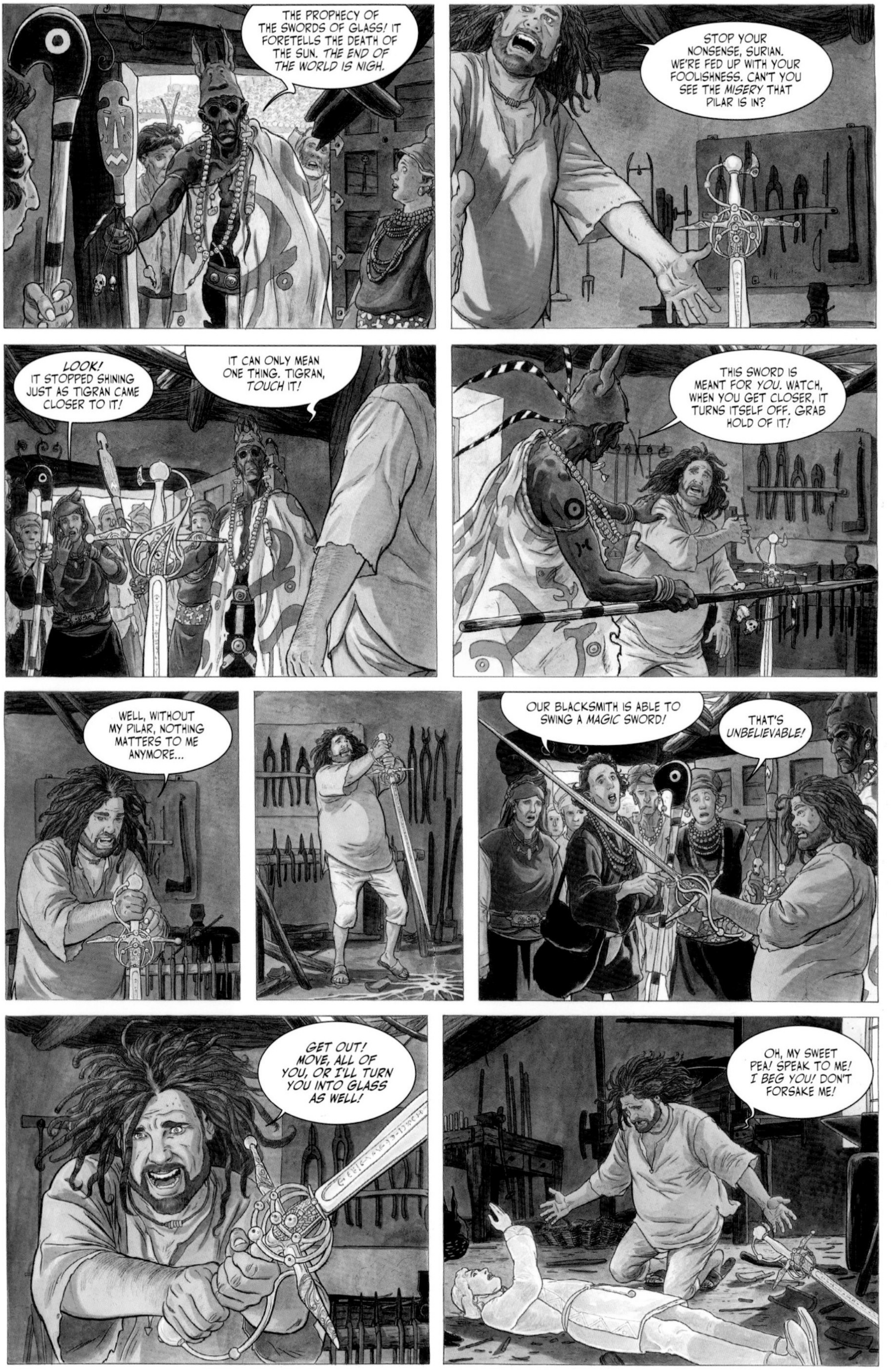
THE PROPHECY OF THE SWORDS OF GLASS! IT FORETELLS THE DEATH OF THE SUN. *THE END OF THE WORLD IS NIGH.*
STOP YOUR NONSENSE, SURIAN. WE'RE FED UP WITH YOUR FOOLISHNESS. CAN'T YOU SEE THE *MISERY* THAT PILAR IS IN?
LOOK! IT STOPPED SHINING JUST AS TIGRAN CAME CLOSER TO IT!
IT CAN ONLY MEAN ONE THING. TIGRAN, *TOUCH IT!*
THIS SWORD IS MEANT FOR *YOU*. WATCH, WHEN YOU GET CLOSER, IT TURNS ITSELF OFF. GRAB HOLD OF IT!
WELL, WITHOUT MY PILAR, NOTHING MATTERS TO ME ANYMORE...
OUR BLACKSMITH IS ABLE TO SWING A *MAGIC* SWORD!
THAT'S *UNBELIEVABLE!*
GET OUT! MOVE, ALL OF YOU, OR I'LL TURN YOU INTO GLASS AS WELL!
OH, MY SWEET PEA! SPEAK TO ME! I BEG YOU! DON'T FORSAKE ME!

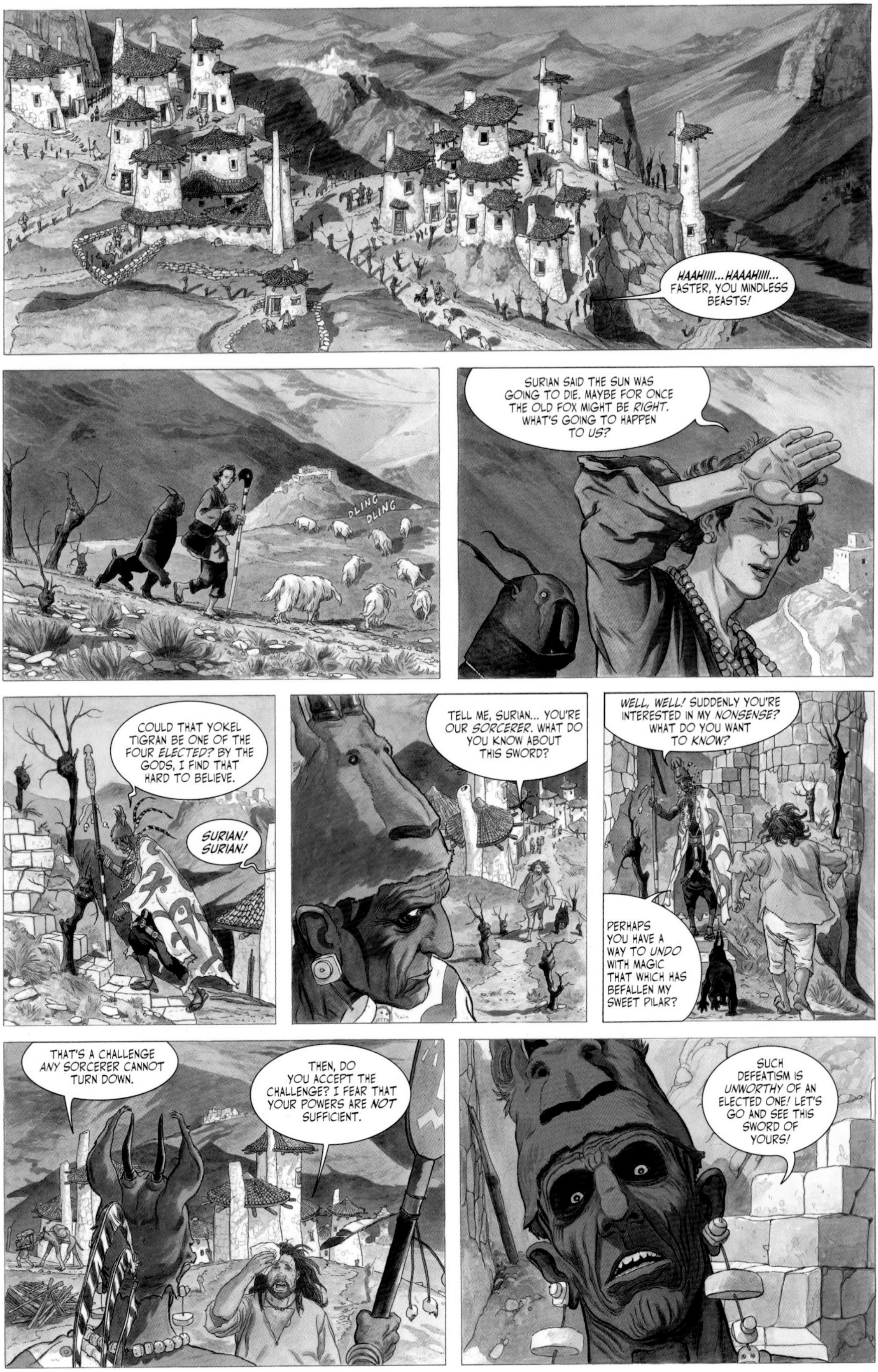
HAAHIIII... HAAAHIIII... FASTER, YOU MINDLESS BEASTS!
DLING DLING
SURIAN SAID THE SUN WAS GOING TO DIE. MAYBE FOR ONCE THE OLD FOX MIGHT BE RIGHT. WHAT'S GOING TO HAPPEN TO US?
COULD THAT YOKEL TIGRAN BE ONE OF THE FOUR ELECTED? BY THE GODS, I FIND THAT HARD TO BELIEVE.
SURIAN! SURIAN!
TELL ME, SURIAN... YOU'RE OUR SORCERER. WHAT DO YOU KNOW ABOUT THIS SWORD?
WELL, WELL! SUDDENLY YOU'RE INTERESTED IN MY NONSENSE? WHAT DO YOU WANT TO KNOW?
PERHAPS YOU HAVE A WAY TO UNDO WITH MAGIC THAT WHICH HAS BEFALLEN MY SWEET PILAR?
THAT'S A CHALLENGE ANY SORCERER CANNOT TURN DOWN.
THEN, DO YOU ACCEPT THE CHALLENGE? I FEAR THAT YOUR POWERS ARE NOT SUFFICIENT.
SUCH DEFEATISM IS UNWORTHY OF AN ELECTED ONE! LET'S GO AND SEE THIS SWORD OF YOURS!

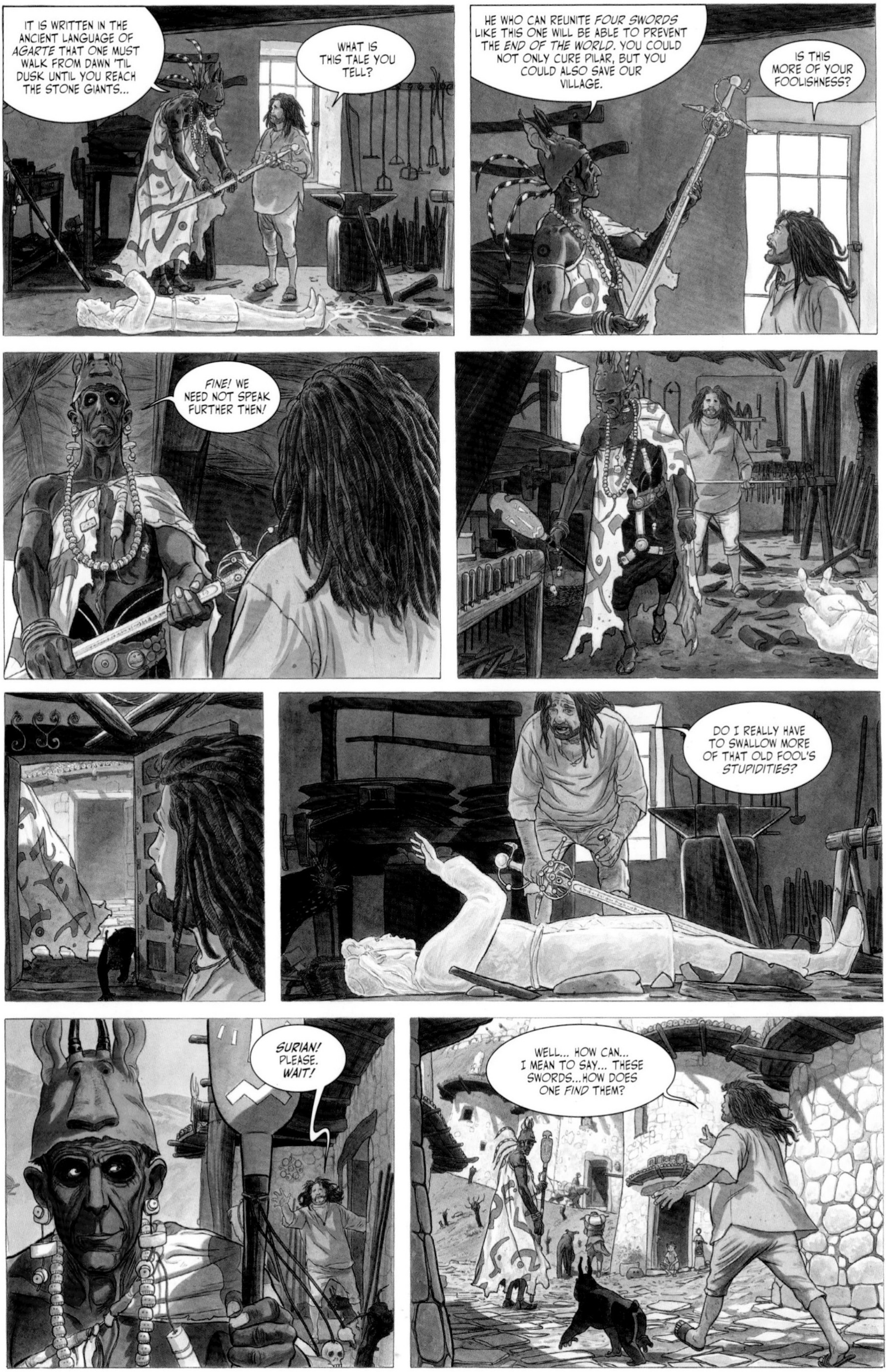

IT IS WRITTEN IN THE ANCIENT LANGUAGE OF *AGARTE* THAT ONE MUST WALK FROM DAWN 'TIL DUSK UNTIL YOU REACH THE STONE GIANTS...
WHAT IS THIS TALE YOU TELL?
HE WHO CAN REUNITE *FOUR SWORDS* LIKE THIS ONE WILL BE ABLE TO PREVENT THE *END OF THE WORLD*. YOU COULD NOT ONLY CURE PILAR, BUT YOU COULD ALSO SAVE OUR VILLAGE.
IS THIS MORE OF YOUR FOOLISHNESS?
FINE! WE NEED NOT SPEAK FURTHER THEN!
DO I REALLY HAVE TO SWALLOW MORE OF THAT OLD FOOL'S *STUPIDITIES?*
SURIAN! PLEASE. *WAIT!*
WELL... HOW CAN... I MEAN TO SAY... THESE SWORDS...HOW DOES ONE *FIND* THEM?

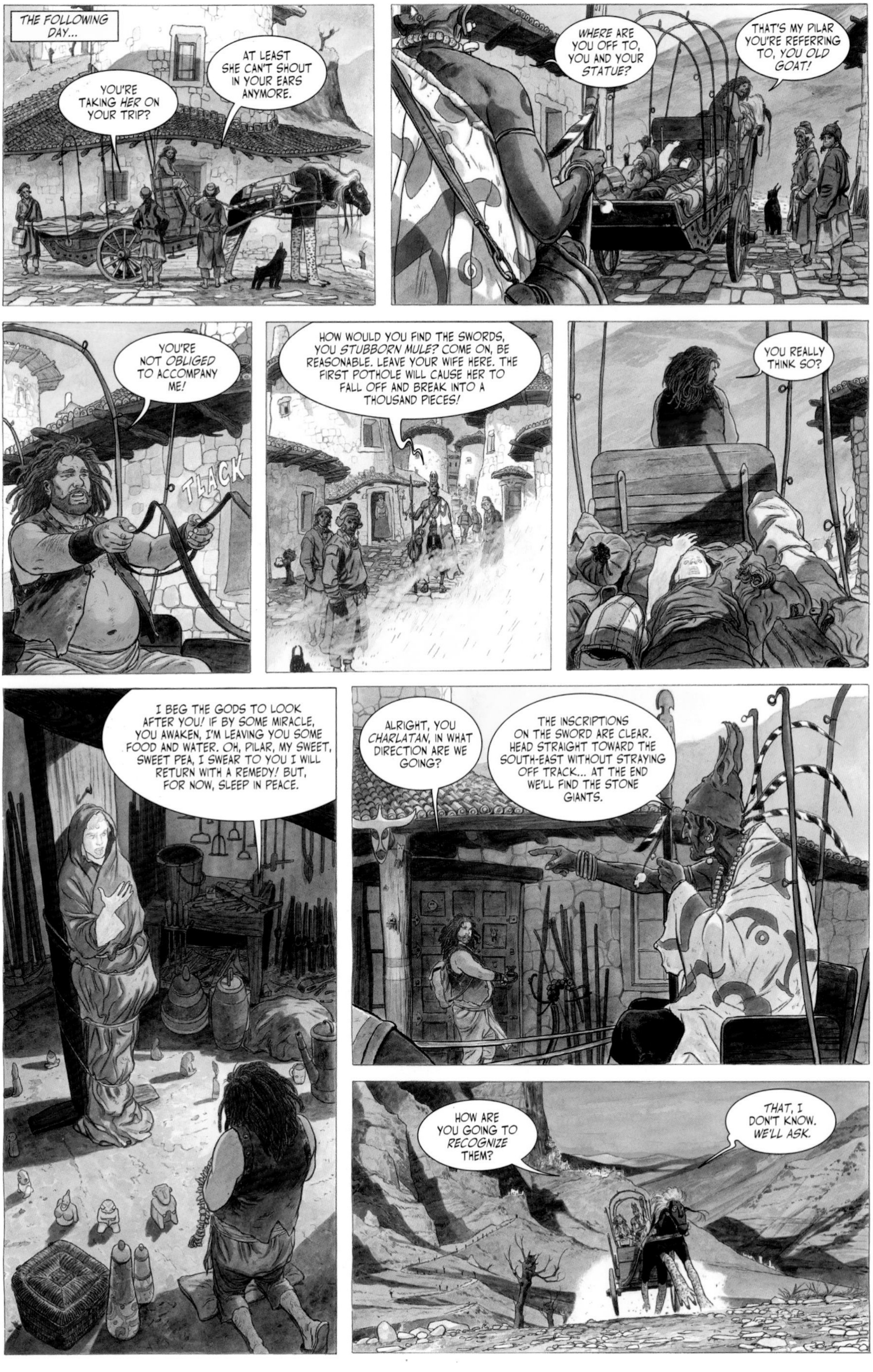
THE FOLLOWING DAY...
YOU'RE TAKING HER ON YOUR TRIP?
AT LEAST SHE CAN'T SHOUT IN YOUR EARS ANYMORE.
WHERE ARE YOU OFF TO, YOU AND YOUR STATUE?
THAT'S MY PILAR YOU'RE REFERRING TO, YOU OLD GOAT!
YOU'RE NOT OBLIGED TO ACCOMPANY ME!
TLACK
HOW WOULD YOU FIND THE SWORDS, YOU STUBBORN MULE? COME ON, BE REASONABLE. LEAVE YOUR WIFE HERE. THE FIRST POTHOLE WILL CAUSE HER TO FALL OFF AND BREAK INTO A THOUSAND PIECES!
YOU REALLY THINK SO?
I BEG THE GODS TO LOOK AFTER YOU! IF BY SOME MIRACLE, YOU AWAKEN, I'M LEAVING YOU SOME FOOD AND WATER. OH, PILAR, MY SWEET, SWEET PEA, I SWEAR TO YOU I WILL RETURN WITH A REMEDY! BUT, FOR NOW, SLEEP IN PEACE.
ALRIGHT, YOU CHARLATAN, IN WHAT DIRECTION ARE WE GOING?
THE INSCRIPTIONS ON THE SWORD ARE CLEAR. HEAD STRAIGHT TOWARD THE SOUTH-EAST WITHOUT STRAYING OFF TRACK... AT THE END WE'LL FIND THE STONE GIANTS.
HOW ARE YOU GOING TO RECOGNIZE THEM?
THAT, I DON'T KNOW. WE'LL ASK.

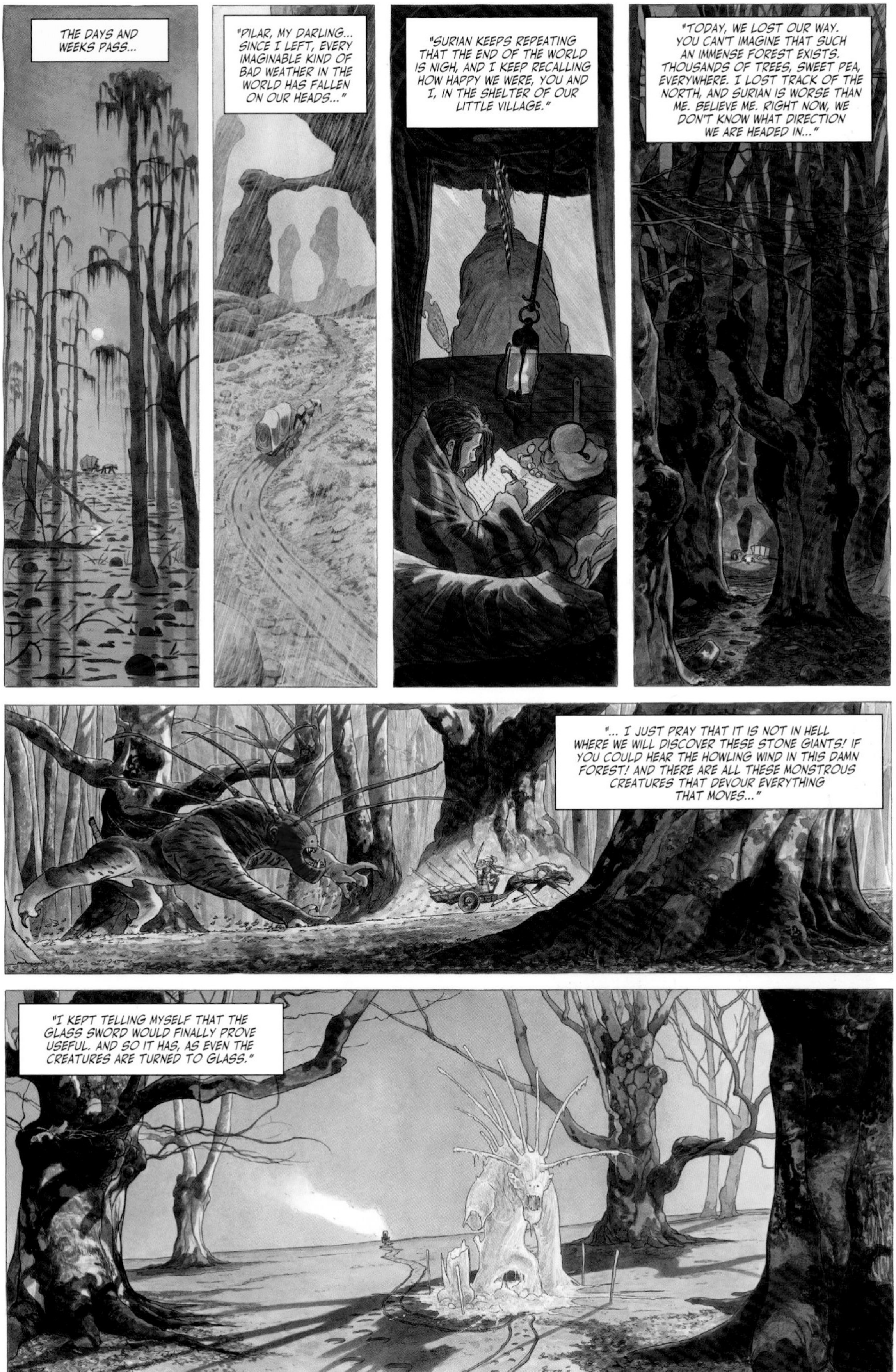
THE DAYS AND WEEKS PASS...
"PILAR, MY DARLING... SINCE I LEFT, EVERY IMAGINABLE KIND OF BAD WEATHER IN THE WORLD HAS FALLEN ON OUR HEADS..."
"SURIAN KEEPS REPEATING THAT THE END OF THE WORLD IS NIGH, AND I KEEP RECALLING HOW HAPPY WE WERE, YOU AND I, IN THE SHELTER OF OUR LITTLE VILLAGE."
"TODAY, WE LOST OUR WAY. YOU CAN'T IMAGINE THAT SUCH AN IMMENSE FOREST EXISTS. THOUSANDS OF TREES, SWEET PEA, EVERYWHERE. I LOST TRACK OF THE NORTH, AND SURIAN IS WORSE THAN ME. BELIEVE ME. RIGHT NOW, WE DON'T KNOW WHAT DIRECTION WE ARE HEADED IN..."
"... I JUST PRAY THAT IT IS NOT IN HELL WHERE WE WILL DISCOVER THESE STONE GIANTS! IF YOU COULD HEAR THE HOWLING WIND IN THIS DAMN FOREST! AND THERE ARE ALL THESE MONSTROUS CREATURES THAT DEVOUR EVERYTHING THAT MOVES..."
"I KEPT TELLING MYSELF THAT THE GLASS SWORD WOULD FINALLY PROVE USEFUL. AND SO IT HAS, AS EVEN THE CREATURES ARE TURNED TO GLASS."

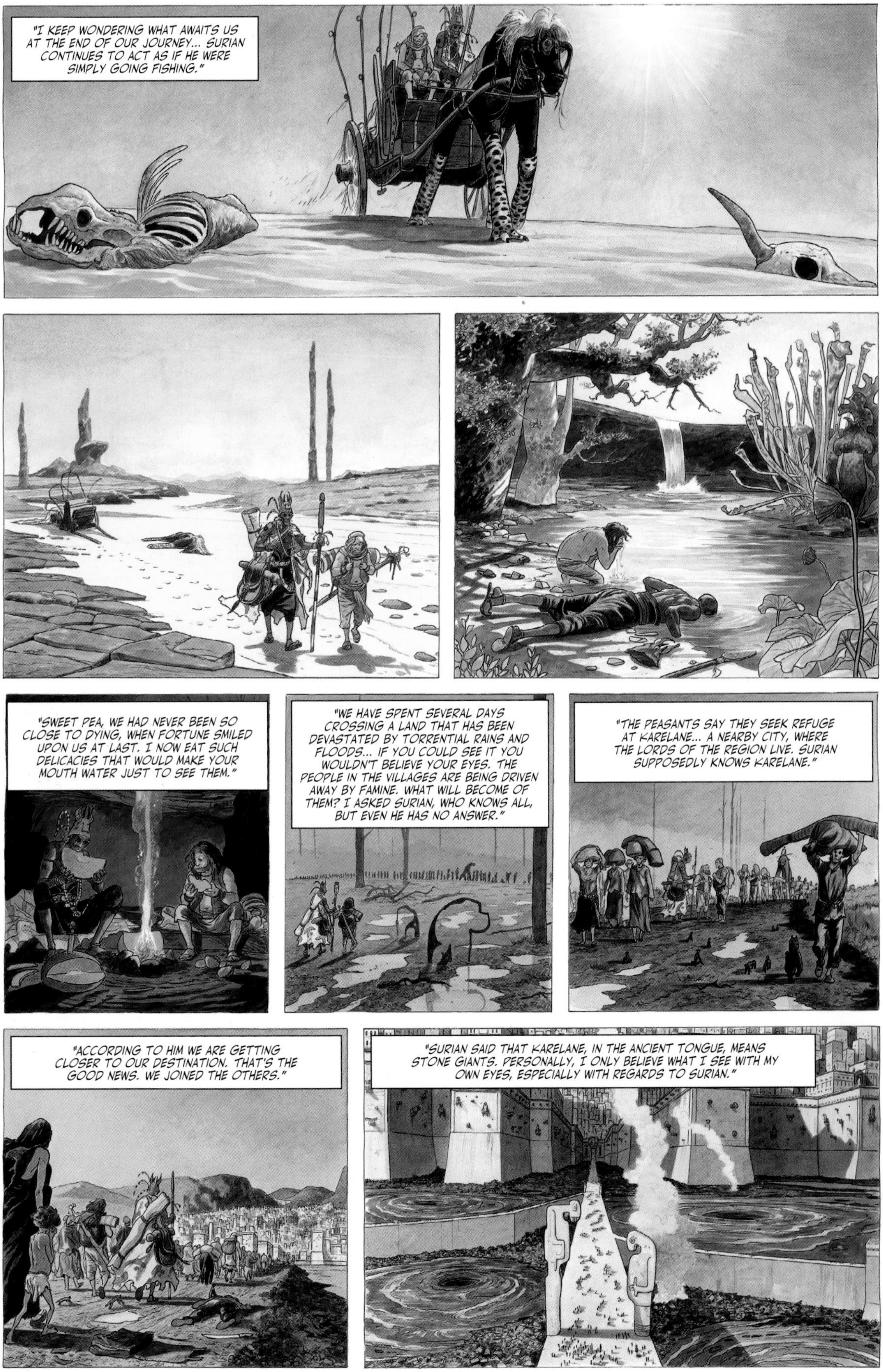
"I KEEP WONDERING WHAT AWAITS US AT THE END OF OUR JOURNEY... SURIAN CONTINUES TO ACT AS IF HE WERE SIMPLY GOING FISHING."
"SWEET PEA, WE HAD NEVER BEEN SO CLOSE TO DYING, WHEN FORTUNE SMILED UPON US AT LAST. I NOW EAT SUCH DELICACIES THAT WOULD MAKE YOUR MOUTH WATER JUST TO SEE THEM."
"WE HAVE SPENT SEVERAL DAYS CROSSING A LAND THAT HAS BEEN DEVASTATED BY TORRENTIAL RAINS AND FLOODS... IF YOU COULD SEE IT YOU WOULDN'T BELIEVE YOUR EYES. THE PEOPLE IN THE VILLAGES ARE BEING DRIVEN AWAY BY FAMINE. WHAT WILL BECOME OF THEM? I ASKED SURIAN, WHO KNOWS ALL, BUT EVEN HE HAS NO ANSWER."
"THE PEASANTS SAY THEY SEEK REFUGE AT KARELANE... A NEARBY CITY, WHERE THE LORDS OF THE REGION LIVE. SURIAN SUPPOSEDLY KNOWS KARELANE."
"ACCORDING TO HIM WE ARE GETTING CLOSER TO OUR DESTINATION. THAT'S THE GOOD NEWS. WE JOINED THE OTHERS."
"SURIAN SAID THAT KARELANE, IN THE ANCIENT TONGUE, MEANS STONE GIANTS. PERSONALLY, I ONLY BELIEVE WHAT I SEE WITH MY OWN EYES, ESPECIALLY WITH REGARDS TO SURIAN."

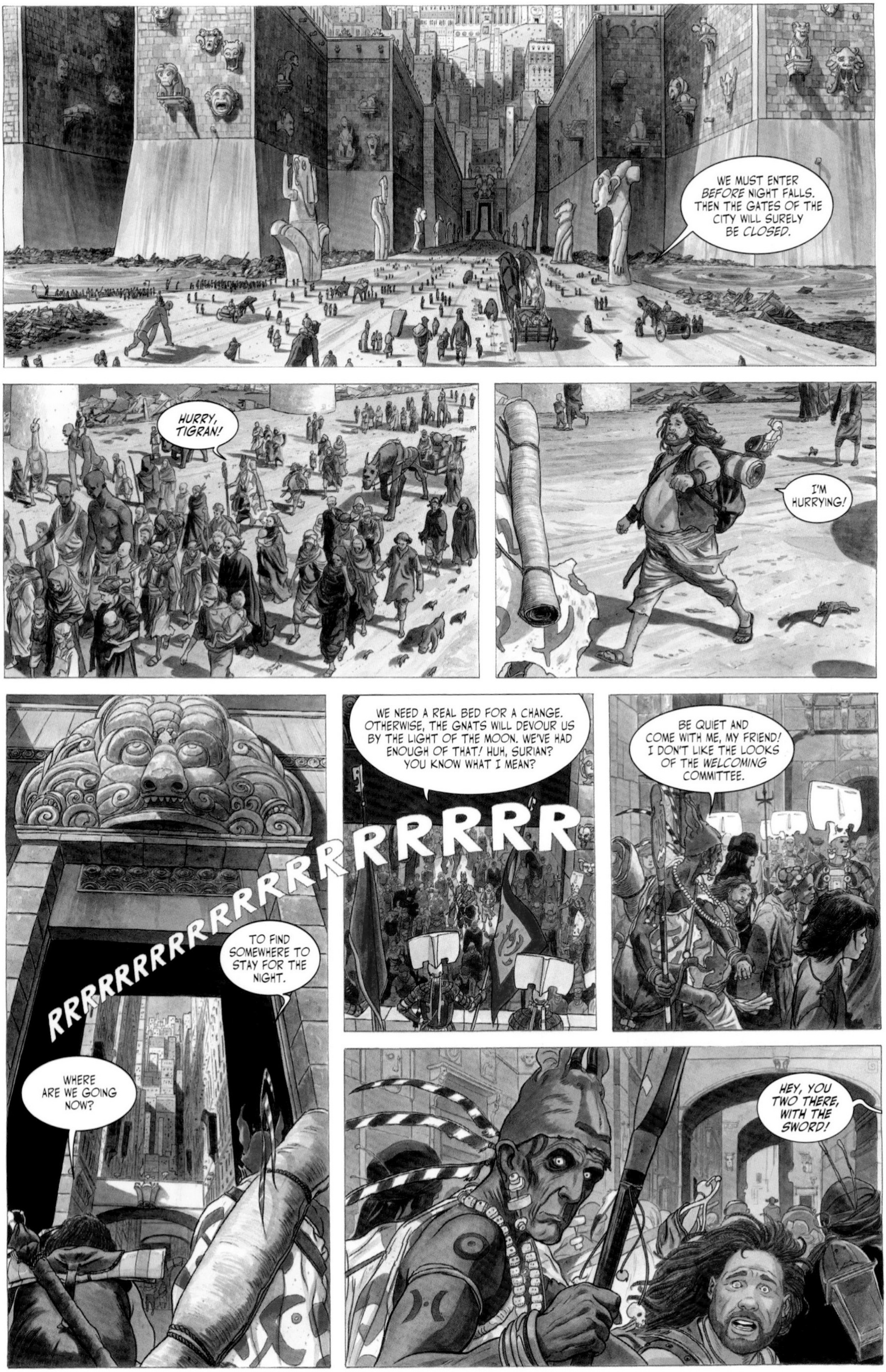
WE MUST ENTER *BEFORE* NIGHT FALLS. THEN THE GATES OF THE CITY WILL SURELY BE *CLOSED*.
HURRY, TIGRAN!
I'M HURRYING!
WHERE ARE WE GOING NOW?
TO FIND SOMEWHERE TO STAY FOR THE NIGHT.
RRRRRRRRRRRRRRRRRRR
WE NEED A REAL BED FOR A CHANGE. OTHERWISE, THE GNATS WILL DEVOUR US BY THE LIGHT OF THE MOON. WE'VE HAD ENOUGH OF THAT! HUH, SURIAN? YOU KNOW WHAT I MEAN?
BE QUIET AND COME WITH ME, MY FRIEND! I DON'T LIKE THE LOOKS OF THE *WELCOMING* COMMITTEE.
HEY, YOU TWO THERE, WITH THE SWORD!

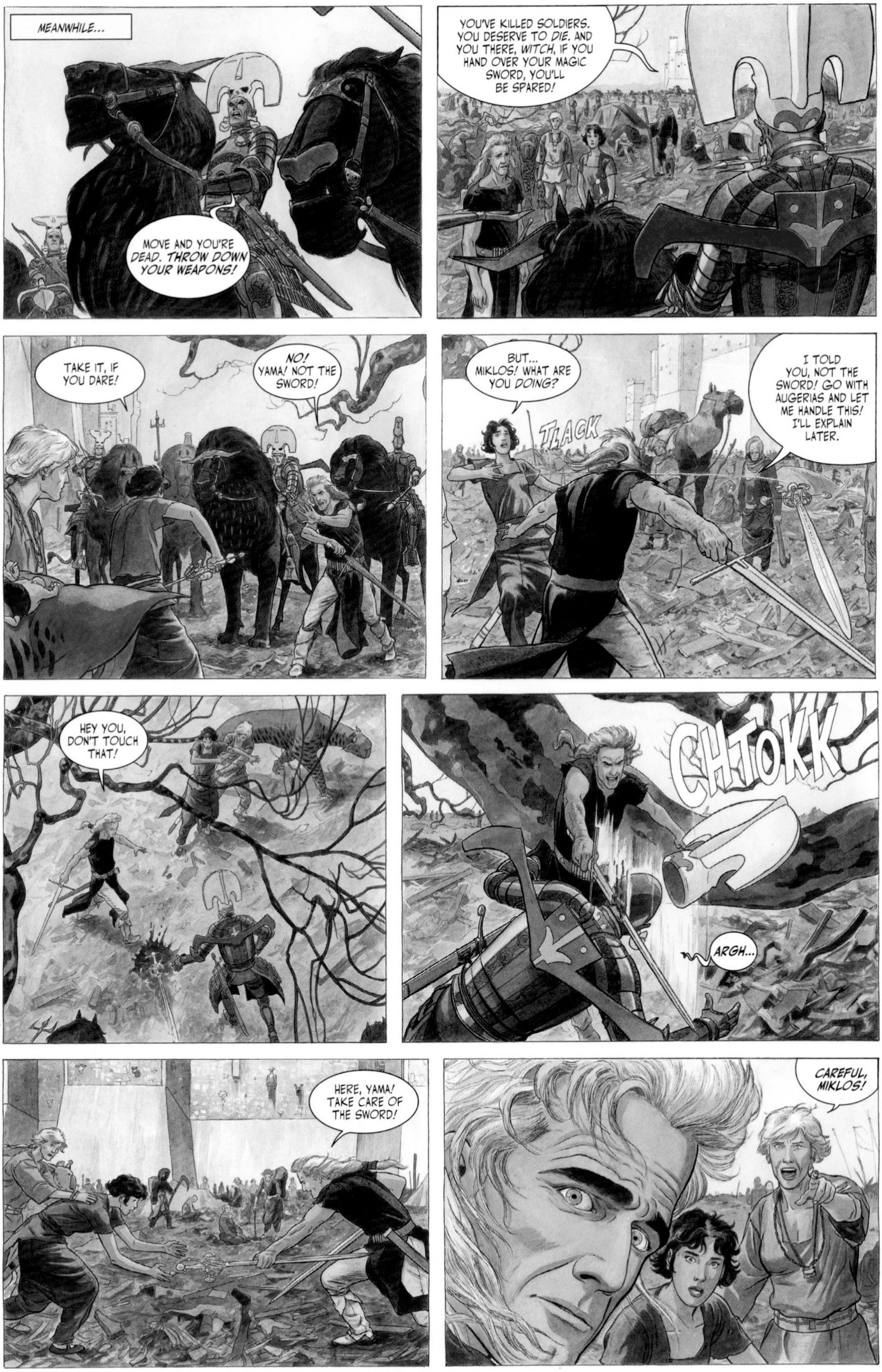

MEANWHILE...
MOVE AND YOU'RE DEAD. THROW DOWN YOUR WEAPONS!
YOU'VE KILLED SOLDIERS. YOU DESERVE TO DIE. AND YOU THERE, WITCH, IF YOU HAND OVER YOUR MAGIC SWORD, YOU'LL BE SPARED!
TAKE IT, IF YOU DARE!
NO! YAMA! NOT THE SWORD!
BUT... MIKLOS! WHAT ARE YOU DOING?
TLACK
I TOLD YOU, NOT THE SWORD! GO WITH AUGERIAS AND LET ME HANDLE THIS! I'LL EXPLAIN LATER.
HEY YOU, DON'T TOUCH THAT!
CHTOKK
ARGH...
HERE, YAMA! TAKE CARE OF THE SWORD!
CAREFUL, MIKLOS!

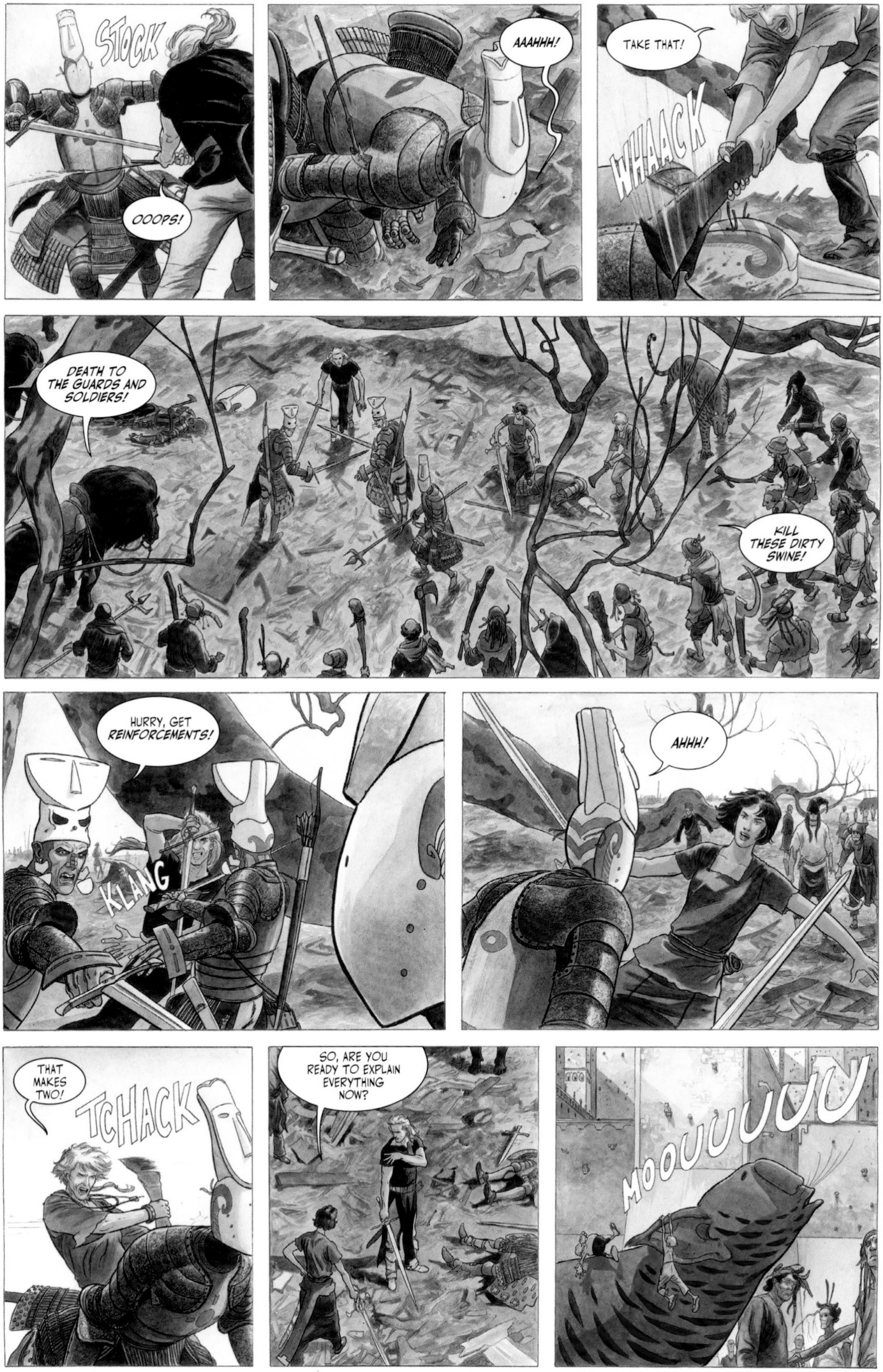
STOCK
OOOPS!
AAAHHH!
TAKE THAT!
WHAACK
DEATH TO THE GUARDS AND SOLDIERS!
KILL THESE DIRTY SWINE!
HURRY, GET REINFORCEMENTS!
KLANG
AHHH!
THAT MAKES TWO!
TCHACK
SO, ARE YOU READY TO EXPLAIN EVERYTHING NOW?
MOOUUUUUU

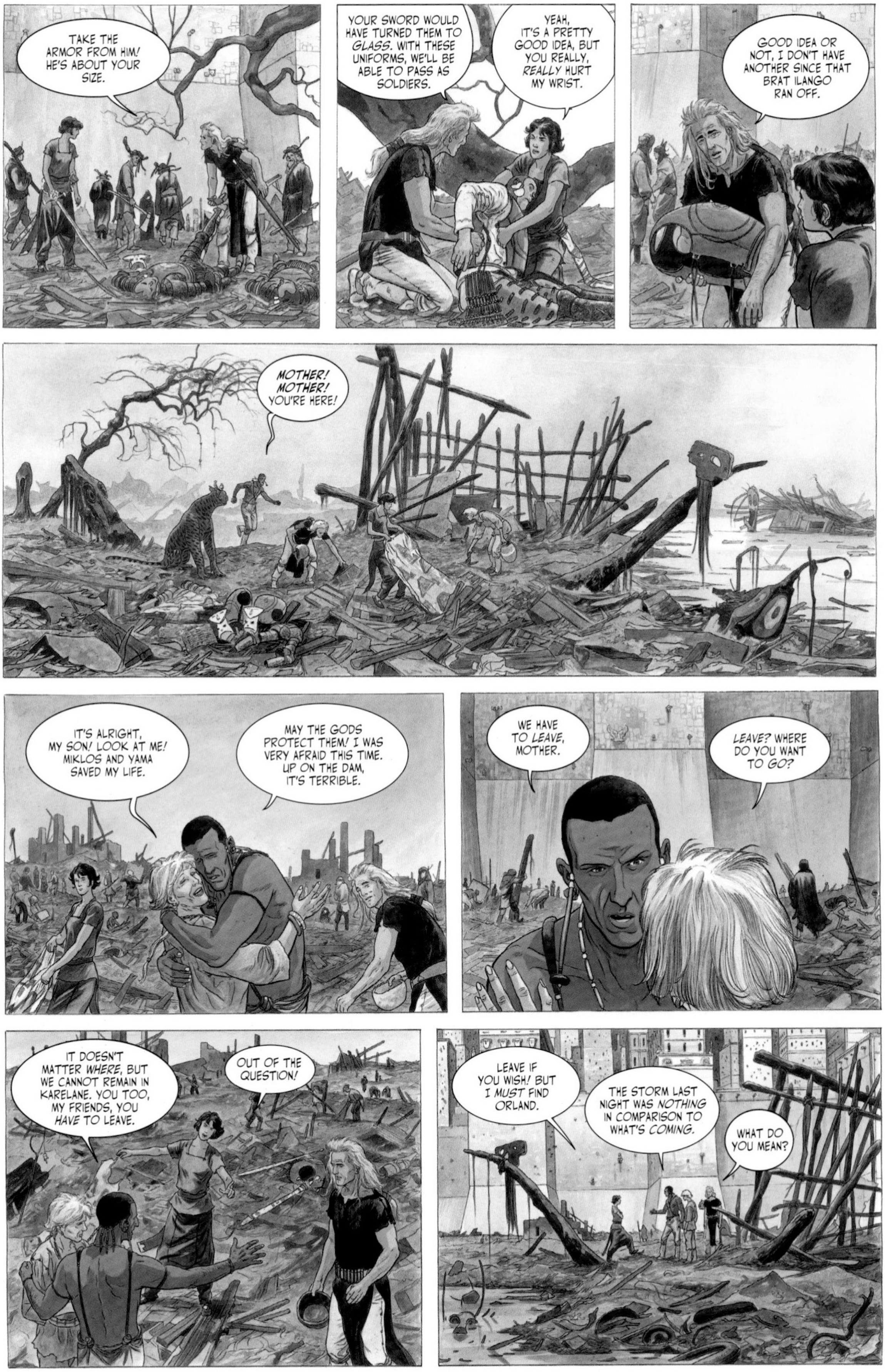
TAKE THE ARMOR FROM HIM! HE'S ABOUT YOUR SIZE.
YOUR SWORD WOULD HAVE TURNED THEM TO GLASS. WITH THESE UNIFORMS, WE'LL BE ABLE TO PASS AS SOLDIERS.
YEAH, IT'S A PRETTY GOOD IDEA, BUT YOU REALLY, REALLY HURT MY WRIST.
GOOD IDEA OR NOT, I DON'T HAVE ANOTHER SINCE THAT BRAT ILANGO RAN OFF.
MOTHER! MOTHER! YOU'RE HERE!
IT'S ALRIGHT, MY SON! LOOK AT ME! MIKLOS AND YAMA SAVED MY LIFE.
MAY THE GODS PROTECT THEM! I WAS VERY AFRAID THIS TIME. UP ON THE DAM, IT'S TERRIBLE.
WE HAVE TO LEAVE, MOTHER.
LEAVE? WHERE DO YOU WANT TO GO?
IT DOESN'T MATTER WHERE, BUT WE CANNOT REMAIN IN KARELANE. YOU TOO, MY FRIENDS, YOU HAVE TO LEAVE.
OUT OF THE QUESTION!
LEAVE IF YOU WISH! BUT I MUST FIND ORLAND.
THE STORM LAST NIGHT WAS NOTHING IN COMPARISON TO WHAT'S COMING.
WHAT DO YOU MEAN?

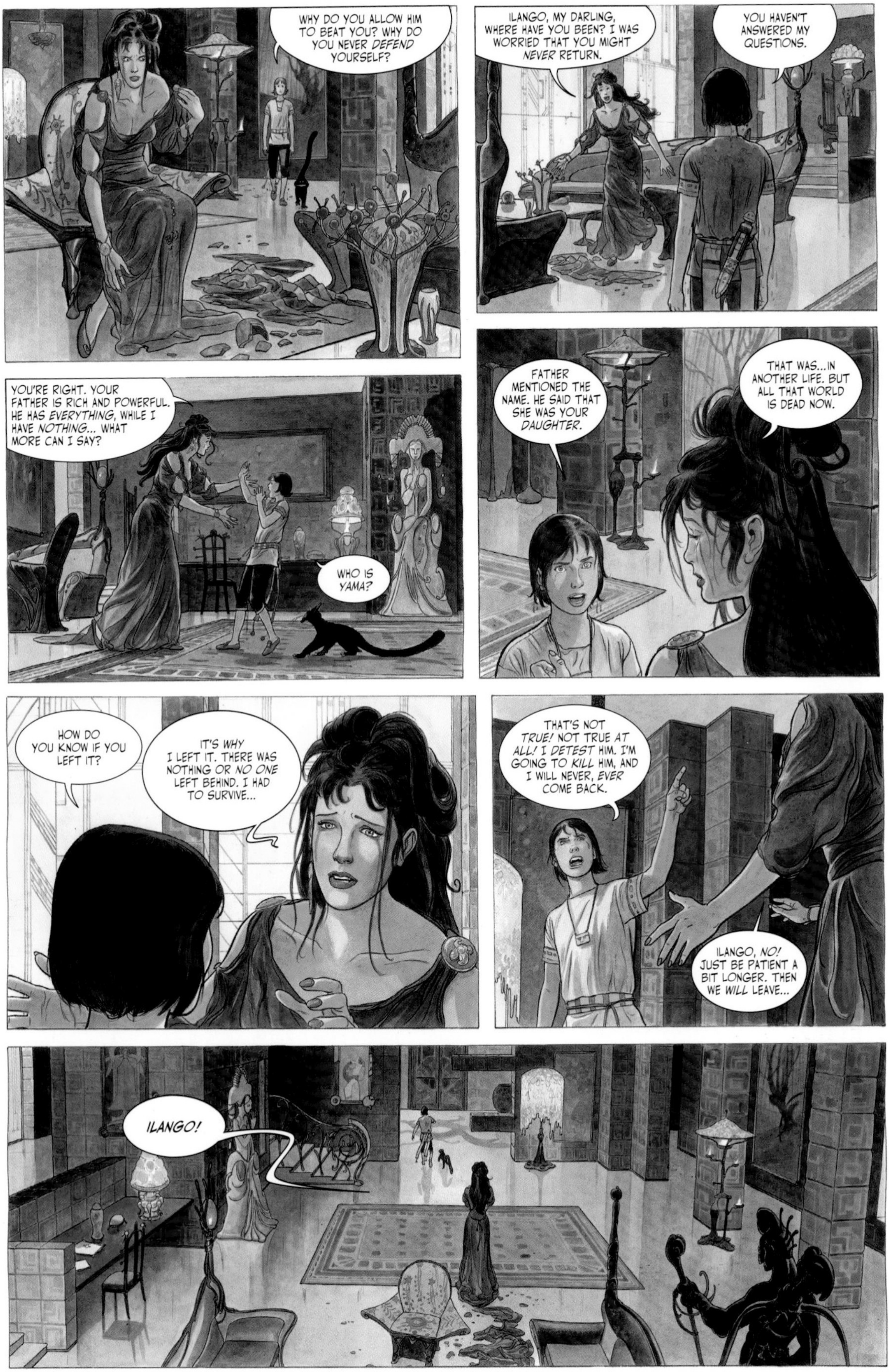
WHY DO YOU ALLOW HIM TO BEAT YOU? WHY DO YOU NEVER *DEFEND* YOURSELF?
ILANGO, MY DARLING, WHERE HAVE YOU BEEN? I WAS WORRIED THAT YOU MIGHT *NEVER* RETURN.
YOU HAVEN'T ANSWERED MY QUESTIONS.
YOU'RE RIGHT. YOUR FATHER IS RICH AND POWERFUL. HE HAS *EVERYTHING*, WHILE I HAVE *NOTHING*... WHAT MORE CAN I SAY?
WHO IS *YAMA?*
FATHER MENTIONED THE NAME. HE SAID THAT SHE WAS YOUR *DAUGHTER*.
THAT WAS...IN ANOTHER LIFE. BUT ALL THAT WORLD IS DEAD NOW.
HOW DO YOU KNOW IF YOU LEFT IT?
IT'S *WHY* I LEFT IT. THERE WAS NOTHING OR *NO ONE* LEFT BEHIND. I HAD TO SURVIVE...
THAT'S NOT *TRUE!* NOT TRUE AT *ALL!* I *DETEST* HIM. I'M GOING TO *KILL* HIM, AND I WILL NEVER, *EVER* COME BACK.
ILANGO, *NO!* JUST BE PATIENT A BIT LONGER. THEN WE *WILL* LEAVE...
ILANGO!

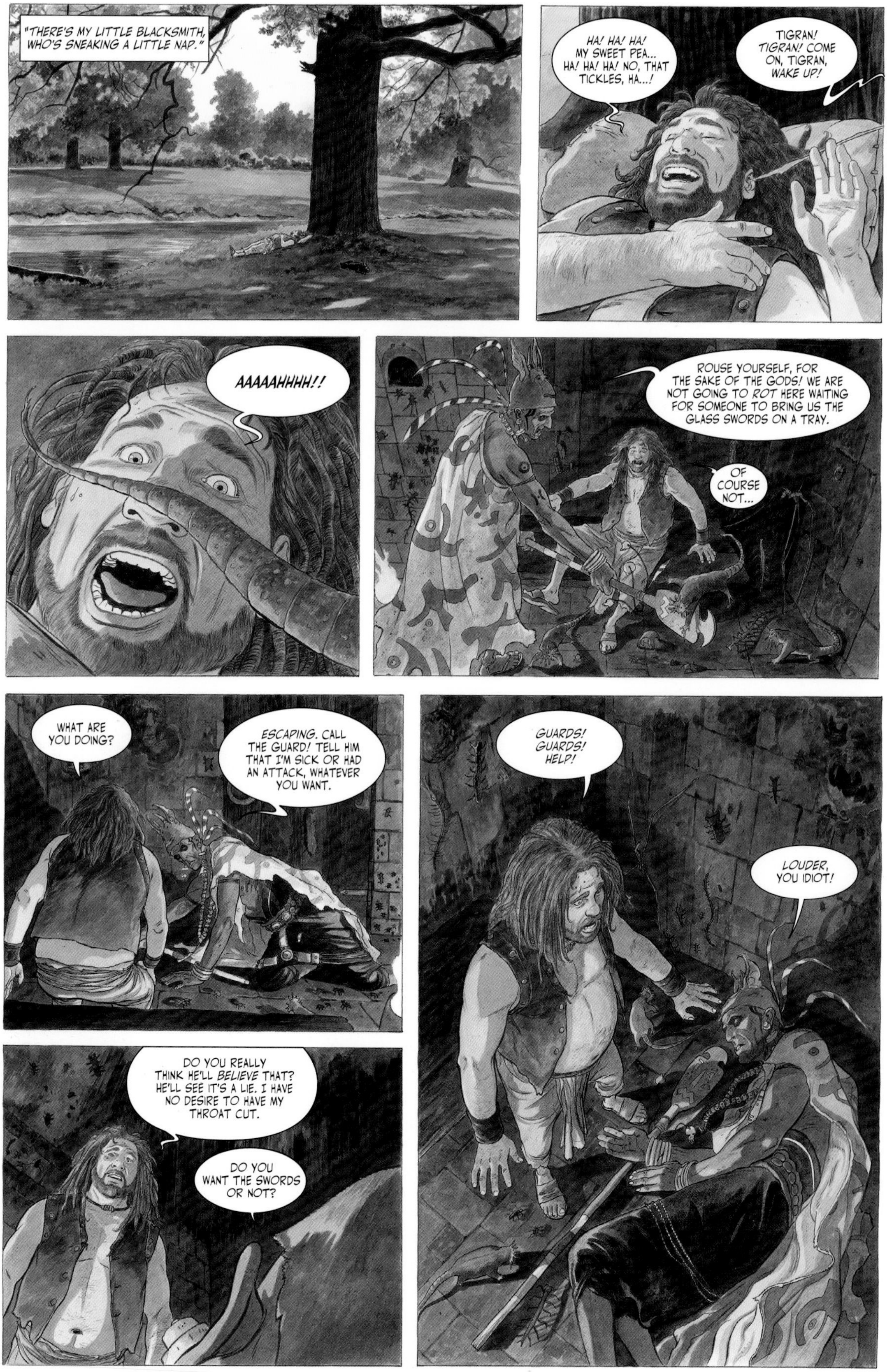
"THERE'S MY LITTLE BLACKSMITH, WHO'S SNEAKING A LITTLE NAP."
HA! HA! HA! MY SWEET PEA... HA! HA! NO, THAT TICKLES, HA...!
TIGRAN! TIGRAN! COME ON, TIGRAN, WAKE UP!
AAAAAHHHH!!
ROUSE YOURSELF, FOR THE SAKE OF THE GODS! WE ARE NOT GOING TO ROT HERE WAITING FOR SOMEONE TO BRING US THE GLASS SWORDS ON A TRAY.
OF COURSE NOT...
WHAT ARE YOU DOING?
ESCAPING. CALL THE GUARD! TELL HIM THAT I'M SICK OR HAD AN ATTACK, WHATEVER YOU WANT.
DO YOU REALLY THINK HE'LL BELIEVE THAT? HE'LL SEE IT'S A LIE. I HAVE NO DESIRE TO HAVE MY THROAT CUT.
DO YOU WANT THE SWORDS OR NOT?
GUARDS! GUARDS! HELP!
LOUDER, YOU IDIOT!

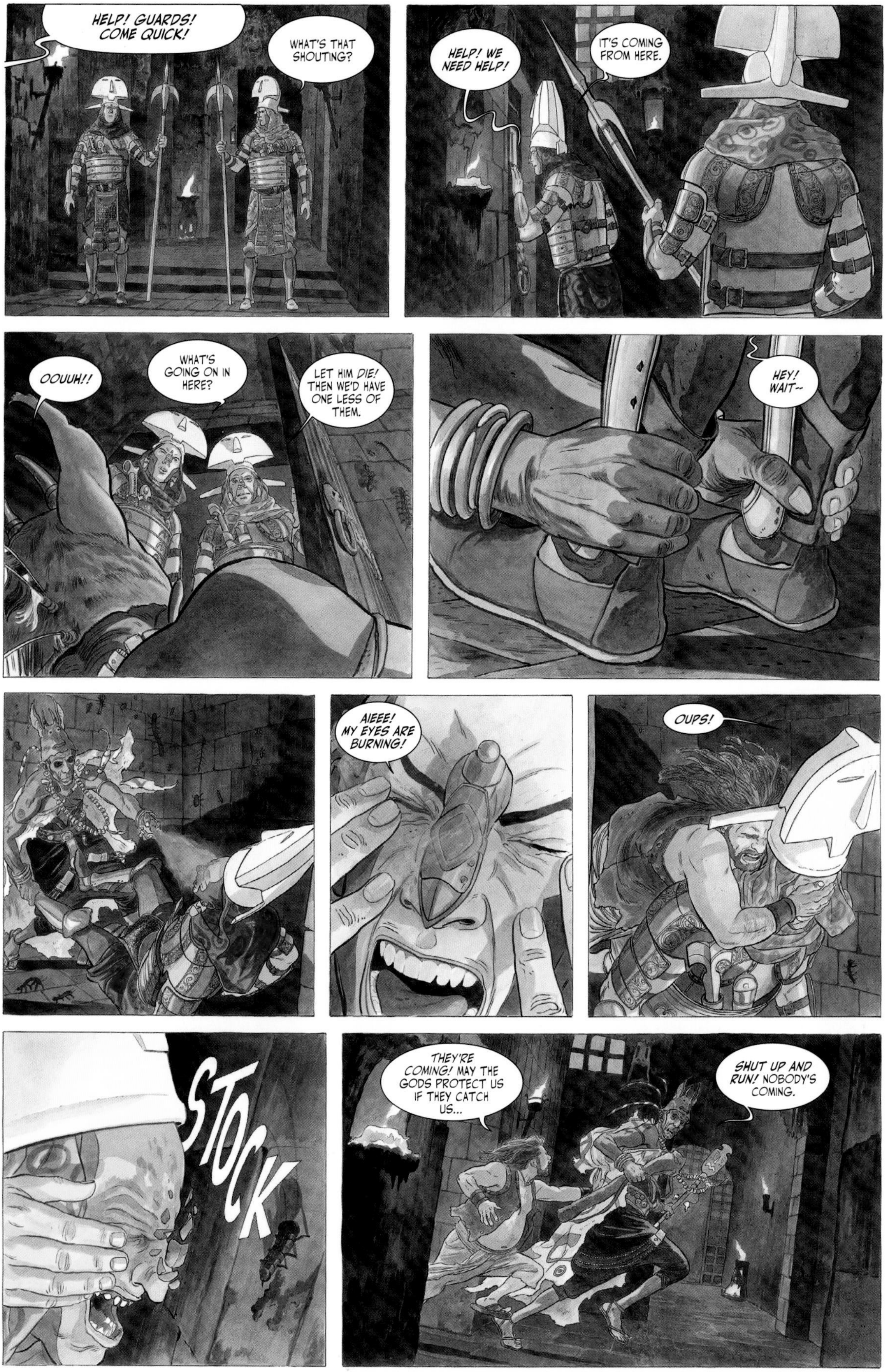

HELP! GUARDS! COME QUICK!
WHAT'S THAT SHOUTING?
HELP! WE NEED HELP!
IT'S COMING FROM HERE.
OOUUH!!
WHAT'S GOING ON IN HERE?
LET HIM DIE! THEN WE'D HAVE ONE LESS OF THEM.
HEY! WAIT--
AIEEE! MY EYES ARE BURNING!
OUPS!
STOCK
THEY'RE COMING! MAY THE GODS PROTECT US IF THEY CATCH US...
SHUT UP AND RUN! NOBODY'S COMING.

"YOU SEE, YAMA, THE HUMAN SPECIES IS PERHAPS UNIQUE IN BEING THE MOST *PERSISTENT* IN ITS FIGHT FOR SURVIVAL."

WHAT PURPOSE DOES THAT SERVE, IF WE ALL DISAPPEAR WHEN THE SUN DIES?

I THOUGHT THE WAY YOU DO... AND I BECAME RESIGNED TO DIE WITH THE OTHERS.

BUT THEN A YOUNG *GIRL* CAME ALONG TO DISTURB MY TRANQUILITY BY RECALLING THE EXISTENCE OF THE SWORDS OF GLASS THAT I HAD TRIED TO FORGET FOR ALL THOSE YEARS.

WHY *YOU*? WHY *ME*? HOW CAN WE LEND FAITH TO THIS INCREDIBLE FABLE! THERE ARE JUST TOO MANY MYSTERIES FOR ME... ALL I KNOW IS I HAVE TO TRY MY BEST TO SURVIVE.

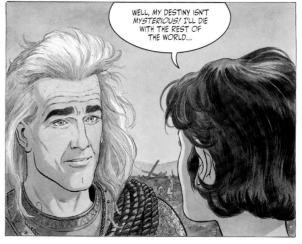

WELL, MY DESTINY ISN'T *MYSTERIOUS!* I'LL DIE WITH THE REST OF THE WORLD...

...BUT NOT BEFORE HAVING TAKEN CARE OF ORLAND.

MAKE YOURSELF PRESENTABLE. YOU'LL NEVER PASS FOR A SOLDIER AS YOU ARE!

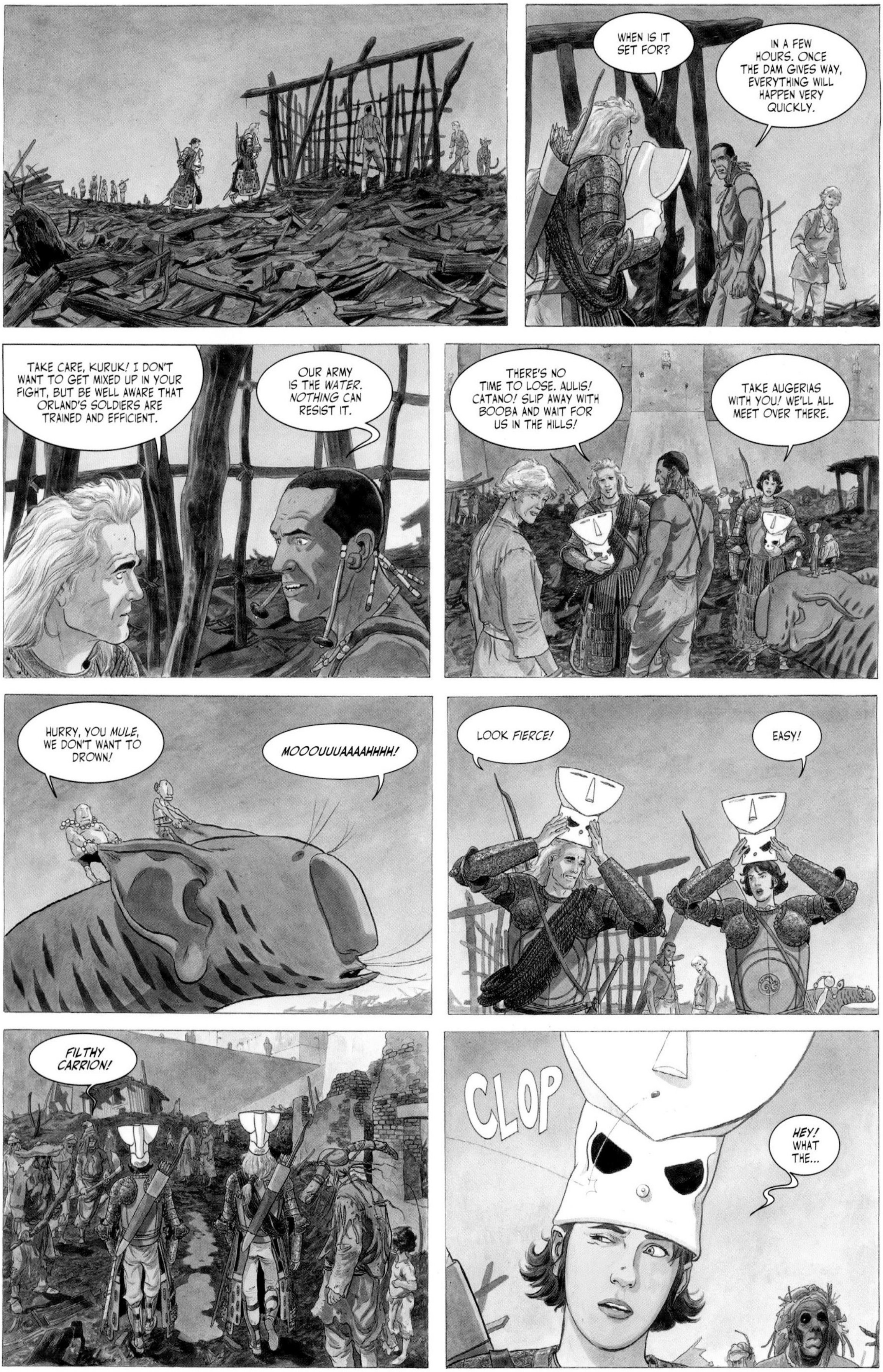
WHEN IS IT SET FOR?
IN A FEW HOURS. ONCE THE DAM GIVES WAY, EVERYTHING WILL HAPPEN VERY QUICKLY.
TAKE CARE, KURUK! I DON'T WANT TO GET MIXED UP IN YOUR FIGHT, BUT BE WELL AWARE THAT ORLAND'S SOLDIERS ARE TRAINED AND EFFICIENT.
OUR ARMY IS THE *WATER*. *NOTHING* CAN RESIST IT.
THERE'S NO TIME TO LOSE. AULIS! CATANO! SLIP AWAY WITH BOOBA AND WAIT FOR US IN THE HILLS!
TAKE AUGERIAS WITH YOU! WE'LL ALL MEET OVER THERE.
HURRY, YOU *MULE*, WE DON'T WANT TO DROWN!
MOOOUUUAAAAHHHH!
LOOK *FIERCE!*
EASY!
FILTHY CARRION!
CLOP
HEY! WHAT THE...

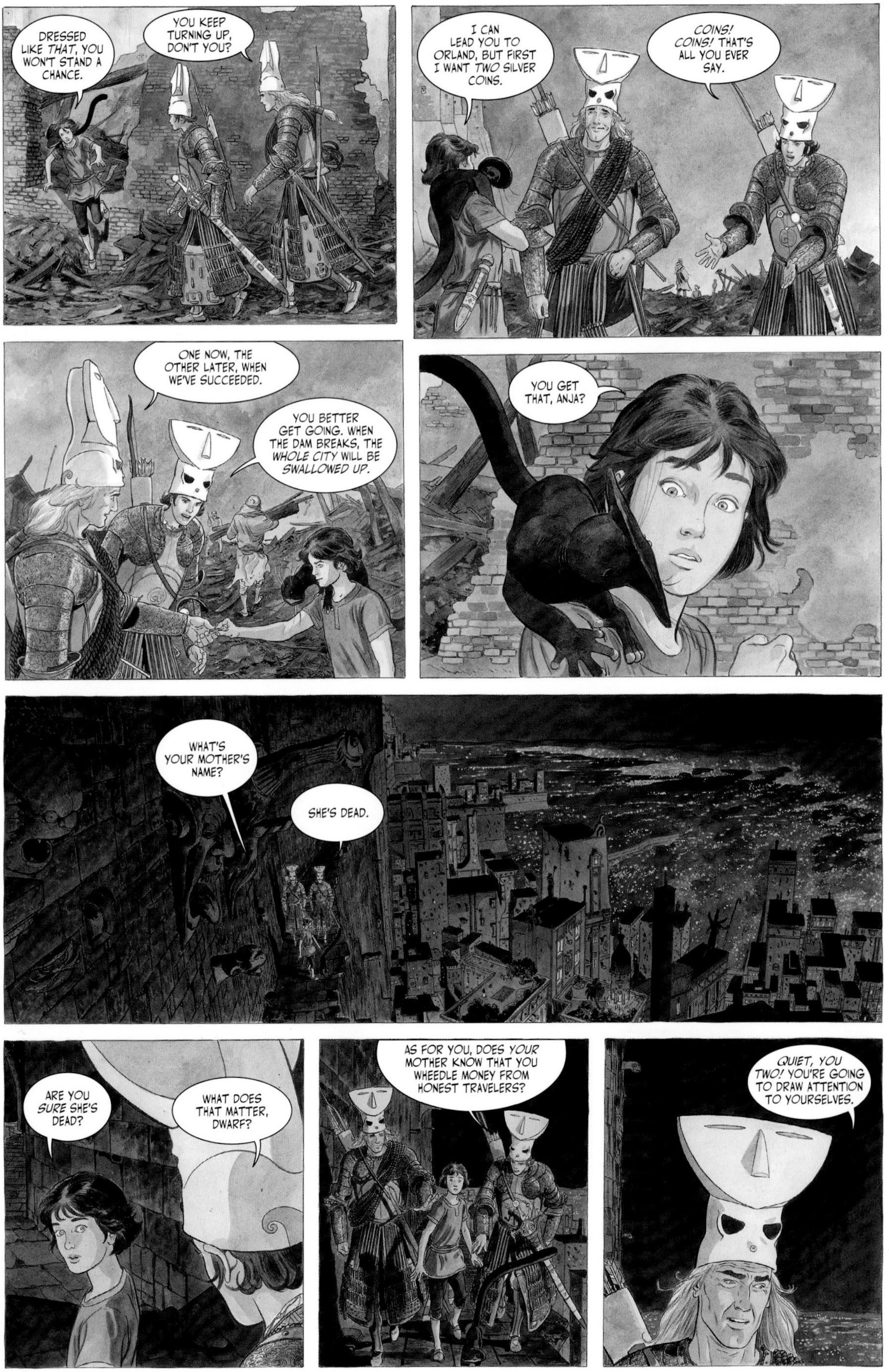
DRESSED LIKE *THAT*, YOU WON'T STAND A CHANCE.
YOU KEEP TURNING UP, DON'T YOU?
I CAN LEAD YOU TO ORLAND, BUT FIRST I WANT *TWO* SILVER COINS.
COINS! COINS! THAT'S ALL YOU EVER SAY.
ONE NOW, THE OTHER LATER, WHEN WE'VE SUCCEEDED.
YOU BETTER GET GOING. WHEN THE DAM BREAKS, THE *WHOLE CITY* WILL BE *SWALLOWED UP*.
YOU GET THAT, ANJA?
WHAT'S YOUR MOTHER'S NAME?
SHE'S DEAD.
ARE YOU *SURE* SHE'S DEAD?
WHAT DOES THAT MATTER, DWARF?
AS FOR YOU, DOES *YOUR* MOTHER KNOW THAT YOU WHEEDLE MONEY FROM HONEST TRAVELERS?
QUIET, YOU TWO! YOU'RE GOING TO DRAW ATTENTION TO YOURSELVES.

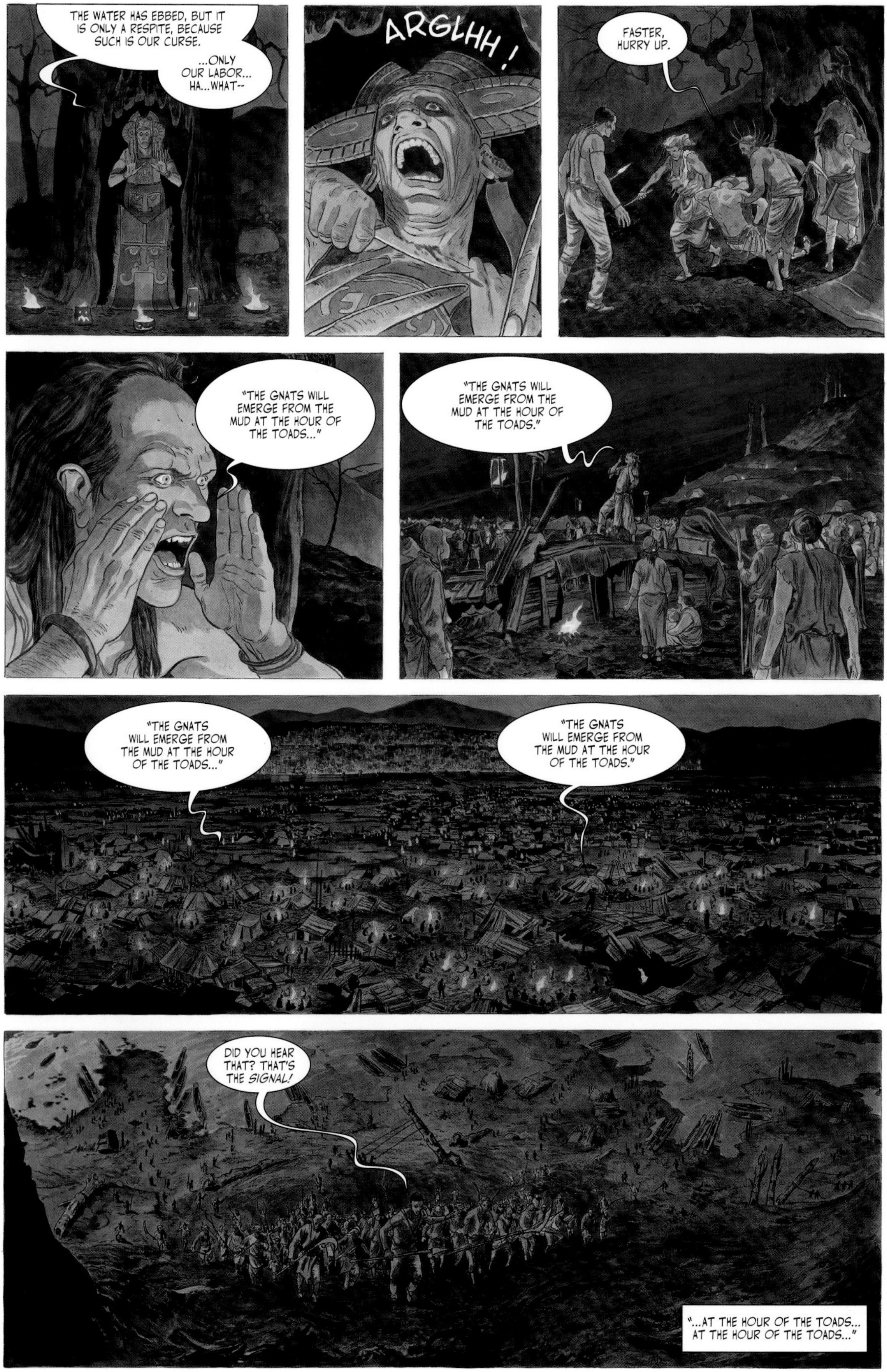
THE WATER HAS EBBED, BUT IT IS ONLY A RESPITE, BECAUSE SUCH IS OUR CURSE.
...ONLY OUR LABOR... HA...WHAT--
ARGLHH!
FASTER, HURRY UP.
"THE GNATS WILL EMERGE FROM THE MUD AT THE HOUR OF THE TOADS..."
"THE GNATS WILL EMERGE FROM THE MUD AT THE HOUR OF THE TOADS."
"THE GNATS WILL EMERGE FROM THE MUD AT THE HOUR OF THE TOADS..."
"THE GNATS WILL EMERGE FROM THE MUD AT THE HOUR OF THE TOADS."
DID YOU HEAR THAT? THAT'S THE *SIGNAL!*
"...AT THE HOUR OF THE TOADS... AT THE HOUR OF THE TOADS..."

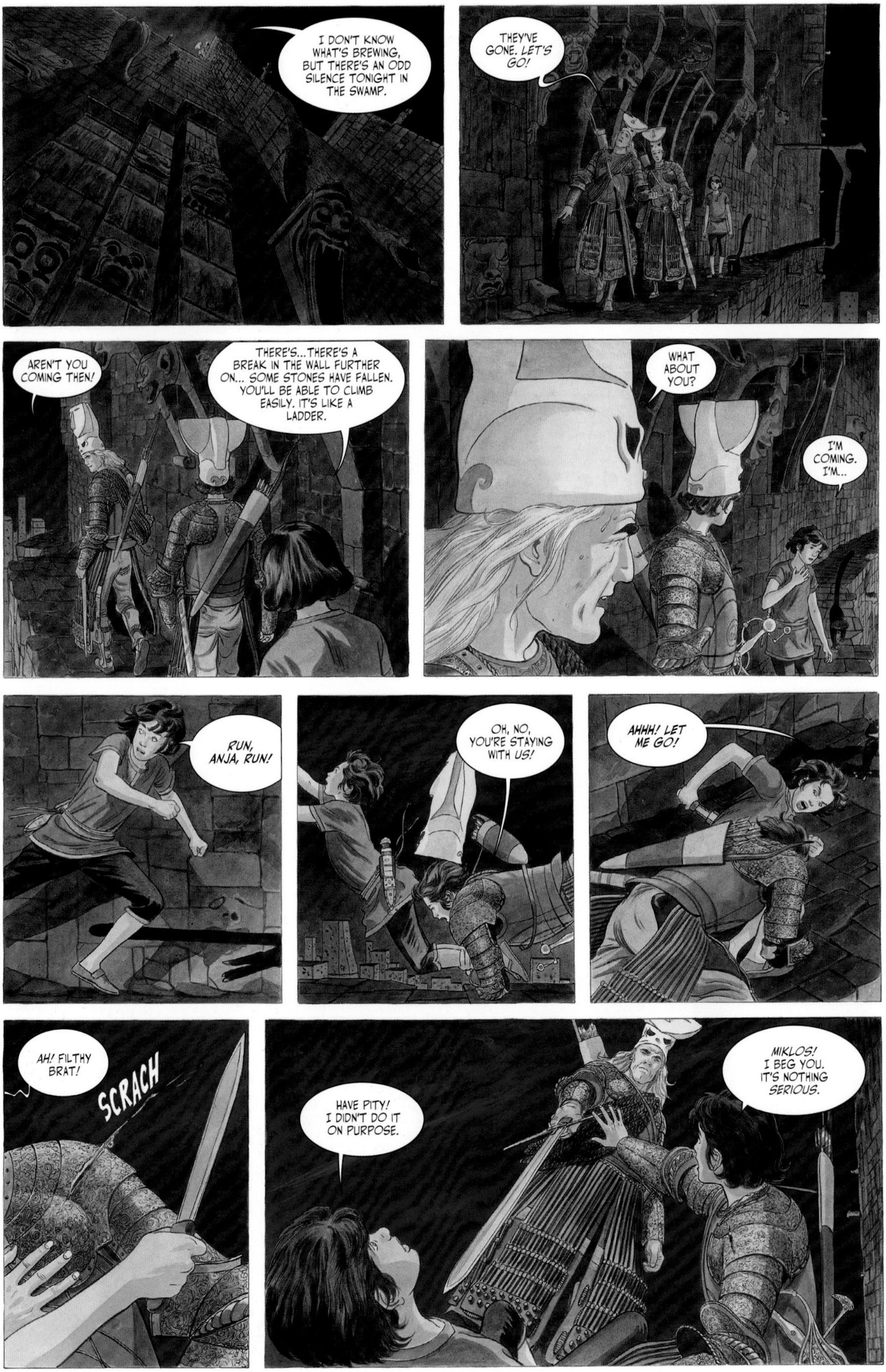
I DON'T KNOW WHAT'S BREWING, BUT THERE'S AN ODD SILENCE TONIGHT IN THE SWAMP.
THEY'VE GONE. *LET'S GO!*
AREN'T YOU COMING THEN!
THERE'S...THERE'S A BREAK IN THE WALL FURTHER ON... SOME STONES HAVE FALLEN. YOU'LL BE ABLE TO CLIMB EASILY. IT'S LIKE A LADDER.
WHAT ABOUT YOU?
I'M COMING. I'M...
RUN, ANJA, RUN!
OH, NO, YOU'RE STAYING WITH *US!*
AHHH! LET ME GO!
AH! FILTHY BRAT!
SCRACH
HAVE PITY! I DIDN'T DO IT ON PURPOSE.
MIKLOS! I BEG YOU. IT'S NOTHING *SERIOUS.*

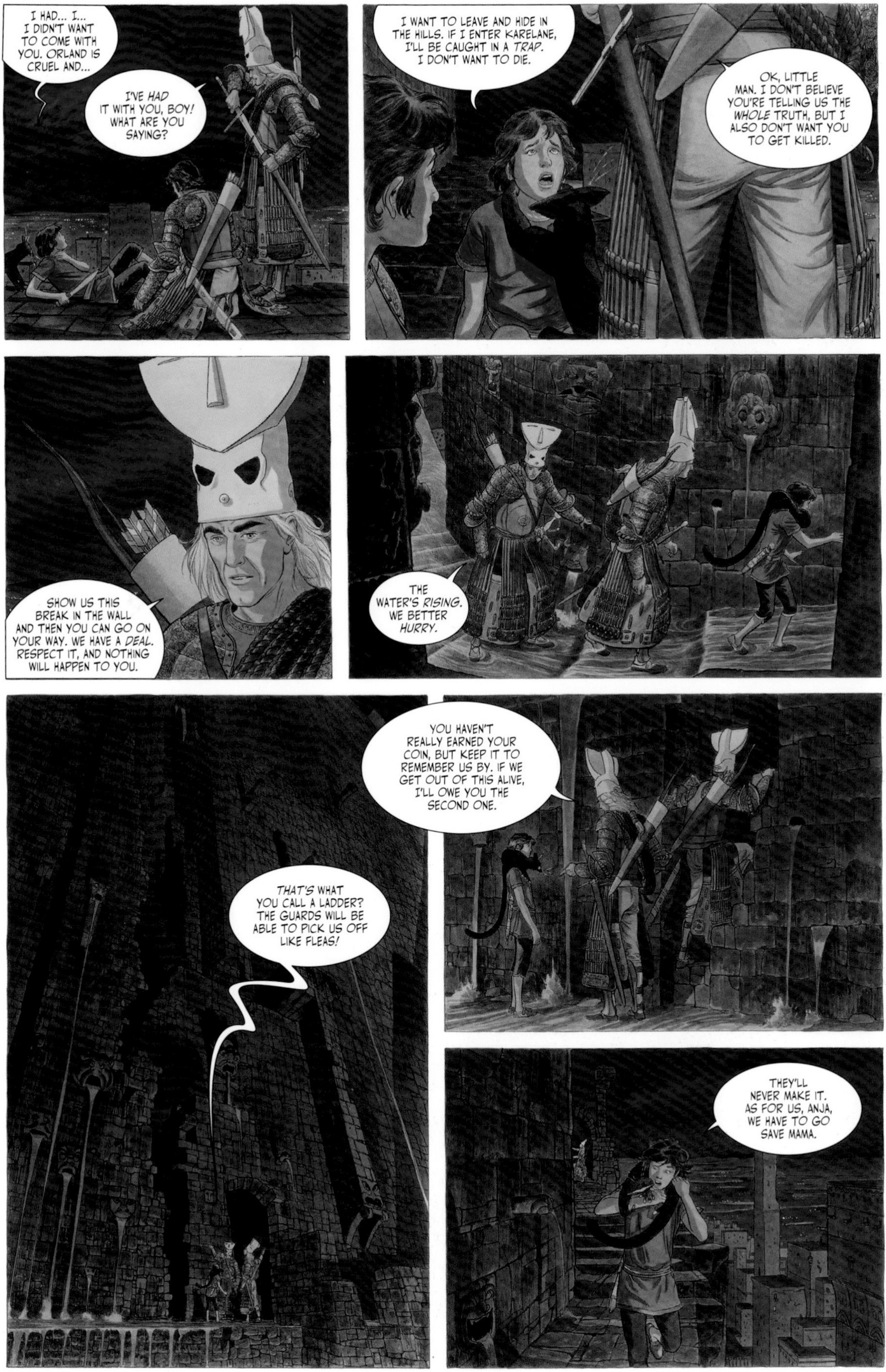
I HAD... I... I DIDN'T WANT TO COME WITH YOU. ORLAND IS CRUEL AND...
I'VE *HAD* IT WITH YOU, BOY! WHAT ARE YOU SAYING?
I WANT TO LEAVE AND HIDE IN THE HILLS. IF I ENTER KARELANE, I'LL BE CAUGHT IN A *TRAP*. I DON'T WANT TO DIE.
OK, LITTLE MAN. I DON'T BELIEVE YOU'RE TELLING US THE *WHOLE* TRUTH, BUT I ALSO DON'T WANT YOU TO GET KILLED.
SHOW US THIS BREAK IN THE WALL AND THEN YOU CAN GO ON YOUR WAY. WE HAVE A *DEAL*. RESPECT IT, AND NOTHING WILL HAPPEN TO YOU.
THE WATER'S *RISING*. WE BETTER *HURRY*.
THAT'S WHAT YOU CALL A LADDER? THE GUARDS WILL BE ABLE TO PICK US OFF LIKE FLEAS!
YOU HAVEN'T REALLY EARNED YOUR COIN, BUT KEEP IT TO REMEMBER US BY. IF WE GET OUT OF THIS ALIVE, I'LL OWE YOU THE SECOND ONE.
THEY'LL NEVER MAKE IT. AS FOR US, ANJA, WE HAVE TO GO SAVE MAMA.

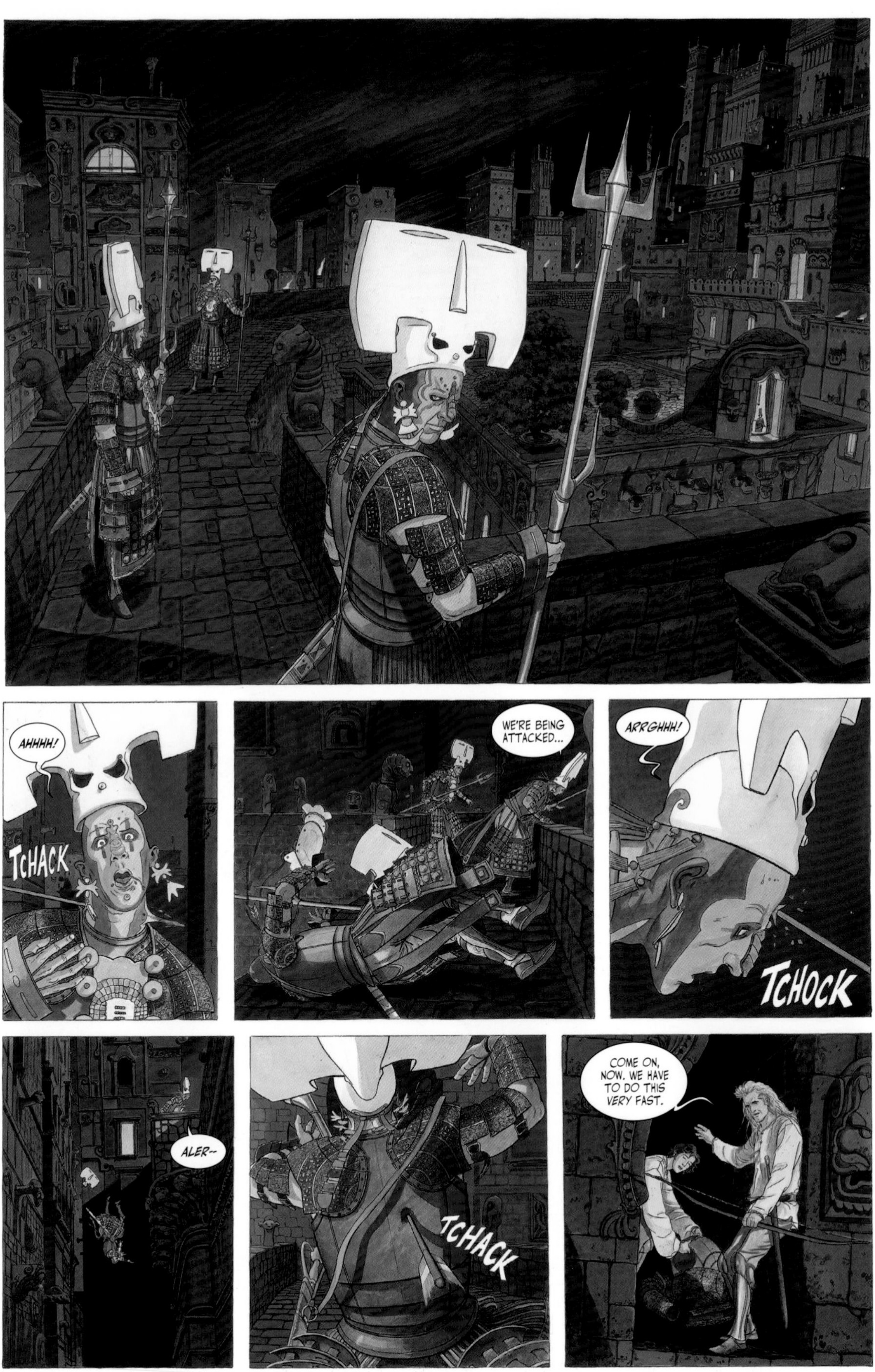

AHHHH!
TCHACK
WE'RE BEING ATTACKED...
ARRGHHH!
TCHOCK
ALER--
TCHACK
COME ON, NOW. WE HAVE TO DO THIS VERY FAST.

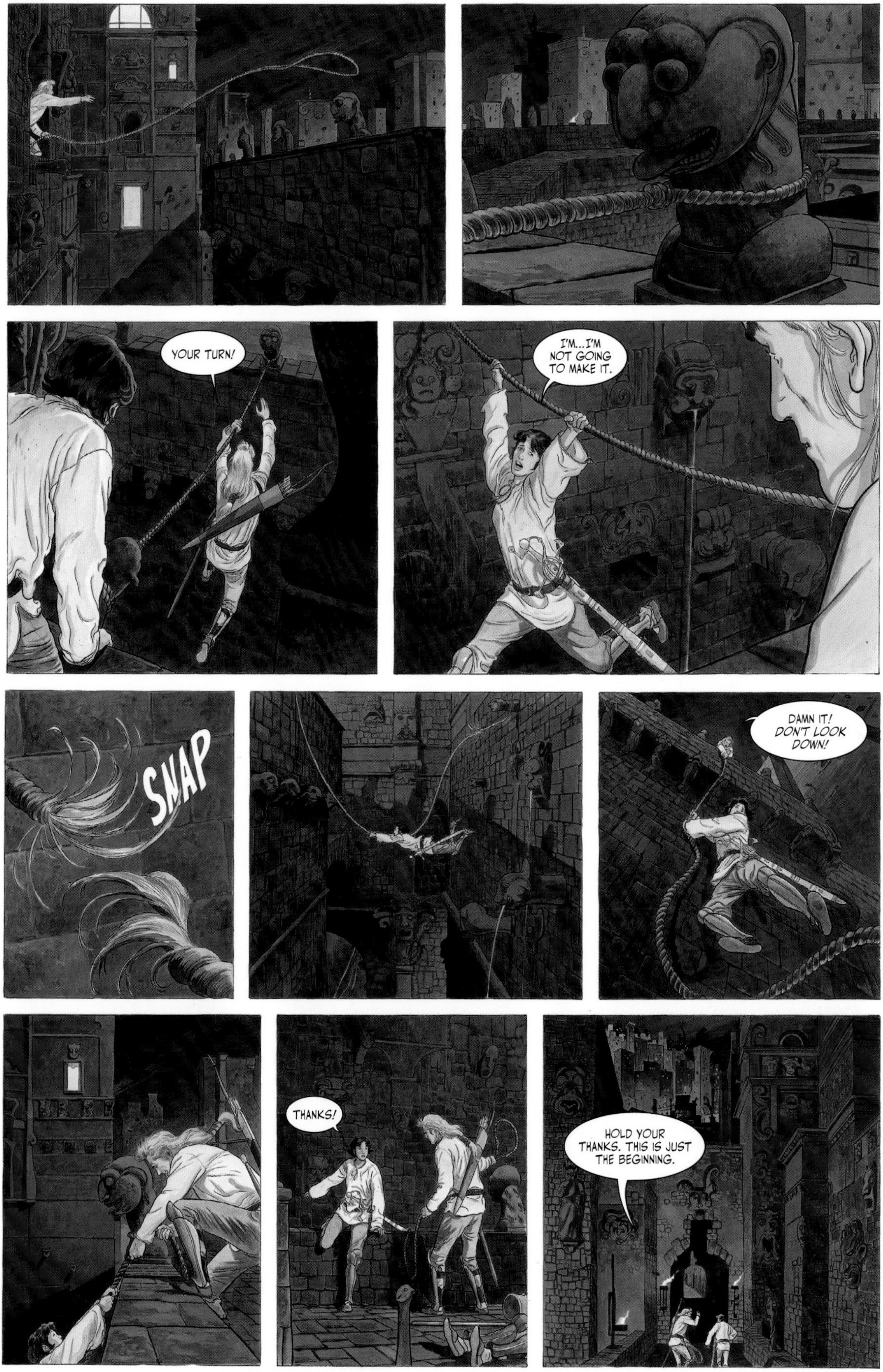
YOUR TURN!
I'M...I'M NOT GOING TO MAKE IT.
SNAP
DAMN IT! DON'T LOOK DOWN!
THANKS!
HOLD YOUR THANKS. THIS IS JUST THE BEGINNING.

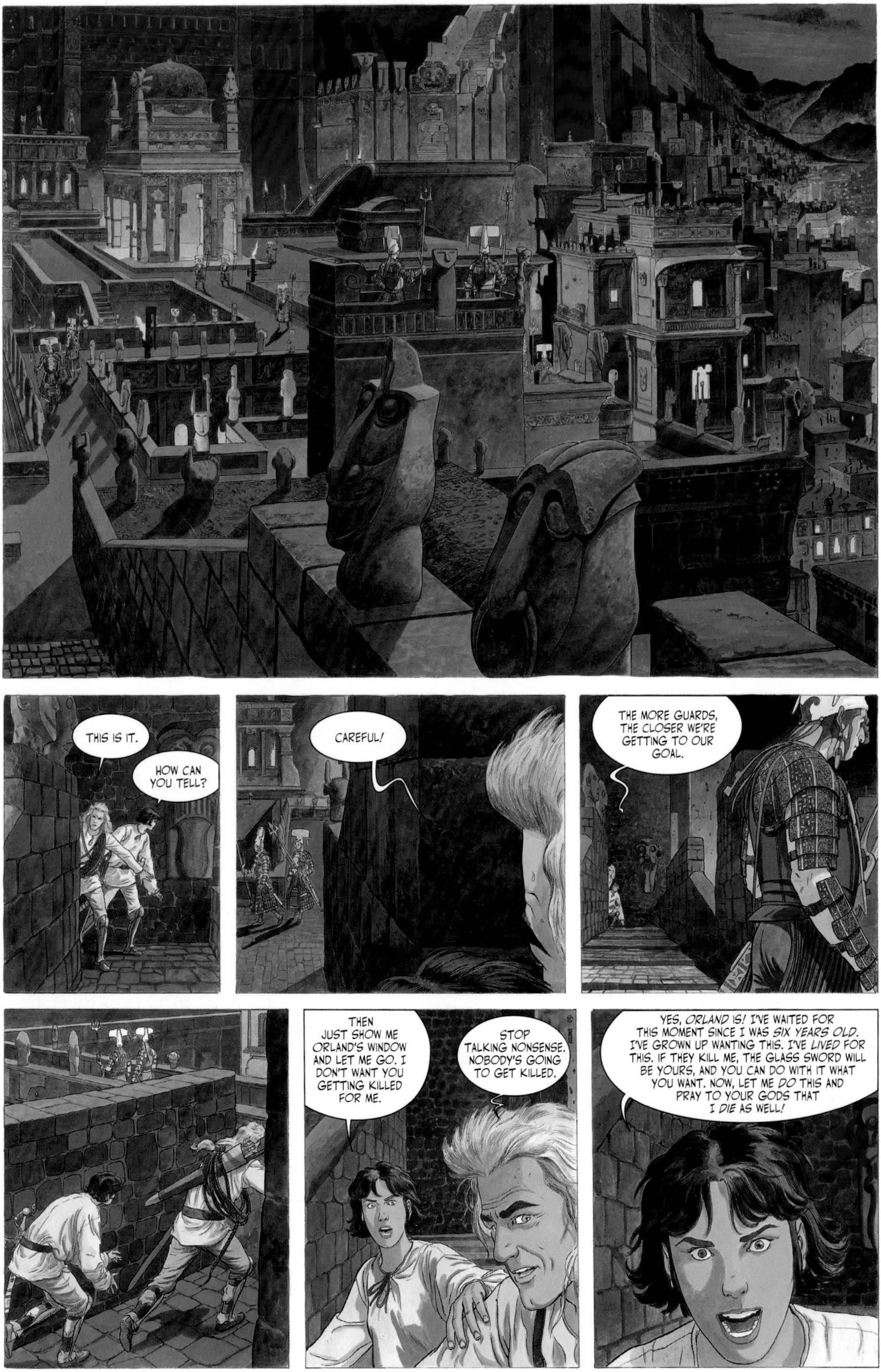
THIS IS IT.
HOW CAN YOU TELL?
CAREFUL!
THE MORE GUARDS, THE CLOSER WE'RE GETTING TO OUR GOAL.
THEN JUST SHOW ME ORLAND'S WINDOW AND LET ME GO. I DON'T WANT YOU GETTING KILLED FOR ME.
STOP TALKING NONSENSE. NOBODY'S GOING TO GET KILLED.
YES, *ORLAND* IS! I'VE WAITED FOR THIS MOMENT SINCE I WAS *SIX YEARS OLD*. I'VE GROWN UP WANTING THIS. I'VE *LIVED* FOR THIS. IF THEY KILL ME, THE GLASS SWORD WILL BE YOURS, AND YOU CAN DO WITH IT WHAT YOU WANT. NOW, LET ME *DO* THIS AND PRAY TO YOUR GODS THAT I *DIE* AS WELL!

SWALLOW THOSE WORDS. YOU'RE GOING TO FINISH WHAT YOU STARTED. DON'T EVEN DREAM OF QUITTING. YOU GOT THAT?

AIE! YOU'RE HURTING ME.

FIRST, THAT LITTLE IDIOT CUTS ME WITH HIS DAGGER, AND NOW YOU TRY TO BREAK MY ARM. WHAT DID I DO TO DESERVE THI--

SHUSH! IT'S DOWN THERE.

I'LL GO FIRST.

YOU SURE THAT IT'S THERE?

THAT'S ONE OF THE WINDOWS OF THE CHIEF GUARD'S APARTMENT. THE GARRISON IS LOCATED JUST BELOW IT.

THEN I SHOULD GO FIRST.

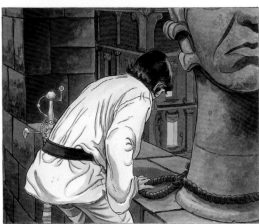

I'VE SEEN PLENTY OF HARD HEADS IN MY LIFE, BUT YOU TAKE THE CAKE!

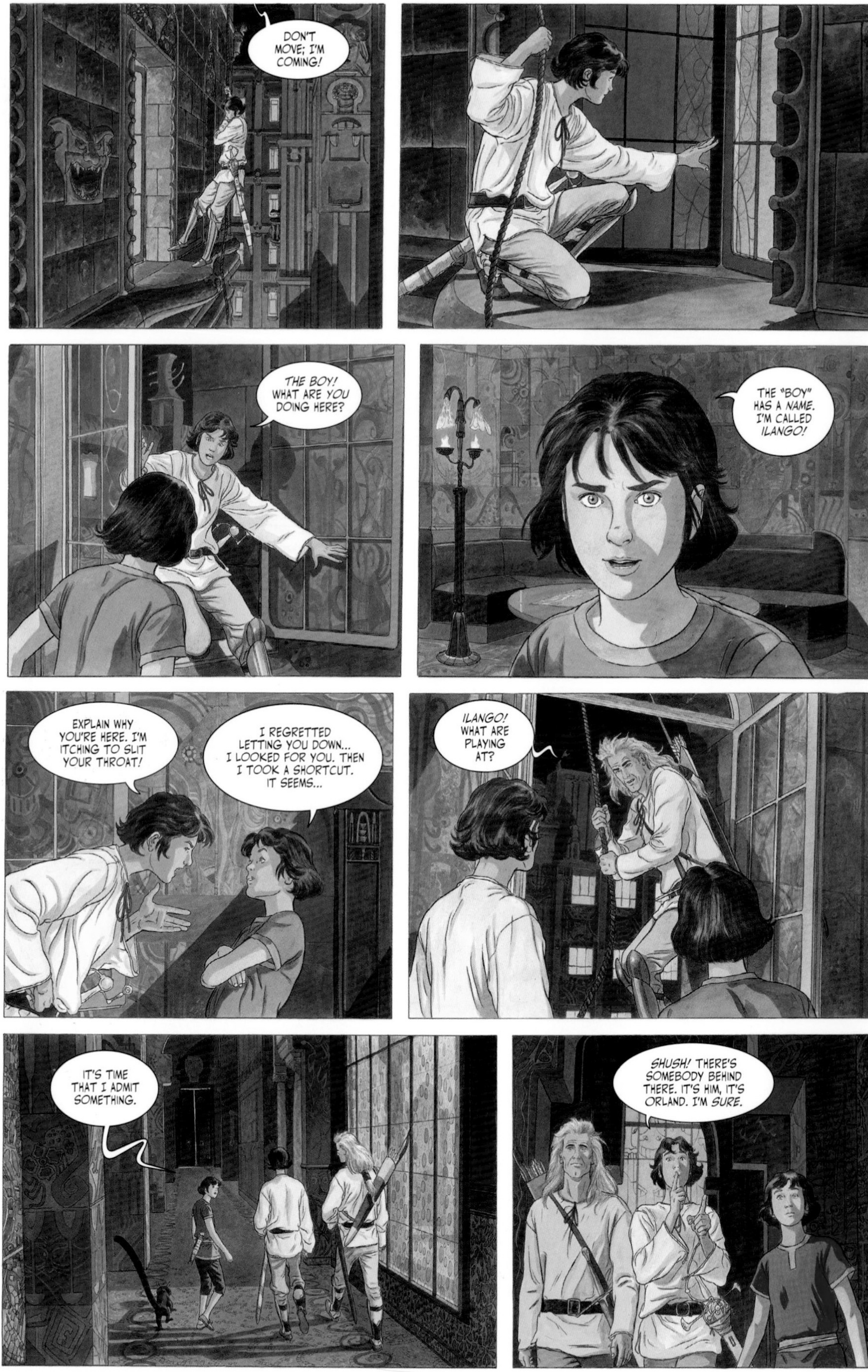
DON'T MOVE; I'M COMING!
THE BOY! WHAT ARE YOU DOING HERE?
THE "BOY" HAS A NAME. I'M CALLED ILANGO!
EXPLAIN WHY YOU'RE HERE. I'M ITCHING TO SLIT YOUR THROAT!
I REGRETTED LETTING YOU DOWN... I LOOKED FOR YOU. THEN I TOOK A SHORTCUT. IT SEEMS...
ILANGO! WHAT ARE PLAYING AT?
IT'S TIME THAT I ADMIT SOMETHING.
SHUSH! THERE'S SOMEBODY BEHIND THERE. IT'S HIM, IT'S ORLAND. I'M SURE.

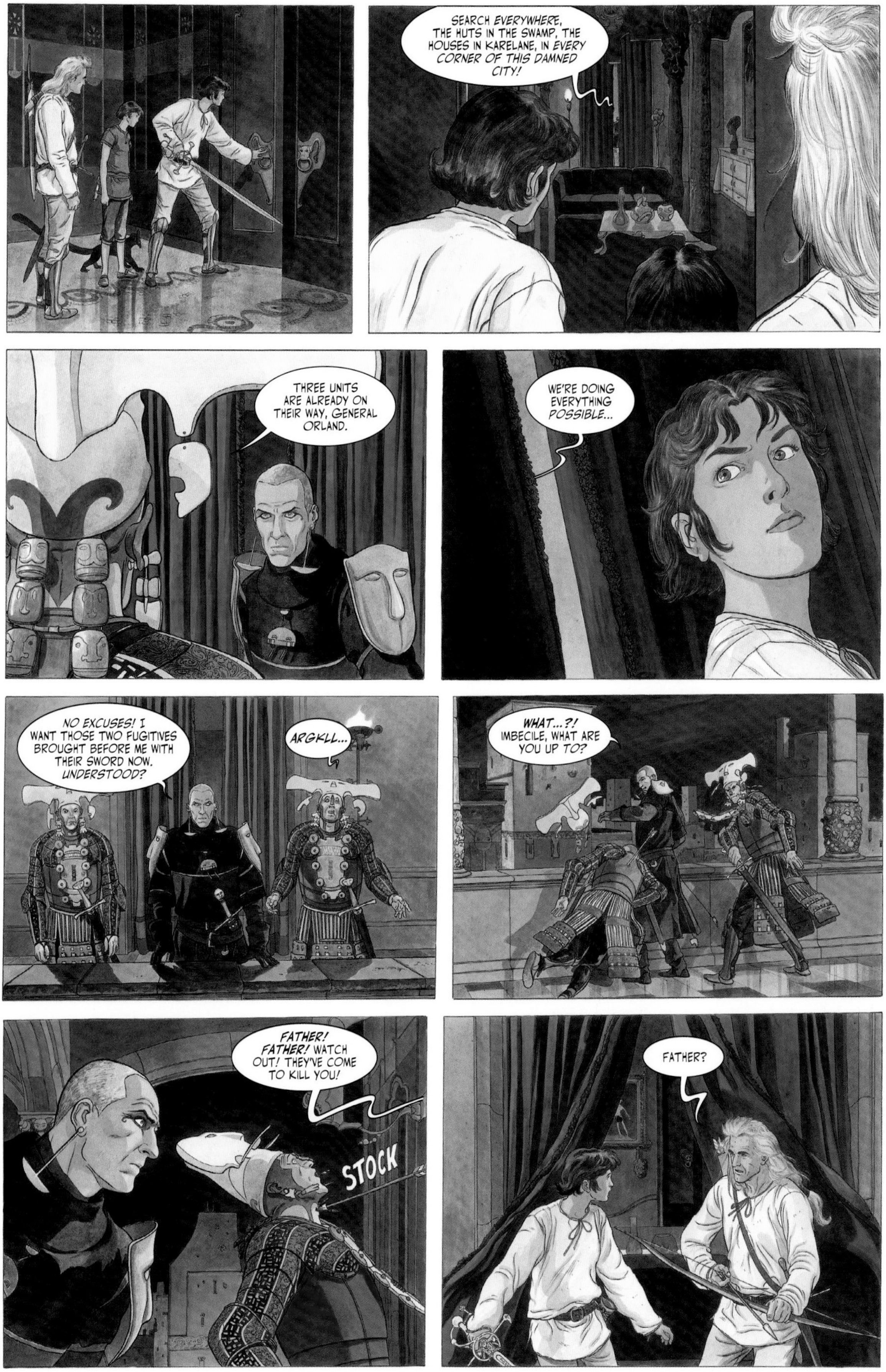
SEARCH EVERYWHERE, THE HUTS IN THE SWAMP, THE HOUSES IN KARELANE, IN EVERY CORNER OF THIS DAMNED CITY!
THREE UNITS ARE ALREADY ON THEIR WAY, GENERAL ORLAND.
WE'RE DOING EVERYTHING POSSIBLE...
NO EXCUSES! I WANT THOSE TWO FUGITIVES BROUGHT BEFORE ME WITH THEIR SWORD NOW. UNDERSTOOD?
ARGKLL...
WHAT...?! IMBECILE, WHAT ARE YOU UP TO?
FATHER! FATHER! WATCH OUT! THEY'VE COME TO KILL YOU!
STOCK
FATHER?

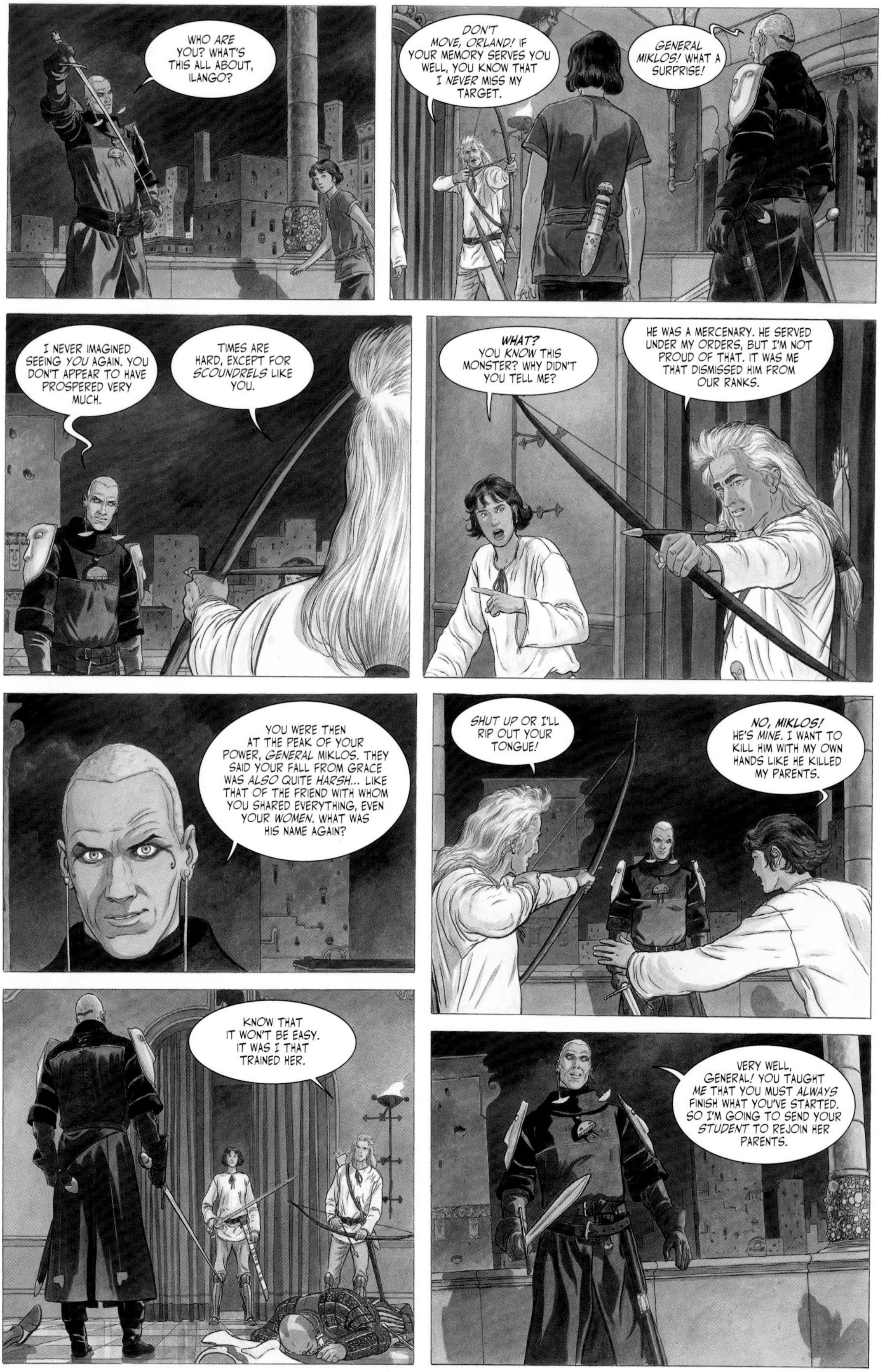
WHO ARE YOU? WHAT'S THIS ALL ABOUT, ILANGO?
DON'T MOVE, ORLAND! IF YOUR MEMORY SERVES YOU WELL, YOU KNOW THAT I NEVER MISS MY TARGET.
GENERAL MIKLOS! WHAT A SURPRISE!
I NEVER IMAGINED SEEING YOU AGAIN. YOU DON'T APPEAR TO HAVE PROSPERED VERY MUCH.
TIMES ARE HARD, EXCEPT FOR SCOUNDRELS LIKE YOU.
WHAT? YOU KNOW THIS MONSTER? WHY DIDN'T YOU TELL ME?
HE WAS A MERCENARY. HE SERVED UNDER MY ORDERS, BUT I'M NOT PROUD OF THAT. IT WAS ME THAT DISMISSED HIM FROM OUR RANKS.
YOU WERE THEN AT THE PEAK OF YOUR POWER, GENERAL MIKLOS. THEY SAID YOUR FALL FROM GRACE WAS ALSO QUITE HARSH... LIKE THAT OF THE FRIEND WITH WHOM YOU SHARED EVERYTHING, EVEN YOUR WOMEN. WHAT WAS HIS NAME AGAIN?
SHUT UP OR I'LL RIP OUT YOUR TONGUE!
NO, MIKLOS! HE'S MINE. I WANT TO KILL HIM WITH MY OWN HANDS LIKE HE KILLED MY PARENTS.
KNOW THAT IT WON'T BE EASY. IT WAS I THAT TRAINED HER.
VERY WELL, GENERAL! YOU TAUGHT ME THAT YOU MUST ALWAYS FINISH WHAT YOU'VE STARTED. SO I'M GOING TO SEND YOUR STUDENT TO REJOIN HER PARENTS.

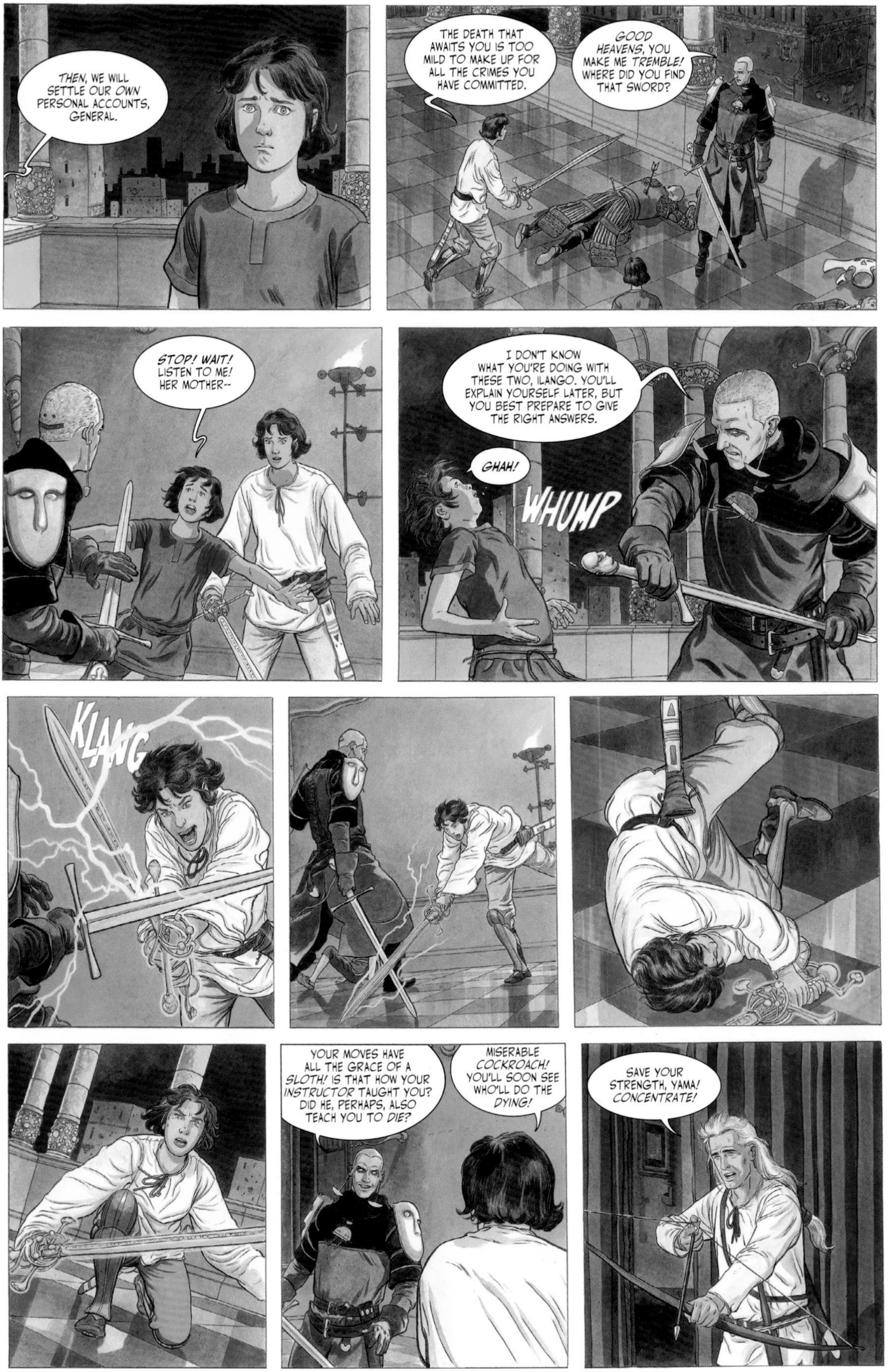

THEN, WE WILL SETTLE OUR OWN PERSONAL ACCOUNTS, GENERAL.
THE DEATH THAT AWAITS YOU IS TOO MILD TO MAKE UP FOR ALL THE CRIMES YOU HAVE COMMITTED.
GOOD HEAVENS, YOU MAKE ME TREMBLE! WHERE DID YOU FIND THAT SWORD?
STOP! WAIT! LISTEN TO ME! HER MOTHER--
I DON'T KNOW WHAT YOU'RE DOING WITH THESE TWO, ILANGO. YOU'LL EXPLAIN YOURSELF LATER, BUT YOU BEST PREPARE TO GIVE THE RIGHT ANSWERS.
GHAH!
WHUMP
KLANG
YOUR MOVES HAVE ALL THE GRACE OF A SLOTH! IS THAT HOW YOUR INSTRUCTOR TAUGHT YOU? DID HE, PERHAPS, ALSO TEACH YOU TO DIE?
MISERABLE COCKROACH! YOU'LL SOON SEE WHO'LL DO THE DYING!
SAVE YOUR STRENGTH, YAMA! CONCENTRATE!

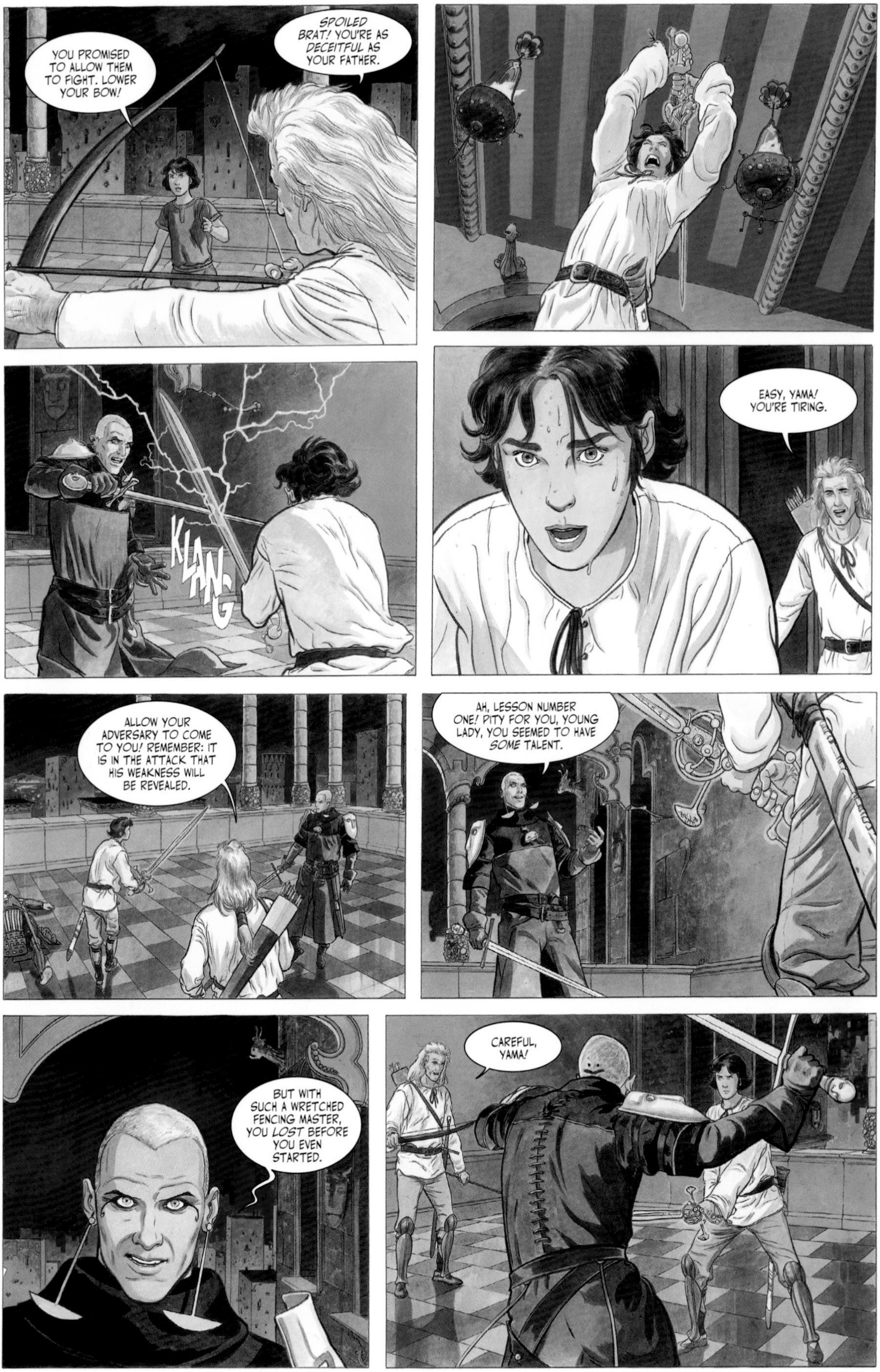
YOU PROMISED TO ALLOW THEM TO FIGHT. LOWER YOUR BOW!
SPOILED BRAT! YOU'RE AS DECEITFUL AS YOUR FATHER.
KLANG
EASY, YAMA! YOU'RE TIRING.
ALLOW YOUR ADVERSARY TO COME TO YOU! REMEMBER: IT IS IN THE ATTACK THAT HIS WEAKNESS WILL BE REVEALED.
AH, LESSON NUMBER ONE! PITY FOR YOU, YOUNG LADY, YOU SEEMED TO HAVE SOME TALENT.
BUT WITH SUCH A WRETCHED FENCING MASTER, YOU LOST BEFORE YOU EVEN STARTED.
CAREFUL, YAMA!

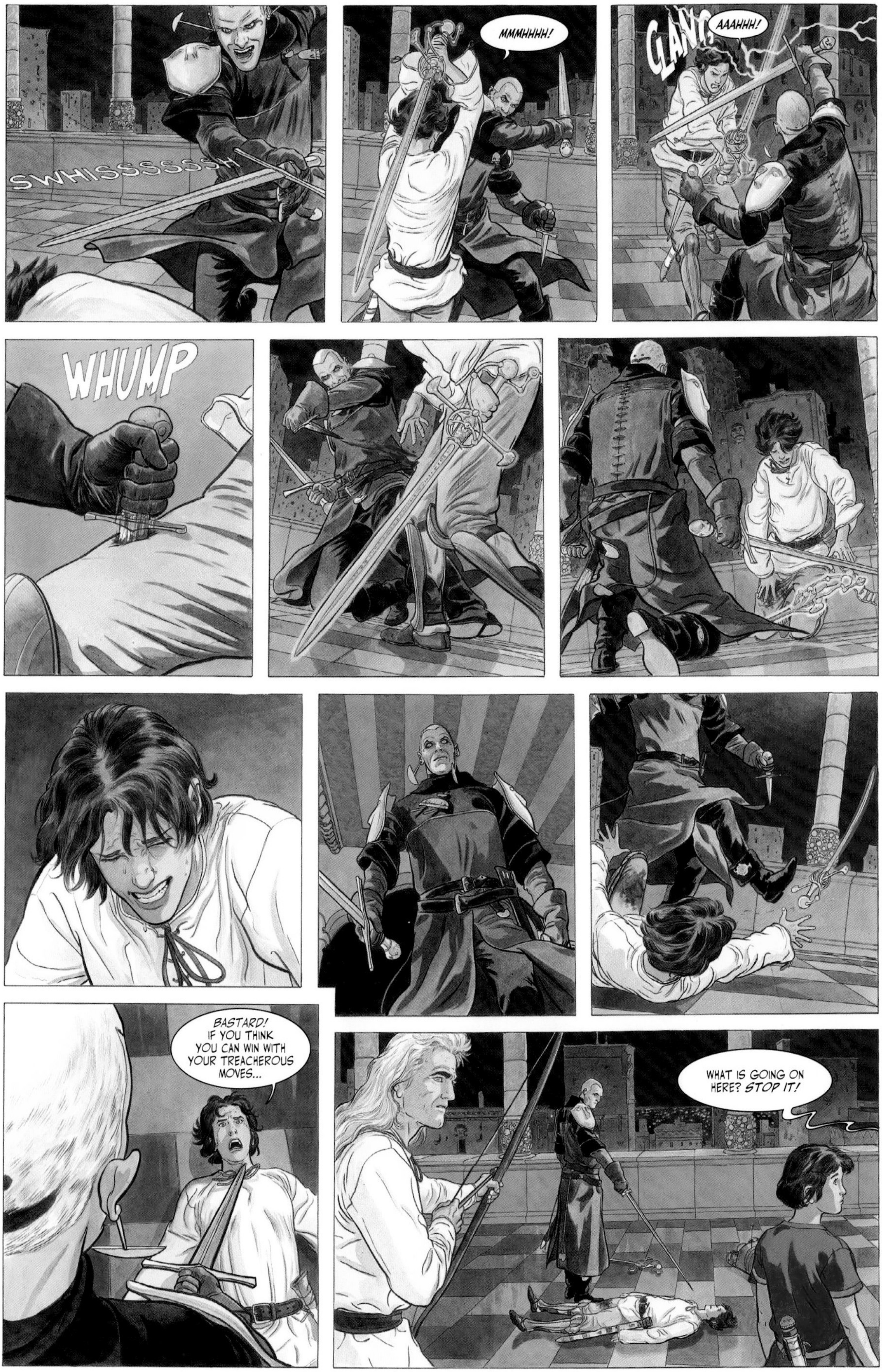
SWHISSSSSSSH
MMMHHHH!
CLANG
AAAHHH!
WHUMP
BASTARD! IF YOU THINK YOU CAN WIN WITH YOUR TREACHEROUS MOVES...
WHAT IS GOING ON HERE? STOP IT!

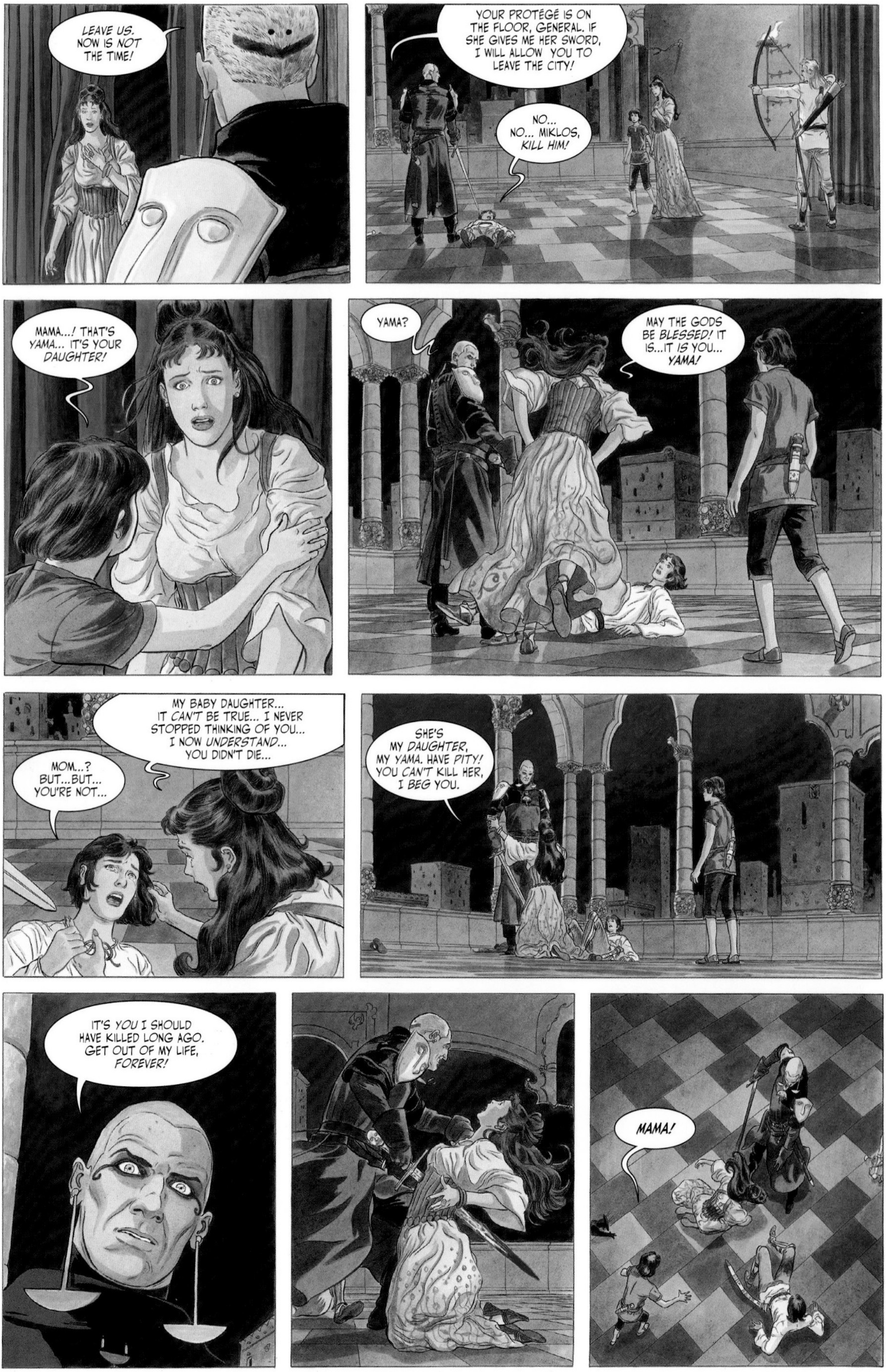
LEAVE US. NOW IS NOT THE TIME!
YOUR PROTÉGÉ IS ON THE FLOOR, GENERAL. IF SHE GIVES ME HER SWORD, I WILL ALLOW YOU TO LEAVE THE CITY!
NO... NO... MIKLOS, KILL HIM!
MAMA...! THAT'S YAMA... IT'S YOUR DAUGHTER!
YAMA?
MAY THE GODS BE BLESSED! IT IS...IT IS YOU... YAMA!
MY BABY DAUGHTER... IT CAN'T BE TRUE... I NEVER STOPPED THINKING OF YOU... I NOW UNDERSTAND... YOU DIDN'T DIE...
MOM...? BUT...BUT... YOU'RE NOT...
SHE'S MY DAUGHTER, MY YAMA. HAVE PITY! YOU CAN'T KILL HER, I BEG YOU.
IT'S YOU I SHOULD HAVE KILLED LONG AGO. GET OUT OF MY LIFE, FOREVER!
MAMA!

YOU'VE KILLED HER!
WHAT THE...?
AHI...! AHIII...! AHIIII...!
MAMA! MAMA! WE'RE GOING TO SAVE YOU.
YA...YAMA...I'VE FOUND YOU AGAIN... YOU'RE...A...ALIVE... I'M SO, SO... HAPPY.

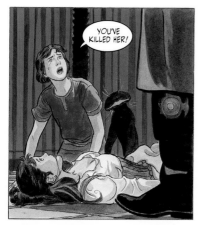

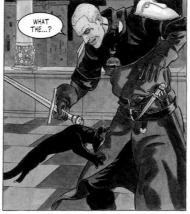

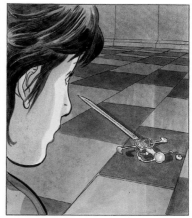

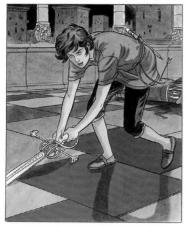

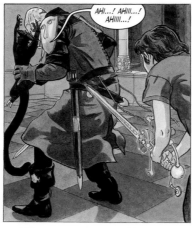

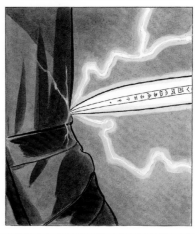

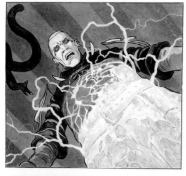

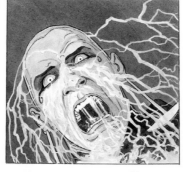

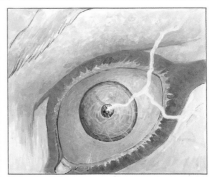

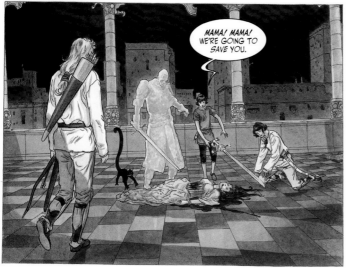

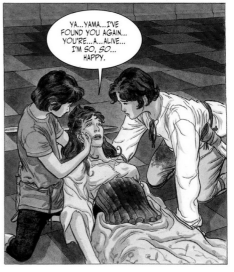

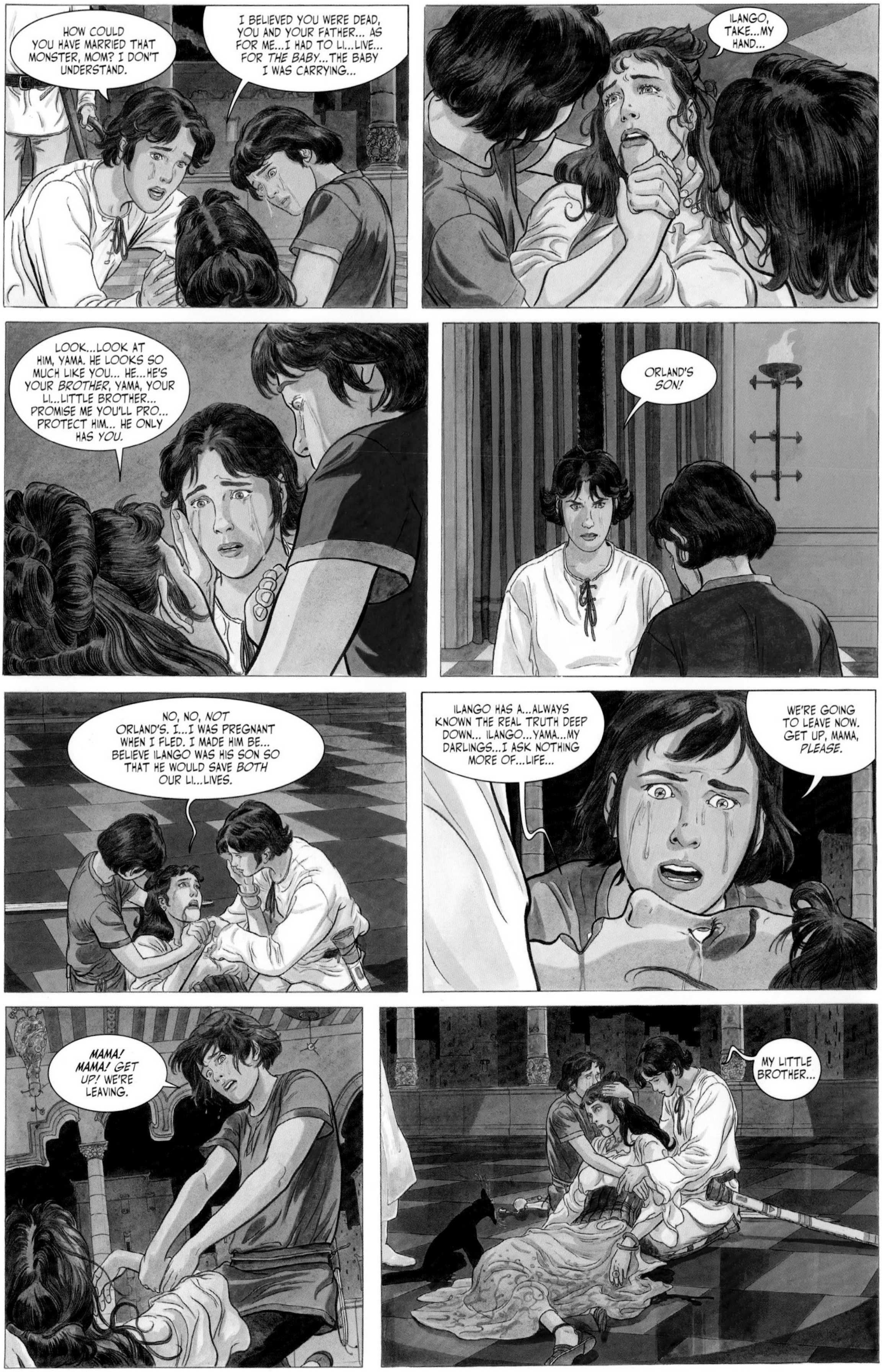
HOW COULD YOU HAVE MARRIED THAT MONSTER, MOM? I DON'T UNDERSTAND.
I BELIEVED YOU WERE DEAD, YOU AND YOUR FATHER... AS FOR ME...I HAD TO LI...LIVE... FOR THE BABY...THE BABY I WAS CARRYING...
ILANGO, TAKE...MY HAND...
LOOK...LOOK AT HIM, YAMA. HE LOOKS SO MUCH LIKE YOU... HE...HE'S YOUR BROTHER, YAMA, YOUR LI...LITTLE BROTHER... PROMISE ME YOU'LL PRO... PROTECT HIM... HE ONLY HAS YOU.
ORLAND'S SON!
NO, NO, NOT ORLAND'S. I...I WAS PREGNANT WHEN I FLED. I MADE HIM BE... BELIEVE ILANGO WAS HIS SON SO THAT HE WOULD SAVE BOTH OUR LI...LIVES.
ILANGO HAS A...ALWAYS KNOWN THE REAL TRUTH DEEP DOWN... ILANGO...YAMA...MY DARLINGS...I ASK NOTHING MORE OF...LIFE...
WE'RE GOING TO LEAVE NOW. GET UP, MAMA, PLEASE.
MAMA! MAMA! GET UP! WE'RE LEAVING.
MY LITTLE BROTHER...

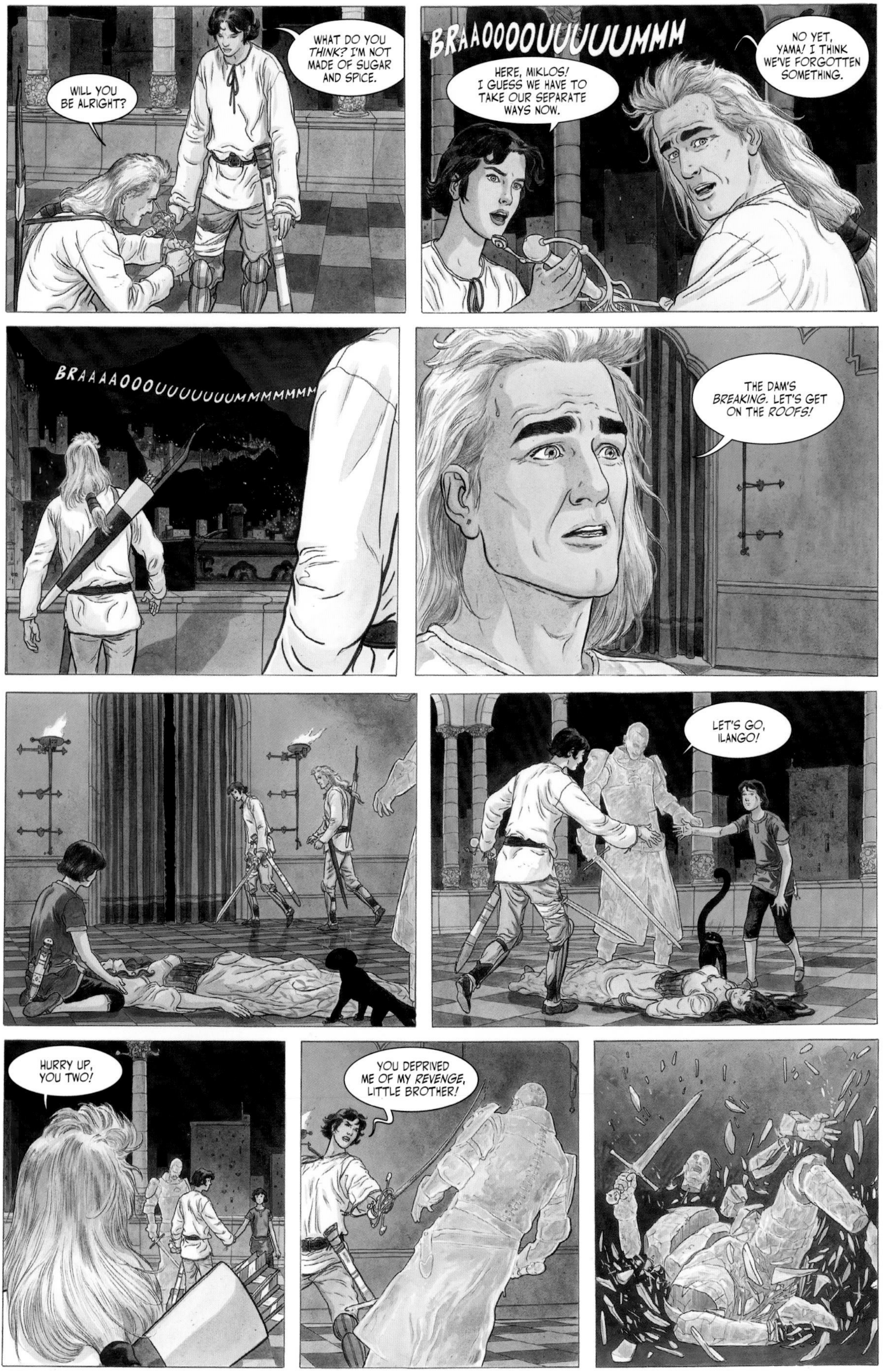
WILL YOU BE ALRIGHT?
WHAT DO YOU THINK? I'M NOT MADE OF SUGAR AND SPICE.
BRAAOOOOUUUUUMMM
HERE, MIKLOS! I GUESS WE HAVE TO TAKE OUR SEPARATE WAYS NOW.
NO YET, YAMA! I THINK WE'VE FORGOTTEN SOMETHING.
BRAAAAOOOUUUUUUUMMMMMM
THE DAM'S BREAKING. LET'S GET ON THE ROOFS!
LET'S GO, ILANGO!
HURRY UP, YOU TWO!
YOU DEPRIVED ME OF MY REVENGE, LITTLE BROTHER!

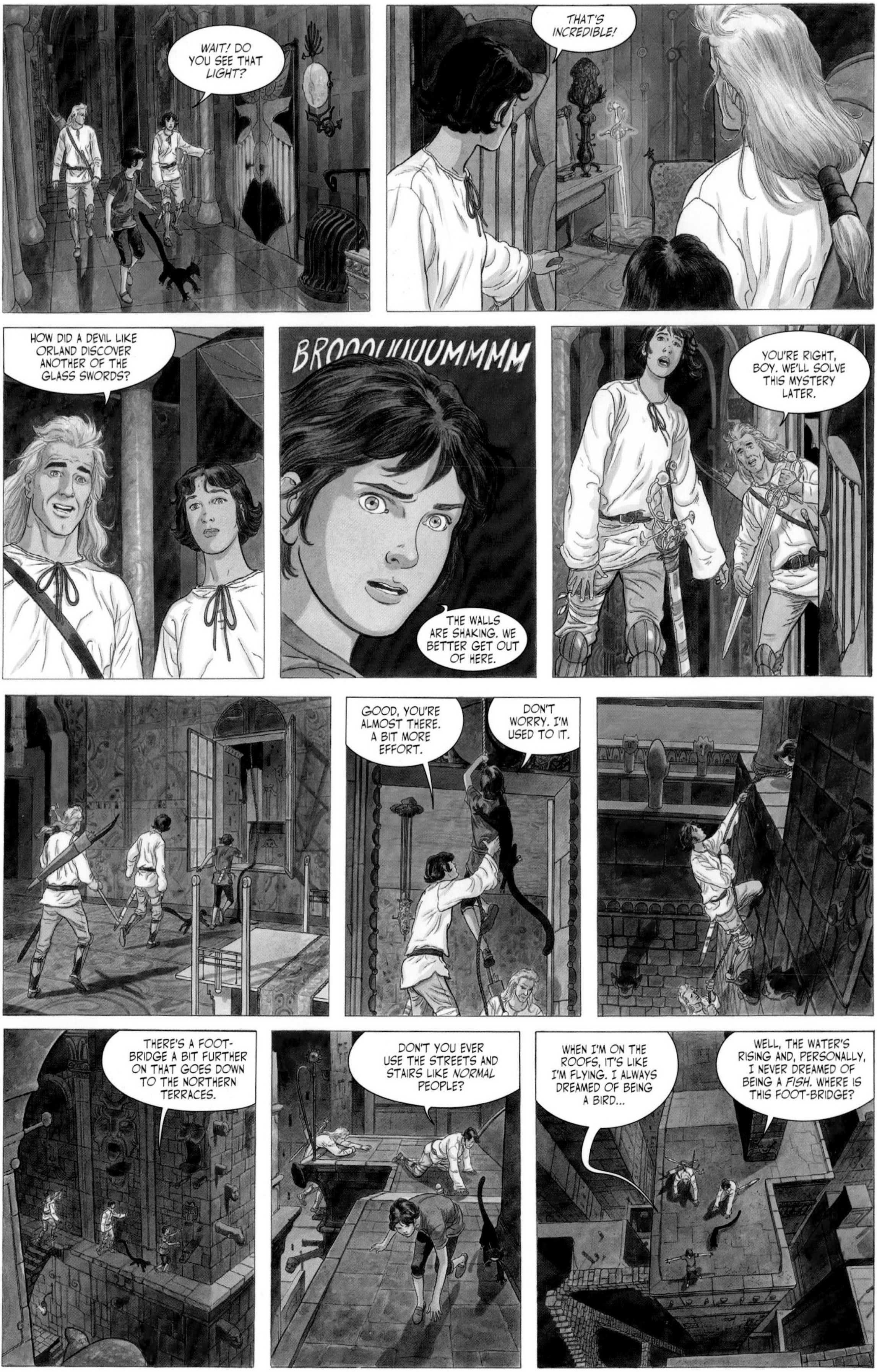

WAIT! DO YOU SEE THAT LIGHT?
THAT'S INCREDIBLE!
HOW DID A DEVIL LIKE ORLAND DISCOVER ANOTHER OF THE GLASS SWORDS?
BROOOUUUUUMMMM
THE WALLS ARE SHAKING. WE BETTER GET OUT OF HERE.
YOU'RE RIGHT, BOY. WE'LL SOLVE THIS MYSTERY LATER.
GOOD, YOU'RE ALMOST THERE. A BIT MORE EFFORT.
DON'T WORRY. I'M USED TO IT.
THERE'S A FOOT-BRIDGE A BIT FURTHER ON THAT GOES DOWN TO THE NORTHERN TERRACES.
DON'T YOU EVER USE THE STREETS AND STAIRS LIKE NORMAL PEOPLE?
WHEN I'M ON THE ROOFS, IT'S LIKE I'M FLYING. I ALWAYS DREAMED OF BEING A BIRD...
WELL, THE WATER'S RISING AND, PERSONALLY, I NEVER DREAMED OF BEING A FISH. WHERE IS THIS FOOT-BRIDGE?

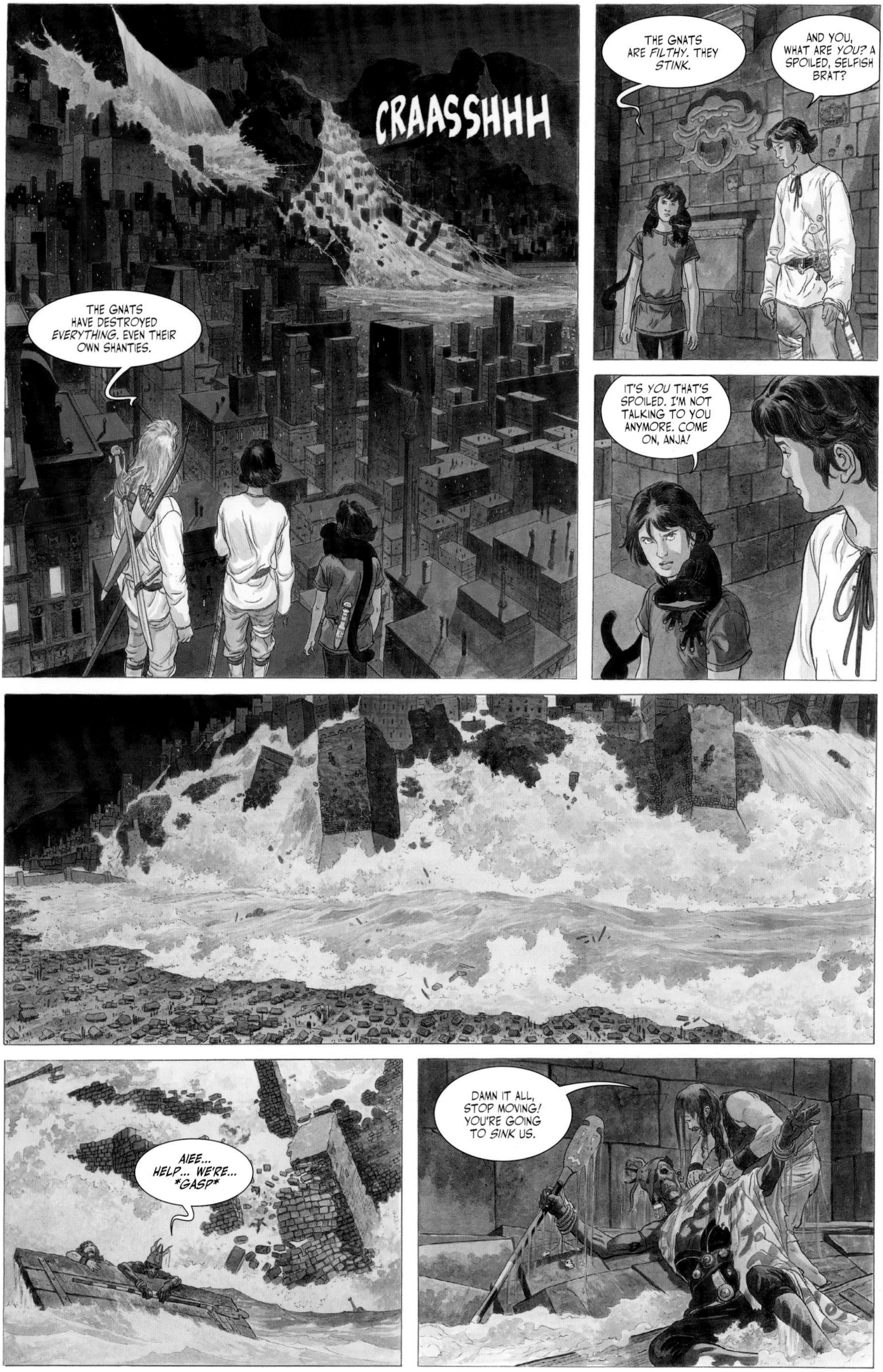
CRAASSHHH
THE GNATS HAVE DESTROYED *EVERYTHING*. EVEN THEIR OWN SHANTIES.
THE GNATS ARE *FILTHY*. THEY *STINK*.
AND YOU, WHAT ARE *YOU*? A SPOILED, SELFISH BRAT?
IT'S *YOU* THAT'S SPOILED. I'M NOT TALKING TO YOU ANYMORE. COME ON, ANJA!
AIEE... HELP... WE'RE... *GASP*
DAMN IT ALL, STOP MOVING! YOU'RE GOING TO *SINK* US.

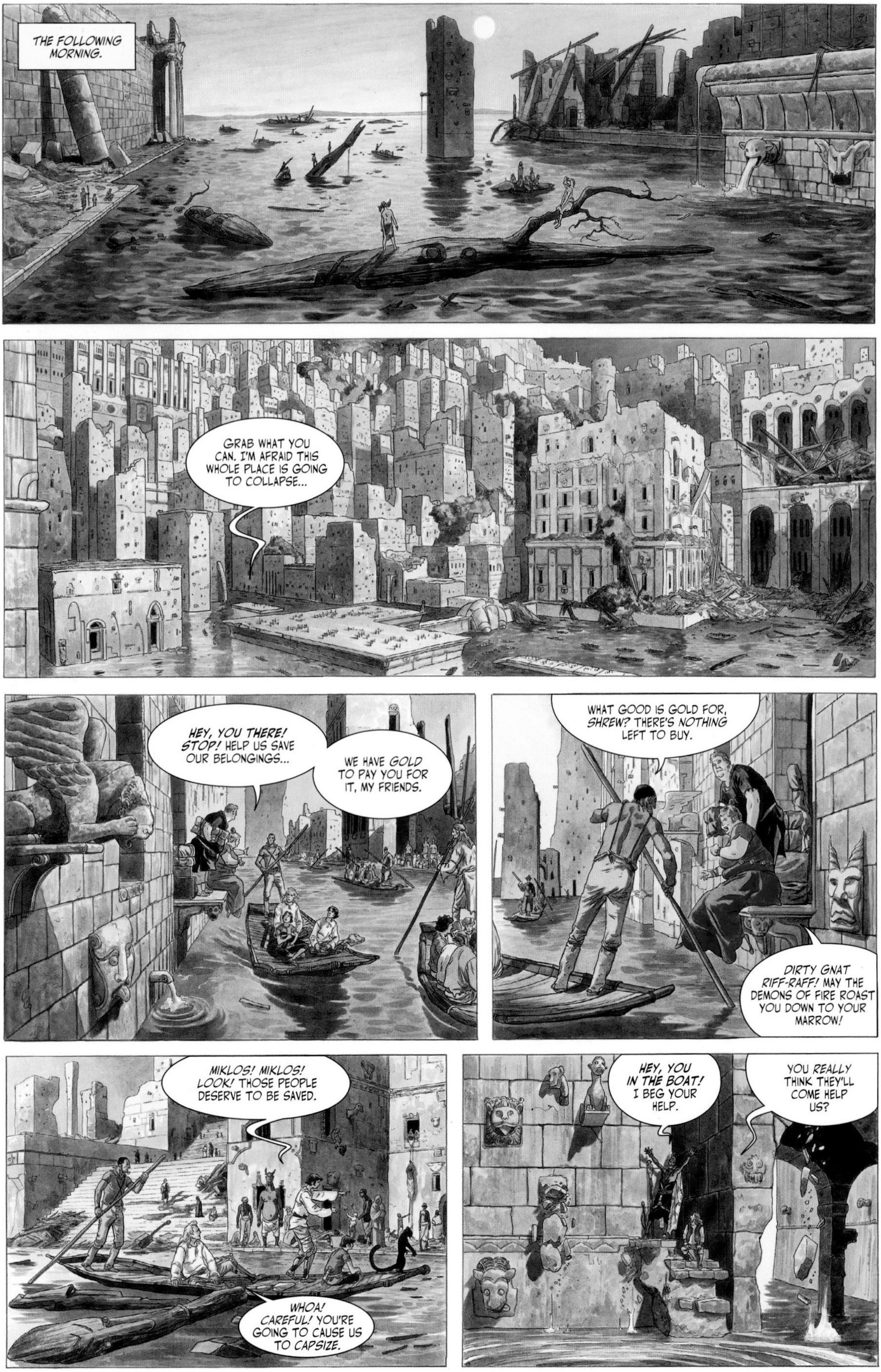
THE FOLLOWING MORNING.
GRAB WHAT YOU CAN. I'M AFRAID THIS WHOLE PLACE IS GOING TO COLLAPSE...
HEY, YOU THERE! STOP! HELP US SAVE OUR BELONGINGS...
WE HAVE GOLD TO PAY YOU FOR IT, MY FRIENDS.
WHAT GOOD IS GOLD FOR, SHREW? THERE'S NOTHING LEFT TO BUY.
DIRTY GNAT RIFF-RAFF! MAY THE DEMONS OF FIRE ROAST YOU DOWN TO YOUR MARROW!
MIKLOS! MIKLOS! LOOK! THOSE PEOPLE DESERVE TO BE SAVED.
WHOA! CAREFUL! YOU'RE GOING TO CAUSE US TO CAPSIZE.
HEY, YOU IN THE BOAT! I BEG YOUR HELP.
YOU REALLY THINK THEY'LL COME HELP US?

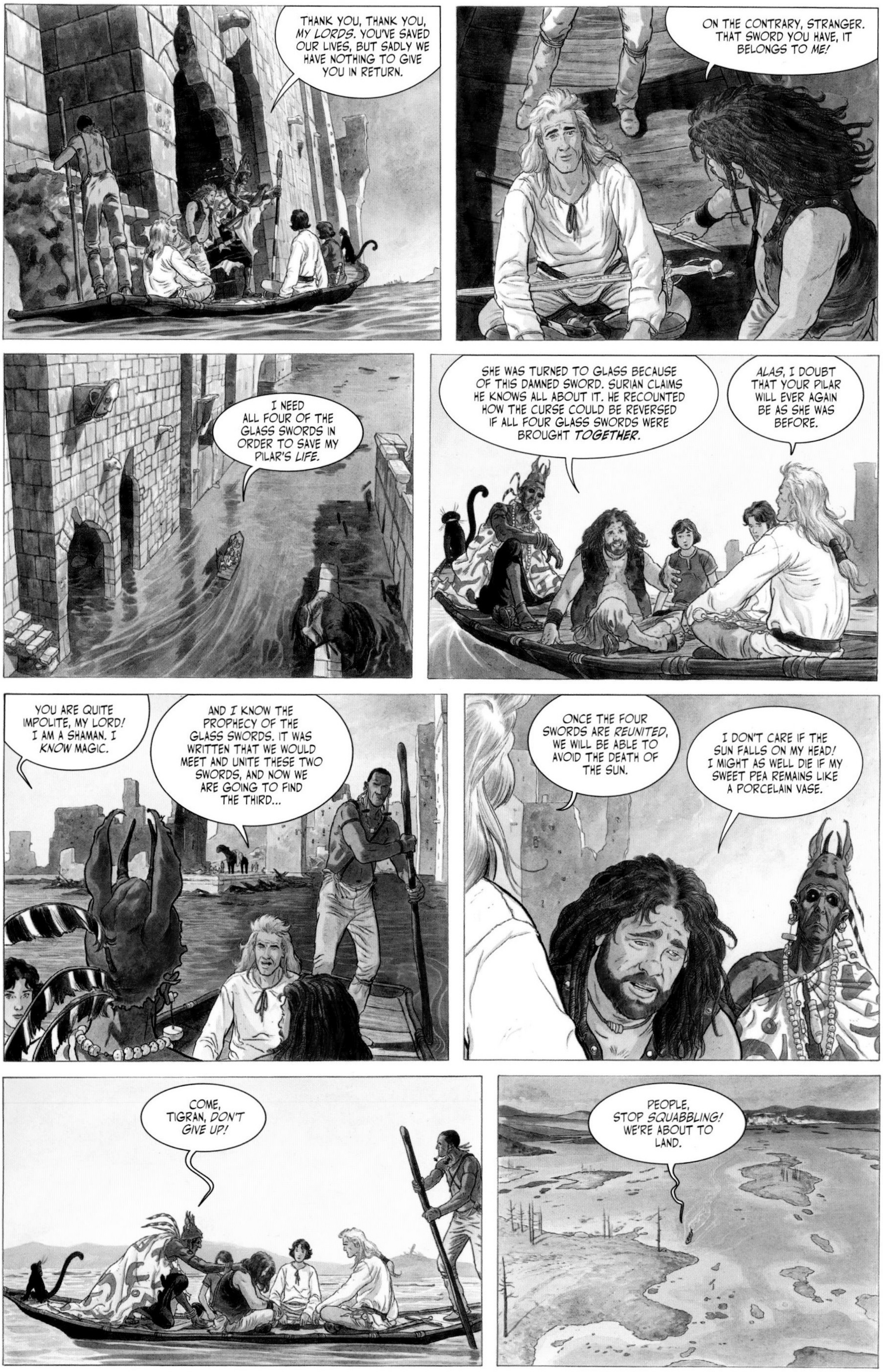

THANK YOU, THANK YOU, MY LORDS. YOU'VE SAVED OUR LIVES, BUT SADLY WE HAVE NOTHING TO GIVE YOU IN RETURN.
ON THE CONTRARY, STRANGER. THAT SWORD YOU HAVE, IT BELONGS TO ME!
I NEED ALL FOUR OF THE GLASS SWORDS IN ORDER TO SAVE MY PILAR'S LIFE.
SHE WAS TURNED TO GLASS BECAUSE OF THIS DAMNED SWORD. SURIAN CLAIMS HE KNOWS ALL ABOUT IT. HE RECOUNTED HOW THE CURSE COULD BE REVERSED IF ALL FOUR GLASS SWORDS WERE BROUGHT TOGETHER.
ALAS, I DOUBT THAT YOUR PILAR WILL EVER AGAIN BE AS SHE WAS BEFORE.
YOU ARE QUITE IMPOLITE, MY LORD! I AM A SHAMAN. I KNOW MAGIC.
AND I KNOW THE PROPHECY OF THE GLASS SWORDS. IT WAS WRITTEN THAT WE WOULD MEET AND UNITE THESE TWO SWORDS, AND NOW WE ARE GOING TO FIND THE THIRD...
ONCE THE FOUR SWORDS ARE REUNITED, WE WILL BE ABLE TO AVOID THE DEATH OF THE SUN.
I DON'T CARE IF THE SUN FALLS ON MY HEAD! I MIGHT AS WELL DIE IF MY SWEET PEA REMAINS LIKE A PORCELAIN VASE.
COME, TIGRAN, DON'T GIVE UP!
PEOPLE, STOP SQUABBLING! WE'RE ABOUT TO LAND.

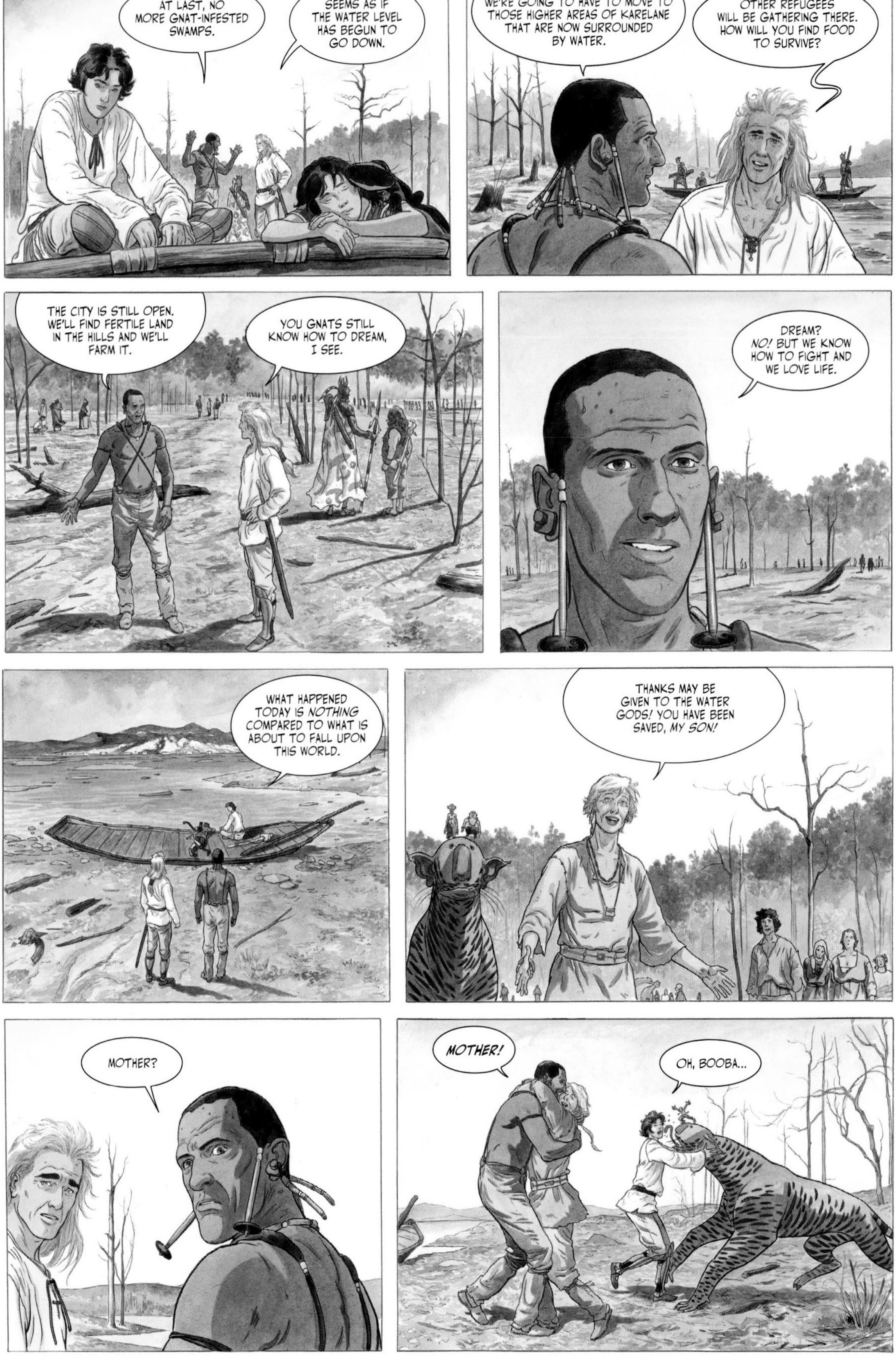
AT LAST, NO MORE GNAT-INFESTED SWAMPS.
SEEMS AS IF THE WATER LEVEL HAS BEGUN TO GO DOWN.
IT WON'T GO MUCH FURTHER. WE'RE GOING TO HAVE TO MOVE TO THOSE HIGHER AREAS OF KARELANE THAT ARE NOW SURROUNDED BY WATER.
OTHER REFUGEES WILL BE GATHERING THERE. HOW WILL YOU FIND FOOD TO SURVIVE?
THE CITY IS STILL OPEN. WE'LL FIND FERTILE LAND IN THE HILLS AND WE'LL FARM IT.
YOU GNATS STILL KNOW HOW TO DREAM, I SEE.
DREAM? *NO!* BUT WE KNOW HOW TO FIGHT AND WE LOVE LIFE.
WHAT HAPPENED TODAY IS *NOTHING* COMPARED TO WHAT IS ABOUT TO FALL UPON THIS WORLD.
THANKS MAY BE GIVEN TO THE WATER GODS! YOU HAVE BEEN SAVED, MY *SON!*
MOTHER?
MOTHER!
OH, BOOBA...

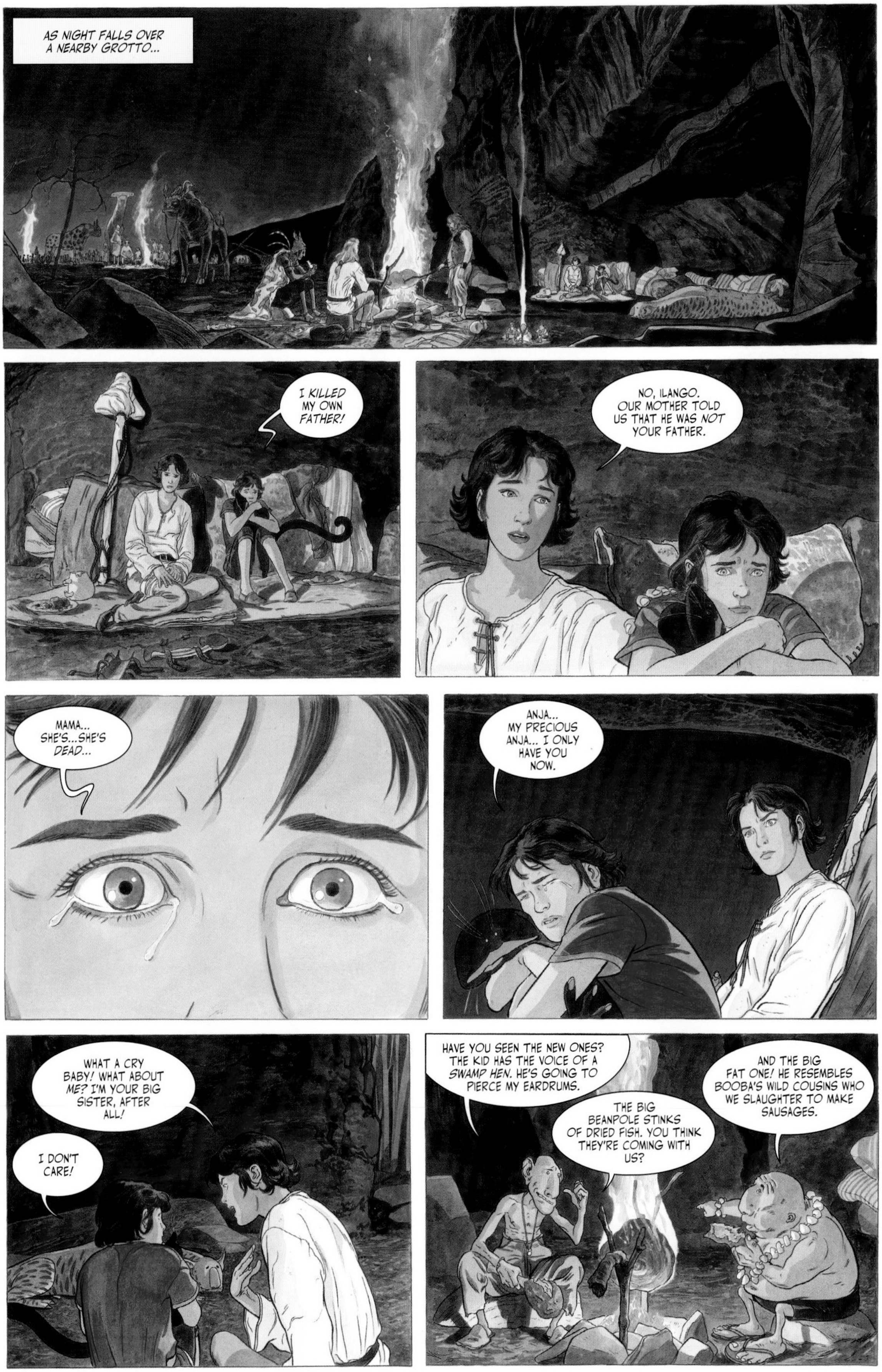
AS NIGHT FALLS OVER A NEARBY GROTTO...
I KILLED MY OWN FATHER!
NO, ILANGO. OUR MOTHER TOLD US THAT HE WAS NOT YOUR FATHER.
MAMA... SHE'S... SHE'S DEAD...
ANJA... MY PRECIOUS ANJA... I ONLY HAVE YOU NOW.
WHAT A CRY BABY! WHAT ABOUT ME? I'M YOUR BIG SISTER, AFTER ALL!
I DON'T CARE!
HAVE YOU SEEN THE NEW ONES? THE KID HAS THE VOICE OF A SWAMP HEN. HE'S GOING TO PIERCE MY EARDRUMS.
THE BIG BEANPOLE STINKS OF DRIED FISH. YOU THINK THEY'RE COMING WITH US?
AND THE BIG FAT ONE! HE RESEMBLES BOOBA'S WILD COUSINS WHO WE SLAUGHTER TO MAKE SAUSAGES.

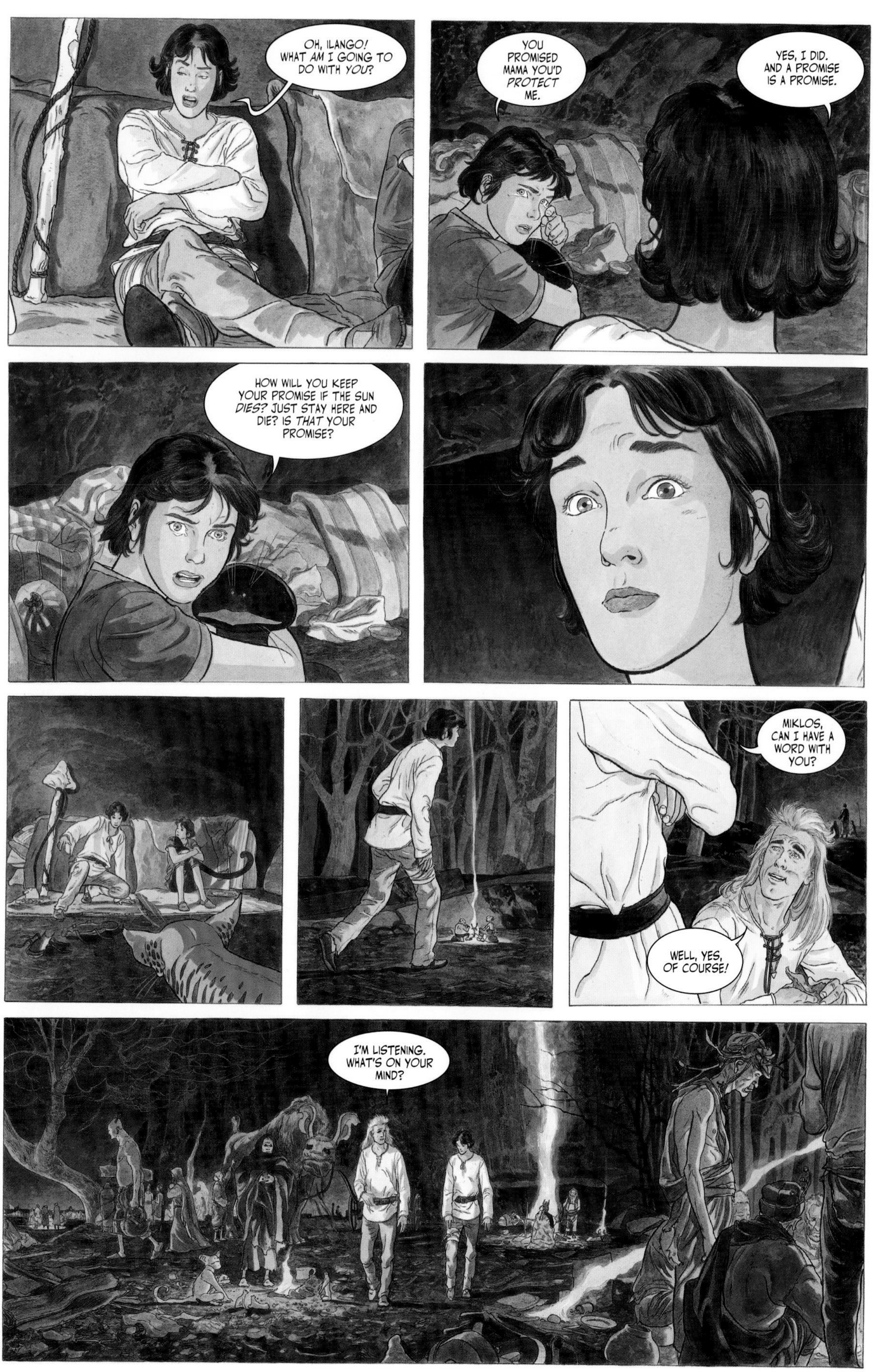
OH, ILANGO! WHAT *AM* I GOING TO DO WITH *YOU*?
YOU PROMISED MAMA YOU'D *PROTECT* ME.
YES, I DID. AND A PROMISE IS A PROMISE.
HOW WILL YOU KEEP YOUR PROMISE IF THE SUN *DIES*? JUST STAY HERE AND DIE? IS *THAT* YOUR PROMISE?
MIKLOS, CAN I HAVE A WORD WITH YOU?
WELL, YES, OF COURSE!
I'M LISTENING. WHAT'S ON YOUR MIND?

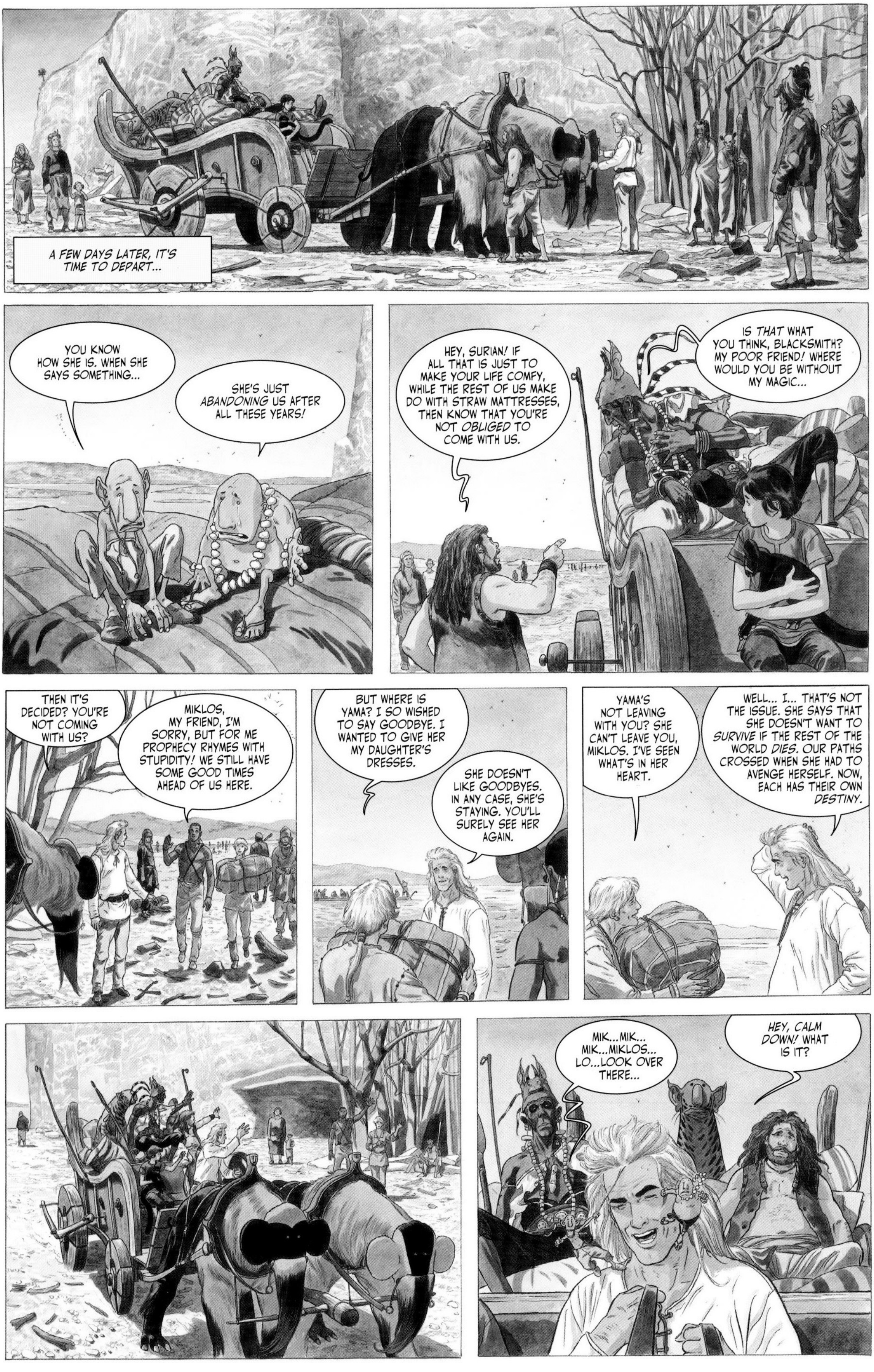
A FEW DAYS LATER, IT'S TIME TO DEPART...
YOU KNOW HOW SHE IS. WHEN SHE SAYS SOMETHING...
SHE'S JUST ABANDONING US AFTER ALL THESE YEARS!
HEY, SURIAN! IF ALL THAT IS JUST TO MAKE YOUR LIFE COMFY, WHILE THE REST OF US MAKE DO WITH STRAW MATTRESSES, THEN KNOW THAT YOU'RE NOT OBLIGED TO COME WITH US.
IS THAT WHAT YOU THINK, BLACKSMITH? MY POOR FRIEND! WHERE WOULD YOU BE WITHOUT MY MAGIC...
THEN IT'S DECIDED? YOU'RE NOT COMING WITH US?
MIKLOS, MY FRIEND, I'M SORRY, BUT FOR ME PROPHECY RHYMES WITH STUPIDITY! WE STILL HAVE SOME GOOD TIMES AHEAD OF US HERE.
BUT WHERE IS YAMA? I SO WISHED TO SAY GOODBYE. I WANTED TO GIVE HER MY DAUGHTER'S DRESSES.
SHE DOESN'T LIKE GOODBYES. IN ANY CASE, SHE'S STAYING. YOU'LL SURELY SEE HER AGAIN.
YAMA'S NOT LEAVING WITH YOU? SHE CAN'T LEAVE YOU, MIKLOS. I'VE SEEN WHAT'S IN HER HEART.
WELL... I... THAT'S NOT THE ISSUE. SHE SAYS THAT SHE DOESN'T WANT TO SURVIVE IF THE REST OF THE WORLD DIES. OUR PATHS CROSSED WHEN SHE HAD TO AVENGE HERSELF. NOW, EACH HAS THEIR OWN DESTINY.
MIK...MIK... MIK...MIKLOS... LO...LOOK OVER THERE...
HEY, CALM DOWN! WHAT IS IT?

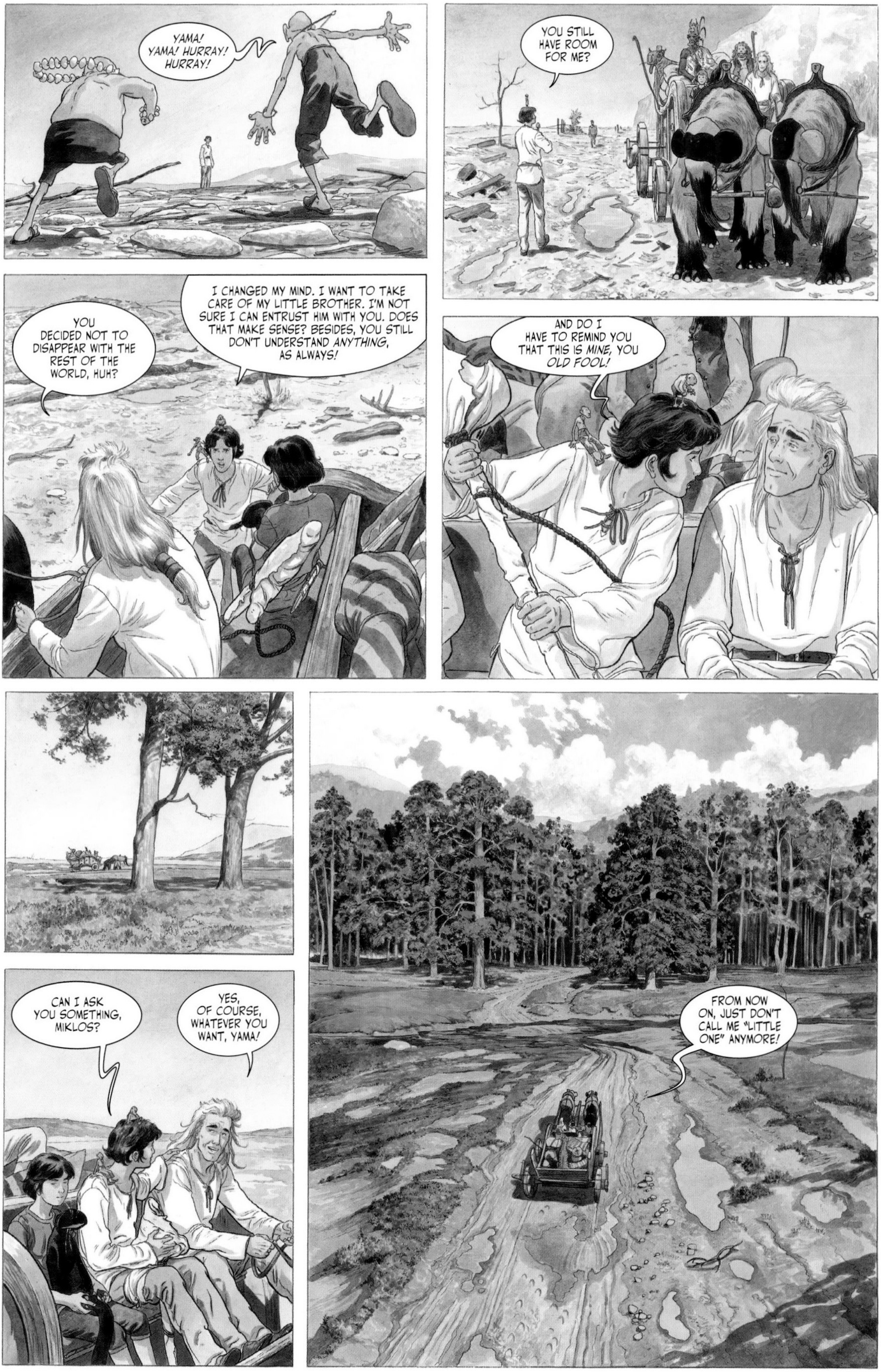
YAMA! YAMA! HURRAY! HURRAY!
YOU STILL HAVE ROOM FOR ME?
YOU DECIDED NOT TO DISAPPEAR WITH THE REST OF THE WORLD, HUH?
I CHANGED MY MIND. I WANT TO TAKE CARE OF MY LITTLE BROTHER. I'M NOT SURE I CAN ENTRUST HIM WITH YOU. DOES THAT MAKE SENSE? BESIDES, YOU STILL DON'T UNDERSTAND *ANYTHING*, AS ALWAYS!
AND DO I HAVE TO REMIND YOU THAT THIS IS *MINE*, YOU *OLD FOOL!*
CAN I ASK YOU SOMETHING, MIKLOS?
YES, OF COURSE, WHATEVER YOU WANT, YAMA!
FROM NOW ON, JUST DON'T CALL ME "LITTLE ONE" ANYMORE!

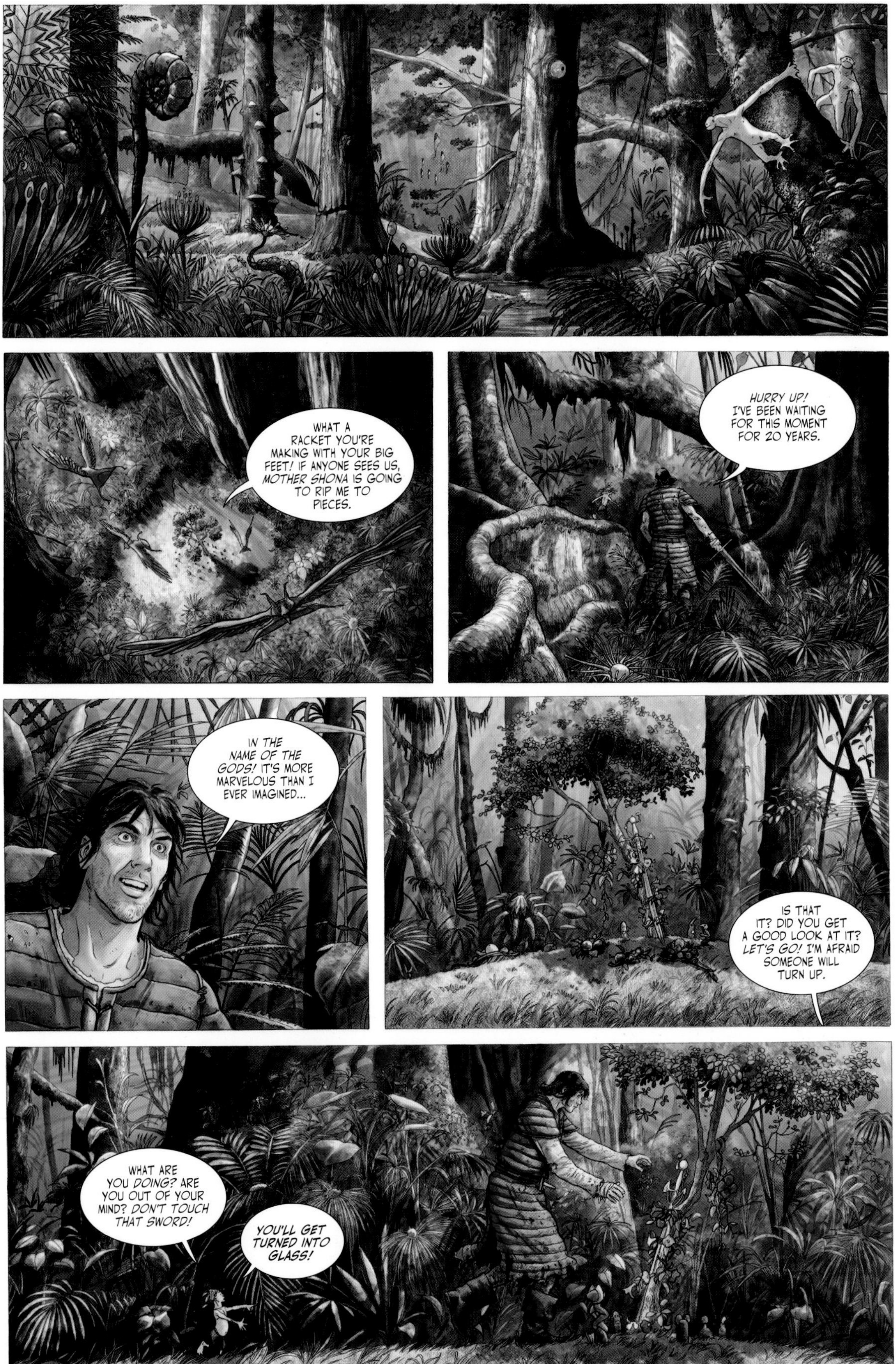
WHAT A RACKET YOU'RE MAKING WITH YOUR BIG FEET! IF ANYONE SEES US, MOTHER SHONA IS GOING TO RIP ME TO PIECES.
HURRY UP! I'VE BEEN WAITING FOR THIS MOMENT FOR 20 YEARS.
IN THE NAME OF THE GODS! IT'S MORE MARVELOUS THAN I EVER IMAGINED...
IS THAT IT? DID YOU GET A GOOD LOOK AT IT? LET'S GO! I'M AFRAID SOMEONE WILL TURN UP.
WHAT ARE YOU DOING? ARE YOU OUT OF YOUR MIND? DON'T TOUCH THAT SWORD!
YOU'LL GET TURNED INTO GLASS!

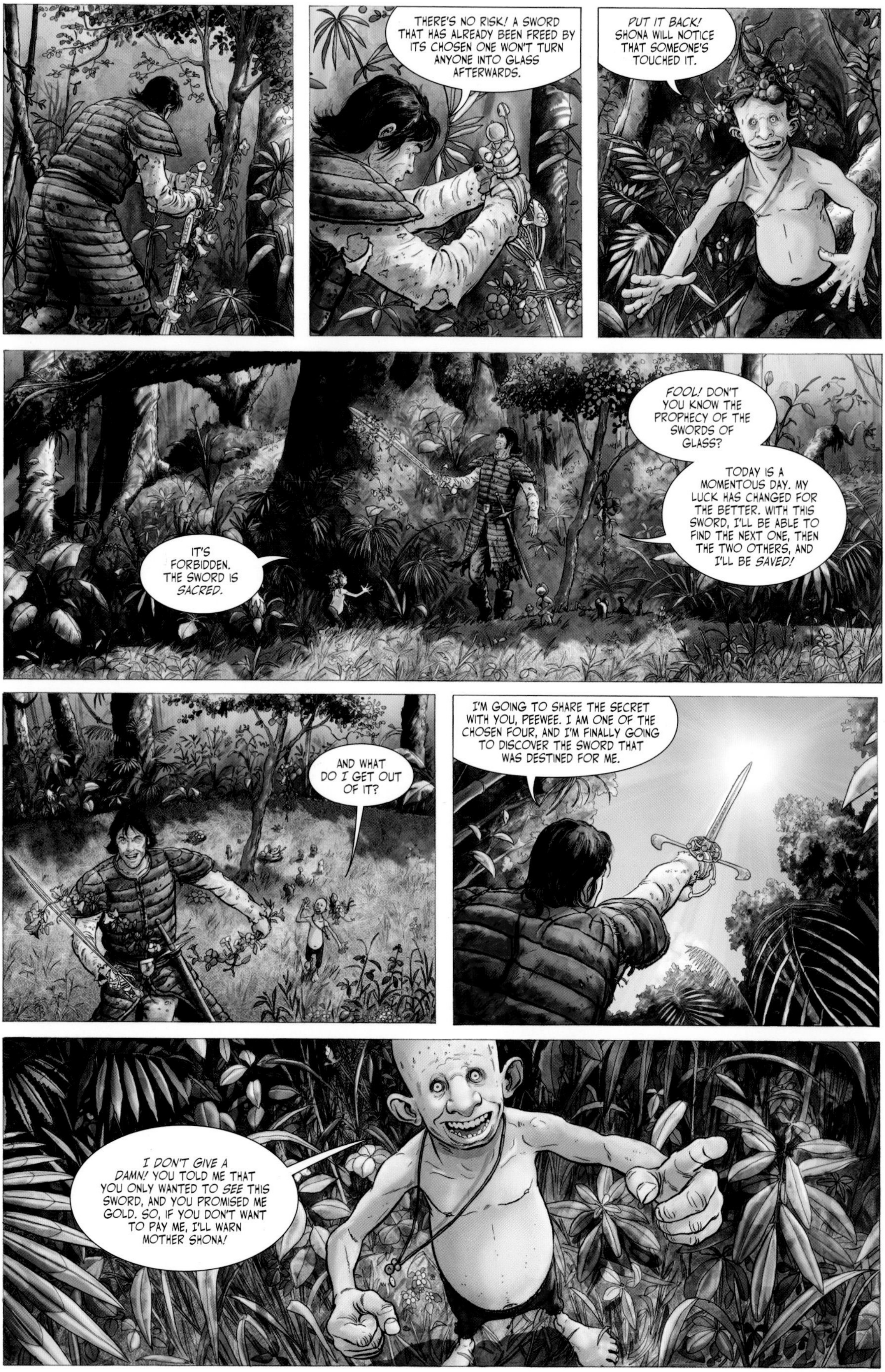
THERE'S NO RISK! A SWORD THAT HAS ALREADY BEEN FREED BY ITS CHOSEN ONE WON'T TURN ANYONE INTO GLASS AFTERWARDS.
PUT IT BACK! SHONA WILL NOTICE THAT SOMEONE'S TOUCHED IT.
FOOL! DON'T YOU KNOW THE PROPHECY OF THE SWORDS OF GLASS?
TODAY IS A MOMENTOUS DAY. MY LUCK HAS CHANGED FOR THE BETTER. WITH THIS SWORD, I'LL BE ABLE TO FIND THE NEXT ONE, THEN THE TWO OTHERS, AND I'LL BE SAVED!
IT'S FORBIDDEN. THE SWORD IS SACRED.
AND WHAT DO I GET OUT OF IT?
I'M GOING TO SHARE THE SECRET WITH YOU, PEEWEE. I AM ONE OF THE CHOSEN FOUR, AND I'M FINALLY GOING TO DISCOVER THE SWORD THAT WAS DESTINED FOR ME.
I DON'T GIVE A DAMN! YOU TOLD ME THAT YOU ONLY WANTED TO SEE THIS SWORD, AND YOU PROMISED ME GOLD. SO, IF YOU DON'T WANT TO PAY ME, I'LL WARN MOTHER SHONA!

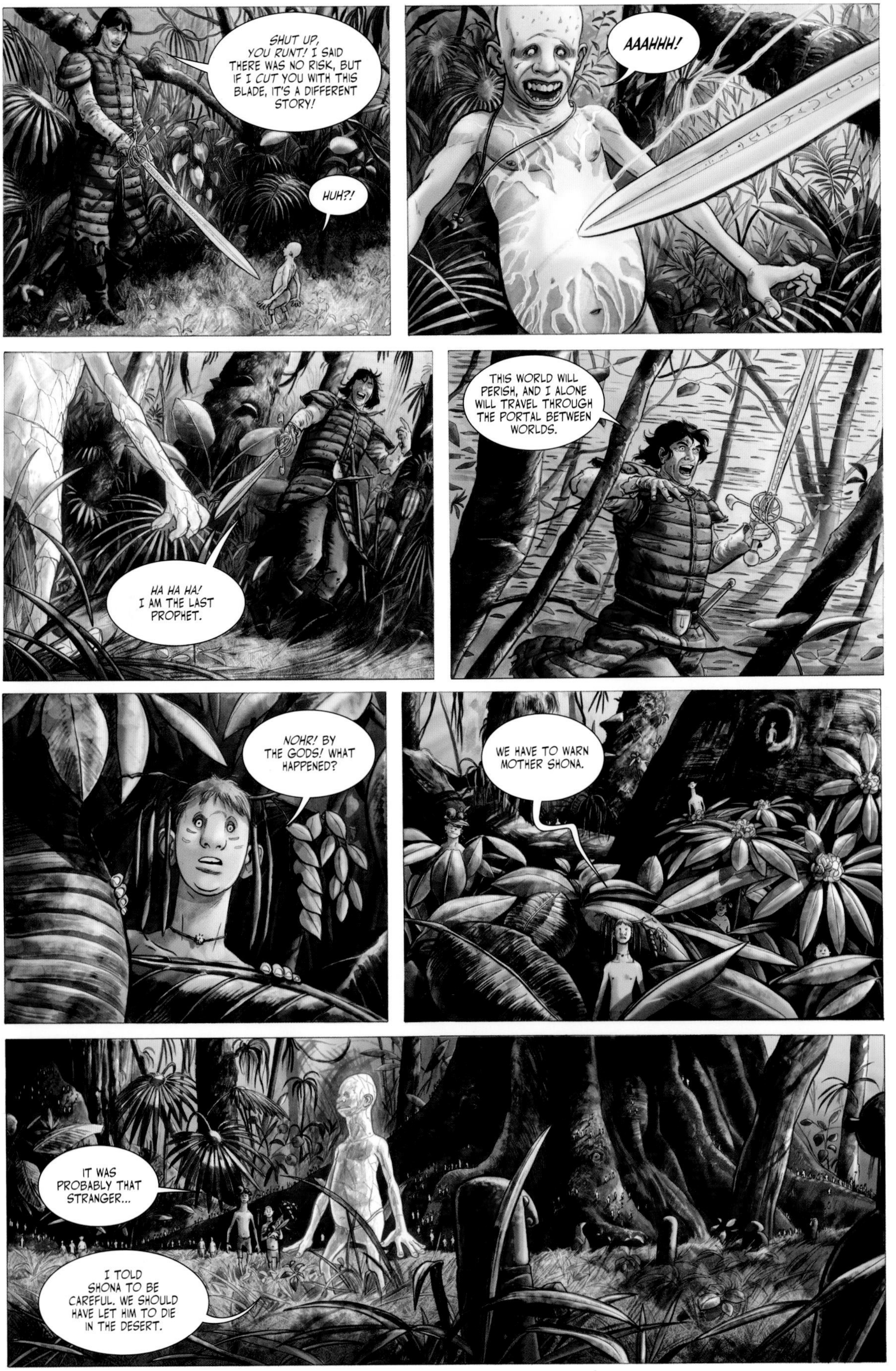
SHUT UP, YOU RUNT! I SAID THERE WAS NO RISK, BUT IF I CUT YOU WITH THIS BLADE, IT'S A DIFFERENT STORY!
HUH?!
AAAHHH!
HA HA HA! I AM THE LAST PROPHET.
THIS WORLD WILL PERISH, AND I ALONE WILL TRAVEL THROUGH THE PORTAL BETWEEN WORLDS.
NOHR! BY THE GODS! WHAT HAPPENED?
WE HAVE TO WARN MOTHER SHONA.
IT WAS PROBABLY THAT STRANGER...
I TOLD SHONA TO BE CAREFUL. WE SHOULD HAVE LET HIM TO DIE IN THE DESERT.

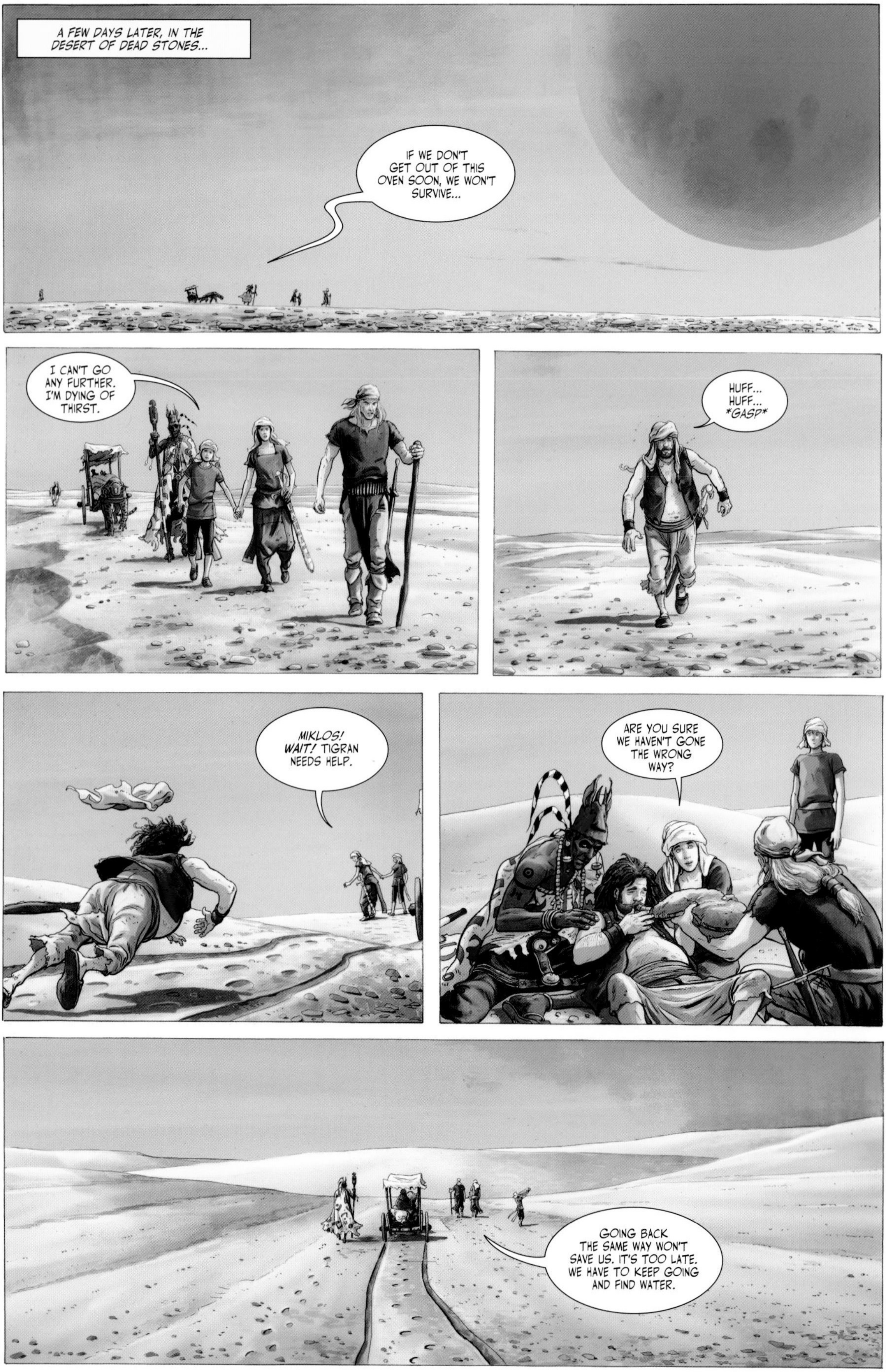
A FEW DAYS LATER, IN THE DESERT OF DEAD STONES...
IF WE DON'T GET OUT OF THIS OVEN SOON, WE WON'T SURVIVE...
I CAN'T GO ANY FURTHER. I'M DYING OF THIRST.
HUFF... HUFF... *GASP*
MIKLOS! WAIT! TIGRAN NEEDS HELP.
ARE YOU SURE WE HAVEN'T GONE THE WRONG WAY?
GOING BACK THE SAME WAY WON'T SAVE US. IT'S TOO LATE. WE HAVE TO KEEP GOING AND FIND WATER.

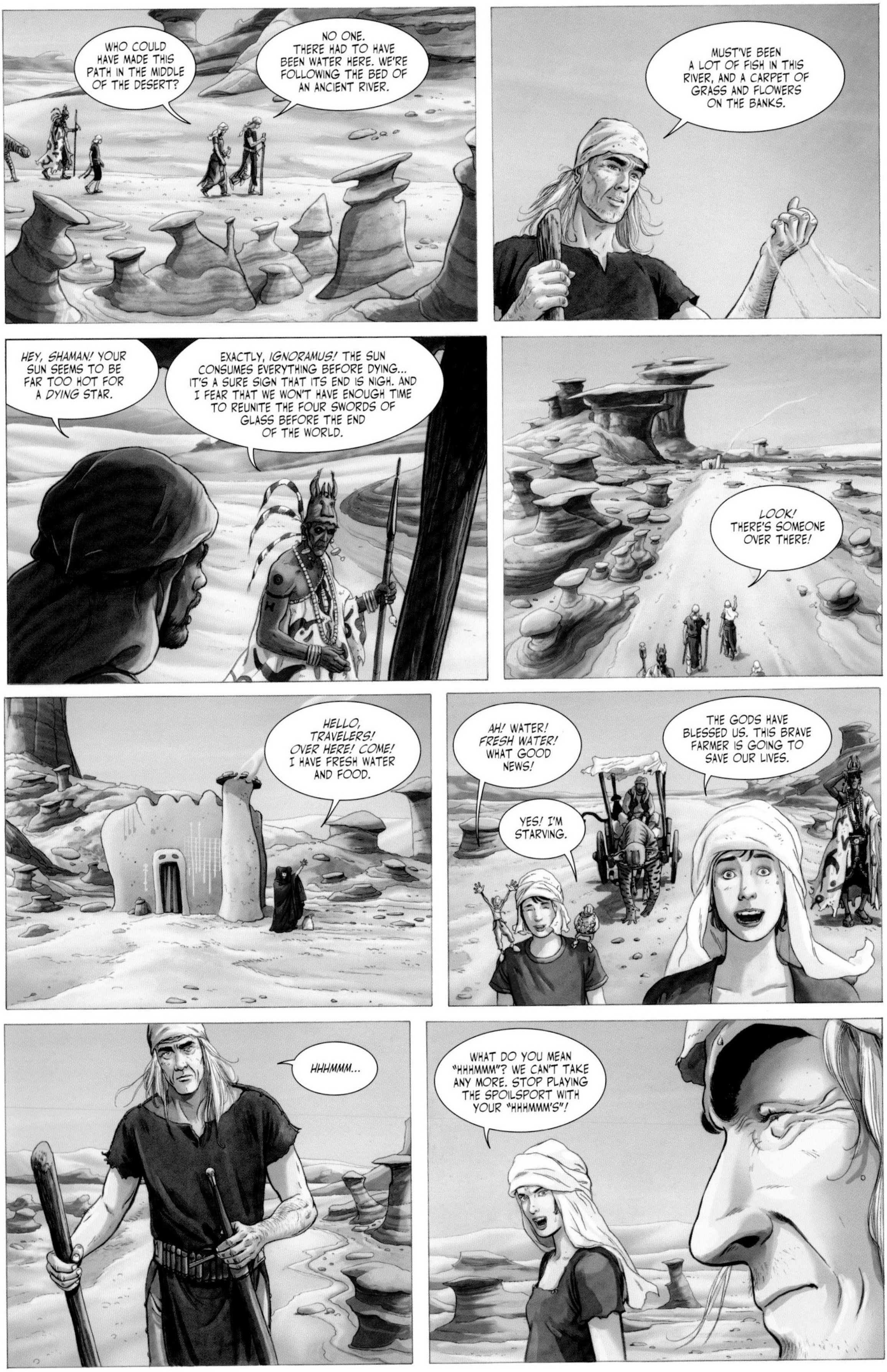
WHO COULD HAVE MADE THIS PATH IN THE MIDDLE OF THE DESERT?
NO ONE. THERE HAD TO HAVE BEEN WATER HERE. WE'RE FOLLOWING THE BED OF AN ANCIENT RIVER.
MUST'VE BEEN A LOT OF FISH IN THIS RIVER, AND A CARPET OF GRASS AND FLOWERS ON THE BANKS.
HEY, SHAMAN! YOUR SUN SEEMS TO BE FAR TOO HOT FOR A DYING STAR.
EXACTLY, IGNORAMUS! THE SUN CONSUMES EVERYTHING BEFORE DYING... IT'S A SURE SIGN THAT ITS END IS NIGH. AND I FEAR THAT WE WON'T HAVE ENOUGH TIME TO REUNITE THE FOUR SWORDS OF GLASS BEFORE THE END OF THE WORLD.
LOOK! THERE'S SOMEONE OVER THERE!
HELLO, TRAVELERS! OVER HERE! COME! I HAVE FRESH WATER AND FOOD.
AH! WATER! FRESH WATER! WHAT GOOD NEWS!
YES! I'M STARVING.
THE GODS HAVE BLESSED US. THIS BRAVE FARMER IS GOING TO SAVE OUR LIVES.
HHHMMM...
WHAT DO YOU MEAN "HHHMMM"? WE CAN'T TAKE ANY MORE. STOP PLAYING THE SPOILSPORT WITH YOUR "HHHMMM'S"!

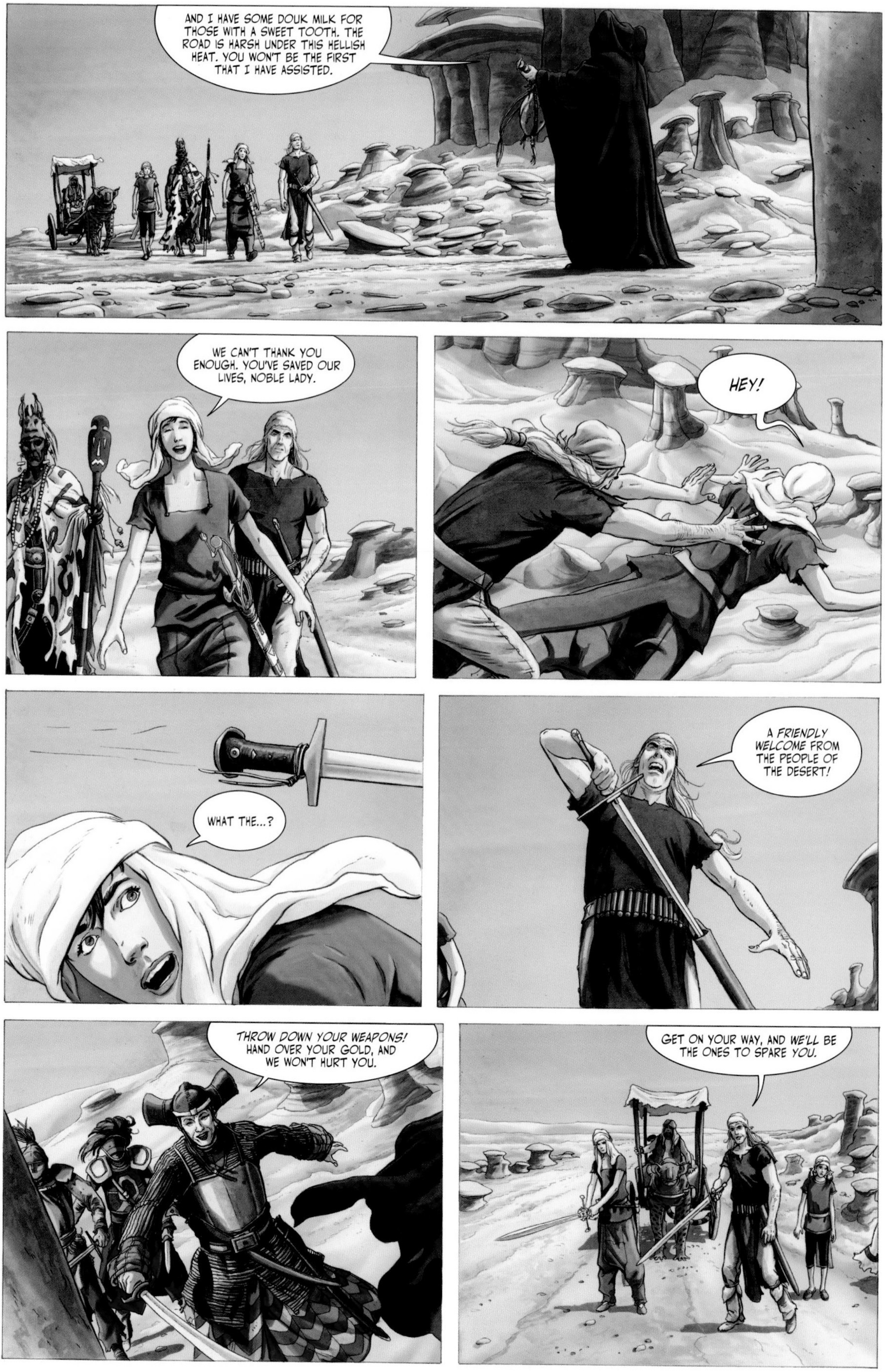
AND I HAVE SOME DOUK MILK FOR THOSE WITH A SWEET TOOTH. THE ROAD IS HARSH UNDER THIS HELLISH HEAT. YOU WON'T BE THE FIRST THAT I HAVE ASSISTED.
WE CAN'T THANK YOU ENOUGH. YOU'VE SAVED OUR LIVES, NOBLE LADY.
HEY!
WHAT THE...?
A FRIENDLY WELCOME FROM THE PEOPLE OF THE DESERT!
THROW DOWN YOUR WEAPONS! HAND OVER YOUR GOLD, AND WE WON'T HURT YOU.
GET ON YOUR WAY, AND WE'LL BE THE ONES TO SPARE YOU.

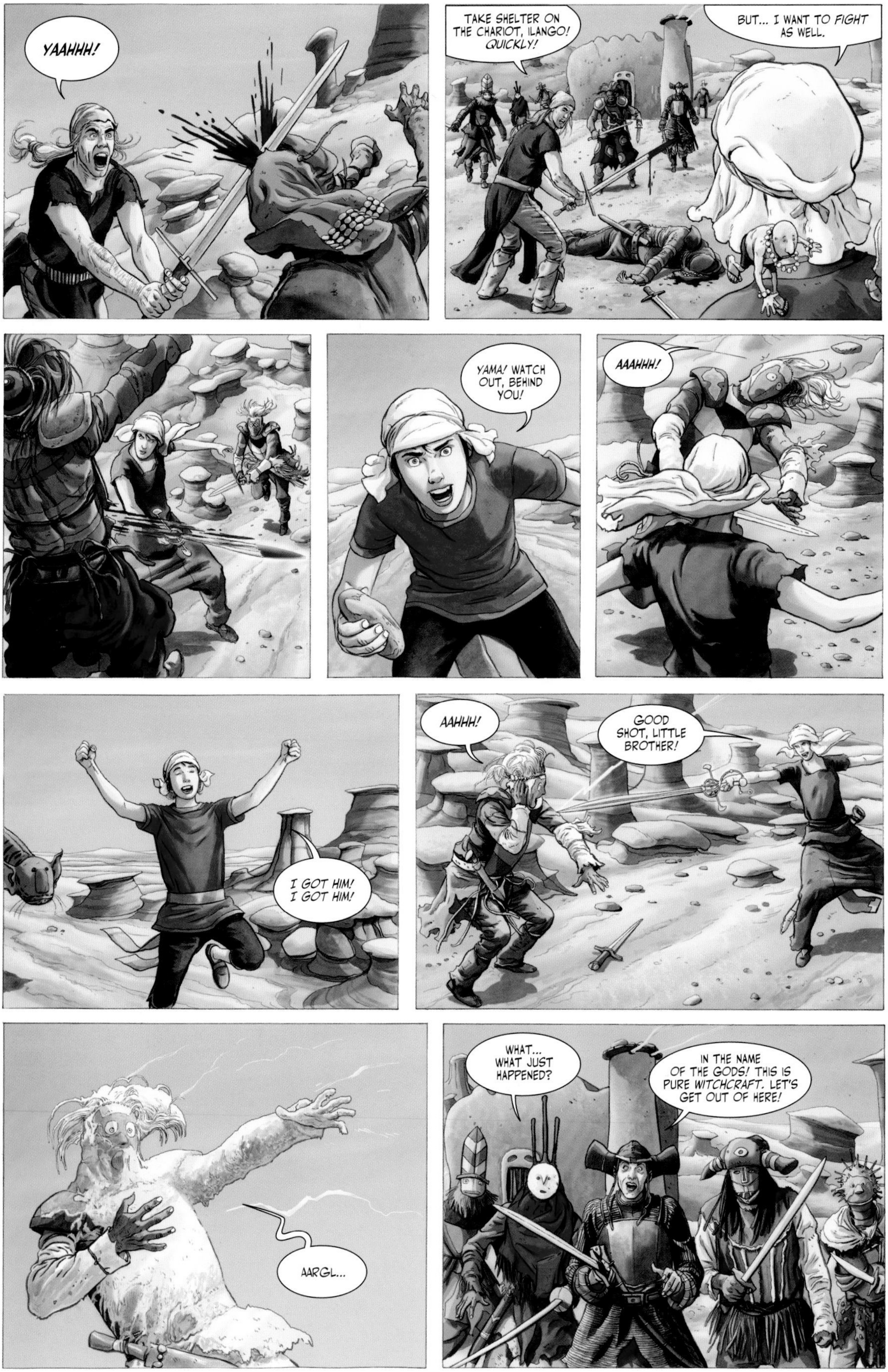
YAAHHH!
TAKE SHELTER ON THE CHARIOT, ILANGO! QUICKLY!
BUT... I WANT TO FIGHT AS WELL.
YAMA! WATCH OUT, BEHIND YOU!
AAAHHH!
I GOT HIM! I GOT HIM!
AAHHH!
GOOD SHOT, LITTLE BROTHER!
AARGL...
WHAT... WHAT JUST HAPPENED?
IN THE NAME OF THE GODS! THIS IS PURE WITCHCRAFT. LET'S GET OUT OF HERE!

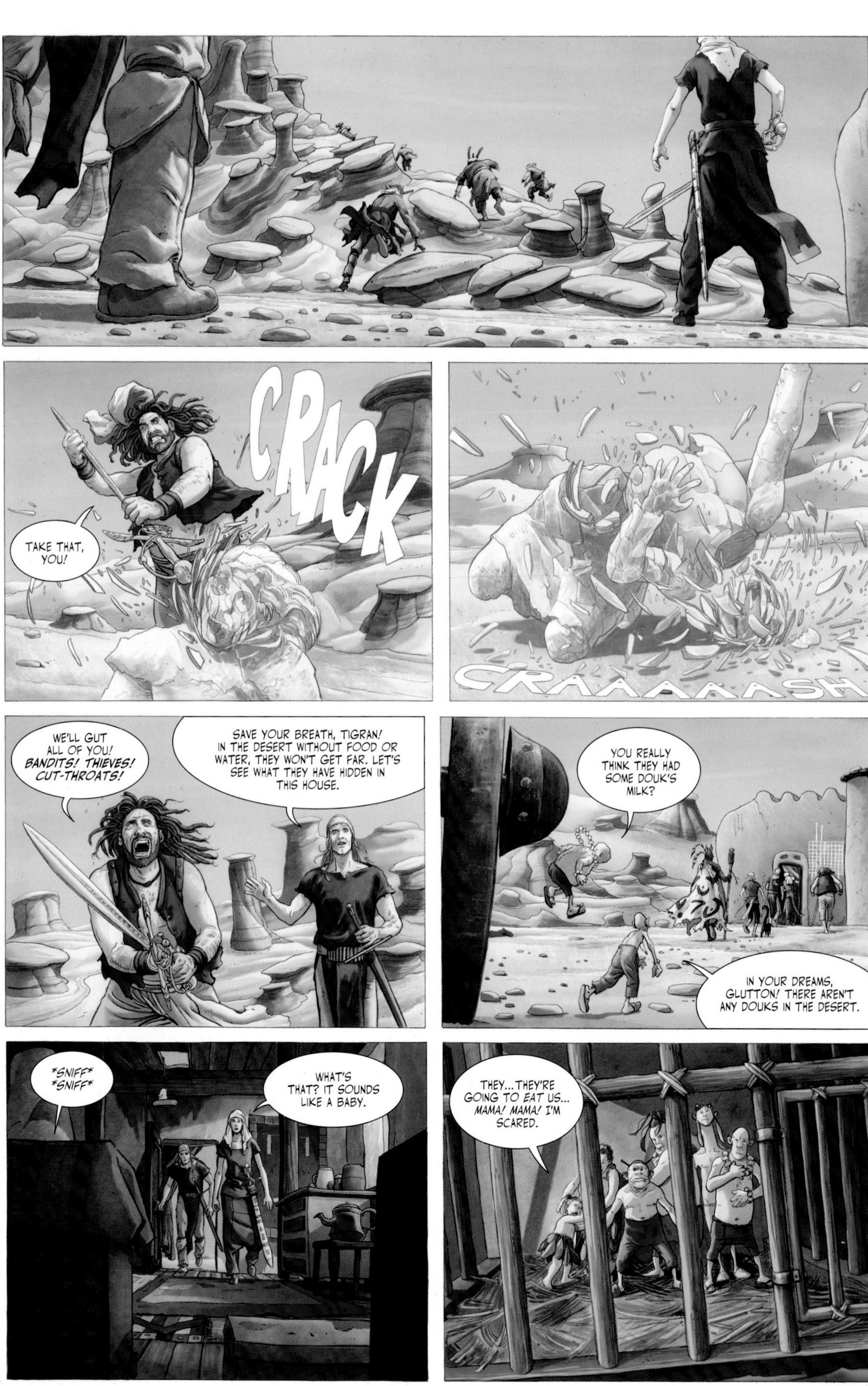

TAKE THAT, YOU!
CRACK
CRAAAAAASH
WE'LL GUT ALL OF YOU! BANDITS! THIEVES! CUT-THROATS!
SAVE YOUR BREATH, TIGRAN! IN THE DESERT WITHOUT FOOD OR WATER, THEY WON'T GET FAR. LET'S SEE WHAT THEY HAVE HIDDEN IN THIS HOUSE.
YOU REALLY THINK THEY HAD SOME DOUK'S MILK?
IN YOUR DREAMS, GLUTTON! THERE AREN'T ANY DOUKS IN THE DESERT.
SNIFF *SNIFF*
WHAT'S THAT? IT SOUNDS LIKE A BABY.
THEY... THEY'RE GOING TO EAT US... MAMA! MAMA! I'M SCARED.

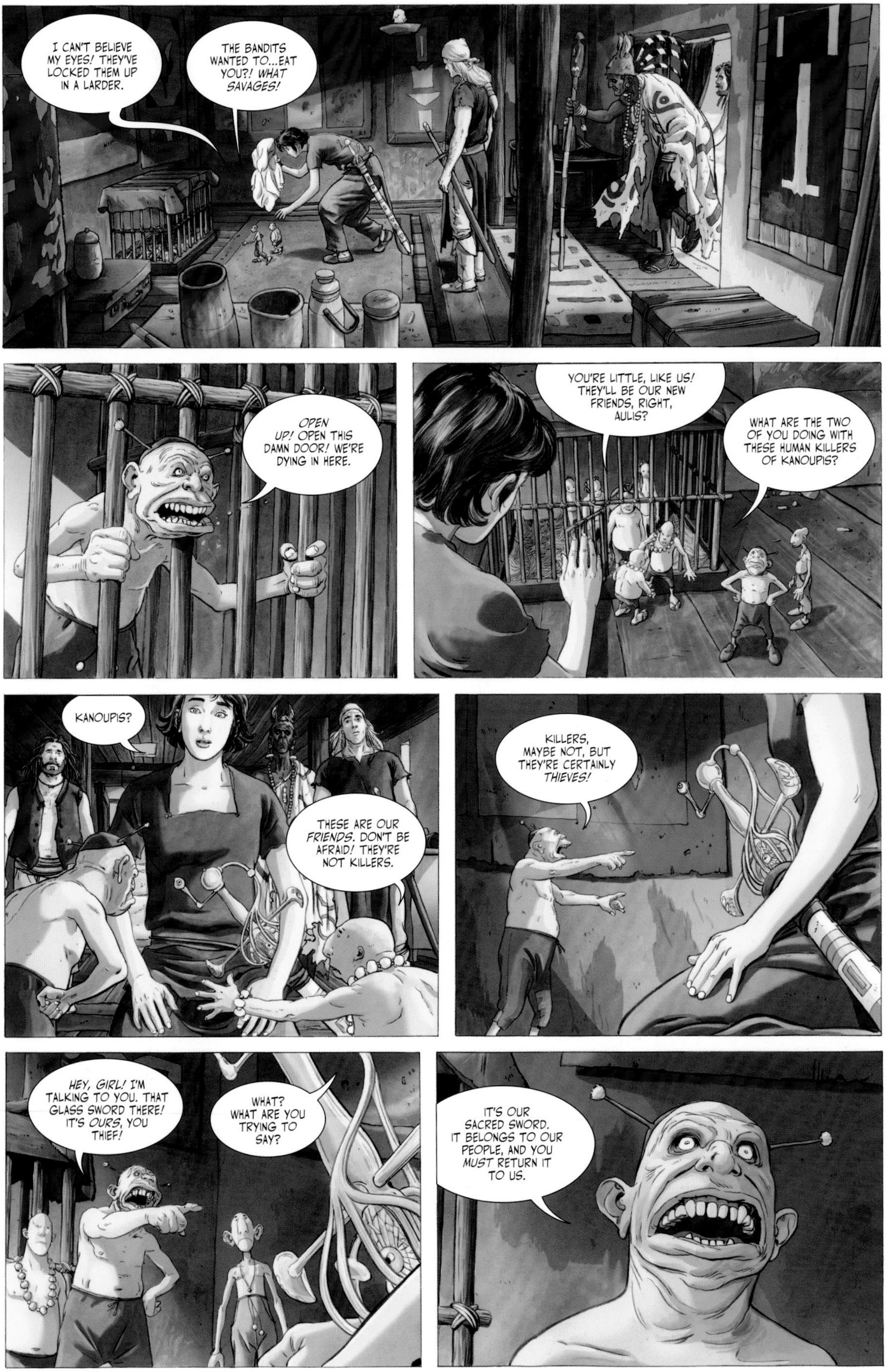
I CAN'T BELIEVE MY EYES! THEY'VE LOCKED THEM UP IN A LARDER.
THE BANDITS WANTED TO...EAT YOU?! *WHAT SAVAGES!*
OPEN UP! OPEN THIS DAMN DOOR! WE'RE DYING IN HERE.
YOU'RE LITTLE, LIKE US! THEY'LL BE OUR NEW FRIENDS, RIGHT, AULIS?
WHAT ARE THE TWO OF YOU DOING WITH THESE HUMAN KILLERS OF KANOUPIS?
KANOUPIS?
THESE ARE OUR *FRIENDS*. DON'T BE AFRAID! THEY'RE NOT KILLERS.
KILLERS, MAYBE NOT, BUT THEY'RE CERTAINLY *THIEVES!*
HEY, GIRL! I'M TALKING TO YOU. THAT GLASS SWORD THERE! IT'S *OURS*, YOU THIEF!
WHAT? WHAT ARE YOU TRYING TO SAY?
IT'S OUR SACRED SWORD. IT BELONGS TO OUR PEOPLE, AND YOU *MUST* RETURN IT TO US.

LONG AGO, WE DWELLED IN THE WOODS, THE PLAINS, EVEN THE MOUNTAINS. WE WERE EVERYWHERE, BUT THEN HUMANS DECIMATED US.

THE LEAST CRUEL OF THEM USED US LIKE PETS. OTHERS ATE US...

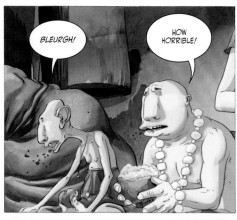

BLEURGH!

HOW HORRIBLE!

OUR LAST GREAT COMMUNITY SURVIVED IN THE OLDEST FOREST IN THE WORLD THAT WE CALL THE *GREAT CRADLE.*

IT WAS THERE THAT KANOUPIS HUNTERS CAPTURED US.

"MANY MOONS AGO, A STRANGE SWORD FELL FROM THE SKY INTO OUR FOREST. A TERRIBLE SPELL FELL UPON ALL WHO ATTEMPTED TO PULL IT FROM ITS STUMP: THEY WERE TRANSFORMED INTO GLASS STATUES AND SHATTERED INTO THOUSANDS OF PIECES."

"NO ON DARED TOUCH IT AFTER THAT, EXCEPT OUR MATRIARCH, SHONA-THE-GREAT. SHE ALONE SURVIVED THE LETHAL MAGIC OF THE SWORD."

WITH YOUR MATRIARCH'S SWORD, WE'LL ONLY LACK ONE MORE SWORD TO OPEN THE DOOR THAT WILL SAVE US ALL.

BY "SAVE US ALL," WE MEAN YOU GUYS AS WELL, OF COURSE. YOU MUST LEAD US TO YOUR FOREST...

SHONA SUCCEEDED IN FREEING THE GLASS SWORD...

SO, THIS TINY CREATURE IS LIKE TIGRAN AND YOU... ONE OF THE CHOSEN FOUR!

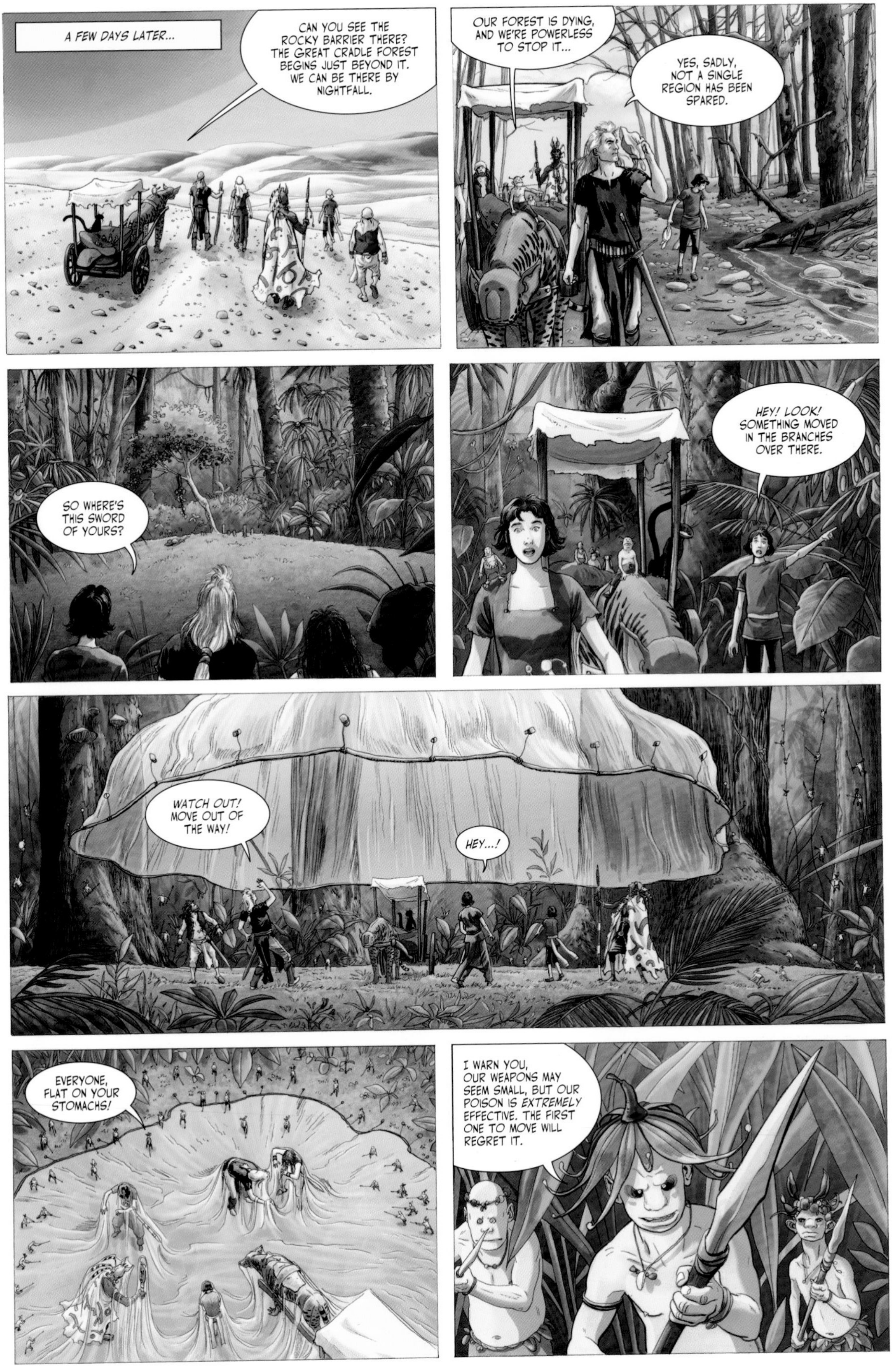
A FEW DAYS LATER...
CAN YOU SEE THE ROCKY BARRIER THERE? THE GREAT CRADLE FOREST BEGINS JUST BEYOND IT. WE CAN BE THERE BY NIGHTFALL.
OUR FOREST IS DYING, AND WE'RE POWERLESS TO STOP IT...
YES, SADLY, NOT A SINGLE REGION HAS BEEN SPARED.
SO WHERE'S THIS SWORD OF YOURS?
HEY! LOOK! SOMETHING MOVED IN THE BRANCHES OVER THERE.
WATCH OUT! MOVE OUT OF THE WAY!
HEY...!
EVERYONE, FLAT ON YOUR STOMACHS!
I WARN YOU, OUR WEAPONS MAY SEEM SMALL, BUT OUR POISON IS EXTREMELY EFFECTIVE. THE FIRST ONE TO MOVE WILL REGRET IT.

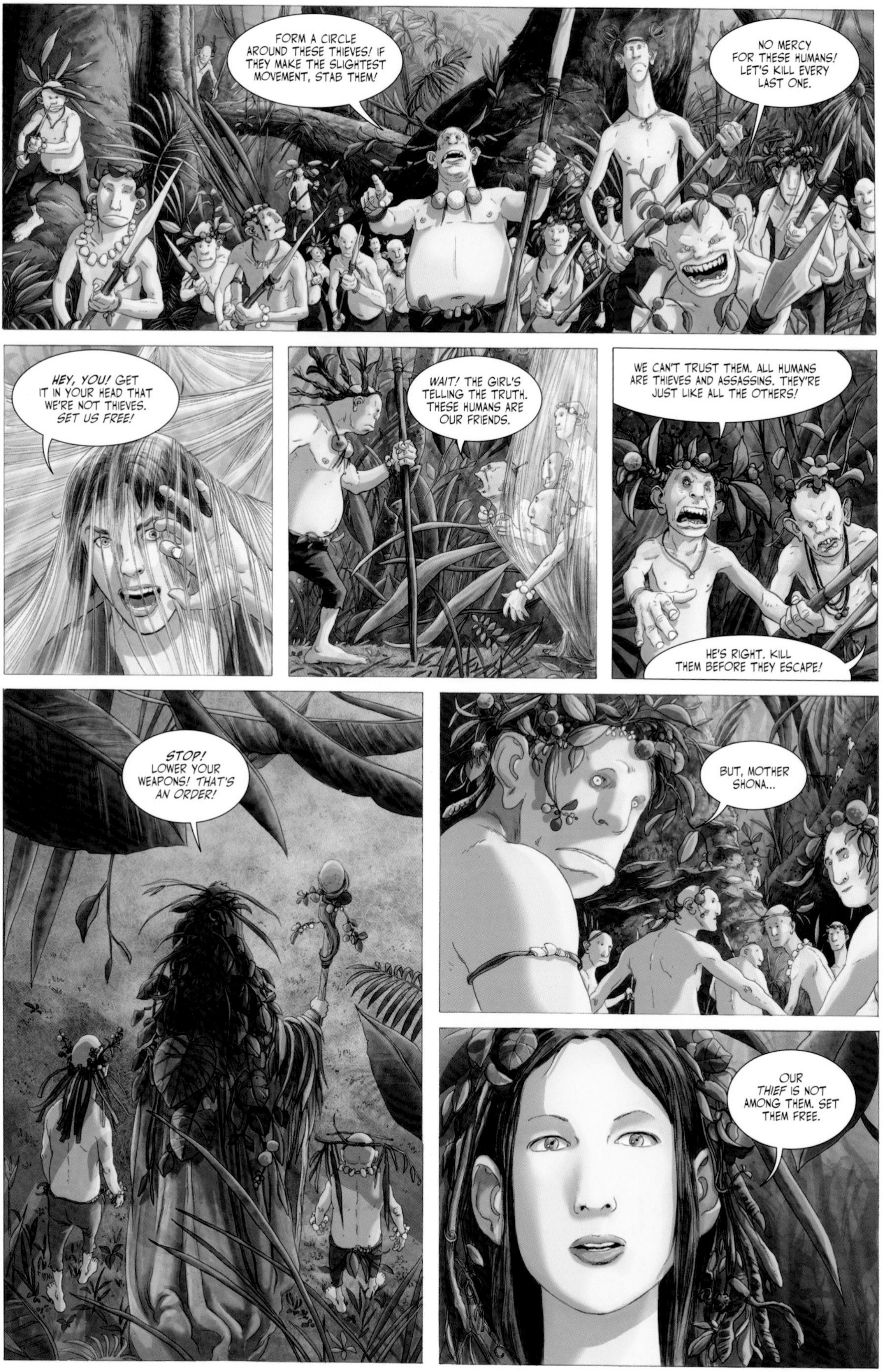
FORM A CIRCLE AROUND THESE THIEVES! IF THEY MAKE THE SLIGHTEST MOVEMENT, STAB THEM!
NO MERCY FOR THESE HUMANS! LET'S KILL EVERY LAST ONE.
HEY, YOU! GET IT IN YOUR HEAD THAT WE'RE NOT THIEVES. SET US FREE!
WAIT! THE GIRL'S TELLING THE TRUTH. THESE HUMANS ARE OUR FRIENDS.
WE CAN'T TRUST THEM. ALL HUMANS ARE THIEVES AND ASSASSINS. THEY'RE JUST LIKE ALL THE OTHERS!
HE'S RIGHT. KILL THEM BEFORE THEY ESCAPE!
STOP! LOWER YOUR WEAPONS! THAT'S AN ORDER!
BUT, MOTHER SHONA...
OUR THIEF IS NOT AMONG THEM. SET THEM FREE.

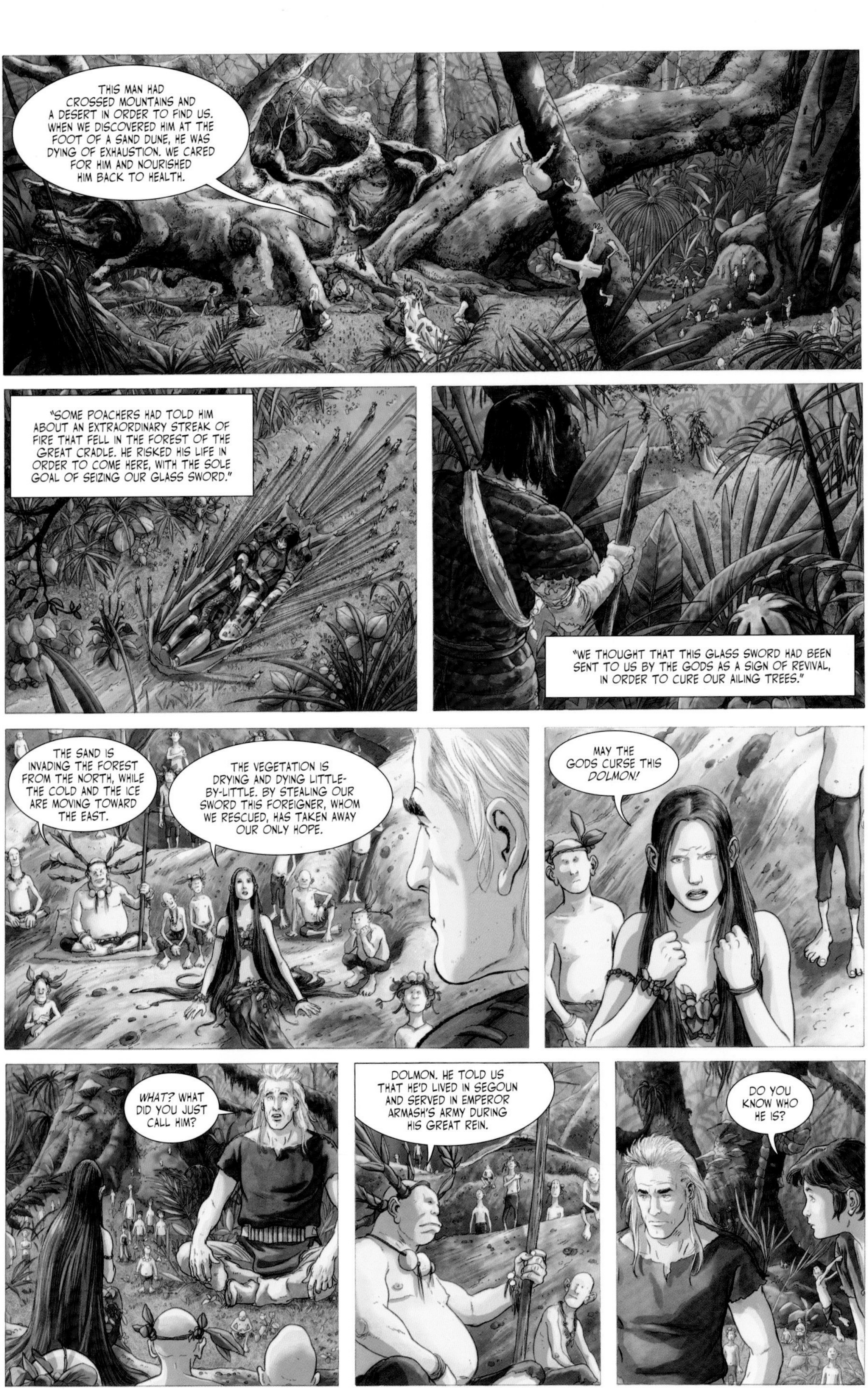
THIS MAN HAD CROSSED MOUNTAINS AND A DESERT IN ORDER TO FIND US. WHEN WE DISCOVERED HIM AT THE FOOT OF A SAND DUNE, HE WAS DYING OF EXHAUSTION. WE CARED FOR HIM AND NOURISHED HIM BACK TO HEALTH.
"SOME POACHERS HAD TOLD HIM ABOUT AN EXTRAORDINARY STREAK OF FIRE THAT FELL IN THE FOREST OF THE GREAT CRADLE. HE RISKED HIS LIFE IN ORDER TO COME HERE, WITH THE SOLE GOAL OF SEIZING OUR GLASS SWORD."
"WE THOUGHT THAT THIS GLASS SWORD HAD BEEN SENT TO US BY THE GODS AS A SIGN OF REVIVAL, IN ORDER TO CURE OUR AILING TREES."
THE SAND IS INVADING THE FOREST FROM THE NORTH, WHILE THE COLD AND THE ICE ARE MOVING TOWARD THE EAST.
THE VEGETATION IS DRYING AND DYING LITTLE-BY-LITTLE. BY STEALING OUR SWORD THIS FOREIGNER, WHOM WE RESCUED, HAS TAKEN AWAY OUR ONLY HOPE.
MAY THE GODS CURSE THIS *DOLMON!*
WHAT? WHAT DID YOU JUST CALL HIM?
DOLMON. HE TOLD US THAT HE'D LIVED IN SEGOUN AND SERVED IN EMPEROR ARMASH'S ARMY DURING HIS GREAT REIN.
DO YOU KNOW WHO HE IS?

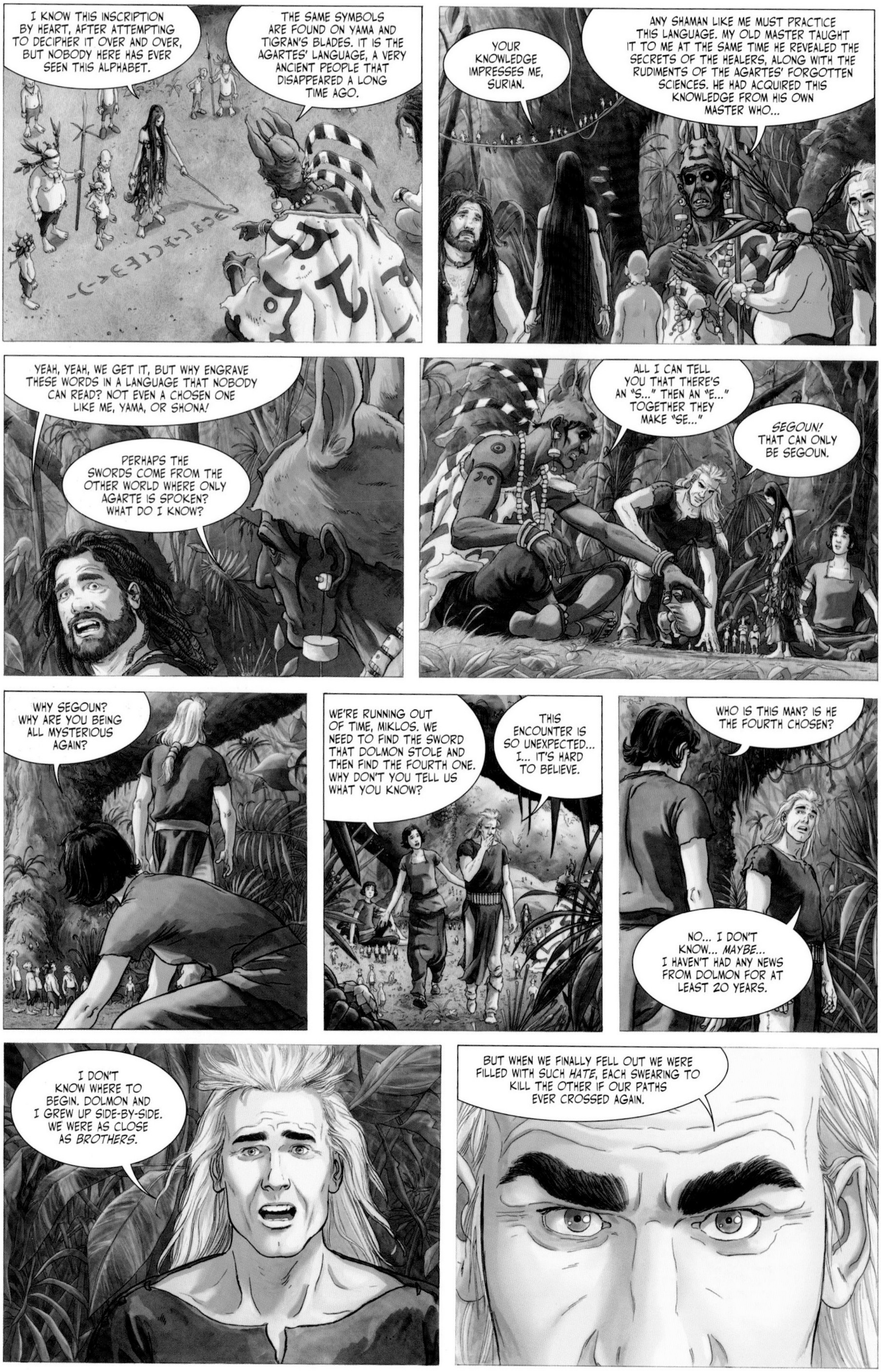
I KNOW THIS INSCRIPTION BY HEART, AFTER ATTEMPTING TO DECIPHER IT OVER AND OVER, BUT NOBODY HERE HAS EVER SEEN THIS ALPHABET.
THE SAME SYMBOLS ARE FOUND ON YAMA AND TIGRAN'S BLADES. IT IS THE AGARTES' LANGUAGE, A VERY ANCIENT PEOPLE THAT DISAPPEARED A LONG TIME AGO.
YOUR KNOWLEDGE IMPRESSES ME, SURIAN.
ANY SHAMAN LIKE ME MUST PRACTICE THIS LANGUAGE. MY OLD MASTER TAUGHT IT TO ME AT THE SAME TIME HE REVEALED THE SECRETS OF THE HEALERS, ALONG WITH THE RUDIMENTS OF THE AGARTES' FORGOTTEN SCIENCES. HE HAD ACQUIRED THIS KNOWLEDGE FROM HIS OWN MASTER WHO...
YEAH, YEAH, WE GET IT, BUT WHY ENGRAVE THESE WORDS IN A LANGUAGE THAT NOBODY CAN READ? NOT EVEN A CHOSEN ONE LIKE ME, YAMA, OR SHONA!
PERHAPS THE SWORDS COME FROM THE OTHER WORLD WHERE ONLY AGARTE IS SPOKEN? WHAT DO I KNOW?
ALL I CAN TELL YOU THAT THERE'S AN "S..." THEN AN "E..." TOGETHER THEY MAKE "SE..."
SEGOUN! THAT CAN ONLY BE SEGOUN.
WHY SEGOUN? WHY ARE YOU BEING ALL MYSTERIOUS AGAIN?
WE'RE RUNNING OUT OF TIME, MIKLOS. WE NEED TO FIND THE SWORD THAT DOLMON STOLE AND THEN FIND THE FOURTH ONE. WHY DON'T YOU TELL US WHAT YOU KNOW?
THIS ENCOUNTER IS SO UNEXPECTED... I... IT'S HARD TO BELIEVE.
WHO IS THIS MAN? IS HE THE FOURTH CHOSEN?
NO... I DON'T KNOW... *MAYBE*... I HAVEN'T HAD ANY NEWS FROM DOLMON FOR AT LEAST 20 YEARS.
I DON'T KNOW WHERE TO BEGIN. DOLMON AND I GREW UP SIDE-BY-SIDE. WE WERE AS CLOSE AS *BROTHERS*.
BUT WHEN WE FINALLY FELL OUT WE WERE FILLED WITH SUCH *HATE*, EACH SWEARING TO KILL THE OTHER IF OUR PATHS EVER CROSSED AGAIN.

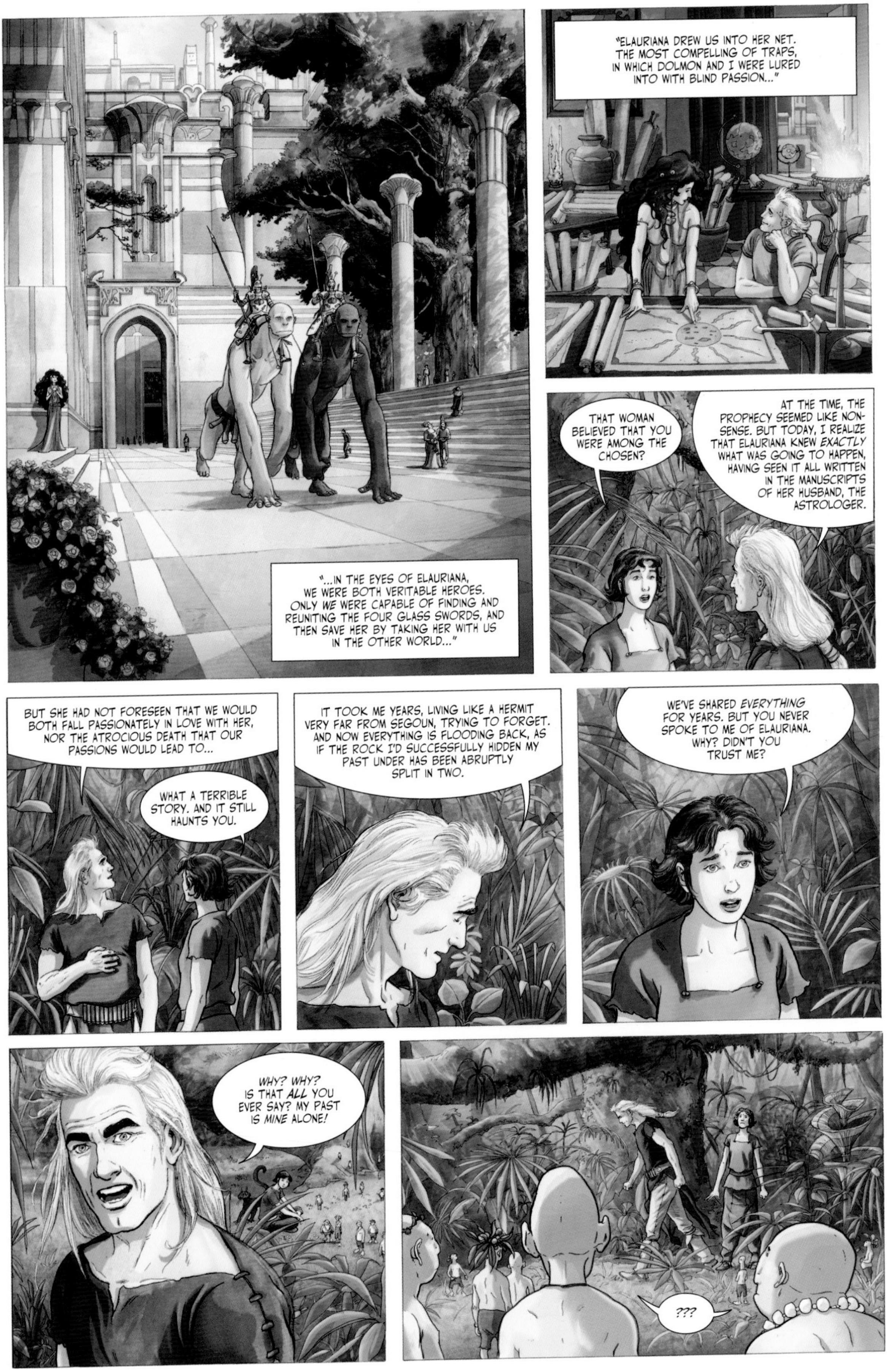
"...IN THE EYES OF ELAURIANA, WE WERE BOTH VERITABLE HEROES. ONLY *WE* WERE CAPABLE OF FINDING AND REUNITING THE FOUR GLASS SWORDS, AND THEN SAVE HER BY TAKING HER WITH US IN THE OTHER WORLD..."
"ELAURIANA DREW US INTO HER NET. THE MOST COMPELLING OF TRAPS, IN WHICH DOLMON AND I WERE LURED INTO WITH BLIND PASSION..."
THAT WOMAN BELIEVED THAT YOU WERE AMONG THE CHOSEN?
AT THE TIME, THE PROPHECY SEEMED LIKE NONSENSE. BUT TODAY, I REALIZE THAT ELAURIANA KNEW *EXACTLY* WHAT WAS GOING TO HAPPEN, HAVING SEEN IT ALL WRITTEN IN THE MANUSCRIPTS OF HER HUSBAND, THE ASTROLOGER.
BUT SHE HAD NOT FORESEEN THAT WE WOULD BOTH FALL PASSIONATELY IN LOVE WITH HER, NOR THE ATROCIOUS DEATH THAT OUR PASSIONS WOULD LEAD TO...
WHAT A TERRIBLE STORY. AND IT STILL HAUNTS YOU.
IT TOOK ME YEARS, LIVING LIKE A HERMIT VERY FAR FROM SEGOUN, TRYING TO FORGET. AND NOW EVERYTHING IS FLOODING BACK, AS IF THE ROCK I'D SUCCESSFULLY HIDDEN MY PAST UNDER HAS BEEN ABRUPTLY SPLIT IN TWO.
WE'VE SHARED *EVERYTHING* FOR YEARS. BUT YOU NEVER SPOKE TO ME OF ELAURIANA. WHY? DIDN'T YOU TRUST ME?
WHY? WHY? IS THAT ***ALL*** YOU EVER SAY? MY PAST IS *MINE* ALONE!
???

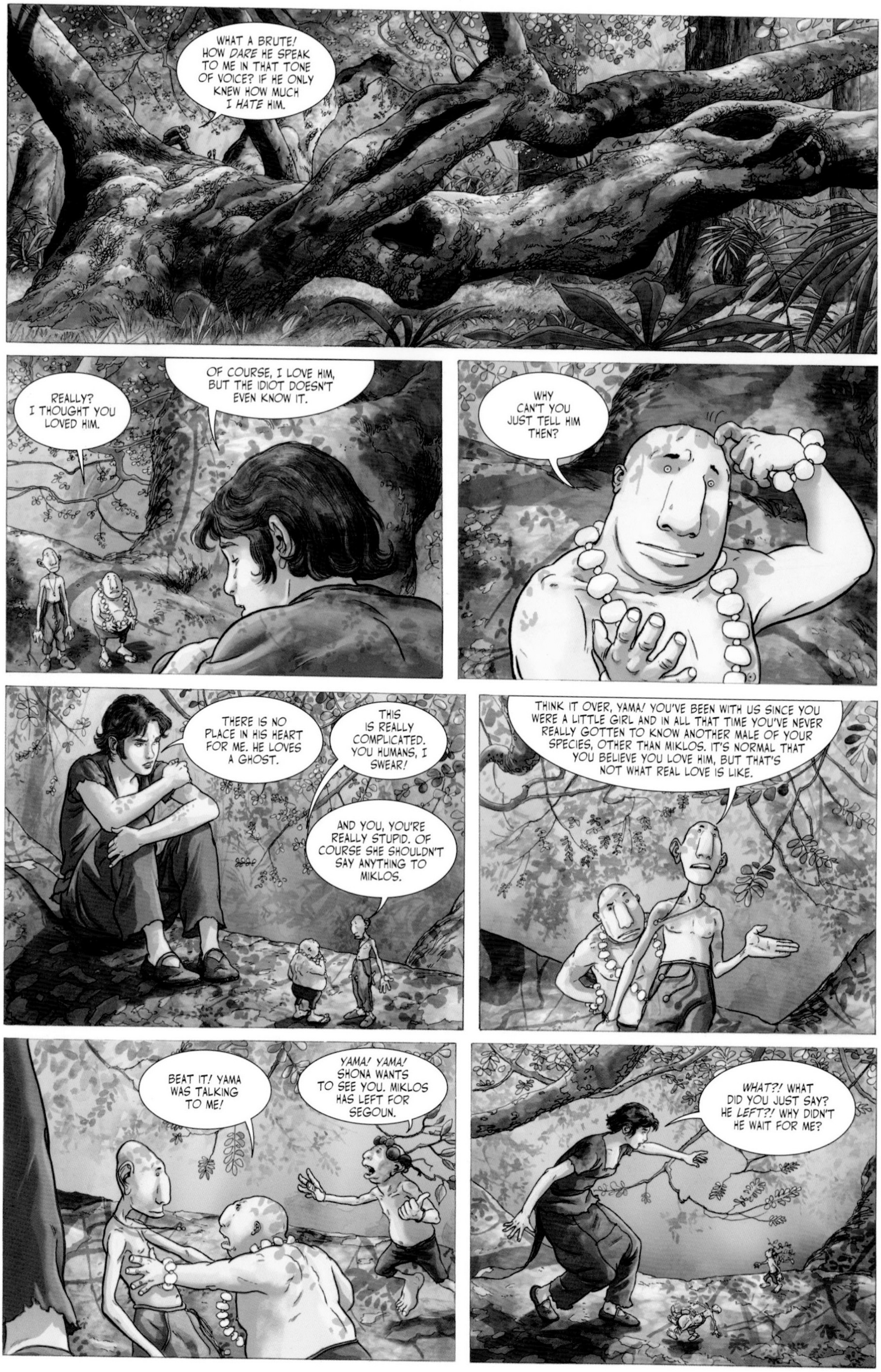
WHAT A BRUTE! HOW DARE HE SPEAK TO ME IN THAT TONE OF VOICE? IF HE ONLY KNEW HOW MUCH I HATE HIM.
REALLY? I THOUGHT YOU LOVED HIM.
OF COURSE, I LOVE HIM, BUT THE IDIOT DOESN'T EVEN KNOW IT.
WHY CAN'T YOU JUST TELL HIM THEN?
THERE IS NO PLACE IN HIS HEART FOR ME. HE LOVES A GHOST.
THIS IS REALLY COMPLICATED. YOU HUMANS, I SWEAR!
AND YOU, YOU'RE REALLY STUPID. OF COURSE SHE SHOULDN'T SAY ANYTHING TO MIKLOS.
THINK IT OVER, YAMA! YOU'VE BEEN WITH US SINCE YOU WERE A LITTLE GIRL AND IN ALL THAT TIME YOU'VE NEVER REALLY GOTTEN TO KNOW ANOTHER MALE OF YOUR SPECIES, OTHER THAN MIKLOS. IT'S NORMAL THAT YOU BELIEVE YOU LOVE HIM, BUT THAT'S NOT WHAT REAL LOVE IS LIKE.
BEAT IT! YAMA WAS TALKING TO ME!
YAMA! YAMA! SHONA WANTS TO SEE YOU. MIKLOS HAS LEFT FOR SEGOUN.
WHAT?! WHAT DID YOU JUST SAY? HE LEFT?! WHY DIDN'T HE WAIT FOR ME?

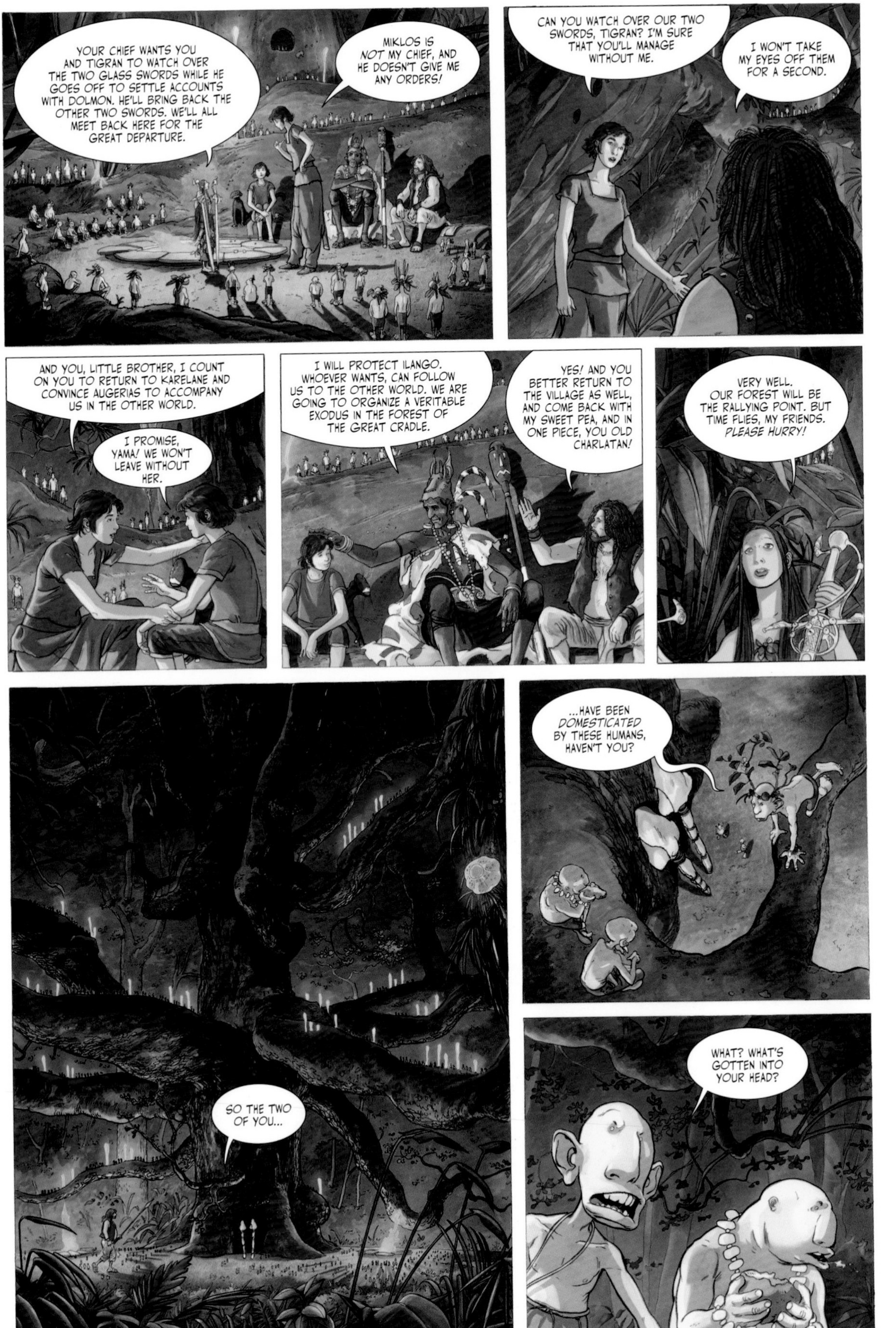

YOUR CHIEF WANTS YOU AND TIGRAN TO WATCH OVER THE TWO GLASS SWORDS WHILE HE GOES OFF TO SETTLE ACCOUNTS WITH DOLMON. HE'LL BRING BACK THE OTHER TWO SWORDS. WE'LL ALL MEET BACK HERE FOR THE GREAT DEPARTURE.
MIKLOS IS *NOT* MY CHIEF, AND HE DOESN'T GIVE ME ANY ORDERS!
CAN YOU WATCH OVER OUR TWO SWORDS, TIGRAN? I'M SURE THAT YOU'LL MANAGE WITHOUT ME.
I WON'T TAKE MY EYES OFF THEM FOR A SECOND.
AND YOU, LITTLE BROTHER, I COUNT ON YOU TO RETURN TO KARELANE AND CONVINCE AUGERIAS TO ACCOMPANY US IN THE OTHER WORLD.
I PROMISE, YAMA! WE WON'T LEAVE WITHOUT HER.
I WILL PROTECT ILANGO. WHOEVER WANTS, CAN FOLLOW US TO THE OTHER WORLD. WE ARE GOING TO ORGANIZE A VERITABLE EXODUS IN THE FOREST OF THE GREAT CRADLE.
YES! AND YOU BETTER RETURN TO THE VILLAGE AS WELL, AND COME BACK WITH MY SWEET PEA, AND IN ONE PIECE, YOU OLD CHARLATAN!
VERY WELL. OUR FOREST WILL BE THE RALLYING POINT. BUT TIME FLIES, MY FRIENDS. *PLEASE HURRY!*
SO THE TWO OF YOU...
...HAVE BEEN *DOMESTICATED* BY THESE HUMANS, HAVEN'T YOU?
WHAT? WHAT'S GOTTEN INTO YOUR HEAD?

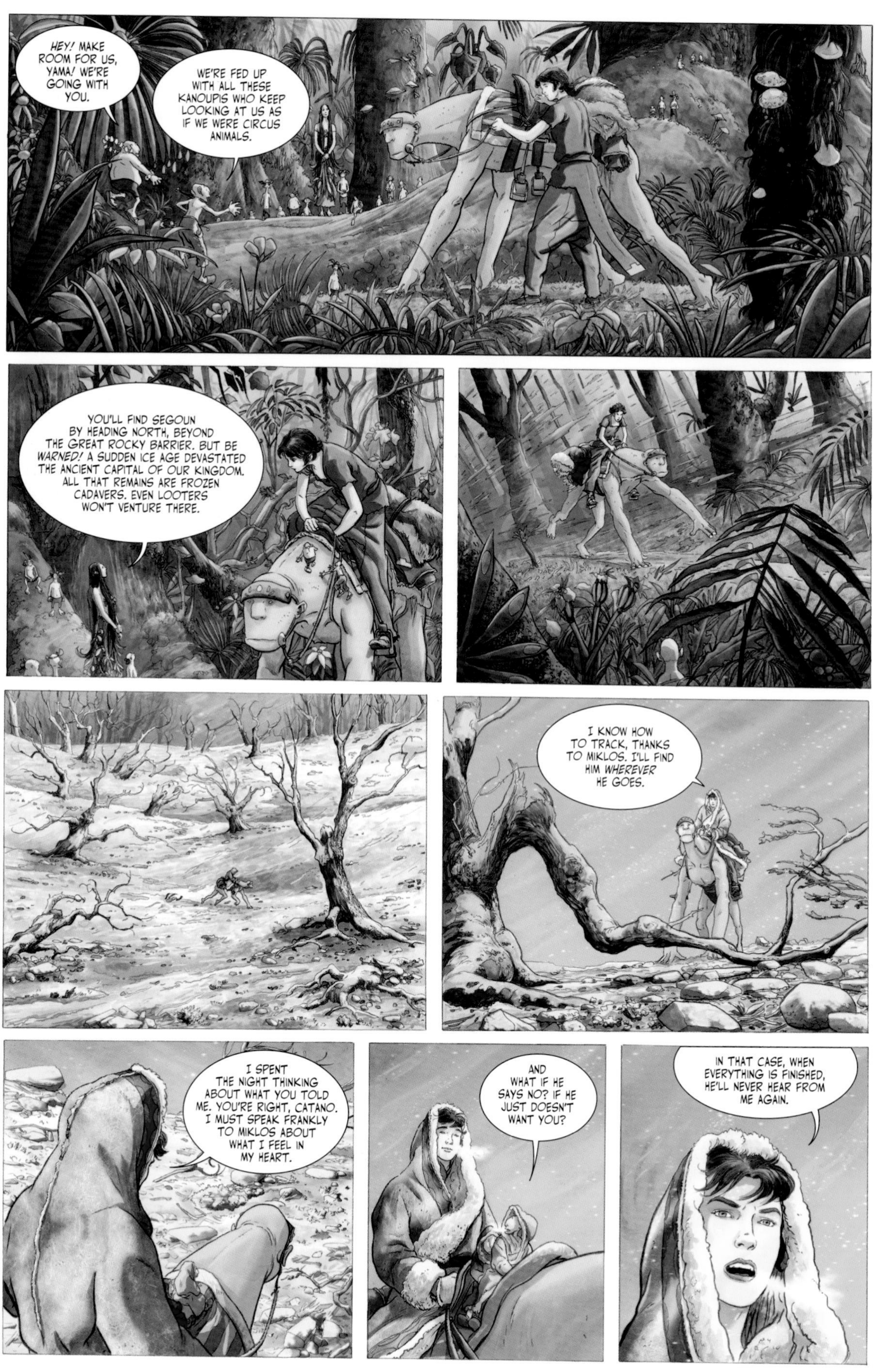
HEY! MAKE ROOM FOR US, YAMA! WE'RE GOING WITH YOU.
WE'RE FED UP WITH ALL THESE KANOUPIS WHO KEEP LOOKING AT US AS IF WE WERE CIRCUS ANIMALS.
YOU'LL FIND SEGOUN BY HEADING NORTH, BEYOND THE GREAT ROCKY BARRIER. BUT BE WARNED! A SUDDEN ICE AGE DEVASTATED THE ANCIENT CAPITAL OF OUR KINGDOM. ALL THAT REMAINS ARE FROZEN CADAVERS. EVEN LOOTERS WON'T VENTURE THERE.
I KNOW HOW TO TRACK, THANKS TO MIKLOS. I'LL FIND HIM WHEREVER HE GOES.
I SPENT THE NIGHT THINKING ABOUT WHAT YOU TOLD ME. YOU'RE RIGHT, CATANO. I MUST SPEAK FRANKLY TO MIKLOS ABOUT WHAT I FEEL IN MY HEART.
AND WHAT IF HE SAYS NO? IF HE JUST DOESN'T WANT YOU?
IN THAT CASE, WHEN EVERYTHING IS FINISHED, HE'LL NEVER HEAR FROM ME AGAIN.

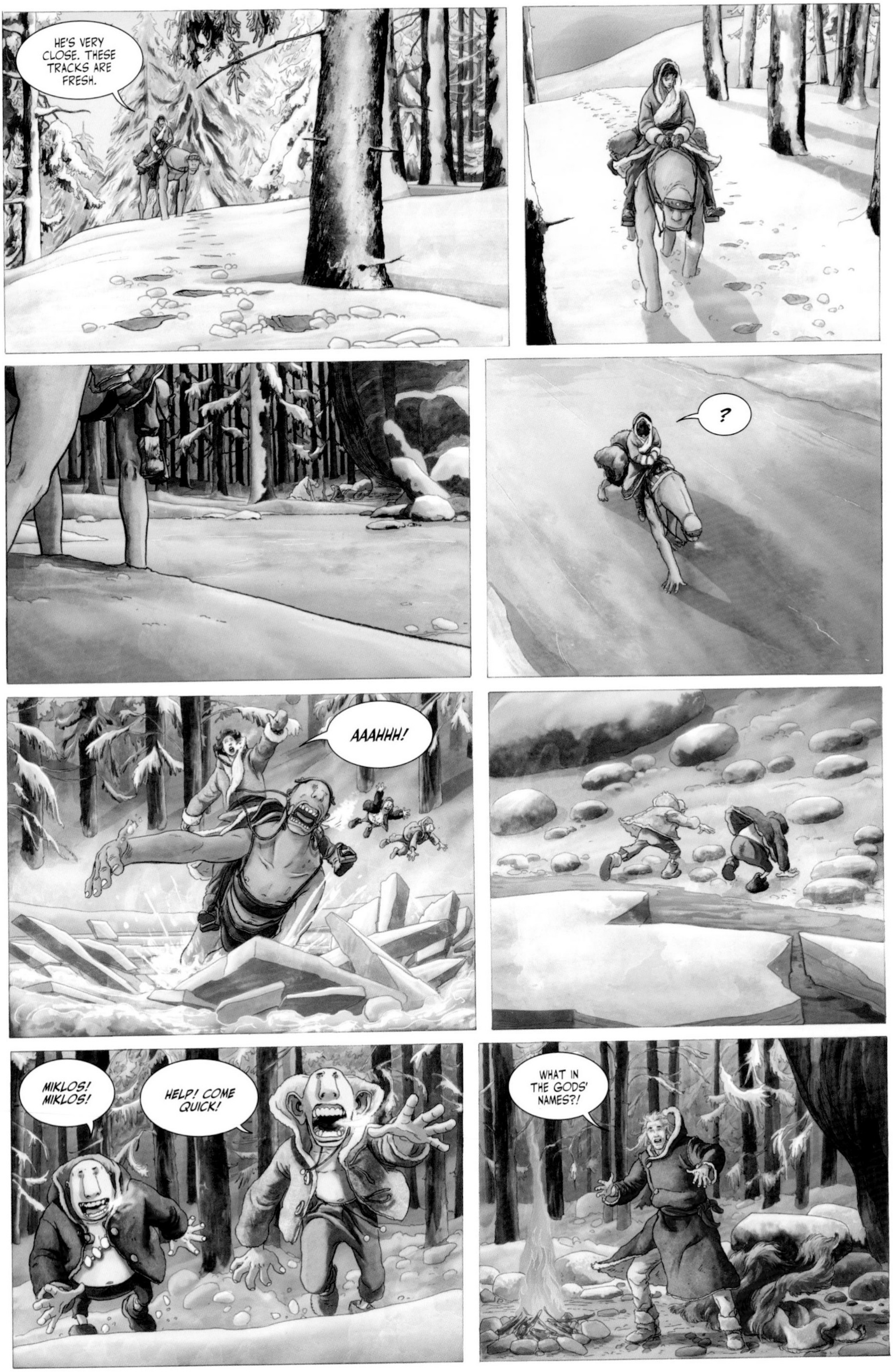

HE'S VERY CLOSE. THESE TRACKS ARE FRESH.
?
AAAHHH!
MIKLOS! MIKLOS!
HELP! COME QUICK!
WHAT IN THE GODS' NAMES?!

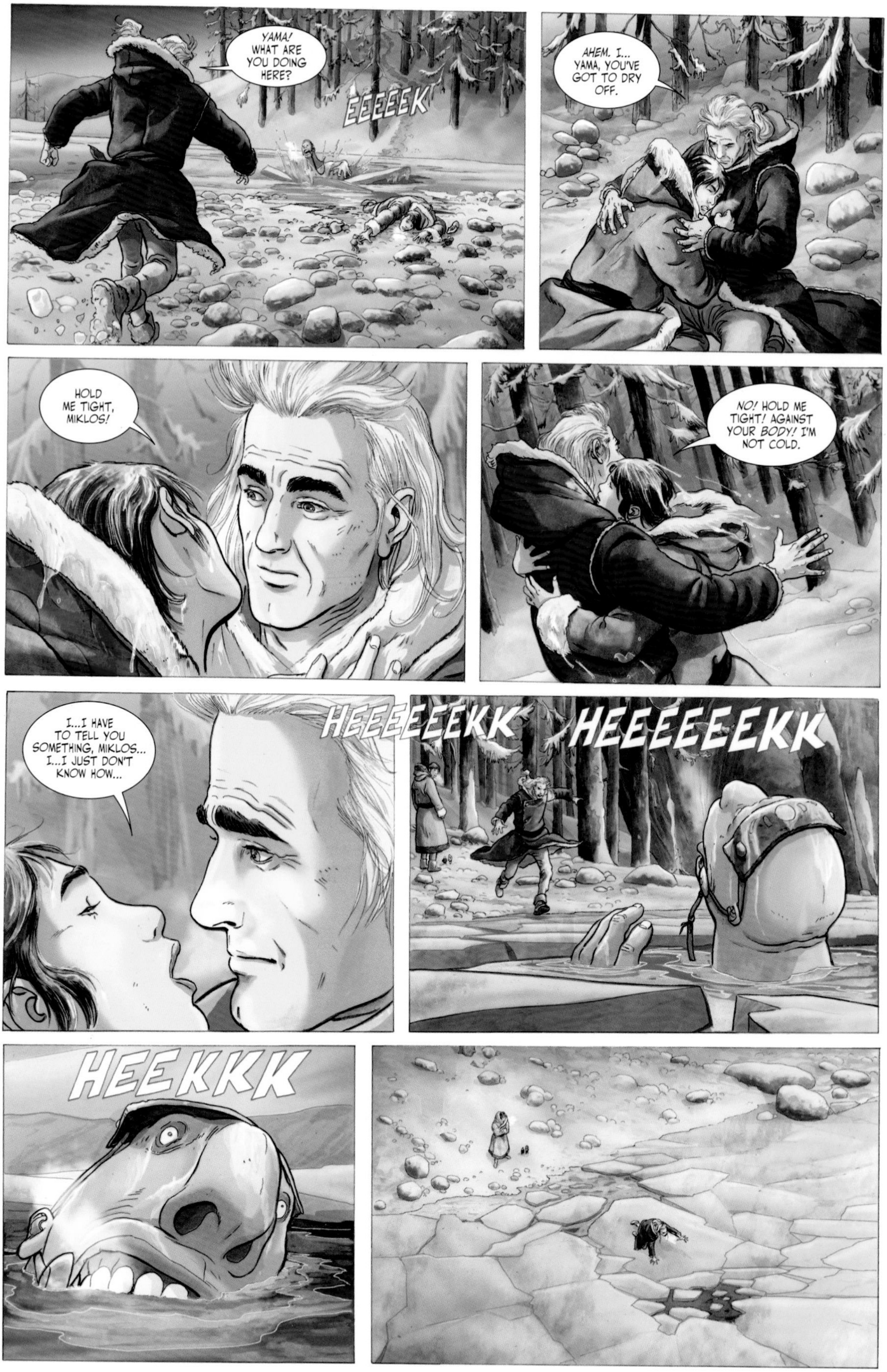
YAMA! WHAT ARE YOU DOING HERE?
EEEEEK
AHEM. I... YAMA, YOU'VE GOT TO DRY OFF.
HOLD ME TIGHT, MIKLOS!
NO! HOLD ME TIGHT! AGAINST YOUR BODY! I'M NOT COLD.
I...I HAVE TO TELL YOU SOMETHING, MIKLOS... I...I JUST DON'T KNOW HOW...
HEEEEEEKK
HEEEEEEKK
HEEKKK

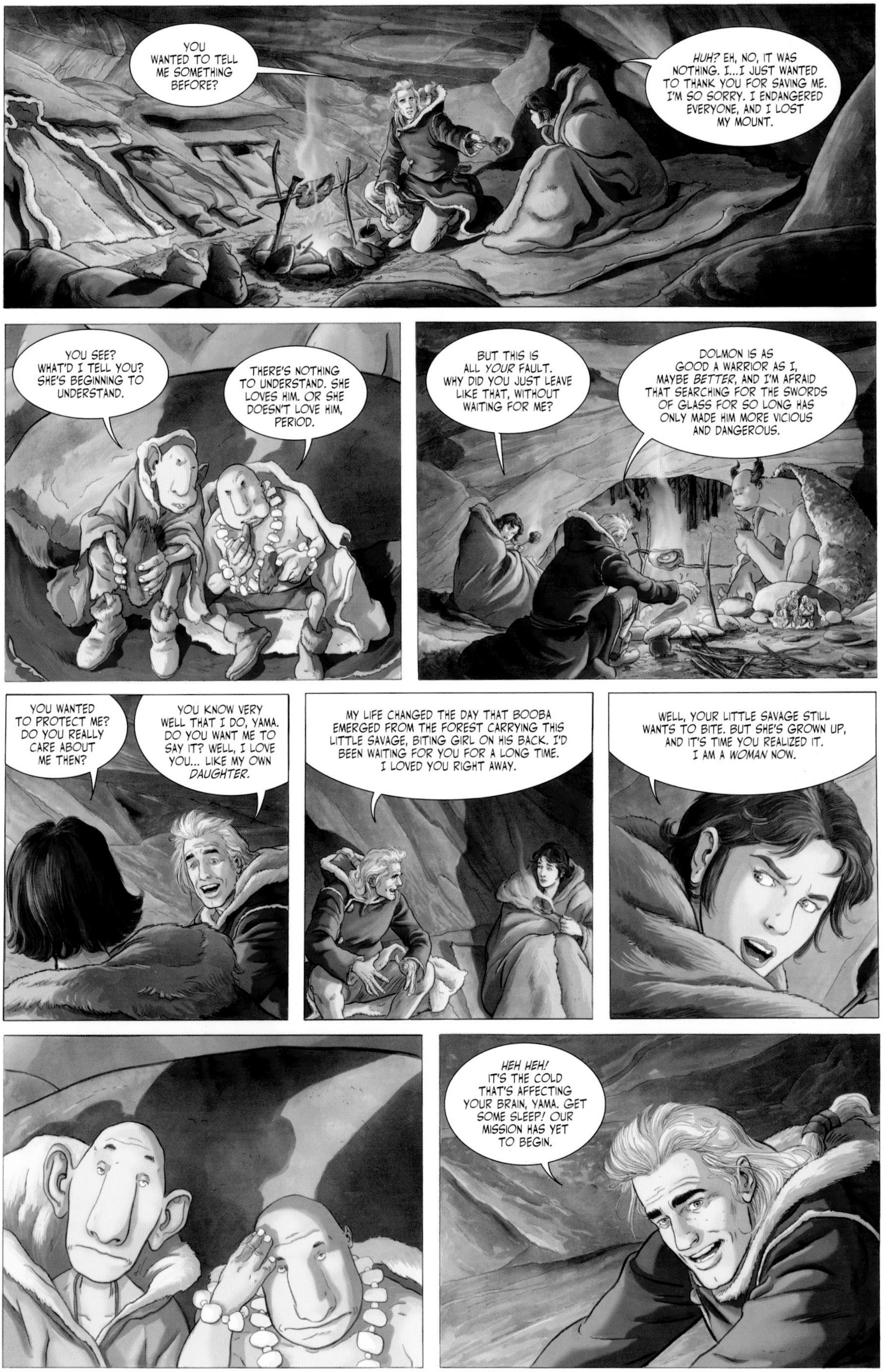
YOU WANTED TO TELL ME SOMETHING BEFORE?
HUH? EH, NO, IT WAS NOTHING. I...I JUST WANTED TO THANK YOU FOR SAVING ME. I'M SO SORRY. I ENDANGERED EVERYONE, AND I LOST MY MOUNT.
YOU SEE? WHAT'D I TELL YOU? SHE'S BEGINNING TO UNDERSTAND.
THERE'S NOTHING TO UNDERSTAND. SHE LOVES HIM. OR SHE DOESN'T LOVE HIM, PERIOD.
BUT THIS IS ALL *YOUR* FAULT. WHY DID YOU JUST LEAVE LIKE THAT, WITHOUT WAITING FOR ME?
DOLMON IS AS GOOD A WARRIOR AS I, MAYBE *BETTER*, AND I'M AFRAID THAT SEARCHING FOR THE SWORDS OF GLASS FOR SO LONG HAS ONLY MADE HIM MORE VICIOUS AND DANGEROUS.
YOU WANTED TO PROTECT ME? DO YOU REALLY CARE ABOUT ME THEN?
YOU KNOW VERY WELL THAT I DO, YAMA. DO YOU WANT ME TO SAY IT? WELL, I LOVE YOU... LIKE MY OWN *DAUGHTER.*
MY LIFE CHANGED THE DAY THAT BOOBA EMERGED FROM THE FOREST CARRYING THIS LITTLE SAVAGE, BITING GIRL ON HIS BACK. I'D BEEN WAITING FOR YOU FOR A LONG TIME. I LOVED YOU RIGHT AWAY.
WELL, YOUR LITTLE SAVAGE STILL WANTS TO BITE. BUT SHE'S GROWN UP, AND IT'S TIME YOU REALIZED IT. I AM A *WOMAN* NOW.
HEH HEH! IT'S THE COLD THAT'S AFFECTING YOUR BRAIN, YAMA. GET SOME SLEEP! OUR MISSION HAS YET TO BEGIN.

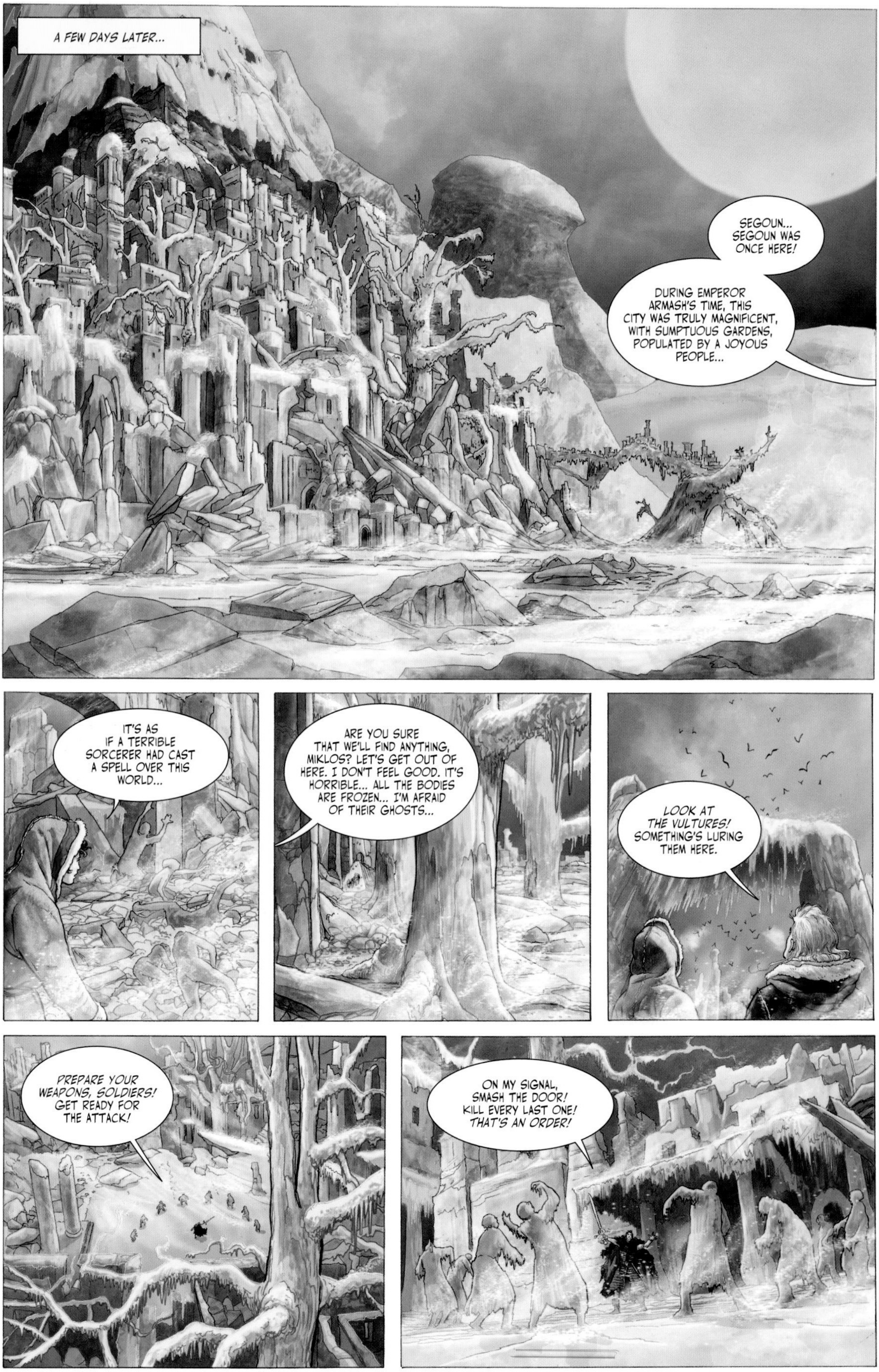
A FEW DAYS LATER...
SEGOUN... SEGOUN WAS ONCE HERE!
DURING EMPEROR ARMASH'S TIME, THIS CITY WAS TRULY MAGNIFICENT, WITH SUMPTUOUS GARDENS, POPULATED BY A JOYOUS PEOPLE...
IT'S AS IF A TERRIBLE SORCERER HAD CAST A SPELL OVER THIS WORLD...
ARE YOU SURE THAT WE'LL FIND ANYTHING, MIKLOS? LET'S GET OUT OF HERE. I DON'T FEEL GOOD. IT'S HORRIBLE... ALL THE BODIES ARE FROZEN... I'M AFRAID OF THEIR GHOSTS...
LOOK AT THE VULTURES! SOMETHING'S LURING THEM HERE.
PREPARE YOUR WEAPONS, SOLDIERS! GET READY FOR THE ATTACK!
ON MY SIGNAL, SMASH THE DOOR! KILL EVERY LAST ONE! THAT'S AN ORDER!

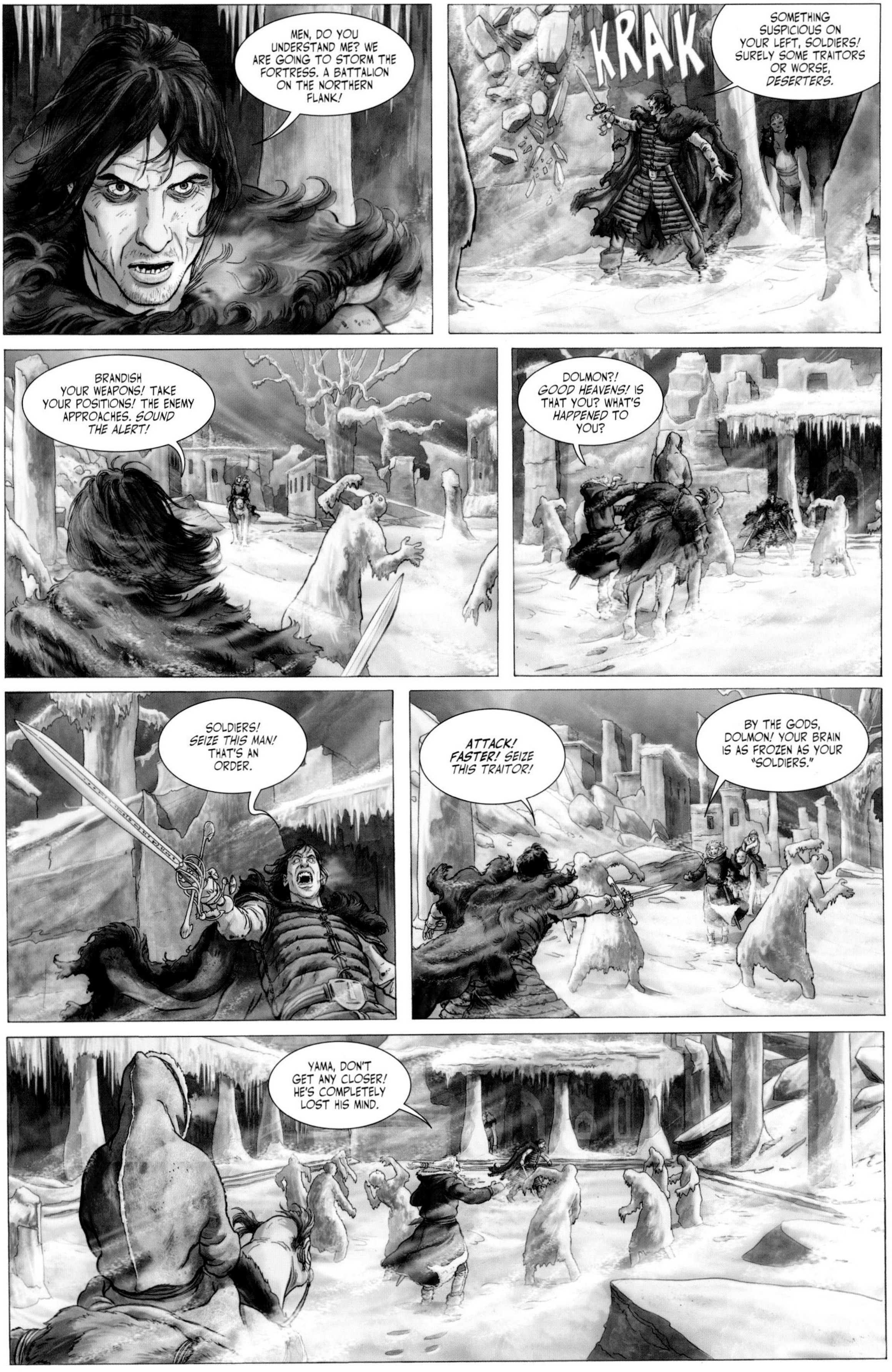
MEN, DO YOU UNDERSTAND ME? WE ARE GOING TO STORM THE FORTRESS. A BATTALION ON THE NORTHERN FLANK!
KRAK
SOMETHING SUSPICIOUS ON YOUR LEFT, SOLDIERS! SURELY SOME TRAITORS OR WORSE, DESERTERS.
BRANDISH YOUR WEAPONS! TAKE YOUR POSITIONS! THE ENEMY APPROACHES. SOUND THE ALERT!
DOLMON?! GOOD HEAVENS! IS THAT YOU? WHAT'S HAPPENED TO YOU?
SOLDIERS! SEIZE THIS MAN! THAT'S AN ORDER.
ATTACK! FASTER! SEIZE THIS TRAITOR!
BY THE GODS, DOLMON! YOUR BRAIN IS AS FROZEN AS YOUR "SOLDIERS."
YAMA, DON'T GET ANY CLOSER! HE'S COMPLETELY LOST HIS MIND.

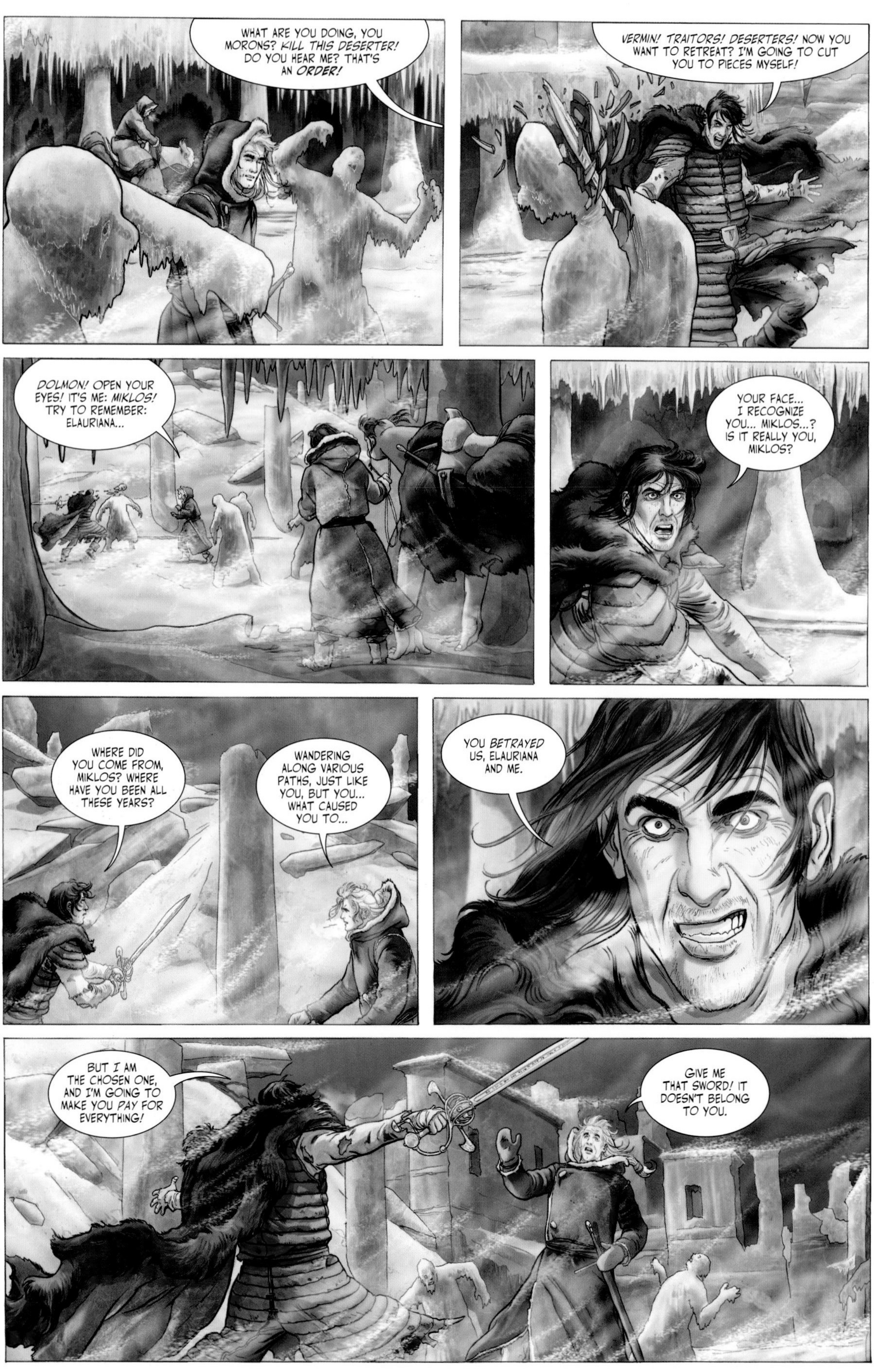
WHAT ARE YOU DOING, YOU MORONS? *KILL THIS DESERTER!* DO YOU HEAR ME? THAT'S AN *ORDER!*
VERMIN! TRAITORS! DESERTERS! NOW YOU WANT TO RETREAT? I'M GOING TO CUT YOU TO PIECES MYSELF!
DOLMON! OPEN YOUR EYES! IT'S ME: *MIKLOS!* TRY TO REMEMBER: ELAURIANA...
YOUR FACE... I RECOGNIZE YOU... MIKLOS...? IS IT REALLY YOU, MIKLOS?
WHERE DID YOU COME FROM, MIKLOS? WHERE HAVE YOU BEEN ALL THESE YEARS?
WANDERING ALONG VARIOUS PATHS, JUST LIKE YOU, BUT YOU... WHAT CAUSED YOU TO...
YOU *BETRAYED* US, ELAURIANA AND ME.
BUT I AM THE CHOSEN ONE, AND I'M GOING TO MAKE YOU *PAY* FOR EVERYTHING!
GIVE ME THAT SWORD! IT DOESN'T BELONG TO YOU.

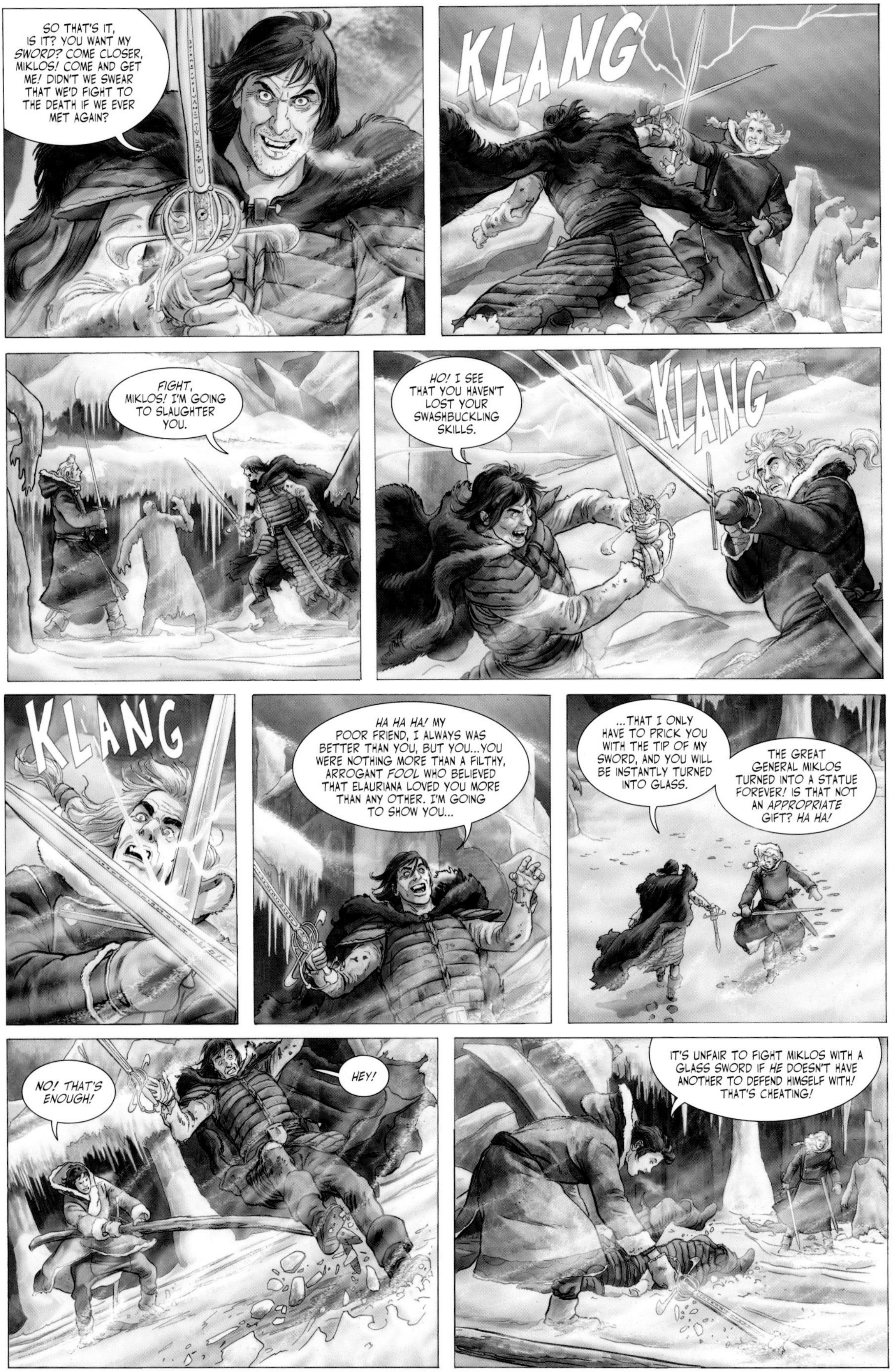

SO THAT'S IT, IS IT? YOU WANT MY *SWORD?* COME CLOSER, MIKLOS! COME AND GET ME! DIDN'T WE SWEAR THAT WE'D FIGHT TO THE DEATH IF WE EVER MET AGAIN?
KLANG
FIGHT, MIKLOS! I'M GOING TO SLAUGHTER YOU.
HO! I SEE THAT YOU HAVEN'T LOST YOUR SWASHBUCKLING SKILLS.
KLANG
KLANG
HA HA HA! MY POOR FRIEND, I ALWAYS WAS BETTER THAN YOU, BUT YOU...YOU WERE NOTHING MORE THAN A FILTHY, ARROGANT *FOOL* WHO BELIEVED THAT ELAURIANA LOVED YOU MORE THAN ANY OTHER. I'M GOING TO SHOW YOU...
...THAT I ONLY HAVE TO PRICK YOU WITH THE TIP OF MY SWORD, AND YOU WILL BE INSTANTLY TURNED INTO GLASS.
THE GREAT GENERAL MIKLOS TURNED INTO A STATUE FOREVER! IS THAT NOT AN *APPROPRIATE* GIFT? *HA HA!*
NO! THAT'S ENOUGH!
HEY!
IT'S UNFAIR TO FIGHT MIKLOS WITH A GLASS SWORD IF *HE* DOESN'T HAVE ANOTHER TO DEFEND HIMSELF WITH! THAT'S CHEATING!

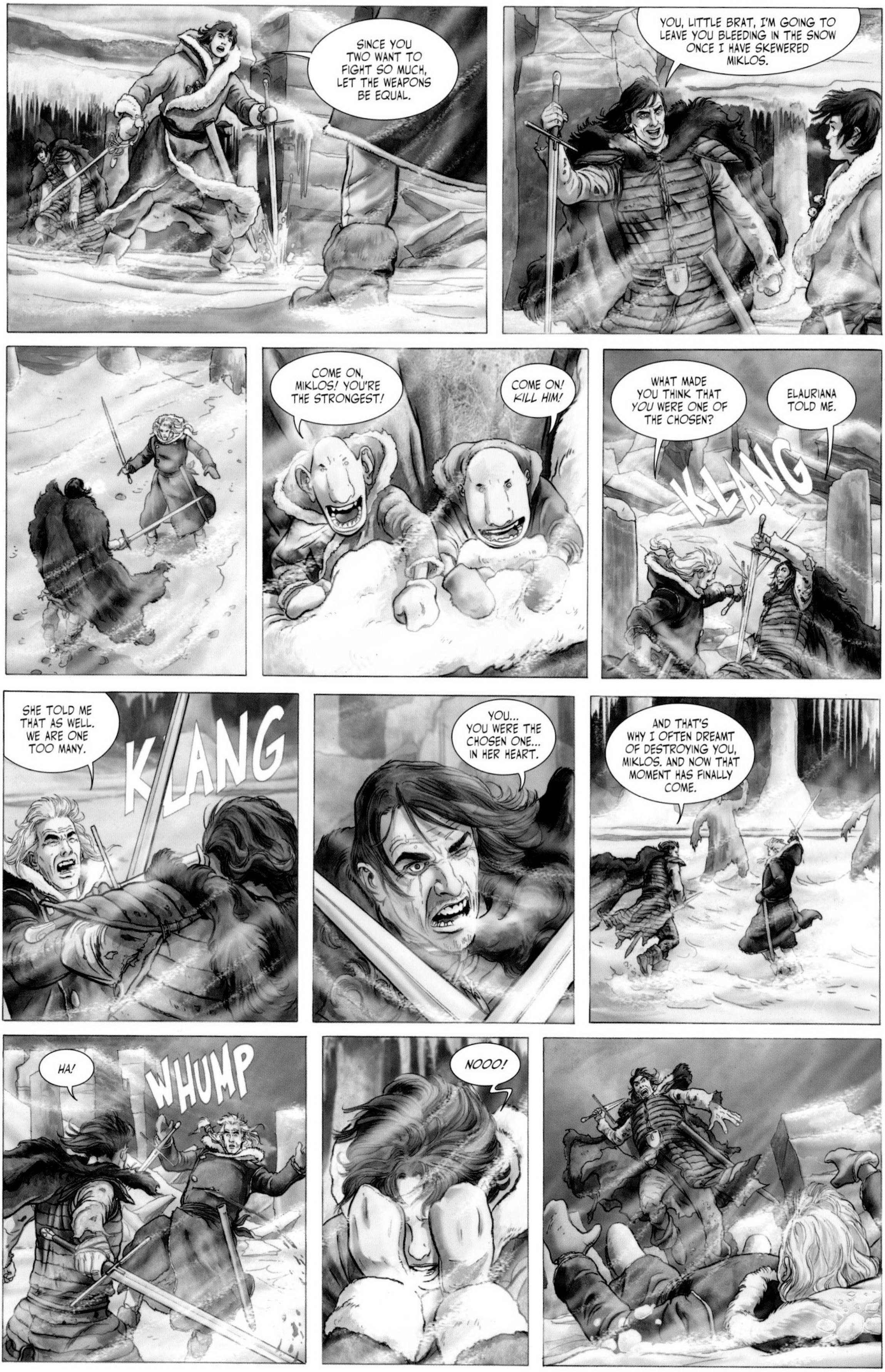
SINCE YOU TWO WANT TO FIGHT SO MUCH, LET THE WEAPONS BE EQUAL.
YOU, LITTLE BRAT, I'M GOING TO LEAVE YOU BLEEDING IN THE SNOW ONCE I HAVE SKEWERED MIKLOS.
COME ON, MIKLOS! YOU'RE THE STRONGEST!
COME ON! KILL HIM!
WHAT MADE YOU THINK THAT YOU WERE ONE OF THE CHOSEN?
ELAURIANA TOLD ME.
KLANG
SHE TOLD ME THAT AS WELL. WE ARE ONE TOO MANY.
KLANG
YOU... YOU WERE THE CHOSEN ONE... IN HER HEART.
AND THAT'S WHY I OFTEN DREAMT OF DESTROYING YOU, MIKLOS. AND NOW THAT MOMENT HAS FINALLY COME.
HA!
WHUMP
NOOO!

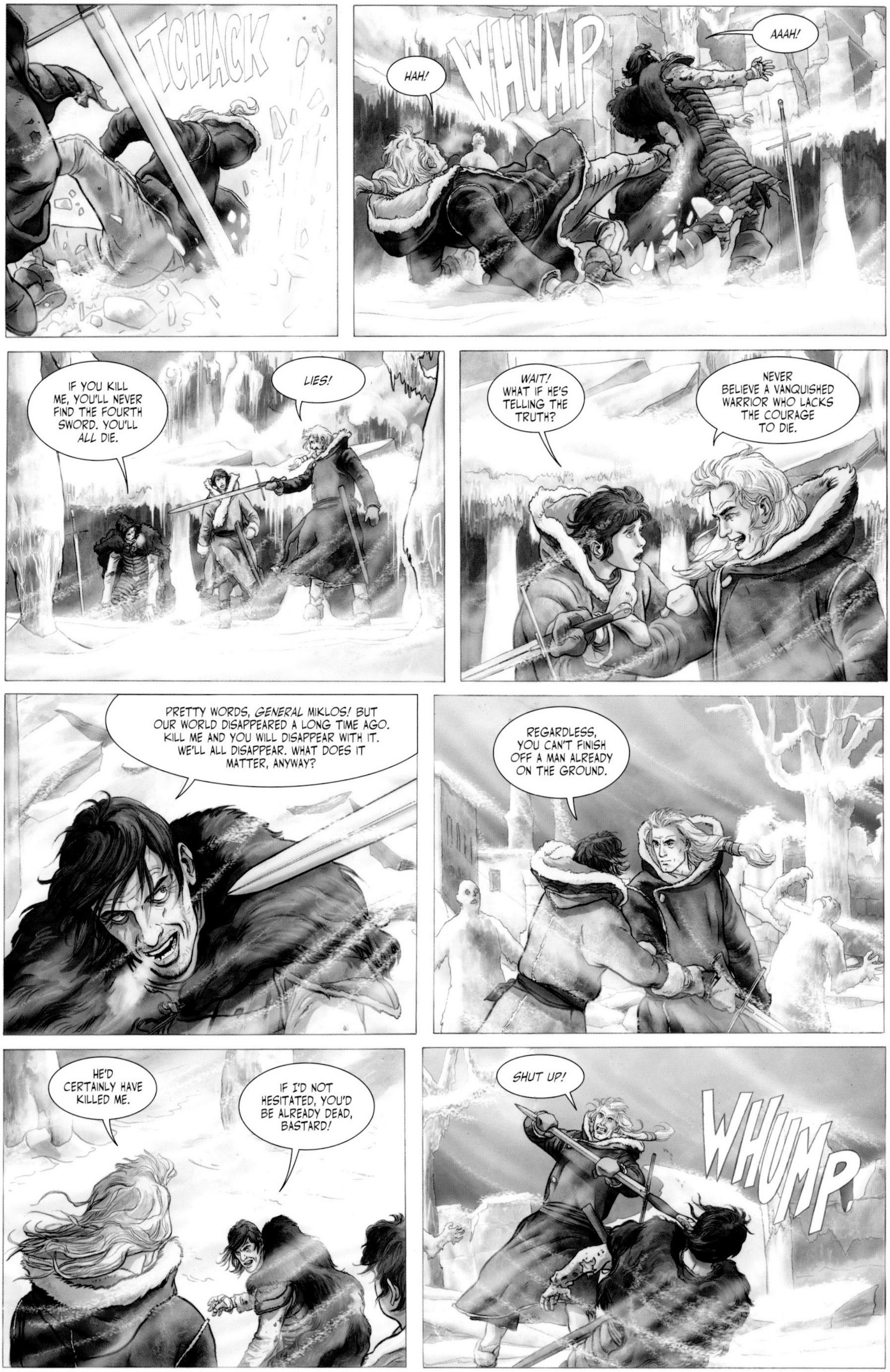
TCHACK
HAH!
WHUMP
AAAH!
IF YOU KILL ME, YOU'LL NEVER FIND THE FOURTH SWORD. YOU'LL ALL DIE.
LIES!
WAIT! WHAT IF HE'S TELLING THE TRUTH?
NEVER BELIEVE A VANQUISHED WARRIOR WHO LACKS THE COURAGE TO DIE.
PRETTY WORDS, GENERAL MIKLOS! BUT OUR WORLD DISAPPEARED A LONG TIME AGO. KILL ME AND YOU WILL DISAPPEAR WITH IT. WE'LL ALL DISAPPEAR. WHAT DOES IT MATTER, ANYWAY?
REGARDLESS, YOU CAN'T FINISH OFF A MAN ALREADY ON THE GROUND.
HE'D CERTAINLY HAVE KILLED ME.
IF I'D NOT HESITATED, YOU'D BE ALREADY DEAD, BASTARD!
SHUT UP!
WHUMP

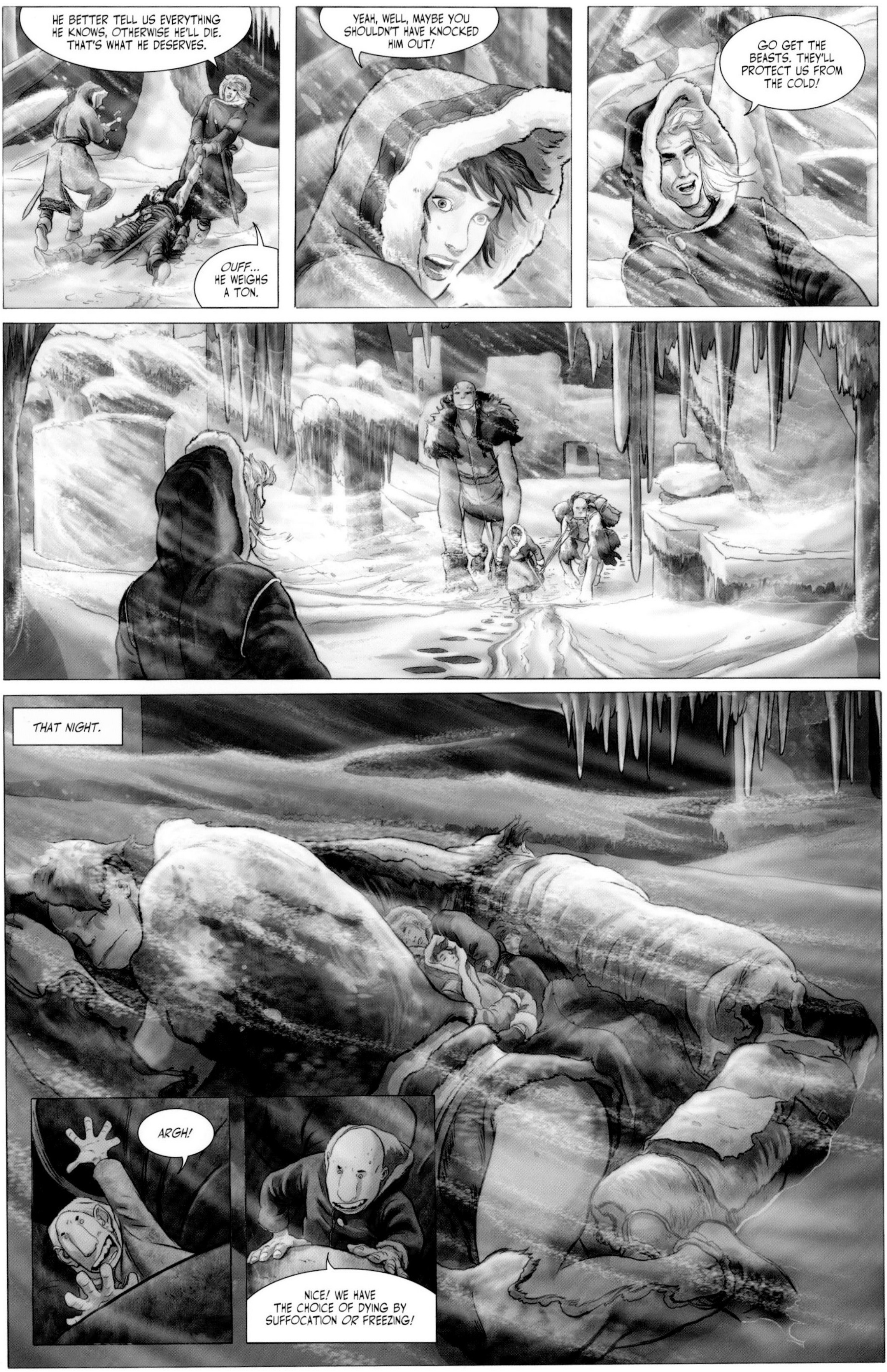

HE BETTER TELL US EVERYTHING HE KNOWS, OTHERWISE HE'LL DIE. THAT'S WHAT HE DESERVES.
OUFF... HE WEIGHS A TON.
YEAH, WELL, MAYBE YOU SHOULDN'T HAVE KNOCKED HIM OUT!
GO GET THE BEASTS. THEY'LL PROTECT US FROM THE COLD!
THAT NIGHT.
ARGH!
NICE! WE HAVE THE CHOICE OF DYING BY SUFFOCATION OR FREEZING!

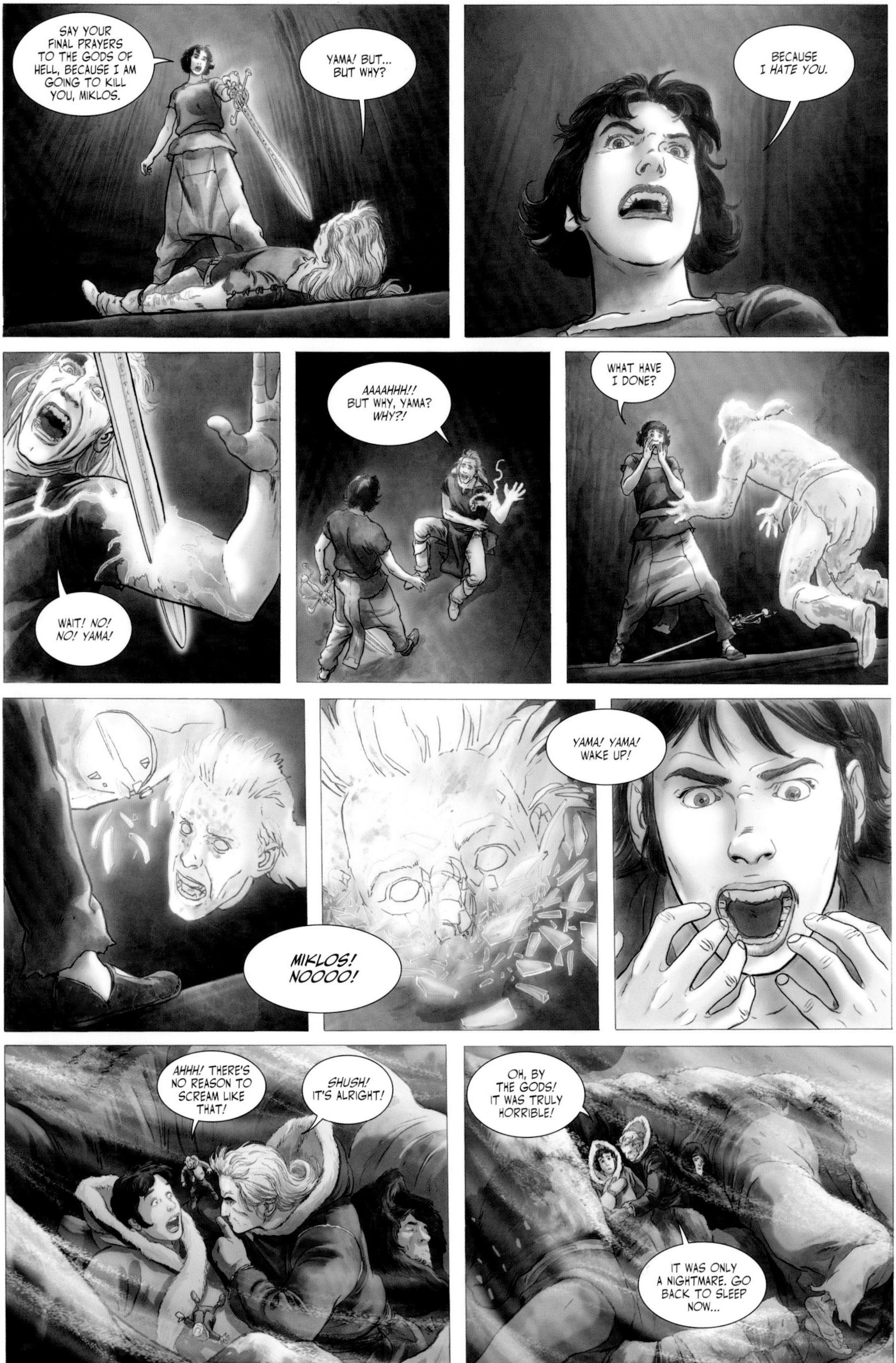
SAY YOUR FINAL PRAYERS TO THE GODS OF HELL, BECAUSE I AM GOING TO KILL YOU, MIKLOS.
YAMA! BUT... BUT WHY?
BECAUSE I HATE YOU.
WAIT! NO! NO! YAMA!
AAAAHHH!! BUT WHY, YAMA? WHY?!
WHAT HAVE I DONE?
MIKLOS! NOOOO!
YAMA! YAMA! WAKE UP!
AHHH! THERE'S NO REASON TO SCREAM LIKE THAT!
SHUSH! IT'S ALRIGHT!
OH, BY THE GODS! IT WAS TRULY HORRIBLE!
IT WAS ONLY A NIGHTMARE. GO BACK TO SLEEP NOW...

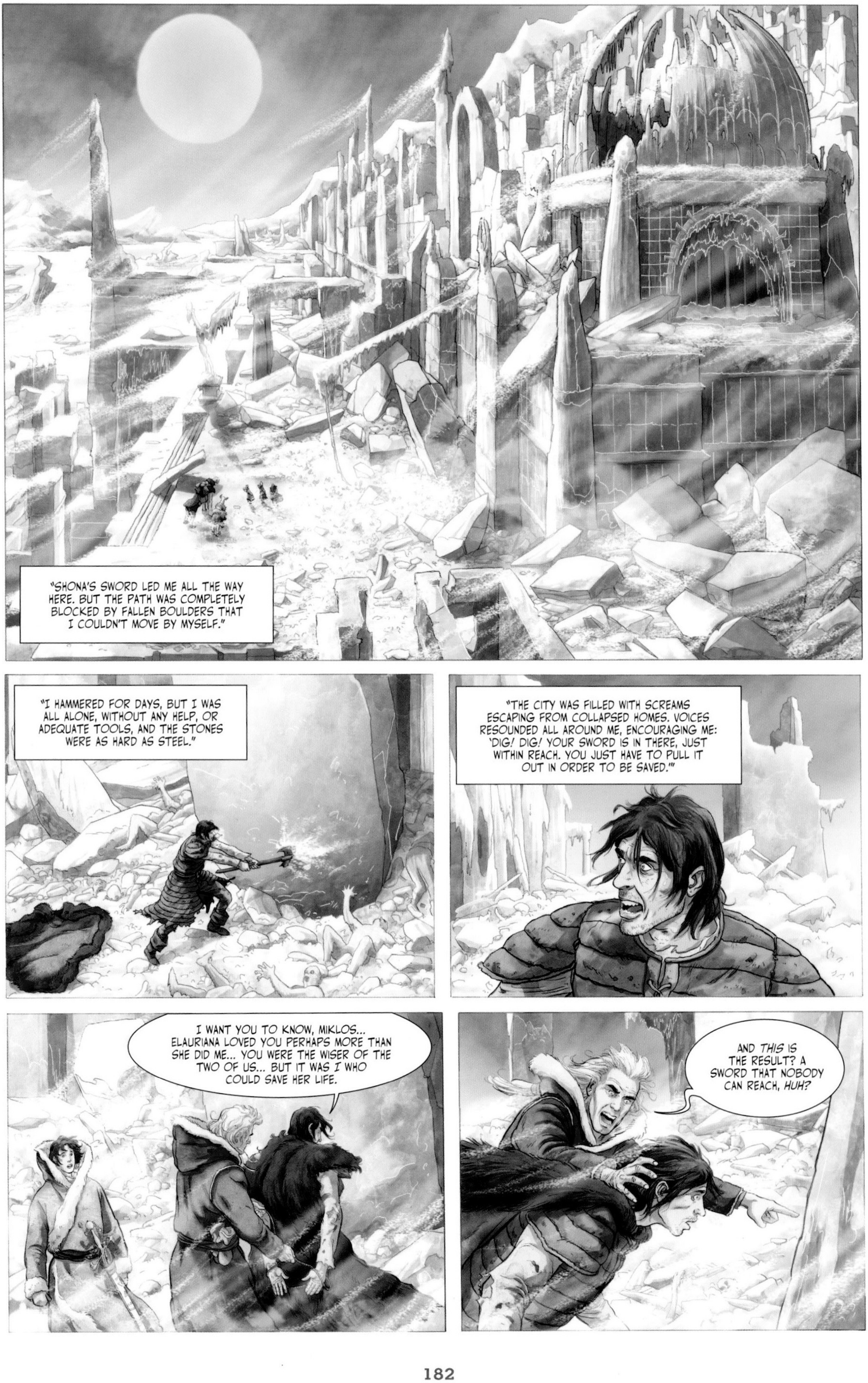
"SHONA'S SWORD LED ME ALL THE WAY HERE. BUT THE PATH WAS COMPLETELY BLOCKED BY FALLEN BOULDERS THAT I COULDN'T MOVE BY MYSELF."
"I HAMMERED FOR DAYS, BUT I WAS ALL ALONE, WITHOUT ANY HELP, OR ADEQUATE TOOLS, AND THE STONES WERE AS HARD AS STEEL."
"THE CITY WAS FILLED WITH SCREAMS ESCAPING FROM COLLAPSED HOMES. VOICES RESOUNDED ALL AROUND ME, ENCOURAGING ME: 'DIG! DIG! YOUR SWORD IS IN THERE, JUST WITHIN REACH. YOU JUST HAVE TO PULL IT OUT IN ORDER TO BE SAVED.'"
I WANT YOU TO KNOW, MIKLOS... ELAURIANA LOVED YOU PERHAPS MORE THAN SHE DID ME... YOU WERE THE WISER OF THE TWO OF US... BUT IT WAS *I* WHO COULD SAVE HER LIFE.
AND *THIS* IS THE RESULT? A SWORD THAT NOBODY CAN REACH, *HUH?*

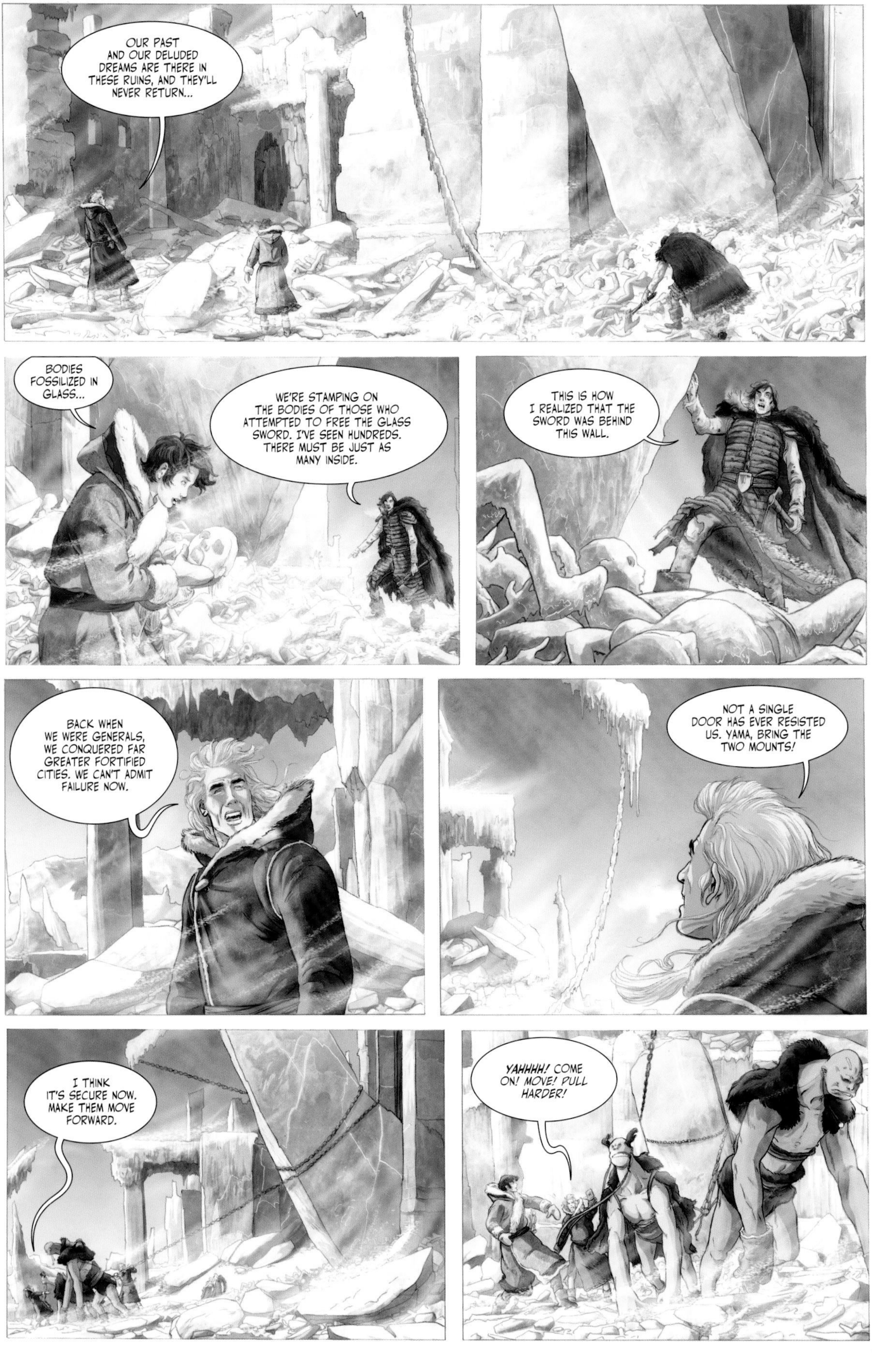
OUR PAST AND OUR DELUDED DREAMS ARE THERE IN THESE RUINS, AND THEY'LL NEVER RETURN...
BODIES FOSSILIZED IN GLASS...
WE'RE STAMPING ON THE BODIES OF THOSE WHO ATTEMPTED TO FREE THE GLASS SWORD. I'VE SEEN HUNDREDS. THERE MUST BE JUST AS MANY INSIDE.
THIS IS HOW I REALIZED THAT THE SWORD WAS BEHIND THIS WALL.
BACK WHEN WE WERE GENERALS, WE CONQUERED FAR GREATER FORTIFIED CITIES. WE CAN'T ADMIT FAILURE NOW.
NOT A SINGLE DOOR HAS EVER RESISTED US. YAMA, BRING THE TWO MOUNTS!
I THINK IT'S SECURE NOW. MAKE THEM MOVE FORWARD.
YAHHHH! COME ON! MOVE! PULL HARDER!

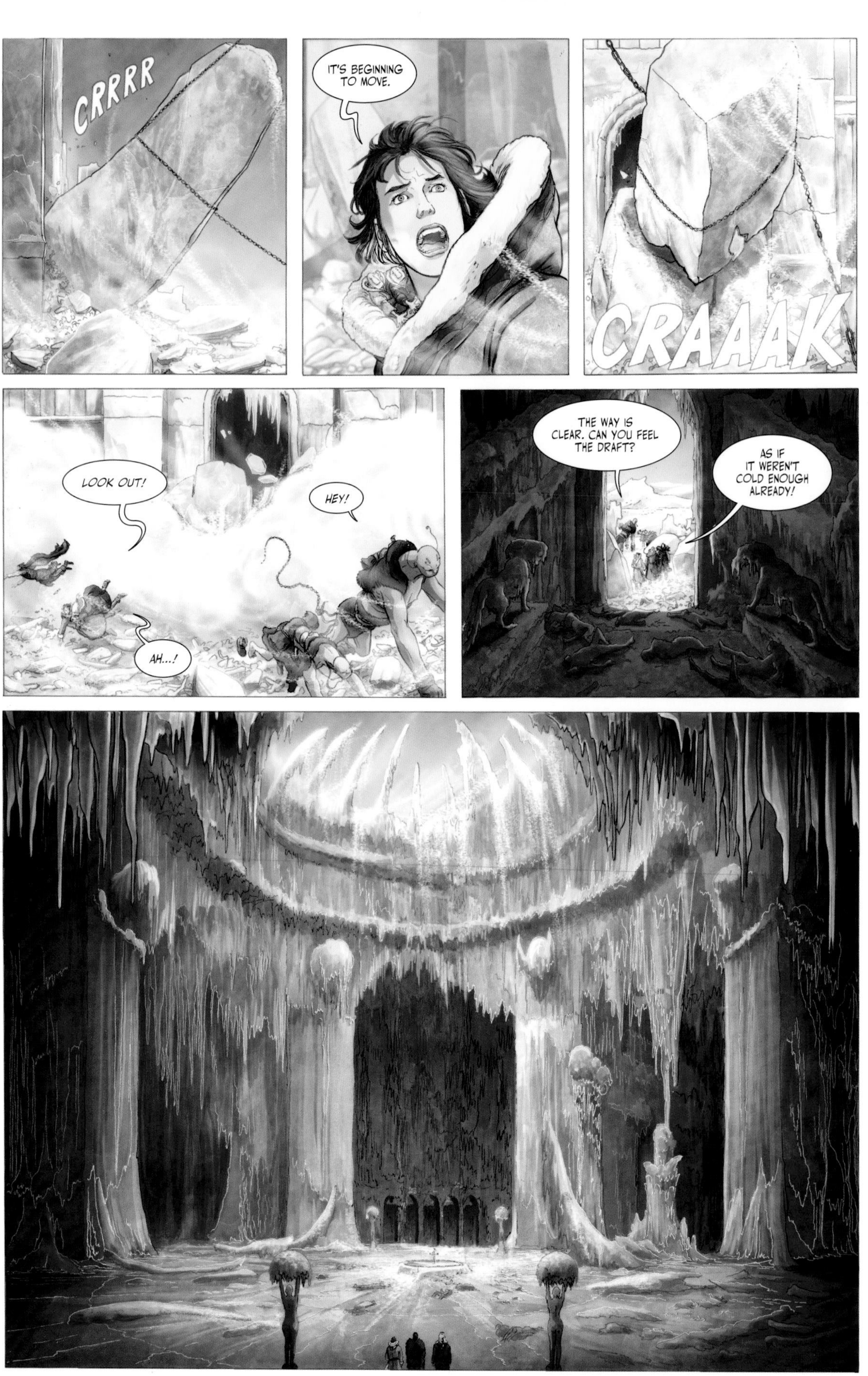
CRRRR
IT'S BEGINNING TO MOVE.
CRAAAK
LOOK OUT!
HEY!
AH...!
THE WAY IS CLEAR. CAN YOU FEEL THE DRAFT?
AS IF IT WEREN'T COLD ENOUGH ALREADY!

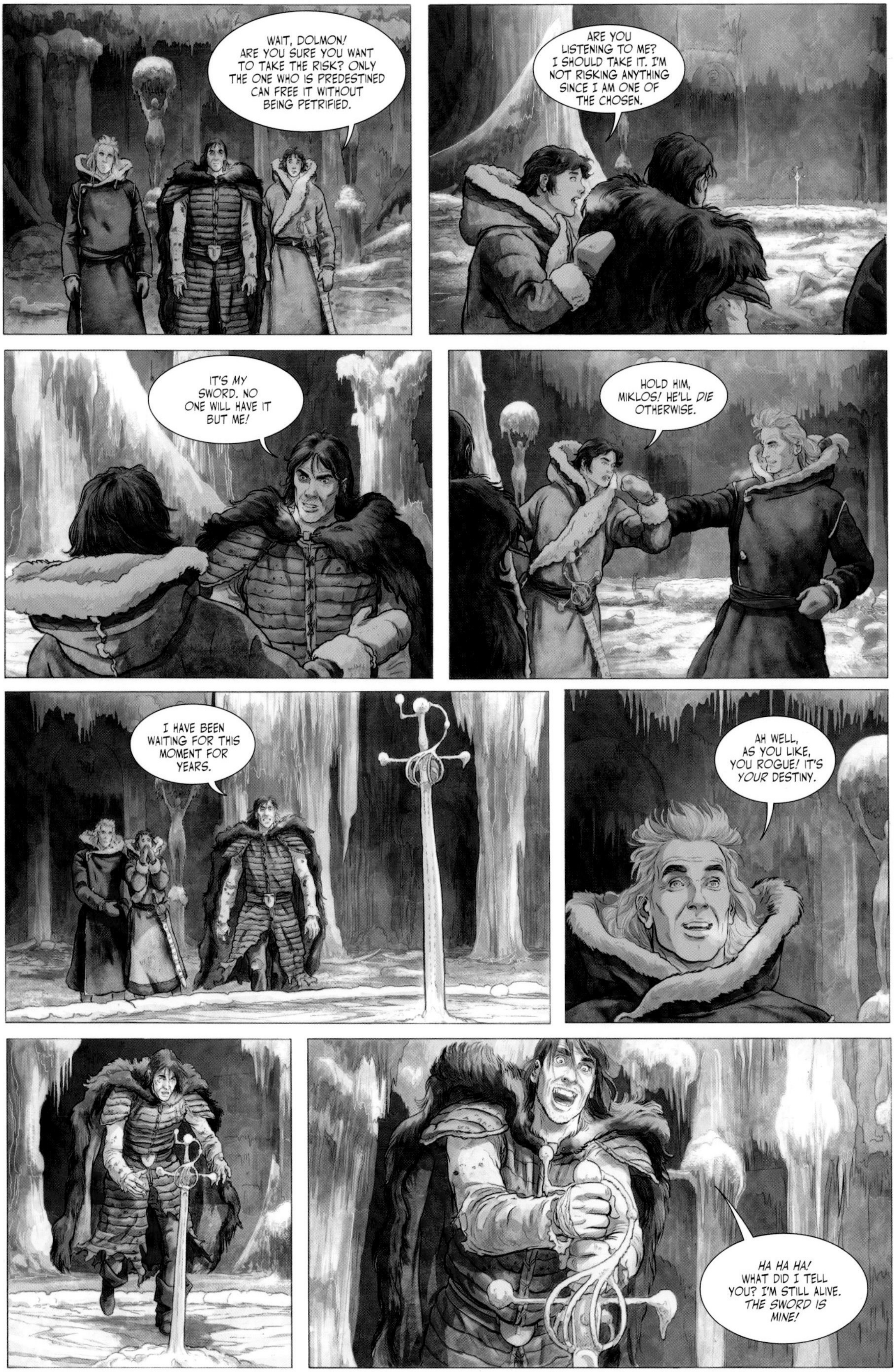
WAIT, DOLMON! ARE YOU SURE YOU WANT TO TAKE THE RISK? ONLY THE ONE WHO IS PREDESTINED CAN FREE IT WITHOUT BEING PETRIFIED.
ARE YOU LISTENING TO ME? I SHOULD TAKE IT. I'M NOT RISKING ANYTHING SINCE I AM ONE OF THE CHOSEN.
IT'S MY SWORD. NO ONE WILL HAVE IT BUT ME!
HOLD HIM, MIKLOS! HE'LL *DIE* OTHERWISE.
I HAVE BEEN WAITING FOR THIS MOMENT FOR YEARS.
AH WELL, AS YOU LIKE, YOU ROGUE! IT'S *YOUR* DESTINY.
HA HA HA! WHAT DID I TELL YOU? I'M STILL ALIVE. *THE SWORD IS MINE!*

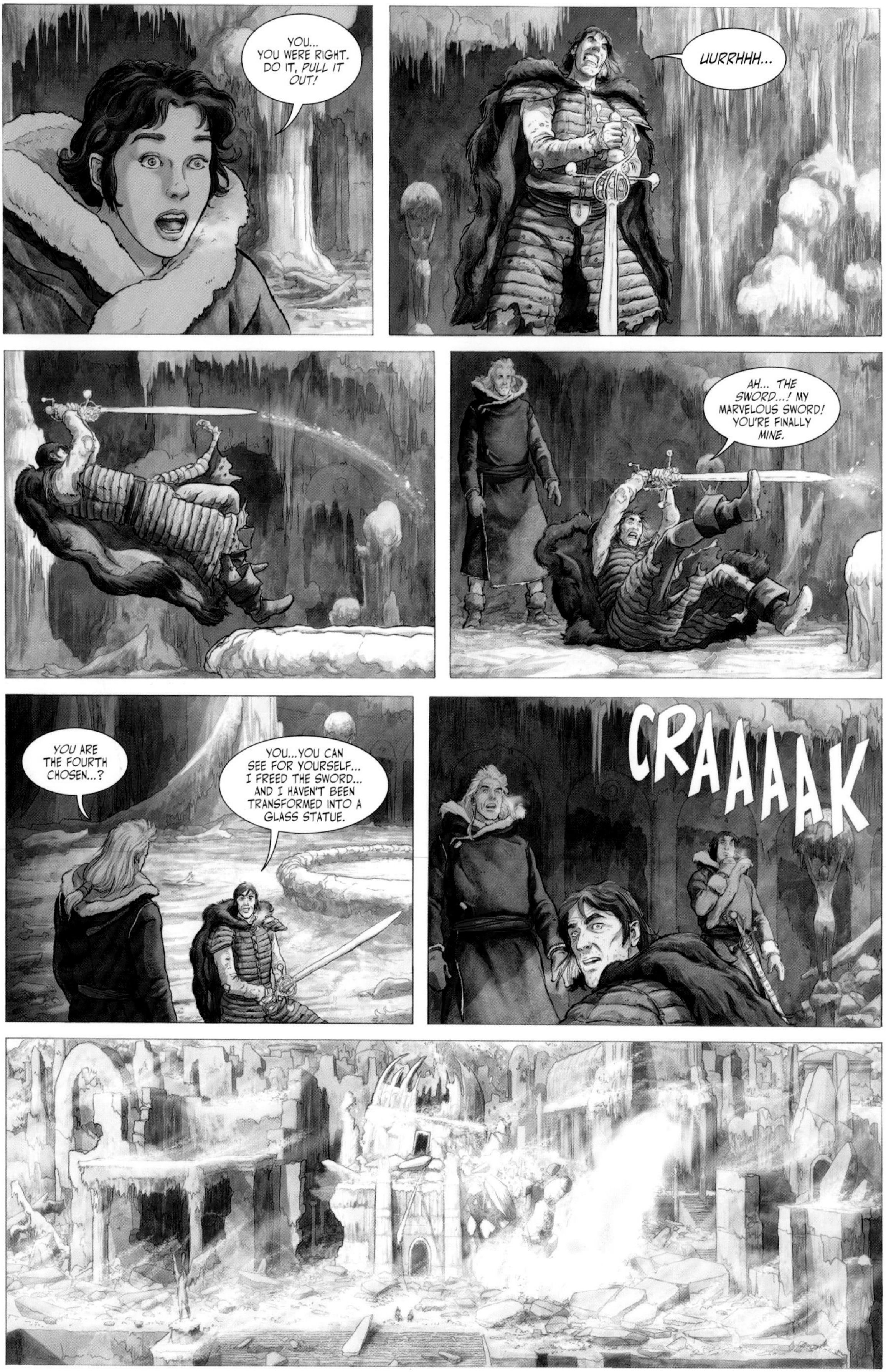
YOU... YOU WERE RIGHT. DO IT, PULL IT OUT!
UURRHHH...
AH... THE SWORD...! MY MARVELOUS SWORD! YOU'RE FINALLY MINE.
YOU ARE THE FOURTH CHOSEN...?
YOU...YOU CAN SEE FOR YOURSELF... I FREED THE SWORD... AND I HAVEN'T BEEN TRANSFORMED INTO A GLASS STATUE.
CRAAAAK

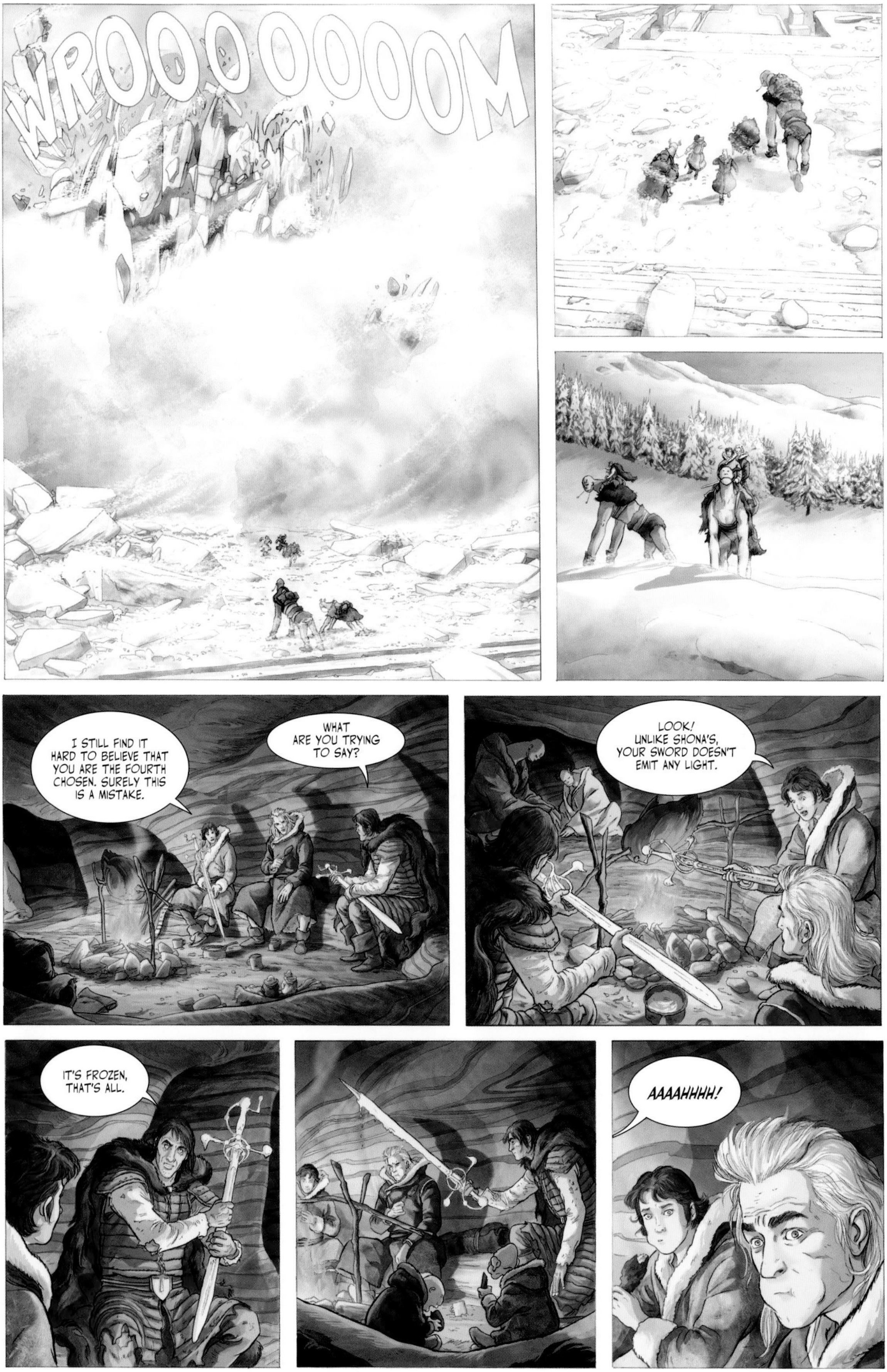
WROOOOOOOM
I STILL FIND IT HARD TO BELIEVE THAT YOU ARE THE FOURTH CHOSEN. SURELY THIS IS A MISTAKE.
WHAT ARE YOU TRYING TO SAY?
LOOK! UNLIKE SHONA'S, YOUR SWORD DOESN'T EMIT ANY LIGHT.
IT'S FROZEN, THAT'S ALL.
AAAAHHHH!

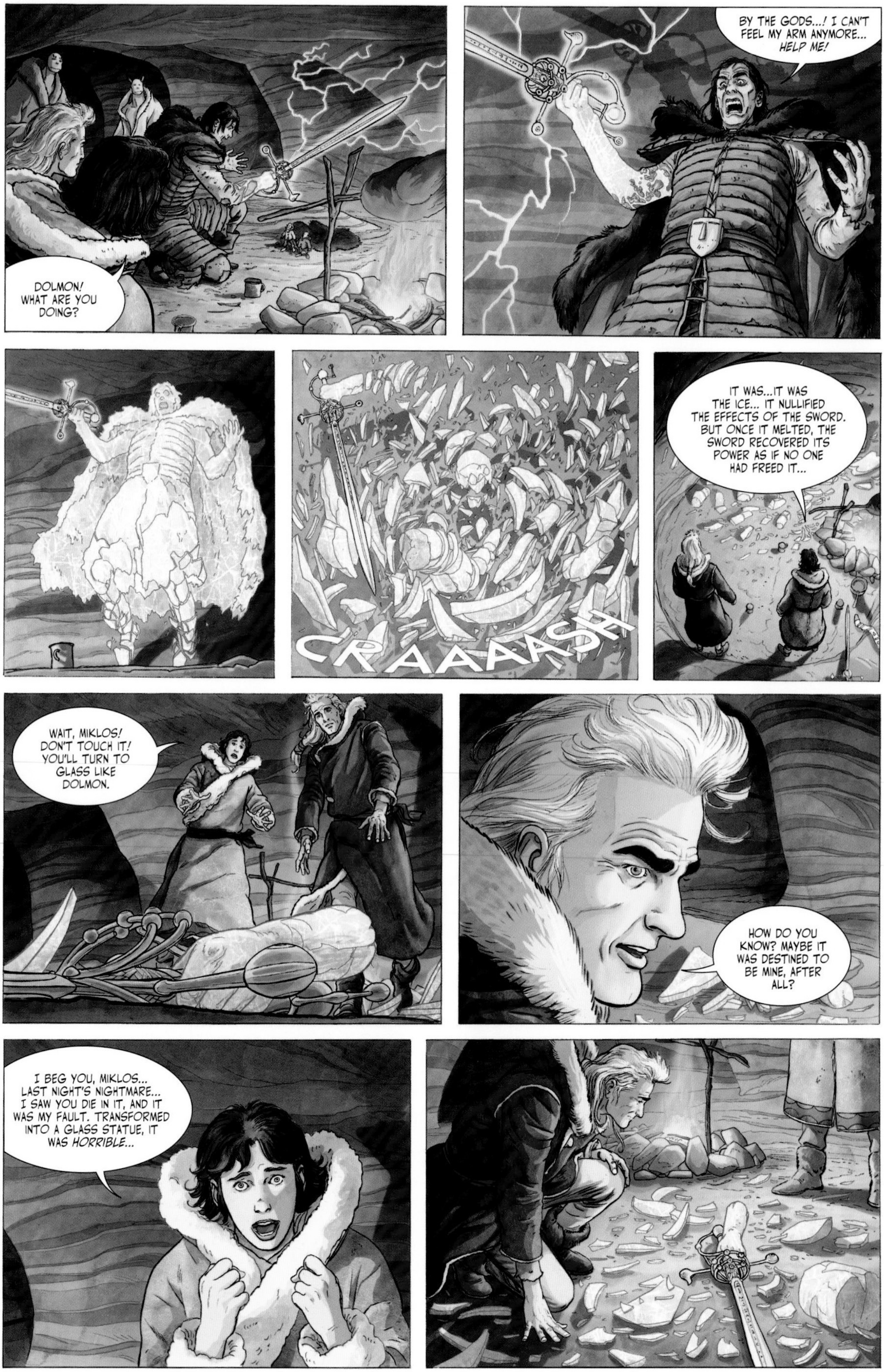
DOLMON! WHAT ARE YOU DOING?
BY THE GODS...! I CAN'T FEEL MY ARM ANYMORE... HELP ME!
CRAAAASH
IT WAS...IT WAS THE ICE... IT NULLIFIED THE EFFECTS OF THE SWORD. BUT ONCE IT MELTED, THE SWORD RECOVERED ITS POWER AS IF NO ONE HAD FREED IT...
WAIT, MIKLOS! DON'T TOUCH IT! YOU'LL TURN TO GLASS LIKE DOLMON.
HOW DO YOU KNOW? MAYBE IT WAS DESTINED TO BE MINE, AFTER ALL?
I BEG YOU, MIKLOS... LAST NIGHT'S NIGHTMARE... I SAW YOU DIE IN IT, AND IT WAS MY FAULT. TRANSFORMED INTO A GLASS STATUE, IT WAS HORRIBLE...

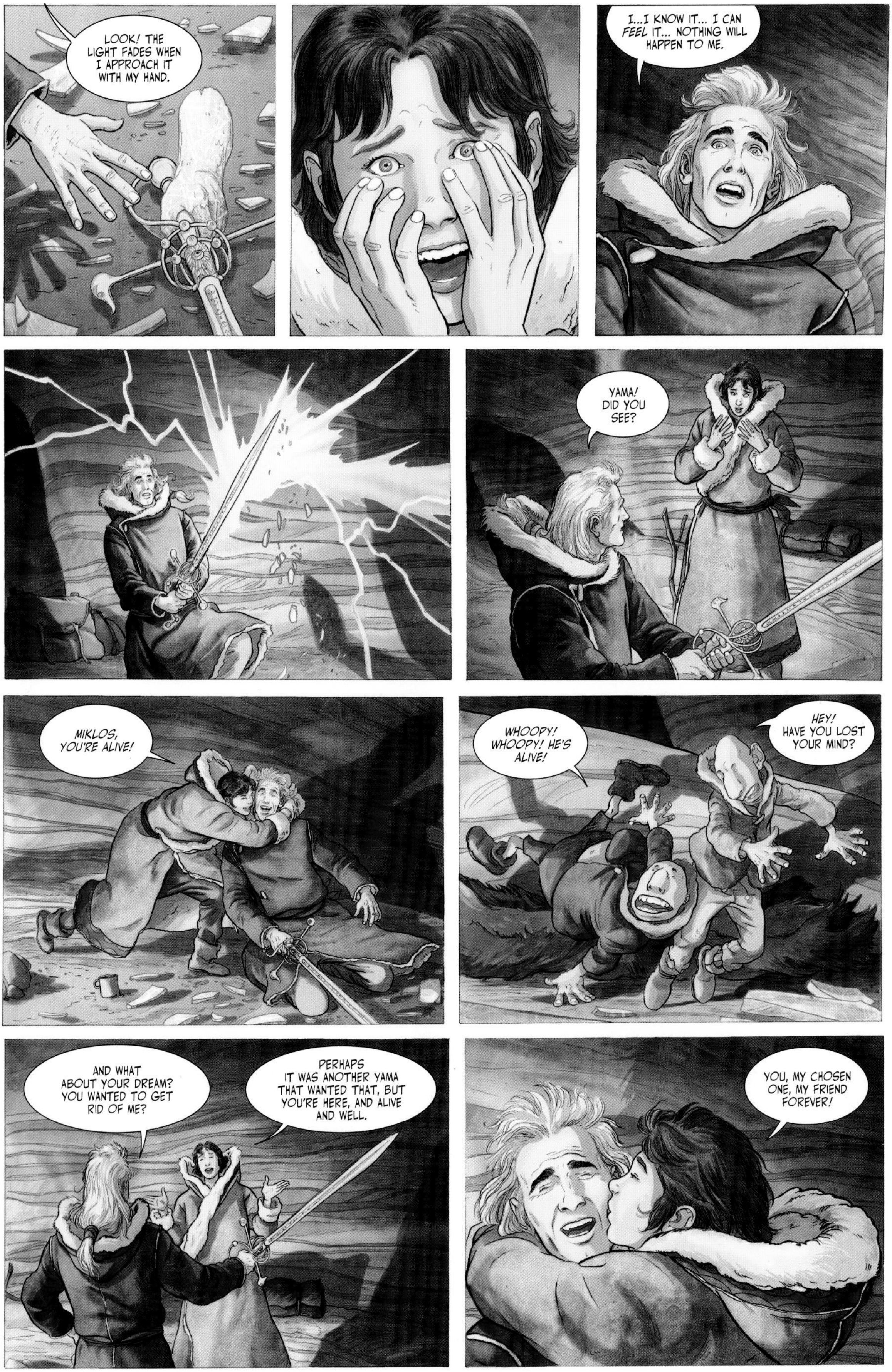
LOOK! THE LIGHT FADES WHEN I APPROACH IT WITH MY HAND.
I...I KNOW IT... I CAN FEEL IT... NOTHING WILL HAPPEN TO ME.
YAMA! DID YOU SEE?
MIKLOS, YOU'RE ALIVE!
WHOOPY! WHOOPY! HE'S ALIVE!
HEY! HAVE YOU LOST YOUR MIND?
AND WHAT ABOUT YOUR DREAM? YOU WANTED TO GET RID OF ME?
PERHAPS IT WAS ANOTHER YAMA THAT WANTED THAT, BUT YOU'RE HERE, AND ALIVE AND WELL.
YOU, MY CHOSEN ONE, MY FRIEND FOREVER!

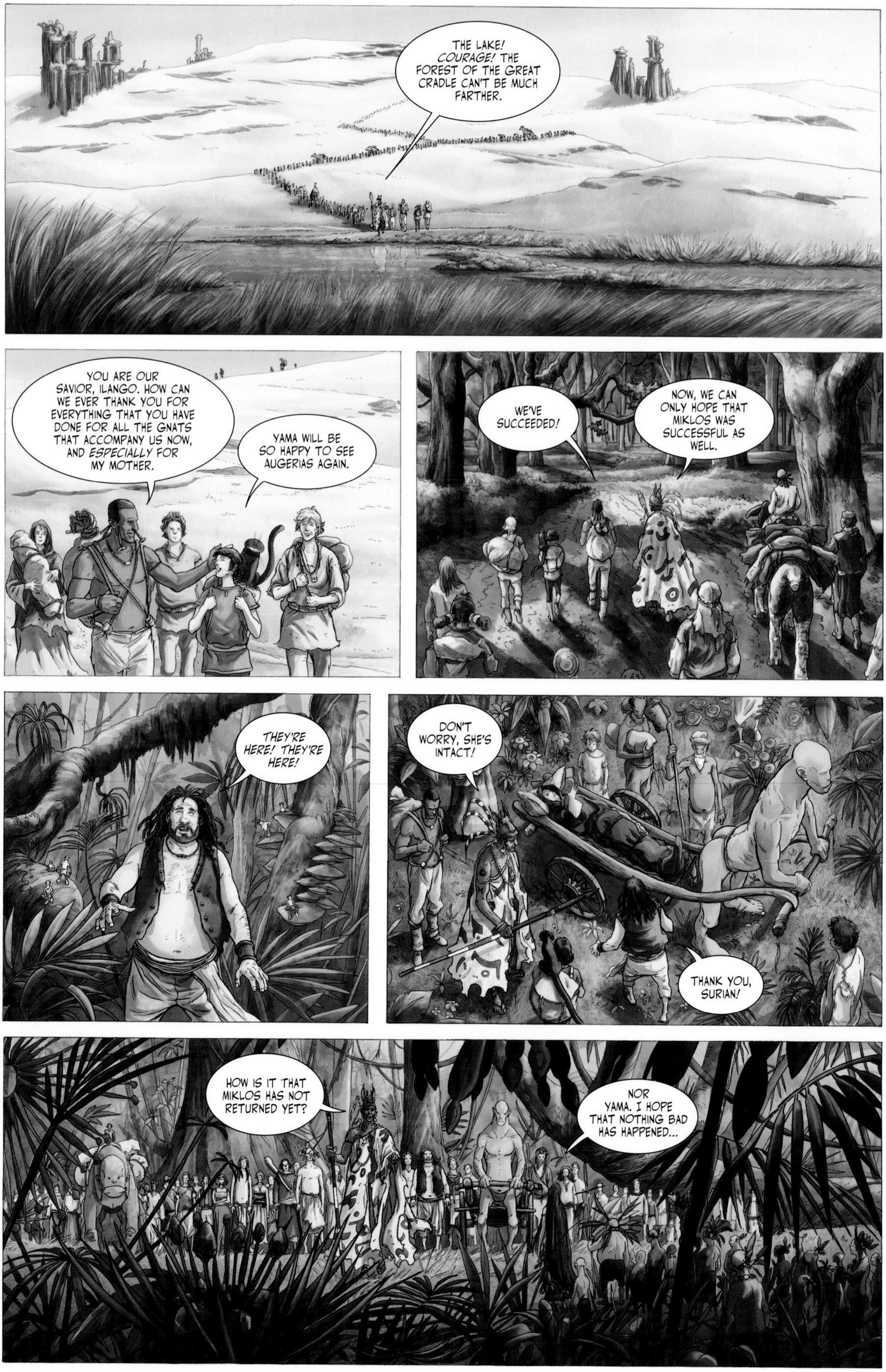
THE LAKE! *COURAGE!* THE FOREST OF THE GREAT CRADLE CAN'T BE MUCH FARTHER.
YOU ARE OUR SAVIOR, ILANGO. HOW CAN WE EVER THANK YOU FOR EVERYTHING THAT YOU HAVE DONE FOR ALL THE GNATS THAT ACCOMPANY US NOW, AND *ESPECIALLY* FOR MY MOTHER.
YAMA WILL BE SO HAPPY TO SEE AUGERIAS AGAIN.
WE'VE SUCCEEDED!
NOW, WE CAN ONLY HOPE THAT MIKLOS WAS SUCCESSFUL AS WELL.
THEY'RE HERE! THEY'RE HERE!
DON'T WORRY, SHE'S INTACT!
THANK YOU, SURIAN!
HOW IS IT THAT MIKLOS HAS NOT RETURNED YET?
NOR YAMA. I HOPE THAT NOTHING BAD HAS HAPPENED...

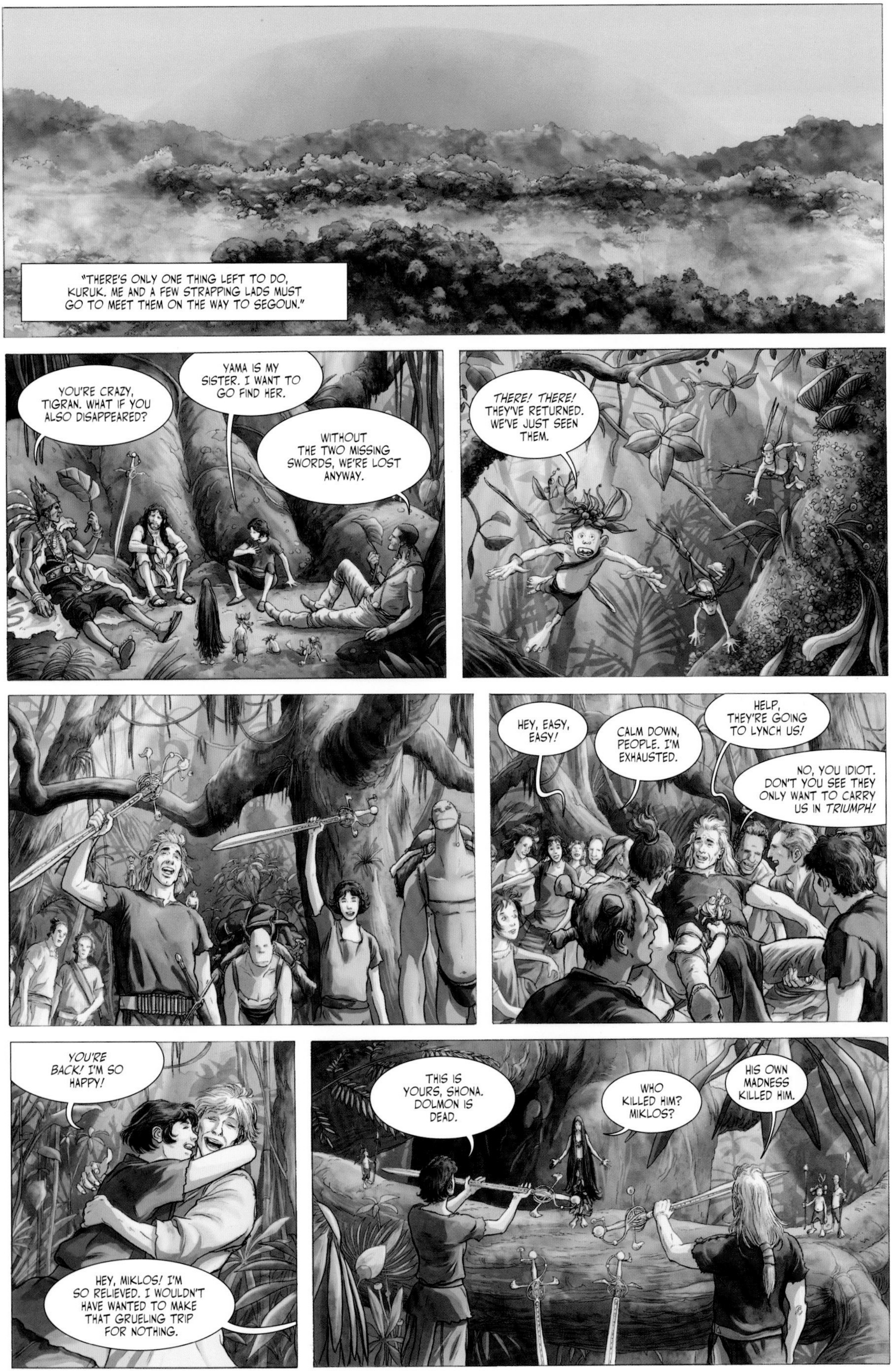
"THERE'S ONLY ONE THING LEFT TO DO, KURUK. ME AND A FEW STRAPPING LADS MUST GO TO MEET THEM ON THE WAY TO SEGOUN."
YOU'RE CRAZY, TIGRAN. WHAT IF YOU ALSO DISAPPEARED?
YAMA IS MY SISTER. I WANT TO GO FIND HER.
WITHOUT THE TWO MISSING SWORDS, WE'RE LOST ANYWAY.
THERE! THERE! THEY'VE RETURNED. WE'VE JUST SEEN THEM.
HEY, EASY, EASY!
CALM DOWN, PEOPLE. I'M EXHAUSTED.
HELP, THEY'RE GOING TO LYNCH US!
NO, YOU IDIOT. DON'T YOU SEE THEY ONLY WANT TO CARRY US IN *TRIUMPH!*
YOU'RE BACK! I'M SO HAPPY!
HEY, MIKLOS! I'M SO RELIEVED. I WOULDN'T HAVE WANTED TO MAKE THAT GRUELING TRIP FOR NOTHING.
THIS IS YOURS, SHONA. DOLMON IS DEAD.
WHO KILLED HIM? MIKLOS?
HIS OWN MADNESS KILLED HIM.

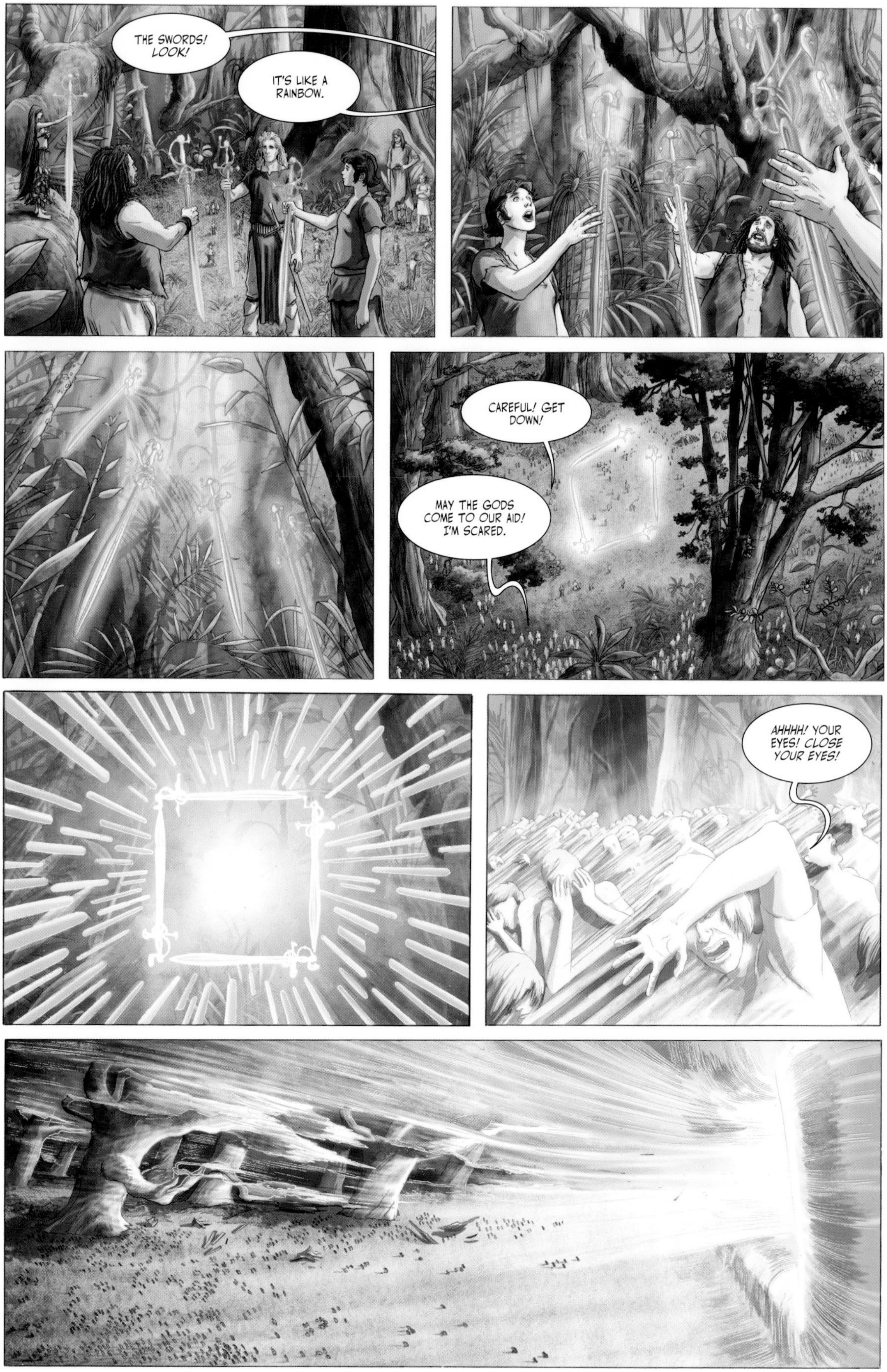
THE SWORDS! LOOK!
IT'S LIKE A RAINBOW.
CAREFUL! GET DOWN!
MAY THE GODS COME TO OUR AID! I'M SCARED.
AHHHH! YOUR EYES! CLOSE YOUR EYES!

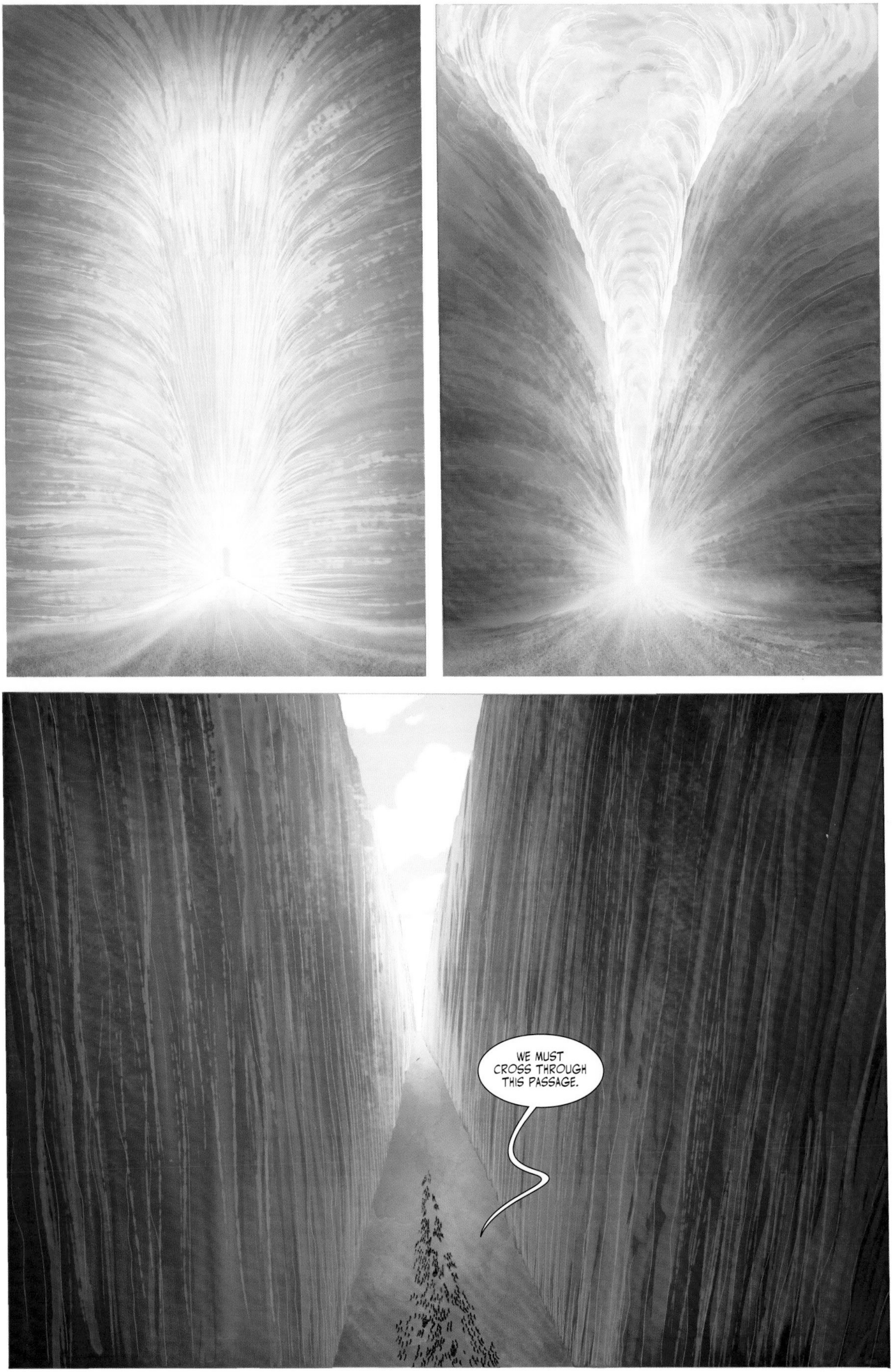
WE MUST CROSS THROUGH THIS PASSAGE.

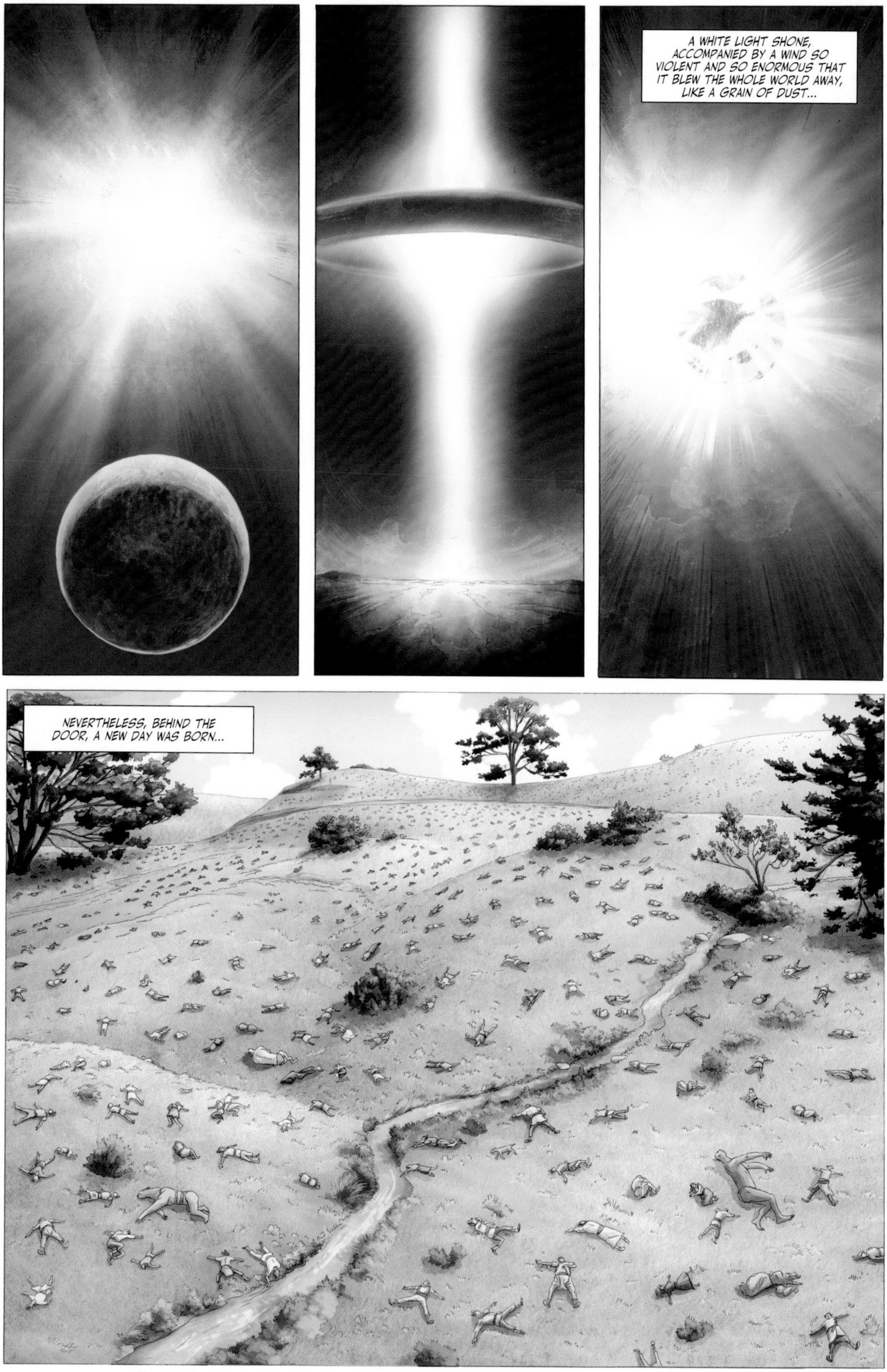
A WHITE LIGHT SHONE, ACCOMPANIED BY A WIND SO VIOLENT AND SO ENORMOUS THAT IT BLEW THE WHOLE WORLD AWAY, LIKE A GRAIN OF DUST...
NEVERTHELESS, BEHIND THE DOOR, A NEW DAY WAS BORN...

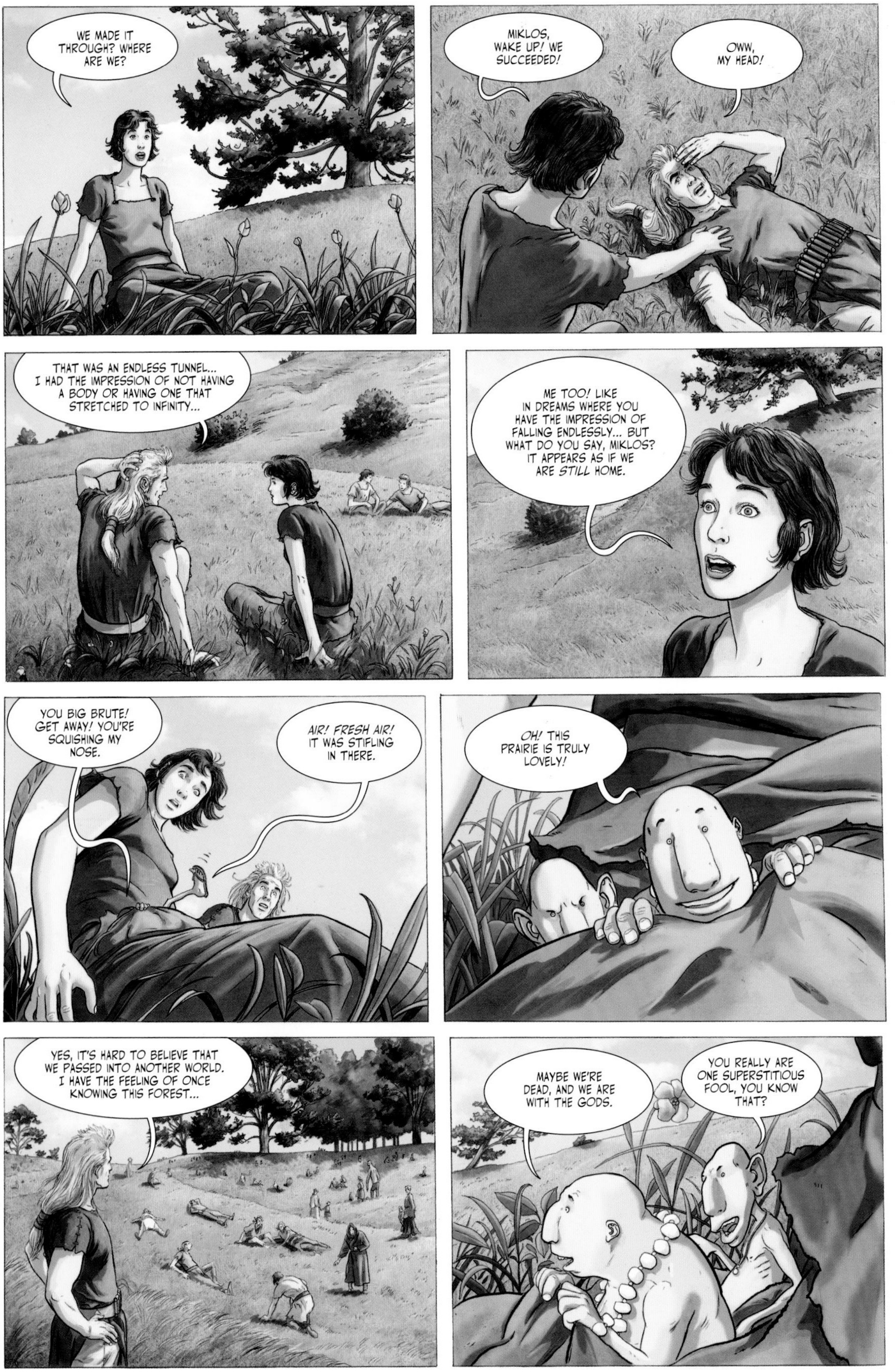
WE MADE IT THROUGH? WHERE ARE WE?
MIKLOS, WAKE UP! WE SUCCEEDED!
OWW, MY HEAD!
THAT WAS AN ENDLESS TUNNEL... I HAD THE IMPRESSION OF NOT HAVING A BODY OR HAVING ONE THAT STRETCHED TO INFINITY...
ME TOO! LIKE IN DREAMS WHERE YOU HAVE THE IMPRESSION OF FALLING ENDLESSLY... BUT WHAT DO YOU SAY, MIKLOS? IT APPEARS AS IF WE ARE STILL HOME.
YOU BIG BRUTE! GET AWAY! YOU'RE SQUISHING MY NOSE.
AIR! FRESH AIR! IT WAS STIFLING IN THERE.
OH! THIS PRAIRIE IS TRULY LOVELY!
YES, IT'S HARD TO BELIEVE THAT WE PASSED INTO ANOTHER WORLD. I HAVE THE FEELING OF ONCE KNOWING THIS FOREST...
MAYBE WE'RE DEAD, AND WE ARE WITH THE GODS.
YOU REALLY ARE ONE SUPERSTITIOUS FOOL, YOU KNOW THAT?

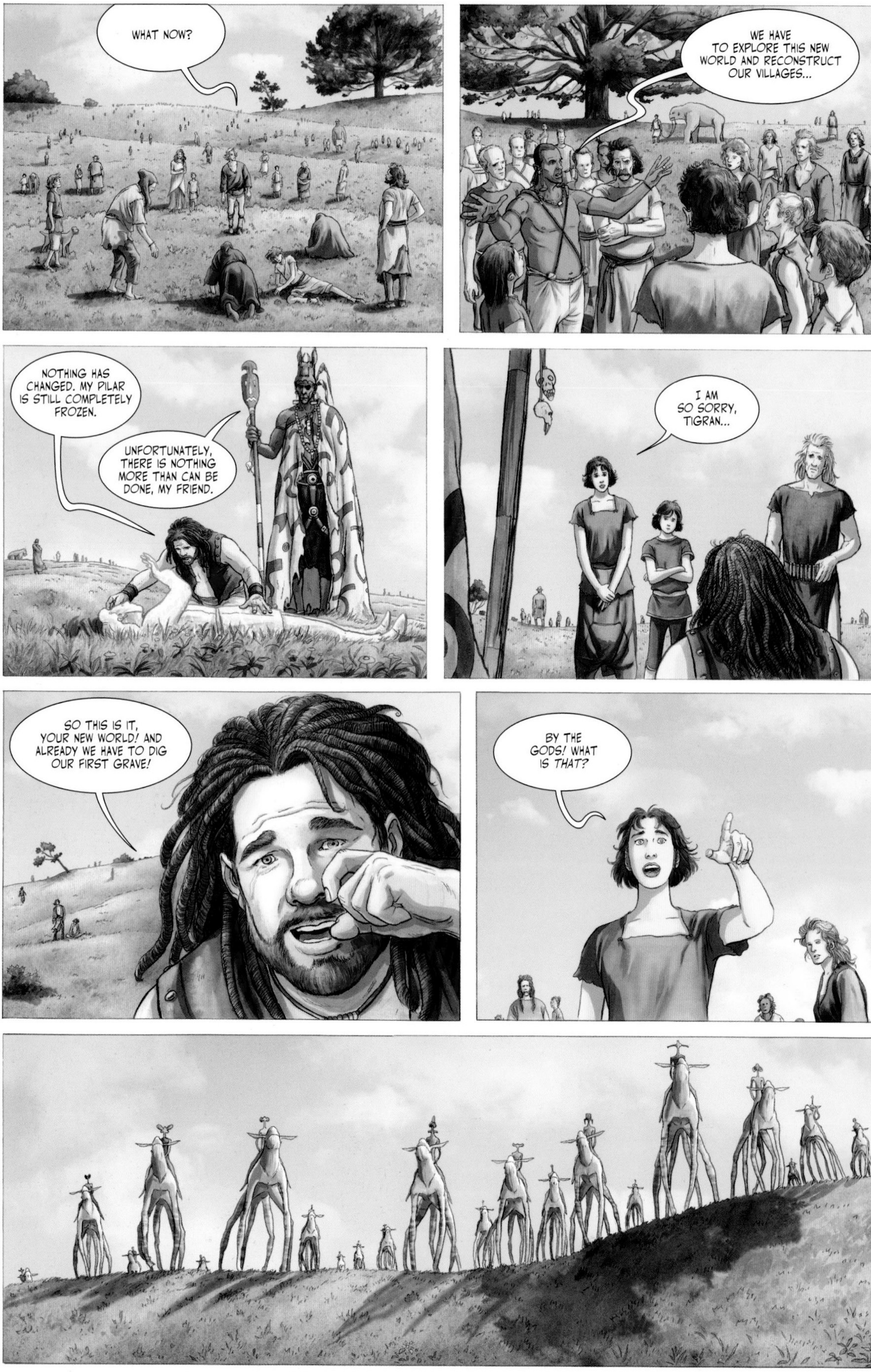
WHAT NOW?
WE HAVE TO EXPLORE THIS NEW WORLD AND RECONSTRUCT OUR VILLAGES...
NOTHING HAS CHANGED. MY PILAR IS STILL COMPLETELY FROZEN.
UNFORTUNATELY, THERE IS NOTHING MORE THAN CAN BE DONE, MY FRIEND.
I AM SO SORRY, TIGRAN...
SO THIS IS IT, YOUR NEW WORLD! AND ALREADY WE HAVE TO DIG OUR FIRST GRAVE!
BY THE GODS! WHAT IS *THAT*?

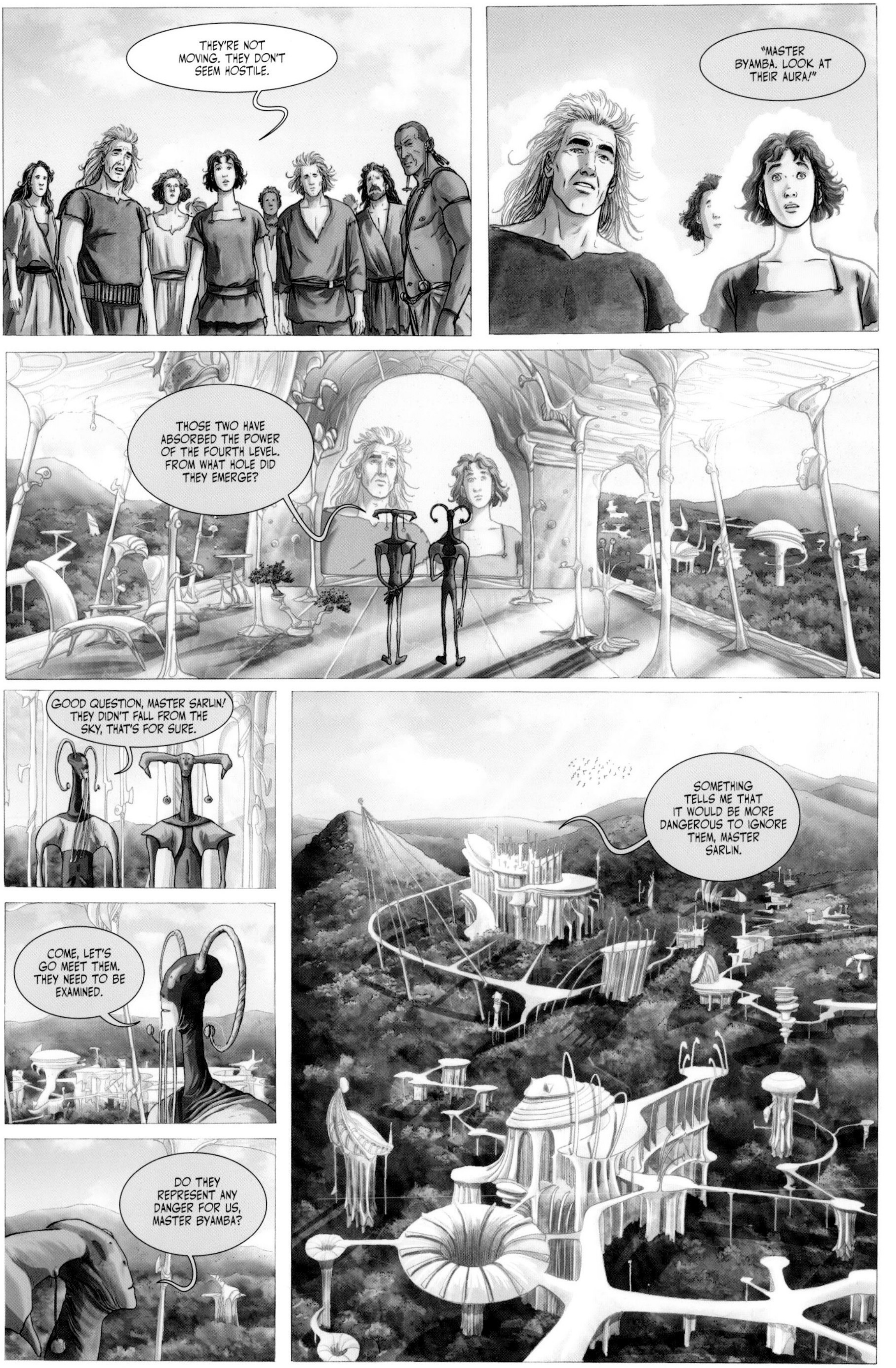
THEY'RE NOT MOVING. THEY DON'T SEEM HOSTILE.
"MASTER BYAMBA. LOOK AT THEIR AURA!"
THOSE TWO HAVE ABSORBED THE POWER OF THE FOURTH LEVEL. FROM WHAT HOLE DID THEY EMERGE?
GOOD QUESTION, MASTER SARLIN! THEY DIDN'T FALL FROM THE SKY, THAT'S FOR SURE.
COME, LET'S GO MEET THEM. THEY NEED TO BE EXAMINED.
DO THEY REPRESENT ANY DANGER FOR US, MASTER BYAMBA?
SOMETHING TELLS ME THAT IT WOULD BE MORE DANGEROUS TO IGNORE THEM, MASTER SARLIN.

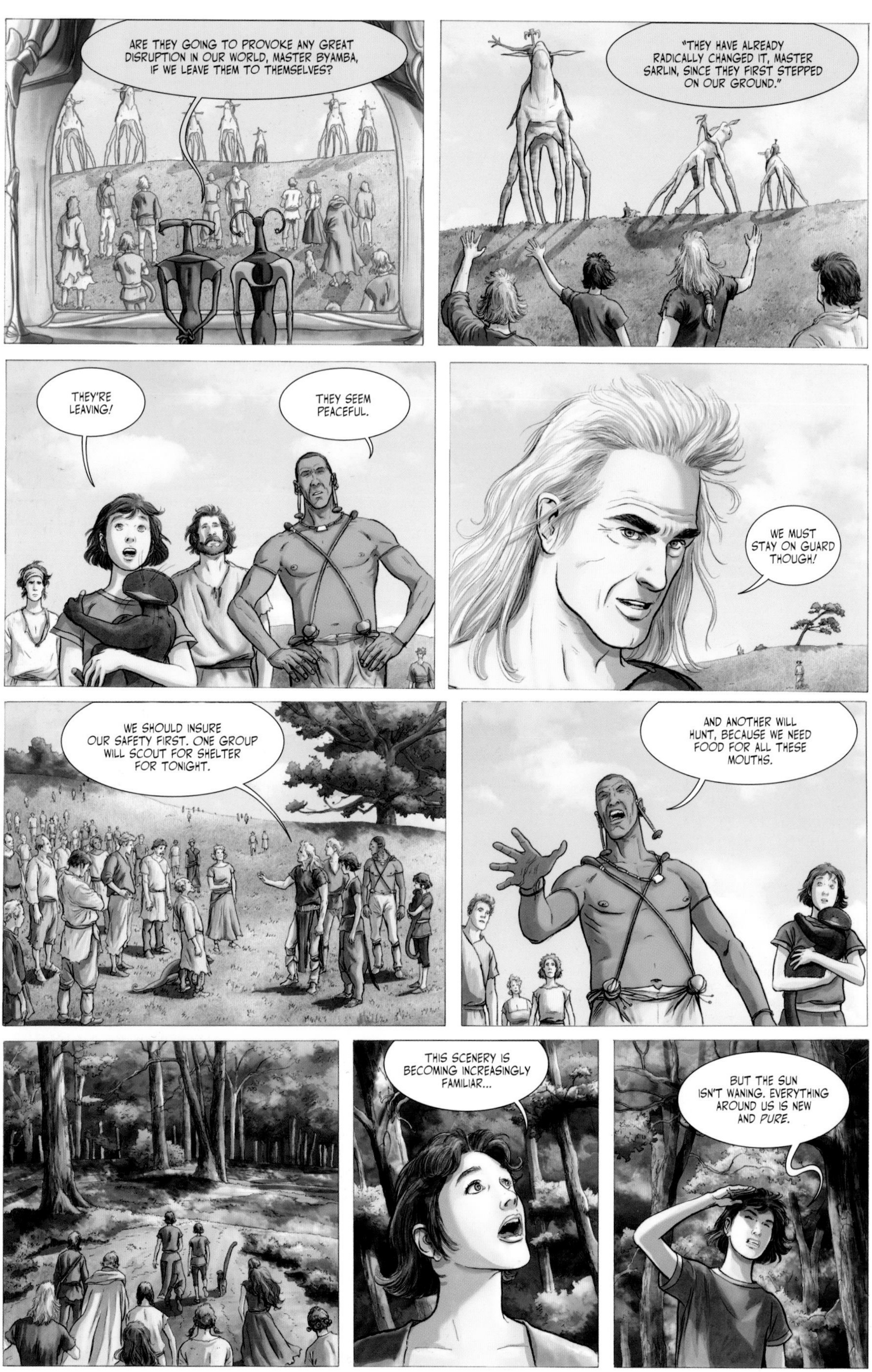
ARE THEY GOING TO PROVOKE ANY GREAT DISRUPTION IN OUR WORLD, MASTER BYAMBA, IF WE LEAVE THEM TO THEMSELVES?
"THEY HAVE ALREADY RADICALLY CHANGED IT, MASTER SARLIN, SINCE THEY FIRST STEPPED ON OUR GROUND."
THEY'RE LEAVING!
THEY SEEM PEACEFUL.
WE MUST STAY ON GUARD THOUGH!
WE SHOULD INSURE OUR SAFETY FIRST. ONE GROUP WILL SCOUT FOR SHELTER FOR TONIGHT.
AND ANOTHER WILL HUNT, BECAUSE WE NEED FOOD FOR ALL THESE MOUTHS.
THIS SCENERY IS BECOMING INCREASINGLY FAMILIAR...
BUT THE SUN ISN'T WANING. EVERYTHING AROUND US IS NEW AND *PURE*.

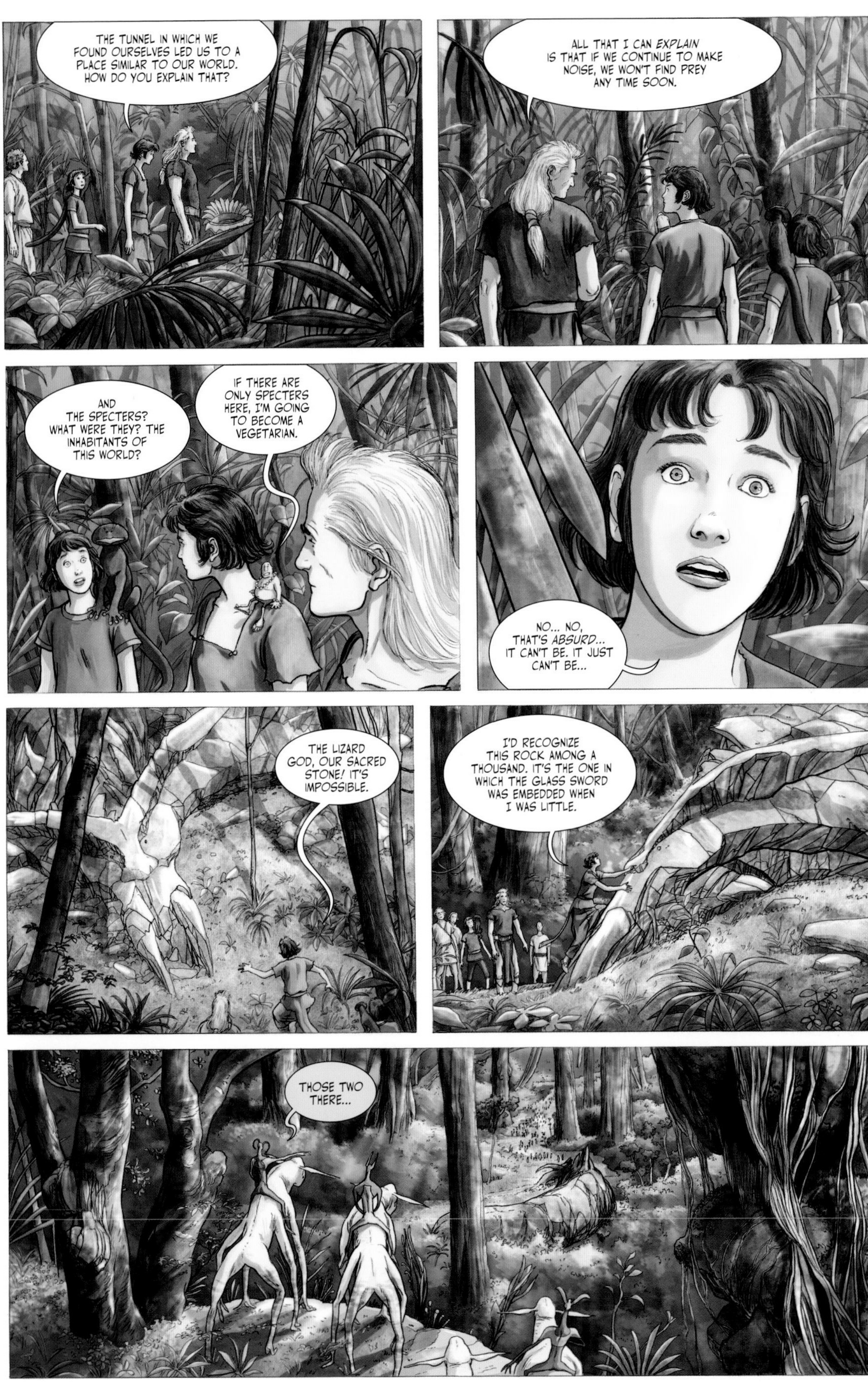
THE TUNNEL IN WHICH WE FOUND OURSELVES LED US TO A PLACE SIMILAR TO OUR WORLD. HOW DO YOU EXPLAIN THAT?
ALL THAT I CAN *EXPLAIN* IS THAT IF WE CONTINUE TO MAKE NOISE, WE WON'T FIND PREY ANY TIME SOON.
AND THE SPECTERS? WHAT WERE THEY? THE INHABITANTS OF THIS WORLD?
IF THERE ARE ONLY SPECTERS HERE, I'M GOING TO BECOME A VEGETARIAN.
NO... NO, THAT'S *ABSURD*... IT CAN'T BE. IT JUST CAN'T BE...
THE LIZARD GOD, OUR SACRED STONE! IT'S IMPOSSIBLE.
I'D RECOGNIZE THIS ROCK AMONG A THOUSAND. IT'S THE ONE IN WHICH THE GLASS SWORD WAS EMBEDDED WHEN I WAS LITTLE.
THOSE TWO THERE...

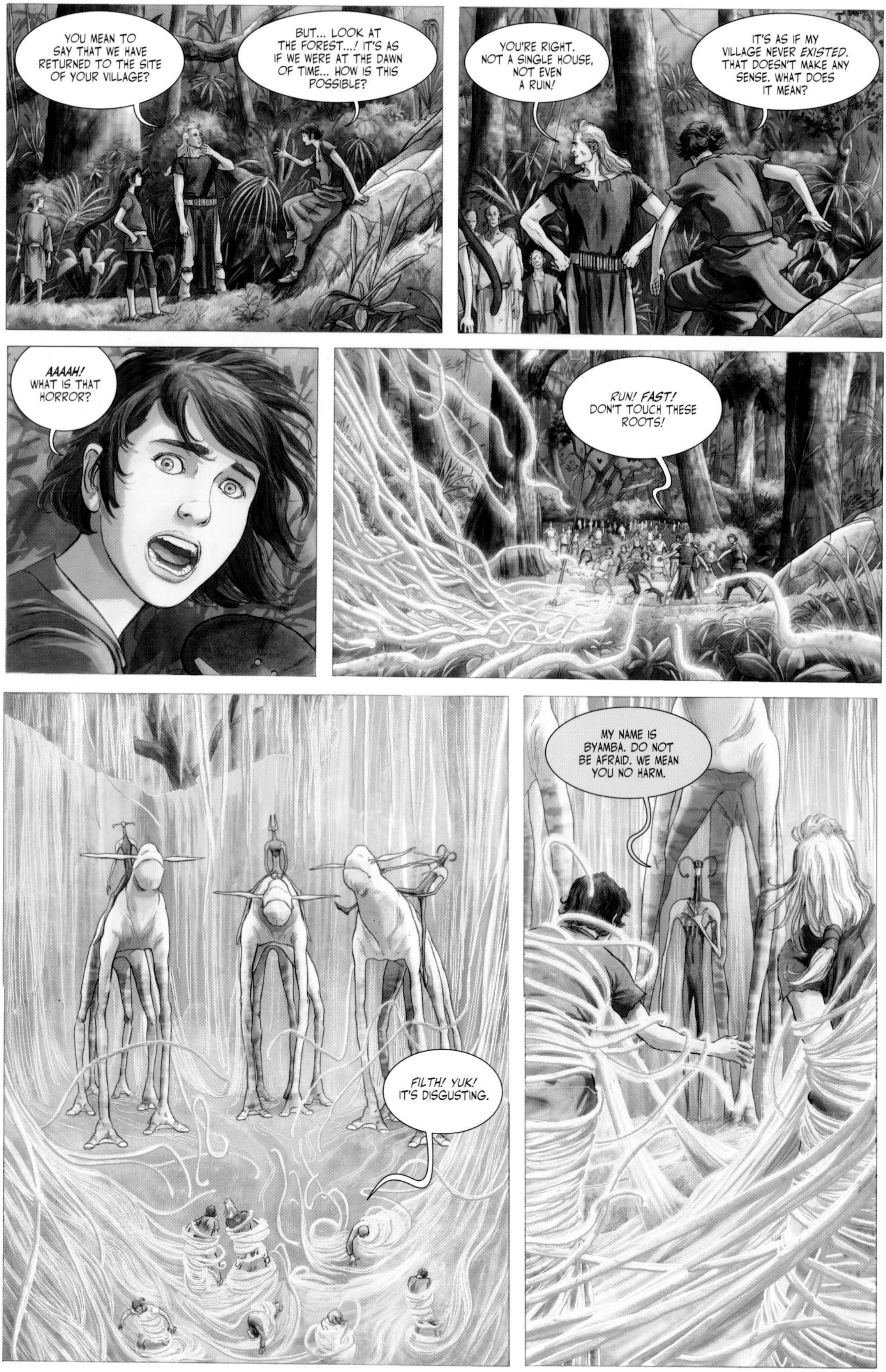
YOU MEAN TO SAY THAT WE HAVE RETURNED TO THE SITE OF YOUR VILLAGE?
BUT... LOOK AT THE FOREST...! IT'S AS IF WE WERE AT THE DAWN OF TIME... HOW IS THIS POSSIBLE?
YOU'RE RIGHT. NOT A SINGLE HOUSE, NOT EVEN A RUIN!
IT'S AS IF MY VILLAGE NEVER EXISTED. THAT DOESN'T MAKE ANY SENSE. WHAT DOES IT MEAN?
AAAAH! WHAT IS THAT HORROR?
RUN! FAST! DON'T TOUCH THESE ROOTS!
FILTH! YUK! IT'S DISGUSTING.
MY NAME IS BYAMBA. DO NOT BE AFRAID. WE MEAN YOU NO HARM.

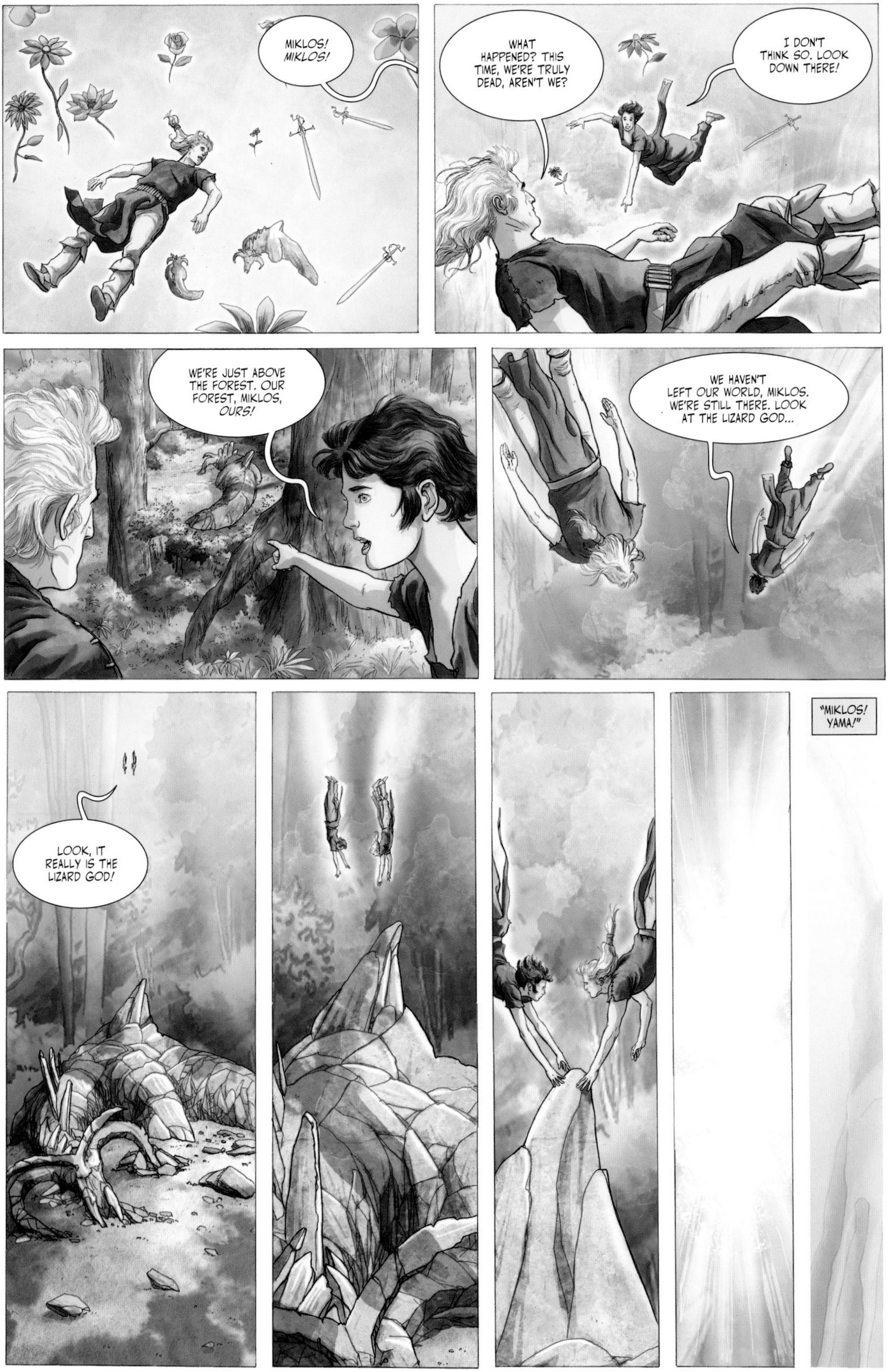
MIKLOS! MIKLOS!
WHAT HAPPENED? THIS TIME, WE'RE TRULY DEAD, AREN'T WE?
I DON'T THINK SO. LOOK DOWN THERE!
WE'RE JUST ABOVE THE FOREST. OUR FOREST, MIKLOS, OURS!
WE HAVEN'T LEFT OUR WORLD, MIKLOS. WE'RE STILL THERE. LOOK AT THE LIZARD GOD...
LOOK, IT REALLY IS THE LIZARD GOD!
"MIKLOS! YAMA!"

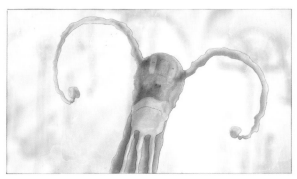

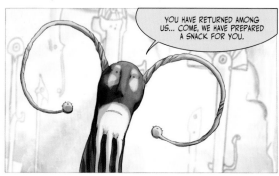

YOU HAVE RETURNED AMONG US... COME, WE HAVE PREPARED A SNACK FOR YOU.

WHERE ARE WE? WHERE ARE THE OTHERS? AND *WHERE* ARE MY CLOTHES?

WE HAVE RELEASED THE OTHERS. IT IS THE TWO OF YOU THAT INTERESTS US. GET DRESSED AND FOLLOW US, PLEASE.

RELAX! YOU ARE SAFE HERE.

I AM NOT REALLY WELCOMING YOU. IT WOULD BE PRESUMPTUOUS OF US... THIS WORLD IS YOURS AS WELL AS OURS. WE ARE SIMPLY GOING TO HAVE TO COHABITATE FOR SOME TIME.

ENTER, AND MAKE YOURSELVES COMFORTABLE! YOU WILL BE HAPPY TO FIND SOME OF YOUR FRIENDS... THEY TELL ME THAT YOU PRETEND TO BE THE FOUR CHOSEN. IS THAT RIGHT?

YOU HAVE MADE QUITE A VOYAGE PRIOR TO ARRIVING HERE WITH US. A VOYAGE THROUGH SPACE.

BUT ABOVE ALL YOU HAVE PASSED THROUGH MANY THOUSANDS OF YEARS IN TIME.

YOU HAVE USED ONE OF OUR TIME PORTALS TO COME BACK FROM WHAT IS, FOR YOU, A VERY DISTANT FUTURE. YOU ARE HERE IN YOUR WORLD, IN AN ERA WHERE THE SUN IS STILL VERY FAR FROM BEGINNING ITS EXTINCTION PHASE.

WHAT IS HE TALKING ABOUT? IT'S...IT'S IMPOSSIBLE.

IT TOOK ME SEVERAL DAYS AND NIGHTS IN ORDER TO ADMIT THE TRUTH. BUT WHEN THE SUN SETS, THERE'S NO DOUBT. THE STARS AND THE CONSTELLATIONS OVER OUR HEADS ARE THOSE THAT WE COULD SEE IN OUR OWN WORLD.

DAYS AND NIGHTS? HOW LONG DID WE SLEEP?

HUH... I HOPE YOU WILL EXCUSE US, BUT READING THE PRESENT DATA IN YOUR, SOMEWHAT DIFFERENT, BRAINS TOOK US QUITE A LONG TIME...

BUT PLEASE, EAT! YOU MUST BE STARVING.

BUT THEN, THE PROPHECY OF THE SWORDS, THE CHOSEN ONES, THE SWORDS THEM-SELVES, WHERE DID THAT ALL COME FROM?

DO YOU NOT HAVE THE SLIGHTEST IDEA, YOUNG WOMAN?

WAS IT YOU? I MEAN, IT'S US WITH YOU... IS THAT IT?

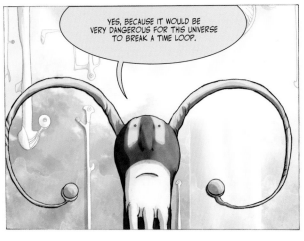

YES, BECAUSE IT WOULD BE VERY DANGEROUS FOR THIS UNIVERSE TO BREAK A TIME LOOP.

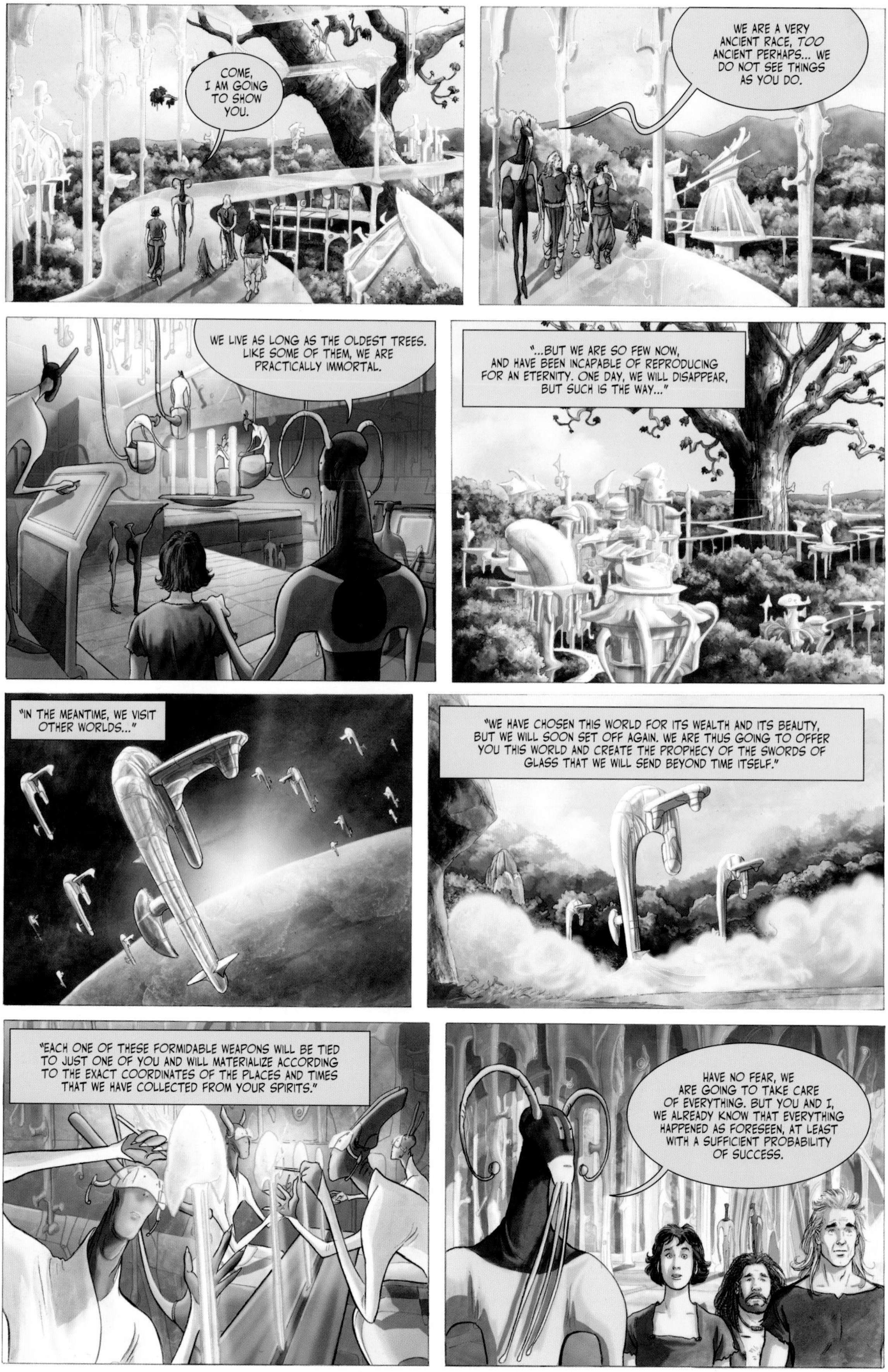
COME, I AM GOING TO SHOW YOU.
WE ARE A VERY ANCIENT RACE, *TOO* ANCIENT PERHAPS... WE DO NOT SEE THINGS AS YOU DO.
WE LIVE AS LONG AS THE OLDEST TREES. LIKE SOME OF THEM, WE ARE PRACTICALLY IMMORTAL.
"...BUT WE ARE SO FEW NOW, AND HAVE BEEN INCAPABLE OF REPRODUCING FOR AN ETERNITY. ONE DAY, WE WILL DISAPPEAR, BUT SUCH IS THE WAY..."
"IN THE MEANTIME, WE VISIT OTHER WORLDS..."
"WE HAVE CHOSEN THIS WORLD FOR ITS WEALTH AND ITS BEAUTY, BUT WE WILL SOON SET OFF AGAIN. WE ARE THUS GOING TO OFFER YOU THIS WORLD AND CREATE THE PROPHECY OF THE SWORDS OF GLASS THAT WE WILL SEND BEYOND TIME ITSELF."
"EACH ONE OF THESE FORMIDABLE WEAPONS WILL BE TIED TO JUST ONE OF YOU AND WILL MATERIALIZE ACCORDING TO THE EXACT COORDINATES OF THE PLACES AND TIMES THAT WE HAVE COLLECTED FROM YOUR SPIRITS."
HAVE NO FEAR, WE ARE GOING TO TAKE CARE OF EVERYTHING. BUT YOU AND I, WE ALREADY KNOW THAT EVERYTHING HAPPENED AS FORESEEN, AT LEAST WITH A SUFFICIENT PROBABILITY OF SUCCESS.

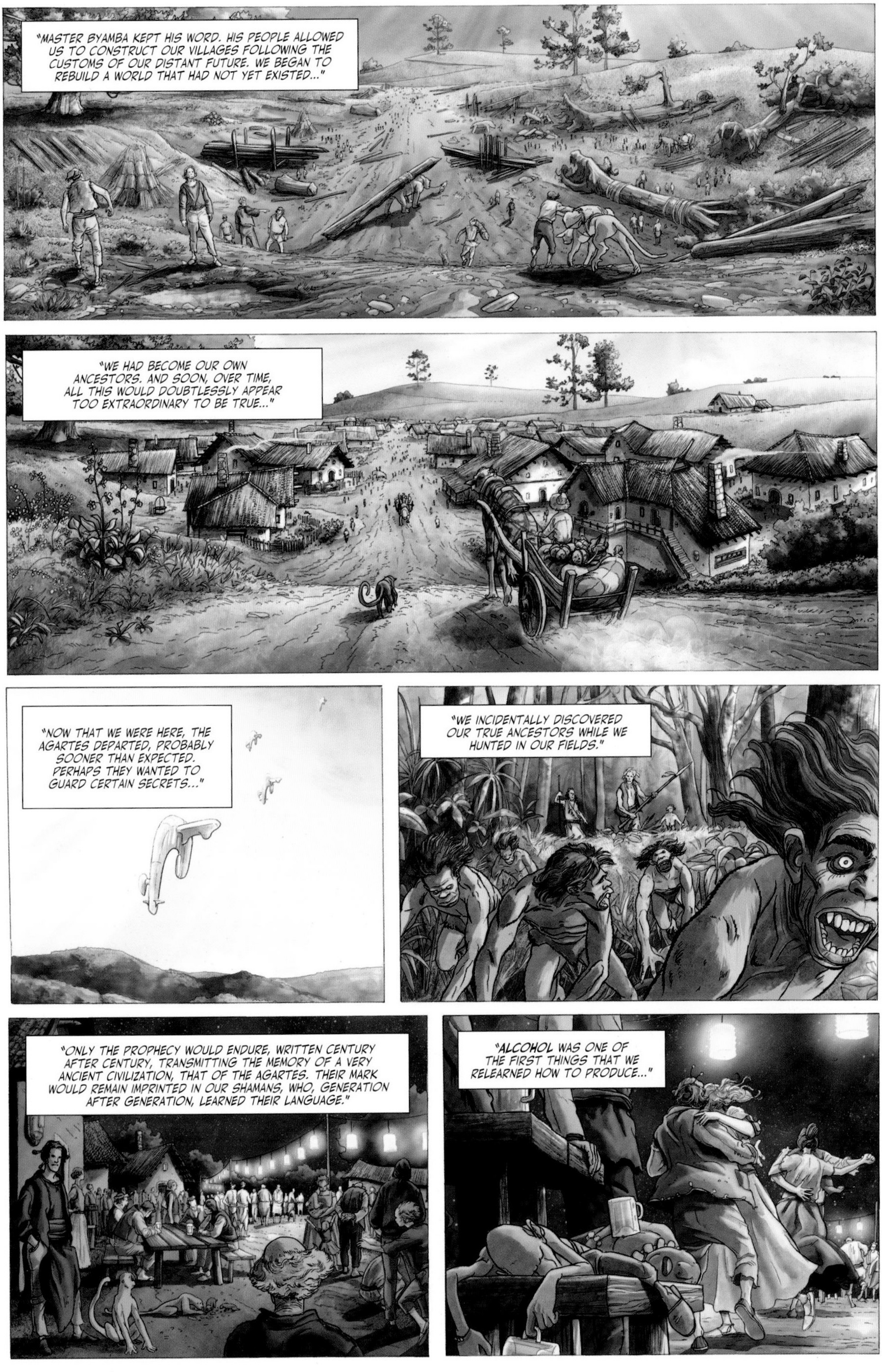
"MASTER BYAMBA KEPT HIS WORD. HIS PEOPLE ALLOWED US TO CONSTRUCT OUR VILLAGES FOLLOWING THE CUSTOMS OF OUR DISTANT FUTURE. WE BEGAN TO REBUILD A WORLD THAT HAD NOT YET EXISTED..."
"WE HAD BECOME OUR OWN ANCESTORS. AND SOON, OVER TIME, ALL THIS WOULD DOUBTLESSLY APPEAR TOO EXTRAORDINARY TO BE TRUE..."
"NOW THAT WE WERE HERE, THE AGARTES DEPARTED, PROBABLY SOONER THAN EXPECTED. PERHAPS THEY WANTED TO GUARD CERTAIN SECRETS..."
"WE INCIDENTALLY DISCOVERED OUR TRUE ANCESTORS WHILE WE HUNTED IN OUR FIELDS."
"ONLY THE PROPHECY WOULD ENDURE, WRITTEN CENTURY AFTER CENTURY, TRANSMITTING THE MEMORY OF A VERY ANCIENT CIVILIZATION, THAT OF THE AGARTES. THEIR MARK WOULD REMAIN IMPRINTED IN OUR SHAMANS, WHO, GENERATION AFTER GENERATION, LEARNED THEIR LANGUAGE."
"ALCOHOL WAS ONE OF THE FIRST THINGS THAT WE RELEARNED HOW TO PRODUCE..."

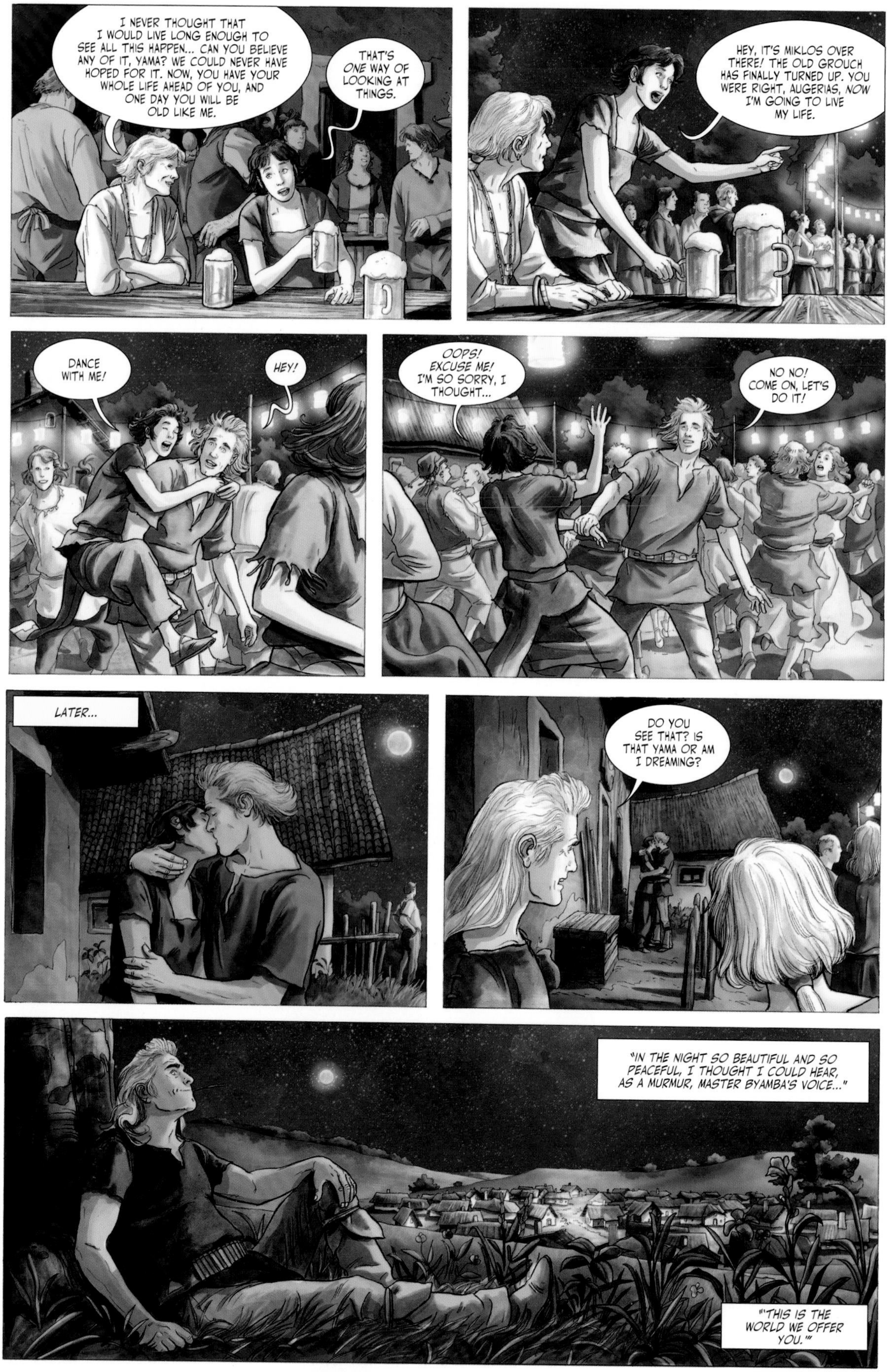
I NEVER THOUGHT THAT I WOULD LIVE LONG ENOUGH TO SEE ALL THIS HAPPEN... CAN YOU BELIEVE ANY OF IT, YAMA? WE COULD NEVER HAVE HOPED FOR IT. NOW, YOU HAVE YOUR WHOLE LIFE AHEAD OF YOU, AND ONE DAY YOU WILL BE OLD LIKE ME.
THAT'S ONE WAY OF LOOKING AT THINGS.
HEY, IT'S MIKLOS OVER THERE! THE OLD GROUCH HAS FINALLY TURNED UP. YOU WERE RIGHT, AUGERIAS, NOW I'M GOING TO LIVE MY LIFE.
DANCE WITH ME!
HEY!
OOPS! EXCUSE ME! I'M SO SORRY, I THOUGHT...
NO NO! COME ON, LET'S DO IT!
LATER...
DO YOU SEE THAT? IS THAT YAMA OR AM I DREAMING?
"IN THE NIGHT SO BEAUTIFUL AND SO PEACEFUL, I THOUGHT I COULD HEAR, AS A MURMUR, MASTER BYAMBA'S VOICE..."
"'THIS IS THE WORLD WE OFFER YOU.'"

END.

AFTERWORD

By MAXIM JAKUBOWSKI

Sylviane Corgiat and Laura Zuccheri's *Swords Of Glass* saga is, paradoxically, both a decidedly old-fashioned bande dessinée and a resolutely modern one. Originally published between 2011 and 2014 in France, it's a rare and likeable attempt to fuse young adult coming of age tropes with the quest and revenge leitmotivs of adult heroic fantasy, while infusing its weaving plot with a powerful sense of wonder which, in the final chapter, cleverly moves into the realm of science fiction and the mystical.

When describing the saga as "old-fashioned," this isn't damning it with faint praise but, on the contrary, celebrating the ligne claire of Laura Zuccheri's ever-realistic illustrations which succeed magnificently in rooting the story in familiar bucolic settings as well as evoking all the myriad wonders of an exotic, if bleak, imagined world full of ferocious deserts, forests, and dizzying cities where excess coexists with extreme poverty and misery. This is the detailed realism we find in many of the classic adventure strips that used to appear in magazines like *Spirou* and *Pilote* before the tsunami of the modern graphic novel and psychedelia intervened in the mid-to-late Seventies. At times, Zuccheri's faces and landscapes are reminiscent of Jean Giraud's western saga, *Blueberry* — before he morphed into Mœbius and embraced the fantastic and the bizarre — precise, etched in life, lovingly detailed, and expressive.

And "modern" because until relatively recently, heroic fantasy was an exclusively Anglo-Saxon genre which was actually spurned in France and Italy, where the influence of Tolkien's *Lord of the Rings* was negligible in the world of books, let alone in comics. Which makes it all the more surprising that, today, works like *The Swords of Glass* are just the tip of a fertile iceberg (and a brilliant one at that...) in Europe, and that so many of them are created by women like Sylviane Corgiat and Laura Zuccheri.

But an important thing happened, the French public finally become aware of the rich stream of heroic fantasy fiction, which had until then been ignored in favor of science fiction, horror, or more traditional fantasy. Soon, Tolkien was reissued in editions no longer targeted to a younger audience (albeit still poorly translated); *Moorcock* was finally made available in French adaptations, as were important precursors like Fritz Leiber, Robert E. Howard, and others. And the readers immediately lapped it up. Within a decade, even French popular fiction writers were tackling the genre with success, to the extent that many even managed the hitherto unlikely feat of being sold back to Anglo-Saxon markets to similar acclaim. Much of this was due to the sterling efforts of innovative editors like Michel Demuth, Jacques Goimard, Patrice Duvic and, later, the setting up of Editions Bragelonne by Stephane Marsan, which remains, to this day, one of the hotbeds of the genre in France.

Born in 1955 in Aix-en-Provence, Sylviane Corgiat's early career as a writer began with crime, SF, and fantasy books (the latter in collaboration with novelist and Les Humanoïdes Associés' long-time editor Bruno Lecigne) published by legendary French pulp imprint Le Fleuve Noir. Her own literary coming of age coincided with the commercial flowering of heroic fantasy in France, which undoubtedly proved a major influence, as both readers and emerging authors simultaneously absorbed both a mass of material previously hidden and began experimenting in the genre, combining English and American influences with their own Gallic touch. At the same time, the genre was also experiencing a new Golden Age in Italy with Valerio Evangelisti, a striking European fantasy author whom illustrator Laura Zuccheri was most likely aware of.

As her writing career progressed, Corgiat was soon in demand as a scriptwriter for film and TV, until she was lured to the world of bandes dessinées in 2004. Her early scripts rapidly proved popular. *Elias The Cursed*, on which she paired up with illustrator Corrado Mastantuono, was a sumptuous fantasy saga involving cosmic fate, magic coins, and a finely drawn anti-hero character in the proper heroic fantasy tradition. *Lune d'Ombre* (*Moon Shadow*) which she worked on with a female illustrator for the first time, Christelle Pécout, was no less imaginative — a neo-feminist take on the world of *One Thousand and One Nights*. A more recent project with Patrick Galliano, *Neferites*, takes its characters back to Ancient Egypt without ever losing the epic sweep by now familiar to Corgiat's scripts.

For *The Swords of Glass*, Corgiat's principal publisher, Humanoids, teamed her up with an up-and-coming Italian artist, Laura Zuccheri. Laura, from the Bologna region, is far more than just a comics artist, and her haunting artwork is a fascinating catalogue of bleak and fantastical landscapes, much of which is glimpsed in *The Swords of Glass*, where the realm of fantasy is so brilliantly brought to life in its beauty and impossibility, without ever taking the focus away from the gripping adventures of the young heroine, Yama. In a world where the sun is dying, Yama seeks vengeance for the death of her father and mother, while embarking on a quest for the swords that — according to the prophecy — might save humanity from extinction.

This accomplished blend of sheer adventure and epic imaginative quest incorporates so many elements of classic heroic fantasy and makes them their own. It is both a large screen coming of age yarn for Yama, as she unpeels the layers of mystery and menace of the world she lives in, and a fascinating unveiling of a world at times familiar and at others unutterably alien and menacing.

And, although Yama's quest for justice forms the backbone of the saga, Corgiat and Zuccheri constantly come up with surprises and plot twists, as other characters momentarily take center stage and we follow their respective adventures and struggles, as the band of sword seekers begins to converge and the overall plot enlarges to the dimensions of the alien intervention they are treading through.

What makes *The Swords of Glass* different from many fantasy tales is the subtle feminine touch that both creators bring to it. Yama is a tomboy who is unaware of her own beauty and the somewhat ambiguous relationship she has with her protector, Miklos, is handled with humor and delicacy. The reader, however, is never allowed to forget the spiky undercurrent of attraction that runs between the two of them. Corgiat cleverly proffers hints of so many other classics of the genre: a zest of John Boorman's *Zardoz* here; the group of outsiders fighting against the odds like in Tolkien's oeuvre; a touch of *Star Wars* in the amusing little alien creatures who populate Yama's world and often act as a Greek Choir, commenting on the action rather than actually contributing to it. There's a trace memory of Edgar Rice Burroughs, and even George R. R. Martin's *Game of Thrones* TV adaptation (although this is quite coincidental, as the first volume of *The Swords of Glass* predates the show by two years) in the unfurling panorama of deserts, walled cities and glass plains, echoes of fair tales and legends and, of course, the world of Camelot given a science fictional spin and turning a single magic sword into four and, in its final major twist, the time travel back to a form of Eden, which concludes the saga like an Ouroboros snake folding upon itself. Multifold elements, which form a new whole, and make *The Swords of Glass* a wonderful accomplishment, a gripping adventure with intriguing characters in all shades of good, evil, and beyond.

The European reading public were quickly convinced by this series and its second volume, *Ilango*, won Zuccheri the Best Illustrator Award at the Lucca Comics & Games festival in 2011.

Having reached these pages you will hopefully be equally convinced and as soon as you have finished reading this you will rush back to the beginning of Yama's story and start reading it again, appreciating all the minor subtleties and beauty you might have missed the first time around when you coasted along the breathless tale, eager to learn whether Yama got her revenge and whether the world was saved. I am confident that you will enjoy the saga even more. Lose yourself in the realm of *The Swords of Glass*, momentarily forgetting this mundane world and perpetually expanding your sense of wonder.

--May 2015

Maxim Jakubowski is a British writer, translator, and critic who began his career in popular fiction in France with a series of anthologies, editing volumes on Michael Moorcock and Brian W. Aldiss. He is a *Sunday Times* bestselling author and still reviews science fiction and fantasy in a monthly column (and has a weak spot for adult graphic novels). Even his erotica work features strong fantasy elements, and when not writing and travelling extensively he lives in London, advising several international film festivals.